Nimāi and the Mouse

The Nimāi Series

Satsvarūpa dāsa Goswami

Second Edition, 2023

This first collected single volume edition of Satsvarūpa dāsa Goswami's popular fictional tales in the Nimāi series, is published as part of a legacy project to restore Satsvarūpa Mahārāja's writings to 'in print' status and make them globally available for current and future readers.

GN Press, Inc., gratefully acknowledges the BBTI for the use within this book of verses and purports from Śrīla Prabhupāda's books. All such verses and purports are ©BBTI.

Illustrations
Nimāi Dāsa and the Mouse: Trivikrāma dāsa
Nimāi's Detour: Satsvarūpa dāsa Goswami
Gurudeva and Nimāi: Satsvarūpa dāsa Goswami
Chota's Way: Keśisudana dāsa

GN Press, Inc.

Oxford | New Delhi | Toscolano Maderno

Nimāi and the Mouse
Four Novels

1. Nimāi Dāsa and the Mouse: A Fable 1

2. Nimāi's Detour: A Story 127

3. Gurudeva and Nimāi: Struggling for Survival 239

4. Chota's Way 381

Appendixes 535

Satsvarūpa dāsa Goswami

1

Nimāi Dāsa and the Mouse
A Fable

vidyā-vinaya-sampanne
brāhmaṇe gavi hastini
śuni caiva śva-pāke ca
paṇḍitāḥ sama-darśinaḥ

—*Bhagavad-gītā* 5.18

"The humble sages, by virtue of true knowledge, see with equal vision a learned and gentle *brāhmaṇa*, a cow, an elephant, a dog and a dog-eater [outcaste]."

"Some of Hans Christian Andersen's best tales are understood at two levels, by the child and by the grown-up person. Andersen himself once explained that his tales 'were told for children, but the grown-up person should be allowed to listen as well.'"

—*Eighty Fairy Tales by Hans Christian Andersen*

To my spiritual master His Divine Grace A. C. Bhaktivedanta Swami Prabhupāda, *jagat-guru* and *founder-ācārya* of the International Society for Krishna Consciousness.

Śrīla Prabhupāda was an erudite scholar who translated many renowned Vedic literatures, including *Śrīmad-Bhāgavatam, Bhagavad-gītā As It Is, Caitanya-caritāmṛta,* and the *Nectar of Devotion*, to name but a few. To these timeless scriptures he authored commentary and purports that captured our present-day mentality, and sparked an insatiable desire to learn more about spiritual life. Prabhupāda was relentless in his compassionate efforts to distribute Kṛṣṇa consciousness worldwide. But beyond his voluminous scholarly writings and serious determination to make these important works available to humanity at large, Prabhupāda endeared himself to us by being a most charming story teller. I hope this book will appeal to that lighter side of him. May he be pleased to accept this humble offering executed in his service.

An Explanation to the Reader

Kṛṣṇa conscious fiction is something of a novelty to members of the International Society for Krishna Consciousness, but it is not unprecedented in the Vaiṣṇava *sampradāya* literature. The most significant example is Bhaktivinoda Ṭhākura's novel, *Jaiva Dharma*, which some consider to be the masterpiece of his philosophical dissertations. Sanātana Gosvāmī's great work *Śrī Bṛhad-Bhāgavatāmṛtam* is another potent example. Even more recently fictional satire has appeared in ISKCON'S *Back to Godhead* magazine, and Śrīla Prabhupāda's followers have started to delight us with novels that are both creative *and* authentic.

Nimāi dāsa and the Mouse is a fable in which the make-believe content is explicit and obvious to the reader. *Hitopadeśa* is an ancient Sanskrit collection of fables that usually involve birds and beasts speaking. It is filled with wise counsel in politics, religion, and morality, similar to the sayings of Cāṇakya Paṇḍita. Some believe *Aesop's Fables* is based on the *Hitopadeśa*.

There are also a few fables in the *Śrīmad-Bhāgavatam*, although *Śrīmad-Bhāgavatam* is mostly *not* fable, and when "animals" like Hanumān Garuḍa and Gajendra speak, we understand that they are actual devotees in advanced spiritual consciousness. In the Eighth Canto King Yayāti tells a fable of a he-goat and a she-goat. He says, "The best of the he-goats, attracted by the many she-goats, engaged in erotic activities and naturally forgot his real business of self-realization." There is a similar story told by a *brāhmaṇa* in the Eleventh Canto about a family of birds. The male bird returned home to the tree and found that his wife and children had been captured by a hunter. At first, he thought to try to save them, but then he decided not to enter the trap. While telling this story Prabhupāda said, "And so the male bird thought, 'Let me take *sannyāsa*.'" The devotees were charmed to hear Prabhupāda tell it that way and no one was dull enough to ask, "But Prabhupāda, how could a bird take *sannyāsa*?"

There is even a fable of a mouse who approached a sage and asked for benedictions to "again become a mouse" (*punar mūṣika bhava*). *Nimāi dāsa and the Mouse* is not a short fable, but novel length, and it is also not so pointed in its didactic moral as the ancient fables.

One may ask, "What is the place of fiction in Kṛṣṇa consciousness?" Some devotees may be perplexed, but as the Kṛṣṇa conscious culture evolves and expands in the world I think that devotees will realize that fiction is as fine a preaching technique as the essay. As with diary writing, fiction centers on an individual's life experience. However, unlike the journal, it is not dependent on the singular view of the journal writer. The author can assume many voices. As the characters are fleshed out and the point of view broadens, so does the possibility of a story. No longer is the writer restricted to literal experience, but he can range as far as the imagination will take him.

Fiction can be a versatile preaching medium because of its ability to draw the reader in. It permits him to experience a life he might not otherwise have access to. So, in addition to conveying Kṛṣṇa conscious philosophy, fiction can absorb the reader in the experiential potency of devotional life. One is reminded of Śrīla Prabhupāda's remark about Kṛṣṇa conscious theater. While watching a dramatic performance of a scene from the book *KṚṢṆA, The Supreme Personality of Godhead*, Prabhupāda said that watching the performance was better than reading the book!

Fiction has the potency to attract a class of nondevotees who have previously been difficult to reach. Fiction is subtle; it entangles the reader and forces him to walk in the shoes of the characters in the book. Fiction offers a non-threatening environment. It affords the non-devotee a glimpse into devotional life, and ISKCON in particular, without the encumbrance of preconceived prejudices. From such a vantage point, the inexplicable mellows of spiritual life can be portrayed, and a genuine taste for Kṛṣṇa consciousness fostered. As for the devotees, benign fictional characters can clearly instruct us in the art of how to take full advantage of the association within our own communities, and how to develop friendships and become more personal in our dealings with fellow devotees. To sum it up, fiction can be a vital form of preaching. Let's welcome an influx of Kṛṣṇa conscious novelists!

I would like to address some questions I have had to face while writing *Nimāi dāsa and the Mouse* and sequels to it. I have already explained to some extent why we may create an imaginary character of a devotee in a fictional setting in order to glorify Kṛṣṇa as we would in the essay format, but with some new opportunities through fiction. In fiction, therefore, the characters are imaginary, but usually the situation is entirely based on realistic life. It should also carry conclusions of Kṛṣṇa consciousness. But, *is it all right to describe something that didn't actually take place historically*?

This question had to be answered in the dramatic works recently produced by my Godbrother Tamal Krishna Goswami. In his plays about Lord Jagannātha and Śrīla Prabhupāda, he made some alterations in history. The author first did extensive research and questioned all available authorities in Vaiṣṇavism before he proceeded. The consensus he received was that a Vaiṣṇava author may sometimes depart from historical incidents in telling his story or dramatic play, provided that the *rasa* or the mood of appreciating Kṛṣṇa is always proper, in line with the authorities of guru, *śāstra* and *sādhu*. In the case of liberated Vaiṣṇava authors like Bhaktivinoda Ṭhākura and Viśvanātha Cakravartī Ṭhākura, we cannot say that their descriptions are "imaginary." When Bhaktivinoda Ṭhākura describes an extended dialogue between Lord Caitanya and Haridāsa Ṭhākura, or when Viśvanātha Cakravartī in his commentary to the Tenth Canto of *Bhāgavatam* gives extended "new" dialogues between Rādhā and Kṛṣṇa, and when Rūpa Gosvāmī does the same, we understand that they are actually meditating on the *līlā* of Kṛṣṇa and it is being revealed to them from the spiritual platform. Because the pastimes of Kṛṣṇa are unlimited, when the pure devotee meditates upon Kṛṣṇa, that meditation is also in the dimension of transcendental reality.

The subject of the pastimes of Kṛṣṇa is a deeper topic than I need to get into in my present discussion. In the "Nimāi" stories there is no treatment of Kṛṣṇa-*līlā* per se, but I wanted to explain why I have taken so seriously the make-believe story of a devotee and a mouse. Many readers will not need the explanation and may even see it as a too-apologetic disclaimer. In a sense, the explanation is anti-poetic. But because some devotee readers may be perplexed, and because one has to be very strict to follow the *sampradāya*, I wish to offer these further explanations.

One reason I have taken the character Nimāi so seriously is because his fancy or fantasy is similar to my own. In addition to the more public life that I share with co-workers in the Kṛṣṇa consciousness movement and in my interactions with nondevotees, I have a private life or "little world" of my own. I think everyone is like this. Some of my private desires are to want to write and publish Kṛṣṇa conscious books. I also like to be alone. I am trying to pray to Lord Kṛṣṇa and my spiritual master, which is a very individual relationship I have with the Lord and His pure devotee. There are also very personal things I do to cultivate my Kṛṣṇa consciousness, such as write poems. We all hope that our own little world is not a mere flight of fancy; that it has some objective significance. In fact, we usually feel that our individuality is something special although the world keeps telling us otherwise. But spiritually speaking, that feeling of uniqueness is borne out by the Vaiṣṇava philosophy. We are each very special persons to Kṛṣṇa.

We hope to improve and purify our individual natures to the point where Kṛṣṇa and the pure devotee will accept the version of ourselves that feels like it's a perfect fit to us. You know when you're on the right track. In this case I feel I am somewhat like my character Nimāi, who people think of as a little eccentric. Nimāi has a special fancy—a spiritual relationship with mice. With this fictional character and his fictional relationship with Choṭa, I can express things about myself and the world which I could not express otherwise.

Authors and critics have also noted that a writer is responsible for any hidden messages that may appear in his works. The idea being that even though the author may not advocate certain activities or flaws in the characters he writes about, he needs to be cognizant of how readers might be affected by his presentation of them. For example, someone may ask me whether I am advocating that a devotee should try to communicate with animals, or am I asserting literally that the devotee Nimāi does talk to a mouse? Do I intend it to be taken as a hallucination? And if it is just make-believe, then what is the importance of it? My answer to these questions is that the Nimāi stories are fables and they are not intended to be taken as reality. In a fable, imaginary things happen "normally." As explained above regarding the power of fiction, it is my hope that this lively fictional format will capture the readers' attention and also act as a medium through which I can express Kṛṣṇa consciousness in a very personal way for my own purification, and in a way, I hope will affect devotees and nondevotees alike.

I therefore take the story of the boy and the mouse very seriously, but it is not historical reality. My wish is that the readers will sympathize with this character in their imaginations. What I am asking is nothing less than what any author asks of his readers. Perhaps in this case the difference is that the characters are not only fictional, but extraordinary—a boy with the ability to communicate and talk with mice. As far as that is concerned, it *is* possible but it *is* a fable. It is fiction with Kṛṣṇa conscious themes and therefore it has a Kṛṣṇa conscious *siddhānta*. More than this I cannot say. I am praying to purify this art and present it for the pleasure of the readers in an attempt to serve my spiritual master.

Chapter 1

Nimāi dāsa was very surprised when the mouse began to speak to him in perfectly good English. At first, he couldn't believe it. But in this strange material world anything is possible! And there was no doubt about it—the mouse had spoken.

Actually, it was Nimāi dāsa who had spoken first to the mouse. He had been feeling dejected when he came up to his attic room. When the mouse appeared Nimāi had blurted, "Hare Kṛṣṇa! What are you looking for? *Prasādam*?"

The mouse, who was small, gray, and nervous in its movements, had replied in a small squeaky voice, "What's *prasādam*?" Nimāi was startled; he looked around. Usually, he had the room to himself. Had someone heard him speaking and answered as a joke? But no. The room was empty as usual.

Nimāi sat down expecting the mouse to flee. The auditory hallucination, or whatever it was, had snapped Nimāi away from his dejection. For the time being he forgot that Vibhu dāsa, the temple president, had just told him that he would not recommend Nimāi as a husband to any of the *brahmacāriṇīs*. Vibhu said that Nimāi was too irresponsible to become a *gṛhastha*. When he heard that, Nimāi had walked away without a word and come up to the little attic space above the *brahmacārī āśrama* ...

The mouse squeaked again, "What's *prasādam*?" and looked up to Nimāi with an earnest face.

Nimāi felt a stirring desire to preach. Despite the absurdity of the situation, he thought that he should answer what seemed like a bona fide inquiry.

"*Prasādam* is food that has been offered to Kṛṣṇa," said Nimāi, and he added, "The Supreme Personality of Godhead."

"How is it that you can talk?" asked Nimāi. Nimāi was now sitting on his sleeping bag on the floor, and the mouse was poised respectfully a few feet in front of him. It twitched its whiskers and sniffed at the floor and replied, "I don't know."

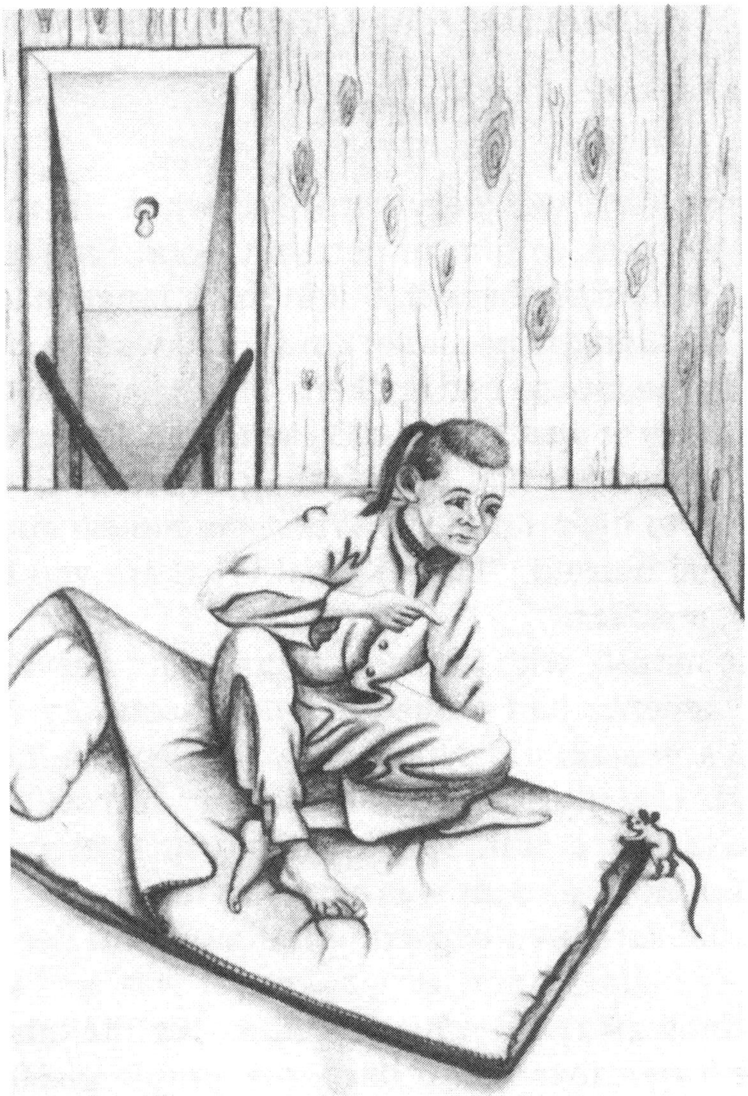

Nimāi flashed on the idea that maybe this mouse, which was after all a spirit soul in a mouse body, had some unusual *karma* and was therefore living in Rādhā-Dāmodara's temple in the association of devotees. Maybe ...

Suddenly there were heavy footfalls on the stairs, the door swung open and the mouse ran for shelter through a crack in the boards.

"Hey Nimāi!" it was Bhīma dāsa. "I heard that Vibhu dāsa just gave you the sauce, huh?" Bhīma dāsa patted Nimāi on the shoulder. "What's the matter? You look like you saw a ghost or something."

Nimāi thought of telling Bhīma dāsa about the mouse, but he decided not to. Who would believe it? They would just laugh and call him crazy. In fact, they already did. They called him Nimāi the Gnome and "eccentric," and someone had said, "He is a sincere devotee, but a little strange."

"Just be patient, Prabhu," said Bhīma dāsa. "Smaller than a blade of grass, more tolerant than a tree, right? If you can't find a wife, that could be Kṛṣṇa's blessing." Bhīma then suggested that it was getting late and they should take rest in order to get up on time for *maṅgala-ārati.*

After Bhīma left, Nimāi kept the light on looking to see if the mouse would come back. But when nothing happened after ten minutes, he turned out the light. Whatever had actually happened he still had to get up at 3:00 A.M. to start his *japa* and morning duties.

When Nimāi dāsa woke the next morning, he wondered whether he had actually spoken with a mouse. Nimāi was not an initiated *brāhmaṇa*, but he assisted the *pūjārīs* in preparing the plates for Rādhā-Dāmodara before *maṅgala-ārati.* He then attended the *ārati kīrtana* with the other devotees. Although they could not induce him to dance, he would stand with his hands in the pockets of his hooded sweatshirt and reverently look upon Their Lordships.

During the *japa* period his mind was filled with distractions, especially the temple president's rejection of him as a candidate for marriage. Neither could he forget the squeaky voice, "What's *prasādam*?" While circumambulating Tulasī and trying to chant *japa*, Nimāi prayed, "My dear Lord Kṛṣṇa, my dear spiritual master, in a state like this how can I pay attention to Your holy names?"

That morning the *Bhāgavatam* class was given by a visiting *sannyāsī.* During the course of his lecture, he mentioned that Lord Caitanya could induce even the lions, tigers, and elephants to chant Hare Kṛṣṇa. When the *sannyāsī* finished speaking and asked for questions, Nimāi dāsa raised his hand.

"Mahārāja," Nimāi asked, "is it possible for an animal to become Kṛṣṇa conscious?" Nimāi had a reputation for asking "mental" or odd questions, although they didn't seem odd to Nimāi.

"Yes, in extraordinary circumstances," the *sannyāsī* replied. "Lord Caitanya once blessed a dog that had also been favored by the Lord's devotee Śivānanda Sena. And that dog soon went back to Godhead. There is also the example of a snake living in the cave of Haridāsa Ṭhākura to whom the Lord in the heart spoke, and then the snake left the cave so as not to disturb Haridāsa."

"Can I ask some more?" Nimāi asked hesitantly. "Your examples are of a great devotee blessing an animal. But could an animal take birth, say in a temple, and have remembrance of living in that temple before?" Some of the devotees in the audience exchanged looks indicating that Nimāi was up to his old tricks.

"Yes, that's possible," the *sannyāsī* answered soberly. "Prabhupāda has said that those people who live in skyscrapers and try to "lick them up" in sense gratification may be born next life in the same building, not as humans but as rats! He has also said that people who are very attached to their country and always want to be Americans, may take their next birth in this land but as cows to be slaughtered."

"But is it possible," asked Nimāi, "that the soul could continue his higher consciousness even in an animal's body?"

"Only if he was a great soul," said the *sannyāsī*. "The prominent example is Mahārāja Bharata who had to take birth as a stag, but kept the higher consciousness and associated only with *sādhus*." The *sannyāsī* looked around the room for other questions, but Nimāi spoke out again.

"Just one more question, Mahārāja," he said. A few of the women tittered and other devotees smiled tolerantly, a bit embarrassed that the visiting *sannyāsī* was getting such a full dose of their Nimāi dāsa. "What if," Nimāi began, "a soul was born in an animal's body because he deserved that lower species? Would it then be possible for him to have any relationship with a human devotee?" Devotees burst out laughing. Nimāi blushed.

"I don't think I can answer a question like that," the *sannyāsī* said. "We should not be so interested in animals, Prabhu. Our duty is to preach Kṛṣṇa consciousness to the human beings. Those human beings who are like hogs, dogs, camels and asses, don't listen to the *Bhāgavatam*, but we have to preach to them. We can give them books. We should try more to distribute Prabhupāda's books; this would be better than speculating about the position of animals."

This remark brought a responsive *"Jaya!"* from some of the men and Nimāi took it as another dig at him. He suddenly realized how foolish he must have sounded.

During the rest of the morning program, Nimāi received a few more jibes for his unusual questions. In reply he nodded silently, although smiling. He was thinking, "There is another reference in the *Bhāgavatam* about this."

After breakfast he went up to his attic room and took down the Second Canto where he seemed to remember something in the *catur-śloka* about animals receiving Kṛṣṇa consciousness. Wasn't there a purport which described Kṛṣṇa consciousness as so liberal that all creatures in the universe can take to it? He finally found this:

> Therefore, the devotional service of the Lord with perfect knowledge through the training of a bona fide spiritual master is advised for everyone, even if one happens not to be a human being. This is confirmed in the *Garuḍa Purāṇa* as follows:
>
> *kīṭa-pakṣi-mṛgāṇāṁ ca*
> *harau sannyasta-cetasām*
> *ūrdhvām eva gatiṁ manye*
> *kiṁ punar jñāninām nṛṇām*
>
> "Even the worms, birds and beasts are assured of elevation to the highest perfectional life if they are completely surrendered to the transcendental loving service of the Lord, so what to speak of the philosophers amongst the human beings?"
>
> —*Śrīmad-Bhāgavatam 2.9.36, purport*

As Nimāi closed the book and sat back thoughtfully, the same mouse came forward from the floorboards and crept slowly before him.

It squeaked, "Who is Kṛṣṇa?"

Nimāi was thrilled. He felt a rush of compassion.

"I'll tell you," he said. What Nimāi had asked in class and what the *sannyāsī* had replied seemed theoretical compared to this moment. To Nimāi, it no longer seemed urgent to know "who" the mouse was or why it was able to talk. It had asked a glorious question, and Nimāi dāsa felt obliged to reply.

Nimāi said, "You have asked a very wonderful question. It is stated in the scripture *Śrīmad-Bhāgavatam* that to answer this question is the perfection of speaking and hearing. I am not very qualified to answer, but I can tell you what I have read in Prabhupāda's books, which are the perfect source of information about Kṛṣṇa. So, try to listen with attention."

The mouse positioned itself comfortably on its haunches and tried to compose the movements of its claws and tail. Its ears were perked outward.

Although the mouse had directly asked, "Who is Kṛṣṇa?" Nimāi dāsa thought it best to begin with the Lord's teachings in the Second Chapter of *Bhagavad-gītā* regarding the identity of the self. This would be particularly relevant for the mouse. Nimāi was eager to use the verses he had memorized, beginning with *dehino 'smin yathā dehe* ... And so, he proceeded logically, describing the transmigration of the soul through the different species. With preacher's instinct, Nimāi dāsa tried to catch the mouse's attention and observe whether it was hearing submissively. Nimāi gave the analogy of a person changing garments that wear out, but then he thought the mouse might not be able to relate to that, so he stressed that all living beings are spirit souls and all are equal. Only due to *karma* do we have different situations where someone is in the body of a human, someone in the body of a dog, and someone in the body of a mouse, etc.

After about half an hour the mouse lost its power of attention and began twitching its nose and running back and forth like an ordinary mouse, as if forgetting the purpose of life. Nimāi dāsa was alarmed at these symptoms. He wanted to nurture whatever trust he had already developed, and so he gently advised the mouse that they should end their discussion and take it up another time. The mouse did not speak further, but seemed to nod in agreement. Nimāi then suggested that they could meet for half-hour intervals twice a day, morning and night.

And so, in the days that followed, they continued to meet as before. The mouse appeared regularly and was always submissive and attentive, as far as was in its power. It continued to ask questions which were short and simple, and yet with a pure and penetrating manner. For example, at the start of the third session the mouse asked Nimāi, "But how can a soul become free of the body's demands?"

Nimāi was accustomed to being the lesser in his relationships with people, and he took well to the fact that the mouse was subordinate and dependent on him. He tried to treat the mouse kindly. By patiently inquiring Nimāi dāsa gradually learned some personal details about his new friend. The mouse told him that he was a male, relatively young, and that he came from a large family. He would not say where he lived exactly, except that it was "somewhere in the temple." The mouse had no interest in the subject of his previous lives, nor did Nimāi care much about it. Nimāi thought of past-life research as Shirley MacLaine stuff, and anyway, what did it matter? Wherever his soul had been before, it was now in a mouse body and that mouse body was interested in Kṛṣṇa consciousness.

The mouse was reluctant to talk about his family and home life, but when Nimāi inquired about his eating habits he admitted that most of their food came from the temple kitchen. Nimāi then explained the principle of eating *prasādam* rather than *bhoga*. The mouse was impressed and squeaked with joy when Nimāi said that he would personally supply *prasādam* for the mouse. Since the mouse's relationship with his family seemed delicate, Nimāi did not pursue the idea that the mouse might bring *prasādam* to his family members.

Within a few days, the mouse was chanting Hare Kṛṣṇa. Nimāi even gave him a name, Choṭa dāsa— "So I can call you," Nimāi said.

Nimāi kept the relationship a secret, but the devotees noticed a great change in him. He was usually morose and irritable, but now he was bright-faced and jolly. He even began dancing in the *kīrtanas*, and one time when one of the *brāhmaṇas* was ill, Nimāi volunteered and gave the *Śrīmad-Bhāgavatam* lecture. He became enthusiastic to describe the glories of the holy name and the philosophy of Kṛṣṇa consciousness. While working at his temple duties or cleaning the grounds, he would spontaneously say to other devotees, "The glories of the holy name are so great we can't even imagine! Kṛṣṇa has such power to liberate us! We should all preach His glories!" This behavior was certainly surprising because Nimāi had a reputation for being a wallflower. He never liked to go out on *harināma* and usually found some excuse to avoid it. He also avoided going to college lectures or speaking to guests who came to the temple. If he did speak to a guest, it usually turned out unfavorably with Nimāi becoming irritable and argumentative.

But now he was a changed man, an asset to the community. Vibhu Prabhu asked Nimāi how he had become so inspired. Nimāi smiled and said, "It's just Kṛṣṇa's mercy."

Vibhu said, "If you keep on progressing like this, maybe I can recommend you to get married." Nimāi laughed with shining eyes, "If I keep up like this, maybe I won't have to get married!"

Chapter 2

Nimāi had twinges of conscience about the fact that no one knew what he was doing. It made him wonder whether his preaching was bona fide. Of course, he knew it was. His relationship with Choṭa dāsa was an unmotivated spiritual friendship. But because it was so unusual, it sometimes led Nimāi to speculate. Was he specially empowered? Should he tell others to try it?

The scriptures clearly state that if one has any doubts, he should approach his spiritual master. Even Lord Caitanya when He felt ecstatic symptoms of love of God thought that maybe He was going mad, and so He placed the matter before His spiritual master Īśvara Purī. Nimāi therefore decided that he should confer with his initiating spiritual master Śrīla Gurudeva.

Gurudeva lived in his own little house on the temple grounds. He was a senior disciple of Śrīla Prabhupāda, and he had initiated hundreds of his own disciples in different places around the world. He often traveled, but he was now observing *cāturmāsya* at the farm and so it was a good time for Nimāi to go and see him.

It took a few days for Nimāi to get an interview through his *guru's* secretary. The last time he had spoken with his *gurudeva* was concerning a fight that he had had with some of the other devotees. Nimāi knew that the temple president sometimes complained to Gurudeva about him and that was why it took a long time for Nimāi to get initiated—why he hadn't yet received second initiation, even though he had been a devotee for five years. And so, their relationship wasn't perfectly harmonious, although Nimāi had an abiding faith that his spiritual master was a genuine link to Prabhupāda and the Gauḍīya-sampradāya.

The spiritual master sat on a cushion behind a low desk and his disciple Nimāi dāsa sat on the floor facing him. Gurudeva was almost fifty years old; Nimāi was less than half that age, and of course, Nimāi was a much less experienced devotee.

"What did you want to see me about?" asked Gurudeva.

Nimāi opened his mouth but then looked down at the floor. He realized this wasn't going to be easy. He began to bring it out gradually so as not to cause a shock of disbelief.

"I have been having some unusual experiences lately," said Nimāi. "I mean, spiritual experiences."

"I see," said Gurudeva. "Do you want to describe them?" Gurudeva had already begun to categorize what Nimāi was saying. As spiritual master to over six hundred disciples Gurudeva had had many dealings with his disciples in person, by letter, and in hearing reports from their authorities. Gurudeva had already encountered many cases of "unusual spiritual behavior." One of his disciples had been put in prison, and when he was released, he told Gurudeva that Lord Caitanya had visited him in his cell and smiled and encouraged him. Another devotee, a young girl, confided in Gurudeva that one day while riding with the other devotees in a van, she had suddenly seen the Universal Form of Kṛṣṇa and after that Kṛṣṇa had appeared before her as a small child with Mother Yaśodā. At first Gurudeva had been completely cynical of these reports, even telling one of the devotees that his experience was bogus. But as he dealt with more cases, he became more cautious. He decided that he should be careful not to commit an offense towards his own disciples who, after all, were devotees of Kṛṣṇa. He didn't want to become a cynical priest. He'd read stories about the lives of the saints and how they often weren't recognized as saints until much later on. He definitely didn't want to be a religious leader who disbelieved in the miraculous visions of devotees who later turned out to be saints. He didn't want to go down in history as another fool and nonbeliever. So, although Gurudeva didn't really have much faith in the visions reported by his disciples, he wanted to play it safe. He had developed some insight into how to deal with such situations.

"Let me just tell you straight, Gurudeva," said Nimāi, "and you can judge for yourself. I don't want to do anything that's not authorized. A few weeks ago, I said some things about Kṛṣṇa to a little mouse who stays in the attic above the *brahmacārī āśrama*. And he actually spoke to me.

Gurudeva suddenly felt thirsty. He reached for his silver drinking chalice and began drinking water the way Prabhupāda did, holding the chalice above his lips and letting the water pour into his mouth.

Nimāi stared fervently at his spiritual master waiting for a response. Gurudeva said, "Go ahead."

"Since then, I've been preaching to this creature and he actually responds. I know it must sound incredible—and I probably would find it hard to believe if somebody told me—but it's actually true. And also, there is some proof in the Vedic literatures, like in the *Garuḍa Purāṇa*, that even creatures like worms and insects, and I suppose mice, can hear the message of Kṛṣṇa from a *[pauses for second]* ... a devotee."

"What were you about to say just then?" asked Gurudeva. "You were about to say a mouse can receive the message from a bona fide spiritual master?"

"Well, I don't think of myself as a spiritual master," said Nimāi. "I am just telling him what I heard from you and what I read in Prabhupāda's books." Since he was not completely sure of himself, Gurudeva decided to encourage him. He was also aware that in recent weeks his disciple Nimāi had much improved in his behavior.

"I'll tell you what I think, Nimāi," said Gurudeva. "I think you should keep this to yourself. I can't say for sure exactly what you are experiencing. Sometimes devotees have special experiences. I think there is even a letter where a devotee said he thought he was having some special reciprocation with the Deity in the temple, and Prabhupāda advised him to keep it to himself. So, the main thing I would advise you is to just be very humble and go on with your duties. Don't become too distracted by this special talking. Your main business is to chant Hare Kṛṣṇa and to hear Vedic knowledge and to serve with the devotees." Gurudeva thought of adding, "And if it's some craziness, it may just pass with time." But he didn't say that. He began instead to advise Nimāi in a general way not to be puffed up about having special experiences. "If we think we are better than other devotees, we'll be guilty of false pride."

Nimāi dāsa nodded respectfully, taking in the instructions of his spiritual master. In one sense he felt that Gurudeva was avoiding the issue, but then he tried not to question the *guru's* authority. His Gurudeva no doubt had reasons for speaking in this way, and Nimāi tried to hear what he was saying. "Actually," Nimāi thought, "my spiritual master is hitting on the heart of the matter by advising me to be humble."

When his meeting with Gurudeva was over, and Nimāi was walking alone back to the temple, he began to feel even better about what his spiritual master had said. Gurudeva had not said that he believed and approved of his preaching to Choṭa dāsa, and in fact, he hadn't even let him tell much more about it. But the important thing was he didn't forbid it. "So indirectly," Nimāi thought, "he has authorized what I am doing. And he put me in my place by telling me to be humble. He even spotted my mentality of trying to act as a *guru* towards Choṭa dāsa. He would try to be humbler, but at the same time, now that he had consulted with his spiritual master, he would try to be more responsible to take on this work. No one else took it seriously, and perhaps no one else could really understand. "It is somehow Kṛṣṇa's arrangement," Nimāi thought, "that I should do this humble work. Who knows, sometime in the future, if I can develop this preaching more, I might convince Gurudeva to take it seriously and I can even introduce him to Choṭa dāsa." By the time he reached the attic room, Nimāi dāsa was infused with the missionary spirit and eager to talk about Kṛṣṇa. He shut the door, sat down, and called softly toward the crack in the floor, "Choṭa dāsa! Choṭa dāsa!"

The relationship between Nimāi and the mouse was like nectar. In many ways the mouse was an ideal disciple. Nimāi convinced Choṭa dāsa to bathe twice daily, which was more than Nimāi himself bathed. He also taught the mouse to count a quota (by a method of pushing pieces of straw) for chanting the Hare Kṛṣṇa *mantra*. Nimāi decided that four rounds daily was sufficient for a start. Nimāi continued to teach from the text of *Bhagavad-gītā*, and he also told whatever stories he could remember about heroes and devotees from the *Śrīmad-Bhāgavatam*. Nimāi liked to tell Choṭa about little creatures, such as the bird who tried to empty the ocean while looking for its eggs and the spider who helped Lord Rāmacandra to build a bridge to Lanka. Not only did Choṭa learn the rudiments of Vaiṣṇava philosophy, but he also began to manifest Vaiṣṇava-like traits.

One time, Nimāi had come to the attic in a grumpy mood after being teased by one of the devotees. It was easy to get a rise from Nimāi. This was done mostly by the school children and teenagers who called him "Nimāi-Fry" and "Nimāi-Knucklehead." But when Choṭa dāsa noticed his instructor's demeanor and asked what was wrong, Nimāi confessed that someone had been calling him names.

"Be tolerant," said Choṭa dāsa. "Isn't that what Lord Caitanya said? 'Think yourself lower than the straw in the street, more tolerant than the tree, and in that way, you can always chant Hare Kṛṣṇa.'"

Nimāi smiled on hearing the encouraging words from his own pupil. He is not merely a pupil, thought Nimāi, but a friend.

Despite occasional dips in his moods, Nimāi was happier since he had begun instructing Choṭa dāsa. Sensing the change many devotees opened up into more friendly exchanges with him. Then one day while he was chanting merrily in the kitchen, Sūrya dāsī glanced at him in a charming way. Unfortunately, this one glance melted Nimāi dāsa just as butter melts in a hot pan, and he at once lost whatever resolve he had about not getting married. He remembered how much he had liked

Sūrya dāsī in the past, and now whenever he saw her, his affection grew. After that glance he couldn't stop thinking about her. She was so pretty!

Sūrya dāsī was the young woman that Nimāi wanted to marry, but he had been turned down by her parents and the temple president. He never heard for sure what her opinion was, but as soon as she had glanced at him in that friendly way, he knew that his feelings for her had not changed. She was nearly twenty years old, and having previously graduated from the *gurukula*, was these days working in the kitchen as quite an accomplished cook. She was also assisting the *pūjārīs* along with Nimāi. Out of all the women he saw at the temple, her *sārīs* always looked the best. She was attractive to Nimāi, with her clinking bracelets and beautiful smiles.

Then Nimāi had a brilliant idea. He decided to tell Sūrya about Choṭa dāsa. He would bring her to the room and call Choṭa out to talk to her! She would be really impressed with Nimāi after that. She would be amazed and look at him with awe. She was a sensitive person and worthy of being included in the secret. He and she could share the secret. It would bind them together. Nimāi daydreamed of Sūrya dāsī looking at him with deep admiration while he asked her if she would marry him. He imagined she replied "Yes."

When they were alone in the kitchen, Nimāi asked her, "Excuse me, Sūrya Prabhu. I wonder if you could come up to the attic room for a minute to look at the Gaura-Nitāi Deities there? They could use a little touch-up with paint and I thought you might advise me on how to go about it." Sūrya agreed. Nimāi dāsa rationalized that it was all right to take her up to the attic room because it wasn't really part of the *brahmacārī āśrama* where women were forbidden. The small attic was not exactly defined. Nimāi slept there because he didn't like staying with some of the other devotees and some of them didn't like staying with him either. Anyway, Nimāi reasoned that he wasn't going to do anything illicit. It was spiritual to share the wonderful secret with the girl who might become his wife.

As they entered the room, Sūrya dāsī asked, "Where are the Deities?"

"First I want to show you something else," said Nimāi. He bent toward the floor and called, "Choṭa dāsa! Choṭa Prabhu!" The mouse scampered out of its hole and headed directly for Nimāi and Sūrya.

"Eeek!" Sūrya screamed. "A mouse!" and she backed up against the door.

The scream aroused Bhīma dāsa, who yelled from the *brahmacārī āśrama*, "What's going on up there?" Sūrya dāsī opened the door revealing herself and Nimāi dāsa standing together. Sūrya felt flustered, and in a guilty mood she left Nimāi's company and went back to her designated place downstairs.

"What do you think you are doing?" said Bhīma, face-to-face with Nimāi. "You know women are not allowed up here." Nimāi blushed and slammed the door.

Within a few moments Nimāi was approached by Vibhu Prabhu.

"A *brahmacārī* is not supposed to be alone with a woman," said Vibhu. "As if you didn't know." Nimāi hung his head with sullen guilt.

"So, what was your intention? Why did you bring her up here?"

"I just wanted to discuss Kṛṣṇa consciousness with her."

"Don't try it again," said Vibhu. "It's a serious transgression. You had better watch your step. I think I know now why they call you

'Nimāi-nonsense.'"

Nimāi was mortified—not so much by the reprimand from the temple authority as from his own inner shame. Now that his brilliant idea had exploded, he saw it for what it was. It was *māyā*! How had he lost his intelligence like that? He still felt that his sentiments for Sūrya dāsī were not wrong, but he had acted so stupidly out of pride.

Nimāi felt especially bad that he had used Choṭa dāsa to show off before a woman. He coaxed the mouse out once again and made his prostrated obeisances. As usual Choṭa was meek and forgiving. "We all make mistakes," he squeaked.

Nimāi resolved never to act like that again. He would be true and loyal to his friend. He would present Kṛṣṇa consciousness and not behave like an ass.

From that day on Nimāi gave up his ebullient displays of joy. He tried to be sober, grave, and always tolerant. He couldn't do it steadily, but he tried. It was especially difficult when some of the teenage boys called after him in sing-song voices,

"Nimāi the gnome
has got a crush on Sūrya,
Nimāi the gnome
has got a crush on a mouse,
Nimāi the gnome
has no home."

Chapter 3

Nimāi was just finishing his last round of *japa* before going up for a scheduled meeting with Choṭa dāsa. Even while chanting the holy names his mind had raced ahead, preparing for what he would say this morning. He decided to instruct Choṭa on the importance of attentive chanting. He would admit, "I am preaching to you, but I am also preaching to myself." Nimāi liked to keep his relationship with Choṭa open and honest. Their friendship continued to amaze him. He'd never heard, even in scripture, of an ordinary *brahmacārī* conversing with a subhuman creature and instructing him in Kṛṣṇa consciousness. "Why has Kṛṣṇa arranged it so this has happened to me?" Nimāi thought. And sometimes he wondered if it was really very significant. Many devotees were meeting hundreds of humans every day. Although some of the humans were like animals, it was much more significant to preach to the humans. What about the injunction to *tell everyone you meet about* Kṛṣṇa, did that include sub-humans? When Nimāi thought like this it bewildered and discouraged him, so he usually put it aside. "Even if what I am doing is not so significant," Nimāi thought, "it's the preaching field assigned to me."

With a humble sense of his mission Nimāi climbed the stairs to the attic, rehearsing in his mind the lecture that he would deliver in a moment. But his heart leaped when Butch, the temple cat, suddenly brushed past him and sped upstairs into the attic. On hearing the sounds of Nimāi's approach Choṭa had come out from hiding, and no sooner had the white tomcat rushed into the room than he spied the mouse and pounced upon it. Nimāi saw his beloved friend clawed and then popped into the mouth of the cat!

Nimāi shouted and kicked the cat, knocking Butch against the wall which dislodged the mouse from his maw. Butch raised his back and snarled as if to attack Nimāi, who then kicked the cat like a football across the room. With an agonized glance towards Choṭa, Nimāi saw that he was dead.

As the *brahmacārīs* were running up the stairs, the tomcat shrieked and streaked past them. Bhīma and several teenage boys entered the room where Nimāi was sobbing. Tears streamed from his eyes as he knelt holding the tiny body of the mouse.

"The cat got the mouse!" said one of the boys.

Nimāi's pet mouse!"

Get out of here!" Nimāi yelled.

Take it easy," said Bhīma.

Why did you kick Butch?" the teenager who used to be called Kṛṣṇa dāsa but was now known as Carl asked. He gave Nimāi a shove. "Hey Nimāi," he goaded. "Why did you kick Butch?"

With blind grief Nimāi put the mouse aside and jumped to attack

Carl. The two of them locked into a wrestling grip and fell to the floor punching. Carl got in a good sock to Nimāi's eye before more men arrived, including Vibhu dāsa, who separated them. Vibhu demanded an explanation but Nimāi picked up Choṭa's body and pushed past everyone out of the room. He was sobbing like one whose best friend has just died.

Gurudeva was reading *Śrīmad-Bhāgavatam* when the phone rang. It was Vibhu dāsa.

Nimāi is on his way down to your cabin," said Vibhu. "He just created a big scene in the temple—kicked the cat and had a fight with Carl. He's bawling and won't listen to anyone but you, so you have to talk to him right now."

"All right," said Gurudeva, "is there any more background you can give me?"

"That's all I know," said Vibhu. "I think Nimāi is not fit to live in the temple. If you want him to stay, you can take responsibility for him. I mean, he is your disciple."

Gurudeva saw Nimāi dāsa coming down the road, sobbing like a baby. He was carrying a small box.

Gurudeva opened the door to receive him.

"Come on in, Nimāi. Sit down. Tell me what's the matter." Gurudeva took his usual position facing Nimāi and slid the box of Kleenex tissues towards his tearful disciple. Nimāi opened the box he was carrying and placed it on Gurudeva's desk. It contained the body of the mouse lying on its back, its four feet pointing upwards. Gurudeva was not fond of mice, but this was not the time to object to the presence of the corpse. He decided to honor Nimāi's grief and try to give him solace, just as he would to anyone suffering from the death of a loved one.

"What happened?" asked Gurudeva.

Nimāi bawled, "This is the mouse I told you about. He's called Choṭa. He talked to me for three months. I taught him Kṛṣṇa consciousness. He is a spirit soul as good as me, as good as the other devotees. Better! He was more submissive. No one understands!" Gurudeva coaxed his disciple to take a Kleenex. Nimāi blew his nose and swiped at the profuse tears that wouldn't stop coming.

Gurudeva came down from his cushion and sat beside Nimāi. He put his arm around him and gradually calmed him.

"I understand," said Gurudeva. "At least I want to understand. I know that you loved this creature, and from what you told me, you fed it *prasādam* and chanted Hare Kṛṣṇa to it. I respect that. A devotee is supposed to honor all creatures." Gurudeva wanted to be sincere. He would have to go beyond formality if he was to give solace to Nimāi. And he wanted to. As far as Nimāi's claim that the mouse could talk, that still seemed pretty crazy. But his being so touched by the death of the mouse was real. It was *bhakti*. Gurudeva had recently been reading that the *guru* is actually the servant of his disciples. If that was true, then Nimāi was definitely in need of his service and guidance. Gurudeva wanted to give it his best.

But he was also amused at Nimāi's *bhakti*. Nimāi was crying over the death of a mouse as if it was a tragic loss. The mouse was the only "person" Nimāi could love. That he could love only a mouse was unfortunate, and yet there was no denying that he showed genuine compassion for the humble creature.

Nimāi nodded and sniffled. Grieved as he was by the loss, Nimāi was also feeling satisfied by his Gurudeva's affection and counsel. He had never sat like this with his spiritual master or seen Gurudeva so personal. Usually, theirs was only an official relationship, but now what Gurudeva was saying entered Nimāi's consciousness like light into darkness. "This is *guru*!" thought Nimāi. "He is saving me!" With full trust, Nimāi listened for more. The pain of Choṭa's death hurt his heart, but there was something beyond the pain. Gurudeva was speaking higher knowledge.

Gurudeva said, "On occasions in the *Bhāgavatam* where some person is sad over someone's death, great sages like Nārada give them important counsel. That counsel should be used by us in these times. It's not theoretical talk. Nimāi, the real person who you loved has received the full benefit of your speaking to him about Kṛṣṇa, and he has gone on. It wasn't just something that the cat did. Everything is arranged by *karma* and higher providence. 'Those who are wise lament neither for the living nor the dead.'

"So Nimāi, don't be like a foolish cow," Gurudeva tried to physically nudge his disciple into a lighter mood, "who cries and wants to stay by her calf's corpse." They both glanced at the body of the mouse whose mouth was partly open revealing its sharp teeth. But while they were looking, one of its feet twitched, and it gave a faint sigh.

"Choṭa! Gurudeva, did you hear that? He just said, "Rāma!" He's alive!"

Gurudeva had not heard "Rāma!" but the mouse was alive. Nimāi gently picked him up and began feeling his body. "He appears to have broken a couple of legs and his body is crushed," said Nimāi, "but he's coming back to consciousness! He was unconscious!" Nimāi was smiling joyfully.

"Just put him back and let him rest," said Gurudeva. He too was excited and concerned to give the mouse a chance to live. "The best thing is to let him rest."

"Wow! Kṛṣṇa's mercy!" While they were talking, Gurudeva's servant entered and asked if he would take his lunch. Gurudeva said yes and that a plate should be brought for Nimāi.

And so, the *guru* and disciple honored *prasādam* together, talking about Kṛṣṇa's mercy and the unusual turns of providence. Choṭa dāsa was breathing slowly and evenly, although he could not move. Gurudeva even placed a tiny bit of curd *sabjī* on his finger and put it to the mouse's mouth. Choṭa gratefully accepted it. When he saw that, Nimāi almost swooned with bliss. Here was Gurudeva, the most important person in his spiritual life, tending to Choṭa dāsa, who was also a very important person in his life.

Gurudeva had caught some of the contagious *bhakti* of Nimāi for Choṭa. He said that they should not bring Choṭa back to the temple as he would be easy prey for the cat. Gurudeva suggested that the mouse could stay at his cabin during its recuperation. Gurudeva was about to leave in a day or so for a three-month tour. Nimāi could come to the cabin once a day to see how the mouse was doing, but it should be kept completely confidential. They would say that Nimāi was looking after the cabin. Nimāi could give the cabin a paint job, and that would be his pretext for staying there during the day.

Gurudeva was always conscientious to follow his exact daily schedule. He had been caught up in the emotions of Nimāi and the mouse but he still had to prosecute his regular duties, so he told Nimāi to take Choṭa dāsa into the next room and find a place where he could stay. Gurudeva then returned to his desk and the page of *Śrīmad-Bhāgavatam* he had been studying before Nimāi's arrival. He read the verse and began making notes in his study book, but it was impossible to remove his mind from what had just occurred.

Chapter 4

The first few days after the attack by the tomcat, Choṭa dāsa remained in critical condition. Nimāi personally bathed him with a wet sponge; spoon-fed him *prasādam* and encouraged him back to health. The mouse was tolerant. As the days went by, he wanted to walk, and Nimāi fashioned two tiny splints for his broken legs. With hobbling steps Choṭa would walk a few feet and then collapse in pain and exhaustion.

"Keep trying," Nimāi urged him. But sometimes he urged him to rest.

On the pretext of painting Gurudeva's house, Nimāi spent hours daily near Choṭa dāsa and oversaw his recuperation.

Nimāi calculated for Choṭa's benefit how soon it might be before he would be well enough to return to his home at the temple.

The mouse said, "If possible, I don't ever want to return there." He then confided to Nimāi about his family situation. Choṭa said there were no secrets in the mouse community, and as soon as Nimāi had spoken with Choṭa, the other mice knew about it. Choṭa's parents became immediately disturbed when Choṭa told them that he had spoken to a man. First of all, they refused to believe that it was possible for a man to speak to a mouse. And just the thought that their son was on friendly terms with a human was madness as far as they were concerned. Humans were the enemies of mice. They set steel traps and took pleasure in poisoning whole communities. They encouraged the cats. So how could he trust a human?

When Choṭa had explained that this was not an ordinary human but a devotee of Kṛṣṇa, the parents of the mouse laughed at the pitiful naïveté of their son. Neither could they understand what he was saying about "a devotee." Choṭa explained to Nimāi that his family observed a primitive form of religion, but the fame, form, and pastimes of Lord Kṛṣṇa were unknown to them. And when Choṭa had tried to sneak out from home to rendezvous with Nimāi, he had increased their anger. Except for the fact that his parents were very attached to him, Choṭa said he would have been completely disowned. "You're as good as dead," his father had said.

"But my younger brother likes Kṛṣṇa," said Choṭa; his tiny eyes sparkled, "and also one younger cousin." Nimāi was fascinated with the accounts of life in the mouse society but troubled to hear them. It was just a miniature version of human society with the same sectarian prejudices. Nimāi had an idea of how to deal with the situation, but he didn't want to force his idea on Choṭa. "What do you think?" he asked the mouse.

"I would like to rescue my brother and cousin and bring them here," said Choṭa. Nimāi was thrilled with the bold spirit of his friend. He was just about to ask Choṭa if the mice in question were of legal age, but then he thought, "Why should I subjugate myself to the laws of mice?" Nimāi had no scruples about taking action, but he didn't want to push his little friend beyond his faith. Yet it was Choṭa who was pushing for action. He wanted to go back to his community as soon as possible and tell his friends that they had a new place where they could live in freedom and practice Kṛṣṇa consciousness without their parents' restraint. He excitedly petitioned Nimāi, "Prabhu, you can carry us all back to Gurudeva's cabin!"

And so, they hatched their plan in full detail and waited for Choṭa to recover enough to play the leading role. Choṭa told Nimāi that on one occasion when his parents were chastising him, they threatened to get large rats to come and attack Nimāi at night. But both Nimāi and Choṭa doubted that the mice actually had any influence over the rats. "Anyway," said Nimāi, "whatever powers they may have, we will just act in the shelter of Kṛṣṇa. Kṛṣṇa says, 'My devotee will never be vanquished.'"

Only a month after he had been attacked, Choṭa dāsa, although still not fully recovered, insisted that they should go and rescue his friends. They chose daylight hours when the mice were more timid in their movements within the temple. Nimāi released Choṭa in the attic room, and within minutes he had gone down into his old neighborhood and returned with the two "boys." They were bright-eyed, squealing fellows, full of young idealism. Nimāi was moved at how Kṛṣṇa consciousness had spread from himself to Choṭa, and from Choṭa to these others. With full trust they allowed Nimāi to scoop them up and put them in a box. He immediately left the room and all three of them were soon back at Gurudeva's house, where they established what Nimāi called a *brahmacārī āśrama.*

Things were livelier now. Because of the increased numbers and the more ideal circumstances, Nimāi instituted a structured *sādhana* for the mice. He set a standard for early rising, performance of spiritual duties, and avoidance of unseemly behavior, like passing stool anywhere and everywhere.

Of course, Nimāi had established the *āśrama* without asking Gurudeva's permission. It was an emergency, and Gurudeva was away on his tour. He definitely would inform Gurudeva about it, and if they had to move out, they would worry about that when the time came. But he hoped that Gurudeva would allow it. In fact, ever since that wonderful meeting where Gurudeva had consoled Nimāi and fed the mouse, Nimāi had begun to hope that one day the mice would actually speak to Gurudeva and that he would give his full blessings and authorization. That was Nimāi's fondest dream. Especially now that there had been success in his preaching, he began to harbor grand aspirations for spreading Kṛṣṇa consciousness in the animal kingdom. He shared some of these ideas with Choṭa dāsa and the new *bhaktas*, and quoted the verse: "By the grace of the spiritual master, the blind man can see the stars in the sky, a lame man can cross the mountains, and a dumb man can speak. And," he added, "mice can become devotees."

They all cheered, *"Haribol!"*

These were happy days for Nimāi and his followers. He kept their activities carefully under cover and went on with his own duties, incurring a minimum of displeasure from his authorities.

But Nimāi dāsa had doubts. He worried that what he was doing was small-time. It was certainly a miniature world that he was absorbed in. The mice were physically tiny (about five inches long including their tails, and no more than an ounce in weight). Also, their service didn't seem to amount to much. He seemed to be mostly training them to clean up after themselves, to chant a very small number of rounds daily, and to learn only the basic philosophy. And the two new mice, although sincere and happy to be living as *brahmacārīs*, were not of the same caliber as Choṭa. They were rather frivolous. So, what was the preaching value of all these activities?

By contrast, the devotees at the temple were preparing themselves for the austerity of the Christmas marathon. Some of the men would be traveling for two months in a van, distributing books in the cities. And some of the householders were going out to sell paintings in an effort to raise large amounts of money, both for their family needs and for meeting the year-end temple expenses. Vibhu Prabhu had asked Nimāi to go on the book distribution party, but Nimāi had refused. He hadn't accepted such austerities so far in his devotional career and he didn't think he could begin now. Vibhu had then asked Nimāi to join with a householder couple selling paintings, which would also require traveling for a couple of months. Again, Nimāi had said he could not do it. He had agreed, however, to take on extra duties at the temple while most of the devotees were on the road. Nimāi admired the men who went out to preach. He was disappointed with himself and his inability to surrender. Nimāi thought, "Am I training up Choṭa and the other mice in the same unsurrendered attitude that I have?" The small-time and inward nature of the mouse *āśrama* troubled Nimāi, and yet he did not see how he could express these thoughts to Choṭa. He didn't want the mouse to get an inferiority complex. Nimāi knew how depressing *that* could get.

Choṭa had become quite sensitive to the different moods of Nimāi. Sensing that something was troubling his teacher, he inquired about it.

Nimāi confessed, "Sometimes I think I am not qualified to lead you. I am not a preacher. Beyond what I can teach you, there is a whole realm of Kṛṣṇa consciousness, which encompasses the bold missionary spirit that is the essence of Lord Caitanya and His disciplic succession. Nowadays, there is heavy pressure for devotees to take part in preaching if they want to please their spiritual masters. But since I can't take that pressure myself, I'm afraid to put it on you. The result is I am not so enlivened when I think of how none of us here are doing big service. Do you understand?"

"We mice are very little devotees," Choṭa said. "We know that it's only by your kindness and willingness to put up with us that we know anything about Kṛṣṇa consciousness at all. Yes, it's a fact that we can't do much, but there is another way to look at it."

Choṭa then began to tell Nimāi the inside story of a mouse's existence. He said that the life of a mouse is very fearful and precarious. "We are always living in fear of a predator. House mice, who usually live in close association with human beings, can come out only at night, and even then, we risk our lives just to get our basic meals. We never know when we are going to be pounced upon by a cat, or when the next step we take will set off a trap that snaps our neck. And the most pleasing foods, like oats or peanut butter, are often mixed with deadly poison. And then, even if we do manage to escape all these dangers, our lifespan is very short. We only live for a few years.

"Now," said Choṭa, "I have learned that life is meant for something more than eating, sleeping, mating, and defending, but what kind of service can I actually render in this condemned body? By your grace, I have learned the art of devotional service to the Supreme Lord Kṛṣṇa. Fortunately, from what you have taught us—if I understand it correctly—it's not the bigness of the service that Kṛṣṇa appreciates, but the devotion in which it is done."

Choṭa usually spoke in smaller bursts, and both he and Nimāi had been kneeling, but now Nimāi sat back, as he did in *Bhāgavatam* class, and listened with appreciation.

"Besides," said Choṭa, "by your words you have also instilled in us a preaching spirit. I simply repeated your words and now two of my kinfolk have joined us, and other mice at the temple are also chanting and talking about Kṛṣṇa. Maybe you think three is small. But if you desire, you could also introduce us to a more ambitious preaching program. There are mice everywhere!" squeaked Choṭa. "In every house, restaurant, factory, warehouse, and barn, as well as in the grain fields and sand dunes, you'll find mice. They are at least as numerous as human beings. Couldn't Kṛṣṇa consciousness be introduced everywhere?"

"I am not sure," said Nimāi. "I mean yes, we could expand our program. What you said about the spirit of devotion and the difficulties of devotional service in a mouse body, I never realized that. I think I have offended you by saying that you were small-time. Please accept my obeisances." Nimāi knelt down to make prostrated obeisances and the mice reciprocated.

"It is you to whom *we* must make obeisances," said Choṭa.

"Yes, you delivered us," said Choṭa's brother. "We were living in a dark hole."

"We were three blind mice," said Choṭa's cousin.

"We are eternally indebted to you," said Choṭa. "At least we think your activities with us are definitely not 'small-time.'"

"It is not small-time," said Nimāi. "That was just my foolishness. The service that we are doing right here in this *āśrama* is being seen and appreciated by Kṛṣṇa. There is no doubt about it! At the same time, we can also increase it."

This discussion had a serious effect upon Nimāi. From that day on he began to appreciate more that the mice were undergoing rigorous austerities just to perform their basic *sādhana*. In his mind, Nimāi began to liken them to the Hare Kṛṣṇa devotees in Russia in the days of the Soviet Union, who risked their lives just to gather together and chant or distribute Prabhupāda's books. Of course, the mice were nowhere as great as the human devotees. But in their own way—just like the spider who worked for Lord Rāma—they could be very pleasing to the Lord. Nimāi sensed unlimited opportunity and benefit for the mice, as well as for himself. He wanted to put aside his neurotic scruples and help them to the best of his ability. Their spunky spirit would help him to become more surrendered.

Nimāi changed not only in his dealings with the mice, but also in his dealings with the devotees. He increased his efforts to surrender, at least in little ways that were within his power. When the teenage boys began to tease him and call him names, Nimāi thought of the bravery of the mice, and it enabled him to take this teasing as something sweet. By not becoming ruffled at the teasing, Nimāi could offer the austerity to Lord Kṛṣṇa.

Nimāi looked forward to opportunities where he could counter his pet peeves with an attitude of acceptance and devotion. He took a more submissive approach in his exchanges with Vibhu, and tried to see him as a representative of Kṛṣṇa and the spiritual master. As the winter progressed and he had to sometimes work outside in freezing weather, he endured the cold as pleasurable, thinking, "My dear Lord Kṛṣṇa, please accept my service."

As the Christmas marathon approached Nimāi had to do the work of several other devotees, spending extra time cleaning in the kitchen, mopping the temple floor, and staying up late to tend to the furnace. He also had to drive into town to buy supplies and help with milking the cows in the barn. But he did it all without grumbling. "The mice have taught me a great secret," he thought, "if I can only remember it. Kṛṣṇa just wants our devotion."

Chapter 5

Vibhu Prabhu again asked Nimāi dāsa to go on traveling *saṅkīrtana* for the Christmas marathon.

"If you could just be the driver of the van," Vibhu requested, "and do back-up services for the book distributors, that would be a great help. It would free one of the other *brahmacārīs* to do book distribution. You could drive and do things like purchase and prepare *prasādam* and be the treasurer and do the laundry. What do you think?"

In his new mood of surrender, Nimāi agreed to do it. "I have never lived outside of the temple," he thought, "but that's what boldness is—to just try."

"Let me think about it overnight," said Nimāi. "I'll tell you for sure tomorrow." In the evening, while distributing hot milk in tiny *loṭās* to the mice, Nimāi asked them what they thought of traveling *saṅkīrtana*. The two new *bhaktas* were goofing off and spilling their milk, but it was really only Choṭa dāsa from whom Nimāi expected a serious response.

"It sounds exciting," said Choṭa, looking up from his milk with a white-stained snout. "But what would we actually do?"

"Well, I am supposed to be the driver," said Nimāi, "so most of the time we'd just be on our own. I suppose you'd all have to live in some kind of box or cage. I'll tell the other men that you are coming along as my pets."

From this initial description of traveling *saṅkīrtana*, Choṭa's brother and cousin looked frightened.

Nimāi continued, "Sometimes we will park the van in a campground or a parking lot while the men are distributing books. I'll run errands during the day for them. And then sometimes we will stay at the homes of friends and life members of Kṛṣṇa consciousness."

"If we went to people's houses," said Choṭa, "then maybe I could visit the mouse communities there and tell them about Kṛṣṇa."

And so Choṭa and Nimāi discussed all the managerial details and spiritual implications of their going on traveling *saṅkīrtana*. They also asked the newcomers to honestly speak their minds on whether they wanted to go or not. The brother and cousin of Choṭa said that it sounded a bit "tough," but if Choṭa Prabhu thought that they could do it, they were willing to try.

"Well, that's exactly how I feel about it," said Nimāi. "If it gets too much for me, or for any of you, then we can just come back. Although I don't think the other devotees would be very pleased if we did that."

On this occasion the new mice asked Nimāi if he could give them devotee names. "The names I give," said Nimāi, "will not be your initiated names. They are just spiritual nicknames. Because you both came to Kṛṣṇa consciousness together, and because you seem to me to be like twins, I'll give you the names Yamala and Arjuna, which are the names of the twin trees that were directly touched by baby Kṛṣṇa."

Afterwards, Nimāi and his little group celebrated the new names by drinking sweet milk. The young mice drunk so much that they became intoxicated and fell asleep. While they slept Nimāi made a wooden box, about three feet by two feet with caging and plenty of air holes. He finished it off by stuffing it with plenty of shredded paper, according to Choṭa's directions. This would be the traveling *āśrama* for the mice. "You'll be a bit cooped up," said Nimāi, "but the men will also be cooped up in the van. That's the austerity of travel."

Nimāi reported back to Vibhu that he was willing to be the *saṅkīrtana* driver on the condition that he be permitted to take his pet mice with him in a box. Vibhu's eyes rolled when he heard that, but he was desperate to get another book distributor out on *saṅkīrtana*. If this was what it took to get Nimāi to surrender, then why not?

But some of the *brahmacārīs* strongly objected.

Vīra dāsa said, "It's bogus! They're filthy creatures. I hate mice! I am not going to sleep in the same van with them."

Dhṛṣṭaketu dāsa, who was the leading book distributor, also objected. "What if one of them gets out of the box?" he asked. "I don't want one of those things running along my leg at night! It's weird and has nothing to do with Kṛṣṇa consciousness!"

Bhīma dāsa was the second biggest book distributor. He also thought that the pet mice were *māyā*, but he shared Vibhu Prabhu's reasoning about doing the needful, and he also had tolerance for Nimāi's eccentricities. Bhīma told the other men, "It takes all kinds of people to form a Kṛṣṇa consciousness movement." He reminded them of how Śrīla Prabhupāda had tolerated so much when he first came to America, sometimes abandoning the strict rules and regulations of a *sannyāsī* in order to preach. Prabhupāda had even lived for a while in an apartment with cats, and he had to put his *sattvic* food in the same refrigerator with meat. Why couldn't they also tolerate a little inconvenience to push on the *saṅkīrtana* movement?

"Tell that to the knucklehead," said Vīra dāsa. "Why should we adjust to his madness? He should just drive and give up his stupid attachment to rodents."

"Of course, you are right," said Bhīma. "But devotional service is voluntary. Nimāi said he'll come with us only if his pets can come also."

Eventually Bhīma dāsa prevailed, and the men accepted it for the ultimate sacrifice of *saṅkīrtana*. They were prepared to face hundreds of insults daily from the nondevotees when they attempted to give them Prabhupāda's books; they were already enduring freezing cold weather, threats of violence, and police arrests, so they figured they could also tolerate Nimāi dāsa, who was, after all, a kind of devotee.

And so the party of six men and three mice set out in the Dodge Ram van for a scheduled month and a half of traveling *saṅkīrtana*. The first day away from the temple was difficult for the whole *saṅkīrtana* party, but Nimāi and the mice were particularly unaccustomed to it. They all slept overnight in the van at a national park. In early morning they took cold showers in an unheated bathroom where the temperature was below freezing. Bhīma dāsa was in charge of the party. He arranged a morning schedule that allowed two hours for *japa* and half an hour for *Bhāgavatam* class, after which breakfast was to be served immediately. Then the men would go out to distribute books. Since Nimāi was the cook, he had to spend most of *japa* period, as well as class time, preparing a full meal of *dāl*, rice and *sabjī* for six men. He had to cook outside the van, setting the Coleman stove, vegetables, and pots of water on a picnic table. The first morning, his fingers became so cold he could hardly feel them. Nimāi's mind was screaming to him, "I can't do this! This is too hard!"

Ever since Nimāi had met Choṭa, he had been able to find solace in their talks, especially at difficult moments. But now that wasn't possible. Although the men had reluctantly agreed that the pet mice could come along for the ride, none of them realized that these mice were actually practicing Kṛṣṇa consciousness and that they often talked with Nimāi. It remained a mystery to both Nimāi and the mice, why the mice could communicate only with Nimāi and not with other humans. For the most part, Nimāi and the mice preferred it this way. But even if they had wanted to include others, it was not possible. At least for now, theirs was a confidential relationship known only to themselves—and it was their fervent hope that their relationship was also known to Lord Kṛṣṇa. Because of the confidentiality of their friendship Nimāi could not speak with the mice, either to help them out or to derive benefit from their friendship. He was allowed to be with them only in ways that would not seem too outrageous to the other men. He could perform only minimal maintenance of their needs and show minimum affection, or else he would risk incurring the disgust of devotees like Vīra and Dhṛṣṭaketu. But when Dhṛṣṭaketu saw Nimāi cleaning out the mouse *āśrama* while singing Hare Kṛṣṇa, even he made a remark of begrudging approval.

"I guess they are not ordinary mice," said Dhṛṣṭaketu. "Otherwise, how could they be hearing Hare Kṛṣṇa and taking Kṛṣṇa *prasādam*?"

"Yeah," chuckled Vīra, "maybe they were human devotees in their last life and they had some big falldown."

"You better be careful," said Bhīma dāsa to Nimāi. "If you think too much about these mice, you will think of them at the time of death like Mahārāja Bhārata, and then you could come back as a mouse and go out on traveling *saṅkīrtana*."

In this way the men derived some comic relief from the otherwise ridiculous and inconvenient presence of the mouse *āśrama*. But as long as Nimāi performed his austerities along with them, they respected him and did not push their teasing too far. And they appreciated Nimāi's simple but decent cooking, especially his hot buttered *capātīs* and strongly spiced *dāl*. Nimāi was happy to be with such highly qualified devotees and to be accepted by them. Although he was suffering, in another sense he was experiencing the highest state of Kṛṣṇa consciousness he could ever remember. The book distributors were very dear to Lord Caitanya because they took all risks to carry the message to the conditioned souls, as desired by the Lord and His pure devotees. They were like frontline soldiers in the battle against *māyā*. Even when they teased him or sometimes behaved not exactly like pure devotees, Nimāi always tried to remember their exalted position. He took great pleasure in serving them.

After breakfast everyone was very busy, and Bhīma dāsa gave Nimāi a list of his duties for the day. It took Nimāi over an hour to wash all the pots and clean up from breakfast, and no sooner was that done than they had to break camp and drive into the city. Nimāi dropped each man off at his designated spot, either a busy parking lot or in front of a supermarket or shopping mall, where they would distribute books all day. Nimāi focused on remembering where each spot was so that he didn't get lost when he returned in a few hours to see if they needed to replenish their book stock or needed any other assistance. Along with the books, he would bring each man a lunch of juice and fruit. After making the lunch rounds, he would somehow find time to do the book-keeping, carefully tallying the numbers of Prabhupāda's books that had been distributed and count the money collected. Washing everyone's clothes at the laundromat had to fit into his day as well. Carried along in the swift current of his duties, Nimāi had no time to spend with the mice. He hardly had time to even think of them.

Nimāi had hurriedly purchased groceries for the next morning's cooking and was driving on a highway to deliver more books to the *saṅkīrtana* men, when he thought that he had better stop to see how the mice were doing. So, he pulled the van off to a rest area and opened their box. The little ones, Yamala and Arjuna, were shivering together in a far corner. They seemed to have reverted to animal consciousness and they cringed when Nimāi reached to touch them. Choṭa said "Hare Kṛṣṇa" on seeing his friend, but he looked wan and cold. Only by Choṭa's talking to the other mice in their native mouse language did Yamala and Arjuna gradually look up and assume a slightly receptive position for greeting Nimāi.

"How is it going?" Nimāi asked.

Choṭa admitted it was difficult, and Nimāi admitted that it was difficult for him too. They spoke of how they might improve things. Nimāi had bought some little woolen pouches to be used as sleeping bags. The mice laughed, since they were accustomed to fending for themselves with whatever nature provided. But maybe the pouches would help. They especially liked the fact that Nimāi had thought of them. After all, their Kṛṣṇa consciousness depended on encouragement from Nimāi. He sensed again, with a greater awareness, the responsibility he had taken on in convincing these creatures to dedicate their lives to self-realization. At first, he had thought that it would be a simple thing to convince them that they were not actually mice but pure spirit souls, and then the rest would be up to them. But since they were so limited, it seemed he would have to guide them closely for a considerable while. "Sooner or later," thought Nimāi, "they will have to get fixed up to be able to serve on their own, in separation."

Nimāi revived the mice with the warmth of his Kṛṣṇa consciousness so that they became more cheerful and joking. Then suddenly he remembered his own difficulties. "This is too much," he sighed. "I'm on the go all day long and I haven't even finished chanting my rounds. I don't think I can last. It's too much."

"Just keep trying," said Choṭa. "It's very important for you to do the back-up work for the *saṅkīrtana* party."

"Yeah," said Nimāi, "it's ecstatic. I finally feel like I'm part of Lord Caitanya's movement. Those book distributors are like great heroes. Do you realize that if somebody takes a book, Prabhupāda said that his life could become perfect by reading one page? Now I can better see that the *karmīs* are just rushing back and forth completely in *māyā*. At any moment somebody could die and then descend to a lower form of life. The book distributors are tossing them a lifeline."

"But how are we part of the *saṅkīrtana* movement?" asked Yamala dāsa. His question expressed doubt, but because it was the first thoughtful question that he had ever asked Nimāi, Nimāi was very pleased.

"You are also part of *saṅkīrtana*. Don't you feel that Choṭa? Tell Yamala."

"Yes, I do," said Choṭa. "By supporting the frontline preachers, Nimāi Prabhu feels that he is part of the *saṅkīrtana*. So, if we can serve him, then we are also connected."

Arjuna, who had seemed the most fearful of the three, moved into the midst of his brothers and asked, "But how are we serving you?"

"To be honest," said Nimāi, "I need your association, especially Choṭa's, because he helps pick me up when I'm about to fall into *māyā*. It's a mutual loving exchange. And it's not that you have to serve me. I am just trying to help you to serve Kṛṣṇa. Your austerity, or *tapasya*, is to remain in higher consciousness even when you are in the dark and cold of this box when there is nothing else to do but chant. So far you haven't been able to do that, have you?"

The mice all looked down shyly, admitting that they had seriously reverted to lower consciousness ever since they had come into the van. But they would try again. Nimāi had to cut their meeting short. He closed the box, drove back onto the highway and soon reached Lakṣmaṇa dāsa, although he was fifteen minutes late.

Chapter 6

By 7:00 P.M. Nimāi dāsa had picked up the last book distributor. He then drove the van out of the city to a national park. While the men sat close together on the wooden platform in the rear of the van talking over the day's experiences, Nimāi carefully served each of them bread, *sabjī*, and cups of hot milk. As they took *prasādam*, Nimāi tabulated the number of books each man had distributed. It had been a good day, especially for Dhṛṣṭaketu Prabhu who had distributed fifty *Bhagavad-gītās* and ten *Śrīmad-Bhāgavatams*.

"I met this far out couple today," said Dhṛṣṭaketu. "It happened as soon as I got out there. I stacked about ten *Bhāgavatams* on a newspaper stand outside the store and went to the bathroom in one of the restaurants. When I returned, I saw a man and woman looking at one of the *Bhāgavatams*."

As soon as Dhṛṣṭaketu began talking, Nimāi reached down, picked up the mouse *āśrama*, and placed it on top of the platform.

"What are you doing?" said Dhṛṣṭaketu.

"Nothin'," said Nimāi, ignoring the fact that the mouse cage was now in the midst of the men.

"You're not going to let them out, are you?" asked Vīra dāsa.

"Of course not," said Nimāi.

"He just wants the mice to hear the *saṅkīrtana* nectar, right Nimāi?" said Bhīma.

Nimāi said, "According to Śrīla Prabhupāda, even a cockroach in the wall of the temple can benefit by hearing Hare Kṛṣṇa."

Bhīma Prabhu allowed Nimāi his whimsy and the other men let it go.

Dhṛṣṭaketu resumed his story. "So, this couple had taken one of the books and walked a distance away from the stand. The man was wearing a blue pinstriped, three-piece suit, and the woman was also wearing a business suit. They both were carrying briefcases. They looked as if they were feeling a little guilty about picking up such a nice hardbound book, so I approached them and said, 'The book you are holding in your hand is the *Śrīmad-Bhāgavatam*. It's one of the first volumes in a sixty-volume series.'

"'Do you know anything about it?' the man asked me, and the woman also looked interested.

"'Yes, a little bit,' I said. This *Bhāgavatam* begins with Mahārāja Parīkṣit who was emperor of the world at the time. He got news that he was going to die in a week, so he approached a great saintly person, Śukadeva Gosvāmī, and asked him, 'What is the duty of a person who is about to die?' I then showed them the picture of Mahārāja Parīkṣit with his folded hands in front of Śukadeva Gosvāmī. 'This *Bhāgavatam* is what Śukadeva spoke,' I said. 'He spoke continuously for seven days, and it's all recorded here.'

"Then the woman asked me, 'And what did he say?'

"I told them, 'Well, you would have to read it for yourself! But to cut it short, Śukadeva Gosvāmī told Parīkṣit that the goal of life is to render devotional service unto God. And in these pages of the *Bhāgavatam* it is elaborately explained how to render service to God. It has been presented very nicely by the author, A. C. Bhaktivedanta Swami Prabhupāda. He is a renowned scholar.'

"Then they asked me who I was. I told them that I was a member of the International Society for Krishna Consciousness, which was founded by Śrīla Prabhupāda. I encouraged them to read the books and if they had any questions, they could write to me. I wrote my name and address on the inside of the book. They wanted to talk more, but I knew they had to rush. Then the man said, 'I hope you don't mind if I offer you something for this book.' I said I didn't. He said he wanted another copy."

The men in the van were delighted. Nimāi was not only delighted but thrilled to be in their company.

Dhṛṣṭaketu continued, "So I was about to go back to the newsstand to get another book, but the guy beat me to it. In the meantime, I was telling the lady how we live a monastic life, and how we have temples around the world. I asked her to visit one of the temples and showed her the addresses at the back of the book. The man returned and paid me for both books. Then before he left, he asked, 'What do they call you?'

"I said, 'My name is Dhṛṣṭaketu dāsa.'

"He said, 'What is your title?'

"I was a little embarrassed, but I said, 'His Grace.'"

Bhima guffawed, "His Divine Grace Śrīman Dhṛṣṭaketu Prabhu!"

"Just listen to this!" said Dhrstaketu. "The man took my hand and bowed down from his waist a few times and said, 'Thank you your Grace, thank you your Grace.' And the woman did the same thing!"

"That sounds like one for the believe-it-or-not book," said Bhīma dāsa.

Nimāi went around with second cups of milk and more bread, and everyone took some.

Vīra said, "I met three Catholic Fathers today, dressed in black with little white collars. They all seemed to be about forty years old, but the short one in the middle seemed to be a little more hip. I greeted them like I usually do, 'How are you doing? I consider you to be gentlemen of God, servants of God,' and I folded my hands. Right away the middle one said, 'Yes, yes, we are servants of God. What are you doing?' He was antagonistic from the beginning. I said, 'We're passing out our books. Are you familiar with them? This is the *Bhagavad-gītā*.' He said, 'Oh! You are Hare Kṛṣṇas? No, we don't want that.' But the Father on the right said, 'Oh! *Bhagavad-gītā*? Yes, I am interested in that book. I have been interested to know what you believe in.' I said, 'As you know, God is the Supreme Person, and we all have a relationship with Him. The *Bhagavad-gītā* explains how that relationship has to be taken up by everyone, whether he be Hindu, Muslim, Christian, or whatever. In this book Kṛṣṇa is speaking to His pure devotee Arjuna, and explaining to him how he is not this body but the soul within the body. The duty of every individual is to surrender to the Supreme and go back to the kingdom of God.' The other two Fathers walked off. They didn't want anything to do with it. But this one on the right side, he was quiet, so I was really just talking to him. But that short one was bitchy. He kept saying, 'No, no, we don't want that!'

"I concentrated on the quiet one and said, 'Different scholars have praised our books, and we simply try to encourage people to read them.'

"He said, 'Okay, thank you.'

"As you know we don't sell them, but we do take contributions so that we can continue distributing our books."

Vīra continued, "It was a difficult show because the one guy was really upset. I mentioned our regulative principles to the quiet one and the short one snapped back, 'Well! We are celibate too!' But then he took out a cigarette and bit it defiantly. I couldn't believe it, right there he took out a cigarette! Anyway, the friendly one was smiling, and he took the *Gītā* and gave a donation."

"Haribol!" cheered the *saṅkīrtana* devotees.

Nimāi glanced furtively at the cage behind him. They could say what they liked; he knew the mice were hearing. It wasn't the duty of the *saṅkīrtana* men to know or believe that the mice could actually hear and understand, and Nimāi didn't resent their skepticism, but at the very least, the mice should be given the opportunity to hear.

Bhīma dāsa said, "A man approached me today and straight off asked me for a *Bhagavad-gītā*. I started explaining to him that it was the science of the soul and the relationship of the soul to God, who is the Supreme Soul. But he was in a real hurry. He was with two other business people who were women. They were dressed very professionally. I was sad to think that he had shown some interest in the *Bhagavad-gītā* but didn't have time to talk. In fact, the two women were already walking ahead. He offered me ten dollars and then he said, 'You know, I was a devotee years ago. My name is Narayana. I want to present this *Bhagavad-gītā* to my companions. I'm sorry I can't talk with you now, but good luck. *Haribol!!*' Then he rushed back to the two women, and while I looked on from a distance, he presented the book to one of them, opened it, and apparently explained what it was about. It all happened so quickly. It made me think that devotional service never stops. Once our devotional spirit has been awakened then no matter what we do, Kṛṣṇa makes arrangements for us to keep rendering service unto Him. I mean, what nondevotee would think of giving someone the valuable gift of Kṛṣṇa consciousness? But this man still wanted to distribute books to his friends."

As soon as Bhima dāsa finished, Ranchor Prabhu began talking. Nimāi served more helpings of *prasādam*, but most of them refused to take more. He kept trying until the men forcibly put their hands over their plates to stop him.

"I was standing on a busy corner of the shopping mall," said Ranchor, "distributing a book to an old soldier. Along comes this guy; I think he was a pilot or something. He looked official anyway, walking between another man and a woman. He shouted out to the soldier, 'Don't take that book! He's ripping you off!' I said, 'That's not true!' He responded by maintaining that I wasn't allowed to be there. I said, 'That's another lie! I have as much right to be here as he does. And I'm not ripping anyone off. I am just presenting him with one of my books. How dare you say that I have no right to do that!' He smirked and replied that he said what he said just because he felt like saying it! I said, 'Well, you're a liar!'"

"Wow!" said Dhṛṣṭaketu. "Fired up! You really let him have it."

"You are lucky he didn't punch you out for talking like that," said Bhīma.

"I couldn't help myself," said Ranchor, "when the guy bragged that I didn't make the sale because of him, I shot back that he was afraid to explore the subject matter of the books in any depth. He snarled, 'I *know* what's in those books. I've watched you guys ripping people off for years.' I challenged, 'No! You are afraid to hear about what's in these books. You're afraid that what you read might dull your passion for material sense enjoyment. If you're really not afraid, just stand there and listen for a moment. I'll blow your mind with the truth of what's actually in these books.'

"So, then this pilot, or whatever he was, said, 'You are just into it for the money!' That really got me mad and so I laid into him. I said, 'We're not into it for money, but we're not shy to ask for a donation to help with the printing costs. But that isn't the problem. The real problem is that you are afraid to discuss these books because you're envious of what we are doing! But in spite of that, I'm still willing to be your friend. Just take a brief moment to listen.' He said, 'Nah, I have to go.' He started to walk away, but before he left, I asked him his name. He told me his name was John and I introduced myself. 'I'm Hari. Happy to have made your acquaintance.'

"Ten minutes later the same man came back, walking between two women. As he passed, he called out to me, 'Hey Hari, did you get any more books out?' 'Not yet,' I replied, 'but it's going to happen. Are you ready to talk to me yet, or are you still afraid?'"

Nimāi laughed with appreciation. He was trying to remain very quiet, but he couldn't help himself. "I didn't know you were so strong," he said to Ranchor.

Ranchor continued, "So the lady says, 'Go on John; talk to him. Talk to him.' He says, 'Nah,' and they walked on down the other way and into a bar. About half an hour later, they came back by me again. John came over and said, 'Actually, you know, I'm sorry.' I said, 'I'm sorry too. I didn't want to speak to you harshly but I felt that what you were saying was wrong and if I didn't speak up, you would just go on thinking the way you did without clearing up your doubts. But I can tell you're a nice person.' Then the lady came up and began asking me about Prabhupāda's books. I said, 'You've seen us around. We are here to tell people to become lovers of God. We believe in the simple truth that everyone is a servant of God, and it's our duty to take up our relationship with Him. Whether we like it or not, that's the purpose of life—to reestablish our relationship with God. So, I am going to stand on this corner and pass out these books to anyone who will take them. If no one takes them, I'll still be here, because that's my duty.'

"Then the woman said, 'Let me see that book.' So, I gave her a *Gītā*. Then John said, 'You know, I like what you guys are doing. I met a bad guy here once, but in general you don't give anyone trouble. I have been watching you. It's just been a bad day, and I figured I'd let off some steam.' She says, 'These pictures are beautiful, John! I want this book!' The guy says, 'No, come on!' 'No,' she says, 'I want this book!' He says, 'Hari, can you believe it? She wants this book! What are you going to charge me for this book? I can't believe it. I can't buy this book!' I said, 'I can't sell you this book. I'm glad she likes the book, but I can't sell this book to you. Even if you gave me a million. He said, 'No, no, what do you get for these things? I see you ripping off the soldiers, what do you get, five? Ten?' I said, 'Well, we get a lot of tens.' He says, 'I'll give you five.'"

"*Haribol!*" arose from the devotees.

Bhīma ended the talking by 8:30 P.M. The only light was the dim interior bulb of the van. They sat on their sleeping bags and read silently. Nimāi placed the mouse cage back under the platform, trying to avoid making the slightest noise. But as he pushed the box out of sight, the devotees could hear lively squeaking.

Chapter 7

Gurudeva was at the ISKCON center in Puerto Rico where a two-day conference of animal rights groups was being hosted by ISKCON. Two hundred international animal rights delegates were attending, living in tents on the twenty acres of the ISKCON property and receiving pure vegetarian *prasādam* from Govinda's restaurant. The devotees were blissful, but they had to work hard to make the program run smoothly. Gurudeva had been invited as one of the speakers. ISKCON's public relations minister and other interested devotees, including special cooks, had also flown in for the event.

The devotees had constructed an outdoor stage, installed a sound system, and spread hundreds of folding chairs on the lawn. This was the scene for the main lecturing. Different groups had set up tables with their books and propaganda. On the first day of the event after several persons had delivered lectures, the leader of the coalition for animal rights groups introduced Gurudeva by announcing, "So far, we have heard the facts and statistics about cruelty to animals and some suggestions for political action. Now let's hear the spiritual side."

Gurudeva began with obeisances to his spiritual master and then quoted the *Bhagavad-gītā* verse:

vidyā-vinaya-sampanne
brāhmaṇe gavi hastini
śuni caiva śva-pāke ca
paṇḍitāḥ sama-darśinaḥ

"The humble sages, by virtue of true knowledge, see with equal vision a learned and gentle brāhmaṇa, a cow, an elephant, a dog and a dog-eater [outcaste]."

— *Bhagavad-gītā 5.18*

He pointed out the need for analytical knowledge as a foundation to animal rights. The animals are as much living beings as are humans, and *all* living beings are pure spirit soul equal in their nature. If a human being unnecessarily tortures or kills any living creature, he will be subject to the laws of karma. Gurudeva gradually injected the idea that there should be a theistic basis to animal rights and not just well-intentioned vague sentiment. The ultimate reason for recognition and protection of the rights of all living beings is that we are all sons and daughters of the Supreme Father, and the Supreme Personality of Godhead does not allow His so-called intelligent sons and daughters to slaughter innocent creatures on the grounds that non-humans are less intelligent or have no souls. Gurudeva had carefully prepared for this talk by gathering whatever he could find from Prabhupāda's preaching on the subject and drawing from the verses of the *Śrīmad-Bhāgavatam*. He presented the knowledge in a form that he hoped the audience would accept. He concluded with a resounding *Hare Kṛṣṇa!* and thanks for listening. There was a moment of silence and then a burst of strong applause.

Being one of the senior devotees, Gurudeva was expected to socialize as much as possible. Most of the devotees were engaged in the logistics of the big event. They were driving nonstop to the airport to pick up guests, acting as stewards by conducting the attendees to their temporary living quarters on the temple grounds and familiarizing them with the program schedule. Others had been working all night setting up tents and making sure that water and other necessities were available. Many were cooking. Only a few devotees were expected to meet with the animal rights representatives for more extended talks.

Gurudeva had done his share for a few hours and then retreated to his tent, which offered some welcome seclusion. The preaching was rewarding but tiring. He was sitting on his cot chanting to reach his minimum quota of *japa* when his secretary interrupted to inform him that his disciple, Nimāi dāsa, had phoned from somewhere in Pennsylvania. Nimāi had said it was urgent that he speak with Gurudeva ASAP. He had requested an appointment to talk to Gurudeva "just for five minutes." Gurudeva's secretary said, "I advised him to write a letter but he said, 'I don't know if I can last that long. Why can't I speak to my spiritual master?' He sounded a little bit hysterical."

Gurudeva sighed but agreed and told his secretary to try to arrange a time when he could use the phone. That would not be easy since there was only one phone located in the temple president's office, and it was always swarming with delegates making long-distance calls. It was Gurudeva's practice to avoid such phone calls, even when disciples threatened that they might bloop unless their guru spoke to them personally. But, by coincidence, Gurudeva had been thinking of Nimāi at the moment his secretary had come to tell him that Nimāi was phoning, and so he thought he should respond.

Nimāi had also come to his mind earlier in the day when he'd been speaking to Flora, an animal rights representative from Santo Domingo. She had been telling him that she appreciated his lecture, especially the part where he said that animals are as good as humans, and we should consider all material bodies to be just like clothing that covers the real self. Flora had significant personal knowledge of the ability of animals to communicate with people. She considered their ability to communicate as proof that there is an intelligent self within all creatures. She told Gurudeva about a dog named Strongheart, who had been able to communicate with people through telepathy and inform them how they, in turn, could commune with him. She said she knew a man who lived in the desert who used to have all kinds of animals coming and staying with him. He told her that the way to communicate with animals was to stop thinking about them as dogs or pigs and to understand that "somebody is there inside."

Flora had spoken to Gurudeva in Spanish, and so he wasn't sure if he was getting all the details right through the translator. Also, Flora was very effusive and fluttery, and Gurudeva hadn't been so comfortable during the chat, although he was interested. Flora had gone on to say that if people could stop being arrogant and cocky, they could actually allow the "channels" to clear and be able to receive messages telepathically from animals. She enthused, "It's a very rewarding experience. It convinces you that there is a further dimension of intelligent life. If you can actually communicate with them, then you know that this is a living entity with a soul standing in front of you, although it may be wearing an animal suit."

The alliance between the animal rights people and the Kṛṣṇa devotees was intriguing, but Gurudeva reserved his judgment as to whether Flora's telepathic communications were actually true. It could be true, and he especially liked it when she said humans were too puffed up and therefore not interested in communicating with the lower species. But Gurudeva thought that even if this were true, it didn't seem to be of such crucial importance. We already know from the Vedic literatures that animals are spirit souls, and therefore they shouldn't be killed. They should be allowed to live out their natural life cycle in their preferred habitat. Animals can be given *prasādam* whenever possible, but the devotees' main purpose should be to focus on establishing relationships with other humans. The human race is the main target for the distribution of Lord Caitanya's *saṅkīrtana.* In Kali-yuga the human populace is hard enough to reach, let alone the animal kingdom! Sadly, sometimes it almost requires mystic potency to be able to connect with an embodied human being as so many are behaving on the animal platform. Case in point, on one occasion when Śrīla Prabhupāda heard that a fashionable clique in Manhattan was eating human fetuses, he declared, "Then we are preaching to animals!"

"Hello, Gurudeva?"

It was Nimāi on the phone. After several unsuccessful attempts Nimāi and Gurudeva had finally connected. Gurudeva had been to the office several times only to find the phone busy, and even now the room was filled with a lot of chatter.

"Please accept my humble obeisances, Gurudeva," said Nimāi. "I've been out on *saṅkīrtana* for four days, and I don't think I can take it any longer. What should I do?"

"Did you speak with Vibhu Prabhu?" said Gurudeva. He put his hand against his left ear so that he could hear Nimāi better.

"Yes, I spoke to Vibhu on the phone. He said that he was disturbed with me. He said it would mean a loss of hundreds of books distributed and hundreds of dollars that wouldn't go to the book fund. He said I should talk to you. He said that maybe I shouldn't be a *brahmacārī.* So, I don't want to disturb you, Gurudeva, but I just don't think I can go on. I like it, but it's too hard on my body and mind. It's too cold, and I don't have any time to myself. I am sorry to admit this."

"Can't you just stick it out a little longer? It's only for about a month and a half," said Gurudeva.

Gurudeva tried to concentrate despite the noises in the room. He couldn't help overhearing a man arguing with a devotee about milk. He was saying that milk produces cholesterol and is dangerous to health, and the devotee was making a counter-argument about a balanced-protein diet. Gurudeva tried to focus on Nimāi's predicament and to decide whether to ask his disciple to stay out longer and do the austerities or go back to the temple. Sometimes in the past Gurudeva had used the full force of his authority as spiritual master to insist that a disciple continue to do *saṅkīrtana*, and as a result, a few of them had left Kṛṣṇa consciousness and later blamed him. On the other hand, if he was soft Vibhu would criticize him. What was best?

On his end of the line, Nimāi wasn't thinking very clearly. He had just presented an insistent plea that he be allowed to return to the temple, but when Gurudeva asked him to explain more about it, there were many more things Nimāi wanted to say. He was agitated by Vibhu's remark that maybe he shouldn't be a *brahmacārī*. But why did Vibhu say that since Vibhu wouldn't let him get married? Did Nimāi have to get married just because he couldn't live in a van? Nimāi also wanted to tell Gurudeva something about Choṭa, how he had fully recovered from his attack and that he was a good devotee. And now there were two new mice who had become devotees. But how could he bring up such things in a conversation like this?

"It's hard for me to know what's best Nimāi," said Gurudeva. "Let me think about it. Can you hang on for a few more days at least?"

"I guess so," Nimāi answered.

"Good," said Gurudeva. Now the pressure was off for an immediate decision. Gurudeva and Nimāi shared the line in silence waiting and thinking if there was something more they wanted to say. Gurudeva flashed on other things Flora had said. She had talked about autistic children who played with dolphins and somehow picked up on the noises which dolphins made to each other. There was also a gorilla who had learned sign language and for its birthday had asked to be given a pet. And chimpanzees had become so accustomed to associating with humans that they were later unable to associate normally with other zoo chimps. She'd spoken about Dian Fossey, who had intimately learned the ways of gorillas, and a woman named Joy Adamson who lived with lions. She had said, "Right now there are a lot of people experiencing these kinds of things." Gurudeva thought of asking Nimāi about the mouse. But he hesitated.

Nimāi also wanted to say at least something about Choṭa, at least mention his name, before hanging up. If anybody could understand, it was Gurudeva. He had already been kind to Choṭa, and Choṭa thought him to be a very advanced devotee. He wanted to tell Gurudeva how the mice were on *saṅkīrtana,* and they too were having great difficulty. That was another reason Nimāi wanted to come back. In fact, it was a very important reason, and yet Nimāi couldn't bring himself to say it.

"So, then I can call back in two or three days Gurudeva? Will you be there?"

"Yes, I'll pray to Kṛṣṇa to help me know what He wants you to do, and you pray also to try to be able to follow His will. All right?"

"Yes, Gurudeva. Thank you very much. Please accept my obeisances."

"All glories to Śrīla Prabhupāda."

The day after Nimāi phoned Gurudeva it snowed all over Pennsylvania. Nimāi had great difficulty driving the van, and the outdoor cooking seemed ridiculous. He couldn't believe that Bhīma was going to keep them all out on *saṅkīrtana* in such weather! Even a few of the *brahmacārīs* complained that it was too cold in the van. More snow was predicted.

In between a run to the bank and the laundromat, Nimāi stopped to talk with Choṭa.

"I feel bad for you guys," said Nimāi. "I would like to take you somewhere warm."

Choṭa admitted that it had been a very difficult night. "My Godbrothers have some serious doubts," said Choṭa, "so they agreed that I could present our situation to you." The two new mice stayed huddled together in a corner of the cage, twitching their whiskers and looking exactly like two ordinary house mice in a bad situation.

"They were thinking of some things that our parents said to us. They feel like they have committed a mistake by submitting to you. Because here we are now in a prison, just as if we had been trapped by some human being who wanted to kill us or torture us. Last night Yamala dāsa said to me, 'What's the difference between what Nimāi is putting us through and what we've heard about mice being captured by humans and kept in a cage to run on a treadmill until they die? Who knows that he won't get tired of us or think that we are in the way and just kill us?'" Choṭa looked up at Nimāi imploringly.

Nimāi was about to ask him, "And what do you think?" but he didn't want to insult his friend's loyalty. No doubt Choṭa had preached to them, and he himself was also feeling strained.

"There is no question of force," said Nimāi. "If you want, I'll just bring you right back to the temple and you can go to your old home. But I don't think you really want that, do you? It's just this austerity. I think it's too much myself! And I can understand that it's too much for you. My Gurudeva asked me to wait just a couple of days, but I don't know now. At least I could bring you all back to Gurudeva's house."

"The problem with that," said Choṭa, "is that we are not yet able to sustain ourselves in Kṛṣṇa consciousness. We can't read on our own, and unless we see and hear from you regularly, I can't even chant my rounds. So, bringing us back to our home in the temple or leaving us at Gurudeva's house without you being there would be just about the same. We'll all fall into *māyā*."

"Maybe not," squeaked Arjuna. "At least we would be warm."

Nimāi wanted to speak some high inspiring philosophy to them. He remembered how Gurudeva would give the example of Arjuna in the *Bhagavad- gītā*. No one was asked to do as difficult a task as was Arjuna. We don't have to kill our relatives on the battlefield, do we? Arjuna didn't want to fight, but Kṛṣṇa convinced him. So, we have to do the same. But Nimāi didn't have the conviction to say such things. How could he tell them to forget their bodily pains and their mental agitation when he himself almost agreed with what they were saying? He was torturing them by keeping them out here in the cold, confined to a dark box, and he wasn't spending adequate time with them to see to their *sādhana*. Since the mice had been out with him, they had had no regular classes of philosophy and no *japa* or *kīrtana* together. The two new mice hardly even knew what Kṛṣṇa consciousness was about, so they naturally judged things by how they were being treated. All they could see was that they were being abused. Nimāi felt abused also, although he was supposed to know better.

"It's difficult for me to decide," said Nimāi, "whether to ask you to stay out on *saṅkīrtana*, or whether to tell you to go back. If it was up to me, I'd just bring you back immediately and I'd go back myself. So, what if they don't distribute as many books without me? I have to consider your survival. I heard that Prabhupāda once said, 'Most important of all is to save yourself.'"

"I think we could wait two more days," said Choṭa, "till you call Gurudeva again."

"But what if he says to stay out?" said Yamala.

Nimāi thought to himself, these mice are no dopes.

"All right," said Nimāi decisively. "I won't wait to call Gurudeva. He wants me to use my own intelligence. I'll tell him there was a snowstorm, and I just had to go back. He wants me to stay fixed in Kṛṣṇa consciousness, not go crazy trying to do some impossible austerity and then fall down."

Choṭa made no objection, and the other mice didn't change their grumpy looks, although Nimāi guessed that they felt relief from what he'd said. So, he drove the van straight to Bhīma's *saṅkīrtana* spot and told him that he couldn't take it any longer and he was going back to the farm.

"You don't have to do that, Nimāi," said Bhima. They were both standing outside in the parking lot of the supermarket. Snow was falling again, adding to the already fallen six inches. "I just phoned my old *saṅkīrtana* buddy Keśava Prabhu," said Bhima. "He's got his own house in the suburbs. He said that we could stay there and use it as our base of operations for *saṅkīrtana*. Most of the time you can stay indoors. It will be a break for all of us. Okay?"

Nimāi felt bad that he was complaining since he had so little austerity to perform compared to Bhīma and the other men. Still ...

"When can we go there?" asked Nimāi.

Chapter 8

Keśava's house was in the suburbs on a block where the houses weren't too tightly packed together. Keśava, who was a large man, and his wife who was wearing a sari, greeted them at the door. Their two young daughters, about five and six years old, were wide awake, although it was about 9:00 in the evening. Keśava said their baby boy was sleeping, so the *saṅkīrtana* party tried to enter the house quietly, although that wasn't possible given their numbers and the excitement of the little girls. Keśava knew all the devotees and they sat together telling *saṅkīrtana* stories. Keśava told a few of his own from the old days while Nimāi carried in the travel bags, groceries and other paraphernalia, including the mouse *āśrama*.

The *saṅkīrtana* party was given the guest room, and Nimāi claimed a large closet in the room as the exclusive domain of the mouse box. He

planned to take rest there as well if no one objected. By 10:30 P.M. the excitement had quieted down and almost everyone was ready to take rest for the night. Nimāi had phoned Gurudeva's secretary earlier and asked him to tell Gurudeva that the *saṅkīrtana* party had made some new arrangements, and so now he would be staying out on *saṅkīrtana*. He would write to Gurudeva soon.

Nimāi relished the comfortable, warm temperature and thick rug in the closet space. He had cleaned out the cage and fed the mice, but there had been no time to speak with them while moving in. Now, in the semi-privacy of the closet, he opened the box and whispered, "Choṭa are you awake?"

"Hare Kṛṣṇa!" chirped Choṭa.

"Prabhu," said Nimāi, "just see how Kṛṣṇa is taking care of us. We should have had more faith."

"You mean, we shouldn't have quit?" said Choṭa.

"Yeah. I mean, I don't think we could have lasted another day out there. But ... I just wish that Kṛṣṇa had made this nice arrangement without our being so weak-hearted."

Nimāi was lying down in his sleeping bag, his head resting on his hand and elbow. Yamala and Arjuna were sleeping peacefully. Choṭa had crawled up to the top of the box to be able to speak quietly without being overheard. They were only inches apart.

"It's hard to figure out what to do, isn't it?" said Choṭa.

"If we had only held out a little longer," said Nimāi. "Austerity is good for us. If we tolerate a situation for Kṛṣṇa, then He will make arrangements one way or another."

"What did we do wrong?"

"I think we should have prayed more and just chanted Hare Kṛṣṇa. We forgot. At least I forgot."

"Nimāi Prabhu?" Choṭa asked. "Could you tell me how to pray? I don't think I understand."

Nimāi often forgot that he was supposed to be a preceptor and not just a friend. He liked the feeling of being honest, at least with Choṭa, and he liked the benefit of the equal friendship. But after all, he was in the superior position.

"Prayer is ..." Nimāi paused. "Prayer is when you very sincerely call out to Kṛṣṇa. The Hare Kṛṣṇa mantra is a prayer, but you really have to put yourself into it. Prabhupāda said it's like a child crying for its mother. So, you have to ask Kṛṣṇa, who is like our mother and father, 'Please accept me. Please engage me in Your service.'"

"Is that all?" Choṭa asked.

"Yes," said Nimāi. "It may seem easy, but it's not. We get distracted. We forget that Kṛṣṇa is actually there, and He is our only friend. I wish I could just believe and remember that I am a tiny soul and sometimes just talk to Kṛṣṇa as my protector and friend. Just like we are talking together. Kṛṣṇa is the Supreme Friend."

"I think I can remember doing like that once," said the mouse. "But not in the last few days, when I really needed it."

"Hey Nimāi!" Bhīma banged on the closet door. "Did you do the laundry?"

"Oh! I forgot." Nimāi resolved not to get agitated by extra austerities. "I'll do it right away." And he got up singing a Hare Kṛṣṇa tune.

The next morning by 10:00 A.M., Nimāi was on his own. Bhīma had asked Nimāi to stay back and get the treasury books in order and prepare a deposit for the bank while Bhīma dāsa drove the men to their *saṅkīrtana* spots. Nimāi wanted to finish his business quickly so that he could read the *Bhagavad-gītā* to Choṭa and the boys, so he was a bit exasperated when Keśava Prabhu stopped in to chat before going to his place of work.

"I hear you've got pet mice," said Keśava. He sat down, and his two daughters sat with him, one on his lap and one holding his hand.

"Yes, they're in a box," said Nimāi, fearing that Keśava might object.

"Sītā dāsī, would you like to see the mice?" said Keśava.

"Yes! Yes!"

"We have a rabbit of our own," said Keśava. "My wife Pārvatī really loves animals. Don't worry; we won't let the rabbit up here."

Nimāi was usually reluctant to show the mice. Most people thought they were repulsive. But Keśava seemed different.

As Nimāi went to get the mouse box, Keśava called his wife in. Nimāi became so much at ease that he began speaking to the mice. "Prabhus," he said, tapping on the mouse box. "There are some devotees here who would like to see you."

The whole family seemed delighted as they peered in and exclaimed. "They seem so friendly," said Pārvatī. "That's very unusual." She confidently reached in and picked up Yamala. Then, carefully supervising her two girls so that they would not be rough, she directed them to lightly pet the mouse's head. In the same way she picked up Arjuna and Choṭa and then put them back.

"If you like," said Mother Pārvatī, "I can fix up their box a little bit and put in some new stuff for their nests."

Nimāi was deeply moved; he could hardly believe it.

"I used to keep a hamster," said Pārvatī, "and I still have his cage. You can put your mice in there and let me take your box; I'll make some improvements on it. All right?"

Nimāi thought, "This is a real mother," and he submitted to whatever she said.

Keśava Prabhu then lingered a few moments alone with Nimāi.

I've got to talk with Bhima," said Keśava, "but maybe I'll mention it to you too. I think there's going to be a problem with you all staying here."

"I'm sorry I broke the washing machine," said Nimāi. "It was really Ranchor's fault for insisting that I put his sneakers in."

"No, that's not it," said Keśava. "Or, maybe that's a little part of it. There is just a basic conflict between the *brahmacārī* and *gṛhastha* way of life. Some of the men were up at 2:00 A.M., and they woke the baby. I guess we could adjust ... But partly it's a matter of attitudes. Like this morning Bhīma was preaching to me real heavy, telling me that household life is *māyā*."

"He said that?" asked Nimāi.

"Yes. But that's not what Prabhupāda says. It's *māyā* if you live like a *gṛhamedhī*, but Prabhupāda didn't expect everyone to live in the temple. Sometimes devotees think that because you're married and have a family and you move out of the temple that you've blooped or you are not a devotee anymore."

Nimāi wondered why Keśava was saying all this to him, since most people considered him to be too inconsequential for serious topics.

"I don't think householder life is *māyā*," said Nimāi. "But I suppose you have to expect someone like Bhīma to be a little bit defensive or whatever. I used to think that the *brahmacārīs* were too fanatical for me, but since I've been out with them, I've grown to really appreciate the tremendous austerities they are doing."

"I know that," said Keśava. "I was on traveling *saṅkīrtana* for ten years. Maybe I am just feeling guilty. But I guess we all like to be encouraged. It's not easy doing business all day long, but I see it as service to Prabhupāda and Kṛṣṇa. I just wish Bhīma and the others could see it that way too."

Nimāi felt flattered that Keśava Prabhu was talking with him in a confidential way. He made a few suggestions on how the *saṅkīrtana* party could adjust their behavior so that they would not cause so much disruption to Keśava's home. Nimāi also expressed his genuine appreciation for the friendly Kṛṣṇa conscious atmosphere.

"I feel more Kṛṣṇa conscious here," said Nimāi, "than I did freezing outdoors in the park. And it's not just the heating in your house; it's the nice warmth in your whole family life. It just seems very spiritual and good to me."

Keśava laughed and gave Nimāi a hug. "Watch out Nimāi, if you get too enamored you may become a householder yourself. But it's really not so wonderful. The best thing is to remain *brahmacārī* if you actually can."

Before he left for work Keśava gave Nimāi a cable knit sweater "to keep warm on *saṅkīrtana*."

"I don't even go on *saṅkīrtana*," Nimāi mumbled.

"Sure, you do," said Keśava.

By late morning Mother Pārvatī returned Nimāi's mouse *āśrama*. The wood part was stained with preservative, and it now had a carrying handle as well as a lock. The inside had separate rooms and fresh nesting paper. The little girls had even drawn colored pictures of Nārada Muni with some animals and devotees and pasted them on the walls. In one of the pictures some small animals were looking up to Nārada and saying, "Hare Kṛṣṇa! All glories to Prabhupāda!"

"I hope we didn't make it worse," said Pārvatī.

But Nimāi thought it was great. "I'm sure they'll like it," he said enthusiastically. He was very pleased, but embarrassed, to be talking to such a chaste, affectionate mother.

"Mice eat anything," she said, "but there are some things they especially like. I'll show you later." Then, with Pārvatī's assistance, Nimāi put the mice back into their refurbished cage. He had been standing respectfully the whole time Pārvatī had been present, but as soon as she left, he sat on the floor, opened the treasury books and spread out the money.

"I've got to get to work now, Choṭa," said Nimāi, but after no more than ten minutes he was asleep on the rug dreaming that he had become a householder. His beautiful wife, Sūrya dāsī, was offering incense to their household Radha-Kṛṣṇa Deities. In the dream, Nimāi saw himself playing a harmonium. He had several sons and daughters beside him ...

Bhīma had to shake Nimāi several times before he woke up. When Nimāi gained consciousness, he began telling Bhīma how Keśava Prabhu was somewhat disturbed by the *saṅkīrtana* party's behavior and some things that Bhīma had said.

"I'll have to apologize," said Bhīma. "I shouldn't be so puffed up about being a *brahmacārī*. I don't think I said anything that's not in Prabhupāda's books, but it wasn't right according to time, place, and person."

"But doesn't Prabhupāda make a distinction," asked Nimāi, "between *gṛhamedhī* and *gṛhastha*?"

"Sometimes. But sometimes he says *gṛhastha* is almost the same. If you take to the *gṛhastha āśrama*, your spiritual advancement is almost nil."

"That doesn't sound right to me," said Nimāi.

"I don't want to argue with you, Nimāi," said Bhīma. "I'll talk to Keśava though; he's my old friend. Time to get to work on these treasury books."

Nimāi knew that the mice were happy in the warmth of the house, but he did not have much chance to talk with them during the day. Only at night when the lights went out did he speak to them in a whisper within the closet. "You got some nice *prasādam* today," said Nimāi.

Mother Pārvatī had made chocolate chip cookies and peanut butter and almond pies, just for the palates of the mice. This was in addition to a big feast she cooked for the men. The mice were visibly plumper.

"We are very satisfied, by Kṛṣṇa's grace," said Choṭa. Yamala and Arjuna were sleeping, faintly snoring.

"I am feeling pretty good too," said Nimāi. He couldn't think of anything more he wanted to say, and so he was prepared to finally get some sleep. But Choṭa had something to say.

"Nimāi? I would like to take Yamala and Arjuna and try to do some preaching to the mice within this house."

Nimāi was shocked to hear it. His first reaction was disappointment. How could Choṭa think of something like that on his own? How could he go preaching without Nimāi? What would Nimāi do without them? Nimāi felt hurt, but he realized such emotions should be controlled.

"Really?" he asked. "Do you think it's safe?"

"Sure," said Choṭa.

Nimāi could see that Choṭa had thought about it a lot and that he was intent.

"Mice are pretty much the same anywhere," said Choṭa. "I know their mentality. Me and Yamala and Arjuna can go and see them and bring them some of the delicious *prasādam* we got today. I kept a stash."

Nimāi was about to say, "*But can you preach?*" but he held his tongue, realizing his words were ill-chosen. Maybe they weren't the greatest preachers but they could do something, even if it was only to go and chant Hare Kṛṣṇa and distribute *prasādam*. Why should he doubt them or hold them back?

"I'm mostly concerned for your safety," said Nimāi. "If you really think it's not dangerous."

"We'll be all right. Kṛṣṇa will protect us. Can we leave in the morning? We want to stay out for two days."

"Two days!"

"I think it would take that long to visit all the mouse places. I can hear them even now in between the walls. But we can only go with your blessings."

Nimāi muttered his consent, and Choṭa returned to his *āśrama*, his head filled with plans and the spirit of adventure.

By morning Nimāi had accepted that Choṭa was actually going off to preach, but Nimāi requested that one of the little mice stay back. Arjuna was selected. Nimāi wanted to give the preachers last minute instructions and practical advice. He tried remembering something that he'd read by Bhaktisiddhānta Sarasvatī when he sent preachers off to Europe. Didn't he tell them to be very humble, thinking themselves lower than a blade of grass and not to feel superior to anyone they met? Nimāi told them they should be very fixed and not fall into *māyā*. He described Śrīla Prabhupāda's brave preaching; how he came to the West all alone on the Jaladuta with only a few dollars spending money and no patrons. Choṭa's work was pioneering, so it would catch Prabhupāda's merciful attention. Nimāi said he was very impressed that just when the mice were being comfortably treated and well fed, they were ready to go off preaching and live austerely, detached from sense gratification.

Yamala, who had been selected to go with Choṭa, had mixed feelings. He didn't want to leave the new, comfortable situation, nor was he delighted at the prospect of visiting unfamiliar mice to tell them about Kṛṣṇa. But he, Choṭa, and Arjuna were all from a particularly aggressive breed of mice, so he looked forward to the idea of roaming and assisting Choṭa in "attacking the *māyā*" of the mouse communities. Nimāi also had mixed feelings, but he managed a good send-off for the preaching party. Again and again, he emphasized that they should come back, no matter what, after no more than two days.

Choṭa packed up his stash of *prasādam* for distribution. He said he had also hidden some in the walls. "This is only the beginning," he said optimistically. "Maybe someday in the future there will be something equivalent to books for mice." Nimāi felt proud of his student, but he was also feeling somewhat distant. He was sad to see them disappear into a hole in the wall which he had never noticed before.

Chapter 9

Choṭa and Yamala proceeded for a few minutes without meeting any life in between the floorboards. Then they saw a mouse coming towards them.

"Excuse me, sir!" Choṭa called out in his native mouse tongue. The other mouse stopped, indicating that he had heard, but then hurried on his way.

"Want me to catch him?" asked Yamala.

"No, there's plenty more," said Choṭa. But as they explored the house, they did not find any other mice, although they saw their droppings. When they reached the kitchen, they met a mouse coming in their own direction. "Excuse me, sir," said Choṭa, while Yamala discreetly blocked the path.

"What is it?" asked the mouse, who was darker than they were.

"We are new to this house," said Choṭa, "and we want to know where the main mouse community is located."

"You will find them in the barn," said the dark mouse. "Only one family lives in the house. Most of the others live in the barn and commute here every day through a passageway. Where are you from?"

"We live in the Rādhā-Dāmodara temple, which is about one hundred miles from here. We're traveling on a mission to help others and we wanted to share some of the nice things we've learned at the Rādhā-Dāmodara temple. If you have a minute I'd like to explain."

But the mouse was in a hurry. He asked Yamala to step aside. Yamala first offered him a piece of *prasādam*, which the mouse sniffed at and immediately devoured. He then tried to devour their whole stash, but Choṭa and Yamala prevented him. When he saw that he couldn't overpower them, the dark mouse ran away.

"What a jerk," said Yamala. "They are all like that. Simply interested in eating. Stupid fools."

"It's not his fault," said Choṭa. "We were in ignorance too. Remember?"

They proceeded to the barn, but Choṭa began thinking, "This isn't going to be easy." He sensed that he was out of touch with his animal instincts and while that was good from the spiritual perspective, he knew he would have to approach the barn mice not from an elevated consciousness but as a mouse-to-mouse equal. He thought of the big, strong, reassuring presence of Nimāi Prabhu, but for now they were on their own.

Yamala dāsa, who trailed close behind Choṭa, was treading on even thinner spiritual ground. All he could think about was eating. "My teeth keep growing," he thought, "and so I need to eat for my health. My belly wants food." He knew theoretically that he was supposed to be above just eating, sleeping, mating, and defending, but he needed to hear constantly that there was something else to life besides those things. What kept him going was that he liked Choṭa better than anyone else he knew, and he had come to see other mice as stupid and useless—in illusion. Mainly, Yamala thought of the delicious peanut butter, almonds, and cookies they had enjoyed at the *āśrama*, and he hoped they would go back soon and have more feasts. Yamala couldn't help thinking, "Why are we running in the opposite direction of the feast?"

As Choṭa and Yamala entered the passageway between the barn and the house, they saw the busy traffic of mice. Some of the mice were carrying bits of food in their mouth to bring back to their nests, and some were carrying nesting material. Choṭa positioned himself slightly to one side of the thoroughfare and had Yamala stand behind him guarding their *prasādam*.

"Excuse me, sir," said Choṭa, gesturing with his front paw. Most of the mice paid him no attention and kept going on their way without even glancing in his direction. Occasionally he was able to draw one off the path, usually because of the aroma of the *prasādam*. But basically, it would turn into the same old exchange that they had had with the first mouse they met, where the mouse would take a tiny bit of offered *prasādam* and then attempt to steal the whole cache. Only by Yamala's strong defensive postures, were they stopped from devouring everything; there were even a few scuffles in which Choṭa had to help push off a greedy mouse.

"If these mice could only use their natural aggression in Kṛṣṇa consciousness," said Choṭa, "they'd be great devotees."

The rejections and scuffles began to exhaust the preachers. What was the use of it?

"At least they are all taking a little *prasādam*," said Yamala. "That in itself gives them spiritual benefit, doesn't it Choṭa?"

"Yes, indirectly," said Choṭa. "But so far none of them know what it is, and they don't appreciate it."

After a fight in which three mice almost overpowered the preachers in order to take the *prasādam*, Choṭa decided they should try a different tactic. They would perform *harināma* for the benefit of the passersby. So, they began to chant the sound vibration they had learned from Nimāi, "Hare Kṛṣṇa, Hare Kṛṣṇa, Kṛṣṇa Kṛṣṇa, Hare Hare / Hare Rāma, Hare Rāma, Rāma Rāma, Hare Hare." They made a little tune of their own and swayed and danced sedately by the side of the busy road. Those mice who had things in their mouths continued hurrying by, even though they glanced with great surprise at the unusual phenomenon. But soon other mice began to gather around. The response was mostly hostile. "What's this? What's going on?" some mice asked the chanters and then asked each other.

"Stop that stupid singing and tell us!" said a big mouse who had already fought with them.

"I know what that is!" said another. "They've been hanging around humans!"

"It sounds awful! You don't even sound like mice!"

"They don't even look like mice. They are traitors!"

"Look at all that food. Ask them where they got that food."

The preachers were encircled by about fifteen squeaking, chattering mice, some of whom displayed threatening bodily postures. Choṭa noticed that one or two in the crowd were quiet, perhaps even thoughtful. But the threat of attack seemed so imminent that Choṭa told Yamala to take up the *prasādam* and get ready to withdraw. Continuing to sing the Hare Kṛṣṇa mantra Choṭa moved forward and the mice parted, letting him through. The crowd jeered after them but eventually dispersed and continued their work in the busy to-and-fro traffic of the passageway.

"Maybe mice as a species can't take to Kṛṣṇa consciousness," said Yamala. He and Choṭa had found a secluded place in between the walls that was only a few minutes' walk from the main passageway. They had calmed themselves from the threatening encounter and were finishing up chanting their quota of *japa* for the day.

"Don't say that," said Choṭa. "What about us? We are mice, and we have taken to Kṛṣṇa consciousness."

"Well, maybe we're rare exceptions," said Yamala, but he laughed out loud at the suggestion that he was something special. "I suppose if I have taken to it," said Yamala, "anyone could."

"Kṛṣṇa is testing us," said Choṭa, "to see how sincere we are about helping others to spiritual life."

"But Nimāi even said something about preaching where it's favorable," said Yamala. The two continued discussing their situation from the philosophical point of view and eventually agreed that they had done enough for one day, but they would try again in the morning. They decided to attempt a nest-to-nest approach to avoid a mob scene where the antagonistic mice could take advantage of their numbers. At least they had discovered that all mice were willing to "take" *prasādam*. But *prasādam* was also risky because it agitated their senses and awakened their instinct to steal.

"I remember Nimāi once mentioned that in Sanskrit the word for mouse is *mūṣaka*, which means thief," said Choṭa. With that thought, Yamala and Choṭa summed up their strategy for the next day by deciding they would distribute *prasādam* in a more civil, controlled way while speaking to the mice in the comfort of their nests. In preparation, Yamala went off to gather the *prasādam* stashes that they had hidden in several locations. After eating a bit, they wrapped the *prasādam* in tiny cloths and then closed their eyes to sleep.

In the middle of the night the preachers were attacked by six or seven *mūṣakas* emitting high-pitched cries. The thieves jumped on the bodies of the sleeping mice and began clawing and biting at their faces and necks. Quickly overcoming the sluggishness of slumber, the two preachers valiantly fought back. Choṭa and Yamala were both good fighters, but eventually they were overcome by the concerted efforts of the thieves who were fighting to kill. Yamala fought back so furiously that one of the thieves bled profusely from his nose and the others temporarily backed off. But they soon regrouped, and three more joined them leaping out of the darkness onto the backs of the preachers. Choṭa signaled Yamala that they should run for their lives, and they both fled. The thieves greedily seized the *prasādam*.

The attack was a great shock for Choṭa and Yamala. They considered returning to Nimāi a day early. Their faces showed gashes, and Yamala's eye pained him where a mouse had tried to scratch it out.

"It's not unusual," said Choṭa, "for devotees to be attacked. Even Lord Nityānanda was hit in the head when he tried to preach to Jagāi and Mādhāi." Although they were dispirited, neither of them wanted to give up.

"Let's try something else," said Choṭa. "I have an idea." They were speaking together in a hideout they had discovered in the basement of the house. "Remember when we were regular house mice how our community used to go outside and invade the field mice in their nests? We overpowered them because they were less aggressive. Now we can use that knowledge to our advantage, but in the service of Kṛṣṇa and not to hurt them."

"Yeah!" Yamala sat up erect. He was soaking his injured eye with water but he grinned, baring his incisor teeth. "And some of them are hibernating now so they will be slow. I mean, more receptive."

At dusk the two left the shelter of the house and made tracks across the snow. They darted into the open spaces only when they were sure there were no cats, rats, or other predators lurking about. By instinct they quickly uncovered a nest of Meadow Jumping mice, which they knew were hibernators. Removing the entrance to an underground nest, they found a closely huddled group of small yellowish mice. Most of them were lying dormant with their heads rolled between their hind legs, and their tails curled around their bodies. But a few disengaged themselves from the huddle as Choṭa and Yamala entered. The preachers recognized the breed by their long hind legs and oversized hind feet. They also knew them to be docile creatures.

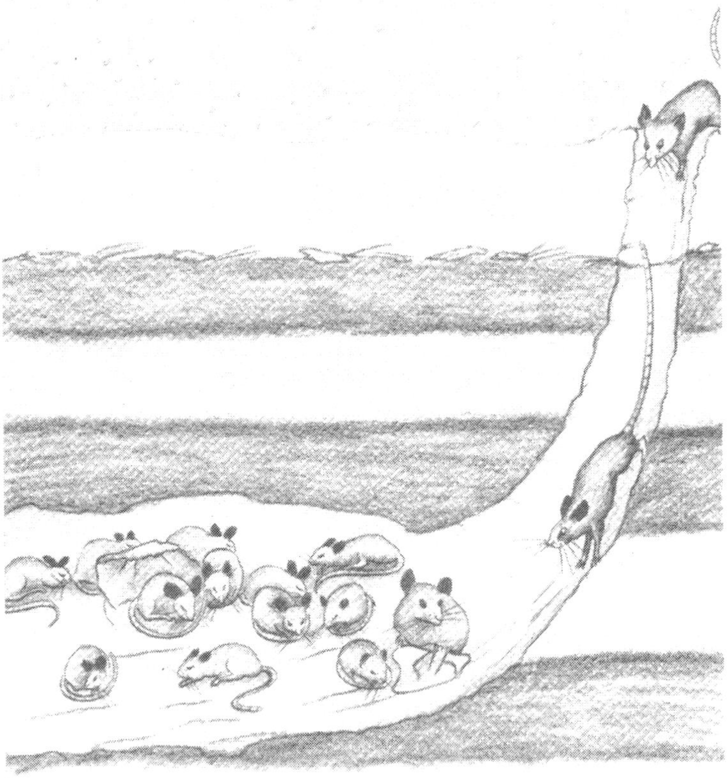

"Hare Kṛṣṇa," said Choṭa. "How are you?"

"Can't you see we are hibernating? Don't bother us," said one of the Meadow clan, stretching his body and squinting his eyes in the darkness.

"We just want to tell you something that will help you to be less fearful. Just spare a minute and let us share with you some spiritual knowledge."

"No," said the Meadow mouse, "just go away. If you want to be kind to us, leave us alone."

"All right," said Choṭa reluctantly. "Hare Kṛṣṇa."

The Meadow mouse turned back to his group but stopped to ask, "What's that you said?"

"It's called a mantra," said Choṭa. "It can protect you from snakes and birds."

"Hmm," the Meadow mouse said. "Hare Kṛṣṇa," and he returned to sleep. Choṭa and Yamala proceeded through the snow to find other nests.

"We've so much to learn," said Yamala. "I'm sure there are better ways to approach them to make the philosophy sound more interesting. But at least he chanted."

They next visited a nest of Oldfield mice. They were smaller than house mice and docile like the Meadow mice. The Oldfield mice were in fact favorite pets of humans because they didn't bite and they got on well even in captivity. Yamala found their nest by noticing mounds of soil at the entrance to an underground tunnel. He removed the plug and then entered. When the mice understood that the visitors had no malicious intent, they received them well and offered them some food in the form of insects. But the preachers refused it, explaining that they were vegetarians.

"Vegetarians? Why is that?" One question led to another and soon the preachers found themselves explaining Kṛṣṇa consciousness. The Oldfields didn't seem to understand spiritual teachings, but they remained sociable and even sang the Hare Kṛṣṇa mantra with their visitors, finding it a pleasant way to spend a cold evening underground. When they left the Oldfield community after several hours, Yamala and Choṭa were jubilant. They had forgotten their wounds and wanted to go visiting nest-to-nest without stopping to eat or sleep.

Their other visits were not as productive but they were at least received by the Deer mice, who talked fearfully about their predators—skunks, foxes, weasels, hawks, owls, and snakes. Even if the Deer mice couldn't understand much of what the preachers were saying, they seemed to respect the calm and confident attitude of their visitors and sensed their nonviolent intentions. In each of these places, the preachers made sure to chant and give an explanation of the mantra. They left each nest with the hope that maybe someone would remember, perhaps at a time of danger, or at the time of death. Most of the mouse species lived only for a few years, so the preachers tried to emphasize the urgent need to understand the purpose of life and how to be spared from rebirth in lower species.

In a bold mood they even entered the nests of the Cotton mice, who were larger than Yamala and Arjuna. Despite their size, the Cottons were a fearful, endangered species, preyed upon by many birds, snakes, and carnivorous mammals. With confidence the preachers spoke of overcoming fear in all situations, and they recommended chanting as a means to do that.

Staying up all night preaching, Choṭa and Yamala returned from the woods at sunrise. They had to wait outside for several hours while a cat prowled nearby before they could finally dart back inside by taking a new route through the garage. In the rafters of the garage the preachers came upon some Albino mice. As Choṭa began to explain his mission, one of the white creatures became quite interested.

"Some of my brothers," he said, "used to be pets of humans. One of them even returned to live with us, so I have heard different things, but never this. You learned this from the humans?"

"Yes," said Choṭa, "but this is not human culture. Spiritual culture is for all living beings. All living creatures are equal as spirit souls. The difference is in the bodies. Bodies are just like coverings of the real self."

"What do you mean?" the Albino asked. "How can a creature be different from his body? All I know are the instincts of a mouse; whereas the cat, our enemy, only knows the instincts of a cat. So how can you say we are the same?"

"What you are describing," said Choṭa, "is material consciousness. And that's all most creatures know. But there is higher knowledge. Certain advanced human beings have received this knowledge, but it can be understood by any creature because we are all spirit soul within. Only in ignorance do we live out a life just thinking of mating, sleeping, eating, and defending. When we die without any other knowledge the purpose of life is defeated."

Another Albino who had overheard the talk moved closer with friendly curiosity. He said, "But how can this help us in a practical way?"

Choṭa was thrilled by the intelligent inquiries. He had never imagined that mice could be so receptive, although he had heard that the Albinos were an advanced race. Yamala was also feeling blissful and he tried to contribute with an occasional intelligent remark. Mostly, however, he left the preaching to Choṭa. But he knew that his demeanor was being carefully watched by the others, so he tried to remain composed and controlled.

The discussion with the Albinos continued all morning. Several of them seemed quite impressed with the philosophy spoken by Choṭa, and with the preachers themselves. The Albinos were sorry to see their friends go, and before they parted company, they made promises to try and meet again sometime. The Albinos agreed to practice the chanting.

"If you simply practice the chanting every day, even a little bit," said Choṭa, "your consciousness will change from material to spiritual and you will feel so many other good benefits."

"Thank you very much for visiting us. I think this is a very important day in our lives," said the Albino leader, and he personally escorted the preachers to the exit of their hidden nest.

Tired as they were, Yamala and Choṭa scampered with joy across the roof beams into the house, racing between the walls and down the pipes before they finally reached their temporary home in the closet. There they took a blissful breath, eager to report their results to Nimāi.

Chapter 10

Nimāi sat anxiously in the closet hoping that Choṭa and Yamala would soon appear. They were three hours late. Nimāi had not been able to converse much with Choṭa's little brother, but Arjuna had managed to suggest that he could go off and look for the other two. Nimāi was considering what to do when he heard the familiar sounds of tiny feet. And then they appeared from the hole—their ears were a bit ragged and their bodies bore gash marks, but both Choṭa and Yamala were beaming with bliss. Nimāi went to embrace them, but before he could reach them, they leaped into his arms. Nimāi and Arjuna were sorry to see their friends' wounds and immediately began to clean the preacher's bodies.

"What happened?" asked Nimāi.

"We got attacked by the mice in this building," said Choṭa. And he began to tell the whole story of their adventures while Nimāi listened with rapt attention. He knew better than anyone how difficult it was for the mice, and he knew their limitations.

"What you are doing," said Nimāi, "is just as important as the *saṅkīrtana* men. And you are no less heroic. You are no less dear to Kṛṣṇa than any human devotee!" The mice were jumping with glee, but then they became embarrassed by the praise.

"You guys must be hungry," said Arjuna. "We've got a feast ready."

"Oh, I might be able to nibble at something," said Yamala.

Nimāi brought forth a spread which Mother Pārvatī had prepared for them which included their favorite seeds and grains, oat-and-peanut-butter balls, almond pies, and different varieties of raw vegetables.

While the mice feasted, Nimāi asked further questions until they had given him an hour-by-hour account of all their deeds, words, and thoughts from the preaching tour.

That afternoon Nimāi went out shopping and returned in the early evening with the *saṅkīrtana* men. The mice had spent the afternoon resting and recuperating. By late evening, Nimāi was alone again with Choṭa while the others slept.

"Choṭa Prabhu," Nimāi said, "I would like to tell you about my activities while you were gone. I hope you will approve of what I am about to say. I think ... I think I am going to get married."

"I am not sure what that means," said Choṭa. Choṭa had trouble distinguishing ordinary mating from "marriage," and so Nimāi had to explain.

"It means taking a wife. I confided in Keśava Prabhu and Pārvatī Prabhu that I had been thinking of getting married. So, they phoned the parents of this young *mātājī*, Sūrya dāsī! —the one who screamed when she saw you. But her parents said they would definitely not let her marry me. I don't blame them. Then Mother Pārvatī had this idea that I could marry a *brahmacāriṇī* from Guyana. Guyana is a country in the Caribbean thousands of miles south of here. Keśava Prabhu has a brother who is married to a devotee from there. Keśava also sends profits from his business to Guyana so they can distribute books and *Back to Godhead* magazines. Devotees from the North sometimes go to Guyana to get wives because the girls there are simple-hearted and raised in Hindu families."

Nimāi was speaking rapidly and most of it was going over Choṭa's head. When Nimāi realized Choṭa wasn't getting it, he slowed down and described the complexities of marrying in the Kṛṣṇa consciousness movement, and what "Hinduism" was, and what it would mean to all of them in a practical way. The immediate result would be that Nimāi—and the mice—would soon be going on a trip to the Caribbean where Nimāi would meet a potential wife, and if all went well, he might even get married while down there and come back with his new wife.

Because Choṭa was an intelligent mouse, he soon grasped the concept of marriage and how it could impact their immediate situation, although much of it remained abstract. He couldn't comprehend distances of thousands of miles or what it was like to travel that far. And marriage, the way Nimāi described it, was baffling. But he had implicit faith in Nimāi, and as long as he was going to be able to go along, it sounded just fine.

"I'm glad you approve," said Nimāi. "I wouldn't want you to think

I am in *māyā*. Keśava Prabhu said a wife could help me in my Kṛṣṇa consciousness, but I don't want to stop working with you and the other prabhus in our *āśrama*. To me that's still the most important thing, especially now that you have started this preaching. I think you could continue preaching even in the countries we visit. There are plenty of mice there! I may not be much good for preaching myself, but if I can assist you in missions like the one you just performed, maybe that's my niche."

Bhīma dāsa couldn't help but show his disappointment to Nimāi. "Why are you getting married?" he asked.

"I figured it would happen sooner or later, so why not sooner?" said Nimāi.

Why *am I* getting married? Nimāi thought for a moment and then answered himself, "Because sometimes I am agitated. Because I am lonely." He also had an idea that maybe it would be nice to have a wife like so many devotees did and just go on doing devotional service, but with double the strength. Nimāi had no deep illusions that marriage was the answer to all problems, but it was something he probably should do. People often told him that some of his habits were not those of a strict *brahmacārī*. Even keeping pets, one of the *saṅkīrtana* men had said, was an indication of that. Nimāi knew his willingness to marry was a symptom of being less spiritually advanced, but he accepted it and was willing to see the bright side. The idea of marrying a simple, chaste Hindu girl was appealing to him. He didn't like disappointing the *brahmacārī*s, but what could he do?

Keśava phoned Nimāi's temple president and explained the proposal to him, and Vibhu reluctantly agreed. He had just been about to tell the *brahmacārī* party to go out again on the road, but he knew Nimāi wasn't up to it. He agreed that Keśava could take Nimāi down to the Caribbean and try to find him a wife.

Nimāi prayed to Kṛṣṇa, "Please don't let me be in *māyā* about this." He wanted to convince himself it was all right, and yet he knew it wasn't the highest standard. "But since when," thought Nimāi, "have I ever conducted devotional service at the highest standard?"

"What do you think?" Nimāi asked Choṭa.

"We can at least go to that place, Guyana," said Choṭa. "You don't have to absolutely decide now."

"But if I go, it's expected I'll do it," said Nimāi. "I wish I could just be a pure devotee and not have to worry about such things. But I am not."

Choṭa couldn't imagine anything like Kṛṣṇa conscious marriage among mice. For him and the other mice, becoming Kṛṣṇa conscious meant giving up association of the opposite sex.

"From what you've told me," said Choṭa, "there is no big objection to a human marrying in Kṛṣṇa consciousness. As you said, Kṛṣṇa was married, Lord Śiva was married, Lord Brahmā was married ..."

And so Nimāi consoled himself with the assistance of his friend, but the incident had raised some doubts in Choṭa's mind. Choṭa was usually very simple and he didn't doubt Nimāi's decision, but he began to wonder again whether mice could get married in Kṛṣṇa consciousness. It made him more aware that there were many unsettled areas in regard to the mouse species and spiritual life.

"How am I supposed to figure these things out?" Choṭa asked.

"We can't figure everything out at once," said Nimāi. "This is all new and I don't know the answers. Mouse preaching has never been done before. Even human beings in the West have only taken to Kṛṣṇa consciousness for about twenty years, since Prabhupāda came. So, there are still unsettled questions, like how to develop the social system of *varṇāśrama*. Don't trouble yourself about it."

"But there is one thing that does trouble me," said Choṭa. "A mouse only lives for a year or so. As young as I am, me and the other boys are more than two thirds finished. What if ... What if we have to leave our bodies before any other mice become interested?"

"That's also a speculation," said Nimāi. "Everything is in Kṛṣṇa's hands. But thinking like that is good. We should all think that we don't have a minute to spare."

With Nimāi's permission, Choṭa made another visit to the favorable Albino and Oldfield mice communities. He took Arjuna with him and distributed *prasādam* and chanting.

Nimāi was busy preparing to leave with Keśava for the Caribbean, but his mind kept reflecting on what Choṭa had said and the reply he had given as a dutiful preceptor. It was true: not a moment should be wasted. Seeking a wife should also be undertaken in that spirit. It was all right to get married and to travel for that purpose, but the main thing was to always remember that Kṛṣṇa consciousness is the goal of life.

On the evening of their journey Nimāi felt sad and somewhat fearful to be leaving his native land and his home temple. He prayed to Kṛṣṇa for protection, for himself "and for my devotee friends, and for the short-lived mice, and for everyone. Please engage us in Your service."

Mother Pārvatī said that she would take care of Nimāi's mice while he traveled abroad. "It would be difficult to pass through Customs and Immigration with the mice," she said. But Nimāi flatly refused. "It may not be so difficult getting into those countries," said Keśava Prabhu, "but getting back into the U.S. could be a problem."

Nimāi said he was willing to take his chances. And so, he fashioned a lunch box into a mouse carrier, punching small air holes in it and draping a shirt over it as camouflage. He briefed the mice on how they should be quiet during the travels and of the risks that they would encounter.

"A mouse's life is nothing but risks," said Choṭa. "If we are in our nest, or if we are out in a field, or at any given moment without our hearing it, a cat or owl could strike. So why shouldn't we travel with you?"

"Kṛṣṇa is our protector," said Arjuna. Nimāi noticed that the mice had become increasingly fearless since their preaching tours. Choṭa had been making remarks that "death can come at any moment," but he didn't say it in a morbid way. He said it to remind himself and whomever he spoke to, that everything depends on Kṛṣṇa. As he liked to tell everyone he met, "Life is short. Just chant Hare Kṛṣṇa."

"It only appears that I am taking care of you," said Nimāi. "Your association is what keeps me going."

Keśava was aware that Nimāi was very fond of his pets, and he made no objection. To him, Nimāi was a child, like one of his young daughters. He was aware that "Nimāi the gnome" was a bit of a laughing stock in the movement, but he saw him as an innocent.

During the five-hour flight to Santo Domingo, Keśava told Nimāi what he could expect on entering householder life. "You should consider how to make money," said Keśava. "What kind of work is suited to you. That might even mean getting further education." Nimāi didn't want to admit it, but he had never even thought of such things. His own mother and father were 1960s hippies, and he himself had dropped out of high school. When he joined the Movement, he assumed that he would be a full-time devotee and not be involved at all in "materialistic life." But as he listened to Keśava, it seemed like all that might have to change.

"Couldn't I get married," asked Nimāi, "and just live in a simple way with my wife in the temple?"

"Yes, you could be a poor *brāhmaṇa*," said Keśava. "That's one way. But to do that you and your wife would have to agree to accept whatever the temple gave you. What if you needed some money? And what about when you have children? What if you or your wife wants to have an apartment? And besides, the temple authorities might tell you that they couldn't maintain you even as a poor *brāhmaṇa*." Nimāi felt bewildered. It sounded almost as bad as living in the freezing van.

Keśava was traveling with Nimāi in order to help him find a wife as well as to do some business in the Caribbean countries. He had brought devotional paintings and jewelry with him, and he would show the devotees how to sell them. Nimāi would also try to learn by assisting Keśava.

"Didn't Prabhupāda say that selling his books was the best business?" asked Nimāi.

"Yes," said Keśava, "if you can live off a percentage of the profits. I did that for ten years, but then I couldn't keep it up. Do you think you could become a book distributor?"

Nimāi didn't think he could. Whenever he had tried to distribute books, he had found it very difficult to face people's rude remarks and constant rejections. Even when he stayed out all day, he didn't make a profit. He was grateful that Keśava was introducing him to the realities of householder life in a gentle way, but he wasn't completely convinced that he'd have to become a businessman. He preferred not to think about it and looked out the plane window, softly chanting on his beads.

After a few hours in the air Nimāi had covertly slipped *prasādam* to the mice, and they were content. Most of the people on the plane were watching the in-flight movie, so Nimāi had time to kill. He began to write a letter:

Dear Gurudeva,

Please accept my humble obeisances. All glories to Śrīla Prabhupāda and to you. I want to keep in touch with you about my devotional life because unless one pleases the spiritual master, he cannot make advancement in Kṛṣṇa consciousness.

I think I am getting married. I hope you approve. I know this means I am less intelligent. I haven't gotten married yet, though. Kṛṣṇa consciousness is still most important to me. Please tell me what to do.

I would like to tell you more about the mouse that I brought to your *āśrama*. I think you remember how he almost died, but then in your room he came back to life, and you fed him some *prasādam*. Now there are two more mice. Do you remember what I told you about how I was having a spiritual exchange with them and talking to them about Kṛṣṇa consciousness? You never really said definitely what you thought about that, except that I should be humble. I have not told anyone else about this. No one knows it or understands. But I thought that I should tell you. I want to let you know everything I do so that you will approve, or else it is useless.

The mice actually go out and preach to other mice. I know it sounds crazy, but it says in the *Garuḍa Purāṇa* that they can be given Kṛṣṇa consciousness too. It is all happening by Kṛṣṇa's grace. Please let me know what you think, Śrīla Gurudeva.

Trying to be your servant,
the most fallen, Nimāi dāsa

P.S. Is it all right that I write to you like this? I will write to you again from Guyana where I am supposed to meet a wife. Keśava Prabhu is taking me there and teaching me about *gṛhastha* life. You once told me that if I thought I should get married I should go ahead. Is that right?"

Chapter 11

They sat on the roof of the ISKCON temple in Santo Domingo. To Nimāi, the tropical dawn seemed more relaxing than other skies he had seen, especially because the weather was so warm and everything was so new. Although he could hear an occasional motor scooter and cars in the distance, he felt as if he were way up on a solitary mountain top. It was a small, flat roof which he had reached by a metal ladder, and no one had noticed him. Nimāi let the mice out of their cage, and they ran about for exercise and to satisfy their insatiable curiosity. But after a few minutes, they sat close to Nimāi and asked him to tell them Kṛṣṇa conscious stories.

Over the months Nimāi had discovered that the mice were more receptive to stories than to straight philosophy. Memorizing Sanskrit verses was very difficult for them. But stories! He had told them all the pastimes he knew of Hanumān and the monkeys and had begun to study the Rāmāyaṇa to find new ones. They especially liked stories involving how God and God's pure devotees showed kindness to the animals, or narratives in which animals displayed higher consciousness. Hanumān and the Vānara soldiers were subhuman, but they were great fighters, eloquent speakers, and staunch devotees. And then there was Garuḍa who appeared to be only a bird, but of whom Prabhupāda had written, "Garuḍa is the greatest of all Vaiṣṇavas."

Nimāi also liked to tell them about the old bird Jaṭāyu from the Rāmāyaṇa, because that was one of his favorites. Devotees were usually victorious in their fights with demons, but Jaṭāyu was defeated by Rāvaṇa. Even in his defeat, however, he was glorified by Rāma, who performed his funeral ceremony. Nimāi had even heard Prabhupāda mention Jaṭāyu in a lecture. Prabhupāda said that even if the devotees are sometimes overcome by demons, like Jaṭāyu was, they are never defeated. Nimāi liked that because he himself felt that he was often defeated, and yet, he could still be a victor in Kṛṣṇa's eyes.

"Tell us again," said Choṭa, "about the dog that was sent back to Godhead by Lord Caitanya."

"Śivānanda Sena was a devotee," Nimāi began, "who used to escort all the other devotees when they traveled from Bengal to see Lord Caitanya in Jagannātha Purī. So, one time he allowed a dog to go with them, and he supplied the dog with food and took care of it. Once when they were crossing a river the boatman would not allow the dog, but Śivānanda Sena paid its toll."

"That's like you, Nimāi," said Arjuna, "you are taking us on the plane even though it's risky."

"I'm no Śivānanda Sena," said Nimāi. "So, one time, Śivānanda Sena was detained by a toll man, and he forgot to feed the dog its cooked rice and the dog disappeared. Śivānanda Sena stayed up all night fasting and unhappy, but he couldn't find the dog. Śrīla Prabhupāda has written a very interesting purport on this. I have it written down in my notebook:

> There are many other instances in which the pet animal of a Vaiṣṇava was delivered back home to Vaikuṇṭhaloka, back to Godhead. Such is the benefit of somehow or other becoming the favorite of a Vaiṣṇava. Śrīla Bhaktivinoda Ṭhākura has also sung *kīṭa-janma ha-u yathā tuyā dāsa* in *Śaraṇāgati*. There is no harm in taking birth again and again. Our only desire should be to take birth under the care of a Vaiṣṇava.... We may conclude that even as dogs we must take shelter of a Vaiṣṇava. The benefit will be the same as that which accrues to an advanced devotee under a Vaiṣṇava's care.
>
> —*Cc Antya, 1.24 purport*

When Nimāi read passages like that, both he and the mice felt completely confirmed. Even if no one else understood or believed that *jīva* souls could become devotees while in their animal bodies, Śrīla Prabhupāda knew it, and he had written about it in his books.

"Prabhupāda says," said Choṭa, "that there are many other instances in which the pet animal of a Vaiṣṇava went back to Godhead. What are some others?"

"First let me finish the story of the dog," said Nimāi. "When all the devotees got to Jagannātha Purī to meet Lord Caitanya, He was taking His lunch *prasādam*. And there, with the devotees, they saw that same dog. The dog was sitting a little apart from the Lord. Lord Caitanya was throwing him remnants of green coconut pulp and saying to the dog, 'Chant the holy names of *Rāma*, Kṛṣṇa, and Hari.' The dog was eating the pulp and chanting, 'Kṛṣṇa, Kṛṣṇa,' again and again, to the great surprise of all the devotees. Then when Śivānanda entered, he humbly offered his obeisances to the dog just to counteract his offenses to it. And the next day no one saw the dog because it had obtained its spiritual body and left for Vaikuṇṭha. There is another purport to this that I have written down:

> This is the result of *sādhu-saṅga*—consequent association with Śrī Caitanya Mahāprabhu and promotion back home, back to Godhead. This result is possible even for a dog, by the mercy of a Vaiṣṇava.... It is therefore requested that all our devotees in the ISKCON community become pure Vaiṣṇavas, so that by their mercy all the people of the world will be transferred to Vaikuṇṭhaloka, even without their knowledge. Everyone should be given a chance to take *prasāda* and thus be induced to chant the holy names of Kṛṣṇa and dance in ecstasy. By these three processes, although performed without knowledge or education, even an animal went back to Godhead.

"Is that possible for us also?" asked Yamala.

"Yes, definitely," said Nimāi. "Even though I am not really a Vaiṣṇava myself, by telling you what Prabhupāda said and by our chanting Hare Kṛṣṇa, you are getting the association of the topmost Vaiṣṇava. There was once a rat who went on the altar looking for food in a Viṣṇu temple. He saw the flame on a ghee lamp before the Deities. He mistook the flame for some food and went to eat it. Now, that ghee wick was buried in the candle and it was just about to go out, but when the rat touched it, the flame burned his whiskers and the wick flared up brightly again. So, the Lord recognized that as favorable service to Him, and the rat was liberated. That shows how the power of devotional service can work even on animals."

"He was liberated!" cried Choṭa. "Are there any mice stories?"

"I don't know all the stories," said Nimāi. "The one I do know of a mouse is not so favorable. It's called 'Again become a mouse.' A mouse went to a *yogī* who had mystic powers. The mouse asked to be transformed into a cat. Do you know why he asked that?"

"So that he wouldn't be attacked by the cat," said Arjuna.

"Yes, so the *yogī* turned him into a cat, but then a big dog chased him. So, he went back again and asked to be changed into a dog, and the *yogī* changed him. But then a tiger chased him. So, he asked to be changed into a tiger, and the *yogī* did it. Then once he was a tiger, the former mouse looked at the *yogī* and wanted to attack and eat him. So, the *yogī* said, 'Again become a mouse!' And he turned him back into an insignificant mouse. Who knows the point of that story?"

All three mice raised their tails, and Nimāi pointed to Arjuna. "We shouldn't approach Kṛṣṇa or His devotee for material things," said Arjuna.

"It also shows," said Choṭa, "what will happen to us if we misuse the benedictions that you are giving us in Kṛṣṇa consciousness. If we forget and become puffed up, we'll again be reduced to mindless mice."

"Can you tell us more about animals in Kṛṣṇa consciousness?" asked Arjuna.

"Not only animals can receive Kṛṣṇa consciousness," said Nimāi, "but even plants, which have lower consciousness. Lord Caitanya wanted all fallen souls to be delivered. He asked Haridāsa Ṭhākura how the non-moving living entities could be given Kṛṣṇa consciousness. Haridāsa said that when a devotee loudly chants Hare Kṛṣṇa and there are trees around, it sounds like an echo comes from the forest. But actually, that's not an echo. That's the chanting of the trees and plants and creepers. Therefore, Haridāsa was describing how human beings can bless the lower creatures and give them Kṛṣṇa consciousness by the loud chanting of Hare Kṛṣṇa."

"Mostly humans," said Choṭa, "think it's useless to help animals. They think we have no souls. Little do they know."

"But the great devotees know," said Nimāi. "And that's why Lord Buddha came, just to protect the animals who were being slaughtered by the priests of the *Vedas*. All devotees are meant to be nonviolent to animals. Prabhupāda used to say we should offer respects even to an ant."

As they spoke, the soft rosy hue of the sky changed into bright sunshine.

"We should go down now," said Nimāi, "and take *prasādam*."

Nimāi liked the devotees in Santo Domingo, although he couldn't converse much with them, since he didn't know Spanish and they didn't know English. When the Spanish devotees saw that he was carrying pet mice they laughed, but it wasn't malicious, and Nimāi laughed with them. They called him "*Ratón Bhakta*!" (mouse *bhakta*). Nimāi wasn't sure whether "mouse *bhakta*" was a name for him or for his mice devotees. The Dominicans were more curious about the mice than the North Americans, and Nimāi allowed them to handle them gently. They warned Nimāi that there were rats in the temple and he should not let the mice out. But they told him that there was a special mouse that had been living in the temple building ever since the devotees had been there. This mouse, who they called *Raton Devóto*, had some unusual habits. He would come out in view of the Deities, but would not climb on the altar or attempt to take food from the Deities' plates. Therefore, they had spared its life and allowed it to move somewhat freely, especially during the *kīrtanas* and *āratis*. Nimāi saw the *ratón devoto* for himself when, during a *maṅgala-ārati*, a dark house mouse ambled into view near the altar, stayed a while, and then disappeared.

Keśava had scheduled their stay for only three days in Santo Domingo, and then they were planning to fly to Trinidad. Keśava wanted Nimāi to assist him and learn some of the tricks of the jewelry selling trade. He had asked Nimāi to assemble some jewelry, placing stones into earrings, but the work was too fine and detailed for Nimāi. He knocked over a box containing small pieces of ornaments, and it took him an hour to place them all back in their right order again.

Keśava then asked Nimāi to accompany him on wholesale purchases from dealers in the city, so Nimāi tagged along. He watched carefully and tried to help. The dealers were not supposed to know that they were devotees, but in one shop Nimāi took off his cap and the man saw his *śikhā*. As blunders like this added up, Keśava began to wonder whether Nimāi could actually become a businessman. This led to more talks about *gṛhastha* life. "We are not just on a holiday spree," said Keśava. "Getting married doesn't mean just picking out a pretty girl. You will have to learn to be responsible in many ways." Nimāi listened and didn't say much.

As for the mice, they wanted to preach. "Let us go out," said Choṭa. But Nimāi was worried about the rats in the building.

"Maybe you shouldn't be so bold," said Nimāi. "You can't exactly imitate the human preachers. It is difficult enough to go out as a human, but we are not being preyed upon by murderers on every block. Why take such chances?"

"If we stayed at home," said Choṭa, "we would be equally in danger. Did you ever see a cat sitting without moving in front of a mouse hole? A mouse can hear very well, and he can see movements, but the cats just sit there quietly and without motion. We come out and don't even know they are there. And if we are outside, owls suddenly come down on us. They have wings that we can't hear flapping. Sometimes a killer comes right into our nest. So, we might as well preach while we can."

Nimāi had mixed feelings, similar to what he had felt in the beginning when the mice went out for the first time. He was supposed to be their protector, but he didn't want his own lack of boldness to affect them. After keeping them in the cage for two days he relented and agreed to a twelve-hour preaching tour. Within minutes, the three chattering mice scampered out of the cage and into the nearest crevice in the wall.

Choṭa had Yamala and Arjuna drag along some *prasādam* in a cloth, because *prasādam* was the most immediate way to attract a spirit soul—especially among the animals. But it presented the same problem as before. A mouse would accost them in an attempt to capture the *prasādam*. The preachers wanted to give just a little piece of *prasādam* to each mouse, so that more mice could benefit, but it usually turned into a scuffle. Now that there were three preachers stamping their feet and making defensive postures, they could chase away the intruders, but they had not come out for that. They wanted to distribute mercy.

It was very difficult. Just the fact that three male mice were wandering into the territory of other mice was bound to bring them an unfriendly reception. Choṭa was well aware of the mouse practice of scent marking by urinating around its territorial perimeter. According to the law of the mouse kingdom, a male mouse would never cross the urine-marked border of another buck. For preaching, they did it. But when their attempts initiated frequent angry encounters, Choṭa abandoned the *prasādam* and continued without it.

And then they were discovered by a rat. He was huge and mangy and leaped at them when they were pausing for a breather in the corner of the room. The mice scattered in three directions. The rat chased

Yamala who went up a potted palm tree like an acrobat and jumped onto a window ledge and down the outside wall. The rat couldn't follow, and when he turned to chase the others, they had escaped. But it had been a close call, and the rat continued sniffing their trail.

The three preachers regrouped in between the walls. They stayed undercover, still looking for a chance to spread the holy name. But how was it possible? Walking and walking, they approached a wall near the Deity room. There they met an old dark mouse who stood near an opening that led right onto the altar of Gaura-Nitāi.

"Who are you? Where are you going?" asked the old mouse. He was slightly bigger than the preachers, but his dull coat, slightly arched back, and lumpy skin indicated he was aged.

Choṭa briefly explained their mission, but the mouse couldn't seem to understand. The preachers were attracted, however, by his peaceful movements and considerate advice. "Don't go out this opening," said the old mouse. "The altar is here."

"And the rat?" asked Yamala. He was still shaking from the chase.

"No, the rat doesn't go on the altar," said the old mouse. "They would kill him if he did. Only I go."

"What do you mean?" asked Choṭa.

"They allow me to go because I don't crawl on the altar or eat the Deities food."

"Do you know about Kṛṣṇa?" asked Choṭa.

"Not much," said the old mouse. Choṭa was surprised. He had thought that he was the only mouse who knew anything about Kṛṣṇa.

"All I know," said the old mouse, "is that I don't want to crawl on Their altar or eat Their food. I like it that way, and the humans do too. And I come to hear the singing."

"You are a devotee!" said Choṭa. He tried to explain as simply as possible that all living beings were actually servants of God, spirit souls. All three preachers were so eager to share their knowledge that they began to speak at once, telling bits of stories and different aspects of the philosophy. But the old mouse could barely understand. It may have been his old age, but he was also somewhat dull. Choṭa decided that he was definitely a devotee with a service attitude about guarding the temple altar and being reverent to the Lord and the devotees. Choṭa asked the old mouse, "Would you come back with us and meet our teacher?"

"I'll just stay here," he said." There is no need to go anywhere else. This is my place."

"At least let us bring you some *prasādam*," said Arjuna. The old mouse agreed, although he didn't seem excited even by that. Despite limited communication, the preachers and the old mouse stayed together for two hours. The old mouse then invited them to come to the entrance of the hole and see the next *ārati*. "But don't try to run out or take any food," he said.

"We would never do that," said Choṭa.

It was *sundara-ārati,* and very few devotees were in the temple room. As the *pūjārī* methodically performed his *ārati*, he glanced down and saw the old mouse come out, but he did not notice three other mice pressed eagerly at the entrance to the hole, watching the holy offerings and the golden forms of Gaura-Nitāi.

Chapter 12

Their plane left for Port of Spain, Trinidad, at 7:00 P.M. Nimāi tried sleeping through the in-flight movie, but Keśava woke him to explain the immigration card and what they should say when questioned at the immigration desk.

"It's a bit complicated," said Keśava, "so listen to me carefully. Trinidad is an easy country to enter for American citizens. The government has no objection to devotees of the Hare Kṛṣṇa movement, but there are particular bureaucratic formalities which have to be observed. Since a devotee is considered to be a preacher or missionary, he is expected to obtain a preacher's permit."

Keśava had already phoned the temple and told the devotees to get the permits, but that usually took two weeks, and he wasn't sure whether the temple would have received them yet. If they did have the permits, the devotees would be standing behind the immigration officials and would come forward at the right moment and present them. But in order to use a permit, the country required that the preacher also have a visa, although ordinarily Americans didn't need visas. But that wasn't so important either, because you could just fill out a visa-waiver form and pay ten dollars. But if they knew you were a devotee, and if you said that you were going to preach but you had no permit, then you could actually be denied entry.

"So the simplest thing," said Keśava, "is just to go in as tourists. Say you're going to the carnival, or that you're going to see your girlfriend." Nimāi said that he couldn't grasp all the rules, but he would do as Keśava suggested. Keśava then filled out the cards while Nimāi went back to sleep, his camouflaged mouse box held securely on his lap.

It was past ten o'clock when they landed. Nimāi was groggy, and the unknown country made him uneasy. They stood in a long queue facing advertising billboards while officials in tropical uniforms questioned the passengers and stamped passports. Nimāi's main concern was the mice and his fear of what might happen to them. There were no devotees from the Trinidad temple present with permits, so Keśava signaled to Nimāi that they should just go through without mentioning they were devotees.

After half an hour it was Nimāi's turn to face the immigration man. "Why you comin' to Trinidad?" The man gave him a quick but penetrating look.

"To see places," Nimāi said, and he suddenly became flustered.

"What places?"

"Like museums and churches," said Nimāi. He recalled Keśava's advice to say he was going to see a girlfriend, but it seemed too crude.

"Churches?" asked the man. "What religion are you?"

"Hare Kṛṣṇa," said Nimāi. "We're going to visit our temple."

Nimāi was aware that he had just shifted his identity, but he didn't think it would do any harm to speak the truth. He saw Keśava Prabhu get his passport stamped and go through into the luggage area.

"Do you have a speaker's permit?" asked the man.

"They said they would get one," said Nimāi, "but I don't see them."

Nimāi sensed that his interview was going poorly, but he decided not to care. He wasn't a clever talker, so there was no use trying to make up stories. The man asked Nimāi to go into an office for another interview. There he was told that as a missionary worker he should have had his friends in Trinidad secure him a preacher's permit. The man at the office desk was polite with Nimāi but very official. There were rules to be followed, and he had not followed them.

At one point the head agent seemed to waver, as if he might let Nimāi enter. He then asked, "If you go into the country without a speaker's permit, would you preach?"

Nimāi wasn't sure exactly what he should've said according to Keśava, but he said, "Yes." Although he didn't usually preach, he knew that he should preach, and after all, maybe the mice would do some preaching at least.

"You see," said Nimāi, "even if we don't preach as an official speaker, a devotee of the Lord should always tell people something about God, because the purpose of life is to develop love of God." The agent heard these words politely, almost approvingly, but now he had decided the case. There were too many contradictions and so Nimāi could not enter. He would have to return to America on the next flight.

Nimāi could hardly believe what the man was saying. He tried explaining that he had friends in Trinidad, and they were waiting for him. But he could not produce a speaker's permit and he couldn't undo the contradictions he had spoken in the interview. The man then explained what would be done. Nimāi would be escorted by a police guard and given a room, free of charge, at the airport hotel. The guard would stay in the hall just to make sure that Nimāi wouldn't try to enter illegally. Nimāi would stay overnight in the hotel room and at seven o'clock in the morning he could catch the flight on the same airlines back to Miami.

The policemen were sympathetic with Nimāi's dilemma, but they had made their decision and it would stick. A police guard, not much older than Nimāi, escorted him in a taxi to the nearby airport hotel. As they rode, Nimāi asked the guard if he had ever seen the Hare Kṛṣṇa devotees in Trinidad. "Ya man," the guard replied, "I seen dem shantin' in Port o' Spain."

Nimāi locked the hotel door from the inside and let his mice out of the lunch box. At least they had entered the country without any difficulty.

"What demons!" squeaked Yamala. "Why don't they let you in like everyone else?"

"If they send you away, will you come right back?" asked Choṭa.

Although Nimāi was as anxious as the mice, their agitation aroused his paternal feelings. "Whatever Kṛṣṇa desires," said Nimāi. He had packed a few *samosas* for the flight, and he broke them up and shared them with his friends. He then began reading and explaining from *Bhagavad-gītā As It Is.*

Nimāi was surprised at how well he was making the best of a bad situation. If he could keep on talking about Kṛṣṇa, it would be all right. But he was nervous in the unwholesome surroundings. A calypso band was playing in the garden of the hotel. Everyone Nimāi had met in the lobby seemed drunk, and the whole place was in a party mood. At least he had his own police guard.

Despite the loud music, Nimāi fell asleep on the hotel bed. But soon he was awakened by a knock on the door. He thought it was the police guard, but when he opened it, it was a young woman. She was a Trinidadian Hindu.

"Are you de guy dats bein' deported?" Nimāi could tell that she was drunk.

"Yes," said Nimāi. He wanted to get rid of her as soon as possible.

"De guard left," she said and laughed. "So, I t'ought you might want to come out and have some fun."

"No thank you," he said and began closing the door.

"How old are you?" she asked.

Nimāi didn't want to shut the door in her face so he paused and said, "I'm twenty-one."

"Me too!" she said.

They both heard sounds of persons approaching. She took this opportunity to push Nimāi's door open and step inside. Her quick move surprised and frightened Nimāi. In the light of his room, he saw her for what she was. She was slightly built and wore gaudy lipstick and a cheap blouse and short skirt. Nimāi was used to seeing Hindu ladies as chaste mothers, dressed in *sārīs* with *tilaka*. Whenever he saw one like this, he felt disgust and pity. "My friends at de bar said, 'tell dat guy why don't you join us?' If you have to leave the country, you might as well have some fun first."

"I don't go into bars," said Nimāi. "I'm a devotee of Kṛṣṇa." Nimāi felt confident, partly because she was young and a Hindu. "You are a Hindu?" he asked.

"Ya," she replied, changing her tone. "But I don't believe in dat anymore. So, you're a Hare Kṛṣṇa. Dat's why you had trouble with immigration. So come to de bar and have some fun."

"That's not my idea of fun," said Nimāi. "Getting intoxicated and having a big headache in the morning is no fun. What do you mean you don't believe anymore? I bet no one ever taught you about Kṛṣṇa. Did you ever read the *Bhagavad-gītā*?"

"No," she said. "Do you want to teach me?" Nimāi saw she was in no condition to hear *Bhagavad-gītā*. "You're a funny lookin' boy," she said smiling. "What is your name?"

"Nimāi," he said. "What's yours?"

"My name is Mina," she said.

Nimāi felt that she was getting the upper hand. There was no use trying to preach or tell her about Kṛṣṇa, so talking for too long was dangerous. He suddenly thought of his mice and how they were listening to all this.

"If you don't want to go to de bar," she said, looking around the room, "maybe I can bring you somethin'. Would you like a cold beer?" She then sat down on the edge of his bed. The calypso band was so loud that the bass notes were vibrating the walls.

"I think you'd better go," said Nimāi. "I don't want anything. I'm a *brahmacārī*. Do you know what that is?"

Mina said she didn't know what a *brahmacārī* was, and by now Nimāi didn't feel like telling her. He knew he was vulnerable—there was no devotee around and he was thousands of miles away from home. If he did desire sinful activity, this would be the time and the place to do it; no one would know. But he didn't want to. He thought again of Choṭa and the other mice. It wouldn't be possible to do any nonsense, he realized, because he could never do it in their presence. He also thought of Gurudeva, who seemed strongly present. "All I have to do," thought Nimāi, "is be firm and get her out of the room." He knew what he wanted, but she was taking advantage of his politeness.

"You should go now," he said. "Please," and he indicated the door.

"What's de matter, Nimāi? Are you afraid to have some fun?"

Her words seemed so stupid to Nimāi that he regained confidence.

"Yes, I'm afraid of *māyā*," he said. "You should also be afraid. Look at you. You're a mess. You can hardly think straight because you drink so much. Don't you know that human life can end at any moment? You say you have forgotten Hinduism, but you probably never learned the right thing. In *Bhagavad-gītā* Kṛṣṇa says that the material world is a dangerous place, but a human being can use his life to understand he's eternal soul. And if we understand that, then at the time of death we can go back to Godhead for a life of real happiness, with God, Kṛṣṇa. If you just waste your life drinking, partying, and hanging around with people who really don't care for you, then you're wasting your life. You should be afraid."

The girl made a bitter expression with her mouth and got up to leave. "OK, Mr. Preacher," she said, "you're no fun."

Nimāi knew he had been heavy, but she was a Hindu and could probably understand under all her nonsense that she was wrong. As he let her out the door he said, "Hare Kṛṣṇa." In a mocking tone she replied, "Hare Kṛṣṇa, Nimāi," which sounded a lot like the old "Nimāi the gnome" cracks from the temple boys.

Nimāi locked the door, turned off the light, and went back to bed. He was proud that he had protected his *brahmacarya*, but he felt his heart pounding loudly. He grew afraid and began praying in his mind, "Kṛṣṇa, please save me." From the concert raucous going on downstairs, he heard the announcer shout, "Let's have a big round of applause for the Mighty Sparrow!"

Nimāi dozed fitfully until he was wakened again by a knock on the door. It was Keśava Prabhu. Nimāi embraced him with a cry, and Keśava hugged him warmly.

"What happened?" Keśava asked. "What did you say that they didn't let you in?"

Nimāi explained that he told the man he wanted to enter Trinidad to see the museums and churches, but then he had admitted that he was a Hare Kṛṣṇa devotee. "And then he asked me for a speaker's permit."

"But actually a devotee doesn't need a permit," said Keśava.

"But I told him I was going to preach."

"Why?"

"He asked me."

Keśava shook his head and said, "Nimāi." He had guessed as much. Like a foolish moth Nimāi dāsa had become caught in the web of immigration bureaucracy, because "he asked me."

"Anyway," said Keśava, "Mr. Persad, who's a good friend of the temple, is an officer in the immigration department. We think we'll be able to get your passport back, and you'll be able to stay in the country for a week. I have to go now to see him, and either bring him here or get him to write a letter. But if anyone asks you, say that you're coming to visit the temples; you're not coming as a speaker. Do you understand? Don't say you're coming to preach."

Nimāi thought, "But I have already been preaching." And he told Keśava about the girl who had come to his room. Nimāi said, "It was a close call, but Kṛṣṇa saved me."

Keśava restrained his own exasperated feelings and remembered that Nimāi was just a simple child who had been through a difficult night. So Keśava sat down with him and spoke in a more relaxed way. He asked about the mice, and Nimāi brought them over for Keśava's inspection. They both began to speak about Mother Pārvatī as a well-wisher of Nimāi's pet mice. Both Keśava and Nimāi praised her ways with children and animals. Keśava said that Nimāi's "close call" was another proof that he would be much better off in the security of a marital relationship.

"In the *Bhāgavatam*," said Keśava, "a wife is described as protection. She's like a fortress. One sage says that as a fort commander easily conquers invading plunderers, so by taking shelter of a wife one can conquer the senses, which are unconquerable in other social orders. Prabhupāda says that the householder is on the safe side."

Nimāi admitted that he certainly didn't feel on the safe side. They shared some fresh *prasādam* which Keśava had brought from the Trinidad temple, and then Keśava left. Nimāi's deportation time was only three hours away.

The letter which Keśava fetched from Mr. Persad was convincing enough for the immigration officials to waive Nimāi's deportation. They had no serious objection to Nimāi, except that he kept failing his verbal interviews. Nimāi was spared a further interview, so when Keśava came back to the hotel everything had been accomplished. They left together to go straight to the temple.

On their way out of the hotel lobby, the girl who had come to Nimāi's door approached him in the lobby. She was dressed more modestly and was sober. "I want to apologize," she said, "for how I acted last night."

"That's all right," said Nimāi. He couldn't help showing that he was moved and pleased with her regret. "Why don't you come and visit our temple?" he said. "We have a feast every Sunday." He wrote down the address on a notepad and gave it to her.

"Will *you* be there?" she asked shyly.

"Yes," said Nimāi, but he thought, *That's not the point, Mina. The point is for you to see Kṛṣṇa and meet the devotee women at the temple.* "I'm just visiting for a week."

And so, they parted, nodding and showing respect with folded palms.

Chapter 13

As soon as they arrived at the Trinidad temple, the temple president drew Keśava Prabhu into his office for a private conversation. Nimāi was considered a very junior devotee, and so he was excluded from the serious talk, but he managed to listen from the hallway. The temple president asked Keśava Prabhu if he could help by talking to two different groups of devotees who were engaged in a controversy. One group was the black Trinidadians and the other was the Hindus. Their differences were similar to the differences of the nondevotees. The Hindu devotees were saying that one couldn't be a Kṛṣṇa conscious leader if he was a non-Hindu, and the other devotees were saying that the Hindu Hare Kṛṣṇas were like other hodgepodge Hindus. And so, for the next few hours Keśava was engaged behind a closed door talking to first one group and then another, trying to settle their differences.

Nimāi wasn't much interested in what was going on, and he also had other duties to perform, but occasionally he would come to the door and hear Keśava preaching. He was inspired to hear Keśava speaking so decisively, emphasizing that there should be no bodily differences in Kṛṣṇa consciousness. Devotees were on the spiritual platform; they should not think in designations like Hindu or non-Hindu. When he overheard the devotees challenging Keśava, Nimāi mostly heard character assassinations and tales of how one group was prejudiced against the other. They politely heard what Keśava had to say and admitted that his arguments had good logic and *śāstric* evidence, but when they left the room, they seemed to maintain their old opinions.

As for the mice, they all wanted to go out preaching. This time Nimāi was surrendered to their request. He began to see himself not as their proprietor or grand protector, but as a training coach. He knew he couldn't expect to keep them in a cage all day. Even the devotees who did not know his spiritual relationship with the mice sometimes remarked that he was cruel to keep them caged up so much. They also thought that keeping pets was whimsical sense gratification. Of course, Nimāi knew that wasn't true, but if all he did was keep the mice in a cage, then what was the point? It would be foolish. They were not his pets; they were devotees and that is why he cared for them.

As each mouse increased in their own conviction about Kṛṣṇa consciousness, Nimāi began to feel that he was becoming redundant. He didn't want to mention it to Choṭa because he knew that Choṭa would say no, they all depended on him. But Nimāi could see that the mice were becoming motivated by the simple desire to mix with other mice and give them an introduction to spiritual life. And although the mice would never say to Nimāi that they resented his treatment of them, they *had* openly said that their life duration was short and they wanted to spend it out on *saṅkīrtana*. Nimāi could see that despite his own good intentions, he was too often playing the role of a benevolent jailer. And so, rather than lamenting their request to get out and distribute the knowledge, Nimāi put aside any misgivings he had and shared their enthusiasm.

"Come back with some good news, Prabhus," he said, as they scurried single file into a hole in the temple wall.

The Trinidad temple mice were brown but of the same house mouse species as Choṭa.

"Where are you from?" asked a temple mouse. Just by sniffing and feeling the sound vibrations, Choṭa and his brothers sensed that these mice were not vicious. But neither were they very friendly.

"We come from up north," said Choṭa. "We're visiting temples."

"Well, you can't serve here," said the temple mouse. "Only mice born in the temple can serve." Choṭa was glad to at least hear the mouse speak of "service" and "the temple," since most mice had no such conceptions.

"*Jāyā*!" said Choṭa. "You know, then, that this is a temple? Do you know the purpose of a temple?"

"Of course," said the temple mouse, "It means we are special. Other buildings don't have incense and statues or a big kitchen and a big hall. Only we who live here have these."

"A temple is more than that," said Arjuna. "It's where God is worshiped."

"Yes, exactly," said the mouse.

Choṭa and his brothers didn't know whether to jump for joy or scratch their heads in puzzlement. This temple mouse was obviously concerned with more than just eating, mating, sleeping, and defending, but they had never come across a mouse with such pride before.

"You worship God?" asked Yamala.

"No," the temple mouse said, "the humans do that. We are the temple mice."

"We have heard from our teacher," said Choṭa, trying not to be proud of his own learning, "that in *Bhagavad-gītā*, the book which is kept in all the temples, God is the Supreme Person and all living creatures, including humans, as well as mice and other animals, differ only in their outer dress or bodies. We're all equal as spirit souls." By now several other brown temple mice had stopped to talk. One of them, who was older and plumper, smiled to hear Choṭa's spirited words.

"You can't know," said the plump mouse, "anything about a temple. Because, as you said, you come from the north. Only a temple mouse born here can know the activities of the temple. And you cannot stay here or eat the food. It's only for temple mice."

Choṭa assured them that they had their own food and were only visiting. With mousy shrewdness, Choṭa and his boys began to size up the situation. They did not feel the threat of physical attack, not like what they had encountered at Keśava's house in Pennsylvania. But at the same time, these temple mice were certainly different from the humble old mouse in Santo Domingo. They were civil, but quite unreceptive to hearing *Bhagavad-gītā*.

The temple mice brought Choṭa and his brothers to see their leader. He was a large mouse and sat on a raised nest surrounded by female mice as well as male attendants. The temple mice explained who the visitors were to the leader, who then asked, "What do the visitors want?" (He didn't ask Choṭa directly but communicated through the attendants.)

"Tell him," said Choṭa, "that we would like to chant the holy names of Kṛṣṇa for your pleasure."

The leader agreed that they would listen if the singing wasn't too long or too loud. The temple mice told Choṭa that he should also consider it a great honor to sing for their leader and for the assembly of temple mice.

The mice "from up north" then began singing the holy names in earnest, as they had learned from Nimāi and which they knew to be the same chanting that had been handed down from Lord Caitanya. After a few minutes the brown mice said, "That is all, please stop now."

As the visitors were escorted from the chambers, a few younger ones went with them to the door. Pressing close to Choṭa they spoke softly, "That was wonderful! We never knew that mice could chant like that. We thought it was only for humans."

"It's for everyone," whispered Choṭa. "That's the whole point. We are not actually mice, neither northern nor temple nor gray nor brown. We are spirit souls, and everyone should chant to develop love of Kṛṣṇa."

"Thank you, thank you," whispered another young mouse. "But I don't think they will ever do such chanting here. We listen through the walls when they chant."

"That's also good, just to hear," said Choṭa. "But both chanting and hearing is best. At least you can chant in private for your own benefit."

The temple mice had made it clear that Choṭa and his friends should return to where they came from. Choṭa decided to comply with their request, because the politeness with which they had been treated seemed thin. So, they returned to Nimāi Prabhu and asked his permission to go out into the fields to find less puffed-up mice.

But Nimāi wanted to hold an *iṣṭa-goṣṭhī* with him and the mice. Many things had happened recently, but they had not been able to have any heart-to-heart talks about them. An opportunity came when almost all of the Trinidad devotees went into town to distribute books at a Hindu festival. Nimāi volunteered to stay back to maintain the temple.

"We will make an agenda for an *iṣṭa-goṣṭhī*," said Nimāi. "Do you have any topics?" They were sitting on the back porch on the second story of the temple building. It was evening, and the sound of frogs filled the air.

Choṭa said, "I would like to hear you discuss, Nimāi, how a devotee can develop humility." Nimāi wrote the topic down and asked for others. Arjuna asked if Nimāi would tell them about upcoming travel plans. Yamala said he would like to give a report on their preaching.

"I have a couple of topics," said Nimāi. "I would like to speak a little bit about *gṛhastha* life, at least my own plans for it. I would also like to discuss the topic of our relationship and hear your views about it."

It was actually this last subject which had prompted Nimāi to hold the open meeting. He felt that his relationship with the mice was going through a significant change, and he wanted to face the truth of it.

"What do you want to say about humility?" asked Nimāi.

Choṭa cleared his throat. "I just wanted to say," he spoke softly, "that I have been guilty of great pride. When we met that old mouse who watches the *āratis* in Santo Domingo, I saw that he was actually a devotee. I was shocked because I thought that I was the only devotee among all the mice in the world."

Nimāi and the mice laughed at Choṭa's realization.

"Even Lord Brahmā," said Nimāi, "once thought that he was the only Brahmā, or controller of a universe. But Kṛṣṇa showed him that there are trillions of Brahmās, and in fact, the four-headed Brahmā is the smallest of all."

"I realize a little better now," said Choṭa, "that Kṛṣṇa can reveal Himself, and does, to many different mice and to any creature He wishes, anywhere in the world."

"But that should not diminish your desire to spread Kṛṣṇa consciousness," said Nimāi.

"Oh no!" said Choṭa intently. "I can see that there are very few devotees. For example, Yamala Prabhu, why don't you tell Nimāi about our *saṅkīrtana* in this temple?"

Yamala then told of the mice within the temple. "Just because they live here," said Yamala, "they think they are superior to everyone and that they know everything about temple life. Actually, they didn't know anything about higher consciousness, but when we tried to tell them, they said whatever we knew was unimportant."

Nimāi was no longer amazed to learn that whatever strange phenomenon existed in human society, a similar version was carried on in the lower kingdoms. But the mice wished to tell Nimāi all the details, and he was eager to hear from them.

When it was Nimāi's turn to talk about *gṛhastha* life he no longer felt inclined to say much. He mainly wanted to explain what had happened in the hotel room the other night and how it had been a very dangerous situation. Keśava Prabhu had said that marriage would protect one from temptation. The mice were respectful of Nimāi's personal plans for *gṛhastha* life, but it was not a subject that interested them very much so he dropped it.

"As for our travel plans," said Nimāi turning to Yamala, "I'm just following Keśava's schedule. We're supposed to leave here in a week and go to Guyana. That's a country in South America. It's mostly a big jungle, but there's a large Hindu population there, and the people are very pious and receptive. It will be an exciting place to pioneer your preaching."

"And the last topic on the agenda," said Nimāi, "is about you and me." He took a deep breath and sighed. He didn't know exactly what he wanted to say.

"I am pleased that you are preaching," Nimāi began, "and I wanted to let you know that I don't like keeping you in a cage so much of the time. When we first began to speak with each other you were so helpless ... I thought it wasn't wrong to keep you in the cage and sometimes take you out and give you a class or *prasādam*. What I mean to say is, I'm sorry that you spend so much of your time in 'jail.'"

"It is difficult," said Choṭa, "especially staying in this small travel box. But that doesn't mean our feelings toward you have changed!"

"Maybe we could live," said Yamala, "like we used to in Gurudeva's cabin. We were on our own, but we came to see you every day."

"Or maybe even that isn't necessary," said Nimāi thinking out loud.

"We're always very grateful to you," said Choṭa. The mice waited in silence to hear what else Nimāi wanted to say, but Nimāi decided to stop groping. The mice were no longer completely dependent on him, but he certainly wasn't telling them that he wanted to get rid of them.

"Maybe we can keep things as they are," said Choṭa.

"We'll see," said Nimāi. "Whatever Kṛṣṇa desires."

Keśava sold necklaces with locket-pictures of Rādhā-Kṛṣṇa and Lakṣmī-Nārāyaṇa to the Hindu villagers. He gave half the profits to the temple. Nimāi helped by assembling the jewelry. He was slow, but Keśava said, "At least don't sabotage." Then on the last day when a shipment of expensive silk paintings arrived from India, Nimāi slashed open the box with an X-Acto knife and ruined the six top paintings. He also lost a receipt on the same day. Keśava began yelling at him, but then Keśava stopped and took a long walk to chant his *japa*.

While attending the Sunday festival in the temple Nimāi was surprised to see Mina, the girl from the hotel, sitting with the other women. He said *"Haribol!"* to her and she smiled back. There was no need to talk further because she was mixing with some of the initiated women. They had even placed a *harināma cādar* around her head and shoulders.

The next morning Keśava and Nimāi were scheduled to leave on an early flight to Guyana. Usually, Nimāi walked through the security check with his "lunch box," but this time they asked him to open it. When the man saw the mice, he said they couldn't go. The only way they could possibly be allowed to travel was if they were medically examined, put into the luggage hold, and then re-examined at the port of destination.

"Then I'll just leave them behind with a friend," said Nimāi. He walked back into the airport terminal and returned ten minutes later smiling. He showed the guards the empty lunch box and they waved him through. Not even Keśava noticed that Nimāi had put one mouse in each of his *kurtā* pockets. Keśava also hadn't noticed the slight bulge at Nimāi's waist under his T-shirt where Choṭa was hiding "quiet as a mouse".

On the plane Nimāi returned the mice to the lunch box. The transaction was very upsetting for both him and the mice. It was also upsetting to Keśava who kept saying, "It's too much," while rubbing his temples with his fingertips. Furthermore, since Nimāi had made it through airport security several times without detection, he decided that the Trinidad capture had been a fluke. From there he concluded that it was safe to keep the mice in the lunch box, which he tried to disguise to look like he was carrying a very small suitcase containing an extra shirt and *cādar*.

But they caught him again in Guyana. This time Nimāi was sent to an office. The agent said that the mice must be confiscated, but when he left the room for a minute Nimāi popped the mice into the hidden places on his body. He then began crying out that the mice had escaped and run into the hall. The ruse was successful. But they kept the mouse box.

After these ordeals, they were relieved to get through customs and meet the devotees. Nimāi was anxious to find a new box for the mice. Keśava was wondering whether he could keep traveling with Nimāi.

"Guess who's here?" beamed Viṣṇudāsa, the Guyana temple president; then he gave his own answer. "Gurudeva is here!"

"Really?" Nimāi replied. At first, he couldn't really absorb how auspicious that was for him, but then his inner voice said, *He's your spiritual master; ask him what to do.*

Chapter 14

Gurudeva had come to Guyana to take part in the *padayātrā*. Modeled after the *padayātrā* in India, it was a walking tour of devotees, village to village. Gurudeva loved the simplicity of it: far away from the pressures of North America he could walk behind an ox-pulled cart and chant Hare Kṛṣṇa with simple devotees. And every evening hundreds of Hindus, sometimes thousands, gathered in a makeshift tent and attentively heard Gurudeva speak from the *Bhagavad-gītā* and *Śrīmad-Bhāgavatam*. And there was massive *prasādam* distribution. The plan was to stay out on the road for a month. During this time Gurudeva preferred to sleep in a tent, which took only a few minutes to set up in a field at night and could be dismantled quickly in the morning.

Gurudeva's secretary informed him that his disciple Nimāi had arrived and hoped to get an appointment for a private talk. Gurudeva had already seen him join the *padayātrā* with Keśava Prabhu. He was the same gawky but likeable Nimāi dāsa, only now, instead of one mouse he had three. He had smuggled all three mice into the country, and for want of a better cage he kept them in a cardboard box. But while an ordinary mouse would quickly gnaw its way through the cardboard, these unusual mice stayed quite content within and responded to all sorts of gestures from Nimāi.

Gurudeva thought that Nimāi probably wanted to talk about what he had written in his last letter, about marriage and his "spiritual experiences" with the mice. Coincidentally, in the same mail in which Nimāi's letter had arrived, Gurudeva had received another letter from a disciple who said Lord Caitanya had begun to speak to him and was sometimes even speaking through him. At least Nimāi's claim was more modest. Rather than believing that the Lord was talking to him, he thought he was talking to mice! Still, it was an extraordinary claim. Gurudeva knew Nimāi's reputation as a blunderer and not being very surrendered, but he liked the boy's genuine sincerity and frankness. Whenever Gurudeva spoke with Nimāi, he felt that he wanted to protect and guide him. Maybe someday Gurudeva thought, Nimāi could travel with him and they could get to know each other better. It was hard to penetrate into someone's heart in such short meetings, especially when such mysterious topics as talking animals were the items of discussion.

From his side, Nimāi was very pleased to see his spiritual master once again. He could tell that Gurudeva was happy and satisfied to be leading the *padayātrā*. It was also encouraging for his disciples to see him away from his office computer and walking barefoot on a country road, singing, dancing, and lecturing. Nimāi thought, "Maybe someday I can travel with him." Seeing Gurudeva engaged in *sādhu* life also made Nimāi aware that he was sadly lacking in dedication to his spiritual master. He wished he could more closely follow what the *ācārya* Viśvanātha Cakravartī had said: "Make the order of the spiritual master your life and soul." Nimāi thought, "I'm too independent. I'm acting like a *guru* with my mice." But if Gurudeva would authorize it, he could work with the mice in a more surrendered way.

But what had especially excited Nimāi when he heard that Gurudeva was in Guyana was the realization that he could (and should) ask Gurudeva what to do with the mice. He had serious doubts about whether he should continue to keep them at all. Traveling with the mice was becoming extremely difficult; only by Kṛṣṇa's grace had he escaped from the last two international borders. If he didn't free the mice, they might be confiscated. Besides, what good was he doing them by keeping them in a cage for most of the day, even if they did humbly accept it? But Choṭa, Yamala, and Arjuna were devotees, and so it wasn't just a matter of "letting them free" like wild beasts. Maybe they should stay with him for more training? In order to present all this for Gurudeva's consideration, Nimāi wanted to be able to explain his ideas better. But organizing his thoughts was difficult. And even if Nimāi could make him fully understand, would Choṭa *ever* be able to communicate with Gurudeva?

They met in Gurudeva's tent where there was just enough room for the two of them to sit on opposite sides of a small trunk. Gurudeva looked relaxed and tanned, and although he was thinner than usual, he beamed with well-being.

"Did you get my letter, Gurudeva?" Nimāi asked.

"Yes. I've been thinking about it. So, you've come to Guyana with Keśava to find a wife?"

"What do you think, Gurudeva?"

"I think it's good that you're facing it as a responsibility," said Gurudeva. "But do you think you're ready for all that marriage entails?"

"Keśava Prabhu has been training me," said Nimāi. "I'm not so good at business. But Keśava said it is possible to live as a simple *gṛhastha* within a temple."

"Yes, if you can do it, do it," said Gurudeva. "And if your wife agrees." Nimāi thought to ask if there was a way that he could avoid marriage, but he knew the answer himself so why bother his spiritual master? Gurudeva had once told him, 'Just the fact that you talk so much about marriage indicates that you're not a strict *brahmacārī*.' "If I want to escape it," Nimāi thought, "I would have to become a very staunch celibate, not someone who chats with loose girls in a hotel room."

"I really wanted to see you," said Nimāi, "not to talk about marriage, but about my mice. What did you think of my letter?"

"Honestly, I don't know what to say," said Gurudeva. Gurudeva knew that he was supposed to be very definite when talking with a disciple, but Nimāi inspired his candor. "It's a very personal thing," said Gurudeva. "Therefore, I told you to keep it to yourself. Other people won't believe you, and then you'll get disturbed by that. I will go so far as to acknowledge that some kind of spiritual communication between you and the mice is possible. I looked up the *Garuḍa Purāṇa* verse, and there are others too. Here's one from *Śrīmad-Bhāgavatam*. In the purport to Kapiladeva's teachings in the Third Canto, Prabhupāda is discussing how a *sādhu* is merciful and friendly to all living entities. He does his preaching despite all obstacles. Then Prabhupāda writes as follows:

> One of the qualifications of a *sādhu* is that he is very tolerant and is merciful to all fallen souls. He is merciful because he is the well-wisher of all living entities. He is not only a well-wisher of human society, but a well-wisher of animal society as well. It is said here, *sarva-dehinam*, which indicates all living entities who have accepted material bodies. Not only does the human

> being have a material body, but other living entities, such as cats and dogs, also have material bodies. The devotee of the Lord is merciful to everyone—the cats, dogs, trees, etc. He treats all living entities in such a way that they can ultimately get salvation from this material entanglement.
>
> —*Śrīmad-Bhāgavatam, 3.25.21 purport*

So, things have happened. But usually, it's by the influence of an empowered devotee. So that's all I will say. Is that enough for you? I honor you and your intentions."

Nimāi's first impulse was to want to say, no that's not enough. But Nimāi was also afraid of his own motives. Maybe he only wanted to take credit. If Gurudeva believed in what Nimāi was doing, he would be more pleased with Nimāi—and he would see that Nimāi was responsible for brilliant, earthshaking preaching. Who had ever done what he had done except great saints? But Nimāi knew that direction was spiritual suicide. Why should he want his Gurudeva to think that he was a great preacher? Gurudeva was already accepting him even if he didn't know about the mice. He should be content that Gurudeva didn't forbid him from talking and acting with the mice and let it go at that.

"Whatever you say, I accept," said Nimāi, "because you're Kṛṣṇa's representative. But I need your advice. The mice are very dear to me and they're devotees. I'm thinking that maybe I shouldn't keep them in a cage anymore. Maybe I should let them free?"

"Yes, do it," said Gurudeva. "Even accepting that they are devotees, it is better to let them go. Don't be attached. You are not their protector. Don't be like Nārada's mother who bound him to her by the knot of affection." Gurudeva felt confident to speak as if the mice were devotees. "That's what I think," he said, "but the decision should be left up to you."

Gurudeva had still not heard from Nimāi about how the mice were preaching. And he had not yet heard Nimāi's real concern: "How will the *parampara* preaching to the mice be continued?" But Nimāi sensed that he would sound like a crazy man if he brought up such topics. Gurudeva had already said enough. Nimāi bowed down before his spiritual master.

As Nimāi stood, Gurudeva was smiling. "Try to stay with us on *padayātrā* as long as you can," said Gurudeva. "It's very purifying."

"I hope I can," said Nimāi. "I need it."

Nimāi loved the *padayātrā*. He thought again and again, "This is just what I needed!" It was easy because all you had to do was walk along and sing Hare Kṛṣṇa. The weather was nice, and the sides of the road were filled with coconut trees. When they passed houses or small towns, people would come to their front yards and wave or look on at the parade of about twenty devotees and two carts. One cart held Gaura-Nitāi Deities, and the second cart carried luggage. The devotees also held a banner with the Hare Kṛṣṇa mantra splayed across it in big bright letters. *That* was *padayātrā!* They were fulfilling Lord Caitanya's desire that the holy names of Kṛṣṇa be heard in every town and village.

Almost every evening they had a program, sometimes in a tent set up by villagers and sometimes in a Hindu temple. For the first time in a long while Nimāi felt inspired to dance during the *kīrtanas*. He even went into the middle of the circle and spun around while the others laughed! Although it was his custom to fall asleep during *Bhāgavatam* class, Nimāi felt quite alert during Gurudeva's evening lectures along the *padayātrā* route. Some people said *padayātrā* was difficult because of so much walking and having nothing special to do, but Nimāi liked it fine.

Keśava Prabhu mentioned to Nimāi that he had arranged for a likely marriage. It was with a eighteen-year-old girl who was as yet uninitiated, but who was a serious devotee. When they returned from the *padayātrā*, Nimāi would have an interview with her parents. Nimāi thanked Keśava and accepted the arrangements, but he didn't feel very excited about it. He was having too much fun walking and chanting to think much about married life.

The mice were also blissful. They spent most of the time out of their box. They even traveled with the *padayātrā*, staying undercover in the meadows on a path parallel with the devotees. Or sometimes, if they were too tired, they would sneak onto the luggage cart for a ride. Nimāi

was relieved to be able to allow them more freedom. They maxed it to the limit, energetically running and jumping in acrobatic leaps after their long confinement in the lunch box.

Choṭa told Nimāi that the preaching in Guyana was the best ever. Whenever the devotees stopped for *kīrtana* and a lecture, Choṭa and his brothers would seek out the mice of that locality. In one place, while the humans were all attending the meeting in a tent, Choṭa gathered a whole village full of mice who patiently heard him speak in the acoustical soundwaves which can be heard only by mice. The Guyanese mice were already familiar with the Hare Kṛṣṇa lively tent *kīrtanas*, and they positively basked in bliss with the delicious *prasādam* remnants that followed. For many generations they had attended religious ceremonies held by the Hindu priests, but they found them dry in comparison.

Sometimes they were so busy on *padayātrā* that they exchanged only a few words all day long. Fortunately, Nimāi no longer had to prepare special meals for the mice, because while they were on *padayātrā* the mice could forage enough *prasādam* on their own. Nimāi was happy for the mice and happy within himself.

One morning Nimāi was left to guard the luggage cart while most of the devotees went bathing in a river. He happened to meet Choṭa and his brothers, who were also just returning from a dip in a roadside pond.

"Nimāi Prabhu, this is the best preaching ever," said Choṭa. "I think it's also good that we are living with the local mice. They see that we're not any different from them and then they listen more when we tell them about Kṛṣṇa."

Nimāi had been waiting for an opportunity to tell Choṭa about his talk with Gurudeva. Now seemed the time to do it as they were relaxed and sitting leisurely outdoors.

"I spoke more to Gurudeva about us," said Nimāi. "He had a very definite opinion that I should not keep carrying you around in boxes; you should go out on your own."

"But he does not know," said Choṭa, "how much we mean to each other. Does he?"

"He knows something," said Nimāi. "We can't try to read the mind of the spiritual master. He spoke as if he did know everything about us and he said, 'Even if you and the mice have a spiritual relationship, don't think that you're their protector. Kṛṣṇa is the protector.'"

"So, is this Gurudeva's order?" asked Choṭa.

"Not exactly an order," said Nimāi.

"What do you think, Nimāi?" asked Choṭa.

Nimāi drew in his breath and gave a heavy sigh. "I think it's best," he said.

"Then so do we," said Choṭa.

"I know Yamala and Arjuna like to daydream," said Nimāi, and he touched them affectionately on the back of their necks. "They dream that we could all live together in a place like Gurudeva's house. But it never seems to work out that way. Instead, I'm stuffing you into my pockets or keeping you in a dark box for twenty-four hours."

Nimāi was afraid that the mice might think he was rejecting them, but they trusted his word. It did seem time for them to separate. Nimāi suggested that when he left in a few weeks for the United States they could stay on in Guyana, which seemed an ideal place for them. The mice accepted his decision without objection. They all observed a sad silence, but then the mice's natural liveliness overcame them and they began chattering about the big tent program scheduled for that evening.

"It will be so much fun!" said Choṭa. "Especially after the humans go home, hundreds of mice will come out, and it will be a perfect occasion to tell them about the mercy of *prasādam* and to engage them in some service."

"What kind of service will they do?" asked Nimāi.

"I don't know," said Choṭa. "At least we can clean up all the crumbs from the feast."

Like all things in this world, the two-week *padayātrā* came to an end. But not a permanent end, because the devotees intended to do it again within a few months. Returning to the temple, Nimāi went with Keśava to meet the parents of the girl that he might marry. The father was a factory worker and he had six other children. He did most of the talking, asking Nimāi how he intended to support a family and what were his plans and ambitions. Nimāi gave simple replies and emphasized his transcendental aspirations for himself and his wife, both in this life and the next. Later in private, the father told Keśava that he was not very impressed with Nimāi. He frankly admitted that he was mainly interested in the opportunity to marry his daughter to an American so that she could escape her limited fate in their own country. Nimāi was in high spirits from the austerity of the *padayātrā* and so he did not feel emotionally attached to the marriage. To him, the girl looked similar to all the devotee girls in Guyana. They all reminded him of the roadside lotus flowers which grow everywhere in Guyana, and the roadside flowers all looked like the lotuses in the pictures of Kṛṣṇa in Vṛndāvana. The girls were like that.

Since his daughter was young, and since he was not overly impressed with Nimāi, the father decided that it should be an engagement rather than a marriage. As Keśava explained it to Nimāi, "We can come back in a year or six months and you can meet with her and her parents. In the meantime, maybe you can get your act more together." Nimāi agreed, and almost felt relieved that everything wasn't finalized and he had more time to think about it.

Nimāi brought the mice for a last meeting with Gurudeva. He carried them in an empty *Back to Godhead* box. The mice always cleaned themselves carefully, but for this occasion Nimāi had also washed them himself. They were shiny.

Gurudeva looked down into their box and tried to think what it might be like for a mouse to be a devotee. He had heard from Flora about the art of telepathic communication between humans and animals. She had said the important thing was to identify with the animal and try to understand what it was like to be that creature. In the case of the man who owned the intelligent dog Strongheart, the man said that one day he suddenly saw the dog not from the human perspective, but from the dog's point of view.

Gurudeva thought, "If a mouse were a devotee, what would he be like?" He tried removing some of the more immediate barriers, such as his repulsion for mice, which he was sure he had inherited from his mother who was terrified of mice. Gurudeva looked at the mild but twitching creatures and noticed that they were alert and cautious. They had delicate large ears. They were nervous and timid, but he knew they could fight if cornered, and they could subsist in difficult conditions.

Gurudeva reached in and softly stroked their heads. They were extremely tame, he thought, as he touched them and as they lowered their bodies and touched their heads to the floor.

"They look like they're making obeisances," said Gurudeva.

"They *are*," said Nimāi. "They know who you are."

Nimāi then dared to try what he had always hoped for—a communication between Choṭa and Gurudeva.

"Choṭa Prabhu," said Nimāi, "would you like to speak to Gurudeva?"

The mouse looked up and made a small sound. "Did you hear, Gurudeva?" asked Nimāi. "He said Hare Kṛṣṇa."

"Yes, I think I heard," said Gurudeva. And then Gurudeva spoke to the mice, "Hare Kṛṣṇa, Choṭa and Prabhus. Nimāi has been very kind to you. It is your turn to be kind to others, and Kṛṣṇa will be pleased. Now go and spread Kṛṣṇa consciousness to your own group."

Nimāi was satisfied, and he took the mice back while making repeated obeisances as he left the room. He knew that Gurudeva had not only approved of the mice, but had recognized the service of his eccentric disciple Nimāi.

Nimāi wanted to avoid any mushy sentiments in his last meeting with the mice, so he read to them from his notebook where he had gathered relevant scriptural passages about animals receiving Kṛṣṇa consciousness. "This is from a lecture," he said, "that Prabhupāda gave in Vṛndāvana in 1972:"

> (A devotee is reading from *The Nectar of Devotion*): "Śrīla Rūpa Gosvāmī has given a definition of auspiciousness. He says that actual auspiciousness means welfare activities for all people of the world!"
>
> Śrīla Prabhupāda: "Yes. Just like this Kṛṣṇa consciousness movement. It is welfare activities for all the people of the world. It is not a sectarian movement. Not only for the human beings, but also for the animals—birds, beasts, trees—everyone. This discussion was made by Haridāsa Ṭhākura with Lord Caitanya. In that statement, Haridāsa Ṭhākura informed Him that by chanting the Hare Kṛṣṇa mantra loudly, the trees, the birds, the

beasts—everyone will be benefited. This is the statement of *nāmācārya* Haridāsa Ṭhākura. So, when we chant Hare Kṛṣṇa mantra loudly, it is beneficial for everyone."

"... If we chant the Hare Kṛṣṇa mantra, it benefits everyone, not only human beings. My Guru Mahārāja used to say if somebody complained that 'we go and chant and nobody attends our meetings', Guru Mahārāja would reply, 'Why? The four walls will hear you; that is sufficient. Don't be disappointed. You go on chanting if there are four walls, they will hear. So chanting is so effective it benefits even the animals, beasts, birds, insects, everywhere.... This is the best welfare activity in the world.... Spread Kṛṣṇa consciousness."

"How will we be able to hear these things when you are not here?" asked Choṭa.

"Hear as many classes as you can. Go to the place where they are speaking and hear the *kīrtanas*. Just teach whatever I have told you," said Nimāi. "You know better than I do how to preach to mice. But repeat what I've said. Don't invent anything."

"And what if we just want to hear from you?" asked Yamala.

"I'll be back in six months," said Nimāi. "I don't know where you'll be traveling then, but you might come back to the temple when I come."

"*Might* come back?" said Choṭa. "We *will* come back."

"Another thing," said Nimāi, "is that you might try speaking to other human devotees. I don't know how this works that we were able to talk to each other, but it happened by Kṛṣṇa's grace, so maybe you can talk to others too."

After speaking for a last time, Nimāi went down and got into the car with Keśava Prabhu. It was time to drive to the airport. Choṭa and his brothers were alone again, just as they had been many times before when they went on their preaching tours. But this time was different. They climbed up to the windowsill and watched Nimāi's car leave. Nimāi waved toward the building in the direction of all the devotees. The mice continued to stand on the windowsill stretching forward to see the street until the car had completely disappeared down the dusty road. They began to softly cry in the grief of separation from their teacher and longtime protector.

After a desolate silence Choṭa took the lead, "All right Prabhus," he squeaked. "Let's go out on *saṅkīrtana*."

2

Nimāi's Detour

A Story

Preface

(By N.d.b)

My name is Nimāi dāsa brahmacārī, and I was written up in the book *Nimāi /Dāsa and the Mouse,* which told about my friendship with three devotees in mice bodies. I was with them for six months until I left them in Guyana. Now my Gurudeva has asked me to write my own account about the stuff that has happened to me in the last six months ending with my coming to be his servant. (Mercy!) Gurudeva thought that if I write down exactly what happened I'll be able to see where I went off and prevent it in the future. He said maybe it would also be helpful for others.

The writer, Satsvarūpa dasa Goswami, said he also wanted to write more about me. I don't know why so much attention should be paid to an insignificant *jīva*-soul, but I suppose it could be instructive. There's a *Bhāgavatam* section that says even animals can be seen as gurus. For example, we can learn from the dog because he's faithful and we can learn from the bees because they are after the nectar. As for the story, I'll tell some and S. d. g. will tell some. My main concern is to do the right thing and follow my superiors. So that's what I'll do by writing this.

It all starts when I left Guyana after I let Choṭa, Yamala, and Arjuna (my mice) free to preach. But before I go into the details of who I met, where I went, and what happened, I want to admit that I've really been in *māyā.* I'm not trying to blame anyone. Somebody said I'm a victim of bad association. But I don't think that the people I met are bad. They're not. The fact is they didn't know much more than I did, and yet they acted as if they did and so they influenced me. That's one thing I think I've learned: it's better to stick to myself and my *guru* and not get swept up in other people's trips. Anyway, I admit that I've been in *māyā*. But I was looking for the right thing, and I still am. By now you're probably wondering, "What has this to do with Kṛṣṇa consciousness?"

Chapter 1

(by S.d.g.)

It took Nimāi dāsa about a day to discover what he had lost. When he said good-bye to Choṭa, Yamala, and Arjuna, he did not expect to be so devastated by their absence. At first, he was preoccupied with travelling. He and Keśava Prabhu had to wait three hours at the Georgetown airport, due to the usual Guyanese delays, before the flight departed. Then he was busy talking for an hour with Keśava. Keśava was going to disembark in Trinidad to do more business, and Nimāi would continue alone. They spent their time talking about Kṛṣṇa consciousness, and especially how Nimāi could improve himself to merit his wife.

"It's not just material qualifications," Keśava said, "but it's getting ready for a serious lifetime's service. Somebody who thinks he's ready to get married just because he's sexually agitated is not at all ready. You have to be sober and prepared to expand your service and in a practical way take care of other living beings, starting with your wife and family."

These talks, as well as sharing *prasādam* with Keśava, kept Nimāi occupied until Keśava left. But then it hit him. The plane was on the ground, and Nimāi was completely alone in the rear section. Previously whenever he was by himself, he would turn to Choṭa. But now he was alone. Choṭa, Yamala and Arjuna were not there. The first thing that occurred to Nimāi was that he had lost his best friend. Then it occurred to him that he had lost his devotional service, which was to train the mice and supervise their preaching. He also felt as if he had lost his inner life. Talking with Choṭa had been Nimāi's method of introspection as well as his prayer to Kṛṣṇa and Prabhupāda. By cheering up the subordinate mice, Nimāi was always able to pull himself out of depression. In intimate friendship with Choṭa he could speak his heart. Now that was all gone, and he didn't know what to do. He could not check his tears.

"I should have asked Gurudeva about this," Nimāi thought. "I didn't know everything would change! What should I do now?" He thought of writing a letter, but his emotions and thoughts were too jumbled.

When the plane landed in Miami, Nimāi decided not to take the ongoing flight to Pennsylvania. He felt too empty and would not be able to explain himself to Vibhu Prabhu and the other devotees. Neither did Gurudeva or Keśava prabhu order him to return to the farm; they just assumed that he would. Nimāi thought of his friend, Bruce the Hermit, who lived in the Florida everglades. Bruce used to live with the devotees on the farm where he was known as a hard worker, but he had some disagreements and decided to live alone. He had found a place deep in the everglades where he was employed as a caretaker and was mostly left undisturbed. Bruce lived like a hermit, chanting fifty rounds daily, writing his Kṛṣṇa conscious observations in a diary, and sometimes sending letters to friends like Nimāi. Nimāi thought maybe he could go to Bruce's for a while, chant extra rounds, and read Prabhupāda's books while waiting to recover from the empty feeling. Nimāi phoned and Bruce agreed, although he said it would take him a full day to paddle a canoe from the swamps out to the nearest bus stop.

"You're the first devotee I've ever brought here," said Bruce, as they paddled back into the everglades. "Mostly I spend my time alone, chanting my rounds, working in the garden, or building for the owner of the place. But I like it that way. I feel more peaceful now than I ever have."

Bruce was in his forties and about 6'4" tall. He had spent most of his life in Florida, where he held jobs similar to the one he had now, care-taking for remote campgrounds or boating outposts. He said the local people tolerated him and even accepted his "religious ways." Although he was living by himself, Bruce wore the shaven head and *śikhā* of a Vaiṣṇava, and he dressed in saffron pants and a saffron T-shirt. Nimāi felt at ease listening to Bruce's assertions of peace and God consciousness in the solitary life. They approached his residence via waterways with names like "Alligator Way" and "Canal #3." Bruce stayed in a one-room wooden shack. He told Nimāi that he was welcome, but the owner probably wouldn't want him to stay there very long.

On their first night together, Nimāi told Bruce how he had been keeping some mice and how they were like devotees, and now that he had set them free, he was feeling lonely. You could talk like that to Bruce. Nimāi regarded him as soft-hearted. If you said something the wrong way, Bruce would get hurt and be silent. That was why he had left the farm up north.

"I am at home with the animals here," said Bruce, "you'll see. The birds fly right in the window, and they're not afraid of me. I even let the alligators walk around. I don't hurt them, and they don't hurt me."

In the morning, they chanted *japa* together for four hours, and then Bruce went out to work in the garden and on the house he was building. Nimāi stayed indoors and read *Śrīmad-Bhāgavatam.*

Nimāi was drawn to read the story of Nārada Muni in the First Canto. He had always liked that story, and Gurudeva had mentioned it during their last talk. Nimāi was looking for a particular purport he seemed to remember, how Nārada had been close to the Lord, but then had lost the vision, and felt bereft. He found it in the Sixth Chapter, eighteenth verse:

> The transcendental form of the Lord, as it is, satisfies the mind's desire and at once erases all mental incongruities. Upon losing that form, I suddenly got up, being perturbed, as is usual when one loses that which is desirable.

Although he was only five years old, Nārada had learned from visiting sages how to meditate on Kṛṣṇa. After Nārada's mother died, Nārada was all alone, and when he meditated on Kṛṣṇa, he directly saw the transcendental form of the Lord and felt great ecstasy. But when he tried to meditate again, the Lord did not appear. Prabhupāda had written, "Nārada Muni had gotten a glimpse of this, but having not seen it again he became perturbed and stood up all of a sudden to search it out. What we desire life after life was obtained by Nārada Muni, and losing sight of Him again was certainly a great shock for him." Nimāi couldn't help but compare himself to Nārada, although he knew any exact resemblance was ridiculous. Nārada had seen Kṛṣṇa, and Nimāi had seen only a small miracle of Kṛṣṇa's. "It was by Kṛṣṇa's grace," thought Nimāi, "that I was able to talk with those mice and now by His grace, it's gone."

Nimāi read on. The *Bhāgavatam* explained that the Lord did not appear again to Nārada but spoke and said, "I regret that during this lifetime you will not be able to see Me anymore. Those who are incomplete in service and are not completely free from all material taints can hardly see Me." It was just to increase Nārada's hankerings for Kṛṣṇa that Kṛṣṇa disappeared from him, and when Nārada understood it, he felt grateful. After that, Nārada began chanting the holy name and traveling all over the earth "fully satisfied, humble, and unenvious."

"Easier said than done," thought Nimāi. "I'm no Nārada. I don't even know what I should do." Nimāi did know that sooner or later he should write his spiritual master for directions, but he didn't want to do that yet. He thought that Gurudeva might like him to think this one out for himself so that he would have a deeper realization.

After a quiet week in the swamps, Bruce remarked that the owner would be coming to check up and Nimāi had better move on.

Chapter 2

(N.d.b.)

I heard that Prabhupāda said in a letter we should not eulogize *māyā* so much but should praise Kṛṣṇa. I should follow that because I'm always writing about how *māyā* bewildered me, so if you listen to me, you'll just be hearing about *māyā.* But I don't want to do that. I wish I could just talk about Kṛṣṇa and think about Him and that's all. But I can't imitate.

I would like to explain more how I felt after Choṭa left. I dreamt of them. I dreamt the mice were being chased down a road by a big hog and Choṭa was calling to me and I was trying to help them find a hole to run into. When I remembered the good times we had together, I would sometimes cry. When I lost my association with the mice, I reverted to what I was before, and I started remembering how people used to bother me at the farm. (That's why I didn't want to go back there.) I also started thinking of stuff from over three years ago before I was a devotee, like rock music I used to listen to, and I thought of my mother and father. I was even about to phone them, but I didn't. No one would be able to understand. But I needed to talk to someone. I could only go so far with Bruce. He thought that all animals were nice and should never be killed and that they were as good as humans. He was much fonder of animals than I am. I was never really that close to animals, just to Choṭa. Because he wasn't an animal really, but a spirit soul.

Now I'll tell you something that will make you laugh. I looked into the *Bhāgavatam* section where Arjuna feels bereft after Kṛṣṇa left the planet, because I identified with him. I never had *powers* like Arjuna, but I could identify with the painting where Arjuna is crying and telling Yudhiṣṭhira that he lost his powers now that Kṛṣṇa's gone. Śukadeva Gosvāmī said that Arjuna was overwhelmed and distressed because Lord Kṛṣṇa was out of his sight; his lotus-like heart had dried up and his body had lost all luster. Arjuna said, "I am bereft of the Supreme Personality of Godhead by whose influence I was so powerful."

But Arjuna was a great devotee and so he was able to remember again the instructions of the *Bhagavad-gītā*, and then he got better and found relief for his burning heart. My problem was that I couldn't remember any relevant instructions, so I was in *māyā*. The very thing that was causing me sorrow was something that I could not express to anyone. With Gurudeva in a couple of meetings I'd gotten *close* to saying it, but to no one else.

Actually, it's no mystery what I experienced, and I know I'm not special. If you have ever loved someone in Kṛṣṇa consciousness, and that person went away for some reason, then you know what I'm talking about. Maybe you can also understand now why I didn't want to go back to the farm. They'd have to invent new names to describe the state I was in. "Nimāi the gnome" would be too good for me. Sometimes they call me "Nee-mind." That means my mind takes over; the restless, powerful mind. I hope you don't mind my saying all this. Unless I can relate my life *in some way* to Kṛṣṇa, what's the use? I don't want to eulogize *māyā*, although I know she is supremely powerful.

When I left Bruce's, I met another devotee. He was on his way to India and said he had an extra ticket. He was a devotee of a guru in our movement, but the guru left and joined the Marines. So, this devotee, Pūjā dāsa, was bitter. I met him in Govinda's restaurant in downtown Miami where I went because I didn't know where else to go.

Pūjā said, "You've got to think for yourself." That was his motto. He said, "I blindly followed authority, and look where it got me." I told him what I had been doing, but not about the mice. It's not that I was going around telling everyone *that*. When someone asked me what I was doing, I said, "I've been traveling with my Gurudeva in the Caribbean, and now I am not sure what I'll do. I'm a little burnt out."

I was burnt out, but not like Pūjā and the others I started meeting who said that they were burnt because of following the authorities. But I started getting influenced by him. I told him that my temple president, Vibhu, was a real heavy authority. I think I was offensive to say that about Vibhu but being with Pūjā made me say it. No, I take that back—it was my own fault. Pūjā said, "Grow up, Nimāi." He kept saying *grow up* and that impressed me. He made me think maybe I shouldn't follow authorities.

Pūjā was going to India to do what he thought best, and he said that all devotees should just do whatever they feel in their heart. That way a person wouldn't be misled, and he could grow up.

I asked him what he was going to do in India. He said maybe travel to holy places, but he was thinking of going somewhere to live in seclusion and chant and worship his Deities. He said some far-out things. He said nobody in our movement has really advanced, and that was because we were all agitated from living in the cities in the West, and by too much opulence.

I said, "Prabhupāda says that things can be used in Kṛṣṇa's service, for preaching."

"Yeah, but look," he said. "Look at how many devotees have fallen down. I think if Prabhupāda had seen so many fall downs he would just tell everyone to go to India and chant and live very simply."

I said, "But Prabhupāda writes that we can't imitate Haridāsa Ṭhākura and live alone."

Pūjā had an answer for that too, although I can't remember what it was. But at the time I was affected. I thought, "Maybe this is what I need." It also seems as if Kṛṣṇa was making the arrangements. Here was Pūjā offering me a free ticket to go to India with him, so I thought this might be the best way to get away from my feelings of loss and, as he said, to grow up and find out what I wanted to do.

Pūjā never spoke against *my* spiritual master, but sometimes he generalized about "those guys on a guru trip." I didn't consider that as a blasphemy, but now I see it wasn't good. The proof is I didn't think that I should first ask Gurudeva's permission before going to India. I figured it was too difficult to get in touch with him in Guyana, and I rationalized that it would be okay.

Pūjā carried Deities with him, and I was attracted to them, so that was nice. And Pūjā was serious about reading Prabhupāda's books as well as other Vaiṣṇava books by Prabhupāda's Godbrothers and different Vaiṣṇava *sampradāyas*. I figured if I traveled with him, it might be good for me to learn different things about the Vaiṣṇava philosophy in general. I didn't think much ahead about what I would do in India. At least it was something to do, and it was bold. I admit I liked the idea of being a little rebellious, not that you have to ask five temple presidents and six *saṅkīrtana* leaders and other department heads in a temple for permission before you do something. With the books and with Supersoul, a person ought to be able to decide for himself. That's how I was thinking after spending an afternoon with Pūjā.

Chapter 3

(S.d.g.)

Nimāi could hardly believe that he was flying to India, at night, with no clear destination and no specific devotional service awaiting him. He knew it was reckless, but since there was nothing that he really wanted to do in the United States, or anywhere, what did it matter? At least he had his *japa* beads so he could chant, and he had his *Śrīmad-Bhāgavatam,* and maybe like Pūjā dāsa, he would do solitary chanting in a holy place like India. According to Pūjā, you didn't have to really know exactly what you wanted to do. You just went ahead and explored. Too many devotees, Pūjā said, claimed to know exactly what to do—but they were either lording it over other devotees, or they were victims being manipulated by the authorities. So, to wander and maintain your own Kṛṣṇa consciousness wasn't such a bad thing. The more Nimāi heard, the more he became confused. He couldn't figure things out but thought that Kṛṣṇa would reveal everything in time.

He enquired more from Pūjā about his plans.

"The plane lands in Delhi," Pūjā said, "So we can visit Vṛndāvana."

"We can visit there," said Pūjā. "But if we want to stay there, they'll charge us ten rupees a day, unless we do full time service. I'm not opposed to working, but as soon as you stay at a temple the authorities think that they own you."

Pūjā proposed to ration out his few hundred dollars and stay at an inexpensive *dharmaśālā* where he could conduct his own spiritual program without interference.

"I'll stay with you if that's all right," said Nimāi.

"Sure," said Pūjā. "We can have our own little *kuṭīra*."

When the plane stopped in London, another devotee boarded. He was instantly recognizable by his *kūrta, dhotī* and *śikhā.* He said he was also going to India, and he was also a disciple of a spiritual master who had given up the regulative practices of devotional life. His plane seat was in a different section, but they talked with him for a while. He said he was planning to meet up with a devotee from Italy, and they would visit the temples in South India. Like Pūjā dāsa, the English devotee was not connected to any temple or serving any authority, and he didn't think that he wanted to be connected in that way in the foreseeable future.

Previously Nimāi had only heard briefly about such things as spiritual masters leaving their disciples. He never inquired into such matters, nor were they discussed much on the farm. But now he heard all about them from Pūjā. During the long flight, Pūjā told Nimāi about many scandals in the Movement. He said the leaders took advantage of their power and misspent money and misguided devotees by engaging them in activities like selling paintings instead of distributing books. And he told much more shocking things. He said a whole book had been written by a reporter about the crimes and bizarre misbehavior of the Movement's leaders, and so all of this was common knowledge.

Nimāi was about to say, "None of the devotees I've worked for have done any terrible things," but then he thought that Pūjā might know some things Nimāi didn't and that he might tell stories about Nimāi's own leaders. Pūjā seemed to know all the dirt. No wonder he was disillusioned.

Nimāi didn't want to hear the bad stories that Pūjā might know about the farm, and besides Nimāi hadn't seen any scandals in his three years there. But still, you never knew for sure what was going on....

Nimāi at least spoke up and praised his Gurudeva who was preaching purely on *pāda-yatra* in Guyana. Pūjā conceded that he had heard that Gurudeva was "one of the few exceptions." Pūjā then began to express that he had been badly hurt when his own guru had left. "I really worshiped him," said Pūjā, "just like you're supposed to worship the guru. My faith was shattered. Now I am like a cracked bell, and I don't think I'll ever be the same. How can I fully trust anyone after that?"

By the time they landed in New Delhi, Nimāi was convinced that it wasn't safe to report into a temple for service as a menial *brahmacārī*. If he did that, he could easily be misled. Nimāi had also developed a sympathetic feeling for Pūjā, who was suffering from a hurt that Nimāi felt was similar to his own, or actually much worse. Hearing of Pūjā's sufferings helped Nimāi to get a clearer view of his own. He thought, "I was given a special taste of spiritual life and now it's gone. But at least I wasn't cheated."

Chapter 4

(N.d.b.)

I want to make it clear that I never forgot Choṭa, Yamala, and Arjuna. I always expected to see them again. When we first parted it was a shock, probably for them too, but I started recalling them in substantial ways. If you have a Kṛṣṇa conscious relationship with someone, you benefit even when you're apart. This is the Vaiṣṇava philosophy of separation. Devotees used to joke with me and say I'd become a mouse in my next body for thinking of them, but I don't think of "mice". When I recall Choṭa, I think of preaching to conditioned souls and of valuable instructions for my own spiritual life and Vedic stories of devotees inducing animals to chant Hare Kṛṣṇa. You wouldn't say, would you, that Ajāmila became a child in his next life just because he thought of his own child, Nārāyaṇa? No—because when he said Nārāyaṇa, he said the name of God. (And Viśvanātha Cakravartī says that Ajāmila thought of the original Nārāyaṇa when he said his child's name). So, by thinking of Choṭa, I don't meditate on dumb rodents running out of holes to scavenge food. Thinking of them turns me from my usual *māyā* to more responsible devotional behavior and a spirit for spreading Kṛṣṇa consciousness. I know that sounds odd (or crazy) but that's how it works.

For the first few days after I left my mice, I missed being with them all the time. But when I saw how truly empty Pūjā dāsa was, it helped me count my own blessings and pick up the positive side of my feelings of separation. For example, it was Choṭa who helped me to appreciate that you can think of Kṛṣṇa and render service to Him even in little ways. I learned that lesson when I had been thinking that the mice were small-time devotees. Choṭa was tiny in size, and the others were even more untrained and unable to do much. So, I thought, "What is the preaching value in this?" I told Choṭa that I was depressed because none of us were doing big service. He then told me how hard it was to live as a mouse, with danger at every step. And then he started to preach to me in a wonderful way. He said it's not the bigness of the service that pleases Kṛṣṇa, but our sincerity and devotion. It was from that point that Choṭa also began to express his desire to preach to other mice. He had great hopes even though his body was so limited.

When I'm in a bad situation, or just in the normal routine, I think of how Choṭa was grateful to have *any* Kṛṣṇa consciousness, and how he tried to do little things for Kṛṣṇa. We can't imagine, for example, what a big thing it is for a mouse to control his sense gratification while eating. To "honor" *prasādam* instead of just ripping it open and eating it is itself devotional service. And if a person can chant Hare Kṛṣṇa nicely, that also is very pleasing to Kṛṣṇa. So, no service is "small time" if by "small" you mean stupid and displeasing to Kṛṣṇa. I usually forget how to render even little acts in a way to please Kṛṣṇa and *guru,* but when I do remember, it's usually by remembering how Choṭa preached in little ways. When I think of the mice, I think of their humble, grateful, enthusiastic service. Does it sound like I'll become a mouse by thinking of Choṭa? I don't think so. Whenever I think of them, I get fired up to pray to Kṛṣṇa and remember that I want to be His friend and servant. At least I realize better how insignificant I am.

Those mice are devotees. Kṛṣṇa allows some creatures in lowly species to teach us valuable things. You can learn devotion even from snakes, dogs, birds, and butterflies, so what to speak of, as sometimes happens, a creature who is able to chant and hear. It's possible.

I like the way Gurudeva deals with me in this regard. He has never said, "Nimāi, you have to prove to me scientifically that these mice can talk to you. Until I hear it, I won't believe it, and I forbid you to keep these mice or think about them." No, he just saw the gold in the filthy place (me). It did not seem important to him *how much* Kṛṣṇa consciousness was being communicated between me and the mice. But Gurudeva knew that something good was there. So, I want to be like that. I mean, I just want to be happy with the ability Kṛṣṇa has given me to remember Him and serve Him, even in some little ways, and *all the time* if possible. And when I think of Choṭa, that helps me to be Kṛṣṇa conscious. So why should anybody object and why should I think I have to *prove something*?

When I first parted from my mice, it was hard because I couldn't talk with other devotees about my feeling sad. Everyone thought of me as someone who missed his pet mice. I became too attached to wanting people to understand me and appreciate me. But if I know my relationship with Choṭa is Kṛṣṇa conscious and that it can continue in separation, why is it so important that I convince others? It's not. If I learn something Kṛṣṇa conscious, I should share it rather than try to prove to them that I have a wonderful, unusual relationship with Kṛṣṇa, as if He has empowered me and everyone should listen to me.

There was no need for me to feel devastated in separation from the mice. I agreed to go back to see them after six months. And I should have known that I could always think of their encouraging example. I'm sure that Choṭa also thinks of me and when we meet again, he'll want to tell me many things in Kṛṣṇa consciousness that he has saved up. And when we're apart, if we are faithful, we can keep up a definite kind of communication. I don't think Kṛṣṇa will object, but of course I can't say for sure. I *would* like to talk more to Gurudeva about this, but he has already blessed us, and I personally saw him accept Choṭa's obeisances and say to the mice, "Be good devotees. Nimāi gave you Kṛṣṇa consciousness, so go preach to others."

This was more important to me than all the scandals in the Movement that Pūjā dāsa was talking about. Even when I get overwhelmed by external things (And I always do! That's why I'm in *māyā!)* I usually manage to retain some inner direction, and *that's* why thinking of Choṭa and communication with him is valuable.

Chapter 5

(Nimāi d. b.)

When I arrived in India, though I was much further away from Choṭa by physical miles, I felt closer. I think we have some kind of mental telepathy between us. It's not like a telephone you can talk back and forth on, but Choṭa is sometimes present in my thoughts. So, he was suddenly right there when I was waiting for the luggage in the Delhi airport while all these crazy things were going on around us at two in the morning.

I am unsure of this, and so I intend to confirm later when I meet with Choṭa, whether he experienced the same thing at the time. It seems that if two people are intently thinking of each other, they can connect.

Since it was unusual, and I don't want to get into trouble, I thought again of the remark that Bhīma made once in the *saṅkīrtana* van. He said that I would take my next birth as a mouse, just as Mahārāja Bharata had to take birth as a stag because he was thinking of a deer at the time of death. So, while waiting with Pūjā dāsa for the luggage, I got out my one-volume edition of *Śrīmad-Bhāgavatam* and looked up the story of Mahārāja Bharata.

First of all, Mahārāja Bharata was a great devotee; all of India was named after him and I'm named "gnome". So, there's no comparison. And yet as elevated as Mahārāja Bharata was, his relationship with the fawn wasn't auspicious. The fawn used to butt him with its head when Mahārāja Bharata was meditating, and then he would stop his devotional service and play with the little deer. He stopped all his religious regulative duties because of this deer. When Mahārāja Bharata was preparing a sacrifice, the deer would come and pollute the *kuśa* grass. But with me and Choṭa and Yamala and Arjuna, our friendship was spiritual. Maybe there was some "pollution" because they couldn't do everything as nicely as human brāhmaṇas, but they tried their best according to time and circumstances. With Mahārāja Bharata, when the deer went away, the Mahārāja became extremely attached and lamented. Well, *that did* happen to me, and I realize it's illusion. Mahārāja Bharata worried that the deer might be killed by ferocious animals, and I do that too. But at least I don't carry them with me anymore and try to protect them. We're just doing our service and depending on Kṛṣṇa. But Prabhupāda writes something very heavy on this point of attachment:

> Even such an exalted personality as Bharata Mahārāja, who had attained loving affection for the Supreme Personality of Godhead, fell down from his position due to his affection for some animal. Consequently, as will be seen, he had to accept the body of a deer in his next life. Since this was the case with Bharata Mahārāja, what can we say of those who are not advanced in spiritual life but who become attached to cats and dogs? Due to their affection for their cats and dogs, they have to take the same bodily forms in the next life unless they clearly increase their affection and love for the Supreme Personality of Godhead.
>
> —*Śrīmad-Bhāgavatam 5.8.12, purport*

So, it's risky. But the test is whether I am Kṛṣṇa conscious. And I think that whatever little Kṛṣṇa consciousness I have, it is helped by preaching to the mice. Even the devotees at the farm noticed that when I first met Choṭa. I've just got to be very careful not to get sentimental or on the bodily platform.

I want to be perfectly honest in this writing because, dear Gurudeva, I am actually writing this for you. You're the one who asked me to write it. So, in order for this to be helpful to you in judging my case— whether to tell me I'm a complete nonsense or whatever—I should really state all the facts. Therefore, another thing I sometimes do is talk out loud. It's really a simple thing, and I've noticed other people do it. It's thinking out loud, that's all. It especially happens when you're in anxiety, or if you're lonely, and of course most people only do it when they are alone. If you do it around other people, they think you're crazy. I've heard that even great and famous people have been known to do this. And the *gopīs* did it also. I was just about to write down, "Lord Caitanya did it also," but if I do that, it will look like I'm trying to say I'm like Him. What I'm saying is, I regard Choṭa as a Vaiṣṇava. If a devotee sometimes has a favorite devotee and when they're not together one of them thinks out loud about the other, is that so wrong? So, I did it, not at length but I just said spontaneously, "Well Choṭa, here we are in India."

I've been defending all these activities, but now I want to admit that I know they need to be judged by a higher authority. Because, even if it's true that my mental telepathy with Choṭa is not bogus and even if talking out loud is spiritual affection between Vaiṣṇavas - the question still remains, *"Why don't I just do all these activities directly in relation to* guru *and Kṛṣṇa?"* I think that's a good question that I have to face and try to answer.

I'll leave the decision up to Gurudeva. But I *can* say that just because I think or even "pray" to Choṭa, doesn't mean that I don't also pray to the Lord and to my spiritual master. Talking to my devotee friend is a natural thing that can lead to higher thinking. Maybe this is all pride and mental madness, but if anybody who doesn't know me is reading this and hasn't quit so far, I ask that you please consider my situation kindly, because I don't mean harm and I'm talking about someone very dear to me.

There was a long delay waiting for the luggage. I sat alone while Pūjā stood in line to change his money. Then I decided to write a letter to Choṭa and put all these feelings of separation into a concrete form of communication. Here's my letter:

February 20,

2:30 A.M.

Dear Choṭa, Yamala, and Arjuna Prabhus,

Please accept my humble obeisances. All glories to Śrīla Prabhupāda.

How are you? I have been devastated by losing the spiritual taste of associating with you. This especially happened almost immediately after I was alone on the plane from Guyana. Now I have started to recover by cultivating feelings of separation. Choṭa, tonight you were present in my thoughts. That is one reason I'm writing this letter, just to put down the date and time so that when we meet again, you can see if you were also thinking of me.

I think you will be surprised to know that I have come all the way to India, for the first time in my life. It happened very fast, when a devotee offered me a free ticket. I don't know exactly why I'm here, except I didn't want to go back to my old temple. I am hearing some different things about the Movement, and I think I just have to work out my own plans for a while.

In case you are feeling sad (like me) about our not being together, I have some advice. Remember the teachings about *vapuḥ* and *vāṇī?* The Vaiṣṇava conclusion is that although being personally present with a devotee is very relishable, it's more important to be with them through instruction. Prabhupāda has said that we live together through the sound vibration. That means the instruction and, of course, the chanting. When we chant, even if we're in different parts of the world, we're together. Which is more important, the *vapuḥ* or the *vāṇī?* I'm sure you'll give the right answer, and this will help you when you apply it.

I think of your preaching activities. Sometimes I feel very protective, but I know there's nothing I can do and that Kṛṣṇa is protecting you. You are very brave souls, braver than me. I don't know why it is that Kṛṣṇa puts me in the position of giving you advice, since I should follow your example. Actually, I do follow your example, especially when I think how you are very tiny creatures, but you have big hearts like *mahātmās* and you risk your life for Kṛṣṇa by going out to preach. Even though I take heart in the fact that even if you are in one sense doing little things, you are offering them sincerely to Kṛṣṇa. I am limited in a different way, due to my own timidity (I don't know why they say mice are timid!), but I'm hoping that I can be sincere and that Kṛṣṇa will accept me and help me to improve.

Anyway, I know you'd like to hear some advice which I can pass down because I've heard it from the older devotees and Prabhupāda's books. So Prabhupāda would sometimes advise preachers not to over endeavor. You should always stay peaceful and do the types of *sādhana* that I taught you, especially in the morning. Don't become so passionate about preaching that you just run here and there. Also, you don't have to unnecessarily risk your lives. Try to do things in a calculated way. There will be dangers enough without your making wild risks. Prabhupāda used to quote, "discretion is the better part of valor." Another thing I thought of is that if you do find favorable response among the mice there, you should try as soon as possible to find a more serious one and train him up. If you can train up at least one local devotee-mouse, then the mission can be assured of continuing, even if something should happen to you.

Maybe when I come to Guyana, we can go somewhere else and stay together permanently. Maybe we can do as Yamala suggested and stay on the farm and you can live free, but we could be together.

Have you talked to any other humans? Or do you have any better understanding of how it works? I haven't. But when I see different animals, I am much more aware now that they can hear the holy name and so I chant to them. And I feel more inclined in that way towards humans also. That is the mercy of your association.

I'll let you know what happens with me. Here is another passage I found from the scriptures. It's from the *Caitanya-caritāmṛta* section describing Lord Caitanya's chanting to the animals. When Lord Caitanya saw that the tigers and deer were following Him, He quoted a verse describing Vṛndāvana. It goes like this:

Vṛndāvana is the transcendental abode of the Lord. There is no hunger, anger or thirst there. Though naturally inimical, both human beings and fierce animals live together there in transcendental friendship.

—*Śrīmad-Bhāgavatam* 10.13.60

In the same section, it's described how Lord Caitanya was followed by peacocks and different birds who were all maddened by the Lord's chanting the holy name of Kṛṣṇa. And when He chanted, "Haribol!" even the trees and creepers became happy to hear Him. In this connection Prabhupāda writes the following purport:

The loud chanting of the Hare Kṛṣṇa mantra is so powerful that it can even penetrate the ears of trees and creepers—what to speak of animals and human beings. Sri Caitanya Mahāprabhu once asked Haridāsa Ṭhākura how trees and plants can be delivered, and Haridāsa Ṭhākura replied that the loud chanting of the Hare Kṛṣṇa mantra would benefit not only trees and plants but insects and all other living beings. One should therefore not be disturbed by the loud chanting of Hare Kṛṣṇa, for it is beneficial not only to the chanter but to everyone who gets an opportunity to hear.

—*Caitanya-caritāmṛta Madhya-līlā* 17.45 purport

Bye for now, I'm thinking of you in the service of *guru* and Kṛṣṇa,

Nimāi dāsa

Chapter 6

(S.D.G.)

Nimāi entered Vṛndāvana like many other pilgrim-tourists, filled with awe and excitement for everything new. Even the little things thrilled him and enlivened his senses, such as the odors of the earth and the dung smoke and the sight of big black hogs walking the streets, and the monkeys! And almost everyone you met was a devotee of Kṛṣṇa. If you greeted them with, "Hare Kṛṣṇa," they would call back, "Jaya Radhe!"

With little trouble Pūjā and Nimāi entered into a comfortable routine. The room they rented in the *"Prema Bhakti Asrama"* was very inexpensive. It had no toilet, but they would pass stool in the field like many Vṛndāvana residents, and they planned to do all their bathing in the Yamunā. They would be supplied dāl and capātīs once a day at the *āśrama*. Although life was austere, the new arrivals were ready to embrace it. Pūjā dāsa had been to India once but only for a three-week visit, so he didn't claim to know much more than Nimāi. But he was quick to point out the advantages of living on their own, rather than reporting in to the Movement's temple.

"You'll see," said Pūjā, "it will be very peaceful here without temple pressures. In a few weeks when the Movement's devotees come for their pilgrimage, the town will be filled with them, and you'll see men and women mixing together and devotees shopping constantly in the bazaars. And politics. But this is the real Vṛndāvana that we've come for.

Nimāi agreed. "I think I'm *really* going to like it," he said smiling. "Just the fact that all the people recognize you as a spiritual person and they're all carrying bead bags and wearing *tilaka*. You feel like you'd like to stay here forever, like you're home."

"Maybe we can stay a long time," said Pūjā. "But it's up to Kṛṣṇa. You can only stay in the holy *dhāma* by His permission and the permission of Rādhārāṇī."

Pūjā and Nimāi kept similar schedules, with allowances for their particular tastes. Nimāi planned to spend at least two hours a day reading Prabhupāda's books and maybe extra time chanting. These were the most important things, and for years he'd never been able to do them with attention. Pūjā was keen to go out and see the holy places and Nimāi wanted to go too.

"The last time I was here," said Pūjā, "there was a nice *bābājī* named Gopīdāsa Bābājī and he used to show the devotees around. I think I know where he lives."

Nimāi had been warned about *bābājīs* in India and how they could mislead you. He had heard Prabhupāda in his lectures mention *prākṛta-sahajiyās,* or persons who took the *līlā* of Kṛṣṇa very cheaply and led people to assume that they could also very quickly enter a relationship with Rādhā and Kṛṣṇa.

"This *bābājī* isn't a *sahajiyā* is he?" asked Nimāi.

"No, he's nice," said Pūjā. "He has some of Prabhupāda's books. Anyway, it's not like he's our guru. He'll just show us around, and he doesn't charge money. Anyway, he's one of the few who speak good English. We can just be careful in case he says anything strange." Pūjā went on to encourage Nimāi to be broad-minded and not to think offensively toward any of the sages living in the *dhāma* and that he shouldn't think that the devotees in the Movement are the only Vaiṣṇavas.

"Prabhupāda has written," said Pūjā, "that for the people who live in Vṛndāvana, their guru is Kṛṣṇa."

"Yeah, I've heard that," said Nimāi.

And so, the two new pilgrims prepared themselves to love Vṛndāvana.

Nimāi didn't think he was ready yet for a systematic study of Prabhupāda's books, so he turned to sections that particularly interested him. He wanted to understand more the proper attitude that he should have toward Choṭa and toward Gurudeva. He also hoped that by reading he could get inspiration from Kṛṣṇa and Prabhupāda as to what he should do, now that he had no regular service. Maybe *this* could be his service, living in Vṛndāvana and reading and chanting. But then, what about preaching? When he was with Choṭa, Nimāi had been more involved in preaching than he had ever been in his life. That was probably another important reason, Nimāi thought, why he felt so bereft. How could he ever expect to reach the peak of preaching as he had when instructing the mice, or when guiding them in the preaching? As hints of topics came to his mind, Nimāi tried to find them in the indexes and from whatever he could of his reading of the *Bhāgavatam* and *Caitanya-caritāmṛta.*

He remembered a purport that he wanted to read about preaching and seclusion. It was after a verse where Lord Caitanya had said that He wanted to stay in a very solitary room at Jagannātha Puri:

> At the present moment we see that some of the members of the International Society for Krishna Consciousness are tending to leave their preaching activities in order to sit in a solitary place. This is not a very good sign. It is a fact that Śrīla Bhaktisiddhānta Sarasvatī Ṭhākura has condemned this process for neophytes. He has even stated in a song: *pratiṣṭhāra tare, nirjanera ghare, tava hari-nāma kevala kaitava.* Sitting in a solitary place intending to chant Hare Kṛṣṇa *mahā-mantra* is considered a cheating process. This practice is not possible for neophytes at all. The neophyte devotee must act and work very laboriously under the direction of the spiritual master, and he must thus preach the cult of Śrī Caitanya Mahāprabhu. Only after maturing in devotion can he sit down in a solitary place to chant the Hare Kṛṣṇa *mahā-mantra* as Śrī Caitanya Mahāprabhu did.
>
> —*Caitanya-caritāmṛta, Madhya-līlā 11.176, purport*

When Nimāi read this purport, he wanted to get up at once and show it to Pūjā dāsa who was also reading, sitting outside. But then Nimāi thought that, of course, Pūjā would have his own interpretation. Maybe it was better to read on his own and keep some things to himself. At least Nimāi was sure what Prabhupāda was saying: *a devotee shouldn't give up preaching.*

Nimāi then tried to think if there were any sections he could remember which would give him some encouragement about his relationship with Choṭa. It was hard to think of more sections about human devotees with animals because there weren't so many of them. But if he just thought of Choṭa as a devotee—maybe there were some encouraging things about friendships.... Of course, there was an important verse and purport in *Upadeśāmṛta* about the six loving exchanges among devotees. But Nimāi didn't have that book with him. The entire *Caitanya-caritāmṛta* was about friendships between devotees and Lord Caitanya and friendships among Lord Caitanya's devotees. Could his friendship with Choṭa qualify at that? Nimāi turned to "friendship" in the index to *Bhagavad-gītā As It Is* and found items like "between Arjuna and Kṛṣṇa," "between Paramātmā and *jīvātmā*," and "a devotee with Kṛṣṇa." What about "ordinary devotees among themselves?"

Nimāi turned to the famous verse in the Tenth Chapter, where Kṛṣṇa says that His devotees dwell in Him and derive bliss "enlightening one another and conversing about Me." Prabhupāda had written there and the purport that followed:

> Devotees of the Supreme Lord are twenty-four hours engaged daily in glorifying the pastimes of the Supreme Lord. Their hearts and souls are constantly submerged in Kṛṣṇa, and they take pleasure in discussing Him with other devotees ... the association of devotees and a bona fide spiritual master are important. We should know that the goal is Kṛṣṇa, and when the goal is assigned, then the path is slowly but progressively traversed, and the ultimate goal is achieved.
>
> —*Bhagavad-gītā 10.9–10, purports*

Friendships among Godbrothers was very important. Nimāi reflected how he was never good at making friends. Maybe, he thought, that was why he so highly valued his relationship with Choṭa. Choṭa was maybe the first and best friend he ever had. So, it was natural that he was missing him and thinking of his good Kṛṣṇa conscious friend.

When Nimāi had read the phrase "the association of devotees and a bona fide spiritual master are important," then he turned to different sections about the importance of a disciple's relationship with his spiritual master. And he thought fondly of his recent meetings with Gurudeva. It seemed as if his relationship with his spiritual master was only beginning, and he should do what he could to deepen it.

Nimāi was happy to read Prabhupāda's books in a personal way in the atmosphere of Vṛndāvana. Everything seemed more meditative, you could think more clearly and you felt close to Kṛṣṇa. The *japa* was also like that, much better than when he was agitated by the teenage boys teasing him on the farm, or when he thought of women or marriage or authorities in the temple.

At the end of their first day in "Prema Bhakti Asrama," when Nimāi was alone for a moment, he said out loud, "No doubt about it, Choṭa, Vṛndāvana is a great place for devotional service."

Pūjā dāsa brought Nimāi dāsa to see Gopīdāsa Bābājī. He had his own room within an old *āśrama* and temple that housed about twenty or thirty inmates, mostly old men. Gopīdāsa Bābājī was an alert, brown-skinned *sādhu* with bright eyes and some missing front teeth. He greeted Nimāi enthusiastically with folded palms and said, "*Daṇḍavats.*"

"See? He's got Prabhupāda's books," said Pūjā gesturing to two shelves of tattered-covered *Śrīmad-Bhāgavatams* and *Caitanya-caritāmṛtas.*

"Some books are missing," said Gopīdāsa Bābājī. "If you could kindly help me to get the other copies, then I will be complete."

The Bābājī produced an old ledger and asked Nimāi to sign his name and place of residence. Bābājī pointed to the names of many important leaders in the Movement who had signed endorsing the services of Bābājī as a good guide in Vṛndāvana. As Nimāi was signing, he noticed, in a corner of the dark room, a small photo of the Bengali monk Rāmakṛṣṇa. "Who's that?" asked Nimāi. "I thought you were a Vaiṣṇava."

"Oh, I *am* a Vaiṣṇava!" Bābājī laughed. "This picture is Rāmakṛṣṇa, because when I was a youth, I first entered spiritual life by hearing about him. This is called *vartma-pradarśaka-guru.*"

Nimāi was confused, because he had never heard of that kind of guru. He knew that Śrīla Prabhupāda had said Rāmakṛṣṇa was a Māyāvādī. But maybe it wasn't so important if this man had only met him in his youth, something like an old relative of the family. Besides, you never knew what to expect from some of the *sādhus.* And Pūjā had said they should be respectful "to all the sages."

They gave Bābājī a donation, promised to try to get him more of Prabhupāda's books, and set out with him for a morning tour of Vṛndāvana.

Bābājī was good at bargaining for a rickshaw and getting a man to wait while they visited different temples. Nimāi thought their guide talked too much, but at least with him they knew where they were going, and they heard different stories of the places and saints.

Nimāi found something attractive and wonderful at each holy place. On their first day they visited some of the major old temples. Nimāi's favorite Deity was the small, almost dapper Kṛṣṇa at Rādhā-Ramaṇa temple, and he liked the walk up the cobble-stoned hill with the Madana-Mohana temple tower looming in front of them and he liked the story Bābājī told there of the well used by Sanātana Gosvāmī.

They visited the Rādhā-Dāmodara temple and bowed before many of the *samādhis* there and peeked in the windows of Prabhupāda's room, which was locked. Before the sun set, they went bathing in the shallow Yamunā River. Then they visited the Movement's Kṛṣṇa-Balarāma temple just at the time when evening *ārati* was beginning. Along with a surging crowd of Indian pilgrims they went forward to see the Deities. Nimāi was glad to be lost in the crowds because he didn't want to meet any devotees he might know and have to explain himself. The Deities of Kṛṣṇa-Balarāma were the most beautifully formed and most beautifully dressed and garlanded of any he had seen that day. And almost everywhere they looked there was a *mūrti* of Śrīla Prabhupāda—Prabhupāda seated on the main *vyāsāsana* in the *kīrtana* hall with marble lions on either side, and Prabhupāda in his rooms, and the sacred room itself, where Prabhupāda spent his last days and passed away to Kṛṣṇa Loka. Nimāi bowed down before the *mūrti* of Prabhupāda sitting at his desk with his hand in his head bag. "Prabhupāda, please," Nimāi prayed, "help me understand what to do."

After their first tour with Bābājī, they sat with him in his room for a while. Pūjā dāsa asked him about the different *rasas* with Kṛṣṇa but Nimāi had trouble staying awake, which he thought was probably due to jet lag. When they finally returned to their own room and were eating some bananas and nuts they had purchased, Pūjā dāsa said, "That was interesting, what he said about the *rasas*, wasn't it?"

"I didn't hear much," said Nimāi.

"He said that in most of the Gauḍīya Vaiṣṇava *sampradāyas,*" said Pūjā, "a person is told his *rasa* with Kṛṣṇa at the time he gets initiated."

"Well, we're not told that," said Nimāi. "I thought that was something you only realized when you were perfect."

"I know, I know," said Pūjā. "Prabhupāda has written against something called *siddha praṇālī*. This isn't exactly the same. Bābājī said it's not exactly your full, eternal *rasa*, but it's a kind of practice."

"I think I better just practice to stay awake during *Bhāgavatam* class," said Nimāi. "Then later I'll find out about my *rasa*, if Kṛṣṇa wants."

"I'm going to ask him more about it tomorrow," said Pūjā, "there's no harm in trying to make advancement. I'm sure Kṛṣṇa wants us to know our eternal relationship with him, and the sooner the better." Nimāi sensed that Pūjā was somewhat displeased with him for his slowness and sleepiness, and for not agreeing. So Nimāi sat up and tried to be a more agreeable companion. After all, it was only by Pūjā's generosity that he'd been able to come to India. "Yes, we can find out more tomorrow," said Nimāi. "I feel very grateful to be here in Kṛṣṇa's abode."

Chapter 7

(Nimāi d. b.)

Don't worry—I didn't find out my *rasa* with Kṛṣṇa from the *bābājī.* I never asked him. But I think Pūjā did. He had a long talk with him alone. I didn't do it, but by being with Pūjā I condoned it, I suppose, and other things like that. My mood was, "Persons have to find out on their own what they want to do." But of course, there are authorized ways to do things. It's not that any path is okay as long as you're sincere. But when I was in Vṛndāvana I was a little like that. My attitude was, "Leave me alone, and I'll leave you alone." Even now, it's not my business to criticize someone like Pūjā personally. He is sincere. But on the other hand, if in the name of experimenting you make a mistake, it can be very costly. It could cost you your life. So, we need good guides in spiritual life. And the fact is, I had come to India without the blessings of any guide, except I knew the Lord is with me in any case, and my spiritual master is always my well-wisher. But that didn't mean that everything I did was approved by them. No, actually I was running away from them. I'm still trying to understand it all, although it's becoming clearer. If you read this, you probably can see it a lot clearer than I could at the time.

At least I didn't inquire into my *rasa* with Kṛṣṇa. I was, however, feeling closer to Kṛṣṇa in Vṛndāvana, and I don't think *that* was wrong. Even if you're a nonsense and you may have some wrong motive for being in Vṛndāvana, you can benefit. But they say it's a dangerous place to commit offenses. If you die doing sinful activities in Vṛndāvana (I heard Śrīla Prabhupāda say this on a talk he gave in Vṛndāvana in 1972), next life you may be born as one of Vṛndāvana's hogs or dogs. That's how dangerous it is to do something wrong in Vṛndāvana. *But,* although you are condemned to be an animal in Vṛndāvana, in your following life you get liberation from birth and death. So, the stakes are high in

Vṛndāvana; it's not a place where you can fool around or experiment in. Even Lord Brahmā learned that, when he came to Vṛndāvana and tried to test his mystic power against Kṛṣṇa's. But when I was there, my activities in themselves weren't sinful—I read a lot and chanted what I thought was improved *japa* and lived austerely—but the basic reason as to why I was there wasn't clear.

When the devotees from the Movement began arriving, the way Pūjā and I were living outside the temple on our own became more of a contrast. Pūjā started increasing his critical talk when he saw so many devotees. It was all because he was so shattered on account of his guru leaving. He had lost faith in the entire Movement. And he took out his hurt in a general way. We would be riding a rickshaw and maybe we would pass a devotee doing something wrong, like arguing with a local person, and Pūjā would say, "Just see." And even when we saw a large group of devotees visiting a temple he said, "How can you go on a peaceful *parikramā* with so many people?" And we kept congratulating ourselves that we had free time with no authority to pressure us.

Then one day a devotee I knew from the farm came to see me at "Prema Bhakti Asrama." He was Nanda dāsa, a devotee I never got along with. I wish Kṛṣṇa had sent someone I liked better, because from the start, Nanda and I started arguing.

"What are you doing in this place?" he asked. "Who authorized you to come to India? Do you know that Vibhu thinks you're still in the Caribbean with Gurudeva?" Everything he said was accusative, so I tried to be peaceful.

"We're just living in Vṛndāvana," I said. "What's wrong with that?"

"If you're not authorized," said Nanda, "there's plenty wrong with that."

Then Pūjā said something in my defense, and he and Nanda got really heavy with each other. In a few minutes they were shouting, and I thought for a moment that they would have a fist fight. Indians in the *āśrama* were gathering around looking and even people from the road heard it and stopped to look from a distance.

"You're bogus!" Nanda would say, and Pūjā would shout back, "No, *you're* bogus!" And then Nanda would say, "You're going against Prabhupāda!" And Pūjā yelled back, "I'm following him more than you do! I read his books two hours a day!" Then Nanda said, "Oh yeah? Well, you can read ten hours a day and still be in *māyā*. The proof is that you're living in this bogus *āśrama* and seeing a bogus *bābājī*!"

The whole thing was very unpleasant, and I was glad when it was over. It didn't help me to want to leave Pūjā and turn myself in at the temple. The whole time they were arguing I was half-thinking, "If I am doing something wrong, why doesn't Kṛṣṇa send someone better able to convince me?" But He sent Nanda, or at least it was Nanda who came, and he was the only devotee in Vṛndāvana at that time who knew me from the farm. I couldn't figure it out, but I felt bad. Afterwards I tried to calm Pūjā down and get us back into our peaceful routine. But despite his criticisms, what Nanda had said did have an effect on me. I wasn't so sure anymore, because I know that I'm not above making mistakes, sometimes big ones.

My relationship with Pūjā dāsa became strained because I didn't follow him with the "*rasa* practice," or whatever it was. Whatever he was thinking about it, he kept to himself, because he couldn't share it with me. But one day while we were both reading, he showed me a verse in *Caitanya-caritāmṛta* where Kṛṣṇadāsa Kavirāja mentions something about serving Kṛṣṇa in Vṛndāvana in a particular way.

> When an advanced, realized devotee hears about the affairs of devotees of Vṛndāvana—in the mellows of *śānta*, *dāsya*, *sakhya*, *vātsalya*, and *mādhurya*—he becomes inclined in that way, and his intelligence becomes attracted. Indeed, he begins to covet that particular type of devotion. When such covetousness is awakened, one's intelligence no longer depends on the instruction of *śāstra,* revealed scriptures, logic or argument.
>
> … The advanced devotee who is inclined to spontaneous loving service should follow the activities of a particular associate of Kṛṣṇa in Vṛndāvana. He should execute service externally as a regulative devotee as well as internally from his self-realized position. Thus, he should perform devotional service both externally and internally.
>
> Actually, the inhabitants of Vṛndāvana are very dear to Kṛṣṇa. If one wants to engage in spontaneous loving service, he must follow the inhabitants of Vṛndāvana and constantly engage in devotional service within his mind.
>
> The devotee should always think of Kṛṣṇa within himself, and one should choose a very dear devotee who is a servitor of Kṛṣṇa in Vṛndāvana. One should constantly engage in topics about that servitor and his loving relationship to Kṛṣṇa, and one should live in Vṛndāvana. However, if one is

physically unable to go to Vṛndāvana, he should mentally live there.

—Caitanya-caritāmṛta, Madhya-līlā 22.155,158–160

There were no Bhaktivedanta purports to these verses, and so for me, since I didn't understand it, I took them as something to ask an older devotee about, or to write to Gurudeva about. But with Pūjā dāsa, since there was no one he trusted, he wanted to do things on his own, or find a different authority of his own choice.

"Maybe this is a very advanced stage," I said, "and we're not supposed to try it."

"Then why did Lord Caitanya teach Sanātana Gosvāmī to put this in his books?" said Pūjā. "This is the whole point of coming to Vṛndāvana: to try to go beyond the mechanical stage of rules and regulations and develop spontaneous attraction. But you can't do it by yourself. So, he says here, according to your choice, you should choose a very dear devotee who is a servitor of Kṛṣṇa in Vṛndāvana and think about him. That means one of the liberated servants of the Lord in one of the *rasas*. You choose it according to your taste."

"But how do you know your taste?" I asked. Sooner or later, I knew he would have to say, "Because Bābājī told me," and I was afraid of that because I didn't want to challenge or upset him like Nanda dāsa did. I mostly wanted to drop the subject and, for myself, just put it on file and ask someone like Gurudeva at a later time. Pūjā must have sensed what was on my mind because he didn't push it any further. He did say that you can know your relationship with Kṛṣṇa if you think about it and pray in Vṛndāvana for Kṛṣṇa to reveal it to you later.

What struck me later when I thought about this was that *I also* was thinking of something that I couldn't share with Pūjā, something confidential and strange—my friendship with Choṭa. I was thinking to myself that he was "off" with his "*rasa*" with the Lord, but he didn't even *know* the strange things I thought of. For a moment I even thought, "Maybe everyone has a strange thing that to them is special and that others can't believe in." But then I thought no, many people may not have anything like that. Or they may have something less unusual: they may think no one appreciates how nice they are or that no one knows how much they suffer. In that sense, everyone has a feeling of self which is theirs alone, and they think no one else can really know that feeling.

But Kṛṣṇa knows what everyone thinks.

Out of this, I decided I ought to write to my Gurudeva. There were several important things that I wanted to ask him.

I continued to go around seeing Vṛndāvana with Pūjā and Bābājī and sometimes just with Pūjā, and sometimes by myself. I liked watching the people and the animals, and I liked thinking how, according to scriptures, every living being in Vṛndāvana is very special. Of course, you have to be on your guard, or people will steal things or cheat you, and you just can't walk up to a filthy hog and embrace him because he's a Brijbasi. But still, whatever they do, you have to remember that they're living in the dust of Vṛndāvana. And there are so many people besides the ones who live there. Hundreds and thousands of Indians come to Vṛndāvana every day, and especially when there are festivals. You see them walking on the trails on *parikramā* and in one sense they're ordinary, but again they're special because they've come to Kṛṣṇa's land just to be near Him. I began to realize that I couldn't stay permanently in Vṛndāvana, but I tried to imbibe some of its mercy. In fact, for people like me they say it's best not to stay long in Vṛndāvana, or you'll become an offender. I hadn't come to Vṛndāvana with an authorized purpose, and I was committing offenses to devotees while staying there, but even I was getting some benefit, or I felt like that while walking barefoot on the soft, sandy *parikramā* trail where thousands of others had come and gone. When I would be forced to leave Vṛndāvana, I thought, at least I could do as Kṛṣṇadāsa Kavirāja stated and live in Vṛndāvana in the mind.

Vṛndāvana, India

My dearest Gurudeva,

Please accept my humble obeisances at your lotus feet. All glories to Śrīla Prabhupāda.

You may be surprised to hear that your insignificant son, Nimāi dāsa, is writing to you from Vṛndāvana, India. At least I am here physically, although they say you can't enter Vṛndāvana just with a travel ticket. You have told us disciples that we will all eventually go to visit Vṛndāvana. So now I have come, as you wished, although not on direct order.

After I left Guyana and you, I felt depressed about giving up my devotee-mice. I can say this to you because you know of my attachment for them. And as a pure devotee you also blessed them as we parted. Maybe you did it in a spirit of kindness to my own whims, but I also appreciate that you have done that.

I met a devotee who had a free ticket for me to go with him to India. So, I just took it. What I should have done was to call up my temple president, Vibhu Prabhu, and ask him what he wanted me to do. But I didn't, and I'm also feeling a little guilty about that.

The devotee I am with, Pūjā dāsa brahmacārī, is a disciple whose spiritual master has gone away. He's a sincere devotee, but he's very bitter now and doesn't trust any authorities in the Movement. Maybe in certain respects he's not good association, but he's pretty strict in his *sādhana* and we have been getting along well so far.

One reason I am writing to you is to tell you my situation so you can decide what you want me to do. Also, here in Vṛndāvana we met one Gopīdāsa Bābājī who was teaching something about practicing our *rasa*. Pūjā has taken him seriously and he showed me a section in *Caitanya-caritāmṛta* where it says that you should follow a resident of Vṛndāvana. I thought that this was probably something only for very advanced devotees, but Pūjā said we should aspire to this and think of our relationship with Kṛṣṇa. So, I am asking for your authoritative decision on this. At this time, I am not practicing my *rasa* or anything like that.

But I am not going to the Krishna Balaram Temple except to visit. One of the devotees from the farm, Nanda dāsa, is here and he came and chastised me for living outside the temple. He was probably right, but he did it in such a harsh way. Anyway, I feel obliged to stay with Pūjā dāsa to keep him company, since he bought me my ticket. So that is my report, in case anybody asks you about me.

Your wayward son who needs to be corrected,
Nimāi dāsa

Chapter 8

(S.d.g.)

One day Nimāi was feeling particularly calm and in touch with Vṛndāvana *dhāma*. He had spent an afternoon sitting on the bank of the Yamunā reading *Śrīmad-Bhāgavatam* with a *gāmchā* wrapped around his head to prevent sunstroke. He also thought a lot about Choṭa and even sometimes spoke out loud.

That evening Nimāi and Pūjā talked together, avoiding any controversies. They had spent some of their dwindling funds to purchase milk and had a small feast of milk and bananas.

"Maybe someday," said Pūjā, "my wounds will heal. I should be grateful that I came in contact with Prabhupāda."

"Yes," said Nimāi, "if we can just serve in Vṛndāvana, all our wounds will be cured."

Before taking rest, Nimāi remembers to say a prayer. He knew that in many ways he was an irregular student, but he didn't see any way to get rid of his whimsical ways. So, he prayed to Kṛṣṇa, the Lord of Vṛndāvana, to help him. Nimāi thought that it was almost in response to his prayers that, during the night, he contracted a high fever. He woke with sweat covering his body. He had flu-like aches, and pains throughout his body. By morning time, he found it difficult to rise from the floor to go to the bathroom. He was stricken with extreme diarrhea and vomiting. Nimāi thought this was his "karma" and he mentally braced himself for illness. His consciousness seemed to retreat within his body while the pains became dominant. He lay helpless on the floor and endured the passing of the hours.

Pūjā told Gopīdāsa Bābājī about Nimāi, and together they put him into a rickshaw and took him to a doctor recommended by Bābājī. The "doctor's office" was a small temple amidst the congested population of inner Vṛndāvana. He was a *sādhu,* similar to Bābājī, but even more unshaven, and more jolly. He embraced Nimāi with both his arms and invited him, as an initial treatment, to lie down on his back in full view of a Kṛṣṇa Deity.

The Deity was a crude plaster statue, but still, it was bluish Kṛṣṇa smiling and with a flute. Nimāi slightly groaned but was pleased although somewhat embarrassed to lie down before Kṛṣṇa. He thought that even if this wasn't a physical cure, it was good to come here and submit himself, or his sick body, as evidence of his faith. The doctor poked him in several places, looked at his eyes and mouth, and decided that Nimāi had a fever and dysentery, which was what they had all previously guessed. Nimāi sat up and watched through bleary eyes as the doctor put tan-colored powders into newspaper wrapping and gave it to Pūjā as Nimāi's medicine. The doctor then looked at Nimāi's palm and studied the lines a few moments.

"Very nice *bhakta*," he chuckled and gave Nimāi a merry wink. "You will live a long time," he said, "and do big preaching as a follower of Prabhupāda."

"*Jaya*!" said Pūjā and Bābājī, while Nimāi grinned shyly. In spite of his desire to be humble he thought, "Maybe he knows."

Pūjā left a donation at the altar of the Kṛṣṇa Deity, and he and the doctor packed a painful Nimāi back into the painful rickshaw. Nimāi could barely control his bowels while they traveled, and they had to stop once for him to vomit. He felt himself a fool and an offender.

"That's all right," said Pūjā patting him on the back. "He said you're a nice *bhakta*."

After taking the bitter tasting powders, Nimāi thought he was getting better. Since it was the appearance day of Lord Nityānanda, he very much wanted to go with Pūjā and visit the Kṛṣṇa-Balarama temple for the evening *ārati*. Pūjā was reluctant at first to mix with so many Movement devotees, but Nimāi persisted.

They entered into the midst of hundreds of Western devotees from different countries, as well as many Vṛndāvana pilgrims, all of whom had gathered for the festival. It was a few moments before the opening of the doors for the evening *kīrtana*. As they waited, Nimāi and Pūjā felt guilty and thought that they were being looked at critically. Nimāi had not been shaving regularly, and his clothes were not so clean, and he imagined that devotees may have been looking at these things. He decided that even if they were criticizing, he wouldn't care. As the doors were opening and the *pūjārīs* blew the conch shells, a cheer went up from the devotees.

And as the *kīrtana* began, Nimāi and Pūjā were able to forget their self-consciousness. Everyone's attention was fixed on the forms of the Deities, Gaura-Nitāi, Kṛṣṇa-Balarama, and Rādhā-Śyāmasundara, or on the chanting and dancing of the devotees. The dancers moved in files back and forth before the Deities and then broke into a large circular dance. When some dancers left the circle to twirl about in the center,

Nimāi joined them. He was too weak to do any fancy dancing, nor was he ever able to do anything graceful. But he moved as best he could, a clumsy shuffle accentuated with leaps up and down as if on a basketball court.

The lead singer was skilled, but his voice was piercingly loud over the microphone. There were also many drummers and *karatāla* players. Those Indian devotees who were regular members of the Movement took part in the wild dancing, but others packed the walls and outer borders as curious spectators. The dancers changed into different patterns and the lead singer varied the melodies of the Hare Kṛṣṇa mantra and sang *bhajans* specially chosen for the appearance night of Lord Nityānanda. Sometimes all the dancers grouped themselves in front of the altar of Gaura-Nitāi, who were dressed in the high standard of the Kṛṣṇa-Balarama Mandir, tonight in tones of red and green. The Deities' upraised arms showed Them clearly as the leaders of all the dancing and chanting, and sitting at Their feet were the unique forms of Śrīla Prabhupāda and Bhaktisiddhānta Sarasvatī, both wearing soft silk saffrons, and smiling mildly. The dancers moved to the middle altar and beheld the large forms of Kṛṣṇa and Balarāma. Everyone knew that Balarāma was also Nityānanda, and relished, at least theoretically, the connection between the two Deities, and the way Lord Balarāma leaned jauntily on the shoulder of His younger brother, Lord Kṛṣṇa, the Supreme Personality of Godhead. The dancers moved to Rādhā-Śyāmasundara in *mādhurya-līlā,* and then back again to the middle of the floor where they could see all the Deities at once.

The formal *ārati* stopped after the blowing of the conch shells, but the *kīrtana* players continued. The leading *kīrtana* men were shining with perspiration and beaming with energy. Nimāi recognized only one or two devotees from America, but he felt he was with his family. They were all followers of Prabhupāda and shared the confidential understanding of Kṛṣṇa conscious philosophy. And at least in the *kīrtana,* disagreements were put aside.

After a full hour, some of the ladies and gentlemen retired from the *kīrtana,* but a large core of singers and dancers continued. Nimāi felt faint. He had deliberately ignored his bodily pains in order to join the fun, but now the discomfort came back persistently—aching joints, a loose feeling in the bowels and stomach, and nausea. He sought out Pūjā dāsa and asked if they could go back. Pūjā had been standing in the more staid ranks, but nonetheless he had been chanting the whole time. At Nimāi's suggestion, they left.

As they rode on their rickshaw through the mystical night, Pūjā remarked, "You dance pretty well for a sick man."

"It was nice to be with all our Godbrothers," said Nimāi.

"Yes," said Pūjā. "But I saw hardly any of the leaders. They were probably up in their rooms making politics."

On returning to their *āśrama* they found their room had been robbed. The door locks were broken and their possessions—tape recorders, sleeping bags, and suitcases—had been cleared out. Pūjā cursed and lamented at the loss of their return plane tickets, travelers' checks, and his passport, which he had left in a suitcase. Pūjā decided to go at once to tell the police. Nimāi lay down on the cement floor and covered himself with his *cādar.* But within minutes he had to rise and go to the latrine because of diarrhea. When he returned, he was shaking with chills. "Well, Choṭa," he said, "at least we got to go to *kirtana.*"

Chapter 9

(N.d.b.)

If I go ahead and tell about my delirium, you'll really think I'm eulogizing *māyā.* When I was trying to decide whether it would serve Gurudeva's purpose for me to write what happened, I concluded that it would probably help, just like a patient who tells his dreams (I've heard) for a psychiatrist to analyze them. Even to this day it scares me to think of it, but if Kṛṣṇa shows you things that frighten you and then you want to reform, that is also beneficial.

The worst thing is that I was alone. Pūjā went to Delhi to try replacing his tickets and passport, and no one in the "Prema Bhakti Asrama" spoke English or cared that I was sick. They probably see people getting sick all the time, and with me they thought, "There's another one." In India everyone is expected to get these sicknesses, and you just have to go through it on your own, so no one is going to hold your hand and ask you every hour, "How are you, prabhu?" But when it happens to *you*, and you lie there all alone, you feel neglected.

First, I woke up completely covered in sweat, but then a little later I was shivering with chills. I saw things that weren't actually there. It's like having a waking nightmare. I heard the running of mice's feet, and then I saw them. It wasn't Choṭa but ordinary rodents. I thought I saw them, but I wasn't sure. Then I thought I saw Gopīdāsa Bābājī standing over me and he was laughing, not nicely but like a demon, and he said, "Your *rasa* is to be a mouse! Ha! Ha! Ha!"

I felt that I was being judged and that I was guilty of worshiping mice. Somebody was saying that my friendship with Choṭa was like a perverted, black-art religion, and so I was getting what I wanted—reincarnation as a mouse. I felt terrible guilt that I was a deviator. "You prayed to mice instead of to Kṛṣṇa, so this is your reward. Ha! Ha! Ha!" So, this was it—I would actually have to become a mouse for my deviation and now the mice were coming and running up and down my body. I felt a presence of evil and that I had done wrong—it was all a joke on me because I was a mouse worshiper instead of a Kṛṣṇa worshiper.

I saw angry faces—Gurudeva and Vibhu and my mother and father and lots of Indians looking down and accusing me, *"This is what you are."*

I probably called out, but nobody came. Or sometimes men came and looked in the room and said something in Hindi and then went away ignoring me like a dead object. When it got really bad, I heard the running steps of something heavier than mice, and I thought the room was being overrun with rats, and I was helpless because I couldn't even get up from the floor. I was either sweating or shivering. I was very thirsty. I saw worms come out of the floor. I saw green grass suddenly wither and turn yellow and die and I smelled stool everywhere.

I couldn't collect myself to think deeply about what was happening, but mostly was helpless against the delirium and pain. But I did feel bad and guilty that I had misplaced my worship and that I was not a devotee of Kṛṣṇa. One nice thing happened though, when I was suffering. I heard a *kīrtana* coming from within the *āśrama*. It wasn't a big rhythmic *kīrtana* like we usually have, but it was definitely the *mahā-mantra*:

Hare Kṛṣṇa Hare Kṛṣṇa Kṛṣṇa Kṛṣṇa Hare Hare
Hare Rāma Hare Rāma Rāma Rāma Hare Hare

And it gave me a feeling of security and appreciation for the Hare Kṛṣṇa *kīrtana*. I couldn't move from the floor, but my spirit or mind went out to that *kīrtana* and took shelter. I was crying and thinking, "Kṛṣṇa, Prabhupāda, Gurudeva, forgive me. I don't want to be a mouse. I didn't mean to pray to them. I want to pray to You. Please forgive me."

But mostly it was a nightmare. I don't know how long I lay there like that, but it was day after day, night after night. Once or twice an old man came in and offered me something to eat, but when I did eat, my body rejected the food almost immediately. And that left me even weaker and dehydrated.

Finally, Pūjā dāsa returned, and at least I had companionship. He assured me that I would get through it. But it didn't go away. He took me to see the *sādhu*-doctor again, who said that I had jaundice or malaria or both. Without telling me, I knew I had something else—boils. One was on my buttock, and it was like my whole consciousness became focused on it as it gradually swelled and grew more uncomfortable and painful.

One week went by and another. I was sick and losing weight. I couldn't chant all my rounds although I tried, and the ones I chanted weren't very good. I was thinking, "What happened to sweet Vṛndāvana?" But devotees say that this is also a regular part of Vṛndāvana: the purification. Okay, I thought, then let me be purified.

When I was out of the delirium, I tried to understand it. It made me want to be more attentive to Kṛṣṇa and Prabhupāda as the objects of my worship. I didn't think it meant I had to reject Choṭa. But I can never mix up the two—my worship is to the Supreme Lord and everything else is a service to Him. I have to be always detached, ready to give up anything that's detrimental to His service. That's what I got out of it.

While lying on the floor day after day, I often thought of being back at the farm. I remembered it in a very favorable way, instead of my usual complaining I desired to be there again and to be a simple servant of Rādhā-Dāmodara. I remembered back to even before I was talking with Choṭa, how I used to feel sorry for myself. But now I just felt grateful to have lived with the devotees, and I wished I could go back. With so much time to pass, I was able to meditate on all the different moods of the farm. I mentally entered the barn and saw the friendly cow Lalitā with all the other cows lined up beside her, and the small pens where the newborn, white calves are kept, and then some heifers down at the end, and the bull who grinned when you petted him. In my mind I walked out into the corn fields and watched men plowing with oxen, and I walked up to the hill where you can see the whole farm with the twin silos and the barn with the slightly sagging roof. And then in my mind I walked down by the creek toward Gurudeva's house, and then I went to the temple and bowed before Prabhupāda and saw the Deities, who were wearing outfits of a chocolate brown color with white Irish lace. I felt grateful and fortunate to have ever been there, and I wanted to go back even if it meant being teased or chastised, which is, after all, what I deserve.

But although the sickness had made me realize I was part of the

Movement, it had created another detour, and it wasn't easy to get off it. They all expected me to recover my health after a few days or a week, but when I continued to have diarrhea and vomiting and to lose weight, they took me again to see the doctor with the Kṛṣṇa Deity. This time he shook his head. He didn't like what he saw, and he said I was seriously ill. He said I had malaria, jaundice, and dysentery, and even today I'm not sure whether I had one of them or all of them. My boils were also increasing—one of them had opened and was very messy, but others were growing in new parts of the body. After lying down in front of Kṛṣṇa, which I liked to do, the doctor suggested that I should go for special treatment under another doctor he knew in South India. He straight-out said that otherwise I might not live. We paid a donation, and Pūjā and I went back to the *āśrama* to talk about it. The place where I was supposed to go was called the Hindu Naturepath Sanatorium, and it wasn't inexpensive. Pūjā was very kind and lent me some money, and he even went over to Kṛṣṇa-Balarāma temple and borrowed some money from Nanda dāsa, although it must have been hard for him to ask. Pūjā said he couldn't come with me because he still had to go to Delhi to try to get his passport and ticket replaced. So, one day, when I really wasn't any better in health, he took me to the train station with instructions on how to travel on trains for the next few days, and he left me alone.

Chapter 10

(S.d.g.)

Nimāi arrived at the Hindu Naturepath Sanatorium in Kerala, South India, after a week of travel. The journey had been prolonged because he had missed a few train connections owing to his inexperience. His mind was half-delirious from his being crushed in the third-class train compartments and having to answer innumerable persons who wanted to test out their English on the Westerner. He had not been able to keep any food down for more than a few hours and had to regularly endure the stench of the train latrines, the ruthless push for seating spaces, and the helplessness of trying to communicate when no one spoke his language. On the last stretch of the trip, he had met some English-speaking Malayalis, both students and Marxists. They were very curious to know why Nimāi had changed from his former life to become a Kṛṣṇa *bhakta*. By talking with them, Nimāi was able to forget his bodily pains as he had during the *kīrtana*. He stood with them for more than an hour debating about God, the *Vedas*, and communism. When he finished speaking with one set of students, someone else approached him for more of the same. They stopped only when they saw that Nimāi was about to faint on his feet, and so they helped him sit down and drink some water.

Dr. Jyotir Anand's sanatorium consisted of ten small cement huts in a hillside grove, plus his own house where he lived with his wife, children and pet dog. His patients stayed in the huts, where for ten thousand rupees per month, Dr. Anand's family provided them with meals and the doctor administered the Naturepath cure.

When Nimāi arrived, it was obvious that he needed treatment, but since his clothes were torn and dirty and he had no possessions, the doctor wasn't sure if he could pay. In the awkward first moments, while standing at the doctor's front door, Nimāi said that he had been recommended to come by the *sādhu*-doctor in Vṛndāvana.

"Did he inform you of our fees?" Asked Dr. Anand.

"Oh yes," said Nimāi, and reaching into his money belt he produced ten thousand rupees as a first installment and placed it into the doctor's hand. "I will write to my father for more," said Nimāi. "He's got money."

The doctor then became pleasant and friendly. "I'm shocked at your appearance," he said with concern. "You need emergency treatment. But don't worry. You will be perfectly well in a month." Nimāi was always ready to hope for the best, and since he wanted to believe in the doctor's words, he resolved the become a submissive patient.

Dr. Anand was a mustached man of medium height, with straight black hair and a droll, wily smile. He immediately took charge of Nimāi with a confidence that seemed to go beyond mere medical treatment, as if he were prepared to give spiritual guidance as well. He assigned Nimāi to a hut and the doctor's sons brought in sheets for the cot, drinking water, and a bottle, which they told him was for thrice daily enemas.

After Nimāi bathed and rested for a few hours, the doctor paid him a visit and sat at his bedside. He began explaining Hindu Naturepath treatment. He said it was a great science—he called it "Vedic wisdom"—and said it couldn't be explained all at once. Some of the basic precepts were that there is only one disease and only one treatment; diseases are all forms of a low state of health, and by raising the health level through natural methods, any disease can be cured. "But actually, Kṛṣṇa will cure you, not me," said the doctor. Nimāi noticed that the doctor was acquainted with the Movement and knew some words from Prabhupāda's books. It turned out that a few Western devotees had been treated in his sanatorium.

"This is actually Prabhupāda's teaching," said the doctor. Nimāi was somewhat skeptical to hear that, but his main desire was to get well, he felt as if he had been beaten all over and maybe was near death. "I'll be like his disciple," Nimāi thought, "and just do what he says, just to get better. No arguments." Nimāi was told he would be put on a diet of raw vegetables; he would take frequent enemas and special baths. There would be prescribed times for sun-bathing, *yoga* exercise, and rest.

"Good," said Nimāi, "I'll follow it strictly."

In a few days, Nimāi began to feel slightly better but from instinct it seemed to him that his disease was abating by itself, but he thought it would be good to recuperate under care and try this interesting system of "Vedic wisdom." As far as Dr. Anand was concerned, Nimāi's cure was entirely due to Hindu Naturepath methods. Nimāi willingly accepted the daily regimen, which included, at least for the beginning, an hour's talk with the doctor. Thinking that it would help their relationship if he took the traditional position of the student, Nimāi offered obeisances and touched his head to the floor when Dr. Anand entered. After the first day, the doctor asked Nimāi if he had written his father to send money. Nimāi said it was a little difficult since he hadn't communicated with his father in several years, but he would try. They next day the doctor asked him again, but still Nimāi had not written. Finally, he wrote the letter although there was not much to say except, "I am very sick in India, please send one thousand dollars for my sanatorium fees."

Dr. Anand said that the mind had a great deal to do with physical disease, and he told Nimāi that he would help him to develop a totally optimistic outlook towards life. "In this world," the doctor said, "your body is *the* vehicle for obtaining spiritual life. You must make it healthy and happy. Health comes from the powers within, which are actually the source of everything. And life is for living, so be happy."

Nimāi was accustomed to hearing Kṛṣṇa conscious philosophy, which he accepted as the Absolute Truth. What Dr. Anand spoke to Nimāi is what Prabhupāda called "hodgepodge Hindu philosophy." Nimāi had heard some of this on the train in an argument he had with a man who said that all gods were equal, and everything was one. Dr. Anand spoke in a similar way, but added, "This is the same thing Prabhupāda says." Nimāi began to dislike the daily talks. He felt like saying, "Just tell me about health treatment, but don't mix in your philosophy,"—but he didn't want to abandon his position as a submissive patient. If Nimāi wanted to know more about the science of Hindu Naturepath, he could read some books which the doctor provided.

One day the doctor taught Nimāi a method of total relaxation. Under the doctor's verbal commands, Nimāi relaxed one part of his body after another and then he was told to relax his mind. At the doctor's request, Nimāi began to intone the word "Oṁ" and he also repeated, following the doctor's instructions, "Every day in every way I am getting better and better." Nimāi was so embarrassed to say this that he almost snickered out loud. What if one of the devotees heard him saying these things? The doctor then asked him to say, "The source of good health is Mother Nature, I turn to her, turn to the sun, and I turn to the source within. I love my body and I want it to get well. Everything is peace."

Since Nimāi was in a state of relaxation which had taken them a half hour to develop step-by-step, he didn't wish to rudely break it, and so he repeated the words. But he promised himself that at the beginning of their next meeting he would tell the doctor that there were certain things he couldn't do.

At their next meeting, when Nimāi brought this up, it gradually developed into an argument. Nimāi asserted that Lord Kṛṣṇa was the Supreme Personality of Godhead, and the doctor disagreed. Dr. Anand said that the demigods were the source of health and happiness.

"But they are the servants of Kṛṣṇa," said Nimāi, "that's what it says in *Bhagavad-gītā*."

"I know they are the servants," said the doctor condescendingly, "but they are one with the source. He is God for some and for others, as for me, our deity is Gaṇeśa. Everyone worships and thinks his God is supreme and all are supreme in the Brahman."

"NO," said Nimāi, "Kṛṣṇa says, '*brahmaṇo hi pratiṣṭhāham*,' the impersonal is subordinate to Him."

"You may think that to enhance your worship," said the doctor, and he smiled to pacify Nimāi's intense look. "You may say that, but in the *Upaniṣads* it is said that all gods come from the one. One God in many forms *Tat tvam asi*, you are also that."

The phrase *tat tvam asi*, spoken by the doctor, set off an alarm within Nimāi. He felt he was in danger, because now he knew that Dr. Anand was an impersonal Māyāvādī and if one listened to a Māyāvādī he could lose his devotion to God.

Dr. Anand saw that Nimāi was likely to bolt and run

"We should not discuss these philosophic technicalities," he said. "I may not have expressed myself so well, but I am actually Kṛṣṇa conscious. I am a devotee of Kṛṣṇa, too." Nimāi and the doctor at least agreed that they should not discuss these topics but stick to the treatment, which Nimāi admitted was a *sāttvic*, harmless cure. So, they made a pact of conduct. If Dr. Anand would refrain from speaking Māyāvādī philosophy, Nimāi would remain and take the treatment and follow faithfully what the doctor prescribed.

After that, Dr. Anand visited Nimāi less frequently. His sons performed the ordinary functions of bringing the one meal a day of raw vegetables and supervising Nimāi's participation in daily sunbathing, exercise, and enemas. Dr. Anand stopped by only for brief, cheerful visits and inquired whether Nimāi had received a letter in which his father said he had wired the money. It became a complicated matter, involving much discussion daily, as to where the money had actually arrived and how they could get it. Finally, it was processed through a bank, and the doctor received the Indian equivalent of one thousand dollars, for a month's stay at the sanatorium.

"Your case was more serious than I thought," said Dr. Anand. "It may take a few months before you're one-hundred percent fit. It all depends on your mental attitude. Relax more and learn not to worry. Turn to Mother Nature and the sun. This is what we do in our Vaiṣṇava culture." Nimāi smiled wanly and lay his head back on the pillow. "This is too much," he thought. "How did I ever get *here*?"

Chapter 11

(N.d.b.)

Once I knew that the doctor was a Māyāvādī, how come I didn't leave? I couldn't—I was too ill, but I knew it wasn't good. At least the situation drew out of me a strong attachment for Kṛṣṇa consciousness. I had to preach (at least to myself) in order to survive. Although the doctor kept asking me to relax, I was becoming more alert and appreciative of Kṛṣṇa consciousness. But I also felt lost and far away from where I was supposed to be. I thought this must be my karma, to be sick and living in such a place. I thought, "I secretly want this, but now I have to reverse it and go back to straight Kṛṣṇa consciousness." I wanted to live in a favorable place under the direct shelter of Gurudeva. But I had discovered that once I went off little bit, *māyā* threw me on a long orbit going away from Kṛṣṇa consciousness, and only by special mercy could I come back. I was swimming against a strong current.

I'll tell you some little deviations (and some not so little) I started doing under this new influence. For example, they wouldn't let me drink milk. At first, I thought that's all right, maybe I'm too ill. But the doctor and his books and other people I met at the sanatorium all said that milk was no good. They were supposed to be Hindus, but they were against drinking cow's milk. So, I was not taking any milk products at all and thinking that maybe it was good not to. And yet I knew that Prabhupāda said without at least a little milk, how can you develop fine brain tissues to understand Kṛṣṇa? And the food I was eating, although the ingredients were harmless, wasn't offered to Kṛṣṇa. They would allow me to offer it to Kṛṣṇa when they brought it to my room, but I didn't have any Deity, just a picture of *guru* and Kṛṣṇa, and the food wasn't really *prepared* for them. The doctor and his staff just humored me and allowed me to offer the food, but they weren't doing it themselves. I even started getting lax and not always offering it. Sometimes

I would be embarrassed to do it in front of someone, and I would think, "All right, I'm a devotee so it must be already offered."

Their whole attitude was non-Kṛṣṇa. The doctor said he was "a Vaiṣṇava," but that was a joke. He probably told other patients he was whatever *they* were just to keep them satisfied. And he could do that because he believed everything was the same anyway.

I could make a whole list of the things I did there that were deviations, and maybe I will let you know the full extent of it, but the main point is, it was not a Kṛṣṇa conscious environment. There was no temple program, no *kṛṣṇa-kathā,* no nothing—nothing but health and relaxing and bogus philosophy.

I had thought when I was with Pūjā dāsa that it was nice not being pressured to attend the morning program, but now I missed it and understood the need for it. I did my own reading and chanting, but it wasn't as good as when you're with like-minded souls. Some devotees may do well living away from others, but at least for me I saw that I wanted to live with devotees.

I didn't even have much time to myself, what with doing enemas, exercises, and talking. Even when I was relaxing it was their kind of relaxation, and it didn't feel right. I knew that what they really would like me to do was relax and forget Kṛṣṇa and maybe not be so strict about following the four rules. The doctor even said he thought my vow to chant sixteen rounds was not so important, that it was better to say one round slowly. He had his own opinion about everything and yet he claimed his opinions were "our *Vaiṣṇava* way" or even "what Prabhupāda said." I had to choose either to argue with him all the time or overlook everything that was going on.

Another way I deviated was to stop thinking so much about Choṭa, Yamala and Arjuna. The delirium had made me unsure of my feelings of separation for Choṭa, because in the hallucination I thought I was punished for "worshipping" mice. I didn't know whether the delirium was just that or whether there was some truth to it. But as a result, I became somewhat detached from thinking of Choṭa. And in the sanatorium, I couldn't go past that doubt. It was another thing I wanted to talk with Gurudeva about. In one sense I thought maybe detachment isn't bad. I wish them well and I would have been happy to see them, but what could I do for them now? Let Choṭa be under Kṛṣṇa's protection in Guyana, and let me be here. We can prosecute our own duties with no undue attachment.

While I was staying in the sanatorium, I also received a letter from you, dear Gurudeva. You wrote it from Guyana and it was forwarded from Vṛndāvana. You may remember it, but I want to quote some of it here:

> Yes, I am surprised that you have gone to India so suddenly and without permission from your temple president. I can understand that you were in a disturbed state of mind, but there will be so many disturbances in life, and we are still expected to act soberly and not fly off when there are troubles. This is the whole message of the *Bhagavad-gītā*. Arjuna was upset and wanted to leave the field of action, so Kṛṣṇa spoke the *Bhagavad-gītā* to him just to direct him back to his duty. If this becomes an established pattern with you, that whenever you feel troubled you act on your own, then what will happen to you? Of course, I am pleased that you have entered Vṛndāvana *dhāma* and that you appreciate the atmosphere. I promised you you would go one day, and so somehow it has come to pass. But I am concerned about the person you are associating with who does not trust any authorities in the Movement. Are you going to become like that too? You know you have a tendency to be easily impressed by others. This tendency can serve you well if you are impressed by the leadership of Lord Kṛṣṇa Himself, and by His devotees, and want to emulate them. But you have to protect yourself and not become influenced by every wind that passes in one direction or another. I'm concerned that your nice attitude towards serving the devotees and serving in Prabhupāda's movement does not become spoiled by those who have themselves unfortunately been victims of bad examples.
>
> As for the Vṛndāvana *bābājī*, the "practice" of the *rasa* which he may be teaching is not bona fide. The real practice is to serve the spiritual master and the Vaiṣṇava. We should keep ourselves fixed up in the lower position and, if Kṛṣṇa likes, He will bring us up. It is not our business to invite ourselves into the eternal *rasa* by speculation or listening to the advice of another person who himself is unqualified to speak of *rasas*. Anyway, there is no question of *rasas* for a conditioned soul. Now in the name of being interested in this, you are loosening your attachment to

> *kṛṣṇa-seva*, or service, in which you were properly fixed up. I refer to your ongoing service at the farm, which you have now abandoned.
>
> I will be going to India myself in a few weeks, and if necessary, I will seek you out and speak with you. I like your association, and I'm sure whatever disturbance has occurred can be cleared up. In the meantime, I suggest you go to live at the Krishna Balaram Temple and take up some service there. Go on with your reading and chanting and now that you are in Vṛndāvana take full advantage of the wonderful atmosphere. But don't act in an independent way.
>
> While writing this letter and thinking of you, I was just about to ask you, "How are your devotee-mice?" But then I realized that you have left them to go free here in Guyana. Perhaps the *bhakti* which they received from you in the form of chanting and *prasādam* is now being transmitted to others. What do you think?

Of course, I was happy to receive such nice chastisement from my Gurudeva. It was like pure nectar relieving me from the nonsense influence of Dr. Anand's *āśrama*. I knew I would do what Gurudeva said, as soon as I got well again. But what struck me most of all was what he wrote at the end. I could hardly believe it. Here I was suspecting my relationship with Choṭa as being a deviation, and Gurudeva asked in such an interested way, "How is your devotee-mouse? ... What do you think?"

Gurudeva, I wish I could have spoken with you right then and there. The mice whom I knew in a Kṛṣṇa conscious way may not be benefited from further association with me, but I am *your* eternal "mouse" in need of constant protection. You won my heart once again by your letter and your thinking like that about the mice-devotees. It made me feel that I wasn't going to be condemned to hell for whatever I had done. I still couldn't see my relationship with Choṭa so straight, and I wished I could have talked with you more (although since then I have gained a better understanding). When I got that letter, I began to think that maybe if my spiritual master came to India, he would come and rescue me just as Lord Caitanya once rescued His servant Kṛṣṇadāsa in South India when he left the Lord and went to live with some gypsies. I began to cherish that idea, although know it wasn't proper to think of my spiritual master coming to serve me in my distress. But it was a solace during the time I became influenced and when the detour I was on seemed to increase in a tangent away from the true path. I would think that when I am at the last gasp, my spiritual master will come and grasp me by the hair and save me.

I also wrote a letter to my dad. He wasn't pleased that I had asked him for money. I never asked him for money in the three years that I've been in the Movement, because I knew he would think that that's all I wanted from him. So, I felt bad that now I had asked for money just to put it in Dr. Anand's pocket rather than having it help the Movement. Therefore, I wrote him a letter explaining Kṛṣṇa consciousness in terms that I thought he might appreciate. Dad calls himself eclectic, which means a mixture of different philosophies, so I tried to appeal to him that Kṛṣṇa consciousness is another very interesting way. I put in some quotes from the *Bhagavad-gītā* and wrote an essay just suited for my dad. It was fun and made me think I ought to preach more like that.

I thought I should also train myself against Māyāvādī philosophy. So, in my daily reading of Prabhupāda's books, I looked at the *Caitanya-caritāmṛta* section where Lord Caitanya talks with the Māyāvādī in Vārāṇāsī. Dr. Anand wasn't a classical Māyāvādī follower of Śaṅkara. In fact, most Māyāvādīs that I have met are a mixture of many different things, including Māyāvādī. For example, I met a hippie on the plane when we were going to India who said he was a Christian. I thought "All right we can agree that God is a person, and we all worship Jesus Christ as the Son of God." But once he started talking, I realized he wasn't actually a Christian. He said that Christ says God is in your heart, and since God is love, then we are also Love and we are also God. I think that's what he said. Whatever it was exactly, it was impersonal. Pūjā dāsa explained to me later that what this "Christian" was actually saying was when he enjoyed sex life, that was Love, and therefore he has attained love of God. I don't think Pūjā dāsa was concocting, because later I saw the hippie in the back of the plane with his girlfriend, kissing and embracing in front of everybody.

Even if most people aren't classical Māyāvādīs, it's good to understand what Śaṅkara said. In India, they're a little more inclined to Śaṅkara because they quote from the *Vedas*. That's what Śaṅkara did.

He avoided the direct meaning of the *Vedas* and gave his own indirect interpretation. His philosophy is so dangerous that the *Caitanya-caritāmṛta* says, "Śaṅkara has misled the world by commenting that Vyāsadeva was mistaken. Thus, he has raised great opposition to theism throughout the entire world." It could be that all the hodgepodge impersonalism that we find also comes from Śaṅkara, because he was so potent, being an incarnation of Śiva. As I read this, I began to think of myself as a representative for Kṛṣṇa consciousness in a Māyāvādī camp, but I wasn't so sure of my own powers to convince anyone. Prabhupāda writes:

> The Māyāvādī philosophers have presented their arguments in such attractive flowery language that hearing Māyāvādī philosophy may sometimes change the mind of even a *mahā-bhāgavata,* or a very advanced devotee. An actual Vaiṣṇava cannot tolerate any philosophy that claims God and the living being to be one and the same."
>
> —*Caitanya-caritāmṛta, Adi-līlā 7.110, purport*

I couldn't argue with some Sanskrit *paṇḍita,* but at least I know a Māyāvādī when I hear one, and I *should* know enough to stay clear of them. In reading Prabhupāda's books, I also looked for references about cows' milk. Dr. Anand said he was once giving a lecture and a man challenged him and said, "Why do you speak against milk, since Kṛṣṇa recommends it in the *Bhagavad-gītā?"* Dr. Anand said he replied, "I have read the *Bhagavad-gītā* fifty times and I don't find that Kṛṣṇa says you should bring milk." I pointed out to Dr. Anand that Kṛṣṇa says the *vaiśya* should protect the cows, and in another chapter Kṛṣṇa says that He is the *surabhī* cow. Dr. Anand said that that still didn't mean that we should drink the cow's milk, because her milk was only for her calves. Hearing these things was contaminating for me. Then I remembered that the *Bhagavad-gītā* is the philosophy in brief, and we can't expect everything to be there. If you look in the *Bhāgavatam* there are different references to milk and milk products. There's one reference where Lord Viṣṇu says that He's very pleased by offerings which are made to him by feeding *brāhmaṇas* with food that has ghee in it. And in the *Kṛṣṇa* book, Kṛṣṇa is always drinking milk and yogurt and giving an example in that way. You often read of *sādhus* drinking cows' milk, like Śukadeva Gosvāmī, who drank only cows' milk. Dr. Anand says that if there's any milk to be drunk it should be goats' milk, but

Śukadeva drank cows' milk and so did Prabhupāda.

I was thankful I still had my books, because I was able to find some good quotes:

> Human civilization means to advance the cause of brahminical culture, and to maintain it, cow protection is essential. There is a miracle in milk, for it contains all the necessary vitamins to sustain human physiological conditions for higher achievements. Brahminical culture can advance only when man is educated to develop the quality of goodness, and for this there is a prime necessity of food prepared with milk, fruits and grains.
>
> —*Śrīmad-Bhāgavatam 1.16.4, purport*

> The mercantile class is also required to give protection to the cows in order to get sufficient milk and milk products, which alone can give the proper health and intelligence to maintain a civilization perfectly meant for knowledge of the ultimate truth.
>
> —*Śrīmad-Bhāgavatam 2.5.37, purport*

Sure, too much milk or too much *anything* can make you sick. But it's not "our Vaiṣṇava way" to avoid cow's milk. When I got my quotes together, I think the doctor became a little leery of me, especially when I talked to other people at the sanatorium.

I also looked up some references about health. I remember seeing in Prabhupāda's letters how he often encouraged the devotees to stay healthy. He used to end all his letters "I hope this meets you in good health." On the other hand, Prabhupāda indicated there was a limit to how much you should strive to maintain your own health. He said just lead a regular life and you'll be healthy. But at Dr. Anand's place the ideal of staying in good health was like a religion. They weren't interested in offering food to Kṛṣṇa; they only wanted to eat to satisfy the demands of their primitive nature. That's why they didn't like to cook. I was able to find quotes where Prabhupāda shows how you can overdo health consciousness.

At a Bombay *paṇḍāla* in 1977, a well-dressed, middle-aged Indian man stepped forward and asked, "Swamiji, what is the importance of health and life, and how do you advise people to maintain health? And how does it connect to your mission?"

> Prabhupada: What is health? First of all, you have to understand that however healthy you may be, you must die. So, what problem will you have

> solved? *Janma-mṛtyu-jarā-vyādhi-duḥkha-doṣānudarśanam*, Kṛṣṇa says. It is not my manufacturing although you may try to remain very healthy, nature's law is that you must die. How can you help yourself? After all, you have to meet death so as long as you have got this material body, there is no question of health. You must suffer. Foolish persons bewildered by false egotism think, "I am improving my health, I am improving this ...". He is improving nothing. He' s completely under the clutches of material nature.
>
> —*Śrīla Prabhupāda-līlāmṛta, Vol. 6*

I became fired up when I started researching these things in Prabhupāda's books, but I didn't always follow what they said myself. I was very weak in health and since I was paying (or my dad was paying), I thought I should take the full treatment. But the problem was, it was hard to take the nectar of bona fide teachings out of the pot of Māyāvādī poison. When I started becoming a little bit stronger, the doctor insisted I participate in some of the group functions. So, I did it. I began to do yoga *āsanas* including *prāṇāyāma* and even "meditation." I worshiped the sun, avoided all milk products, and talked a lot about health – but I didn't become a Māyāvādī (I hope).

Chapter 12

(Nimāi d. b.)

If anyone reading this thinks I'm a sincere devotee, he'll have to revise his opinion. I'm telling this part only because Gurudeva said the *māyā* should be exposed.

The sanatorium wasn't so bad as long as I was very sick and allowed to rest all the time in my hut. But when I started to recover a little bit and I went outside and saw what the sanatorium really was, I became disturbed. There were different kinds of people living there and they were all doing their own thing. I usually met the other inmates only at the two times for compulsory group exercise. We were also supposed to eat together outdoors under the banana trees, but I insisted on staying alone, and I paid Dr. Anand's son some money to bring my meal indoors. People soon learned that I was a Hare Kṛṣṇa devotee, and they also regarded me as a bit anti-social, just as they do in the Movement. So, they humored my eating alone. But sometimes people would drop by to see me, and after a while I also sometimes looked in at the other huts and chatted with the guests.

Another time you met with people was during sunbathing or when soaking in the special tubs which were to improve your spine. Since there were some women attending, I sunbathed on my own, although everyone else mixed. Dr. Anand liked people to mix and be happy and share good vibrations. Probably I didn't fit so well with the vibrations, but at least I was quiet, and I was paid up for one month, with another letter on the way to my father for another month's rent. As for the exercise, we did it in a circular dirt clearing, in the morning and at sundown, and Dr. Anand led us. I liked the bending and stretching, but disliked anything that sounded like meditation, because I figured he was trying to get us to become one. I don't think anyone else there even understood my objection. Their attitude was, "It's okay if you're a devotee of

Kṛṣṇa and we're a devotee of something else. But when we get together, we can transcend our different gods and become One." If I tried to explain that the Supreme God is Himself a transcendental person and the source of the impersonal oneness and that our meditation should be to seek union with Him person to person, they would think that was "another idea." What they really wanted was to enter the impersonal One in a short meditation and then come out again and be themselves. I don't think I'm being unfair to say this; it's just what they wanted. They didn't want God in any overwhelming way. Unfortunately, I didn't want Kṛṣṇa in an overwhelming way either (*laulyam*), but I know that *that* is the goal. Any other practice which goes by the name of meditation is cheating. So, either I stayed in my room, which was not allowed, or I came out but kept interrupting Dr. Anand and everyone else by saying, "No, that's speculation," or I sat with them and became an accomplice of the Māyāvādī tinged exercises—which is what I did most of the time. I suppose there were other alternatives open to me, such as leaving the place, but I wasn't up to that.

In order to tell you how I became influenced, I have to describe a little about who it was that influenced me.

My hut was centrally located. In the hut next to mine was a very old lady from Switzerland. She spoke a quaint kind of English. She took an interest in me and my *japa* chanting. I know you're not supposed to sit alone even with an old woman, but at this place it was impossible to follow all the rules. So, I would sometimes sit with her on the bench in front of her hut. She knew about auras, the energies that some people can see emanating from a person's body. She claimed that by seeing someone's aura and then meditating on it very deeply—which she said she could no longer do because it was so physically taxing—she could tell all kinds of things about a person's past lives and what their present weakness or strength was. I thought, "Uh-oh, she's going to tell me about myself." Whenever I meet a person like that who knows astrology or some psychic art, I half want to find out about it and half want to run away. But she was my next-door neighbor. "You have a very pure aura," she said, "many brilliant colors." She told me that I was a master *yogi* in my past life and long ago I had even been a personal associate of Gautama Buddha. That seemed interesting because the *Bhagavad-gītā* also says that if one practices Kṛṣṇa consciousness in this lifetime he must have been a spiritualist in a past life.

But when I talked with Brenda (that was her name) I became puffed up. I tried to tell her about Kṛṣṇa and how to chant. Although she seemed amused to watch me chant, she thought that she knew all about it and that I was just a kid. But she liked my aura and would sometimes tell me how "it" looked or when I had a problem. She said I had special abilities to communicate, but I wasn't using them. Brenda also ate a special supplement that she had brought with her which was a rare alga that grew only in Iceland and would guarantee long life. She used to give me some. All in all, Brenda was a mild influence, but if I tried to influence her by asking if she'd like to hear *Kṛṣṇa* book or chant, she didn't want to do it.

A stronger influence was my next-door-neighbor on the other side, Bud, who was thirty years old, from Denmark. He had been suffering from bronchitis his whole life, he said, but after one month with Dr. Anand, he was making an amazing recovery. Bud also pursued some supplementary activities. Dr. Anand officially disapproved of anything but the strict Naturepath, but he allowed people to do what they wanted, and he himself ate food which he advised others not to take. Bud lifted weights so he was very muscular. He advised me to try. Just to be sociable I started working out with a ten-pound barbell he lent me, and I watched the progress on my biceps.

He also knew about massage and had a portable, battery-run machine that sent a low frequency electric current into your body for healing the cells. He said it would help my diarrhea problem, and so I tried it a few times, but I didn't notice anything except a dull shock.

I didn't get very far in talking with Bud about Kṛṣṇa consciousness. When I asked him what his philosophy was, he said, "I don't have one. I just live." He took a supplement of special bee pollen which he said will give you extraordinary energy. I was particularly low on energy, and so I tried some of it. But I never noticed anything. Whatever special thing I take, I never get the result that people say you're supposed to get.

In two other huts were respectable Indian businessmen. They used to sit together between their huts and smoke cigarettes when Dr. Anand wasn't looking. Apparently, they made a visit to the sanatorium every couple of years to overcome hypertension. I think sometimes at night they would also drink liquor.

There was also a young man and woman from France, who lived together in one hut, and who played music on their tape recorder. The music was very interesting, such as Bach or Mozart or sometimes Bob Dylan, but they didn't ask anyone whether they wanted to hear it or not. They played it loud. I mentioned it to Dr. Anand, but he smiled and said he couldn't do anything.

Everyone knew I was a devotee, but it didn't seem to make much difference. I wore my Vaiṣṇava *tilaka* faithfully, but eventually I stopped wearing a *dhotī*. Most of the men there, as advised by Dr. Anand, went around wearing a *gāmchā* and no shirt. One of the doctor's books even recommended nudity. At least at this sanatorium things didn't go that far. But you were supposed to wear as little clothing as possible so that the air could circulate on your body, and you could get the sunshine. And as part of the back-to-nature mood, most of the men didn't bother shaving. Just by association I also stopped shaving. I had never grown out a beard, so I became curious to see what I could do. We each had a little wall mirror in our hut, and I began watching my beard's progress and flexing my muscles. This all goes to prove that Hiraṇyakaśipu was right when he said that association is like crystal glass; it reflects the color of whatever comes near it. Although my intentions were always to regain health so that I could return to devotional service, I was becoming subtly and grossly transformed by my association outside of the society of devotees.

Chapter 13

(Nimāi d. b.)

I am making this a separate chapter because it's the worst. I hoped that S.d.g. would write it because I am ashamed. But he and Gurudeva thought it would be better for me to tell it from the inside. I've read adventure books where people get in a lot worse jams than I got into, but my life has been pretty sheltered. At least since I became a full-time devotee, I've been in the shelter of Kṛṣṇa. As stated by Prabhupāda in the heading of his *Back to Godhead* magazine, "Where there is Godhead there is no nescience." The opposite is also true. As soon as you step a little bit out of the shelter of the Kṛṣṇa-sun, you get thrown into the darkness.

Because it's painful for me to talk about my falldown, and I don't see any real profit in describing the details, I won't dwell on it. But I won't minimize the facts either.

What happened is that Bud put some intoxicant in a drink of juice he gave me. Before I became a devotee, I tried some drugs and so I think what he gave me was LSD. I'm surprised that he did such a malicious thing or maybe he thought it was fun or wanted to give me a good time. But he knew my strict principles, so there was something destructive in his mind. Maybe he thought I was too highfalutin.

At first, I thought I was becoming delirious again, but there was no fever. It didn't make sense, why I should feel all these rushes of power and perception. But it was all material, *māyā*, and I recognized it from the past. Then Bud came into my hut and told me what he had done. I told him to get out and leave me alone. He looked like he was deciding whether to beat me up, but then he left. He said something blasphemous that I won't repeat.

I've read in the *Nectar of Devotion* that when a gentleman gets intoxicated, like Lord Balarāma, he lies down. But a low-class man shouts and is sometimes violent. I used to wonder why the *N.O.D.* spoke of a gentleman being intoxicated. Not that I am a gentleman. Then, again, I didn't purposefully take this, but it was acting on me. So, I thought maybe I should lie down. However, that didn't work because everything was spinning around, and I felt an urgency to *do* something and prove myself.

I was very sorry. I felt as guilty as if I had willfully taken it myself. That was the worst part of it, feeling guilty. I felt as if all the pious activity I had accumulated was just being thrown away within a few hours. I had heard of some devotees in the past taking things like LSD or mushrooms in an attempt to get full realization of Kṛṣṇa. I knew that that was stupid. I would never do such a thing. Prabhupāda says you can't know Kṛṣṇa by taking a pill. He told that to Allen Ginsberg who was trying to argue that maybe Kṛṣṇa came in the form of a pill in Kali-yuga. Prabhupāda said Kṛṣṇa is spiritual not material, and He doesn't reveal Himself to someone just because he takes a pill. So, whatever anybody sees in a drug state is hallucination.

In one sense I wasn't doing such a bad job controlling myself if I could have just stayed in bed. I knew it would wear off in a few hours, or at least the worst of it. But one feeling was getting stronger and stronger, and that was a fear that I was in bad association, and I should leave as soon as possible. When I looked in the mirror and saw that I had a beard, I knew that I was in complete *māyā* from staying in this place. So, whether it was by rational decision or by exaggerated fears, I decided I had to go at once. I was just wearing *yogī* pants and a T-shirt and I just gathered up the few other things I had with me and left the Hindu Naturepath Sanatorium without talking to anyone and with the intention of never coming back.

By Kṛṣṇa's grace, the effects of hallucination started to diminish sooner that I thought they would. I began to chant with more sincerity than usual,

Hare Kṛṣṇa, Hare Kṛṣṇa, Kṛṣṇa Kṛṣṇa, Hare Hare
Hare Rāma, Hare Rāma, Rāma Rāma, Hare Hare

That always happens when you are afraid. We don't ask for fearful situations, but when they happen, we immediately become more dependent on Kṛṣṇa. I was definitely afraid and was also depending on Kṛṣṇa, or at least I was chanting to Kṛṣṇa to please help me.

I didn't have much money and I couldn't think straight about where I should go. If there was a Prabhupāda temple nearby I definitely would have gone there, just like you read in Prabhupāda's biography, how the hippies used to turn themselves in at the temple in Haight-Ashbury. I was ready to turn myself in not just for the night, but for good, for life. I was ready to serve in a menial way for the rest of my life if someone would just let me work in the kitchen or in some way serve the other devotees, whatever they wanted. I wanted to be part of the Movement. I thought of Pūjā dāsa and how he had influenced me, but I didn't want to be like that anymore. Within my heart I didn't have any big cynicism towards leaders. I had my spiritual master and as for the other devotees I had served, they had never done any horrible scandalous things to me, such as written about in anti-cult books. So why should I pretend that I was better off outside the Movement?

I was paranoic as I walked into the nearest town. I realized that, with my beard and non-devotee clothes, I looked like a vagabond and not like a brahminical devotee. I kept thinking, "This is what you wanted." Otherwise, why was I dressed like this and with a beard? No one forced me. Definitely I was getting kicked by *māyā*, I knew that. But at least now I wanted to be a devotee, if it wasn't too late.

Since I had so little money and it was getting late, I decided to just lie down somewhere and sleep. Then in the morning when I could think more clearly, I would plan where I was and maybe find someone to talk to and find a way to get to a Prabhupāda temple. At least I could tell people I was a devotee although they might not believe it to look at me.

I knew in India it wasn't such a big deal as in America to just lie down outside somewhere for the night. Many poor people sleep just on an open cart or on the ground under a *cādar.* So, I walked off the road aways in the dark and tried that.

I was lying down but not asleep when four men came up to me. When they got close, two of them took out knives and grabbed at me. I gave them all my money. They took my passport too and then one swung at me and hit me in the face with his fist. They weren't much bigger than me, so I tried to scare them and fight back, but I don't know how to fight, and they could see that. One of them cut me on the arm with his knife. I thought, "They're *gundas*!" They pushed me down and kicked me in-between the legs and in the head. Then they went away.

After that, it was like when I was very sick in Vṛndāvana. I couldn't think much except to see how badly I was bleeding and how badly I was hurt. I sensed that it wasn't so bad, so I sat up and chanted Hare Kṛṣṇa.

When it was daylight, I went into town and asked for the police. No one in the police station spoke English. It was a foul place. Then they put me in jail.

Chapter 14

(S. d. g.)

Gurudeva arrived in Māyāpur, India, just a few days before Lord Caitanya's appearance day. Once again, he mixed with old friends among his Godbrothers, and with devotees from all over the world. The Māyāpur festival always leveled him and made him aware that he was just a tiny devotee in a world movement. He may have been a leader of the *pada-yātrā* in Guyana, but when he was thrust into the assembly of many preachers, it was a painful but welcome blow to the false ego. The festival was also a time of intense socializing. While walking from the temple to the Ganges, he would stop dozens of times to talk, sometimes making promises for future visits or business exchanges.

While fasting and bathing in the Ganges on Gaura-pūrṇimā day, Gurudeva met his Godbrother Nanda dāsa, who had just come with a group of devotees from Vṛndāvana. Nanda told him how Gurudeva's disciple Nimāi dāsa had been "acting like a rascal," hanging out with one Pūjā dāsa who was associating with a *bābājī*. Gurudeva already knew this from the letter he had received from Nimāi and so he toned down the alarmist edge to the report given by Nanda. But then Nanda said, "Nimāi got very, very sick. They had to take him to a sanatorium in South India."

Gurudeva listened sympathetically. Getting sick in India was par for the course, but it sounded like Nimāi had gotten an extra dose. "Where is the sanatorium?" Gurudeva asked, but Nanda didn't know. So, there was nothing to do about it but depend on Kṛṣṇa. Probably Nimāi would get well.

That same evening, Gurudeva stood on the roof of the guesthouse overlooking thousands of pilgrims filing into the Māyāpur Mandir. He was watching the sky for the appearance of the full moon. A smiling *brahmacārī* approached Gurudeva, greeted him, and said that he was a member of the Movement's temple in Trivandrum, South India.

"Do you have a disciple named Nimāi dāsa?" the *brahmacārī* asked. Gurudeva replied, "yes," and the *brahmacārī* told him that Nimāi was in jail in Trivandrum. He had been arrested as a "vagrant," and there was a rumor that he was a C.I.A. agent.

It sounded too incredible to believe, but the *brahmacārī* showed Gurudeva a photo of Nimāi dāsa in jail.

"He has a beard!" cried Gurudeva.

"Is he your disciple?" the *brahmacārī* asked.

"Yes, that's him, but...."

The *brahmacārī* said that the police had contacted their temple, but when they went to see Nimāi in the jail, their temple president was a bit doubtful. Was this young American with the beard and *karmī* clothes actually a devotee or someone trying to take advantage of them? When they talked with Nimāi, he *sounded* like a devotee. But the police were serious about holding him as a criminal, and the Trivandrum devotees were hesitant to get one of their life members to vouch for Nimāi. So Nimāi asked them to try to see his spiritual master, Gurudeva, or some devotees who knew him, such as Pūjā dāsa or Nanda dāsa.

"Now that we know he's your devotee," said the *brahmacārī,* "when we go back, we will try to get him out."

The news distracted Gurudeva for a while, and he wondered whether he should become directly involved. Should he send someone to South India? Should he go himself? But as the Gaura-pūrṇimā evening swelled to its auspicious climax, with the appearance of the moon of Gaurāṅga, and when the devotees insisted that he go join the *mahā kīrtana* in the temple, Gurudeva put Nimāi in the back of his mind.

The next morning, Gurudeva woke thinking of Nimāi dāsa. That boy was really getting his kicks from *māyā*. Gurudeva couldn't meddle with *māyā*, but still, he had his duty as spiritual master. As the *Caitanya-caritāmṛta* stated, "If by chance a servant falls down and goes somewhere else, glorious is that master who captures him and brings him back by the hair."

He considered flying to Trivandrum and dovetailing it with a visit to some Viṣṇu temples. That wasn't so important, but Nimāi ... Gurudeva wrote a letter on official letterhead and brought it to the Trivandrum devotees in Māyāpur. Maybe this would be enough, and he wouldn't have to go personally. But then he decided to go. Getting Nimāi out of jail was only the first step. "Why was he wearing a beard? Why was he a "vagrant?"

Nimāi sat in a small jailhouse cell. Materially speaking, he was at the low point in his life. But he felt better and had confidence that things would turn out all right. At least he could think more clearly and more deeply into the issues which had confused him for months. He knew he had committed a falldown by taking intoxication, he had broken one of the four prohibitions of his vow. But he had not done it willfully. Yet he was implicated by living in such a strange place. He knew his own guilt and was sorry but felt assured of Kṛṣṇa's forgiveness. Being isolated and misunderstood in a South Indian jail was no picnic, but Nimāi felt resigned to it. "Eventually I'll get out," he thought, "and then I will go back and join a temple. Or I'll go to Gurudeva first and ask him what he wants me to do."

On his second day in jail, Nimāi was questioned by a police officer, who threatened to beat him. It had taken them two days to speak to him in English. He told them that he had just come from the Hindu Naturepath Sanatorium and that he was a devotee of the Hare Kṛṣṇa movement and an American citizen. His father was a lawyer and worked in New York City. The police returned him to his cell and checked out his story at the Hindu sanatorium. Dr. Ananda said that Nimāi had been staying there, but he could not vouch for his character. Nimāi had left abruptly leaving no notice and owing two weeks fees. The police officer informed Nimāi of this through the bars and said that it was another point against him. "How will you pay your fees at the sanatorium?"

"My father will pay."

"Your rich American father?" they laughed. "Where is he now?" Why did Nimāi have no ID, no passport? If he was a Hare Kṛṣṇa devotee, why didn't he look like the *bhaktas* in Trivandrum, with shaved head and *śikhā*? No, they would not allow him to use the phone. No, he couldn't not shave his face. They would keep him in jail as long as they liked, they said, until he decided to tell them the truth about his purpose in India.

But mostly they left him alone, and he only overheard from his cell the bureaucratic dealings of the police office routine from morning to night. Nimāi turned to his inner resources; he had no others.

His chanting of *japa* had been markedly improved ever since he left the sanatorium. Now he clung to the holy names with quiet fervor. His thoughts were reverent and fairly steady, considering the aridity and anxiety of living in jail. He thought of his spiritual master, and he thought of different sections from Prabhupāda's books.

On the first day in the cell, Nimāi was visited by a small gray mouse. Nimāi placed a bit of bread in his palm and eventually coaxed the mouse to come into his hand. The mouse sniffed out Nimāi's body scent, cautiously approved it, and consented to be fed. Since food was not so plentiful elsewhere, the mouse began to appear at mealtimes. Even when there was no food it walked about without timidity. Nimāi chanted and spoke to the mouse, and although it never made a reply, its presence filled Nimāi with remembrance of Choṭa. Even if this mouse wasn't special, it was more peaceful and friendly than the humans in jail. "Yes," Nimāi thought, "an animal can take to Kṛṣṇa consciousness. I've done this before."

By the time Gurudeva arrived in Trivandrum, Nimāi had been in prison for five days. Gurudeva, along with the Trivandrum temple president, explained the situation to the vice-mayor of the city, who was a regular visitor to the temple. In the presence of the devotees the vice-mayor phoned the local police station and told them to release the Hare Kṛṣṇa devotee. Gurudeva also reprimanded the police officer and threatened to make an inquiry as to why they had so detained a foreign citizen with no formal charges.

Nimāi suddenly heard the sound of Gurudeva's voice and a police officer replying in courteous tones. He leaped with joy. But then be clutched at his beard. What a humiliation to have to face Gurudeva like this! How to explain it? But Nimāi knew that his spiritual master would accept him. Gurudeva would know that Nimāi had a clear mind to surrender. In the few minutes it took before they came to get him, Nimāi gave his last breadcrumbs to the mouse cell-mate. "If I had more time," he said to it, "I could train you." Nimāi remembered what the old woman had said, that he had a special ability to communicate. But he rejected the idea and thought, "I'm just a jailbird."

As the officer and Gurudeva approached him, Nimāi fell down flat to the floor and spoke his obeisances out loud.

Nimāi didn't have to explain himself at length to his spiritual master. Gurudeva knew Nimāi felt very regretful that he had deviated from his straight and simple devotional service. He had learned a lesson. And so, with minimum words, they took him to the Trivandrum temple where he promptly bathed and shaved his face and head.

Nimāi then appeared before Gurudeva and asked, "What do you want me to do?" Gurudeva said that Nimāi should become his assistant and travel with him wherever he went. Nimāi was happy to receive the order, and he prayed that he could carry it out with fixed determination. He knew that intimate service to Gurudeva would be demanding. He thought that he could do it. Now by the grace of Kṛṣṇa, and the direct supervision of his *guru*, he would learn for good how to stay free of *māyā's* detours.

A few days after Nimāi's release, Gurudeva called him into his room. Gurudeva said, "Nimāi, I know you sometimes think of your mice, Choṭa and the others, right? Do you sometimes think of what they might be doing, whether they're involved in Kṛṣṇa conscious acts and preaching?"

"Yes," said Nimāi. "Or I think of things I did with them or heard from them."

"In either case," said Gurudeva, "I was thinking of a way you could remember them without being distracted from Kṛṣṇa consciousness, a way to dovetail your propensity. Maybe you could fashion some *stories* about the mice or even other creatures. You know, like in *Hitopadeśa*, but for *gurukula* children. What do you think?"

"You mean ... fairy tales?"

"You wouldn't have to call them that," said Gurudeva. "Fables—Kṛṣṇa conscious fables for children."

"Would they be imaginary?"

"You can believe in them," said Gurudeva, "or half-believe that they could happen. But you should take them seriously and make them into some kind of story that a child would like to listen to, and that mothers would like to tell their children."

"They've got true stories," said Nimāi, "of Kṛṣṇa in the Kṛṣṇa book."

"Yes, they're the best," said Gurudeva. "But they want more. Stories about people nowadays who are devotees of Kṛṣṇa and of Prabhupāda. *Saṅkīrtana* stories and Kṛṣṇa conscious stories for children."

"I don't think I could qualify," said Nimāi, "to teach children."

"You wouldn't have to be a teacher," said Gurudeva. "Just write stories and others can tell them to the children."

"What about grown-ups?"

"The stories can be told for children," said Gurudeva, "but the grown-up person may be allowed to listen as well. Or some of them may be more appealing to adults."

"But is it all right," Nimāi asked, "to make up stories for devotees?"

"Yes, I think so," said Gurudeva, "as long as you evoke the Kṛṣṇa conscious *paramparā*, without deviation. And don't 'make up' stories of Kṛṣṇa-*līlā*. You're not so advanced for that, are you?"

"Gurudeva, I'm not advanced at all. I can't do anything unless you empower me. It's a fascinating idea. I'd like to give it a try."

"But don't go on a binge," said Gurudeva. "Just do it sometimes, like when you can't control your mind otherwise, or when the stories just come into your mind almost without asking. Mainly I want you to serve like the other devotees—chant, go to the morning program, read *Śrīmad-Bhāgavatam,* and do regular services. Would you like to go back to the farm?"

"I think I would like to," said Nimāi. "But what about the idea of going back to Guyana? I was supposed to go back in six months to see that girl's father. And also ... I had some agreement with my mice that I would see them again." Gurudeva wasn't ready to answer about Guyana. He had only wanted to express his idea of storytelling. So Nimāi didn't pursue it. Gurudeva wanted him to think over what he had already said.

Nimāi didn't give the storytelling suggestion much thought that day. He mostly felt very satisfied to have had such an open talk with his spiritual master. He remembered a purport where Śrīla Prabhupāda describes the guru as capable of knowing the tendency of his disciples and being expert to assign them a suitable service— "You should work in the editorial department; you should work in the kitchen." It seemed as if Gurudeva had been manifesting some of that potency, and Nimāi was pleased to see it.

The next morning Nimāi woke early, by one o'clock, and the beginning of a story suddenly came to him, just the way Choṭa would sometimes come to him and perch on his knee. The story even had an opening line, "Once there was a *gurukula* boy named Anu dāsa, who could talk to butterflies ...". Nimāi felt a gentle but insistent invitation to get up from bed, put on the light, and write a story for children, as ordered by his spiritual master. So, he did it, and later that day placed it under his spiritual master's door.

Preaching to the Butterflies
by Nimāi dāsa

Once there was a *gurukula* boy named Anu dāsa who could talk to butterflies and flowers. They also spoke back to Anu dāsa, and he could understand them. But they spoke to him so gently that no one else heard it. Or sometimes if a person came very close to where Anu was talking, and if the wind was right, they could hear the soft voices of the yellow and black butterflies and the red roses in conversation with the boy. Although Anu liked to talk of games and silly things and about eating when he was with the other boys, yet when he spoke to the butterflies—and sometimes he would also speak to birds who came and landed in the rose garden—he would speak only Kṛṣṇa consciousness. He liked to preach to them.

Anu's father asked his son, who was only six years old, "Anu, why do you talk to the butterflies?"

"I'm preaching," said Anu, hoping his father would approve.

"You should preach to humans," said his father. "That's more important. What good could a butterfly do as a devotee, even if he could understand you?"

Anu replied, "They're easier to talk to." Anu remembered that he had once seen a man throw a bottle at devotees when they were chanting in a park. It had hit the devotee on the head.

"Anyway," his father said, "I don't mind if you do it. You can talk to the flower and birds as practice. Then when you grow up, you can preach to humans." So, his parents allowed him to talk in the backyard garden, which he often did. In the summer he told the butterflies about Kṛṣṇa, the lifter of Govardhana Hill, who protected all the residents, even the animals, birds, and plants, from the floods of Indra. He also told them of Lord Caitanya's merciful chanting of Hare Kṛṣṇa which even the birds and butterflies appreciated. In the winter months, Anu told the chickadees, who were quite friendly, how to chant and sing Hare Kṛṣṇa. It seemed to Anu that the birds were peeping back to him, "Hare Kṛṣṇa, Hare Kṛṣṇa" just like a parrot that Anu's uncle kept in a cage which actually did say, "Haribol! Hare Kṛṣṇa!" and which everyone heard. Anu's teacher also told him that there were parrots in Vṛndāvana, one of which spoke about Kṛṣṇa and another which spoke about Rādhā.

But when Anu became a couple of years older, and he still only talked about Kṛṣṇa to the lower creatures and not to the humans, his elders became a bit worried.

"He will be retarded," his father said.

But his mother said, "Leave him alone, he's only eight years old."

Anu's father was a very good preacher. He used to speak Lord Caitanya's philosophy in college classrooms and on the streets. He also distributed Prabhupāda's books, even though sometimes people cursed at him, and the police said that they would put him in jail. His father was like Prahlāda, who wasn't afraid because he knew that Kṛṣṇa would protect him. Even if someone did try to hurt a devotee, it was possible only to hurt his body, because the soul can never be cut or soaked or burned or made sad or afraid—as long as a devotee remembers Kṛṣṇa.

Anu's father became more worried when the boy was ten years old and still preferred to talk alone in the garden, rather than in front of people. When Anu did talk to people, he usually only said a few things like, "Please pass the salt," or "Yes, I did my mathematics homework. Five times seven is thirty-five." So, people thought that Anu was funny.

One day when Anu was eleven years old, or maybe twelve, on a beautiful summer day in the garden, several monarch butterflies came to him and fluttered onto his hand.

"You have always been kind to us, to tell us of Kṛṣṇa," they said. And then a robin came by and said, "Yes, that's true." And the flowers nodded in agreement. By now Anu was so friendly with the creatures in the garden that even animals that normally killed each other did not do so by his influence. So, on this day all the creatures were expressing their thanks to Anu. Then a particularly gorgeous red rose opened its petals and said softly to Anu, "The other flowers and birds have asked me to say to you that we think you are practiced enough, and now you can try to tell about Kṛṣṇa to the humans. Whenever you attempt to, if you just remember us, we will help you as best we can."

Anu was very satisfied with the well-wishing words of the birds, butterflies, and flowers that he would be able to preach to humans, although humans were certainly harder to speak to, and they sometimes threw bottles.

Anu's father had been patiently waiting for Anu to come and join him in his preaching, which *he* did every day. Every day his father would go out with a bag of Prabhupāda's books and come back at night with the bag empty or almost empty. By distributing books his father was satisfied in Kṛṣṇa consciousness. Anu knew that the books were meant especially for human beings, and in fact, the birds and animals couldn't understand them. And that was another reason why it was so important to learn to preach to humans.

When Anu told his father that now he was ready to preach, his father asked, "How did you finally grow up?"

"I practiced as you told me," said Anu. "And the butterflies and birds and flowers told me that I should go now and speak to the humans. They said if I became afraid, that they would help me if I remembered them."

"That's a *fancy* story!" said his father. "But if it helps you to preach now, then it's all right with me."

And so, the father and son went out together preaching, and although they did meet with difficult people, and even people who called the police and threatened them, the father and son made a good team. And Lord Kṛṣṇa was pleased with them.

Later that day, Gurudeva passed Nimāi dāsa in the hallway and said, "Not bad for a start. But don't go on a binge."

Nimāi knew that his "fable" was not much of a story. Gurudeva was just encouraging him. But it was good that Gurudeva had warned him. "Don't go on a binge." Because it seemed to Nimāi that once he caught the knack of how to tell Kṛṣṇa conscious stories, he would never want to stop.

Chapter 15

(N. d. b.)

When Gurudeva asked me to try writing some stories for devotees (he called them "fables"), I thought he was just trying to engage me in service. I don't want to second-guess the spiritual master and say why he recommended this for me. He didn't say he thought I was crazy or "hearing things." He just said to do it, although he did bring it up in the context of my experience with the devotee-mice, and at a time when I had just been on a detour into *māyā* and away from devotional service in the company of devotees.

I must admit that when I began the stories, I had to face some basic questions about myself and devotional service—and the role of imagination. I suppose Gurudeva wanted me to face these things. He said a story didn't have to be historically accurate as long as it carried the truths of Kṛṣṇa consciousness, but he warned me not to link my characters or stories to *kṛṣṇa-līlā*, because that's way over my head spiritually. So, I thought maybe it could be stories that showed devotees struggling and succeeding in their attempts to serve the Lord in Kali-yuga. Gurudeva said a fable, if successful, could entertain, refresh, and encourage the devotees and nondevotees.

But as soon as I started to write I thought, "Who am I to play like God or guru and describe what people are doing? I am not a liberated soul who can write transcendental literature." Here's what Śrīla Prabhupāda says about a writer of transcendental literature:

> It is not possible for a common man to write books on *bhakti*, for his writings will not be effective. He may be a very great scholar or expert in presenting the literature in flowery language, but this is not at all helpful.... The secret in a devotee's writing is that when he writes about the pastimes of the Lord, the Lord helps him; he does not write himself.
>
> —*Caitanya-caritāmṛta, Ādi-līlā 8.39, purport*

Does this describe me? No. Then? I'll show the stories to Gurudeva, and if he doesn't like them, he can throw them all away, or maybe save a few. I am working under his direction and trying to tell the truths from Prabhupāda's books. I know it's strange for someone like me to even try. My conditioning is bound to show through even if I try to be a transparent via media to give some interesting stories.

As for imagination or make-believe, that really gets me wondering. If I live in a world of make-believe (sometimes), does that mean I should invite others to do it? Is it escape? Is it bad? When I think about it, I get puzzled. On the one hand I like to make up things in a fable, about talking animals for instance, because it allows me to speak more truthfully and freely. Maybe that's one reason Nārada Muni told such a long, make-believe story about a king who lived in a city of nine gates, and who had a serpent who was the chief of police of the city, and who was finally attacked by soldiers of the days and nights. That's a particular kind of storytelling which is called allegory—it's not the literal truth, but it points to a higher truth.

When I began to write, I had not resolved the questions about whether my stories would be make-believe or realistic, and whether they were really for children—not to mention my other doubts. I just proceeded with the hope that a dumb man could speak Kṛṣṇa consciousness, by the grace of the spiritual master.

Remembering Prabhupāda at 26 Second Avenue

The ISKCON officers in New York considered it a very fortunate day when they were able to once again rent Prabhupāda's old apartment at 26 Second Avenue. Prabhupāda had lived there in 1966 and visited there a year after that, but then the apartment had gone into the hands of nondevotees for over twenty-five years. To celebrate repossession of the apartment, devotees gathered for a Prabhupāda memory night. Their plan was to turn the apartment into a museum. Devotees who had paraphernalia from Prabhupāda's early days had agreed to donate it in an attempt to set up the apartment just as it was when Prabhupāda was present.

Some of the original "storefront boys," like Mukunda Mahārāja, Rūpānuga prabhu, and Brahmānanda prabhu, attended and treated the other devotees to their firsthand experiences of Prabhupāda in the apartment. Brahmānanda recalled how he first met Prabhupāda in this room. He had been telling Prabhupāda about his psychology professor at N.Y.U. who interpreted everything in the Freudian way, and about a girl he met in India. Brahmānanda said that while Prabhupāda spoke to him he was looking over Brahmānanda's head with a loving glance. Brahmānanda then looked up and saw that he was looking at a picture of Lord Caitanya.

As the stories were told in the original setting, the devotees looked at different parts of the room and tried to savor what it had actually been like. Mukunda Mahārāja took the devotees into the second room of the apartment and told how his wedding had been performed there, and how the room had filled up with smoke from the fire *yajña,* but Prabhupāda would not open the windows for fear of disturbing the neighbors. The floor was scrubbed clean, so that it looked pretty much like it had when Prabhupāda walked there and spoke with devotees in 1966.

One of the devotees had donated Prabhupāda's original three-tiered brass cooker, and a meal was cooked on it in Prabhupāda's kitchen. Prabhupāda's small Indian trunk, which he had used as a desk, was also restored to its original place, and a typewriter, which seemed to be the same one he had used, was also there. The New York temple had donated one of its prized Prabhupāda relics, his original white rubber slippers, which had since been gold plated. Remembering Prabhupāda in the association of his followers, and in his first apartment in America, made for a memorable evening. When they left, the devotees promised to have Prabhupāda meetings like this at least monthly.

After all the devotees had left and the lights were turned out and the door locked with a double lock, the rooms fell into silence. But the remembrances of Prabhupāda had been so sweet and intense that Prabhupāda's various paraphernalia began speaking among themselves just to continue the Vaiṣṇava-*kathā*.

The first to speak was the trunk, which was battered and painted yellow.

"It's so nice to be back with all of you," he said. "I remember how Prabhupāda used to sit behind me and sometimes touch me with his lotus feet. The devotees would sit over there by the wall. Everyone noticed me, although I'm just an ordinary Indian trunk. I can never forget those days when I served Prabhupāda as a writing desk and so many other things."

"Yes, I remember you," said Prabhupāda's rubber shoes. "No one knew at that time that later Prabhupāda would have many elegant desks. You were the first, at least in America. Now, of course, my memories range far and wide. I bore the lotus feet of the pure devotee when he walked the streets of New York. It is very extraordinary, because I am just a humble pair of shoes from India."

"I read about you," said Swamiji's spectacles, which were sitting in a glass case on the desk. "There is mention in the biography of Prabhupāda that the lady in Pennsylvania saw her child going to bite into Swamiji's shoes, and she thought, 'Oh, these shoes have been all over India.'"

"Yes, little did she know," said the shoes, "how fortunate I am. Prabhupāda used to walk the streets of Manhattan, sometimes through the snow, and I would get all wet! How I wished I could protect his lotus feet! But he never complained. And you know, Swamiji actually treated all of his paraphernalia very tenderly, he never slammed things down or abused things. Because he saw us all as Kṛṣṇa's energy, something to be used in devotional service."

"I can vouch for that," said the stainless-steel letter opener on his desk. "Swamiji used to open his letters very carefully. He used me in a way that very few letter openers are used. He not only opened the letter but slit all the corners of the letter and turned it inside out and used it later for writing notes. He handled me so delicately and placed me down gently, always in the same place. He was methodical."

"Don't forget us," said the walls. "We have observed so many things. One time, Prabhupāda even said that his spiritual master said if no one else listens, you talk to the four walls. And many times, early in the morning Prabhupāda would get up and speak to the four walls. Actually, he was speaking and chanting and singing to Kṛṣṇa in his heart, but no persons were present except us. So, we were able to see Swāmījī in the very beginning of his days in New York. Before anyone else really appreciated, we heard him, we four walls."

"What a relief it is!" said the floorboards, "not to be walked on by nondevotees! We always languished and were sad, just like mother earth herself, after Prabhupāda left this apartment, and so many disgusting things took place in this room and on these floors. Now to be able to remember with all of Prabhupāda's paraphernalia is beyond expectation. But for the sake of reminiscing, we may remind you how Prabhupāda used to walk so nicely with his bare feet all the time across the floor. Sometimes he would be going into the other room to perform *ārati* which the devotees called "bells," or he would stand in the hall to open the door and let in yet another hippie to sit down and talk with him. His walking in this way, from one room to another, was heaven for us."

"Listen to my story," said the three-tiered cooker calling in from the kitchen. "I am celebrated all over the three worlds for being the original cooker on which Śrīla Prabhupāda made his rice and *sabjī*. How deftly, like a chemist, he put in the right proportions and stacked in each vegetable in just the right place in my compartments. After a while, Prabhupāda began to cook so much that I was not big enough. But I was with him in the early days, and I am a symbol of when Prabhupāda was so much alone that all his meals could be prepared in a single cooker.

In this way, one after another, every object and nook and cranny of the rooms at 26 Second Avenue spoke out in testimony that the pure devotee had lived and walked within these rooms for many months and had begun a worldwide Kṛṣṇa consciousness movement here. The rooms and paraphernalia spoke and heard from each other until it was almost dawn, and then they became quiet again, like dumb objects, but retaining the aura of association which could never be forgotten.

Chapter 16

(S. d. g.)

Dear Nimāi,

Please accept Prabhupāda's blessings from me. All glories to Prabhupāda.

I like your story, especially the fact that you were remembering Prabhupāda. Allowing the paraphernalia of Prabhupāda to speak out is not only an interesting device for the fable, but it moves us to consider also that these paraphernalia are actually valuable and should be considered valuable.

There are statements in the scriptures about the paraphernalia of the Lord, as well as the paraphernalia of the pure devotee. Your story reminded me particularly of a verse spoken by Lord Śiva to Pārvatī in the *Śrīmad-Bhāgavatam*. Lord Śiva said as follows:

ārādhanānāṁ sarveṣāṁ
viṣṇor ārādhanaṁ param
tasmāt parataram devī
tadīyānāṁ samarcanam

—*Laghu-bhāgavatāmṛta 2.4*

The meaning is that the worship of Lord Viṣṇu is the best of all worship, but beyond that is "worship of things in relationship to Viṣṇu." The word *tadīyānām* means things in relationship to Kṛṣṇa, and it has the primary meaning of a person who serves the Lord. But it could also refer to the paraphernalia which are used either by the Lord or by the devotee of the Lord. The devotee himself is a living instrument in the service of Kṛṣṇa. And when he uses other instruments, they become surcharged with spiritual association. Perhaps the best example is Kṛṣṇa's flute. The *gopīs* say that the flute is just a dry wooden stick, a descendant of the trees on the bank of the Yamunā. But because the flute is touched by the lotus lips of Kṛṣṇa, it shares a position which even the *gopīs* envy. Similarly, when Mahārāja Pratāparudra wanted to worship Lord Caitanya, the Lord at first did not want to meet with the king, but He consented to give a piece of cloth to Mahārāja Pratāparudra. The king received this with joy and worshiped it with full faith that it was nondifferent from Lord Caitanya. And this faith was approved by the Lord.

Therefore, the museums which display the personal paraphernalia of His Divine Grace Śrīla Prabhupāda are worshipable *tīrthas*. Those who are followers of Prabhupāda have many things to do to carry out his mission. They are not always sitting and pondering over Prabhupāda's paraphernalia in museums. But there is a time for that too.

I know that you are concerned whether your imaginative flights are bona fide. We are just beginning this little experiment of your fable writing, so I do not want to discourage you, but neither in the beginning do I absolutely endorse it. I think that even if I told you not to think imaginatively, it would not be possible for you to curtail it. So, it is better to find a way to use it in the service of Kṛṣṇa, if at all possible. I've asked you to channel your metaphors and allegories and imaginative flights into Kṛṣṇa conscious fables and show them to me, and later we can see if we want to share them with others. Write as a way to render service to the Lord, not with the thought of becoming a famous writer. Śrīla Prabhupāda has encouraged writers, and he said that whether we know it or not we write for our own purification. That should be the first purpose. By applying your mind to Kṛṣṇa conscious themes, you can purify the quality of the mind and even reject, through the process of writing, materialistic motives.

Write from themes you really care about. Express even your doubts and problems, and then try to defeat them by the weapon of knowledge. But only when writing is purified of flaws, and when it is free from any attempt to surpass the previous *ācāryas*, can it be considered "literature in pursuance of the Vedic version."

I'm looking forward to seeing more of your stories. You may write them at a designated time without disturbance to your other important duties, such as attending the morning program in the temple, chanting your prescribed rounds, hearing the *Śrīmad-Bhāgavatam* (which is the best, all-perfect form of philosophy and narration), and taking part in the preaching of the *saṅkīrtana* movement. Don't be puffed up thinking you are "a writer," but try to think of yourself as a servant of the servant of the servant of those who are trying to serve the Lord. As you write your stories, please send me copies, and I will tell you whether or not I think it would be proper to send them around for the pleasure of the devotees and their children.

Chapter 17

(Nimāi d.b)
The Boy who Wanted to Become a *Gṛhastha*

Once there was a *gurukula* boy who decided that, when he grew up, he would probably get married. After all, his father had been married, and in fact even those sages who never married were themselves sons of married persons. So, it seemed inevitable. This boy, whose name was Dhīra dāsa, was too young to think very seriously about marriage. But if an uncle or older devotee asked him, "Are you going to be a *brahmacārī* when you grow up?" Dhīra would reply, "No, a *gṛhastha* devotee." The parents were amused that a young boy had decided to become a *gṛhastha*.

When he grew up, it wasn't so easy to get himself married. One reason was he belonged to a society for pure devotional service unto Kṛṣṇa. Devotees of Kṛṣṇa don't like to marry persons who have no affection at all for Kṛṣṇa. Sometimes people ask devotees, "Are you allowed to marry people who aren't devotees?" But devotees think, "What a strange question!" It's not that someone forbids them to marry a nondevotee, but how could you love someone who doesn't love Kṛṣṇa? Since there are so few people who love Kṛṣṇa, it is sometimes hard for devotees to find a husband or wife when it is time to get married.

Another reason it was hard for Dhīra to get married was because he wasn't very big or handsome, and girls generally like someone who is at least a little bit like Rāmacandra or Lakṣmaṇa. Although devotees are supposed to love everyone, you can't expect an innocent young girl to marry someone who looks like a Yamadūta or a Ruru. But then there is the history of Vyāsadeva. He was considered ugly. Even some of the women who married Vyāsa couldn't bear to look at him. One wife closed her eyes when she went to see Vyāsa, and as a result she conceived a child who was blind, Dhṛtarāṣṭra. Another wife turned white when she was with Vyāsa, and she bore a child who was very white, Pāṇḍu. But when a *śūdra* woman accepted Vyāsa and served him nicely, she bore a child who was a great devotee, Vidura.

Intelligent girls know that "beauty isn't only skin deep," and so they look for good qualities in a boy they want to marry, such as whether he chants Hare Kṛṣṇa *japa* with attention, and whether he has a good reputation among the Vaiṣṇavas as a surrendered soul. If you could find a husband who was considered a good devotee, even if he wasn't handsome, that would still be fortunate. Ideally, devotees should mainly consider whether the person they marry is a serious devotee. Prabhupāda writes this in a purport:

> A devotee is transcendental and therefore in a marriage between devotees, the boy and girl form a very happy combination.
>
> —*Śrīmad-Bhāgavatam 6.2.26, purport*

Some girls count high in their estimation the ability of a devotee to protect them by strong financial income, or they look for a man who is sensible in how to survive in the material world. For example, if a young man was very good looking and a good devotee but was poor as Sudāmā Vipra (who was so poor that his wife didn't get enough to eat, and they lived in rags), that might be another disqualification in a husband, at least for some girls.

Dhīra dāsa lacked in all these qualifications, and so he couldn't find a wife. Still, he thought that he probably should get married and that there was a girl somewhere who would appreciate him. Maybe there was a girl who also wanted to get married, and who had been passed up by other men, and Dhīra and this girl might just like each other and be what is called "compatible." Sometimes Dhīra became quite concerned about this, especially when he reached twenty years of age, and he still didn't have a wife.

Because too much talking or thinking about marriage is definitely *māyā*, and a devotee should concentrate his thoughts, words, and deeds in the service of Kṛṣṇa, Dhīra decided not to talk about it anymore. But he continued to think about marriage, and sometimes he dreamt about it.

One night in a dream, a Matchmaker appeared to Dhīra dāsa and said, "I have the power to marry you to any girl according to your wishes. As a reward for your devotional service to the Supreme Lord, I will arrange this for you."

Dhīra doubted whether this Matchmaker was himself a devotee of the Lord, because he had never heard of such a person in Vedic literature. He had heard of matchmakers, and there was even such a person who appeared in Caitanya-*līlā* and arranged for the marriage of Lord Caitanya and Lakṣmī-devī. But that was different.

"Will you be able to fulfill my request for a girl who is a good devotee, in addition to other qualifications?" asked Dhīra.

"You request, and I'll comply," said the Matchmaker. "What more do you want?"

Dhīra thought for a moment and then said, "What I mean is, are you aware of the ultimate goal of life?"

The Matchmaker laughed. He was a short, heavy-set man dressed in a business suit. "That's a strange question to ask," said the Matchmaker, "for one who calls upon a matchmaker to arrange a wife for him. If you're so highfalutin', then why are you asking to get married in the first place? As for the ultimate goal, yes, I understand it is to be liberated from birth and death and to become free from the miseries of material existence. But it is a gradual process. By a happy marriage a man may prosecute his *varṇāśrama* tendencies, control his desires, and prosecute spiritual service all at the same time. Now, if you're finished questioning my knowledge, we can proceed. That's if you really want 'the girl of your dreams.' I can't spend all night just on you, you know. There are plenty of other conditioned souls who require my service."

Dhīra was sorry that the Matchmaker was offended, and he didn't want to disturb him further. He was afraid the man might go away, and he would miss a big opportunity. But Dhīra wanted to be cautious about his Kṛṣṇa consciousness. He did have more questions about the Matchmaker's credentials. How could Dhīra trust him with such a highly personal and important matter when he didn't know the man and his position in relation to Kṛṣṇa and pure devotional service? But then marriage was worldly, you were supposed to be unafraid of its worldly aspects, or—as the man had said—why get married? But that remark, about "highfalutin'" had also caused Dhīra concern. The Matchmaker had seemed to slight marriage, as if it were merely "a license for sense gratification for those who are less intelligent." Dhīra liked to think of marriage in a positive light, as something which had been performed by seven out of the twelve Kṛṣṇa conscious *mahājanas* and by four of the five members of the Pañca-tattva. Those *gṛhasthas* were not diminished spiritually just because they became married.

"Well?" asked the Matchmaker, and he glanced at his watch. He had taken out a portable computer and was typing at its keyboard.

Dhīra decided to plunge ahead. Beggars can't be choosers, he thought, which was something his mother used to say.

"I would like a beautiful girl who loves me and who is a devotee of Kṛṣṇa," said Dhīra.

The Matchmaker then pushed some keys on his computer and looked at its screen. He made a tight expression, reminding Dhīra of airline agents when they type your name into the computer and then wait to see if your reservation is confirmed.

"Your case is a bit unusual," said the Matchmaker, sitting back in his chair. "I would suggest you avail yourself of another service which I can perform for you before we try to call up the girl of your dreams."

"What's that?"

"How would you like to be ten times more handsome than you are at present?"

"You can do that?" asked Dhīra. But even as he asked, Dhīra felt himself slipping into illusion. As Dhīra dāsa was dreaming this whole encounter with the Matchmaker, a faint part of him observed the dream and saw it as *māyā*. It was another one of those dreams in which he didn't cry out, "Kṛṣṇa! Save me!"

"What do you want?" the Matchmaker asked.

"All right, do it," consented Dhīra. The next thing he knew he was looking into a mirror and seeing himself as a different person, strong and handsome. He was still Dhīra—or was he? Dhīra became attracted to the features of the young man he saw in the mirror. "He really is good looking! He'll have no trouble attracting women," thought Dhīra. But at the same time, Dhīra was repulsed at what he saw and felt. He had never considered himself a very humble person, but now he realized that although he wasn't an advanced devotee, still he had attained, by the grace of *guru* and Kṛṣṇa, some humility. In fact, he used to feel much humbler than he felt looking in the mirror at this good looking "prince." "Don't look a gift horse in the mouth," he thought, which was a saying he had heard from his father.

The Matchmaker allowed Dhīra a few moments to get used to the sudden transformation.

"Like what you see?" asked the Matchmaker. "I think you can understand now that we don't fool around. We know our business. Now, with your permission, we can proceed to find you a suitable match." The Matchmaker was already typing pertinent information into the computer.

"Wait a minute," said Dhīra.

"What's the matter now?"

"This really isn't me!" Despite his attraction to the handsome form in the mirror—that young man with the square jaw, beautiful teeth, courageous manly demeanor—Dhīra felt an overwhelming desire to return to his former self.

"If you're a real matchmaker," said Dhīra, "can't you just get me the wife I want without changing me? This bodily change seems contrary to the laws of karma."

"Who do you think you are?" said the Matchmaker. He was angry. "Are you implying that I have done something illegal? I'll have you know that my business is fully authorized. I do nothing contrary to the laws of nature! You asked for a beautiful wife, and I made the best logical adjustment for your case. Do you want to get married or not? Just tell me so I don't waste my time."

"I want to get married," said Dhīra. "But I want to be...who I am."

"I already told you that would reduce your chances to find your dream girl," said the Matchmaker. "But if you insist, I'll do what I can." The Matchmaker then consulted a thick reference book. He worked with a pocket calculator for a few moments, resumed typing and peering into his computer screen, and then said, "You must be passing through a good astrological period. I've been able to arrange a wife for you, and she is immediately available for a betrothal interview."

Dhīra went to meet the lady, whose name was Mātājī, in a semipublic place, a park near a temple. As soon as he saw her, he liked her. She was dressed in a *sārī* and was quite beautiful. She was perhaps a bit older than Dhīra, but he thought that was nice too. She was somewhat motherly.

"What I would like in marriage," said Dhīra, "is companionship and all the things that Prabhupāda says in his books. I would like a strict marriage in regard to following the principles, but Kṛṣṇa conscious fun too. It is written that the wife and husband can live together like Lakṣmī-Nārāyaṇa, but if it doesn't work out well, the wife is like a tiger or witch. I prefer the Goddess of Fortune. We would live together peacefully and raise children and keep Kṛṣṇa and the spiritual master in the center. If we have any fights, we would not take them seriously."

"Yes, I think I would like that too," said Mātājī. "But of course, there are many practical aspects to marriage, such as getting to know each other, being compatible, deciding whether to live in a temple or apart from one, how things will be financially managed, and so on. Most of these things can be worked out if the husband and wife are sincere. It shouldn't be too difficult. One of the main things is not to have overly romantic conceptions, but to become actual friends. You know what I mean?"

"Yes," said Dhīra. "I agree. Mātājī, do you like to read the *Śrīmad-Bhāgavatam*?"

"Oh, I love it!" said Mātājī.

Dhīra and Mātājī spoke agreeably for about half an hour, and then she said she had to return to her regular service.

Dhīra walked back to the Matchmaker. He found him with that tight expression around his mouth, which meant things didn't look well on the computer screen.

"I like her," said Dhīra. "I think I'll accept her."

"Unfortunately, she has rejected you," said the Matchmaker. The Matchmaker looked down sorrowfully because he had failed to arrange a successful match. Dhīra was about to blame him, but he didn't. He thought, "At least I didn't know Mātājī long enough to become deeply attached to her."

"This has never happened to me before," said the Matchmaker. "Your case is a real challenge."

Meanwhile, the actual Dhīra dāsa, who was dreaming, wished that he could wake up from the illusion. His limbs and especially his face, eyes, and brain all seemed very heavy, as if he were drugged by sleep. A thought passed faintly through his mind that he should get up and chant the holy names, even if it meant losing sleep. But his body seemed so heavy and helpless that he could not move. His closed eyes moved rapidly, and he continued dreaming.

This time he dreamed of a girl who was perfect in almost every respect. In his dream Dhīra sensed that his life was passing by quickly, and he didn't want to keep getting disappointed before finding the girl of his dreams. So, he didn't even go through the Matchmaker, but by his desire a girl suddenly appeared at a table in Govinda's restaurant, and he approached her. She was young and pretty and lively and, of course, she was a devotee.

"I like you," she said, as girls sometimes do in dreams, "because you're a controller."

Dhīra was amused by that remark. It was mysterious and made him feel cheerful. "Why do you say I'm a controller?"

"Well, you are, you know," she laughed. He sat beside her, and they got on very well together, like intimate friends, although they had just met. She said her name was Māyā.

"That's a strange name for a devotee," said Dhīra. "Why don't you change it?" But she didn't bother to answer.

They soon married and had three children. Dhīra managed to make money without too much endeavor, and everyone congratulated him that he had a nice wife—he was lucky.

Dhīra dāsa, who was dreaming, thought, "This is good," and his eyes moved more rapidly.

But then the girl turned out to be a witch, not a witch who flies on a stick but a very unpleasant, unfaithful person. She was so unpleasant that it's not even pleasant to write about her.

Although Māyā dāsī had seemed nice and even perfect at first, she became inimical to Dhīra and began to find many faults in him (which weren't very hard to discover). She also began to make friends with other men, and she became disinterested in her own spiritual practices. How all this came about, since in the beginning it seemed otherwise, is simply the nature of material life.

"Why did you marry me in the first place?" asked Dhīra.

"Because you forced me!" she said, which really wasn't true.

"I must have been in *māyā* when I married you," she said "You are not exactly Prince Charming, you know."

Dhīra sighed, "Why is this happening?" He wept, but things got worse. The temple could not pay him any longer, and he had to find a job and an apartment. In Dhīra's case, this caused him much difficulty. Then Dhīra's children started having trouble in school. The teacher reported that they were cheating and lying. Dhīra dāsa fell behind in his daily quota of rounds.

He cried, but no one heard him, just as when a man falls into an old well in a field and no one hears his call for help.

Then Dhīra dreamed that he had actually fallen into a well. "Why is this happening?" he called out. The face of a *sannyāsī* appeared at the top of the well and said, "It's happening because you tried to be the controller. If you had been more patient and just accepted things as they happened, everything would have turned out much better. You should have left your marriage up to Kṛṣṇa."

"But ..." Dhīra thought of a million replies in his defense. It all seemed unfair. But it was too late. Dhīra fell down again to the bottom of the material pool.

When Dhīra dāsa awoke from his nightmare, he felt very relieved that it wasn't really happening. He prayed and resolved never to complain about his fate. He saw everything very philosophically and clearly and accepted his life as Kṛṣṇa's mercy. Even after the immediate effects of the dream wore off, Dhīra maintained a better attitude. And that is the result of a good lesson.

Soon after, Dhīra also found a passage while reading a Bhaktivedanta purport, which made him think that God had informed him in a dream. The passage stated:

> "The fulfilment of desires, therefore, should be entrusted to the Supreme Personality of Godhead; that is the nicest situation.... If we depend on the choice of the Supreme Personality of Godhead, we will receive benedictions in greater opulence than we desire."
>
> —*Śrīmad-Bhāgavatam 3.21.28 purport*

Chapter 18

Big-hearted Mice

Once there was a boy named Mānasa, who was fortunate to have a bona fide spiritual master, and so he sought his guidance. But when the boy spoke to his master, the guru noticed, "You talk just about yourself and your own problems. You should try to have a broader vision for helping others, because that is the meaning of *mahātmā*, one whose heart is big in love of Kṛṣṇa."

Although Mānasa was absorbed in his own little world, he tried to expand his vision for the pleasure of his guru.

As he sat down to think of a world beyond his own, Mānasa began to see the activities of some very rare souls who were devotees of Kṛṣṇa, although they were in mice bodies. Mānasa dāsa could not actually see them with his eyes or hear them with his ears, because these mice-devotees lived in a far distant country. But he began to imagine their activities. Mānasa's imagining was not like that of a Māyāvādī philosopher who imagines the nature of God independent from what is stated in the authoritative scriptures. (As for Māyāvādīs, Prabhupāda has said "their imagination only leads to more imagination."). Mānasa's thinking of mice-devotees was different—it was based, as strange as it may seem, on actual experience and was in line with the Vedic scriptures.

This is what Mānasa thought when he tried to expand his heart:

Three devotee-mice were living in Guyana and trying to spread Kṛṣṇa consciousness among the mouse population. These mice had been born in North America, but were brought to South America by their friend, Mīna dāsa, after they had been trained in Kṛṣṇa consciousness. How the mice became devotees of Kṛṣṇa is a story which can be told another time. But in case anyone is wondering how it is actually possible, the answer is "by the inconceivable mercy of Kṛṣṇa and *guru*." As stated in the *Garuḍa Purāṇa*, even lower living beings, such as insects, can become surrendered servants of the Lord.

The mice, named Choṭa, Yamala and Arjuna, were quite lonely when they were first left in Guyana by their human friend, Mina dāsa, but remembering his instructions, they took heart and began preaching. At that time, the human devotees of Guyana were conducting a *pada-yātrā,* or walking tour. So, the mice walked along with the *pada-yātrā,* or sometimes they rode on the carts. Whenever the devotees stopped to hold festivals and lectures, the mice also stopped and tried to preach to the spirit souls of their own species.

One time the devotees stopped at a leper colony which was a hospital. Some of the lepers had lost their hands, and their faces were disfigured by the disease. Hardly anyone ever visited the lepers, and so they were happy when the devotees came with the loud musical chanting of Hare Kṛṣṇa. The lepers freely joined in the singing and even brought their disfigured limbs together in a clapping rhythm. Sometimes when devotees chant, the nondevotees become quickly bored by it. But the lepers were genuinely interested in the *kīrtana,* and even after the devotees had chanted for an hour, the lepers were not bored but continued to sing:

Hare Kṛṣṇa, Hare Kṛṣṇa, Kṛṣṇa Kṛṣṇa, Hare Hare
Hare Rāma, Hare Rāma, Rāma Rāma, Hare Hare

When the *kīrtana* finally ended, a devotee explained the meaning of the names of God and encouraged the inmates to chant every day on their own. When they left the hospital, the devotees felt sure that Lord Caitanya was pleased that they had extended His mercy into quarters which are usually neglected.

The mice had observed this unusual *kīrtana,* and it gave them courage and inspiration to extend themselves and try to reach those who are normally rejected. Among the mice community there is a group known as "waltzing mice." Human beings are sometimes amused to see the way these mice spin around, and they have given them the name "waltzing mice," because the mice look like they are happily dancing in a ballroom. The actual fact is that such mice are suffering from brain damage. Healthy mice sometimes attack the waltzing mice, and they reject them from normal communities. So Choṭa, Yamala, and Arjuna began to include visits to waltzing mice whenever they found them, although they did not neglect approaching normal mice. As Mīna dāsa had informed the mice-devotees, all persons in the material world, whether they consider themselves normal or healthy, are all more or less crazy and diseased, because that is the nature of material life. No one is free of birth, death, disease and old age.

The preacher-mice found that the waltzing mice were more receptive than the normal ones. They heard the chanting and received sanctified food from the preacher-mice with gratitude, and this gave the preachers much satisfaction.

After a day of active preaching, when the devotee-mice were resting and sipping milk, they spoke among themselves about how their *saṅkīrtana* would be pleasing to their human instructor, who was known as Mīna dāsa.

"Mīna dāsa would be very happy." said Choṭa, "to hear that we made some inroads with the waltzing mice."

"Is there some way we can tell him?" asked Yamala.

"It's not necessary," said Choṭa, "and anyway what can we do? But if we actually please him, then even if we are not able to write him a letter or talk to him on the telephone, our purpose is achieved, isn't it? If we try to please him, then Kṛṣṇa, who sees everything, will be pleased. That's what Mīna dāsa told us in the story of the *brāhmaṇa* in South India. Remember? He offered Kṛṣṇa articles like sweet rice within his mind, and the Lord in Vaikuṇṭha was pleased." As the mice spoke, their feelings of separation from their human instructor increased. They became convinced that if they tried to please him, he would somehow know of their activities.

While the mice were thinking of him, Mīna dāsa, who was ten-thousand miles away in India, was also thinking of them. He was busy with his service to his spiritual master, but he had not forgotten his friends in Guyana. As he meditated thoughtfully, he imagined and pictured what the devotee-mice were actually doing. He did not feel that he was superior to them, but that they were his friends. He was therefore inspired by their compassionate activities and their determined preaching. Because Mīna dāsa was a human being and had more access to the Vedic literature, he had shared quotes from the scriptures with the mice. And in their kindness, the mice had invited Mīna to speak to them from his own realizations.

In Guyana, the human devotees were discussing whether it was advisable to attend a festival in honor of an Indian *paṇḍita* who was visiting Guyana.

"I don't think we should attend this festival," said one devotee. "It's dangerous to hear from a Māyāvādī. This *paṇḍita* teaches people not to worship the Supreme Personality of Godhead, but he quotes the *Vedas* in an attempt to prove that "everyone is God" and that we are all one in the impersonal Spirit."

But another said, "We're not going to hear from him, so don't be afraid. Thousands of people will attend, so we should at least go to the entrance and chant Hare Kṛṣṇa and give out books and magazines." The devotees disagreed whether they should go and decided to telephone their regional director, who was at that time in India, but they could not reach him.

They agreed to go to the festival but not enter the tent to hear from the Māyāvādī or his students.

The mice decided they would go also, but in their boldness, they wanted to go inside to hold a meeting of their own.

Usually at these festivals, a stage was erected at one end and the audience sat on folding chairs facing the stage. The devotee-mice would move through the crowd and pass the word among the attending mice (and many mice came because there was food to be found at these meetings) that a special mouse meeting was being held at the other side of the tent. But this time when they entered, they could not find any mice. Finally, one mouse told them, "All the mice are gathered at a *sat-saṅga* in the rear. There's a swami mouse from India who came with the *paṇḍita.* He's the real thing—from India!"

Choṭa, Yamala and Arjuna moved to the edge of the crowd of mice. The "swami" was the first mouse they'd ever seen wearing a beard and turban. He had shiny eyes, and the mouse audience seemed to be in awe of him. Mice in the front row were sitting in a *yoga* meditational pose. Although the mice-*bhaktas* knew that the Vaiṣṇavas should not hear from the Māyāvādīs, they decided to hear a little in order to know what was going on.

The Māyāvādī mouse was finishing up his lecture, advising people to practice daily mediation "to become God in three months." He said that even if they could not actually become Gods, they would be able to increase their life duration by the *yoga* exercises taught in the *Bhagavad-gītā*. He especially recommended deep breathing, head standing, and chanting "I AM THAT TOO." The mouse *paṇḍita* finished his talk and asked if anyone had questions. Choṭa dāsa raised his paw.

"You have just cited *Bhagavad-gītā* as authority." said Choṭa. "But the speaker of the *Gītā* is Lord Kṛṣṇa, and His conclusion is 'surrender to Me.' You have not mentioned Kṛṣṇa." Mice in Guyana are usually familiar with Hinduism, and they respect the *Bhagavad-gītā*, so the mice in the crowd became interested in Choṭa's question. They turned to hear what the turbaned mouse would say.

"It is the One within Kṛṣṇa," said the *paṇḍita* mouse, "that we have to surrender to. The person Kṛṣṇa is a human God for humans to worship. But the impersonal Brahman is for everyone, and that's why it is best for mice to worship the One!" When he said "the One" the *paṇḍita* mouse raised his voice in squeaky fervor, and many mice applauded.

"What you said about Kṛṣṇa is not true!" said Choṭa loudly. "Kṛṣṇa is for everyone!" The *paṇḍita* mouse looked annoyedly at Choṭa, and some mice in the audience began to hiss. Someone shouted to Choṭa, "Sit down!" and they would not let him speak anymore.

When the mouse meeting ended, a few mice in the audience approached Choṭa and said confidentially, "What you said was right. That is the real meaning of *Gītā*." The three *bhaktas* then began to mix among the crowd to distribute Kṛṣṇa conscious magazines. Since the audience was interested in *yoga*, Choṭa said, "Please take this magazine which teaches you about the highest *yoga* and meditation." After they had distributed most of the magazines, each of the devotee-mice met up with one of the trained followers of the Māyāvādī mouse. Choṭa, Yamala and Arjuna were each engaged in separate intense conversations which lasted about an hour.

Late that night, when the mice had returned to the temple, they discussed what had happened.

"That wasn't so bad," said Choṭa. "At least we distributed magazines, and they heard about Kṛṣṇa. But their philosophy is disgusting. It's a shame that all those mice were bring misled."

Yamala and Arjuna didn't have much to say. When they had talked with the Māyāvādī representatives, they had mostly listened, unlike Choṭa who had given many arguments.

"I would never become a Māyāvādī," said Yamala, "but I don't think there's anything wrong with increasing your life duration through *yoga.*"

"Yes, what's the harm in that?" asked Arjuna. And the two mice proceeded to stand on their heads. "You are that too," said Yamala. Choṭa was shocked to see it.

"That's not necessary," he said. "Our life duration will be as long as Kṛṣṇa wants it to be, and we can't extend it."

"But aren't Kṛṣṇa's teachings mostly for humans?" said Yamala.

"What!" said Choṭa, and he hopped up and down. "Kṛṣṇa is the original form of God. He's not a human! He says in the *Bhagavad-gītā*, the 'foolish deride Me, because I appear in human form. They do not know My supreme dominion over all that be.' What nonsense are you thinking?"

"Don't be angry," said Yamala. "A *sādhu* shouldn't get angry. After all, there are many paths to reach the same goal."

"Yes," said Arjuna and he smiled dreamily, "We are all One." Arjuna and Yamala then inhaled deeply and held their breaths with half-closed eyes.

Choṭa became very frightened to hear what his fellow *bhaktas* were saying. They had been infected by the Māyāvādī preaching, which Choṭa knew could be fatal to the spirit of devotion. But when he began to argue with them, they said they did not want to listen. It was late at night, and they wanted to sleep. Although his brother and cousin loved Choṭa, their relationship was quite familiar, so they would not listen to Choṭa as an authority.

While the cousins slept on their straw mats, Choṭa paced nervously back and forth. If only Mīna was here! He would be able to speak to them and show the serious defects in the Māyāvādī philosophy. Choṭa had never felt so alone and vulnerable as he did now. There was no one he could turn to for help among the other humans, and so he prayed to Kṛṣṇa and chanted.

While Choṭa was pacing and chanting, the temple phone rang nearby. After about six rings, one of the women came and picked it up.

"*Haribol.* Who is this? Mīna dāsa! What? Mahārāja is there and he wants to talk to the temple president? Just a minute."

Choṭa's hairs stood on end. As the *mātājī* walked away, Choṭa leaped up to the telephone and spoke.

"Mīna!" Choṭa squeaked. "This is your mouse Choṭa speaking. Please accept my obeisances."

Mīna was astounded and pleased to hear the voice of his mouse friend from thousands of miles away.

"Kṛṣṇa's mercy!" said Mīna. "I never expected to hear you from so far away. All glories to Prabhupāda. How are you and Yamala and Arjuna?"

"We need you, Mīna!" said Choṭa. But before he could say more, the lady returned to the phone. Choṭa had just enough time to hide behind the phone book.

"Hello Mīna? The temple president is sleeping in his house down the block. It's late at night here. Would you like to phone in the morning?"

"No, wake him up please," said Mīna. They both had to shout over the long-distance connection to be heard. "Mahārāja said it's important, so please go and wake him up. I'll hold on the line."

"All right," she said, "it may take me a few minutes." And she ran off.

Choṭa leaped back to the mouthpiece and shouted as loud as he could to Mīna in India.

"We went to a Māyāvādī festival last night to preach!"

"*Jaya*! Wonderful. Did you distribute many books?"

"Yes, but something terrible happened. Yamala and Arjuna became affected after speaking to two Māyāvādīs. Now they want to meditate on the impersonal Brahman! They won't listen to me."

"Bring them to the phone right away." Choṭa ran as fast as if a cat were chasing him. He woke up the two devotee-mice and brought them sleepy-eyed to the phone. All three mice were able to listen together to the sound of Mīna's voice through the phone speaker.

"What are you thinking?" said Mīna. Unlike Choṭa, Mina did not sound angry or excited with the other mice. They were all glad to hear whatever he had to say.

"The swami said that Kṛṣṇa is the god just for humans, not for mice!" shouted Yamala.

"Then he doesn't know Kṛṣṇa," said Mīna. "Kṛṣṇa and His incarnations did associate with the animals. Don't you remember the spider who served Lord Rāma, and the dog that Lord Caitanya liberated, and Gajendra, the king of the elephants, and Garuda? There are many. Besides that, are you a mouse?" Mīna paused to hear their reply.

"No!" all three mice called out. "We're spirit souls!"

"That's right," said Mīna, "we all have spiritual bodies. I'm not a human, and you're not mice. So Kṛṣṇa is not just for humans. In the spiritual world everyone has a liberated spiritual body to serve Kṛṣṇa. The cows serve Kṛṣṇa, and the *gopīs* and the *gopas* and even the grass of the Yamunā. Please don't misunderstand Kṛṣṇa. The Māyāvādī does not know Kṛṣṇa, because he is envious of God. You should learn about Kṛṣṇa from *Bhagavad-gītā As It Is*, not from a Māyāvādī."

"What about increasing life duration by *yoga*?" asked Yamala. The two mice felt ashamed but relieved to get it all out.

"By leading a life of devotional service," said Mīna, "you'll live the longest life possible. *Bhakti* is good for your health too. But in the end, we all have to die. Our energy should be spent in extending our duration of life to eternal life, not in adding a few more years. Just depend on Kṛṣṇa for as long as He wants you to live, and then go back to Godhead. Is that all right?"

"Yes!" all three mice replied. "When are you coming back here? We need you!" shouted Choṭa.

"I don't know. I'm travelling with Mahārāja. Maybe soon."

"Please come soon," said Yamala.

"We're sorry we caused you trouble," said Arjuna. "Don't worry about us. We won't become Māyāvādīs."

"Let's all chant Hare Kṛṣṇa always, and in that way we'll be together. Just see how Kṛṣṇa has brought us together to talk!"

The telephone connection was then taken over by Mīna's spiritual master in India, and the temple president in Guyana. Mīna and the mice were spinning in bliss.

Mahārāja had phoned Guyana because they had phoned him the day before but had not reached him. The temple president explained that they had been trying to decide whether to attend a Māyāvādī meeting, but they had gone ahead and done it. They had chanted outside the meeting and sold many books. Mahārāja was glad to hear this and encouraged them in their preaching.

When the phone call was complete, Mahārāja turned to Mīna dāsa.

"You seem very enlivened, Mīna. Have you been trying to help others as I suggested?"

"Yes, I've been appreciating the preaching of Kṛṣṇa's devotees all over the world. I've been trying to serve some devotees in Guyana by telling them your instructions."

"That's very good," said Mīna's spiritual master. "And you yourself should also preach directly. If you like preaching to others about preaching, you should do it yourself."

"Yes, Mahārāja," said Mīna. In the glow from his talk with mice-devotees, and in the presence of his spiritual master, Mīna felt inspired to surrender. He went down to the temple book table and began distributing Prabhupāda's books. It was a Sunday evening and hundreds of guests were in the temple. Mīna circulated among them and went outside along the street to find more people. "This is the direct way," he thought, "to expand my heart." As he spoke to people on the street, Mīna thought of his friends in Guyana. He hoped that they were also preaching and that he could help them by his example. "If I am chanting and preaching," Mīna thought, "and they're doing the same, we can be together in Kṛṣṇa consciousness wherever we are in the world, and in the next life we'll be with Kṛṣṇa in eternity, bliss, and knowledge."

Chapter 19

(S. d. g.)

Dear Nimāi,

Please accept Śrīla Prabhupāda's blessings from me. All glories to Śrīla Prabhupāda.

I have selected a few stories from those you have written. You can send these to your friends to share as Kṛṣṇa conscious fables. Some of the stories I didn't select, because they didn't seem to have a strong enough Vaiṣṇava conclusion. Even the ones I selected left me a bit puzzled in parts, but I think you have good intentions. You seem to have a knack for telling stories, and I hope you get better at it.

In this connection, I may tell you a story of my own. Once there was a boy who possessed an Aladdin's lamp. The lamp's name was The Mind. The boy's name was Nitāi dāsa. When Nitāi dāsa rubbed the lamp a huge, powerful genie appeared.

"You have called me?" said the genie. "Now give me some task to do. I will do anything you ask, but I cannot remain idle. If you leave me idle, I will attack you."

Nitāi dāsa was both delighted and afraid to see the genie.

"For a starter," said Nitāi, "you can write a big book. Write a book of tales for spiritual life."

Within a moment the genie had composed a book of a thousand pages filled with lively and instructive stories and illustrated with many colorful drawings. Not only had he written it, but it was printed in ten thousand copies.

"Now what else do you have for me to do?" said the genie, with a menacing smile.

"Uh...please clean up the temple and the temple grounds so that there's not a speck of dirt anywhere."

In an instant the genie had scoured the entire area so that it was sparkling clean, like the heart of a pure devotee.

"What next?" asked the genie. "Don't keep me idle. If you do, I'll attack you."

"If I give you something that will satisfy you and that you can never finish, will you leave me alone?"

"Yes," said the genie, folding his arms across his chest. "I have never found an activity that I could not finish instantly, and never anything that could satisfy me. But I will do whatever you say. And try to give me something to do that not only will satisfy you but will be beneficial to the world."

"I know!" said Nitāi. "My dear genie, I request you to please chant the glories of the holy name of Lord Kṛṣṇa. This is something you will never be able to finish. Even the Lord's incarnation as Ananta Śeṣa, who has thousands of heads and is more powerful than any genie, has been trying to glorify the Lord for millions of years and has not come to the end of it. I request you to chant and be satisfied, and I will also be satisfied, and everyone who hears you will benefit."

"What chant is that?" asked the genie.

Then Nitāi gave him the holy name:

Hare Kṛṣṇa, Hare Kṛṣṇa,
Kṛṣṇa Kṛṣṇa, Hare Hare
Hare Rāma, Hare Rāma,
Rāma Rāma, Hare Hare

The genie, whose name was The Mind, then began chanting and soon understood that he was the eternal servant of Lord Kṛṣṇa and that there would be no tiring—and never completion—of chanting the glories of the Lord.

Yours in the service of
Śrīla Prabhupāda

A Kṛṣṇa conscious person does not make any distinctions between species or castes. The *brāhmaṇa* and the outcaste may be different from the social point of view, or a dog, a cow and an elephant may be different from the point of view of species, but these differences of body are meaningless from the viewpoint of a learned transcendentalist. This is due to their relationship to the Supreme, for the Supreme Lord, by His plenary portion, as Paramātmā, is present in everyone's heart. Such an understanding of the Supreme is real knowledge.

—*Bhagavad-gītā As It Is 5.18, purport*

3

Gurudeva and Nimāi

Struggling for Survival

"One must be able to pass the test of the spiritual master, and when he sees the genuine desire of the disciple, he automatically blesses the disciple with genuine spiritual understanding."

—*Bhagavad-gītā*, *4.34 purport*

"Stalking Wolf had told me how young Indian braves would often leave the tribe and survive alone for twelve moons. Through this experience, they would find themselves. The Indians believed that the Great Spirit would bring a special teaching to the isolated brave. Many Indian legends told of great discoveries made by these braves that benefitted the entire tribe."

—*Tom Brown, Jr., The Search*

Preface

My spiritual master, Gauracandra dāsa Swami, is a follower of His Divine Grace A. C. Bhaktivedanta Swami Prabhupāda, the Founder-*Ācārya* of the International Society for Krishna Consciousness. This story is about our struggle for survival when we were stranded in the Canadian mountains, and when we were also fighting for spiritual truth.

My Gurudeva asked me to tell about the ordeal he and I went through, even though it included some offensive mentality on my part. The book also contains excerpts from Gurudeva's diary, which are confessional. My Gurudeva said, "Our story is the real life-and-death struggle in this world." What he means is that a person's attempt to maintain faith in the order of the spiritual master is the most important struggle in his life. We hope this story will help others.

Nimāi dāsa

#1: Guru Reform

When I got myself into trouble in India, my Gurudeva fetched me out of jail and out of *māyā*. It was then that he asked me to travel with him. A statement in the *Caitanya-caritāmṛta* describes what happened:

> "If by chance a servant falls down and goes somewhere else, glorious is *that* master who captures him and brings him back by the hair."
>
> —*Cc. Antya-līlā 4.47*

Gurudeva certainly fulfilled the spiritual master part of that statement by saving me, but I'm sorry to say that I didn't prove myself worthy as a loyal servant.

As Gurudeva's servant, I did all right in the beginning, when things were blissful and easy. Gurudeva and I went together to Gujarat, India, where Gurudeva was received as a worshipable *sādhu* by devotees in their homes. Even though it is the Age of Kali and India has become degraded, many Gujaratis still profess to be devotees of Lord Kṛṣṇa, and they are vegetarians. The Vedic culture is so nice that they were pleased to honor my Gurudeva as a bona fide spiritual representative of the Supreme Lord. They weren't prejudiced against him just because he was born and raised in the West. They invited him to their homes, washed his feet, and gave him an elevated seat while they sat on the floor and listened to his *Śrīmad-Bhāgavatam* discourse and joined in the *kīrtanas*. The *prasādam* we received in those places was tasty cooking like *paratha* and *dhokla* and a sweet *dāl* like I'd never tasted. My appreciation for Gurudeva was enhanced by my seeing him treated like that. He told me he didn't feel worthy of having his feet washed and being offered *ārati* and all that, but he was obliged to respond to their Vaiṣṇava etiquette.

After Gujarat, we went to New Delhi and then we flew back to America. In the West, most people have no idea of Vedic culture and they also lack deep God consciousness. Otherwise, they would recognize a saintly person like Gurudeva as a bona fide priest. Even a Christian priest doesn't get much honor. But at least in Prabhupāda's temple in New York City, Gurudeva was well received and again I became happy to see it.

But I was a fair-weather disciple. When Gurudeva was not well received, which happened when we went to Canada, I became affected—not at first, but gradually. When we arrived at the temple in Victoria, British Columbia, no one received Gurudeva with honors. They didn't even meet us at the airport, although I had phoned telling them we were coming. And there was no foot-bathing ceremony, which I had been accustomed to seeing in India. There was barely a "Haribol, Mahārāja" from a devotee who happened to be standing around the temple when we pulled up in the taxi. I had to ask where we could stay, and at first, they weren't sure but they ended up giving us the use of their guest rooms.

I was aware that a guru reform had occurred in our Movement, but I had never received a full whiff of it. In case you don't know what the reform is, I'll mention it briefly. After Śrīla Prabhupāda disappeared from the world, some of his senior disciples, with the approval of the Governing Body, started initiating disciples. Not every disciple of Prabhupāda was allowed to become a guru, but only a select few. Those who were gurus had many disciples and everyone in the Movement honored them. In many ways the gurus were given the same respect as Śrīla Prabhupāda, while their own Godbrothers sat on the floor. Everyone considered the gurus as pure devotees of the highest standard. But—to make a long story short—some of the gurus deviated and eventually other Godbrothers began a reform movement. Then at the international meeting in Māyāpur, India, the Governing Body voted some changes or reforms. More Godbrothers were invited to become initiating *gurus*, and we stopped worshiping the *gurus* every day on big *vyāsāsanas*, which were now reserved only for Śrīla Prabhupāda.

Those are some of the bare facts of what happened, but there were intense emotions and many arguments involved. I was mostly spared from it because I was never invited to any meetings, and at the farm where I stayed in Pennsylvania, no one talked about it much. When Gurudeva announced to us some of the changes, I just accepted it. He said the Movement had made some mistakes, and he was personally sorry if he had offended any Godbrothers or Śrīla Prabhupāda. We saw that he was acting humbly and for the good of the Movement. I never stopped considering him as a pure devotee and as my spiritual master who connected me to Śrīla Prabhupāda and the *paramparā*.

But in Victoria, some of the devotees were heavy and bitter about the mistakes that had been made, and since I was my guru's personal servant, I had to bear the brunt of some of it. At first, it seemed insulting and unnecessary.

After the first *Śrīmad-Bhāgavatam* class that Gurudeva gave in Victoria, one of his disciples asked what I thought was a strange question. He said, "Now that Śrīla Prabhupāda is gone and there is no pure devotee who can command respect, how can we become enthusiastic to preach to newcomers?" Gurudeva replied that the disciplic succession was still working, and any qualified devotee of Śrīla Prabhupāda could preach on his behalf, and newcomers would get the same benefit as those who had been personally initiated by Śrīla Prabhupāda. He gave an example: You may wonder if a certain light bulb will work, but when you plug it in and it *does* light, then that is proof that it works. So, since we see people are becoming initiated by Prabhupāda's disciples and are serving nicely in Kṛṣṇa consciousness, this is proof. But when he said that some of Gurudeva's Godbrothers raised their hands and challenged. Gurudeva answered them all right.

Then a guest to the temple raised his hand and said, "Can a person just directly worship Kṛṣṇa and offer Him food and prayers?" Gurudeva replied that one has to render service to Lord Kṛṣṇa through the spiritual master. He quoted *Bhagavad-gītā* verse 4.34 where Kṛṣṇa recommends that we approach a spiritual master. But the guest said, "No, I mean, can we just worship Prabhupāda directly?" Gurudeva replied, "Oh yes. Prabhupāda is everyone's *śikṣā guru,* instructing spiritual master. You can take a picture of Śrīla Prabhupāda and offer your food to him even if you are not initiated and you can read his books and accept him as your *guru*." Gurudeva didn't go on to say that the newcomer would have to become eventually initiated by a follower of Śrīla Prabhupāda. I figured that he just wanted to affirm that Śrīla Prabhupāda was a *śikṣā guru* and *jagat-guru* to encourage the guest. Also, most of the devotees there didn't *want* to hear anything more.

Usually when we visit a temple, some of my Godbrothers and Godsisters volunteer to cook for Gurudeva and do his laundry. But when I arranged for this in Victoria, the temple president came to me and said he couldn't spare the devotees. So, I had to cook and do the laundry myself. I didn't mention this to Gurudeva, but I resented that the devotees weren't able to do a little service for their spiritual master. I thought it was important for a disciple to learn the principle of trying to please Kṛṣṇa by pleasing His representative. I've found it's inspiring to do this in the personal presence of the *guru* and felt bad that disciples wouldn't have the same opportunity. Gurudeva discovered that I was doing those duties myself, but he seemed nonplussed. I could understand the temple president's point of view that the Victoria devotees had more important service to do, but I also guessed that he was trying to show that Gurudeva wasn't better than anyone else and should not expect special treatment. As a result, I became agitated and eager to leave the temple.

Then I overheard Gurudeva talking with one of his disciples. I'm usually close outside his door and I eavesdrop if it sounds interesting. This was a confidential talk, but I couldn't resist. The devotee was Subala dāsa and he was asking about his relationship with Śrīla Prabhupāda. Gurudeva was assuring him, "Yes, you have a direct relationship with Śrīla Prabhupāda as *śikṣā-guru.*" But Gurudeva asserted that he too was Subala's *dīkṣā-* and *śikṣā-guru,* as long as Subala was willing to receive instruction from him. Gurudeva said that if a devotee is willing to become a servant of the servant of the servant—a hundred times a servant of God—then this shows his faith and Kṛṣṇa is pleased with him. He quoted Lord Caitanya as saying:

... gopī-bhartuḥ pada-kamalayor dāsa-dāsānudāsaḥ

"I am not a *brāhmaṇa* ... or a *sannyāsī.* I identify Myself only as the servant of the servant of the servant of the lotus feet of Lord Śrī Kṛṣṇa, the maintainer of the *gopīs.*"

—*Cc Madhya, 13.80*

But Subala kept wanting to know more about his right to worship Śrīla Prabhupāda. He said, "I joined this movement by reading Śrīla

Prabhupāda's *Bhagavad-gītā As It Is*, and I actually saw him at an airport in 1977. So, I want to ask your permission to worship directly, because I consider Śrīla Prabhupāda is my main *guru* and my relationship with you is secondary. Is that all right?" Gurudeva said "Yes," but he didn't sound very enthusiastic. "I don't want to be offensive to you," said Subala, "but that is what I think." Gurudeva gave his approval again, and Subala thanked him happily. I ducked away from the door as if I had not been listening, but actually that conversation had a deep effect on me.

Like Subala dāsa, I too had been initially attracted to Kṛṣṇa consciousness by Śrīla Prabhupāda's *Bhagavad-gītā As It Is.* I was in my first year of college (which is as far as I ever got) and a friend gave me a paperback copy of *Bhagavad-gītā As It Is.* The verse and purports completely answered many of my questions and exposed the folly of my dreams and my parents' dreams that I should become a lawyer or businessman. What was the sense of becoming a material success if the body is doomed? What about the success of the permanent self, the spirit soul? I became convinced by studying the Bhaktidevanta purports, and I also began to chant the *mahā-mantra* before I even went to a temple, or met the devotees, or heard about my Gurudeva (whose initiated name is actually Gauracandra Swami).

In Victoria, these thoughts led me to seek out the audience of Śrīla Prabhupāda in the temple room. I went and bowed down before the life-sized *mūrti* of Prabhupāda and then sat before him, savoring my relationship with him. The *mūrti* of Śrīla Prabhupāda is very calm and regal, and I looked with new eyes upon his saffron-dressed form, his hands folded on his lap, and his head ever so lightly tilted to the right. By being with him in the temple room, I felt very close to Prabhupāda, and I thought that if he wanted to he could communicate with me. While looking at him I realized better that Prabhupāda was actually the pure force behind the Kṛṣṇa consciousness movement, because he is an indisputably pure devotee and a highly empowered preacher (*śaktyāveśa avatāra*). So, if Gauracandra Swami had given Subala dāsa freedom to consider Prabhupāda as his most important guru, then shouldn't I too have the freedom to choose? And if I were to choose between Śrīla Prabhupāda and Gauracandra Swami, wouldn't it be obvious that Śrīla Prabhupāda was unquestionably the more advanced devotee and therefore a better shelter for me? Gurudeva had always said that his disciples shouldn't consider that there was a competition between him and Śrīla Prabhupāda. All right, no competition, but still, it was natural to *compare* them and to seek the stronger. But did I have direct access to Prabhupāda? Was I "jumping over" the person I was supposed to accept as my link to Śrīla Prabhupāda? *How vitally did I need my initiating guru?*

My thoughts were interrupted when I noticed Subala dāsa sitting next to me, smiling and looking up at Śrīla Prabhupāda. Subala was slightly balding and had been through a lot of family trouble, such as splitting up with his wife and giving up his job in order to become a full-time devotee. As we sat together, Subala said something about how great Prabhupāda was and so we began talking. I admitted to him that I had overheard what Gurudeva had said to him.

"I am feeling relieved," said Subala, "that he has allowed me to go where my heart is." Subala and I continued glorifying Prabhupāda, his books and his potency.

"Actually, the gurus are not really qualified," said Subala, "if you consider what the scriptures say." I have heard remarks like that before, and usually they set off alarms and red lights inside my head. To speak like that was offensive towards my initiating spiritual master. Whenever I heard such things, I would either argue against them or go away. But this time I stayed."

"Have you read what Śrīla Prabhupāda writes in his books?" said Subala. He had the quotes in a notebook which he took from his book bag. He began to read aloud:

> The *uttama-adhikārī,* or the highest devotee, is one who is very advanced in devotional service. One should not become a spiritual master unless he has attained the platform of *uttama-adhikārī.* A neophyte *Vaiṣṇava* or a *Vaiṣṇava* situated on the intermediate platform can also accept disciples, but such disciples must be on the same platform, and it should be understood that they cannot advance very well toward the ultimate goal of life under his insufficient guidance. Therefore, a disciple should be careful to accept an *uttama-adhikārī* as a spiritual master
>
> —*Nectar of Instruction, text 5, purport*

I have heard that statement before, and I knew it was argued back and forth by devotees. But this time I accepted that it could be applied to my initiating spiritual master—as someone who was probably not an *uttama-adhikārī* or if he was one, his position was contested by his Godbrothers. And anyway, Śrīla Prabhupāda was more than a *mahā-bhāgavata*; he was a *mahā-mahā-bhāgavata*.

Subala went on to make a general statement about "those guys," meaning the initiating *gurus*, and the wrongs they had committed. I told him that he shouldn't lump Gauracandra Swami in with the rest. He agreed but added, "he's guilty by association." I finally figured out that I was indulging in unnecessary talk, and so I decided to return to my duties in serving Gurudeva.

"Where were you?" Gurudeva looked up when I entered the room. I had forgotten to serve him his evening milk. He was calm as usual, but I knew he must have been somewhat annoyed by my absence, especially when I had no good excuse. It then occurred to me that I had also forgotten to do his laundry as well as a few other things I was supposed to do. I decided not to hide the trouble in my mind and so I tried to mention it, indirectly.

"Gurudeva, it's quite different here, isn't it, from the way we were being received in Gujarat?"

"Our Movement is going through some painful transitions," he replied. "Sometimes the changes occur like the swings of a pendulum from one extreme to another."

Within a few moments, I blurted out to him the issues which had possessed my mind, but I tried to conceal that they were of such personal concern to me. I read him the quote from *Nectar of Instruction*, that a devotee who is less than the liberated *uttama-adhikārī* shouldn't become a spiritual master. I asked him what he thought.

Gurudeva replied at length. He said that when this question was asked a few years ago, the gurus used to reply that *uttama-adhikārī* could also apply to ourselves. In the same passage describing the *uttama-adhikārī* as spiritual master, Prabhupāda defines the term by saying, "Out of many *Vaiṣṇavas* one may be found to be very seriously engaged in the service of the Lord and strictly following all of the regulative principles, chanting the prescribed number of rounds on *japa* beads and always thinking of how to expand the Kṛṣṇa Consciousness Movement." So, by that definition even some of Prabhupāda's disciples could qualify. By a similar interpretation, once could note that Śrīla

Prabhupāda sometimes used words like "pure devotee," and "liberated personality" to apply even to his young disciples, provided they were fully engaged in the process of *bhakti-yoga*."

"But that kind of interpretation won't hold anymore," said Gurudeva. "The fact is, we followers of Śrīla Prabhupāda have to act as spiritual master, not based on whether we are *mahā-bhāgavatas*, but because it is our duty. It's the order of Prabhupāda, and we have to undertake it even at great risk."

Gurudeva explained that the major mistake the Movement had made after Prabhupāda's disappearance was to claim that only a few select persons could become spiritual masters. But throughout Prabhupāda's books and letters he advocates that all his followers should become spiritual masters. Lord Caitanya says, "Whoever you meet, tell him about Kṛṣṇa, and you will become a spiritual master." Gurudeva spoke of the pressing need for many initiating and instructing spiritual masters in the world, due to the complete absence of Kṛṣṇa consciousness. Gurudeva's point was that it would be ideal to accept a *mahā-bhāgavata* as your guru, but there are many, many statements indicating that Prabhupāda wanted his followers to become gurus, and not necessarily that they had to wait until they became *uttama-adhikārī*, or until their Godbrothers recognized them as such. Gurudeva showed me a few statements, such as the one in a letter by Prabhupāda where he says, "Generally the spiritual master comes from the group of eternal associates of the Lord, but anyone who follows the principles of such ever-liberated persons is as good as a liberated one. Persons who are less qualified are not liberated but can act as guru and *ācārya* by strictly following the disciplic succession." He also showed me a purport by Śrīla Prabhupāda in the Fourth Canto where he states,

> Although a follower may not be a liberated person, if he follows the Supreme...one can immediately become a spiritual master by having full faith in the transcendental words of the Supreme Personality of Godhead and by following His instructions.
>
> —*Śrīmad-Bhāgavatam 4.18.5*

Gurudeva said the very fact that there are so many warnings in the scriptures and from the previous *ācāryas* about the right behavior of gurus indicates that those who are gurus may be prone to mistakes. For example, a guru is warned not to take too many disciples. Lord

Caitanya said a guru should not accept money or grains from materialists and should not be proud of his position. Lord Caitanya gave these instructions "for all spiritual masters."

When Gurudeva mentioned that we should not jump over our spiritual master in going directly to the previous spiritual master, I tried to listen very carefully, because this was my main concern about my relationship with Prabhupāda. Gurudeva said that over the centuries perfect masters have sometimes appeared who have started *sampradāyas,* such as Rāmānuja and Mādhva, and he also mentioned Jesus Christ and Lord Buddha. Gurudeva said, "Imagine what it was like for disciples of the perfect masters to also become gurus. The direct apostles or followers of the perfect masters are very fortunate, but they must also face the fact that people will be disappointed—because they just missed becoming disciples of the original spiritual master. Still, one who represents the perfect master is acceptable, provided he really represents his teacher."

"The real test is a personal one," said Gurudeva, "whether your spiritual master has actually saved you from material life. If a disciple of a disciple of a disciple of the perfect master actually saves you by giving you the teachings of his previous teachers, and if you feel a debt in your heart to him, then he may be qualified and may actually be in fact your spiritual master."

"What if," I asked, "a follower of a follower of a perfect spiritual master feels that he has a personal debt to the *perfect* master?"

"Then he has to fulfill that debt," said Gurudeva. "But one way to fulfill it, such as the debt we all feel to Prabhupāda, is by serving another follower of Prabhupāda. This shouldn't be imposed on people as an institutional dogma, which I think is another mistake our Movement made. But neither should we make such a swing of the pendulum that we deny that Prabhupāda's mercy comes also through his followers. We shouldn't deliberately try to undermine the faith that may be coming to people's hearts when they meet devotees of Prabhupāda who tell them about Kṛṣṇa, and who explain Prabhupāda's books to them and help them to practice."

There were more questions on my mind, but I felt too confused and contaminated to pursue the topic. I didn't want to ask merely theoretical questions or to challenge. I was thinking of asking, for example,

"Why does someone have to explain Prabhupāda's books to us, why can't we just read them on our own?" From what Gurudeva already had said, however, I could see that there was a need for spiritual masters even after Prabhupāda. I hadn't yet asked my personal question, whether I should consider Prabhupāda my main spiritual master, but I guessed that Gurudeva might have answered it by saying that I had to answer it for myself. When I stopped asking further questions, Gurudeva could see that I was still confused.

"You seemed peaceful before we came here," said Gurudeva, "and now you may be thinking differently. You know, Nimāi, your tendency is to go off on different detours. You go in one way and then become influenced and go in another way. So, consider things carefully."

"Thank you Gurudeva." I bowed down, left his room, and tried to catch up on the duties I had neglected.

But the emotional changes that had occurred when I had heard Gurudeva tell Subala that Prabhupāda could be his main guru and my own awakening of direct attraction to Prabhupāda didn't leave me. Some of those emotions were nice, but some of them scared me. My innocent dedication to Gurudeva was exposed as shallow. As a result of all of this, I remained somewhat disturbed and less enthusiastic. I also forgot to do things in my service to Gurudeva. Some of my mistakes turned out to be very costly.

#2: The Crash

Toward the end of our stay in Victoria, Gurudeva decided he wanted to visit New Naimiṣāraṇya, a community of Kṛṣṇa conscious devotees in northern British Columbia. About six different families had built a home in the wilderness, without phones or electricity, and they were practicing "simple living and high thinking." One of them had written to Gurudeva asking him to visit: "We hardly ever see anyone up here and we'd be encouraged if a *sannyāsī* came and assured us that what we're doing is part of Prabhupāda's movement." A devotee from Victoria agreed to drive us there in his van, but on the day that we were supposed to leave, he canceled the offer in favor of some urgent business. When Gurudeva heard that, he wanted to go without delay to our next scheduled stop, San Francisco.

The man who drove us to the airport was just beginning to learn about Kṛṣṇa consciousness. I had spoken with him at the Sunday feast about transmigration and about his profession—flying. As soon as we got into his car, he proposed that he could fly Gurudeva and me in his one-engine place to New Naimiṣāraṇya. He said he had done it himself half a dozen times and that it was an easy three-hour flight. Gurudeva likes to act with caution and time for deliberation, so I didn't think he would go for it. But he began to ask the man questions as if he were seriously interested in the offer. The man, Bob Gates, said he was a licensed pilot and that his little plane was very reliable. He regularly made much longer flights to the mountains and all the way north into the Arctic region. Sometimes he flew trappers or tourists or parcels or even a dog or calf. He said the devotees at New Naimiṣāraṇya had prepared a level field just for this purpose. "Flying in a plane," said Bob, "is still safer than driving a car on the highway."

And so, before we were halfway to the city airport, Gurudeva decided to accept the offer. Bob changed direction and drove us to a smaller airfield where he kept his plane.

Bob left Gurudeva and me in the car while he went in to check the weather report and prepare his plane.

"What do you think Nimāi?" asked Gurudeva.

"Think about what Gurudeva?" I was still in my confusion over spiritual masters.

"About flying in this plane."

"I think it's all right, if you do." I knew that Gurudeva had flown in little planes before, in Guyana, and he liked the adventure and the convenience. He didn't like long car trips because they gave him headaches.

"I want you to personally inquire about the weather where we're going," Gurudeva said. The sky was overcast. Spring was supposed to begin in a week, but it was still cold. Gurudeva told me to go into the air terminal and make two phone calls, one to the San Francisco temple to tell them we were not coming and one to the Victoria temple to tell them we were planning to go to Naimiṣāraṇya.

I went inside, but someone was using the pay phone. I sat waiting for a while, but I spaced out. At first, I began thinking of the talk with Gurudeva about how someone could be a spiritual master even if he wasn't a *mahā-bhāgavata*. Then I fell into bad consciousness while waiting in the airfield office. I doubted whether my spiritual master could take me back to Godhead. But I also doubted that I could depend entirely on my relationship with Śrīla Prabhupāda. And I doubted myself. I doubted my faith in Kṛṣṇa and the pure devotees. By shaking the foundation of my faith in Gurudeva, my whole spiritual life was being threatened. But now that I had started, it was hard to stop. While sitting and worrying, I began to doze. Then Bob Gates came over and woke me up.

"We're ready to go," he said cheerfully. "The weather report isn't so bad."

I told Bob that I had to make phone calls for Gurudeva and that I would join them in a few minutes. As I dialed the phone, I could see out the window Bob and Gurudeva walking towards the small planes. They stopped before a one-engine white Cessna with a red stripe. It looked fragile, and I wondered if it could carry us with all our baggage. When no one answered the phone at the San Francisco temple, I decided not to bother trying any other phone calls.

I think I should explain why I didn't pursue making those phone calls. It might have been very important if I had been able to tell Gurudeva what I had heard with my own ears. It also could have made a big difference if I informed the devotees where we were going. I can "explain" my action by saying, "I just spaced out." But it was something more. It was minimization of the order of the spiritual master. It just didn't seem that important to me, making these "little" calls that Gurudeva asked for. Hadn't the pilot said that the weather was all right? And why bother calling up different temples? Now that I look back, I think my resistance was connected to a general doubtful state. A faithful disciple would have carried out the order of the spiritual master at all costs and just assumed that the guru would not have asked for something if it were unimportant. I tried a second time to reach the San Francisco temple, but when no one answered I just dropped the attempt to call anyone else and went out to join them at the airplane.

Now I have to describe a very low point. As we stood outside the plane Gurudeva asked, "Did you make the phone calls?" I replied, "Yes." I rationalized to myself that I wasn't lying, because I had tried to phone San Francisco.

"Was it all right?" asked Gurudeva. I knew he was referring to the weather report. He didn't want Bob to hear that we were double-checking on him. At this point, I told a bold-faced lie and said, "Yes." Why? Because I just didn't consider it very important, and I thought that Gurudeva would never find out one way or another. So there, I've said it. Now everyone can know what a rascal I am.

As the plane taxied for the take-off, I noticed that the doors were held shut with less security than a car door. And the plane cabin was very noisy from the engine roar so that you couldn't converse. Gurudeva and I, strapped in small, hard seats, prayed on our *japa* beads.

The Cessna lifted lightly into a hazy sky. As far as I could tell, Bob Gates had very few panel instruments. I don't think he had a radio, and he certainly had no radar, so he was flying by visual reference. He flew at a very low altitude in order to see the ground under the clouds. I guess he was expecting to make the whole trip just by memory. Gurudeva had a road atlas which he took out and showed me what he thought was our route north, over places called Squamish, Garibaldi, Brandy Wine Falls Park, and then passing in between some of the peaks of the Coast Mountains and over Chilko Lake. One-time Gurudeva leaned forward to Bob and said, "Are we over the Squamish yet?" But it was no use because Bob couldn't hear him over the engine. Gurudeva would have had to shout, and he didn't, so he sat back, chanting and holding on. I think we both felt uneasy to be so much at the mercy of Bob and his little plane.

At times like that, you naturally turn to God, at least I do. Death came closer too, like a personal presence, and so I was forced to take shelter of Kṛṣṇa in direct open prayer of His holy names. After a while, a turbulence began and the plane started to shake. We lost altitude and suddenly gained it again. I didn't know whether the pilot was jockeying to get out of the wind currents or whether the gusts were moving us around helplessly. It got so strong that I considered the wings might come off. They were mere wood and fabric, not like when you look out the window on Pan Am and see steel rivets.

The visibility diminished. Then you couldn't see at all, just fog all around. When we noticed wet snowflakes swirling, Gurudeva said to me, "He should turn back." Then he shouted up to Bob, *"Shouldn't you turn back?"* But Bob, with his hands very tightly on his steering shouted back, *"I think it will be all right! I've done it before! If it gets too bad, we can land somewhere!"*

I was feeling relieved that at least I could chant out loud without embarrassment. When traveling in commercial jets, I had often thought that in an emergency it might be very awkward to call out Kṛṣṇa's names in the midst of two-hundred nondevotees. Even if I could do it, they might say, "Tell that Hare Kṛṣṇa to shut up!" But here chanting was expected. Gurudeva was chanting also, although at the same time he was looking outside and glancing forward to the pilot and the control panel.

"How could he have received good weather reports?" Gurudeva said as if he were thinking out loud.

There were some breaks in the clouds, and we could see a huge bulk of a mountain not far to the left. We lost visibility again and when we regained it, we were heading toward another smaller mountain.

Bob suddenly banked sharply. He wasn't consulting us, and so we could only guess what he was attempting. The personal danger was real enough, but I also felt terrible anxiety and regret that I had placed Gurudeva at the mercy of such flimsy protectors. And now we were trapped. It seems that Bob had lost his way.

View of mountain from window

Then the engine started to run rough. I began praying like anything, loud and sincere. I was completely frightened and holding on tight. Gurudeva's chanting was deep and clear and loud. Kṛṣṇa was the Supreme Personality of Godhead, and He would decide. We just tried to remember Him.

The plane began to lose altitude, and Bob switched the engine off. So, he was going to land. The propeller kept turning and he switched the engine on again, but it only ran smooth a few seconds before it acted up. He switched it off and glided, constantly losing altitude but maintaining enough height so we could make an emergency landing and not a nosedive.

"Hold on," he shouted, "this might be a bit rough!" Down we went into a ravine—I couldn't call it a field—amid mountains and trees, toward a somewhat clear space of snow. I was by then in a panic, but at least the holy names were on my lips. We were all three crying out for Kṛṣṇa. The first ground impact was maybe the tail touching down, and it wasn't bad. I fully braced myself. The second jolt was severe. The third was the crash. We were hurled and crushed against the plane, which crumpled and broke into pieces.

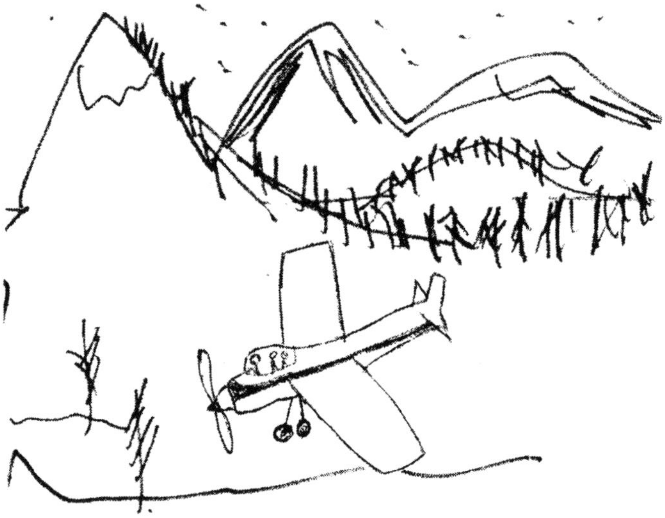

Forced landing in mountains

#3: Gurudeva's Journal

March 14

Pain. Broken leg. Freezing cold. Lost in the mountains. But by Kṛṣṇa's grace we are alive and have found a trapper's cabin, and we have food and a fire.

Yesterday we crashed into a ravine in the Coastal Mountains. We are far from civilization, in a dangerously inaccessible spot. There are big peaks here, each ten thousand feet tall. Mount Tatlow, Razorback Mountain, Taseko Mountain, and all snow-capped—at least I think these are some of the peaks in sight. Who would ever come by here?

I was the only one with a serious injury. Besides the broken bone, I had a cut on my leg which probably would have received about six stitches from a doctor. I'm afraid it may become infected. We started walking (I with a crutch), and after an hour we found this little cabin. The foolhardy pilot insisted on walking off by himself to find help. I thought it better to stay where we are. A crashed plane and smoke from a cabin are more likely to attract attention than a man wandering in the snow. But he insisted, and it is also brave of him to do so.

I have to forcibly restrain my imagination from living in "what might have been"—*if* we had gotten a car ride to New Naimiṣāraṇya, or if I had been more cautious and not jumped into this crazy offer of a plane flight, or even if Bob had had enough sense to turn back when he saw the storm. What actually has happened I must accept as the will of Providence and as the best opportunity for spiritual advancement.

March 15

Freezing cold night. Stripped of all amenities (but not necessities). For how long?

Nimāi dāsa is not much companionship, not yet. He's so young and inside his own head; being with him is like being alone. Something unpleasant came over our relationship in Victoria when he picked up new doubts whether I am a bona fide spiritual master. I thought I had already gone through that. I admitted that I, like the other gurus, had been imitating Śrīla Prabhupāda, and I acknowledged my lesser position. So, I wanted to go on and do the needful, to *serve* disciples by acting as their spiritual master in *paramparā*.

Being thrown here in the mountains has brought me again to face myself for what I am. I don't like what I see. Nimāi is right: He should take shelter of Śrīla Prabhupāda, and I should encourage him to do it. I can't give shelter to anyone, and I don't spontaneously speak the science of Kṛṣṇa. At best, I'm just a clinging, dependent disciple of Śrīla Prabhupāda. Maybe I've not advanced *at all* since I first met Śrīla Prabhupāda and he blessed me to chant Hare Kṛṣṇa, follow the four rules, and follow him.

That's it, bas
Jaya Gauracandra dāsa

Let me admit my disqualifications as spiritual master:

When I "became" guru, one of the biggest changes I went through was my behavior toward women. Previously I was very strict as a *sannyāsī* and wouldn't even look at women's faces if at all possible. But as guru I was supposed to become the protector and intimate guide of many women. I asked one of the other initiating gurus about it, and he said it was no problem, you just have to see them as your daughters. I tried it, on the premise that I was a liberated spiritual father. When an attractive young woman approached me and said that she wanted me to initiate her, or rather when her temple president told her that she had to accept me as her eternal guru, I would ask her to come see me for an initial interview. Sometimes I would sit alone with one of them for more than two hours, while my *brahmacārī* assistant sat just outside the door. The daughters approached me openly and adoringly because according to the system I was as pure as an angel. I was like another Śukadeva Gosvāmī who could walk naked, and when the ladies bathing by the river saw him, they didn't bother to cover themselves because they knew that he had no designs on them. He was purely thinking of Kṛṣṇa. But I can admit to impurity and were not some of the daughters also in the mixed modes? It was only by Kṛṣṇa's mercy that I got through the years of guruship with no gross fall down. Now, it's mostly a series of battles that I somehow survived. But to have put in so much time resisting feminine attraction doesn't speak well of someone who is supposed to be in higher consciousness.

There are many other disqualifications. I really lack compassion to face "the zoo" of nondevotees, and neither do I appreciate the association of Kṛṣṇa. So much envy in my mental life. Maybe that's why Kṛṣṇa has thrown me here— "You want to be alone? Here!"

Just the fact that I still expect to be served hand and foot by servants and followers means that I'm covered over. Once I complained to a Godbrother that my servant had been a few minutes late in serving us lunch. The Godbrother said, "Yes, it's hard to get good servants nowadays." He was teasing me, as if I were some king of patrician or slave owner, and I resented it. But there was truth to that remark. I *expect* to be served. I think I *need* it for *my* service to God! I need a cook, a dishwasher, a toilet cleaner, someone to wash my clothes and sew my buttons, someone to open doors for me, someone to make my phone calls. And I accept a soft pillow, mattress, money, and assistants. I don't drive cars; I ride in them. My servant screens prospective visitors: "You can't see him," is his standard line.

So what? Well, it's just too much covering around the real person. I'm not even able to ask the vital question anymore: *Who am I*? Because the too-ready answer I give myself is, "I'm guru: My name is Gurudeva." But as Bhaktisiddhānta Sarasvati writes, if you think you're a guru, then you are actually *goru*, a cow.

I have received so much honor in this lifetime as *sannyāsī* and guru! Why don't I just refuse it? Because it is duty. I won't blunder like that *sannyāsī*-disciple of Prabhupāda who threw away his *daṇḍa* saying, "I don't want people to bow to me." We explained to him, "They are not bowing to you personally. You are representing the *paramparā*." But if you are possessed of false ego and material desires, if you are cheating, then you had better put down the *daṇḍa*.

Serve as befits a *sannyāsī*. If a householder in Gujarat wants to offer you heavenly sweet rice and a cushion, you may accept it. But then accept austerities equally and accept them with the same pleasure. Lord Caitanya was delighted to walk with one servant through South India singing:

kṛṣṇa! kṛṣṇa! kṛṣṇa! kṛṣṇa! kṛṣṇa! kṛṣṇa! kṛṣṇa! he
kṛṣṇa! kṛṣṇa! kṛṣṇa! kṛṣṇa! kṛṣṇa! kṛṣṇa! pāhi mām

"O Lord Kṛṣṇa, please save me!
O Lord Kṛṣṇa, please protect me!"

O Lord Kṛṣṇa, please be my worshipable Deity, please be my friend, please come to me and save me from my self-inflicted wounds. I want to be your devotee, to serve as a devotee of your pure devotee, but so far, I'm a "farcical Nārada." Please have pity on me and banish my self-pity. Let me stand up like a devotee of the Lord. Better late than never.

As I write this entry, my pen is running out. I have a supply of Sheaffer cartridges in my briefcase, and I am inclined to keep writing. But how long before someone finds us?

March 16

I have to be careful, or I'll lose track of the date. I must be sure to check it off each morning on the calendar.

I'm going to try to talk with Nimāi. We are in this together. I should see him as a spirit soul and as a Vaiṣṇava, not by designation, a "young kid," "neophyte devotee," or "servant." He's trying his best within limitations, which is all I am doing.

So far Nimāi and I have mostly talked about how we expect someone to find us here. They will notice the plane is missing. They will send a search party. They will see the plane's silver landing gear, which we have exposed. They will see the smoke from our chimney. They will send down a helicopter. But we have also admitted that almost no one knew where we were going; it's not like a lost jumbo jet that does not show up in New York. Who knows if Gates even properly logged in, or whatever they're supposed to do at the airport? So, there may not be a deliberate search. Maybe some hunters or trappers will come by. But our Movement is such that one could go weeks without anyone even asking for him. If my name comes up in conversation, devotees will say, "Isn't he preaching in Canada somewhere?" I know when I don't hear of a *sannyāsī's* whereabouts for a long time, I start to wonder: Did he bloop like so many others?" "I heard he got married and has a job as a shoe salesman in Oklahoma."

I'm afraid.

kṛṣṇa! kṛṣṇa! pāhi mām
kṛṣṇa! kṛṣṇa! rakṣa mām

#4: Fears

I could have functioned much better in the woods if I hadn't been so afraid. The actual work was practical—how to maintain a food supply and physical shelter, and how to reciprocate with Gurudeva. But when I became distracted by fear I couldn't concentrate on my work.

While writing this, I've just looked up the word "fear" in the *Bhagavad-gītā As It Is*. If I share some of it with you, it will help me to express myself. Prabhupāda states, "*Bhagavad-gītā* is a transcendental literature which one should read very carefully. It is capable of saving one from all fear." When he discussed the fact that the Kurus were afraid on hearing the sound of the conches blown by the Pāṇḍavas, Prabhupāda comments, "One who takes shelter of the Supreme Lord has nothing to fear, even in the midst of the greatest calamity." There is also an item listed in the index as "fear: freedom from, as requisite for love." This means that a Kṛṣṇa conscious person has to actually be free of fear, as well as lust and anger, in order to advance in transcendental life. Kṛṣṇa finally promises that if one surrenders to Him, He will deliver us from sinful reaction: "Do not fear." Hearing these statements by the Supreme Personality of Godhead, I can conclude that my fear was a combination of being in the bodily concept of life and of not remembering Kṛṣṇa.

I probably had what medical people call shock or trauma after the plane crash, although I wasn't much hurt. I was shocked that Gurudeva was bleeding and that we were freezing in the snow and that we were lost. I didn't want to believe that it was really happening. I kept wanting to be somewhere safe and warm where we all belonged, such as the temple room or the attic room in the Pennsylvania farm. Although I still had something very valuable, my service relationship with Gurudeva, I just freaked out and couldn't face reality.

When we entered the cabin, one of the first things I saw there became another major cause of my fear. There was a photo on the wall and some books, and as soon as we entered, I went right up to them to see what they were. I am like that. Even if I enter a place with a very serious purpose, I have to check out the titles of any books or magazines and look at any pictures or any graffiti on the walls. So, in this cabin there was a photo nailed to the wall. It showed a tall creature walking on two legs in the woods; its face was like a mask or like a werewolf with big teeth. One picture showed him coming forward and the other picture showed him walking away. The caption said, "Pictures hurriedly snapped of an object thought to be a Sasquatch near our cabin at Nahanni Butte, April 1967." Another picture showed footprints in the snow and said, "Alleged Sasquatch tracks." That was all I needed: my imagination filled in the rest. It all happened in about ten seconds, and I don't think Gurudeva even noticed. Although we had immediate urgent duties, most of which fell on me to carry out, such as building our first fire and looking for food, I still managed to find a few minutes in which to pick up another book in the cabin and glance through it. It was a *Guide to the Wildlife of British Columbia*. It featured photos and descriptions of moose, wolves, coyotes, cougars, and bears. On the first page I turned to I read, "WARNING: black bears frequent the area and ARE NOT TAME OR FRIENDLY. A disappointed bear or sow with cubs can quickly kill a human when annoyed or alarmed." The grizzly bear is beautiful in a sense, because of his natural power, but to even think of meeting up with him gave me the jitters. The same with the wolf. And yet we were in their backyard.

The cabin was just one room and had an earthen floor. There were wooden bunks, a stove, a small pile of wood, a hatchet, a knife, but no food. There was another small structure near the cabin, smaller than a room, but well-built and set upon tall posts. Gurudeva asked me to enter it, because as it turned out, it was the food cache. Within half an hour of our arrival at the cabin, I was out again by myself in the snow. I could guess the reason why tin was nailed around the four posts, and why I had to enter the "pantry" with a long ladder. It was built that way to keep out our friends, the wolves and bears. The cache wasn't full: it contained only two cardboard cartons of stuff. There was a 2½ kg bag of whole wheat flour and smaller bags of corn flour, oats, powdered milk, sugar, and powdered mashed potatoes. There were bags of different kinds of beans and a collection of canned vegetables, like corn, peas, and so on. There was also a jar of peanut butter. A fair percentage of it was inedible for a Vaiṣṇava, such as cans of beans with pork and things that were probably considered delicacies, like Brunswick sardines, liverwurst spread, coffee, and cream of mushroom soup. I wasn't sure whether the previous owner had dwindled down the supplies from a larger amount, or whether this cache was left just for people like us who were lost. I didn't even try to imagine how long the food would last. We had no concept of rationing, and so I planned to make a feast to cheer us up.

I made a big mess in the cabin trying to cook, and only a few of my preparations came out edible. I never cooked before, except to help a little, and watch others. My so-called *capātī* dough was all sticky, and when I tried to roll it, it stuck to the rolling pin (a jar) and to my hands. I managed to pound one into shape and put it over the heat, but although I burned the outsides (and also my fingers), the insides of the *capātīs* were raw. So, I gave up on it and turned to other things. This was in full view of Gurudeva, who was lying on the bunk and enduring the pains of his injuries. A few times he sat up and told me something about how to cook. He also smiled as if he were amused.

I figured the easiest thing would be to just boil water and heat things up that way, like steamed vegetables. So, I got some snow from outside and melted it for water and put the pots on the stove. My beans soon boiled furiously. But even after half an hour they were still hard and shriveled up, so they had to be tossed aside. What finally came onto the plate for offering to the Deities was canned corn and string beans which I had not ruined, and surprisingly, a rice which was soft, although a little too soft, and canned pears and canned applesauce, which were impossible for me to ruin (fortunately, the last resident had left a can opener). The peanut butter was also very good. All this was offered to the little Deities which Gurudeva always travels with. He has a small Deity of Gaura-Nitāi and one of Śrīla Prabhupāda and a picture of Rādhā and Kṛṣṇa and one of Nṛsiṁhadeva. I assembled all these on a box and made the offering of prayers.

Although I knew that we could not expect our battery-run tape recorders to last long, I thought it was appropriate to play a lecture tape of Prabhupāda while Gurudeva ate. He asked me to also eat and not wait until he was finished. So, we ate together hearing Śrīla Prabhupāda, who happened to be talking on a verse from *Bhāgavatam* that says if you hear about Kṛṣṇa then your duration of life cannot be taken away by the sun. We both ate quite a bit, and then we were able to sleep, which is one way to ease the trauma of the crash and the desolation of being lost in the mountains.

On the afternoon of our first full day at the cabin, the fuel supply ran out, so I went out with a hatchet to cut down a tree. In one sense, all of this was fun and exciting, like being a Boy Scout again, only this time for the service of *guru* and Kṛṣṇa, rather than for merit badges and scoutmasters. But on another level, it was frightening and hellish, and I would have given anything to have been done with it and back to the world of security and warmth.

I dared not go deep into the woods but went to the edge of the clearing and began working on a small fir tree with the hand ax.

Sasquatch

Whenever I heard the slightest noise, I stopped and looked up, imagining a wolf or bear—or a Sasquatch. My eyes were also overactive. If I looked at a rock or distant tree the wrong way, I suddenly imagined it was a beast. My fears even began to supply imaginary "films" in which a few big wolves came trotting around the bend. I carried the knife at my belt and even took it out and handled it and swung it in the air, as I would have to do if I were attacked. I'm not a physically brave or violent person, and I doubted that I would have the guts for hand-to-hand combat to the death. But if it came to that, I would have to fight rather than be eaten alive. But I thought I probably wouldn't fight well, unfortunately. They say if you're real scared, an animal can tell, and if you run from him, that's even worse. So, in this way, I was nervous and distracted the whole time that I was cutting down the tree and chopping it into logs. It took me hours and it was dark before I finished. When I was carrying the wood back, I saw fresh turds in the snow. And there were dog-like tracks. I was so scared. I decided to tell Gurudeva about it. I didn't want to disturb him by causing unnecessary alarm. Our situation was dangerous enough. But I felt I had to turn to him in my fears.

There was a fireplace, but we decided to burn the fuel in the stove in order to make it last longer. Although it was cold outside, maybe around ten degrees Fahrenheit, at least it wasn't winter. If it had been winter, we might have frozen to death. After I built a fire, I mixed up and heated some powdered milk.

"Gurudeva," I said, "I'm becoming overwhelmed with fears."

Gurudeva sat up on the bunk. "I'm also afraid," he said, "but what can be done? Let us at least turn to Kṛṣṇa with our fear." Gurudeva was wearing an improvised splint for his broken leg. His other leg, where he had cut it, was wrapped in an improvised bandage. With his hands on his wounds, he smiled in a way that comforted me.

"When Arjuna was afraid," said Gurudeva, "Kṛṣṇa didn't exactly tell him his tears or fears were forbidden. But what *was* forbidden was the giving up of duty. Kṛṣṇa told Arjuna to tolerate. In other words, because we're not liberated, we're afraid. Otherwise, Kṛṣṇa wouldn't have to tell us to tolerate, would He? But He knows that we're weak and conditioned, and so He reminds us that everything in this world is temporary and we should tolerate it."

I then confided to Gurudeva my specific fears of the wild animals. Even while we were talking, some animal, either coyote or wolf, started high-pitched howling not far away.

"As far as I know," said Gurudeva very soberly, "they usually won't attack if you leave them alone. But we have to be very cautious. In your case, I think your mind is adding terrors to what is already here. Why add to it?" Gurudeva laughed. "Isn't it fearful enough for you just as it is?" We laughed together and continued sipping our milk. Gurudeva then told some pastimes from the *śāstras* concerning fear. He said that even Kṛṣṇa's father, Nanda Maharaja, was afraid. His fear was for the welfare of Kṛṣṇa, a kind of ecstatic emotion. "But still," said Gurudeva, "the *Kṛṣṇa* book mentions that Nanda was afraid. He was on his way home from Mathura and, based on a warning by his friend Vasudeva, Nanda became afraid that maybe demons were attacking his child."

"You're afraid of this so-called Sasquatch," said Gurudeva, with a glance toward the photo on the wall. "But Nanda had to contend with a *rākṣasī* demon who was twelve miles long and whose only business was to suck the blood of babies. And when Nanda was afraid, what did he do?"

"He began to think very anxiously of Kṛṣṇa," I said.

"And so should we," said Gurudeva. "Very anxiously and prayerfully. Since we've come here, I've been reciting that song,

kṛṣṇa! kṛṣṇa! kṛṣṇa! he

It means, 'Kṛṣṇa please protect me, Kṛṣṇa please save me.' Like that."

Gurudeva asked me to join him in singing the *bhajan* of *kṛṣṇa! kṛṣṇa! kṛṣṇa! he*—We sang it together and then he led into a Hare Kṛṣṇa *kīrtana* which we continued for about half an hour. Gurudeva then sang another song which goes like this:

samāśritā ye pada-pallava-plavaṁ
mahat-padaṁ puṇya-yaśo murāreḥ
bhavāmbudhir vatsa-padaṁ paraṁ padaṁ
padaṁ padaṁ yad vipadāṁ na teṣām

He said the meaning is that the material world is dangerous at every step. But for one who has taken shelter at the fearless lotus feet of Kṛṣṇa, who slays the demon Murāri, the dangerous ocean of birth and death becomes shrunk up to the tiny impression that is made in the earth by the hoof of a calf.

Gurudeva continued talking about Kṛṣṇa as fearless, and about His holy name, of which even fear personified is afraid. I felt pacified and enlivened to hear him speak in this way, and he encouraged me to contribute what I had heard from the scriptures. It was 10 P.M. by the time we stopped and put out the kerosene lamp. I kept on chanting Hare Kṛṣṇa to myself until I fell asleep.

#5: Gurudeva's Journal: Sending Out a Beam

bhajahū re mana śrī-nanda-nandana-
abhaya-caraṇāravinda re

"O mind, please take shelter of the lotus feet of Kṛṣṇa which award fearlessness." If we could do this constantly, there would be no fear.

It's all right if someone actually wants me to serve as his teacher, but he should know who I am. And I should not bluff him.

Why become so hung up? It's the most natural thing in the world that after practicing as Prabhupāda's disciple for twenty-five years I should be able to train newcomers in *how to follow Śrīla Prabhupāda.* But that doesn't make me Prabhupāda. I cannot control what I am within the hearts of those I train up. I can't demand, "Worship me exclusively" or "Don't accept me as a spiritual master." Just teach them how to be a student of Prabhupāda; teach it in words and actions; be absorbed in it and detached from the results.

I used to think that being a guru was a conflict in my mood of worshiping Prabhupāda. That means I was doing something wrong. It's not a conflict. I would think, "At every moment they must see me as perfect and the receiver of their service. But if I'm always a receiver of service, then how can I be a servant? These servants of mine won't let me just serve the guru of my heart!" Much of this has been cleared up by guru reform.

Taking the Lord's Picture

Rādhā-Dāmodara,
if I can remember You
in this far-away place,
the mountains will not freeze me,

and the wolves cannot harm me.
But when I send out my beam
will you accept it?

I focused Your image
in the camera of my mind,
because I *need* You!
But the picture came out faded,
"due to lack of devotion."

I will try again.
There is nothing else.
Please give me suggestions.

Giridhārī

I can see the Coastal Mountains
and I know there must be
a Mountain maker
I have faith
that He will reveal Himself
as the Mountain Lifter
to protect His devotees

March 17

Thinking about our rescue from here is speculation. Maybe *this* will happen, maybe *that*. It's possible that no one will come at all. Then? I'm supposed to be the leader and figure out what to do. But I can't walk far.

The main thing is to maintain (or achieve) Kṛṣṇa consciousness. I can just hear Śrīla Prabhupāda saying, if someone were to tell him about surviving in the wilderness— "Who has survived? No one can survive. This is a bogus idea. First of all, you have to understand that however long you may live you must die. So, what problem will you have solved if you 'survive' *janma-mṛtyu-jarā-vyādhi.*"

March 18

City-slicker vegetarians. Tenderfeet. Untried monks. Fortunate recipients of the highest spiritual knowledge. Poor souls. Unhappy. Blessed.

Lost babes in the woods. Praying men. Connected to the eternal *paramparā* by the mercy of Śrīla Prabhupāda.

Two different souls. Friends. Still trying to learn the beginning lessons.

> "O son of Kuntī, the nonpermanent appearance of happiness and distress, and their disappearance in due course, are like the appearance and disappearance of winter and summer seasons. They arise from sense perception, O scion of Bharata, and one must learn to tolerate them without being disturbed."
>
> —*Bhagavad-gītā* 2.14

Bodies in the mountains, minds wandering the three worlds—souls, "on ice?"

Feet on earth, hearts faltering, "While speaking learned words, you are mourning for what is not worthy of grief. Those who are wise lament neither for the living nor for the dead."

Unwise. Only theorists so far. But belonging to you, Prabhupāda and Kṛṣṇa.

March 19

Built the fire on the evening of this day. "Praised be You, my Lord, through Brother Fire, through whom you light the night, and he is beautiful and playful and robust and strong." I used to think that St. Francis's "You light the night" was quaint and humorous. *Electricity* lights the night, not Brother Fire.

And what is the most important thing we did today? Drank water. Made Bannock, a type of pan bread, for the first time. Ate beans. Evacuated and urinated. Stayed indoors when the wolves howled. Thought a million errant thoughts. The most important thing was chanting the holy names. We did it, me and my "son" Nimāi dāsa. We chanted loud *japa* in this sourdough cabin.

#6: I Discover My Doubts

After one week, we had eaten half of the cache. We had also used up the lamp kerosene and our tape recorder batteries. The firewood was unlimited as long as the hatchet held out, and I counted five hundred matches. But we realized that we very seriously had to ration out things like food and matches and learn as soon as possible how to do things in alternative ways. The weather changed. It was very cold at night but above freezing in the day. We were not so worried. We told each other we would just depend on Kṛṣṇa.

As for the wild animals, I continued to be afraid of them, to think of them, to hear them, and occasionally to see them. I started walking farther away from the cabin to find small trees I could cut down. One sunny day when snow was melting, and the ground was soft I took about a fifteen-minute hike. I was returning, walking down an incline, when I saw less than a hundred yards ahead two black bears passing me from right to left. I said, "Christ!" out loud. This wasn't one of my imaginary "films", and these bears weren't in the zoo. I turned around and started walking quickly up the hill again, although I didn't like going farther away from the cabin. Finally, I came down again, constantly looking around me for signs, but nothing happened and I didn't see any bears again.

Since talking with Gurudeva about fear, I was no longer always in a state of near panic. I noticed that my continual consciousness was less frivolous. I didn't allow myself to fully relax and enjoy different moments but instead I kept awareness that danger could come at any moment. Any little "heaven on earth" I might create could be destroyed in an instant. This thinking helped me to remember to chant more, not just when I was chanting my sixteen prescribed rounds. I thought, "When bad times come, then all you'll have is Kṛṣṇa. And whatever else you have is illusion."

Being in the woods in that condition brought me moments of better clarity and depth than I was used to. Usually, I seem to run around confused and influenced by different people too much. But now many irrelevant things became cleared away. For example, I saw that my relationship with Gurudeva was natural. I was his *brahmacārī* assistant. I did my chores without resentment and looked to him as my spiritual guide. So, then, what was all that stuff I was confused about in Victoria? It didn't seem to matter anymore. In fact, I had to think about it just to remember what it was. One of the issues was whether I had a direct relationship with Śrīla Prabhupāda, or whether anyone was stopping me from that. I could see that my relationship with Prabhupāda was clear and open, and Gurudeva was always inviting me to take it up. No one was in the way between Prabhupāda and me.

After that evening when Gurudeva talked to me about fear and we had a *kīrtana*, I felt more inclined to approach him with things on my mind. He also seemed to welcome it. After all, what else did we have to do except survive together and do our own thinking? But you can only think so much on your own, and then you want to talk with someone else. Although I'm sure I wasn't very elevated company for Gurudeva, yet he still didn't mind my talking, as long as it was Kṛṣṇa conscious.

So, after a few days I told him that I didn't have any more problems about my relationship with him and with Prabhupāda. The reason I brought it up to him was not because I wanted to talk so much about it, but I just wanted him to know that I felt all right. But Gurudeva seemed to have been thinking about it himself, because he began saying humble things about how he wasn't qualified. He said that he personally could not bring me back to Godhead, but Prabhupāda could. And so, he wanted to help me and help himself by depending on the pure devotee. When he spoke like that, I liked him even more and wanted to serve him. Although he was saying that he was unqualified, he wasn't being morbid, or depressing about it. He wasn't artificial. He said, "When there are no big trees, then a castor tree is considered big." That's a saying by Śrīla Prabhupāda. It means that if there is no longer a *mahā-bhagavata* like Śrīla Prabhupāda present, even an "ordinary" devotee will serve as sufficient.

"You are more than sufficient for me," I said.

"That's because you're submissive."

So, I realized that the "guru reform" business really hadn't affected me, and I was glad about that.

But almost immediately after I had expressed my gratitude to Gurudeva, while I was walking towards the woods to cut another tree, Kṛṣṇa suddenly gave me another moment of unusual clarity. It was like He held up a mirror so I could see my own spirituality.

This "clarity" wasn't something wonderful that brought me a vision of Kṛṣṇa in all things. It was just the opposite—I suddenly saw myself as more or less a nondevotee. I still wanted to be a devotee, but I saw that I wasn't one yet. I think what happened was that I clearly sensed how thin and how very recent my spiritual life was and how longstanding was my life of forgetfulness. Something like this is also written somewhere in a purport by Prabhupāda. He says that it is not that we were always devotees. He says that is not to be expected that we are one-hundred percent devotees. Or something like that. We may have very recently become devotees by the grace of a pure devotee, but our being a nondevotee goes back for many lifetimes in different animal species in which our consciousness was never raised above eating, mating, sleeping, and defending. Even in this lifetime, for almost twenty-one years, I had no higher awareness, maybe just sometimes lip service to God, and at other times a definite agnosticism. Even as I write this, I'm not so foolish as to claim, "Now I have higher awareness." But when I was forced to take a closer, unflattering look at myself, removed from the many support systems that make life go smoothly even in a religious institution, I suddenly asked myself, "Do you really believe in God?" And I found I had many doubts. Logically I could have tracked them down, because I *have* been a devotee for a few years. I wasn't happy about this sudden "clarity." I had no intention of "preaching" or advocating that there is no God, but I had reverted to a stage that I thought I had already passed through.

Something like this is described several places in the scriptures. For example, Arjuna said very doubtful things to Kṛṣṇa in the *Bhagavad-gītā*, so that Lord Kṛṣṇa replied, "Arjuna, where are these impurities coming from?" Of course, in Arjuna's case, he was doing it on purpose just so that Kṛṣṇa could teach all mankind and all less intelligent persons by His teaching of Arjuna.

In my case, I wasn't doubting God's existence as much as I was doubting my own convictions. I saw that I was not at all fixed up in even the ABCs of spiritual knowledge, even though I could repeat those ABCs. Śrīla Prabhupāda has described that there are three classes of devotees. The lowest one has not much faith, nor does he understand the scriptures, nor is he able to speak with theological meaning to others. I used to think that I had advanced to the second class of devotee, who is described as possessing good faith and an ability to speak to others. One who is a third-class devotee is advised to move ahead to second class as soon as possible, or else he will soon fall away from the spiritual path. I suddenly saw myself as third class, or less than that. Here I was chopping wood and serving a spiritual master in so many ways, but I didn't really have any conviction. I didn't know what I was doing.

It was shocking to learn this. My fellow devotees in the temples, although they call me names for my eccentric ways, used to concede that I wasn't a bad scholar. If there was a guest, I used to be able to talk to him glibly about Kṛṣṇa consciousness. For example, if some guest to the temple wanted to help me wash dishes in the kitchen, I used to explain to him, "This isn't ordinary work, you know. This is called devotional service, because we're actually serving God even though it looks like we're doing something ordinary." But here I was doing devotional service with less realization than a submissive guest to the temple.

And then another doubt hit me: "Even if there is God, which is most likely, how can we accept the Vedic scriptures' version that Kṛṣṇa is the Supreme Personality of Godhead? He looks like a young boy." Doubts like that "Is Kṛṣṇa really God?"—I had answered years ago when I was a young *bhakta*, either by other devotees or by reading the scriptures. But here it was back again. That meant I never learned it in my heart, or if I did learn it, it was so superficial an understanding that it was torn away in a second. Just as we had to face the rude awakening that we were lost in the mountains, without phones, cars, mail service or nice food, and always on guard for wild animals, so I realized I couldn't count on a profile of myself as a faithful devotee.

But at least I know where to go in this predicament. I thought, "I am definitely going to ask Gurudeva about *this*."

#7: Gurudeva's Journal: Prisoner in a Cave

March 24

N. approached me tonight with doubts in the existence of God. It was late, and I said we could discuss it fully tomorrow. I decided we should start having a daily morning program—rise and attend *maṅgala-ārati* by 4:30 A.M., then chant *japa* together two hours, sing *pūjā* to Prabhupāda, then have a class from *Śrīmad-Bhāgavatam*. I didn't think we would be here indefinitely—and still don't—yet we should live our Vaiṣṇava way as long as we are here. In 1967 Brahmānanda wrote to Śrīla Prabhupāda that the devotees were just about to move from their old temple at 26 Second Avenue to a new address, but that they were also in the process of beautifying the old temple by painting and making improvements. Śrīla Prabhupāda replied that they should go on beautifying the old temple, because even if we are in a place (or in this world) for a short time, our process is to beautify for Kṛṣṇa. Similarly, we should be regulated. Maybe Nimāi wouldn't have been seized with doubts if we had had a regular program of chanting and hearing *Śrīmad-Bhāgavatam.*

Poet Desmond O'Grady asked Śrīla Prabhupāda, "Where does God get His knowledge?" Prabhupāda replied, "First let's ask *what is God*? He's defined as *svarāṭ,* independent. He doesn't 'get' His knowledge from someone else; He's *svarāṭ.*"

Should I prepare notes to talk to N. on the existence of God? Better pray that Kṛṣṇa allow me to convince him and convince myself. N. has heard the answers before, and he actually accepts them, but he wants the *life* of knowledge.

How do broken bones heal themselves? Scientists explain it in bombastic words. It's a *śakti,* an energy given within the living body; dead men's bones don't heal.

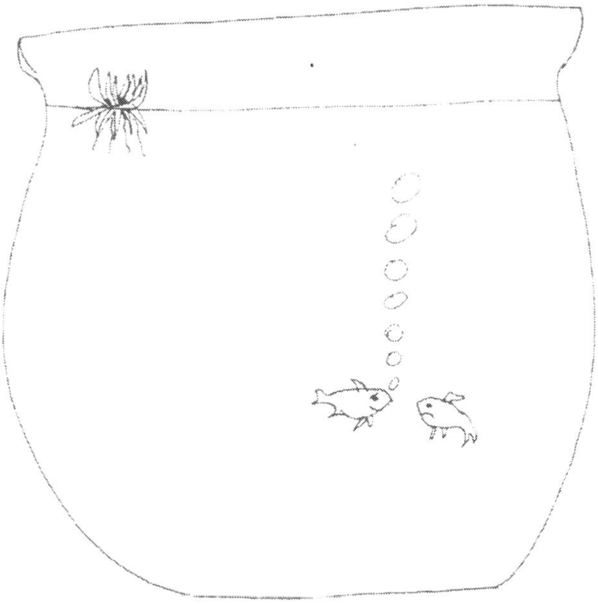

Two little fish in a fish bowl. One says to the other, "Sure I believe in the existence of God. Because, who changes the water?"

Hurt. Sorry. Lost. Lost heart. Kṛṣṇa said to Arjuna, don't be a coward or people will criticize that you are a friend of mine and yet a coward. For one who has honor, infamy is worse than death. Most people think nothing is worse than death. What do *I* think?

I think you should say your prayers and take rest.

March 25, 2:00 A.M.

Good to rise early; good to make this cabin a temple. Improve the altar. Take down Sasquatch and other pictures and put up Kṛṣṇa and Caitanya līlā. Put the animal traps out of sight. I'm somewhat distracted by Nimāi's *japa* which is like "indistinct whirring." I am on my fifth round; Nimāi will be a few ahead of me by now. Why does he pace so heavily with his feet? Maybe I should sleep more. Doctors used to say that I have a bodily constitution which warrants more sleep. How long will we have to stay here? Will we die of starvation?

Swallowing the Forest Fire

His friends look to Him
as a dying man looks at a picture
of the Supreme Personality of Godhead.

They called to Him
across the crackling flames,
"Kṛṣṇa, it's not right
that we should perish like this!"

"Don't worry," He told them, with His eyes.
Then Govinda said to close their eyes
and in less than a moment
He sucked the whole fire
into His mouth.
"Well done! Well done!"
They danced around Him.
It was one of many sports in a day.

All glories to Śrī Kṛṣṇa!
All glories to the spiritual master,
who saves us from the fire
of repeated birth and death!

Saving the Kings from the Cave

20,800 kings
were trapped in a cave
by the demon Jarāsandha.
In the dark for years,
their bodies starved,
their hearts desolate,
their pride smashed.

Śrī Kṛṣṇa killed their tormentor
and came before them.
In the soothing light of His presence,
they bowed and admitted,
"We were proud of our royal opulence,
but now we've been reduced
to prisoners in a cave.
Your rescue and presence are
bliss to our hearts!
We regret our former ways,
please accept us as Your servants.
Give us instructions how to please You,
O redeemer,
who owns the three worlds!"

Lord Kṛṣṇa released them
to return to their kingdoms,
to guide the people
in this world and the next.

Dear Lord,
We too have lost our way
and we call to You.
Give us your assuring presence.
We are proud and unworthy,
but please come and take us back.

#8: Submissive Hearing

In the morning after completing our *japa*. Gurudeva invited me to ask him questions. He was sitting on the bunk, and I sat near him on the floor.

"I don't want to sit so high" he insisted, and so I helped him adjust his legs so that he was sitting on the floor. But then I insisted that he sit on a deerskin mat we had found in the cabin. We joked about that mat, because Vaiṣṇavas usually don't sit on deerskins. *Yogīs* use them in their meditations in the forest, and trappers use them in their own way. But there was nothing else to sit on except the earth.

"So, what are your doubts?" he asked, just as if we were in a normal temple situation.

"Nothing you haven't heard before," I said. "But it's something new to me. Yesterday I suddenly saw that all my God consciousness is theoretical. It's all from the book, with no sign that it's part of me and what I know. Or I only know very little, maybe nothing."

"Maybe that's good," said Gurudeva. As usual, he didn't talk like a know-it-all. He liked to explore questions with you, so that you could find the answers together. But he soon steered things to the Vedic scriptures or something that Prabhupāda had said.

"I don't think *this* is good," I said. "It makes me lose faith in the statements of the *śāstras*. I don't think I have been *truly convinced* yet on basic points. For example, in the *Bhagavad-gītā* Kṛṣṇa says that the self of every person is eternal. But how do I know that? And then He gives an analogy: Just as we pass in one lifetime through different stages or bodies, such as boyhood and youth and old age, so at death the soul passes on to yet another body in a new life. But is the analogy itself proof? And in *Bhagavad-gītā* Kṛṣṇa and Arjuna claim that Kṛṣṇa is the origin of everything, but how do I *know* that? Do you see what I mean?"

"Do you think that Vyāsadeva or Kṛṣṇa are cheating?" Gurudeva asked.

"No, I don't," I said, I don't." It has always been very important for me that great souls, like the Vaiṣṇava *ācāryas* and the sacred teachers in other times and places, like Lord Buddha, or Lord Jesus Christ, actually lived and reached higher consciousness. I never thought that they were cheaters or bluffers, and I resent it when people deride them or psychoanalyze them in mundane ways.

"It's probably not logical," I said, "but I can believe in great souls and in the scriptures on one hand and yet still have a strong voice within me of total doubt."

"Why?" Gurudeva asked.

"I don't know," I said. "Maybe I'm affected by all the skepticism and science that I've been exposed to."

"In other words," said Gurudeva, "you're a conditioned soul. We all are. And as long as we're conditioned, we'll have some kind of doubts, big or small. I do also. So, let's accept that it's not unusual to have some doubts. And accept also that they're not magically going to go away all at once. It's like the bears. We can't *wish* them away. But we don't have to be so petrified that we can't live our own life."

I sensed that Gurudeva was going to be able to help me with this problem. And I think we both knew that it was important. If he and I could talk openly, and if we could succeed in this, we could really overcome anything, including whatever might happen in the mountains.

"Why is it Gurudeva," I asked, "that I can't have these questions answered once and for all? Why does it seem we have to keep learning them over and over?"

"Because we're dull and our will is weak," said Gurudeva. "So *māyā* moves in. But so what if we have to go on hearing and hearing? As long as we have enough sense not to stop hearing guru, *śāstra*, and *sādhu*."

"Okay, but what about my questions? If for me the truth about the soul and the next life, and the truth about God is all in the books and not in my heart or head, then should I just admit that I'm an agnostic?"

"No," said Gurudeva, "Prabhupāda used to consider an agnostic more or less like an atheist. Atheists deny the scriptures; they think they are ordinary books and that the saints and sages are more or less deluded. Is that what you think?"

"No Gurudeva. I accept the existence of elevated souls."

"You *say* that, but why? Why do you believe in them?"

I wasn't sure what to say, but when I paused, Gurudeva continued.

"You accept them because, although you don't know anything yet for yourself, you have been shown God consciousness by them. For example, in my case, my ultimate point of reference is Śrīla Prabhupāda. Prabhupāda represents the *paramparā* teachings, and he is the form in which those teachings came to me and touched me. He's my standard. Whatever I have heard, before or since, which attacks or tries to undermine the God consciousness that Prabhupāda taught and exemplified, does not shake me. I reject it. Prabhupāda is a pure devotee of Kṛṣṇa, and he has created in me the desire to also become a devotee."

"But," I said, "what if someone says that they want objective knowledge. Prabhupāda may be dedicated to Kṛṣṇa, and you're dedicated to Prabhupāda. But where's a proof that everyone can examine for themselves?"

"All right, I'll tell you what Śrīla Prabhupāda says." Whenever Gurudeva thought a challenge was serious, he replied by taking his position as a disciple of his spiritual master. That way he would not bluff anyone, but neither would he get defeated by staying on unsure ground.

"Knowledge about the soul and God," said Gurudeva, "is scientific and open for inspection. But in order to inspect it, you have to become qualified yourself, just as a science student has to become qualified by the austerities of study and practice before he can know for himself the secrets of his science. In fact, no one can judge the science of God except those who actually study it thoroughly."

"With the science of Kṛṣṇa consciousness," Gurudeva continued, "the proof is beyond mental speculation or examination by the senses. That's the big stumbling block for everyone who's a materialist. They refuse to think there's knowledge beyond their senses. But there is. So, when you say, 'How can you prove the soul?', we reply that it's proved by the statement of the scripture, and it's proved by the statement of the Supreme Personality of Godhead. You already know this—it is called *śabda-brahma*—knowledge received by hearing from authority. There's no way to fully understand the soul and God unless you accept bona fide scriptures, and if you then practice their teachings yourself, you gain direct realization. You can't reject hearing from God and at the same time know Him in truth. Prabhupāda would give the example, if a child wants to know who his father is, he has to accept the word of his mother. She's the authority on that subject, and the child has to hear from her. You can't know God by yourself, by the inductive process."

"Is it wrong," I asked Gurudeva "if at every step I feel within myself that I have a choice to either accept faithfully what you say or reject it?"

"No, that's not wrong," said Gurudeva. "This isn't brainwashing. Why should it be threatening to your faith if at every moment you accept what's being said by free choice? But you reach a point where you begin to accept the basic elements of the science. That should never become mechanical for us, because then we get cut off from the root or the very reason why we took to spiritual life in the first place. Doubt is a sign of intelligence, in the beginning. But you can't be doubtful all the time. Still, you should know how and why you overcame those doubts. Then if you have to, you can repeat the reasoning again and again. But eventually you should get a feeling of triumph over the doubts. They're like rascals that you've defeated, so even if they pop up again, you can take the sword of knowledge, as Kṛṣṇa told Arjuna, and kill them. Remember that statement by Lord Kṛṣṇa?"

I tried to quote from memory but fumbled. So I reached for the *Bhagavad-gītā*, turned to the last two verses in the fourth chapter, and started reading out loud.

> One who acts in devotional service, renouncing the fruits of his actions, and whose doubts have been destroyed by transcendental knowledge, is situated factually in the self. Thus, he is not bound by the reactions of work, O conqueror of riches. Therefore, the doubts which have arisen in your heart out of ignorance should be slashed by the weapon of knowledge. Armed with yoga, O Bhārata, stand and fight.
>
> —*Bhagavad-gītā, 4.41–42*

"Is it clearing up?" Gurudeva asked.

"Yes," I said, "but I have more questions." Gurudeva laughed. I knew that he didn't want to go on unendingly if it meant I wouldn't carefully think over what he had already said. But I needed to ask my questions personally. It wasn't enough to just look up "doubt" in the index to Prabhupāda's books. I had to know *why* I should look at the books and believe in them in the first place. I had to hear it from my teacher. Someone who knew me had to catch my rascal mind and remind me of my inclination to accept saintly persons and scriptures and then test me as to why I have that inclination.

"How can we tell," I asked, "if a person is actually in higher spiritual consciousness, and how can we tell that a book, such as *Bhagavad-gītā*, is the absolute truth?"

"There are symptoms for a saintly person," said Gurudeva. "First there are brahminical symptoms like sense control, peacefulness, cleanliness, simplicity, non-duplicity, and religiousness. Beyond that you have to receive the seed of devotion in your heart from someone who is himself a genuine devotee of God, of Kṛṣṇa. Arjuna asked a question similar to yours. Kṛṣṇa told him that a person in higher consciousness doesn't lament over life or death. So Arjuna asked, what is a transcendentalist like? How does he sit and walk? How does he talk? Kṛṣṇa replied that the saintly person understands that he's not the body, therefore he's detached from material happiness and grief. Then later Kṛṣṇa said that to be a qualified person you have to receive the knowledge from a spiritual master in the disciplic succession. When you find a person with all these qualifications, he's a saintly person."

"And the books?" I asked, "How do you know they're perfect?"

Gurudeva replied, "Our acceptance of the books is axiomatic."

"Is that reasonable, Gurudeva?"

"Yes, because the scriptures have been accepted by great authorities of all different schools, and by empiric experience we often find that what the *Vedas* say is true. For example, the *Vedas* say cow dung is pure although they also say stool is impure. So a prominent doctor examined cow dung in the laboratory and found that it has all antiseptic properties. Furthermore, the *Vedas* offer detailed reasonable explanations for phenomena that no other source so adequately explains. If you don't accept the *Vedas*, you have no alternative way to know."

"There's also a statement in the *Mahābhārata*, that things which are inconceivable, such as God, cannot be reached by ordinary logic. We have to approach a realized devotee, a *mahājana*, who has received the knowledge from guru, *śāstra* and *sādhu*."

"I feel better," I said. "I think I've licked my first problem. I have more questions, but should I save them?"

"Yes," said Gurudeva. "Why don't you think over what we said and write it down for yourself. Now we should follow our schedule of other duties."

Gurudeva seemed enlivened by our talk, as if he had been lecturing to a larger audience in an important place. I was also enlivened. We both realized that *kṛṣṇa-katha*, talks about Lord Kṛṣṇa, could overcome all our problems.

#9: Gurudeva's Journal: Turning Inward

March 28

We've been here two weeks. I calculated that if we eat a minimum ration of cache food, we have two more weeks' supply. We have to immediately start finding (and trying to eat) food from nature. It's also my duty in devotional service to think how to be rescued, so that we can join the Movement in our regular service. But since I conclude that there's no use in trying to hike aimlessly (and neither *can* I do it yet), it's my Kṛṣṇa conscious duty to figure out how to live on here, even if that means I have to spend my energy thinking like an animal. Food seems to be the main problem. Prabhupāda says it's no problem: No one should starve to death; it's only the humans who mismanage. So, what are the birds and animals eating?

But I can't think only about how to eat. Śrīla Prabhupāda said the people in India accepted famine, although arranged by the British, as ultimately due to karma and providence. An American visitor to India said, "In our country there would have been riots." Prabhupāda said that the Vedic culture was so nice that people would die of starvation and accept it.

He Was Never Lost

At 70 years of age, entering Manhattan
with no money or home,
only the address of a Māyāvādī *yogī*.
Crossing the street
Against horns and sirens,
to room 307—
His property was stolen.
Moving to the Bowery,

he saw every place
as Kṛṣṇa's mercy.
Kept going.
Another month alone.
No one wanted to hear
talk about Kṛṣṇa.
Just for Lord Kṛṣṇa and Bhaktisiddhānta Sarasvatī,
he recorded *Gītopaniṣad.*
A year later
Kṛṣṇa sent some boys,
and the Movement started.
He was never lost.

This diary is a good place to consider my service to Prabhupāda's Movement. What was I doing before coming here, and what do I intend to do when I get out? I have to think how to maintain the body, but my deeper concern is to maintain the spirit. Let me review it.

After our Society made the changes in guruship, I turned more inward. Since I had been guilty of excesses (imitation of Prabhupāda), I thought I ought not merely "repent," but learn to depend on Kṛṣṇa so I don't fall into excesses again. I decided that too much superficial activism had contributed to my becoming proud of my position. So, I became more interested in prayer. I stopped initiating disciples for a while and dropped leadership in some of the projects I was managing.

This led me to associate with Bhānu dāsa, with whom I shared my thoughts about inner life. We both had collections of statements by Prabhupāda on prayer and constant thinking of Kṛṣṇa. I shared mine with him. He helped me also to see how I had become puffed up by accepting the praise of others, especially my disciples. And he helped me become aware that *we need Kṛṣṇa constantly*; we are helpless without Him. We also found benefit in reading a few of the best Christian mystics on prayer.

That led to my taking time to practice prayer and my trying again to overcome inattentive *japa*. I began "conversing" with Śrīla Prabhupāda and Lord Kṛṣṇa during the day, even while doing "little" things. I spent two weeks in Ireland, with only one other devotee, practicing prayer, and I compiled prayers and my own reflections on them but hesitated to share them with devotees.

I want to print my manuscript, *Seeds for Prayer.* I think it could help our Movement. Although our Movement has corrected itself from the gross egotism of us *guru* leaders and others, there's something superficial in devotees' dealings and in much that goes on in temple life. My hope is that by sharing my own direct cultivation of prayer, to Kṛṣṇa and Śrīla Prabhupāda, it will be a kind of preaching. The inner life is very important. So, I should appreciate it and encourage myself that it's not selfish. I want to bring to the Movement something which I feel is lacking in myself at least.

But I'm afraid they may say I'm too reclusive, a *bābājī.* Śrīla Prabhupāda and his spiritual master Bhaktisiddhānta Sarasvati wrote that one shouldn't attempt to chant Hare Kṛṣṇa in a secluded place in imitation of Haridāsa Ṭhākura. One should work laboriously for the spiritual master and try to spend this mission for helping others.

Another hesitation: When praying to Kṛṣṇa I think, "This is me, this is my personal expression of Kṛṣṇa consciousness." But that might be a self-deception. We're advised—as Kṛṣṇa advised Arjuna—to sometimes change our personal view in favor of what Kṛṣṇa wants. It is difficult always to know what to do and to do it. If I asked three different leading Godbrothers what I should do, each might tell me something different.

March 29

I know what my *Seeds for Prayer* is. It's the beginning of a way of life. If I *want* to keep it up, it will take long commitment and hard work. Do I want to?

The mountain fades in a mist,
and sometimes it's visible,
with crevices, trees, and snow.
Like that is my yearning.
But when I slipped and fell.
He was there.

#10: Krishna, the Supreme Personality of Godhead

There was a wooden chest just outside the front door. It was used to store kindling for the fireplace. I suggested that Gurudeva might like to sit on the chest a few hours a day, around noon, when it was sunny and warm enough to be outside. He took to it and started spending part of every day on the "front porch." I would join him sometimes, sitting at his feet, and we'd both look out at the wilderness.

Often it was windy, and when we were quiet, you could hear the pines and watch the nearby trees move their branches. Of all the creatures in the woods, the ones we saw the most of were the Canadian blue jays. I was used to seeing northeastern blue jays, which are bright, light blue with white in their feathers. These birds were a deeper blue and had black heads and pointy black tufts. Their cry was like other blue jays, just a bit more musical than a crow. The reason they came around was that I would leave out remnants of food. They would swoop down and take the grains and then call loudly to each other. Sometimes six or eight would come around at once, and they would do wild things, like bump into the sides of the cabin or sometimes peck at it just like a woodpecker does.

Gurudeva had learned from Prabhupāda to observe Kṛṣṇa in nature, and he did it often. He quoted Bhaktivinoda Ṭhākura, that nature was like a book which can show you the spiritual world. Gurudeva said that the jays were "stout and strong," and not because of the extra handouts that we were giving them. Their food was supplied by nature, and nature, he said, is under the control of God. Every creature in nature has its own food supply, with no question of shortage or starvation. "But the human being," said Gurudeva, "has developed such bizarre and demoniac tastes that he needs to have his food imported by planes and trucks from all over the world, or else he thinks he'll starve to death."

Our cabin was situated on a small hill which led into the valley where the plane had crashed. Straight ahead from our front door was the face of a big mountain.

Mountain view from window

Over the weeks, Gurudeva said different things about the mountain. He said that, according to Prabhupāda, a mountain has a soul. The proof of the presence of the soul is that a body goes through six stages of life; it's born, it grows, it gives off by-products, it has a certain life duration, it dwindles, and it dies. So, a mountain goes through those stages also. For example, it gives off by-products, like minerals. The Vedic scriptures state that some mountains can even fly, and maybe the ones that we are seeing have landed. Mountains are also mentioned in the *Bhagavad-gītā.* Lord Kṛṣṇa said, "Of immovable things, I am the Himalayas." By appreciating the essential quality of a mountain, you can see Lord Kṛṣṇa, the Immovable.

These talks were good for me to hear, especially because they helped me overcome my so-called doubts about the existence of God. Whatever further doubts I had, Gurudeva continued to clear them up by talking with me. He gave examples that he personally heard from Prabhupāda. Prabhupāda would very often quote a verse from the *Upaniṣads,*

nityo nityānāṁ cetanaś cetanānām
eko bahūnāṁ yo vidadhāti kāmān

This means that each of us is an eternal spirit soul, a person, and the Supreme Being, God, is also an eternal person. But the difference between us and "that One", the Supreme, is that He is supplying the needs of all the other living entities. Mankind doesn't supply the needs of the blue jays or the bears and wolves, the ants, or the elephants. But God supplies—for mankind also.

When Gurudeva spoke his appreciations and convictions of God, he used the words "God" and "Kṛṣṇa" interchangeably. But this was another doubt that had hit me in my "clarity." When I had faced the fact that I was really not a devotee, one of my doubts was then even if there is a God, the Supreme Being, how can we be sure that Śrī Kṛṣṇa is God? My doubt didn't come with a full set of atheistic or anti-Kṛṣṇa arguments. It came more like a sudden drop or loss. The arguments came afterwards. So, one day while sitting together outside the cabin, I explained to Gurudeva my doubts about Kṛṣṇa.

"Gurudeva," I said, "the other week I expressed to you my doubts about God, and you helped me very much. But I didn't ask my question why Kṛṣṇa is God. How can we exclusively accept Kṛṣṇa as the Supreme Being? I remember in high school I once read a book by Carl Jung, who observed that religions have similar elements. So, it seems simplistic to say that only Kṛṣṇa is God. Or do we say that? Maybe I'm revealing my impersonal tendency, because sometimes when I doubt Kṛṣṇa, I also think, 'How could this boy Kṛṣṇa be the Supreme Controller, Maintainer, and Destroyer, as well as the source of the impersonal eternal Brahman?'"

"That's quite a mouthful of doubt," said Gurudeva.

I don't think I would have dared to ask such doubts in front of other devotees, or even of Gurudeva before we had landed in the mountains. But you *should* be able to ask your guru about your real doubts. Neither was I trying to raise some intellectual opposition. I wasn't playing a game.

"First of all," Gurudeva replied, "because we say that God is Kṛṣṇa, doesn't mean we reject other theistic versions of God or other names for God. The first thing is to actually understand God consciousness and to approach it in a nonsectarian way. You can't be prejudiced beforehand that Kṛṣṇa can't be God, or that another name for the Supreme is the only name of God."

"Yes," I said, "but why should God look like a cowherd boy?"

"You're jumping way ahead," said Gurudeva. "God can be many things. He can be anything. But before we think about Kṛṣṇa, His pastimes, His forms and how He's a person with inconceivable energies and so on, we should first consider Kṛṣṇa's teachings of God consciousness. Prabhupāda never liked it when even so-called believers in Kṛṣṇa wanted to jump ahead and just talk about Kṛṣṇa's dancing with the *gopīs*. Neither should you reject Him because you heard someone say, 'He's a cowherd boy.' First, study His *Bhagavad-gītā*."

"A person who is Kṛṣṇa conscious has to be fixed in the basics. For example, when Sanātana Gosvāmī approached Lord Caitanya, Sanātana said, 'People in my neighborhood call me a *paṇḍita,* but I don't even know the basic truth. I don't know my destination and what is good for me.' So, when you inquire about Kṛṣṇa consciousness, rather than just start talking about advanced pastimes of Kṛṣṇa, which you don't really understand, you should ask yourself, 'Why am I suffering? Where have I come from? Where am I going next life? What is God? What is my relationship with God?' But although people claim to be advanced in transcendental and spiritual life, if you ask them these basic questions, they don't know the answers. So, if we want to see how good Kṛṣṇa is, let's go to Him with these basic questions. Let's approach Kṛṣṇa as *jagad-guru.* Kṛṣṇa spoke the *Bhagavad-gītā.* In His book He teaches everything about the science of God in a way similar to other scriptures, but He also gives information that is not found in the others."

While Gurudeva was speaking, the wind was picking up, moving the pines, and making that deep wind-sound. He was taking his time answering, choosing his words, and I was also patiently hearing. It was nice being alone in the wilderness and hearing about Kṛṣṇa in a gradual way.

"You've asked why Kṛṣṇa is God," said Gurudeva, "so I'll answer in that way. But it's interesting that when Kṛṣṇa taught Arjuna, he first started explaining about the nature of the individual soul and transmigration of the soul. Only later did He describe the Supreme Person. What we call God, which is an English word, is explained in *Śrīmad-Bhāgavatam* by the word Bhagavān. In one verse it's stated that there are three aspects of the Absolute Truth. One is the impersonal all-pervading aspect, which is called Brahman. The other is God in the heart, called Paramātmā, as perceived by the *yogīs* in meditation. And the other aspect is Bhagavān, or God, the Supreme Personality of Godhead. All three of these are different ways of looking at the one Absolute Truth. So, we don't say that only Bhagavān is the Absolute Truth, because the other aspects are also, and so are the other incarnations. Other religions point to the Absolute Truth in one form or another, but according to *Śrīmad-Bhāgavatam* and *Bhagavad-gītā*, Bhagavān is the highest manifestation of the Absolute Truth. The other manifestations give eternality, or they manifest all knowledge, but only in Bhagavān do you get *sac-cid-ānanda-vigraha*, or eternality, knowledge, and the bliss of loving exchanges from Him."

"I think I agree," I said, "that Kṛṣṇa and the Vedic literatures are the best teachers of the science of God. But because He's our best teacher, does that mean Kṛṣṇa's God?"

"Kṛṣṇa is a name to describe Him," said Gurudeva. "It means all-attractive. God must be all-attractive. But who qualifies to be God or Kṛṣṇa, the All-Attractive One? All the *Vedas* say that Bhagavān appears in different incarnations and has different names. They're all called Viṣṇu. But among all the forms of Viṣṇu, the original form is Śrī Kṛṣṇa. And if you study Him, He has the all-attractive qualities of the original

Personality of Godhead. To study Kṛṣṇa is an unlimited science. I don't think it's wrong or terrible if you say, 'I don't know Kṛṣṇa yet,' because even the greatest sages and devotees don't claim they know Kṛṣṇa in full. But when you just pop off and say, 'Kṛṣṇa can't be God, He's a cowherd boy,' then this is a foolish doubt, and it's based on ignorance of the science of Kṛṣṇa. Better you admit you don't know Kṛṣṇa, but hear from the scriptures and the spiritual master about Kṛṣṇa. Knowing Kṛṣṇa and fully surrendering to Kṛṣṇa are not so easy."

"So Gurudeva?" I asked. "May I ask you something else? This may sound like I'm changing the subject, but I'm not. I wanted to ask you about Jesus Christ in relation to Kṛṣṇa. Because when I suddenly realized that I'm not even a devotee of God, and then when I had this doubt about Kṛṣṇa, it also took the form of a challenge like, 'Anyway if there is God, why not see Him as Christ, as so many others do in the West? Why take an Indian God? That's how it hit me. And I guess I have sentiment for Christ."

"There's no contradiction between Christ consciousness and Kṛṣṇa consciousness," said Gurudeva. "One time someone asked Prabhupāda about Christ and he replied, 'Christ is Kṛṣṇa consciousness, that's all. So, you become like Christ, Kṛṣṇa conscious.' Another time Prabhupāda was praising the Vaiṣṇavas because they're not only interested in their own spiritual welfare but in helping others and he said, 'Try to liberate all conditioned souls. Just like Jesus Christ. For himself he was the son of God, and so he has nothing to do. He was already perfectly God conscious. He knows everything. But then why was he crucified? Because he wanted to work for others.' And Prabhupāda said, 'This is Vaiṣṇavism.'"

But He's the *son* of God?" I said. "Kṛṣṇa is the Father?"

"Yes. And the Father and son are one in quality. If the theologies or incarnations seem to be saying something different, it's because religion is taught differently according to time, persons and place. The essence is the same, to know God, and render Him loving service, to go back to Godhead."

I had many more things to ask, but I didn't want to push my luck. I wanted to fill myself up with whatever Gurudeva could impart to me. And I felt that I was receiving deeply whatever he said. If I could just keep asking questions in this mood of exchange, whatever I heard would do me long-term or permanent good. Even though his answers were satisfying, they led me to more questions. But I decided to stop.

After I had asked my last questions, I thought that Gurudeva didn't want to talk more and that he would suggest we take up our other duties. But he continued to sit with me. And although he was silent, I sensed that he wanted to say something. We both chanted *japa* for a few minutes as the sky darkened, and the clouds caught the last effulgence of the setting sun.

"Nimāi," said Gurudeva, "may I ask you something?"

"Sure."

"It's something personal about my own service. I have some doubt, and I wanted to consult someone."

When Gurudeva said that I couldn't think of anything intelligent to say, and so I stayed silent. I wanted to serve him.

"You're aware of how I've been trying to practice prayer in recent months, and how I've been talking about it?"

"Yeah, I think it's great."

Gurudeva smiled. He said, "Do you? I'm feeling a little unsure about it. On the one had it's like an important discovery or breakthrough for me. And I would like to print my book on prayer, *Seeds of Prayer*. But sometimes I think I might get criticized by some devotees."

"Oh, Gurudeva, you should print that book!" I said. This was something I was enthusiastic about, and I couldn't help but show it.

"Your practice and your talking about prayer are just what our Movement needs," I said. "With all different controversies and fall downs of leaders, people are looking to an example of a saintly person. Some of the devotees that I've talked to really like it when you talk about how we should always think of Kṛṣṇa and always pray to Kṛṣṇa. You yourself have said that somebody will always criticize no matter what you do."

"That's true," he said, "but aside from what others might say, I'm trying to think within myself whether it's right, whether it'll be pleasing to Prabhupāda and help the preaching. I don't want to make one of these cheap presentations, like people who say they are always talking to God or Jesus, and yet they themselves are nonsense."

"But what you're doing isn't cheap," I said, "you're showing and telling us what many of us have missed. Prabhupāda was always thinking of Kṛṣṇa, and he and Kṛṣṇa want us to practice it. It's so easy for us to just get swept away in our passionate activities and to forget what we're doing it for."

This was a favorite subject of mine, Gurudeva's absorption in prayer. It enthused me, and I could tell that it enthused him. I figured that Gurudeva knew what he wanted to do, but maybe he was using me as a sounding board for his ideas. I felt sorry that he had no one to actually consult with but me, with all my offenses and doubts. But at least I meant what I said. I loved to hear Gurudeva talk of an inner life and how we should be always praying to Kṛṣṇa.

#11: Gurudeva's Journal: Seeds of Prayer

April 5

Nimāi's encouragement for my practice of prayer was helpful. He said that the devotees would benefit from *Seeds of Prayer*. So, whenever we get out of here, I intend to print it in a limited edition and distribute it to those who are interested. Aside from printing a book about prayer, I want to *do* it. As Nārada prays in the *KṚṢṆA* book:

> "My dear Lord, You have kindly asked me what you can do for me. In answer to this I must simply request that I may not forget Your lotus feet at any time. I do not care where I may be, but I pray that I constantly be allowed to remember Your lotus feet.

My thinking and speaking to Lord Kṛṣṇa and Śrīla Prabhupāda waned in recent months, but since coming here they have increased. I see that I am *mainly* praying to He who will protect me from material danger, death, attack, panic, pain, and further worldly adversities. This world remains very real to me, and I'm afraid to be lost in the wilderness. This is the lowest form of prayer and devotion. "Those who when they are in distress, and in need of money . . . turn to Me," are declared by Kṛṣṇa to be pious but materialistic. And yet that's where I am at. I'm grateful too, because just as the world is real and fearful to me, so my prayer for protection is also real and fervent. The more threatened I feel the more fervently I pray and feel intimately within the Lord's presence. It's a bit amusing in an ironic way that as a supposed *guru* and follower on the path of pure, unmotivated love of God I—who have often lectured against "cheating religionists" who pray for daily bread—find myself down on my knees before Lord Nṛsiṁha saying, "Please protect me, I am afraid." The howls of the wolves turn my thoughts to Kṛṣṇa. My lack of higher religious attainment is exposed. Great devotees, like Lord Caitanya or Śrīla Prabhupāda, were in the highest stages of pure devotion, *desiring always to please Kṛṣṇa,* even when they were in danger.

Prayer

My dear Lord Kṛṣṇa, I try to avoid You
when fetching water
or starting another wood fire
and while sweeping the floor again.
These common acts I know,
are *bhakti*,
when done as personal service to You.

To think of You
when I chant Your names
is harder for me.
I'd rather bow down
to start the fire
than to place my head at Your lotus feet.

I worship *whatever* connection
You will allow me—
I'll go on sweeping the dust for You
and throwing it out the door
and surveying the diminishing food stores,
making plans to be "rescued,"
sleeping, evacuating,
and bathing this body of mine.
But I know these are not enough.

When I boil the water
and put on the rice
while mainly thinking of food that pleases me, it's stretching it a bit to say
"I'm preparing this *bhoga* for You."

And when I gaze at our local Himalaya
I'm just a common man, not a mystic.
But I am confident
that You, who are known as Janārdana,
will find some specks of devotion in my acts,
and You'll accept them in Vaikuṇṭha,
where I'm storing up my credits
for my ultimate return.

But Lord, when the little bird

tried to empty the ocean
by taking water in her beak,
You saw it was impossible,
and so You sent Garuḍa
to finish the task.

I wonder,
what will you do with me?
I'm sure you have a plan
to deliver slowpokes.
Please allow me
to take my eternal part
in Your blissful pastimes.

April 8

I'm thinking in a general way of my disciples. Usually, I hear from them by mail. By now there must be a few dozen letters waiting for me somewhere. Some people are wondering where I am. "Maybe he took a retreat, like that time in Ireland when we did not know where he was for two weeks, or like when he's traveling in India." They needn't be alarmed.

Some disciples couldn't care less. I've initiated over six-hundred, and dozens of them no longer practice the rules and regulations or think much of me. They dropped me, and I dropped them. But you still occasionally think of people from your past life: "that person I accepted as my *guru*" or "that person I accepted as my disciple to deliver back to Godhead." Some who write me occasionally may be disturbed if I don't show up for months, and some will become seriously concerned. But their lives will go on, and according to how they approach Lord Kṛṣṇa, He will reciprocate with them. I am not indispensable.

I say these things not without jealousy, a desire to be loved. And I feel some resentment and hurt towards those who have resisted my offers to help. Why don't they give me their attention? After all, we vowed and agreed to function as guru and *śiṣya.* Did I really disappoint them so much, or was it their own reawakening of material desires? Even if they had material desires, why didn't I deliver them from agitations by bathing them in divine love? Why didn't I give them a higher taste of Kṛṣṇa consciousness? And if I can't do that, why did I accept so many "disciples" in the first place? When an ex-disciple said, "You let me down; I couldn't follow you as a guru," is that the truth that hurts, or am I justified to think, "they are just not serious?"

Mail for me piles up somewhere, letters from disciples and a few from Godbrothers. Maybe I've been appointed to some editorial committee, maybe someone wants my opinion. A few steady correspondents will wait for our on-going friendly exchanges. And the book publishers who have my name on their lists will automatically send me catalogs and wait to see if I am still a "live one." Newsletters will pile up, as will "free offers" and first letters from persons writing from faraway places. The Pan Am World Pass has probably written to inform me, "Your opportunity for a free ticket is running out. Contact us today for your free offer." My subscription to *World Press* has already run out.

But although I am functioning here with at least one disciple who is sincere and in need of my services, and who appreciates what I can give him, maybe that is my speed, just one disciple. And if, as they sometimes say it's the example that counts, then I'm continuing at least in basic operations, even though I am "lost." I'm chanting and teaching a disciple. By teaching one can I teach all by example? That's why I'd like to print *Seeds of Prayer,* to share with them.

April 9

Because Nimāi is sincere I should sincerely connect him to Prabhupāda. Because he has some faith in me, I shouldn't think, "Oh, he's my disciple." Spiritual life is meant to conquer repeated birth and death. If one assumes to be guru and actually cheats his disciples, he goes to the world of the faithless, full of darkness and ignorance, and his followers go with him. So bring him to Prabhupāda.

April 11

Today the food supply runs out.

#12: Controlling the Tongue

Now I have to do some confessing. I admitted that I have trouble controlling my mind. But as you probably know, if your mind is agitated, it usually means your senses are also. I have trouble controlling my tongue, and sometimes I become sexually agitated, although I don't usually break the regulative principles. I know many people who have been initiated who have that trouble, but I'm not trying to make an excuse. Also, I'm only twenty-four years old, but that's not an excuse either. Once in a while I've had bad dreams, you know. But nothing deliberate. You might think that being stranded in the mountains would be conducive to less sexual agitation. *Yogīs* leave the city and come to the mountains just to get away from all that. Yet I've also heard that if someone's mind and senses aren't controlled, it doesn't matter if he lives alone and practices meditation in a cave, he will still be plagued by the pushes of the serpent-like senses. Well, it's true.

In my case I think it was a reaction from offensive thoughts toward my spiritual master, and from lying to him and cheating. That's another thing you hear about and you may doubt—that you suffer from offenses to Vaiṣṇavas. It's clearly stated in the scriptures that insults to a Vaiṣṇava are comparable to what a mad elephant will do when he charges into your garden. It's called Vaiṣṇava *aparādha,* and it uproots the creepers of *bhakti.* I had read about *aparādhas,* but it seemed esoteric. Now I know. You do suffer from blaspheming devotees. And one way you suffer, if you're trying to be a *brahmacārī,* is that you find your material desires increase. And there's only one way to get release if your problem is due to insults. You have to go to that person whom you insulted and beg forgiveness. Anyway, I became so agitated in the mountains that I was having dreams, and one time I even committed deliberate self-abuse.

So, I went to Gurudeva to confess it and ask forgiveness. This was about month after we'd been in the mountains.

Gurudeva said, "I thought so. I could see that you were morose the last two days." Gurudeva minimized and overlooked that I had said it was because of my offenses to him. He just wanted to help me overcome the problem, and so he mostly talked about that. But because he knew, of course, that I had committed offenses to him and that I was suffering from them, he looked me in the eyes gently and said, "I forgive you."

"You have a problem controlling your tongue, don't you?" he said.

"Yes, Gurudeva."

"You've also been filching from the cache," he said.

"Yes, Gurudeva."

When Gurudeva is heavy, he's actually gentle. He doesn't have to shout or slam things. He was also sympathetic about my tongue. He said that I had been working much harder physically than he had, and so I needed more food. But in rationing, he had given me twice as much as himself.

"Are you hungry?" he asked.

"Not really, it's my tongue." I hadn't thought that he had noticed that I had stolen things, because I did it like a mouse by just tearing off bits of bannock and peanut butter. But he knew.

"The senses are in a straight line," he said. "Tongue, belly, and genitals. If you don't control the tongue, and then overload your belly, you'll also be more sexually inclined." I had heard that before, but I had never heard it so relevantly applied. To tell the truth, I liked being chastised by Gurudeva, because I knew it was for my good. Everyone should be so lucky to be caught and chastised by his guru. But I was also ashamed and embarrassed. Then he lectured to me in a personal way about illicit sex.

"According to Prabhupāda," he said, "to overcome Mr. Lust, you should chant Hare Kṛṣṇa more. And you may also take more to Deity worship." Once Prabhupāda wrote to a person who was sexually agitated, "Either you can perform devotional service twenty-four hours a day and think of Kṛṣṇa and that will save you, or else you should get married. But don't practice immoral sex. Immoral sex and spiritual life don't go together."

Gurudeva then gave some practical advice how to avoid self-abuse. He was not sympathetic about it, as he was with my tongue. I mean he was sympathetic with *me*, but not with the act. He said it's a deliberate act of misbehavior. He told me not to do it anymore. He said that I should become very carefully aware of my actions leading up to such immoral acts. I should not allow myself to take even the first steps in my mind. He explains that everything happens according to three stages, first thinking, then feeling, and then willing. So, he advised me to be on the alert, because it's a serious mistake to break the four regulative principles. As soon as I think of doing such a thing, I should stop my deliberate plans or get away from that place or do whatever I have to do to avoid going further into the feeling and willing stages. I can honestly say that what Gurudeva said on this occasion has been very effective for me.

After being stern for a while, Gurudeva relaxed and smiled. Something seemed to amuse him. He said, "Anyway, it looks like we're both going to be in for some austerities for a while. We'll *have* to control our tongues because there's no more food."

Gurudeva explained fasting. He said that it was important that we found some weeds or plant or berries to eat, but that we could expect to eat a lot less. He wasn't sure if we could actually find that much to eat. He didn't even mention meat-eating. He said that we should look forward to our fasting in a positive way. We shouldn't think that we are fasting because of famine, or just because of the external circumstances of being stranded on a mountain. We certainly weren't fasting for political reasons to try to prove a point, and we weren't fasting in a mechanical way as therapy under the order of some doctor. In other words, if we had to do without food, we shouldn't keep thinking of different kinds of food we'd like to eat, because this would be depressing to the mind and would hurt the body also. The best way to fast, he said, was to remain in spiritual consciousness. That would be best for the mind and body.

"Almost every day," said Gurudeva, "we think of satisfying the tongue and belly. So, if we don't eat as much and we turn our thoughts more to Kṛṣṇa, there is a spiritual advantage."

Hearing from Gurudeva, I actually became fired-up to start fasting and overcome Mr. Lust.

"It just so happens that in a couple of days there's an Ekādaśī. Would you like to observe the full vow with me?"

Gurudeva had been observing the full Ekādaśī vow for a few years, which meant not eating or even drinking water, chanting at least sixty-four rounds, and staying up all night singing *bhajan*. I had never done the *vrata* with him, although when we visited the temples some of the devotees used to join him, and they said it was great. But now I thought I was ready for it, and since he asked me, I said yes.

Ekādaśī comes every two weeks, on the eleventh day after the full moon and after the new moon, and it's traditionally a time when Vaiṣṇavas fast, at least from beans and grains, and increase their chanting and hearing of Kṛṣṇa. But this was the first time I ever really got into the spirit of it.

The day before, I collected enough wood and cleansed the cabin and everything, so that I would be free to chant all day on Ekādaśī.

For me, the extra *japa* was mostly a matter of counting my beads rather than praying and being in *samādhi* (trance) with the holy names. But as the day wore on, I could not help but surrender to the process. By my determined will, my mind was getting the message, "You have nothing else to do but hear the holy names; you might as well listen and give up your trips." And since it was also pre-decided that we wouldn't eat or sleep, my senses—although they would have liked to rebel—also became subdued to the vow. We offered food to the Deities, because we don't make Lord Viṣṇu fast on Ekādaśī, but to Prabhupāda, Lord Caitanya and Lord Nityānanda, who appear as devotees, we didn't offer grains. We didn't have any grains anyway, so it was easy to avoid. I burned a stick of incense from a remaining pack, and I also decorated the altar with forest greens.

Gurudeva and Nimāi after three weeks

In preparation we also cut our hair and beards, which up to now we were growing like wild men. So, in the auspicious presence of so much transcendental vibration, I overcame the constant heaviness and peril of our situation.

When evening came on Ekādaśī, I went outside for a break. Around midnight as I was chanting, I thought how all the trees could benefit, so I chanted loudly and heard their echo, which Haridāsa Ṭhākura says isn't just an echo but "the *kīrtana* of the non-moving living entities." I am sure many of the moving entities also heard me, and it was good to let them have it, rather than cringe silently when they made their "call of the wild."

It would have been nice if we had had a harmonium and drum for singing *bhajans*, but we did have a pair of *karatālas* and I improvised a drum from an empty flour tin. Gurudeva spoke about Śrīla Prabhupāda and Lord Kṛṣṇa, and we read favorite sections of the scriptures and those which were applicable to our situation. Gurudeva, for example, read and commented on this verse:

nārāyaṇa-parāḥ sarve
na kutaścana bibhyati
svargāpavarga-narakeṣv
api tulyārtha-darśinaḥ

> Devotees solely engaged in the devotional service of the Supreme Personality of Godhead, Nārāyaṇa, never fear any condition of life. For them the heavenly planets, liberation and the hellish planets are all the same, for such devotees are interested only in the service of the Lord.
>
> —*Śrīmad-Bhāgavatam, 6.17.28*

I'm not saying it was all easy and blissful for me, but nevertheless it was a triumph of spirit over matter. Lord Kṛṣṇa has given us a potent method in observing Ekādaśī, and I hope I can remember to observe it as fully as possible as long as I live.

The next day I was in extra good spirits, and Gurudeva said he was also. My mind was clear to consider seriously, but in a transcendental way, how I was supposed to go out and gather food from nature. Gurudeva had previously asked me to do this, weeks ago, but I wasn't able to. But now I got into it. I had been a Boy Scout for a few years when I was a kid, and I tried to remember about eating, what you find in the woods. I thought, if there's anything to extract from the evergreen trees, we ought to consider it because they're all over the place.

But maybe evergreens would be categorized as impious trees, because they don't give fruits or flowers. Of course, they give some sort of fruit or flowers even if they're not in the class with mango and banana and apple trees or *kadamba* and *pārijāta* trees, which are really pious creatures. So, I cut some green pine needles and boiled them into a tea or soup. It was pretty horrible at first, but we drank some. The pine cones also contained some little nuts, and we managed to eat them.

From that day I kept thinking and looking for more edible, nourishing things, and I found that some of the more tender weeds, like dandelion greens were best. They became a staple, along with clear water from the creek. As Śukadeva Gosvāmī said, "Do the trees not give fruit? Do the rivers not give water? Can't you use your soft arm as a pillow? Doesn't the ground provide a bed? Can't you find some rejected cloth for garments? They why do you flatter men and go to passionate sinful endeavors (*ugra-karma*) just to "make a living?"

Evergreen tree

To live as an animal and keep alive as long as possible isn't the same as transcendental consciousness. We were fortunate to be able to do both. I had to keep reminding myself, however, to think as Gurudeva suggested, that we were not merely victims of famine or catastrophe, but we were fasting and practicing *śravaṇam kīrtanaṁ* to voluntarily remember, worship, and serve Govinda in this world and in the next.

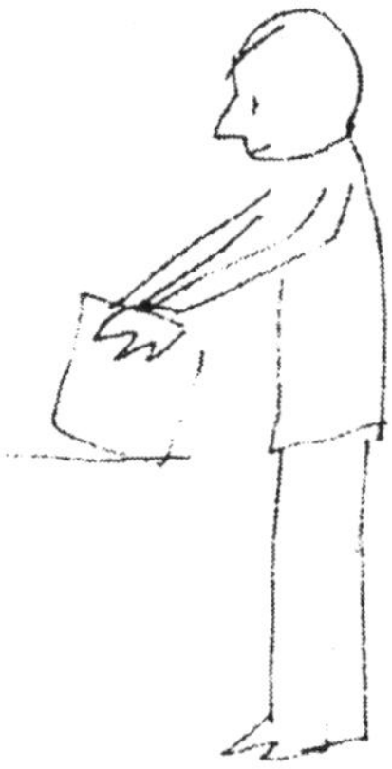

Pot Washer

Japa Walker

Fire Builder

Log Hauler

Slipping on Ice

#13: Gurudeva's Journal: Dreams of Prabhupāda

April 15

I had a dream that we were in a South American city, "Cintron," Colombia, and I was lost. Finally, I was able to return to the Hare Kṛṣṇa temple at the "135 Mohendro" address. I was taken in a taxi driven by an American. Then I was wondering, "Why have we come to this country?" My secretary replied that this was the way our plane itinerary had been planned. My secretary and I both reasoned further that I had traveled here because I wanted to preach. In the dream I said, "I used to travel just to collect disciples." Then through a translator, although he was not very expert, I spoke to some Colombians. What was most notable was that I was fired-up to speak and preach, because I was in a foreign country. I had great gusto to convey Kṛṣṇa consciousness.

This dream left me with a resolution that when I get out of here, I want to preach vigorously and try to spread Kṛṣṇa consciousness on behalf of Śrīla Prabhupāda. I may have been burned by my mistakes as a puffed-up *guru*, but now I want to get out and preach. This is not incompatible with the internal cultivation. I will confide to my disciple here, that this is what I want to do.

Waiting for Nimāi

I am waiting for Nimāi,
who has gone to fetch water.
If I lived alone,
I could fetch it myself,
but I am waiting for
his cheerful, shy appearance
at the cabin door.

Solitude makes you feel
the evening darkness

intensely quiet
and so vulnerable.
You pray more
to your Friend.
But I'm human—
I want to be with Nimāi.

He represents the whole *saṅga*
for congregational chanting
and the six exchanges of love.

As I wait for him
I'm thinking what to say
to ease his passion and confusion.
If I could speak of Kṛṣṇa!

April 17

I dreamed I was with Prabhupāda in a mountain retreat. He arrived by railroad, and I assisted him. "Śrīla Prabhupāda, where is your basket?" I asked. He was coming to write his commentaries to *Śrīmad-Bhāgavatam*, and we had to arrange for batteries for the dictaphone. We set up an arrangement of power from the sun. Śrīla Prabhupāda was bathing in warm water in a room filled with sunlight. Then I was typing his tapes and hearing his voice, "The materialistic demeanor cannot stretch to reach the transcendental autocrat who is ever calling the fallen souls back to His eternal abode." I went to Prabhupāda's room with the typing and some ripe grapes. He was smiling, and the room was filled with sunshine. There were other devotees present. He said, "Gauracandra, this place is very nice."

"When will we go back, Śrīla Prabhupāda?" I asked.

"Why are you anxious to know?" Prabhupāda said. "Let us stay. I can gain strength here. I was feeling tired. Now you can assist me. What are you cooking for lunch?"

I said, "I'm afraid it's just some bannock."

Prabhupāda said, "Cook it nicely for Kṛṣṇa."

Then Prabhupāda was walking suspended over the ground, and many devotees were there. I could see that each person thought Prabhupāda was only with them. We were chanting in a very big *kīrtana* with many devotees and guests. More kept entering by the front door of the cabin and passing out the back door to the other side of a mountain where everyone was crying. "All glories to Śrīla Prabhupāda! All glories to Śrī Kṛṣṇa!" Someone said, "Keep it up until the whole world is here!"

Usually, my dreams of Śrīla Prabhupāda are peripheral and ambiguous. This one was ecstatic and light. I woke up surcharged.

I can't expect to dream like this always. But I heard of an Indian tribe where the children were encouraged to have brave dreams or auspicious religious dreams. Even when my dreams of Śrīla Prabhupāda seem to be insignificant or incomprehensible, I become interested and satisfied, because it helps me to gather my thoughts and ambitions to serve him better, and to re-establish my lost relationship. If someone comes upon an excavation site of a fabulous ancient civilization, *any* genuine artifact he finds there, even a laundry list or a broken jar, would be considered very valuable and would be properly kept.

April 18

Another Śrīla Prabhupāda dream. Are more coming because of my simplified diet of only water and soup?

I dreamed I was feeding cookies to my childhood dog and I saw Prabhupāda from a distance. He thought that I should come to him. But his servant, Kurukṣetra dāsa, was there so I hesitated. Mentally Śrīla Prabhupāda and I communicated. I knew that when Śrīla Prabhupāda would leave that place I would also. So, I kept a humble distance.

Does more dreaming of Śrīla Prabhupāda mean my unconscious self is turning more to him and is more receptive? I hope so. With less distractions here I am noticing it more. When other activities and selfish concerns are reduced, what is left except my relationship with him?

In the morning while Nimāi was out, I napped and dreamed again. It was a dream in which many things occurred. There was very little narrative or scene-setting that I could recall. I woke with this verbal message or sensation: "There are many things short of devotional service to Kṛṣṇa. Even powerful persons do not attain devotion to Kṛṣṇa. But by virtue of my relationship with Prabhupāda, I can enter into that eternal relationship where Kṛṣṇa will accept me. No one else but Prabhupāda can bring me there."

April 19

Last night in a dream I suddenly remembered an old acrobatic trick my father used to do with me. My dreaming self said: "I remember when I was a little boy I would stand, bend down, and place my hands between my legs. With full faith in Śrīla Prabhupāda—I mean with faith in my father—he would then come behind me, take my hands, and pull me into the air into an acrobatic flip, while I screamed in delight 'Do it again! Do it again!" The trick depended on complete trust in him." When in the dream I said that I had full faith in Prabhupāda, I was very surprised that I said "Prabhupāda" instead of "my father". My surprise woke me up.

I confided to Nimāi dāsa that I had been dreaming of Śrīla Prabhupāda. He asked if there was anything I was doing consciously to bring it about. I said, "No, it is just his mercy."

I dreamed I was on the telephone with Prabhupāda. There were devotees with him, and they told me that Prabhupāda would now come and speak to me. I couldn't hear him well, but it seemed that he was saying, "We are transcendental to the teachers of *jñāna*, because we can concentrate on Kṛṣṇa. You have always been a transcendental beggar." The import of his speech was that I should do something big for Kṛṣṇa. He seemed to imply that I should help build a big expensive temple. I wanted to ask the other devotees who were with Śrīla Prabhupāda what he actually said, because I was talking to him from a ferry boat and there was a lot of noise. I thought, "Prabhupāda knows what's best for me. At this time of my life, he has given me this instruction. If he actually did say I had to do something big, like construct a temple, he knows it's the best thing for me to do."

When I woke up, I thought it would be very difficult for the Movement, at this time, to engage devotees in such a project as building a big temple. Whatever Prabhupāda was saying on the phone wasn't clear and cannot be taken as such. But the good impression was that Prabhupāda was watching my career in spiritual life and recommending what was best for me, I also seemed willing to do whatever he said.

Later in the night I had another dream. We were attempting to bring a new Deity into the temple, but He wouldn't fit. It was very hard for the *pūjārī* and he fell down with the Deity. Then Prabhupāda was performing a miracle to lift up one side of the temple. At the time I could not appreciate the miracle. But we all accepted that it could be done.

April 20

A rough dream:

Prabhupāda was in the temple room sitting on a *vyāsāsana* and in the same room, also on a large *vyāsāsana*, was a disciple of Prabhupāda who looked as old as Prabhupāda himself. I was there sitting in the audience slumped over and watched. In Prabhupāda's presence, a devotee asked the old disciple, "How do you feel lecturing in front of Prabhupāda?" He replied, "I have thought about it, and I think I should just be patient." And I noticed that while I was speaking, Prabhupāda glanced at me to size me up. When this was said, Prabhupāda smiled slightly and we all understood that he was fully aware how we were conducting things with the big *vyāsāsana* for his disciple. Prabhupāda saw it as a game, and he gave his permission, and he seemed to approve the remark that we should just be patient with it. Prabhupāda's attitude made a nice atmosphere, and then the ceremonies were over and we all bowed down while Prabhupāda quickly left the room to go about his usual activities. I felt excited and pleased to write down my realizations. While those events were happening, I had been slumped over and tired, but now I felt enlightened because Prabhupāda had revealed his attitude and we were blissful.

April 21

I dreamed that Prabhupāda was carried in a palanquin, as his devotees walked alongside, to a Greek audience at an "Elias" temple which was in the city. The temple was connected to a scene in the Bible. Before the head man of the temple, Prabhupāda spoke in Hindi. We then held *kīrtana*. Everyone knew that Prabhupāda had great faith that the *kīrtana* would cleanse people, even though they didn't understand the language. It was a very large audience, but few people could understand Prabhupāda's lecture, because of the language difference, yet the *kīrtana* was sufficient and important. I sat near Prabhupāda, and as he left, I helped lead the way through a swinging door. Prabhupāda was wrapped in *cādars*.

#14: Appreciating Śrīla Prabhupāda

I became disturbed when Gurudeva spoke to me about his dreams of Prabhupāda. Rather than share his happiness, I became anxious. I was jealous. I thought, "Here we are without food, but Gurudeva got something special to sustain him. And I can't have it." It was nectar to be with Gurudeva, but it was heavy also. He exposed my *anarthas*, my unwanted habits. Prabhupāda warns us about this in his purports:

> The Deity of the Lord and the spiritual master should be seen from a distant place. This is called *maryādā*. Otherwise, as is said, familiarity breeds contempt. Sometimes coming too near the Deity or the spiritual master degrades the neophyte devotee. Personal servants of the Deity and the spiritual master should therefore always be very careful, for negligence may overcome them in their duty.
>
> —*Caitanya-caritāmṛta, Madhya līlā 12.212, purport*

From what I've heard, senior devotees who were close to Prabhupāda also found it hard, as Prabhupāda forced out their *anarthas*.

I didn't reveal my mind about the dreams to Gurudeva because it seemed awful. I was afraid he would be hurt and think he had no one at all to talk to, and I would end up ruining everything. But by not telling him I had to start faking responses when he told me his dreams. My actual response was, "Why can't I have experiences like that?" I knew he wasn't showing off by telling me that he dreamed of Prabhupāda. He was treating me as a confidential friend. But I wasn't worthy of it.

Then I became confused thinking of Śrīla Prabhupāda. Sometimes I used to think that it was fortunate that I came to Kṛṣṇa consciousness after Śrīla Prabhupāda disappeared from the world, because I would be less likely to see Prabhupāda in too familiar a way, or to commit offenses in his presence. I was usually satisfied by hearing of his greatness and achievements. But when Gurudeva started telling of his tangible association with Prabhupāda, I felt left out. Gurudeva seemed to be very interested also in the fact that he was having more Prabhupāda dreams now that we were fasting from regular food. I almost thought that he was getting ready to die if he had to. I thought he was saying, "If we have to die here, that's not so bad, because I can think of Prabhupāda and Kṛṣṇa." But what about me? I wasn't ready. I couldn't think of either Kṛṣṇa or Prabhupāda. Gurudeva was drawing from his years of association with Prabhupāda and, in a difficult time, he was dreaming of him. And I felt bad about it.

After a few days riding on the chariot of my mind, I decided to submit my problem to my spiritual master. Gurudeva was sitting and reading on the front porch chest during a chilly but sunny afternoon. I finished my chores and went and sat beneath him. He put down his book, indicating that he was willing to give me time and attention.

"Gurudeva, can I ask you some questions about Śrīla Prabhupāda?"

"Yes," he replied, "it's your mercy on me if you do."

"I want to know about my relationship with him. Do I have an eternal relationship with Prabhupāda? How can I know it? When will I know it?"

Gurudeva gave me a serious look. "Yes, you have a relationship with Prabhupāda," he said. "But I can't say exactly what it is. It's something that you have to develop more to know. I don't know myself what my relationship is with Prabhupāda. I know him from certain association I've had, but spiritually and eternally I don't know yet. In one song, Narottama dāsa Ṭhākura yearns to meet with his spiritual master in the spiritual world. He says that his spiritual master will appear in the spiritual body of a *gopī* and Narottama dāsa Ṭhākura will be a *gopī's* assistant and together they'll serve Rādhā and Kṛṣṇa. So that's in the liberated stage. This much I can say: that you will recognize and know Prabhupāda more and more; it's just up to you. And you know what? When you meet him, you realize that you have already known him, and that's how you'll recognize him."

"What do you mean?"

"I mean that even when Prabhupāda was present in the world, we might go without seeing him for as long as a year and when we saw him again, I would think, 'Prabhupāda is just like he is in separation, and his tapes and books.' In other words, when we saw him in his personal form, his *vapuḥ*, it made us appreciate even more that Prabhupāda was mostly with us in his *vāṇī*, or his teachings. Being with him personally helped us to appreciate his form in his teachings. You know the difference between *vāṇī* and *vapuḥ*? The *vapuḥ* is the spiritual master's personal presence. When he's present you can serve him by cooking or talking or walking with him, like that. But he's not always available in that form. However, in the *vāṇī* he's eternally available. Therefore, we say about the spiritual master, 'He lives eternally, and his disciple lives with him by following his instructions.' How did Prabhupāda know his own spiritual master, Bhaktisiddhanta Sarasvatī Ṭhākura? He said he only met him a dozen times over a period of about fifteen years. And yet Prabhupāda said that his spiritual master was always with him, was watching him, was pleased with him, was in his heart. That's by the *vāṇī*, the teachings."

"Does Śrīla Prabhupāda know my services to you and my devotional service in general?" I had never asked anyone these exact questions, and Gurudeva's answers were important to me. But I knew I was also avoiding my questions about Gurudeva's dreams of Prabhupāda.

"Yes, Prabhupāda knows," said Gurudeva. "Everything goes through the *paramparā*. Just as when you offer your food in *paramparā*. You offer it to your spiritual master with faith that he will offer it to Prabhupāda, and Prabhupāda will offer it to his spiritual master, and in that way, it is offered to Kṛṣṇa. This same question was once asked by a disciple of Prabhupāda on a morning walk in India. The devotee said, "Prabhupāda. You have thousands of disciples, how can each one be assured that you are aware of his services?" Prabhupāda replied that a devotee would feel enthusiastic about his personal relationship just by following the rules and regulations, such as chanting sixteen rounds. When he serves Prabhupāda by chanting or maybe distributing Prabhupāda's books, a sincere devotee will feel personal contact. He'll *know*, no one else will have to tell him or assure him. So, there are theological explanations of how a past *ācārya* can know or communicate with devotees in later ages. But the test of it is by experience, when you worship or serve that devotee. If you read Rūpa Gosvāmī's book *Nectar of Devotion,* for example, you worship and you commune with him, and you'll feel that you're with him, and that he knows you."

Gurudeva's answers were so transcendental and pleasing to me that I wanted to expose and remove all the dirty things in my heart as soon as possible.

"When you tell me your dreams about Prabhupāda," I said, while looking down to the ground, "I feel left out. I become envious."

When I looked up, Gurudeva was surprised.

"I'm sorry," he said. "It's my fault if you feel that way."

"No, it's *my* fault. I wanted to admit it to you."

"By telling you my dreams," said Gurudeva, "I've made too much of them. They're not on the level with the scriptures. Although Prabhupāda is in my dreams, the dreams are mixed with impurities." I wanted to protest more against his self-effacing statements, but I knew he wouldn't accept it. I also thought that if I could ask more questions and gain more understanding of my relationship with Prabhupāda, that would be the way to free myself from enviousness or feeling left out.

"Could you explain again," I asked, "how Prabhupāda is the *śikṣā*, or instructor *guru*?"

"According to scriptures," said Gurudeva, "a person can have only one initiating spiritual master, but he may have many instructor *gurus*. Since Prabhupāda left the planet before you joined this movement, he could not be your initiating *guru*. But the *śikṣā* and initiating *gurus* are identical in terms of being eternal guides, and so on. And in our *paramparā*, many disciples had their main relationship with their *śikṣā guru*. It can also be done even though many years separate the *guru* and disciple, just as Madhv*ācārya* became the disciple of Vyāsadeva hundreds of years after Vyāsadeva had passed away. Anyone can accept Prabhupāda as his teacher, as his *śikṣā guru*, to the degree that he actually surrenders and follows the *vāṇī* of Prabhupāda. There's no reason to feel left out. When a so-called senior devotee like me toots his own horn by telling stories of how he met Prabhupāda, or by telling his dreams of Prabhupāda, you just have to tolerate it. But it shouldn't intimidate you."

"I'm sorry," I said, "I feel offensive now. I don't want to jump over you to reach Prabhupāda. I mainly want to hear about him from you. Please keep telling me about Śrīla Prabhupāda."

"One of the best ways to come close to Prabhupāda," said Gurudeva, "is to read his books. We also have the full biography of Prabhupāda and different nectarean memoirs that are coming out. So why don't you read more? And also, we have the Deity of Prabhupāda here. I think it would be nice if we worshiped him together. We can bathe him and dress him, why don't you help me more with it? I used to have a higher standard of worship, but since we've come here, I've neglected it."

"Yes, that would be nice," I said. "And I'll try to read. But I especially like it when you tell me about Śrīla Prabhupāda. Could you tell me about the early days when you were with him in New York City?"

Gurudeva laughed. "What can I say? My memory is not so good. Your question is like asking, 'Tell me about the Pacific Ocean.'"

We both became silent and listened to the wind in the trees. After a few minutes Gurudeva spoke again. "It was the beginning," he said. "No one knew of Prabhupāda's greatness by hearing or tradition or advertisement. He had no money, and we were his only followers. But gradually we came to know he was a self-realized pure devotee, and from him we became convinced that Lord Kṛṣṇa is the Supreme Personality of Godhead. He taught us the *Bhagavad-gītā* gave us knowledge and faith. It was the perfect way to become linked to Kṛṣṇa, by Śrīla Prabhupāda personally, in the humble form in which he first came, and at that time and place. I needed it in that way otherwise I doubt that I would've become a devotee or that I would've lived long."

I was ready to put in a few more questions, but I realized that Gurudeva wanted to speak more about the early days.

"He was ... dressed in simple *khādī* cloth from India. No silk. No shirts even, but simple cloth wrapped around him. We began to bring him things, like sweaters and socks, although those also were inexpensive, because we didn't know better. He cooked for us wonderful, tasty *prasādam*, and he insisted that we 'eat more!' He invited us to his apartment. One time I met him on the street after I'd been initiated. I bowed down on the sidewalk ... He would personally lead the singing of all the *kīrtanas* in the storefront temple ... I can't remember well. Just different things ... He saved me."

Gurudeva seemed to be in reverie, as if he was feeling more than he was able to say. Then he, sort of, woke himself from it and spoke more quickly.

"I'm sorry I can't tell you more. I've written some of it down. Maybe someday I can learn how to relive it all and recall it. Because when I think of meeting Śrīla Prabhupāda again I can't imagine that those early days with him will simply be erased. Even Śrīla Prabhupāda used to remember them. He said, 'Those were happy days.' Although in later years he had many disciples to help him, in the beginning he said, 'I was depending only on Kṛṣṇa.'"

"Any one devotee's memories of Śrīla Prabhupāda are fractional. We should always be aware that he was empowered to spread Kṛṣṇa consciousness as no devotee ever did. Before him, *bhakti* was locked in India, and the only swamis who came to the West were *yogīs* and impersonal meditators. At least no pure devotee came who was so empowered. So, if you want appreciate Prabhupāda, appreciate his greatness as *very dear to Kṛṣṇa*, and at the same time be aware of his personal, lenient dealing with every individual. You will find this in his biography and also, as you serve more, you'll find that he's in your own heart."

"How can I really feel grateful," I asked, "or whatever it is I'm supposed to feel, if I never met him?"

"Look Nimāi," said Gurudeva emphatically, "the important thing about Prabhupāda is that he taught us and imbued us with Kṛṣṇa consciousness. He taught us that we are eternal spiritual souls and that Kṛṣṇa is the Supreme Personality of Godhead. And he convinced us to follow the authoritative Vedic literatures and to actually practice Kṛṣṇa consciousness. This is his miracle. In remembering Śrīla Prabhupāda we don't talk of a wizard or mind reader. Many people seem to emphasize that their guru could read their minds or show them lights and visions. Some people even say things like that in connection with Prabhupāda. But I distinctly remember someone once asked him if he could read minds, and he said that doing so was superficial. He said a person couldn't know everything in another's mind, and anyway it wasn't important. What good is seeing lights or even learning subreligious principles if your teacher can't save you from death? Śrīla Prabhupāda taught us that nothing short of complete surrender and love of God can save us from transmigration and enable us to go back to Godhead. He *planted* the seed of *bhakti* in our hearts and taught us how to water and care for that plant by chanting and hearing the holy names. Prabhupāda stayed and, by his personal example and books, gradually developed, in a painstaking way, a society of devotees ... Yes, you can serve Śrīla Prabhupāda, you and people far into the future."

The night after I questioned Gurudeva about Śrīla Prabhupāda, I had a dream in which Śrīla Prabhupāda appeared to me. I was away from the cabin cutting firewood, and Prabhupāda came walking along the path. He observed me working and smiled. Then a second scene followed where Prabhupāda was lecturing in a large temple room, like Los Angeles, before many devotees. He singled me out and asked, "Nimāi, what is the purpose of human life?" I replied shyly, "To serve Kṛṣṇa." This scene merged into a third where Śrīla Prabhupāda again appeared at our cabin looking for me. But this time he was angry and said to me, "Why did you do that?" I woke with a shock but was very pleased to have received his mercy in the form of chastisement. I later told Gurudeva about it and he approved. He said, "So now you know."

#15: Gurudeva's Journal: A Bona Fide Forest Sage

May 1

When Nimāi expressed his innocent arousal of devotion to Śrīla Prabhupāda—and his being peeved that I dreamt of Śrīla Prabhupāda—my first reaction was jealousy. I had been thinking of Nimāi as *my* disciple, and I was hurt to see him want to be Prabhupāda's disciple. But I surrendered to it. If I take full shelter in Śrīla Prabhupāda, why shouldn't he?

Every day I see
the unnamed mountain,
morning, noon, and night
in millions of phases,
although the same hard slope.
Sometimes in black silhouette
against a dark blue sky,
and sometimes rosy with
clouds half-hidden behind the peak
and clouds moving left to right
With the wind.

It doesn't move,
but always changes.
The peak is snowy, bare
and one side of its face
is unshaven with pine trees.

My Lord, Your creation
is mysterious
and when untouched by civilization,
it's more mysterious still.
In this wilderness I pray to You,
succor me with Your nearness,
Lord of the mountain,
O You who move all things.

May 8

Nimāi is taking me on "the palanquin" to see the neighborhood. There's a downhill path to the flooding creek. Ice is thawing. New birds and ducks returning. Spring means life, but also death. This world is *jīvo jīvasya jīvanam.* The strong eat the weak. One living being is food for another. The cheerful singing birds are deadly predators to insects, and they themselves are preyed upon. Near the cabin we saw a pile of feathers and recognized by color that it was a friendly bird who had eaten out of our hand. We saw the meandering tracks of a rabbit, then bigger dog-like tracks covering the smaller tracks, and scuffle marks and blood. Eggs in nests means there will also be egg-robbers. The mating calls of big animals are invitations for the males to fight. We watched the graceful feats of the hawks and eagles in the sky, but when one swooped down, we heard the death cries of a mouse.

We should see this scene for what it is and think, "I must work to get out of this cycle and not descend again into the lower species." The tendency is to forget and to use our intelligence only as cunning for survival and enjoyment in speculation.

Gurudeva in woods by creek

May 10

While chanting *japa*, it occurred to me that I would like to start a little school or *āśrama* if we ever get out of here. One idea could be to hold four- or five-day retreats for busy householders and friends. They could come to a place like the farm in Pennsylvania, and we could have intensive sessions and basics like *japa* or reading and prayer. The goal would be that within a few days some students could actually achieve a significant rebirth and reconciliation with Kṛṣṇa. The sessions could be held yearly to refresh and reaffirm the initial experience of reconciliation. I'm not sure if I'm up to guiding others in such introspection, but at the very least the classes would be helpful for improving *japa*, instilling devotees with improved reading habits, and reawakening them to the fact that we are all about to die and that our purpose is not simply the struggle for survival—which in the cities takes the shape of family maintenance and child upbringing, or for unmarried temple devotees, passionate, external activities with little realization.

Aside from short courses, there could be month-long courses held maybe twice a year. A place like Vṛndāvana, India, might be ideal. There could be courses taught by different *sannyāsīs* and others on *Śrīmad-Bhāgavatam, Bhagavad-gītā*, or *Nectar of Devotion* and special interests, like Vaiṣṇava etiquette, logic, and public speaking, and a course on writing, a course on Sanskrit, and so on. A Vaiṣṇava institute. Of course, such an ambitious plan would involve considerable management, financing, and cooperation of many devotees. It could start with something small. At least I could teach a course myself and gather some of my disciples for it.

While I'm here I may design a syllabus, outline chapters and sections of *Śrīmad-Bhāgavatam*, and even teach the course to Nimāi with homework assignments, class discussion, and exams. It can be like a *gurukula* or *āśrama* here. That will also help us to endure this situation. A course on "prayer" may be controversial or beyond my realization, but it's a challenge. If I could do it in a thoroughly Vaiṣṇava way, who could object?

May 12

I had a dream of Śrīla Prabhupāda last night, but I am not going to talk about it.

May 14

I can't help but think that Lord Kṛṣṇa may have put me here to fulfill my desires. Is there anything morally wrong with an isolated life in the woods? So many sages and *yogīs* have done it, and in cold places too. It's called *tapo-vana,* retiring to the forest for austerity. I remember reading of Pṛthu Mahārāja going to the forest, where he refused to receive any cooked food sent from the city and vowed to live on roots, tree trunks, fruits, dried leaves, or whatever nature provided. Sometimes he ate only dry leaves or only water.

One lesson I have learned here is to slow down. Time no longer has the same meaning that it did in the cities, where everything is divided by hours and minutes and calendar days. I've stopped setting the alarm to my clock or even wearing a watch. You work with the sun and go to bed when you are tired. Now the senses are becoming quieter, without heavy food. Chanting and hearing are becoming clearer. I'm not making so many plans. So, in a certain way I think I am closer to the Supreme Lord in my heart.

But Śrīla Prabhupāda says that Vaiṣṇava sages do not go to the forest for their own benefit only, but to help humanity. Even when in the forest, they gather like the sages at Naimiṣāraṇya, to perform sacrifices for the good of all men. Śrīla Prabhupāda writes, "They are always anxious to perform acts which may bring about peace in the world." They are sincere friends to all living entities, and at the risk of great personal inconvenience, they engage in austerities for the good of all people. In Naimiṣāraṇya this was done by hearing *Śrīmad-Bhāgavatam* from Sūta Gosvāmī and now that *Śrīmad-Bhāgavatam* has been spoken and recorded, it is our duty to distribute it.

Śrīla Prabhupāda tells of two kinds of sages, the *bhajanānandī* and the *goṣṭhyānandī.* The *bhajanānandī* worships mostly for his own benefit and tends to inhabit solitary places for contemplation. The *goṣṭhyānandī* is more often found among many persons with whom he associates in order to guide them in Kṛṣṇa consciousness. The *goṣṭhyānandī* is appreciated as a higher devotee of the Lord. Maybe I wanted to live like this in the forest, therefore Kṛṣṇa has thrust me here, but in any case, I am now forced to stay. Let me make the best of it by not complaining, by living like a bona fide forest sage and readying myself to help others when the opportunity comes again. Maybe my idea of a forest school can help in that way.

#16 :Gurudeva's Forest School

There was a wheelbarrow in a woodshed which I used to carry chopped wood from the forest to the cabin. After a couple of months, Gurudeva still couldn't walk, except very slowly with two canes, and so I began to think that I could make the wheelbarrow into a palanquin for carrying him to some nearby places. I had favorite places which Gurudeva hadn't seen, such as the creek, the lake, a nice grove, and other spots which I wanted to share with him. When I first mentioned my idea, he laughed and scoffed at it. But I kept telling him it would be nice and comfortable and that he would be happy to see more of Kṛṣṇa's wilderness. Then one day I just went ahead and cleaned up the wheelbarrow, padded it with some clothes and a cloth and presented it at the door introducing myself as a *pukka* rickshaw driver. Gurudeva accepted the ride, and I took him along the path I had worn leading into the forest and toward the lake. We were both glad that he took the ride because it opened up new vistas for Gurudeva, who had been cooped up in the one room with all its reminders of trappers and hunters.

A few days after Gurudeva's first palanquin ride, the ice on the lake suddenly broke up. A big piece of brittle ice that spanned the lake was pushed against the shore by the wind. Slowly it drove against the shore in piles of jagged, broken crystals with a sound like thousands of dinner plates breaking. It continued for a few days like that, crashing and crushing on the rocks and scarring trees, until eventually the lake was thawed out. The ducks soon found out about it and began landing on the lake and diving after fish. I also began to notice more animal tracks, either because there were actually more animals walking about, or because I was noticing things better. I *was* noticing details that escaped me at first, and I was becoming at least a little bit attuned to the natural world around us.

By now it was over a month since we had been eating only what we found in the woods. During the first four or five days of "fasting", I had headaches and other bodily discomforts, but then the body seemed to resign itself and allow my mind to be free. It was harder to do chores, but we also didn't burn wood twenty-four hours a day in the stove, and so my work wasn't as much.

One day when we came back from a nature walk, Gurudeva announced that he wanted to start a forest school and that it required my cooperation. I had noticed that he had been writing intensely for a week or so. He said he had prepared a syllabus for different courses that he hoped could be taught by different senior devotees and that he wanted to form a Kṛṣṇa consciousness institute whenever we returned to civilization. I thought it was a wonderful idea, and I told him I would love to help him bring it about once we returned to temples and association of devotees.

"But I want to start it now," said Gurudeva. "We will begin our own experimental school, just you and me right here in the mountains." At first, I couldn't grasp it, until he explained that I would be the only student in all the classes and that he would teach me. I didn't like the prospect. It seemed like too much responsibility for me, but Gurudeva was so excited by it that his voice was extra forceful and his eyes were shining.

"There will be six courses, Nimāi, and you'll be the star pupil in all of them. There is brahminical culture, logic and public speaking, prayer and inner life, Sanskrit and verse memorization, a writing course, and a course on *Śrīmad-Bhāgavatam*. What do you think?"

"I don't know if I can do it, Gurudeva," I replied limply. "But I'll try."

"If you try, you'll succeed," he said. I was glad that Gurudeva was confident in me, but afraid that if I did fail to hold up my end, he might become frustrated in his plan for the institute.

"There will be homework in each course," he said, "and exams." I never cared for academic institutions, and Gurudeva knew that, so he assured me, "It won't be like an ordinary school. You'll like it." I hoped so.

My participation in the courses turned out to be a lot of foolishness, and I would rather not tell about it. I don't know what good it will do unless you want to laugh at me. Gurudeva's forest school has since developed successfully, and so my initial difficulties don't have much significance. But he wanted me to tell about it. He said it's history, and people can benefit from hearing the mistakes of the first blundering pioneer. So only out of duty I'll tell some of it, but I'll make it brief. One excuse for my behavior is that when you go a long time without eating, you daydream a lot due to lightness.

In the course called Brahminical Culture, I became very enthusiastic but imitative. I'm not an initiated *brahmin*, so I had to function as a "blind uncle." In case you don't know what a blind uncle is, it comes from a story told by Prabhupāda. There was once an orphan who was crying because he had no mother and father. His uncle came to him and volunteered that he would act as the child's parent, but unfortunately this uncle was blind. The bereft child accepted the offer, saying, "A blind uncle is better than none." So, I was the blind uncle student at the forest school.

One of the important purposes of the Brahminical Culture course, according to Gurudeva, was to understand the deep cultural and spiritual meaning underlying the different acts which a devotee performs, which we may take as ritualistic unless we know why we're doing them. I missed that point and became more interested in imitating the refined behaviors of a spiritual person. I would end up doing wrong things with flair. For example, no one is supposed to recite the Gāyatrī mantras unless he is an initiated *brāhmaṇa*. But I reasoned to myself that since I was taking the brahminical class, I might be an exception to this rule. As Gurudeva's servant, I used to carry an envelope containing sheets of the Gāyatrī mantra for when he initiated *brāhmaṇas*, although I wasn't supposed to look at it. But I began to recite the Gāyatrī when I became a student in the course for *brāhmaṇas.* Another thing only *brāhmaṇas* can do is worship *śālagrāma-śilā.* This is a form of the Lord like the statues in the temple of Rādhā and Kṛṣṇa, only the *śilā* is worshiped just as it appears in nature, as stone from sacred places in India, like Govardhana Hill. In the brahminical mood, I picked up a rock from the stream nearby and while I didn't actually start anything with it, I was toying with the idea of considering it like a practice *śilā.* Gurudeva must have read my mind, because when he saw me carrying it, he said, "What do you think you're doing?" I tried not to admit what was on my mind, but as I say, he seems to read me, and he reprimanded me strongly. He told a story at that time of a *brāhmaṇa* who put two little balls inside of his pot, and all other *brāhmaṇas* imitated him without knowing what he was doing.

I also had been practicing little things I had seen other *brāhmaṇas* in the Movement do, such as facing the sun when saying mantras and lying down at night facing the East and folding your *dhotī* with special pleats and wearing arm bands, although I didn't wear an earring like some of them do. Although I experimented, I wasn't really sure which direction to face or exactly how to move your fingers in the *mūla mantras* and things like that. Gurudeva got pretty disgusted with my antics and decided that it wasn't a good idea to teach someone like me, who wasn't yet a *brāhmaṇa* in a course for brahminical culture. So, for the time being he dropped that from the syllabus.

The course on logic and public speaking was interesting and very valuable, but I found it hard to take to. If you learn logic and debating you can defeat the nondevotees. I wasn't so much interested in arguing or fighting with others, but I thought it would be helpful for defeating my own mind. But I found it difficult to memorize the different types of false logic, CIRCULAR and ANALYTICAL. I especially couldn't take it when Gurudeva invited me to debate with him. In public speaking I learned many orator's tips, and then I had to prepare my own lecture. At the beginning of my first lecture, I stood fidgeting before Gurudeva. It would have been easier if there were a room full of people, but it was only my spiritual master and some blue jays, who seemed to be making fun of me with their squawks. As I began to speak, I remembered a funny story I had heard a Hindu man tell when I was staying at a health sanatorium in South India. I thought it might be interesting to introduce the philosophy with the story and so I began it. It was about a man who had thirteen wives, and who had a problem remembering their different names. One of the wives suggested that he could tell them apart by an interesting method. "Just speak the *Bhāgavatam*," said Gurudeva, interrupting me. His interruption was quite a shock for me, and I think I learned a good lesson about the importance of speaking *paramparā*. We shouldn't waste people's time but give them straight Kṛṣṇa consciousness. The main purpose for our public speaking was to give *Bhāgavatam* lectures, and since I have always considered the *Bhāgavatam* lecture very important, I felt bad to waste Gurudeva's time with my poor lecturing. I thought maybe some people are better at just hearing, and they should improve their hearing skills rather than just fake it as lecturers, but Gurudeva insisted that I could be taught.

The course in prayer and inner life was something introduced especially by Gurudeva. I wanted to succeed in this so that he would feel confident to introduce it once his school developed. He made it clear that he wasn't teaching any special techniques or methods of prayer but was trying to awaken within us a desire to call on Kṛṣṇa at every moment. He showed me many passages in Prabhupāda's books where this mood is evoked. For example, Prabhupāda writes, "In execution of devotional service one has to submit to Kṛṣṇa whatever distress or confidential problem he has. He should say, 'Kṛṣṇa, I am suffering in this way.'" Gurudeva also emphasizes that prayer didn't mean asking Kṛṣṇa for something we want, or for trying to get Kṛṣṇa to change His mind, but it was to cooperate with God and seek out what He wants for us. Prayer is learning to accept His will. Gurudeva promised that if I developed the habit of regular prayer, it would noticeably change my life. Prayer puts you in touch with Kṛṣṇa.

These were all things that I wanted very much to attain, but although it sounded very good in theory, it was very difficult for me to practice. Practicing prayer assumes that you are actually serious to enter into a deeper relationship with Kṛṣṇa, and that means that you have to surrender in reciprocation. When you start praying, Kṛṣṇa is going to let you know more what He wants of you. And I found that very hard to handle. Because if I sincerely prayed, "Please Lord, tell me what You want me to do," and if Kṛṣṇa actually told me what He wanted and yet I couldn't do it, then what? My reluctance to pray exposed to me that I'm actually afraid of Kṛṣṇa. I think this is the real reason I found it difficult to practice prayer. I invented other reasons which were more like excuses, such as I was embarrassed to bow down and afraid that Gurudeva or other people would see me engaged in prayer. These are silly excuses. Anyway, I tried to do it, and I still haven't given up on the practice of prayer.

Sanskrit and verse memorization was particularly difficult for me. I suppose it's also in the category of an excuse if I say that I have a weak memory, although I think that's a fact. It was hard for me to become so humble and study each word of the scripture carefully and to treasure it so much that I should imprint it within my mind and commit it to memory. At first Gurudeva said that I had to learn one *śloka* per day. When he saw that I couldn't do it, he said do three a week, and finally he asked me to do one a week, which I was actually able to do. My mind rebelled by telling me, "What will you have to do with this memorized verse? What does it have to do with your life?" My reluctance showed me that I was not surrendered to the sound vibration of Kṛṣṇa. And I even thought, uncharitably, of some different devotees I knew who had memorized hundreds of *ślokas*, but who became unserious about spiritual life, and who even broke the regulative principles. It made me think, "What good is learning *ślokas*?" Anyway, I'm not the least bit sorry for those *ślokas* which I did commit to memory, at the rate of one a week. They eventually began to accumulate, and now I see them as an opulence in my life.

My favorite course was *Śrīmad-Bhāgavatam.* Gurudeva treated the *Bhāgavatam* in a systematic way, starting from the First Canto. I loved hearing how the *Bhāgavatam* was put together by Vyāsadeva who told Śukadeva who told Sūta, and how all the different speakers appear. There are stories within the stories. He helped me to see also that Prabhupāda's purports are not as repetitious as they appear to be when you look at them superficially. The purports develop one thought after another and once you start to study them more, they are revealed to you.

As for the writing course, it requires a lot of patience, more than I normally have, especially in learning how to rewrite and correct what you first wrote down. But I tried to work on some pieces. If possible, I will include something I wrote at the forest school within this book.

I've briefly described my own performance at Gurudeva's experimental school in the mountains, and now I'd rather drop the subject and tell you something more interesting. Gurudeva's school is a first-class project, but it is unfortunate that the idea came to him when I was the only person around to participate. Although I complained about the demands of the school, now that I think of it, it was really nectarean because it gave me a chance to directly serve my spiritual master in something that was important to him. I regret that his interests didn't automatically become mine and that I may have been more botheration than help.

Once we began the classes, they continued without interruption and helped us to occupy ourselves for several months even as we grew physically weaker. Being occupied in that way also helped me from becoming panicky or worrying as I sometimes did, about what might finally happen to us unless someone found us soon.

#17: Gurudeva's Journal: Beyond the Mountains

June 16

My dear Lord Kṛṣṇa and Prabhupāda, I want to be your devotee. I want to wake up and do the right things. I want to do what you want me to do. But I am already going in a direction which is, I suppose, the direction of my own will, and I'm trying to dovetail that into acceptable devotional service. Please help me to satisfy You in that way. If the service I'm attached to is really not Your will for me, please let me know clearly. Otherwise, I will continue to try to please You by the service I am doing. But that service also is imperfect, so please improve it, and let me do something humbly that is helpful to the Movement.

I may have my plans, like the forest school, and my claim to be working at prayer and inner life, and my responsibilities as initiating guru to guide disciples, but if these activities should be abandoned instead of perfected, please let me know. You will have to do this in a way which I can understand. I am too much set on my own ways, and I am not able to see them as totally wrong ways. Only You can enable me to see it.

My Lord, this prayer is also made insincerely. It is merely clever and literary. But I hope my intention to address myself to God and guru is not so far off the mark that you do not even hear me.

I am Your servant,
G.C.S.

June 19

Crooked, scarred tree near the cabin:

I noticed him when we first arrived. He had been chopped at a few times. He is as broad as a telephone pole, and taller than that, but his trunk also grows crooked after about 10 feet up. He is not fully branched with pine needles but is scraggly. Although there are millions of trees here, I can't meet them all, but he is nearby. For him I feel some of the pity and wonderment for souls in the bodies of trees. Śrīla Prabhupāda has said that one gets the body of a tree as a result of extreme lust. His punishment is that he can't move and stands naked.

If a person comes to harm the tree it can't protest or go away. It is also very sinful to cut down trees for producing sense gratification newspapers and magazines. In the past, I have seen loggers destroying acres like these in the mountains, felling in a matter of moments by chainsaw a tree which took hundreds of years to reach its stature and dignity in nature. As for the nearby scarred and crooked fir tree, he provides niches for many jays. Without him and his nearby brothers, I also would feel more desolate. Imagine, if when I looked out all I could see was barren rock or sand and dirt. It would tend to make the heart morose.

Stump and fallen tree

I do not wish to be holier than thou when I pass you, scarred tree, or to scorn you because of your sinfulness. As spirit soul, I am not better than you. Although you are silent, you convey to me the message that the proper use of human life is to escape becoming either a tree or once again a misled human being. May our daily chanting of the holy names of Kṛṣṇa penetrate your coverings of bark and your concentric circles of trunk, which obscure the pure soul lodged within.

I know you are tolerant, brother tree. I am no wonder-worker or great saint who can reach you as spirit soul. But at least I can recite here thoughtfully a prayer that you may know the Lord and accept my own respect for your right to live in God's wilderness. He is great, the Lord of all, and He desires to release us from all our reactions to misdeeds. He simply wants us to turn to Him and recognize that we are His lost but loving servants. He wants us to understand Him and begin to do whatever we are doing for His sake. And that can be done even in the forest and even—as recorded in Vedic literatures—by the trees.

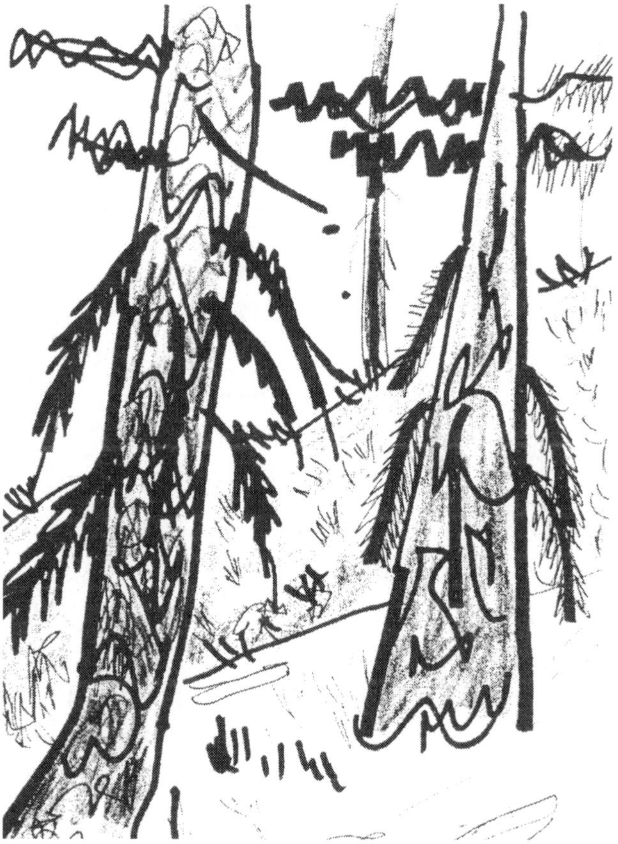

Fir tree, our chimney smoke
blows past you in the Alpine wind.
The calendar says spring,
but it's an Arctic air
that blows from the north.

I am not far away
from the Supreme Lord's presence:
"Of purifiers I am the wind."
Crashing through the forest,
is the wheel of birth and death.

It's up to me to reach Vaikuṇṭha
by a pure God consciousness
that sees right through
the sky and rock

Like a drinking cup,
I can receive clear water
and thank Him.
Because I am not dead,
I can make the choice.

Meditation: Beyond the Mountain

I often look out at this mountain. Maybe I should call it Yearning Peak. I cast my thought beyond it, to where? To a few hundred miles away, where there is civilization. I go beyond the wilderness to cities like Victoria, Seattle, to the south, the east. Maybe I should call it Mount Barrier. But why do I think it's a barrier only to a few cities which I yearn to reach? The mountain is actually a symbolic barrier of what prevents me from going beyond the entire material world, beyond my crippled conceptions of reaching safety and a house in Chicago or Pennsylvania and of attaining the warmth of "society, friendship, and love." I should yearn beyond the mountain for my eternal home in the spiritual world. *That's* what the mountain is preventing me from reaching. That's why we are *lost*: because we have forgotten Kṛṣṇa. These rocks are not preventing me from going there, I'm just caught (like almost everyone else on this planet) within false conceptions and illusions. I can free myself by Krishna's grace.

June 21

While cleaning out my briefcase I found an unopened letter. It was from someone named Bill whom I can't recall meeting. He had read an article by me in which I repeated Śrīla Prabhupāda's example illustrating why many people do not accept Kṛṣṇa consciousness. The example is that diamonds are very expensive, and so one cannot expect to have many customers, but that does not lessen the value of the diamonds. Bill objected to my use of this example and said that I'm claiming that only Hare Kṛṣṇa devotees are the elect of the world, and others are rejected by us as "*karmis*," "demons," and so on.

He said that he knew someone who knew me before I met Prabhupāda and that I was just an ordinary hippie in the 1960s who took L.S.D. and marijuana and had sex with my girlfriend. He wrote, "And you ate meat for the first 20 years of your life!"

Bill started ranting about the whole Hare Kṛṣṇa movement, whose members think they're the only ones who know love of God—and therefore we say that the diamonds cannot be easily purchased. He wrote, "You probably would say that one should not throw pearls before swine and that everyone is swine but you!" His conclusion was that I should wake up and surrender to his guru, Charles Ringo Boddhisattva, who Bill says is right this minute flooding the planet with Love. He included a quote from his guru, who said that his message is not only for his own disciples but for the four billion people on the planet and that this will all be revealed very soon. Bill also said, from what he knew of me, I was a "do-nothing" who never did much preaching or made any sacrifice.

As I read it, I thought that I was probably guilty of sounding smug in the article I wrote. I've done that before and people have caught me on it. I seem to think that there are only a few devotees in the world. If I had Bill's address, I would write him and admit it. But as for spreading Kṛṣṇa consciousness, Prabhupāda said both things—that we cannot expect everyone to become devotees and also that everyone *could* become devotees. Lord Kṛṣṇa states, *manuṣyāṇāṁ sahasreṣu* ... "Out of thousands of persons, few try for perfection and out of those who attain perfection, few know Kṛṣṇa in truth." And yet Lord Caitanya says that the planet will be flooded by love of God, *prema*, and that His holy names will be known in every town and village. I once asked Prabhupāda about this apparent contradiction, and he said it is up to the preachers whether love of God is spread widely.

With all our faults, at least we do have connection to a bona fide *sampradāya* and authorized scriptures. As for my personal history, it is true, I was degraded, but that was a past life. It seems that these fights and accusations will never end. I pray to keep simple obedience to the rules and regulations, and to keep my nose clean. Even if I cannot attain much progress in the inner life, I must at least keep clean behavior and faith in Śrīla Prabhupāda and Kṛṣṇa consciousness.

#18: Heavy Doubts and Heavy Reactions

Now I am going to tell the most dangerous episode that happened to me the whole time we were in the mountains. Or maybe it's the second most dangerous, not counting the time I thought of killing a creature to eat its meat. Before I tell it, I want to give a little preface.

Whether you are lost in the mountains or living in civilization, maintaining your spiritual life is a struggle for survival. Wherever you are, you have to guard against insults to the pure devotee and doubts in God or Kṛṣṇa, and you have to avoid sex agitation and maintain control of the tongue and mind. You have to be always on the alert. And eventually you have to attain a higher taste for spiritual life. The science of *bhakti-yoga* gives all protection if you practice it thoroughly. People sometimes think that *bhakti* is easy and sentimental, only singing and dancing in the temple. They think because it lacks austere meditation that it's just for women and children, not philosophers. Prabhupāda writes on this:

> Although nondevotees declare that the path of *bhakti*, or devotional service, is very easy, they cannot practice it. If the path of *bhakti* is so easy, as the nondevotee class of men proclaim, then why do they take up the difficult path? Actually, the path of *bhakti* is not easy. The so-called path of *bhakti* practiced by unauthorized persons without knowledge of *bhakti* may be easy, but when it is practiced factually according to the rules and regulations, the speculative scholars and philosophers fall away from the path.
>
> —*Bhagavad-gītā 7.3, purport*

So, the reason I fell into danger is clear and simple: I wasn't careful and so I fell into doubts again. I mean doubts in my initiating spiritual master, Gauracandra dāsa Swami. What happened is I read a letter which Gurudeva had left sitting on his bunk. It was a crazy hate letter criticizing him personally and even criticizing the whole Movement. It wasn't constructive, but based on a misunderstanding that because we say Kṛṣṇa consciousness is very difficult and only a few people can attain it, we're snobs. I should've put the letter down and not bothered about it. It wasn't even my business to pick it up and read it in the first place, but as I told you, I'm very nosy.

The personal accusations against my Gurudeva stuck in my mind, and the mind started to work on them. I'm not going to commit new offenses by writing all the details here, but I began to agree with some of the accusations. I began finding faults.

As I understand it now, my fault-finding tendency, and all the trouble I got into, was the destructive power of the uncontrolled mind. I know I have to take the blame for my wrong actions, but if there's to be some benefit from hearing of my activities, I think it's to learn what can happen to you if you can't control the mind. This is described in many places in the scriptures. For example, in the Fifth Canto of the *Śrīmad-Bhāgavatam*, Śukadeva Gosvāmī explains that the great devotee Ṛṣabhadeva was very careful in controlling his mind. Mahārāja Parīkṣit, who was hearing the whole narration of the *Bhāgavatam*, asked Śukadeva why Ṛṣabhadeva didn't use his mind to bring about mystic effects. Here is Śukadeva Gosvāmī's reply:

> My dear King, you have spoken correctly. However, after capturing animals, a cunning hunter does not put faith in them, for they might run away. Similarly, those who are advanced in spiritual life do not put faith in the mind. Indeed, they always remain vigilant and watch the mind's action.
>
> All the learned scholars have given their opinion. The mind is by nature very restless, and one should not make friends with it. If we place full confidence in the mind, it may cheat us at any moment. Even Lord Śiva became agitated upon seeing the Mohinī form of Lord Kṛṣṇa, and Saubhari Muni also fell down from the mature stage of yogic perfection.
>
> An unchaste woman is very easily carried away by paramours, and it sometimes happens that her husband is violently killed by her paramours. If the *yogī* gives his mind a chance and does not restrain it, his mind will give facility to enemies like lust, anger and greed, and they will doubtlessly kill the *yogī*.
>
> The mind is the root cause of lust, anger, pride, greed, lamentation, illusion, and fear. Combined, these constitute bondage to fruitive activity. What learned man would put faith in the mind?
>
> —*Śrīmad-Bhāgavatam* 5.6 2–5

I sometimes think of the expression, "My mind ran with it." It's like we're in a football game, and Māyā is the quarterback. She throws a long pass; the mind catches the football and thinks that it has to run with it. So, after reading that crazy letter my mind started running with the idea that my spiritual master is an ordinary man. I ran and didn't try to check myself although I *could* have. You can always look at things from two different sides. It was always possible to think of the previous life of my spiritual master before he met Prabhupāda, and to consider that he had imperfections and shortcomings. You can do that, but on the other hand, the scriptures warn us not to. Rūpa Gosvāmī states in *Upadeśāmṛta:*

> A devotee should not be seen from a materialistic point of view. One should overlook a devotee's having a body born in a low family, a body with a bad complexion, a deformed body, or a diseased or infirm body.

You're supposed to see a devotee just like the waters of the Ganges, which during the rainy season are full of bubbles, foam, and mud, but are not polluted. But I had caught Māyā's football, and I was running.

I suddenly got the idea that I should leave. I was by myself chopping wood in the forest and my mind said to me, "Why don't you just leave?" Our problem was that we were stuck in the mountains, but why not just leave? What I was actually telling myself was, "Leave Gurudeva." He had always said that we wouldn't be able to get anywhere on our own and that we should just wait until someone found us. But I thought, "That may be his idea, but it's not mine. I could probably just walk right out of here and find civilization within a few days." I was so impetuous that I didn't even want to discuss this idea with Gurudeva, but just carry it out at once. When a person rebels from his spiritual authority or is fed up with living in a temple, he usually thinks like that: "I'll leave." If you're living in a temple or monastery and you want to assert your independence and reject your authorities' hold on you, you *leave*. I wasn't thinking in such a gross way, that I wanted to bloop from spiritual life. But that was part of it. By dwelling on the accusations that my spiritual master was an ordinary man, I began to second-guess him and resent him. I had a better idea than to stay lost in the mountains. I would get out and find the way.

Without any further preparation, I began to walk away. I chose what

I thought was the eastern direction. Partly I thought that I was going to take a little exploratory hike just in case I did want to find my way out in the future. Partly, I thought that I would do myself and Gurudeva a favor and walk to civilization. I'd come back with people and rescue Gurudeva with a plane or helicopter. Still another part of me, the wild uncontrollable part, was walking away in order to disobey the order of the spiritual master.

I had done something similar to this the first few months after I had joined the Movement and was living in a temple. But at that time, it wasn't so serious. The temple was on South Street in Philadelphia, so when I walked out the door, my old world was right there. But I soon got a strong sense that it was just the same old chewing what had already been chewed. It was on a Friday night, and it wasn't long before I got disgusted with the night life, and scared, and so I came back to the temple that same night. But once I got going into the woods, I couldn't get out.

For most of that day I followed an animal trail which led in a general direction. Eventually I wandered off it and began crashing heavily through thick woods and undergrowth. Sometimes I plunged into ravines and sometimes climbed up hills and even mountains. From the very beginning I didn't know where I was going, and when the day began to turn dark, I became emotional: I was lost and afraid. I stumbled upon one of my own footprints and realized that I had been walking in a circle. I wanted to return to the cabin, but I didn't know how. I tried climbing another mountain, because from the top I might be able to see the smoke from the cabin or maybe a sign of civilization in another direction. But I picked out a mountain that was so tall it was above the tree line, and I didn't get far before it turned to night, and I had to stop.

I hadn't prepared myself for a trip and had no equipment or pack. Although it was supposed to be almost summer it became very cold and started to rain. I entered dense bushes, padded down a bed with leaves, and made my "camp" for the night. But because of cold and fear I couldn't sleep. I heard creatures moving about and sometimes the cry of a bird. I thought of the bears and wolves and Sasquatch—who seemed as real as anything to me as I sat crouched in my bush.

And then from partly up the hill came a low howl, which I knew to be a timber wolf. More wolves joined in, starting on a high note, then slowly dropping in tone and volume, Ow, Ow, Owwhoo-oo-oo. The wolves began answering each other from different sides until there seemed to be wolves howling in every direction. Their howls became louder and more intense and then I thought I saw shadows slinking along only a short distance from where I sat. Shivers ran up and down my spine, and I fervently wished that I had stayed back at the cabin with Gurudeva. But it was too late for wishing to do me any good. After what seemed a long time, the wolf pack joined together in one place, all howling, and I guessed that they made a kill, probably a moose.

I desperately chanted Kṛṣṇa's names that night, but I was too panicked to pray for love of God. When dawn came, I got up and continued walking, although didn't know either my immediate direction or my destination. I soon came upon a pile of bones with no hair or flesh, which was all that was left of the wolf attack on the moose. There were wolf tracks all over the muddy ground. That didn't help me any to use cool-headed thinking. I continued to lurch around, tripping over branches, scraping my hands and face bloody from twigs and thorns, and only stopping when I ran out of breath. I don't even want to remember the details of that day, and I hope I never have to go through another one like it.

I was so afraid of the dark by the second night that again I couldn't sleep, and I kept thinking that every sound was a ferocious animal coming to attack and eat me. To protect myself I climbed into a tree and spent the night there. During that night, I started "coming down" from panic and total confusion. I began to understand what had happened and what I had done. I had been so self-centered about the whole thing that only after two days did I feel bad that I had left Gurudeva alone! I began to worry for him and feel sorry for myself. But I checked those emotions too, lest I plunge myself into another turmoil. Instead, I began to consider in a more cool-headed way, "What am I going to do?"

In the morning, I climbed down the tree and remembered some of the Boy Scout stuff I had learned as a kid. I didn't have a compass or anything, but I tried to use common sense. I at least knew that the sun rises in the East. So, if that was the direction that I had started heading out in, probably if I turned the opposite direction from the sunrise, I would be heading somewhat toward the cabin. I definitely decided that I wanted to return to Gurudeva. He was right, that it was probably best not to try hiking out of the wilderness. At least I wasn't the man to do it. As for all the offensive reasons and the half-mad plan to "leave," I just put that out of my mind for the time being. I walked all day concentrating my energies in trying to walk in one direction without going in circles. What I did was line myself up visually with an object ahead, like a particular tree or rock, and then made sure that I reached it. At the same time, I tried to leave a trail by breaking branches or scarring the bark with a rock. Then I could look behind me and double check that I was keeping my straight path. I'm not sure if I remembered that technique or whether I just thought it up, but just the fact that I was using my wits in a realistic way made me feel more cheerful. I thought of myself as an Indian scout, and of returning to the cabin as a contest of my skills in nature. I also began chanting Hare Kṛṣṇa in a rhythmic way to keep from feeling scared or lonely. By the afternoon of that day, I recognized the face of a particular mountain peak and I headed toward it. Just before it started getting dark, I climbed another smaller mountain and from the top I finally saw the column of smoke which I knew was Gurudeva in his cabin. After that sight, I ran nonstop in the right direction and reached home, even though it was completely dark for about the last hour of the hike.

Gurudeva was so happy to see me that he jumped up, called "Nimāi!" and embraced me. He had tears in his eyes, and I was crying too.

"What happened?" he said, but he didn't give me a chance to answer. He said he had been worried and tried walking to find me and that he was praying to Kṛṣṇa. I started to explain a little, but not everything at once. Gurudeva, however, knows me like a book, so whatever I didn't explicitly say he already knew. But neither he nor I wanted to get into it. We were just happy to be united again. He said that I should take a bath and that he would prepare some dandelion soup and salad. So, we did that and for the first time in two days I relaxed and was able to sleep in the warmth of the cabin and in the company of my best friend. I was feeling very grateful to Kṛṣṇa.

Gurudeva didn't reprimand me for what I'd done. He must've thought that I had already received enough punishment. But we discussed it the next day.

"When people criticize the spiritual master," I said, "the mind thinks that at least *some* of it may be correct. But it's so heavy! So how do we deal with it? I was thinking that we should have blind faith in the guru. Is that right?"

"Not blind faith," said Gurudeva, "but unflinching faith. It's blind if you accept the spiritual master sentimentally or dogmatically. You should become educated in the position of your spiritual master and your relationship with him, according to reason and argument based on the scriptures. But once you accept a spiritual master, it should be with unflinching faith. Prabhupāda even said that he didn't know what would come from following his spiritual master's order to print and distribute books, but he said, 'I did it in blind faith.' As for hearing criticism of the guru or Vaiṣṇava, the scriptures say you should argue back or leave that place if you can't argue."

"But what if a spiritual master cheats a disciple who has unflinching faith in him?"

"That is the greatest misfortune." said Gurudeva. "We have to take all care before we select a spiritual master. But you cannot, out of fear that you'll be cheated, refuse to surrender. If a spiritual master misbehaves, he can also be rejected—if he deviates from Kṛṣṇa conscious philosophy or falls down from religious life. Even then, the disciple should first patiently wait and pray to Kṛṣṇa that his spiritual master may be redeemed. Also, the past life of a spiritual master, before he became initiated, shouldn't be held against him. You shouldn't even be curious about it. Nārada says the disciple should be submissive and should have an attitude of firm friendship for the spiritual master. So, he should be able to talk with him intimately about his doubts, and reason them out."

"I hear all kinds of criticisms of the spiritual master," I said, "not just that letter that I read, but in the Victoria temple and almost any place you go you hear things if you're listening for them. Sometimes they say, 'Your guru isn't doing the highest service,' and they quote Prabhupāda. Or they say, 'your guru doesn't preach enough or associate enough with his Godbrothers, or he doesn't take care of his disciples,' and so on. It's heavy!"

"You should be aware," said Gurudeva, "that the statements you just gave are opinions. They're not absolute. He says that your guru isn't doing the highest service, but what is actually highest? Just because somebody criticizes, doesn't mean it's the absolute."

"It seems that this relationship is inconceivable," I said. "Kṛṣṇa is inconceivable, and the guru is His representative. Is that right?"

"Yes, Prabhupāda says, 'The spiritual master and disciple do not need to understand anything more than Kṛṣṇa, because by understanding Kṛṣṇa and by talking about Kṛṣṇa, one becomes a perfect, learned person.' The relationship of guru and *śiṣya* is not within this material world."

As I said before, my tendency is to eulogize *māyā* more than to praise Kṛṣṇa. I'm amazed and bewildered how *māyā* always bowls me over despite my good intentions. So, in spite of myself, I praise her. It's like expressing awe at the power of a hurricane that just tore apart your house. In that mood, I was just about to close this chapter by reminding everyone of the power of the uncontrolled mind. Arjuna says in the *Bhagavad-gītā*:

> For the mind is restless, turbulent, obstinate and very strong, O Kṛṣṇa, and to subdue it, I think, is more difficult than controlling the wind.
>
> —*Bhagavad-gītā, 6.34*

But I just thought of something else Gurudeva said to me that afternoon, after I had returned from leaving him

"Nimāi," he asked, "When you were up in the tree all night, were you praying?"

"Yes, Gurudeva. I was praying I wouldn't be attacked. I was too far gone to pray for anything else."

"Still, you were praying. You turned to Kṛṣṇa."

"Yes, I was chanting. And once I got my bearings, I chanted Hare Kṛṣṇa all the way back to the cabin."

"If you pray and chant," said Gurudeva, "as much as possible, all the time, that will help more than anything else to deal with your mental problem. We all need to do it, but maybe it's Kṛṣṇa's mercy that He is showing you that if you don't chant and pray, you'll be an easy victim for the uncontrolled mind."

How could I forget this most valuable instruction? I only hope that before my life is over, I'll be able to say truly that I have learned to take shelter in the holy names of Kṛṣṇa.

#19: Gurudeva's Journal: Nothing to Do But Surrender

June 28

Ekādaśī: a quiet day with nothing to do but surrender to chanting. At least I surrender my occupation, will, breath, and so on, to the practice of *nāma bhajana*. Prabhupāda encouraged us by the example: If an iron rod is left in the fire, it will eventually become hotter until finally it acts as fire.

Chanting of Hare Kṛṣṇa *japa* is as real to me as the mountains, chimney smoke, and rain. So, mountains *and* chanting; sky *and* chanting; holy name *and* me. *Sarvaṁ khalv idaṁ brahma*: Everything is Kṛṣṇa. Although my realization is junior, I won't deny it; it's my only hope.

Sitting before the firelight with the returned son, Nimāi, up all night singing *bhajans*. As we sing, I conjure up the times when I sat in temple rooms in the U.S.A. and Europe with other devotees. We would warm up with favorites like *Bhajahū re mana* and *Yaśomatī-nandana* ... Hours passed in the most simple and direct consciousness—Lord Kṛṣṇa is the beloved son of Mother Yaśodā, and He is the transcendental lover in the land of Vraja.

To sing *bhajans* with only one other is also satisfying, and tonight we are linked up with all other devotees around the world who are performing this vigil. If this light goes out, we will be immersed in darkness.

From "Vibhāvarī Śeṣa":

O mind, obey these words of mine and sing the glories of Śrī Kṛṣṇa in the form of these holy names which are full of nectarean mellows.

From "Śrī Dāmodarāṣṭaka"

O Supreme Godhead, I offer my obeisances unto You. O Dāmodara! O Ananta! O Viṣṇu! O master! O my Lord, be pleased upon me. By showering Your glance of mercy upon me, deliver this poor ignorant fool who is immersed in an ocean of worldly sorrows, and become visible to my eyes.

Yawning, stretching a leg, languishing in the lake of nectarean *bhajans* by Narottama dāsa Ṭhākura and Bhaktivinoda Ṭhākura. After we sing, we read aloud in English. You're tired, but you stay up. "This is my desire, that birth after birth I may live with those devotees who serve the lotus feet of the Six Gosvāmīs."

In a cabin
by stove light
we stayed awake
feasting on the holy names.
We took no other food or drink
and spoke few words,
only the singing.

The harmonium player pumped
a mixture of reeds,
in tunes from Bengal
in praise of Lord Kṛṣṇa
in the mood of Narottama.

Deep in the woods,
we attracted the attention
of the killer of Keśī,
the enjoyer of the *rāsa*,
He who appeared as half-man, half-lion,
who is worshiped by a *tulasī* leaf.

During the night
we felt we accomplished
the goal of our works.

Outside after midnight—cold, very dark, no moon. The whole sky is filled with stars. They are inconceivable, and no human can entirely figure them out. No one from here can go there. But in another sense, the stars are simple fact: lights in the night. I cannot read the stars, except for the Big and Little Dippers. In some places the stars appear tiny and powdered together thickly, and in other places they are big lights in more space.

Our mountains are hard, black outlines, darker than the dark sky. The sky of stars reminds me of my childhood. Now I am in the *paramparā* of Vedic wisdom, which explains the stars and everything else, but I cannot enter that wisdom yet. The best thing for me is to chant Hare Kṛṣṇa—and not stand out here in the cold. I'm cold enough and lonely, better go in where there's a fire and a human spirit to chant beside.

July 1

Nimāi dropped on me the criticisms that other devotees make of me. I'm not sure whether Nimāi actually heard my Godbrothers saying these things about me, or whether they are general criticisms that he has heard over the years toward many gurus. I suppose some Godbrothers say that I am not doing the highest service. Some would say the highest service is distribution of Prabhupāda's books, and there are letters by Prabhupāda to indicate that. But this old controversy has been termed "childish" by Prabhupāda, and he said it was not worthy of his older students. According to Prabhupāda, each service within the nice processes of devotional service is absolute. A devotee advances according to his sincerity, and not by belonging to a certain department, or by putting down others' service. My service is more in the education of devotees and the literary field, although I've also helped to distribute Prabhupāda's literature. I want to read his literature and serve the devotees who read and distribute his literature. I want to exemplify the life he teaches in his books.

The result of my hearing criticism is that I defend myself. I've given up mating, eating, some sleeping, yet I defend myself at the first sign of attack, just like the forest birds and beasts.

What did he mean, "some say that your guru is not preaching enough and that he should associate more with his Godbrothers, and that's why he's deviating. Some say he's neglecting his disciples, and that's why they are growing independent and drifting away. Prabhupāda didn't stress the kind of things that he stresses."?

The accusations are full of truth-hurts. But I cry back defiantly. "Oh yeah? Oh yeah? We'll see who is pleasing Prabhupāda!" And then I ask, "*Who* has criticized me, tell me who?" I want to know so that I can attack the arguments by the "honorable" method of *ad hominem*: "Oh, *he* said it? Well, who is *he* to speak? He may have distributed some books, but he fell down once really bad, remember? Is *he* the kind you say I should associate with? And does *he* say that I neglect my disciples? But *he* does it!" (Do two wrongs make a right?)

Although I am alone, I have become restless hearing the voices of others criticizing me. In *Śrīmad-Bhāgavatam*, hearing criticism is compared to the harsh sounds of crickets. He who hankers for prestige works hard for it, but when he doesn't attain it, he suffers. The proud religionist wants to be known as a Vaiṣṇava, and when he doesn't receive the laurels which he thinks he deserves, he claims sour grapes. He thereby exposes his lack of humility. But Lord Caitanya said humility was the first requisite for chanting the holy name constantly.

As Nimāi dumped it on me, I am now dumping it on you, and so the world is polluted by garbage disposal. Let me not dump it on others but cleanse my polluted mind and heart which are always harassed and which are so prone to strike back in the struggle for survival. Let me cleanse myself in chanting the holy names and humbly admit my wrongs. Pray, when I get the chance to associate with Godbrothers and to serve Prabhupāda's movement directly. I will be kinder, more grateful, and more active a soldier—if He will allow me.

#20: The Last Month

I don't mean to give the impression that every day was a crisis, with me falling into illusion and Gurudeva pulling me out by the hair two seconds before I drowned to death. Many days were quiet and peaceful.

Gurudeva began writing Kṛṣṇa consciousness portraits called "Persons and Places I Met in the Mountains." I would go with him and sit in some spot to wait for animals, or just to be quiet until I could start noticing things. He and I could sit for hours that way, Gurudeva occasionally making notes, or both of us reading *Śrīmad-Bhāgavatam* silently, or chanting softly. When an animal or hawk would suddenly appear, we would both notice without commenting. Just to give me service, Gurudeva also asked me to draw simple pictures of whatever we saw. Some of the birds became unafraid of us, and jays would eat from our hands. There was also a marten, which is like a small fox only more mildly tempered, and he became tame around us. He had shiny eyes and sleek black fur, and day by day he came closer to us until he would eat from our hands and allow himself to be petted.

The forest school continued in an informal way. I would memorize verses and study the scriptures, but without any pressure. Although I've recorded a few of the talks with Gurudeva, we had innumerable other talks. Sometimes we discussed what we would do when we re-entered society. I said I would like to continue traveling with him, but if he ever decided otherwise, then I'd like to open my own preaching center. I was only daydreaming, but Gurudeva didn't mind. I thought that I would like to get a small house in the country and grow a garden and have *brahmacārīs* come and live there. We would eat simply, work on the land, and read and chant. I imagined that such a place would have preaching value too, because people would come and want to spend time with us. We would have a guest room, but everything would be on the austere side, and there would be no nonsense or talking politics or fault-finding. Gurudeva said it sounded nice.

He said that he would like to start an institute and offer courses for devotees. Or he would like to travel around the world and preach to people in their homes. He would visit devotees who had become married and who didn't have much connection with the Movement anymore. But he would also visit the temples in every country and go with the devotees in the street for *hari-nāma*. Or maybe he would go to India and spend years there learning the culture. Mainly he wanted to live as a simple *sannyāsī* and to preach.

We did many little things in the mountains which I'll probably never get around to telling, but some of them were memorable in their own ways. For example, cutting wood. I got to be quite expert at it. It seemed like years had gone by since I had chopped that first tree when I was so afraid and incompetent. I never lost my fear of bears, but it was just something you lived with, and none ever attacked us. Or wolves either. We did sight them a number of times, but they went about their business and we went about ours.

It was always quiet in the mountains. The ground froze up at night and then became soft in the day. There were many wonderful things there, and even when you became familiar with them, they didn't disgust you. It was a wonderful place. But I probably would have a completely different opinion if I hadn't been there in the company of my spiritual master, who allowed me to see everything in a spiritual way.

In the last month I had a problem with not having enough to eat. There *was* enough, but my mind and tongue couldn't accept it. We had been eating whatever nature provided for several months, and I had already passed the first tests where the body and mind react in extreme ways. I knew we had enough food to sustain life and that it was even beneficial for health and spirituality. Since that time, I've also heard how people are able to continue fasts for a very long time without suffering, as long as they have water. You just have to learn to separate the intelligence from the mind and the body. The intelligence has to dominate and tell the body and mind what to do. I accomplished that for a while. All my bodily demands—eating, sleeping, mating, and defending—were reduced. I was able to guide the body and the mind without them so much engaged in a tug-of-war with me. I became more peaceful and could read and chant with attention. I was physically weaker, but that only meant that I had to work in a restrained and thoughtful way. And there were other benefits from our diet, but as time wore on, I lost my patience and Gurudeva had to help me out.

We were eating mostly roots and greens, either boiling them or eating them as salad. Although some of the roots were starchy, we never found enough to have what I would call a satisfying meal. Sometimes we ate dandelion leaves, cattails, and wild strawberries (but the other animals gave us heavy competition for these). There was also a berry I've since found out is called cloudberry, but we couldn't find many, and then there were thistle roots, miner's lettuce, and silverweed roots. We had experimented with most of the local weeds, flowers, and tree products and had settled on these items as most edible and nutritious. I thought I had already accepted the bland taste of the food and the lack of bulk, but sometimes I would start daydreaming of foods that I used to like. Then with the gradual weakening of my body, I began to think that I needed more strength. A line came into my head: "The sage Viśvāmitra once ate a dog." I didn't know where this statement came from, but I attributed it to Śrīla Prabhupāda. Viśvāmitra was supposedly in a desert and unless he ate the dog's flesh he would have died. This was called "emergency *dharma*." I had also heard that *kṣatriyas* sometimes ate meat. Someone said that Bhīma ate meat and in one translation of the *Rāmāyaṇa* it states that Lord Rāma hunted deer. I thought, "I'm not a *brāhmaṇa*. So maybe I'm a *kṣatriya*."

When I thought like this, I began to look at the living creatures with a different eye. I had often seen fish in the creek from which I drew water. There were some big ones, like carp, and probably if somebody wanted to, he could catch them in the clear water with just a little endeavor. But other animals, like rabbits or marten, would require more skill to kill. *"And Viśvāmitra once ate a dog."*

I didn't get very far before Gurudeva caught me. I had gone as far as to think of how to make a fishing hook by carving it from wood. I made a few drawings and maybe Gurudeva saw them. By this time, he and I had such a close relationship that we could almost read each other's minds. At least he could read my mind, and I was often able to know what Gurudeva wanted before he spoke to request it. Without accusing me of planning to hunt and eat animal flesh, Gurudeva began talking about it one day. His main point was that we were not dying, and we had sufficient food from the vegetable kingdom. He said that all the other animals were being provided their needs, so why should Kṛṣṇa neglect us? The Lord wasn't neglecting, He was supplying us. It was not as if I were already a meat-eater that he had to preach to me about vegetarianism, but Gurudeva actually spoke to me like that. He said that the human body has teeth and intestines designed for vegetarian eating. And more importantly, the scriptures forbid eating of flesh and killing of creatures. If the human kills fish or animals just to satisfy the senses, he incurs very bad karma and has to suffer as a result. So, we shouldn't cause any living entity unnecessary pain.

Gurudeva emphasized that we were all right and that Kṛṣṇa was taking care of us. He told a story that Prabhupāda had told him one day in Bombay during a general strike. Because of the strike many people were without food, and they were in anxiety. But Prabhupāda noted that somehow the devotees in the *āśrama* had sufficient food. He said that this was a sign that Kṛṣṇa was taking special care of them. But Prabhupāda said that even if they did not get food, they would then take the opportunity to sit down and just chant Hare Kṛṣṇa. That is what Gurudeva wanted: for us to be assured that Kṛṣṇa was supplying sufficient food from nature and that we would not starve to death. But even if such a thing were to occur, we should accept it as His mercy. When I mentioned to Gurudeva the line about Viśvāmitra, he said that did not apply to our situation. After that, I stopped complaining and Kṛṣṇa released me from that anxiety. And as the weather grew warmer, we began to find new varieties of edibles, and life was easier.

On a few occasions during our stay in the mountains we saw planes flying overhead. But they were very far away, like stars in the sky, or we would see the trail of a jet or its shimmering lights. One time a prop plane came closer, but the pilot didn't notice us or didn't know we were in trouble. Then one day, after we had been there for almost five months, a small plane came over close when we were cooking and there was a tall column of smoke rising from our chimney. When I head the plane engine, I ran outside and waved to it with both my arms. The pilot then moved the wings in recognition. I thought he wouldn't know we actually needed help, so I threw myself on the ground in a spread-eagle position and again he flipped his wings. He circled around our camp and then landed on the lake. The lake was about a hundred yards long and he used almost every foot of it to come to a stop. By this time Gurudeva and I were completely excited and happy, shouting and running toward the plane. When we came near enough, the pilot shouted, "You guys need help?"

Within an hour we had packed our belongings in the plane, made quick farewells to our "home," and crawled into the plane for take-off.

"It's about an hour to Squamish," the pilot shouted over the engine's roar as we leveled and flew south. "You can tell me all about it," he said.

Gurudeva let me do the talking so I spoke up loudly, and told about our experiences, including some Kṛṣṇa conscious topics, as we flew through mild weather and clear skies over the Alpine region of British Columbia.

"That was a good story; maybe you should write a book," the man said as we unloaded at a dock near Squamish. He gave me a hearty slap on the back that sent me reeling, and then he taxied down the lake for another take-off, leaving us waving and thanking him for the rescue.

At Squamish, Gurudeva phoned to find out what happened to Bob Gates. We were disappointed to learn that the airport in Victoria didn't know anything of Gates' whereabouts. No one had been even looking for him or his plane because he had not logged out the day we flew five months ago. We later learned that none of the devotees have seen him, although there was a rumor that someone met him on a street in Seattle.

We took a bus to Victoria. At first everything we saw brought a shock. We had become so attuned to living alone in the mountains. When we approached the first city, the car traffic seemed incredibly fast, and the congestion and noise were unnerving. We were glad to be rescued, but we had some mixed feelings too.

They gave us a nice reception at the temple in Victoria, and that night they had a big feast in our honor. I was overjoyed to be able to taste real *prasādam* again. One of the important reasons I had joined the Movement was because of the taste of *purī* and *halava* and sweet rice and vegetable preparations when they're expertly cooked, the way the Indians can do it. So, we feasted and everybody kidded me about eating and gaining weight, and they gave me a lot of attention. The temple president invited the media, and men came from the television and newspapers for a press conference. Gurudeva and I explained our adventures, how we crashed in the mountains and lived there. It was a good opportunity to express some Kṛṣṇa consciousness realizations. This time Gurudeva did most of the talking. But unfortunately, the TV and newspaper reports that came out were more or less twisted and unfavorable. They mostly told about a court case in which an ex-devotee was suing the Movement for "brainwashing" him. For ten minutes they talked about that, and only at the end did they talk a little bit about our being stranded in the mountains. There was a close up of Gurudeva saying that he was disappointed when returning to civilization to see the amount of pollution and waste of energy compared to the peace of nature in its unspoiled state. But the newscaster made a wise crack, "While nature tests our endurance by physical hardship, civilization has her own tests. And on their emergence from the wilderness, two Hare Kṛṣṇas may have to ask whether they are among the fittest to survive in this environment." When I saw the TV show and the stupid remarks I thought, "It's the same old world."

Some of Gurudeva's disciples who lived on the U.S. East Coast were so happy to hear that he'd returned that they flew out to West Canada just to greet him. And they were planning a big homecoming for us at the farm in Pennsylvania.

One day in the Victoria temple they even asked me to give a special talk to the devotees. In my talk I was praising Gurudeva for being courageous and resourceful and mentioned, for example, how he learned to cook using wild plants. One of the devotees laughed and said, "You don't have to be a 'Gurudeva'—*anyone* would have thought of *that*." And then another said, "What do you expect from a Gurudeva groupie?" That brought me down to earth again. Things hadn't changed that much since we were away.

Gurudeva said that he and I really hadn't done anything very wonderful, and so we shouldn't expect to be praised. It's good that he said that, because I was beginning to feel that I had become a very serious devotee. I was surprised when we first arrived at the temple to see how some of the *brahmacārīs* were talking frivolously. It was harmless, but I wasn't used to it. Yet within a few hours, I was also being frivolous. I had thought that I had become more serious than other devotees, but it really wasn't true. And then when I began noticing the women, it was clear to me that I was as much attracted to them as ever. Within a few days I had given up some of the best parts of my daily schedule from the mountains, like my early morning studying of Prabhupāda's books. And I lost my momentum on careful *japa* too.

Gurudeva was probably especially glad to get rid of me as his only companion. I tried not to presume anymore that I should take up all his time, but one night when we were still in Victoria, he called me to his room. As we spoke together about the "old times" in the wilderness, we both realized that our isolation had been in many ways a very nice opportunity.

"Don't regret being back," said Gurudeva.

I don't regret it, and neither do I regret whatever we went through. For me, the main benefit was that I enjoyed a serious relationship with a serious person, my spiritual master. Before this time, I was not used to being with him, but now that I know more what he's like, my intention is to serve him. I hope he doesn't kick me away.

Appendix

"Persons, Places, and Things I Met in the Mountains"

by Gauracandra dāsa Swami
(Drawings by Nimāi dasa)

1: Patience

I tried meeting patience. To meet her you have to first get past Quick Cheap Victory, and you also have to get past the conviction that you have many things to do on time. I found it better to approach Patience by sitting rather than standing. So, I sat on the hill in the forest overlooking a deep ravine, and I watched and waited. Because I was not able to overcome all the obstacles, I didn't fully meet with Patience on my first try. But she came near at one point, and I think I heard her say, "Don't expect anything but participation. Just participate in *bhakti-yoga* and everything will be revealed to you." So, I sat for an hour, and although I saw no animals and I only brushed with Patience, I thought, "If I can carry this with me, I'll perform devotional service much more peacefully." Lord Kṛṣṇa says, "Among women I am ... patience."

2: Juniper

I met a dull green juniper with its small gray berries bunched on the branches. It was about six feet tall with a thin top, like a Christmas tree. Next to it was a brighter green fir tree with straight stiff needles. When I saw them, both trees swayed on their hill in the pushes and tugs of the wind.

Why and for whom does the juniper produce those berries? Not for *me*. How much bigger will it grow? How long will it live? I can scarcely conceive that within the tree there is a soul as good as mine. If I sat here longer, I would learn more.

By meeting the creatures, one meets oneself. Ferocious beasts make us afraid, or they make us ferocious to fight back. And the swaying, forbearing juniper loaded with bitter berries makes me think of the origin (*janmādy asya*), from which everything comes.

Juniper and Evergreen

3: Old Tree Trunk

About a hundred yards from the cabin, I met an old tree trunk, two feet high. I don't know the story of when it was chopped down. But if I could count the rings, I would know how old it was when it was cut. The exposed part is ancient gray, with holes gouged by birds or animals. By *karma* the soul of this tree had to leave, but in the abandoned hulk new life has entered in the form of tiny green lichen.

The dead stump still dominates the scene. A piece of it sticks upright forming a crude sun dial. It is a page in Nature's Book, but in order to read it one needs a special literacy.

4: The Evening Sun

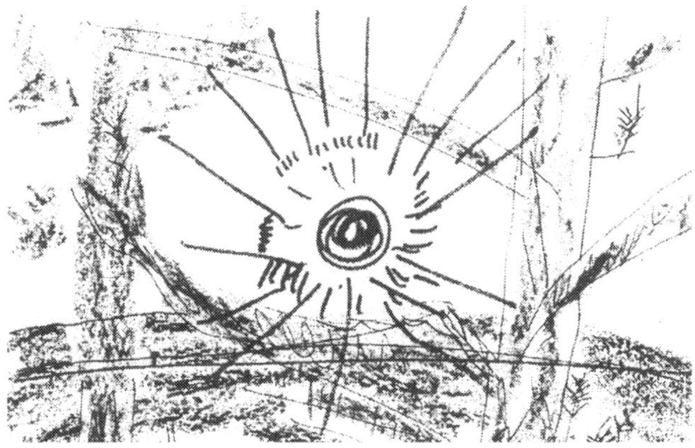

I sat in a spot where I could see the evening sun blazing above a hill, and the sky was clear blue. The sun blaze was so glaring you couldn't look at it. Only through the fir branches could you watch it indirectly.

When you meet a creature or thing in nature, it's not just you and that entity in a vacuum, but you enter a harmony. Like now, it's not me and the sun, but me and the sunshine, and the fir branches, and the cool breeze, my own body relaxed, the constant whoosh and no other sound (thank God), the steady earth, the dirt, weeds, rocks — everything. It's all Kṛṣṇa and His energies and His parts and parcels. Just as we can't meet the sun directly, so we may not see the Supreme Lord face to face, but He's here in all this.

5: Rotting Log

In a ravine I saw a reddish, rotting log. It was open and shredded, worked on by animals, but mostly by time. The log was once a solid object, but now it is turning to mulch, returning to earth. Even the hill is disintegrating. I can't detect the hill's decay because my eyes are untrained, but I can't miss the work of time on the log.

In the *Śrīmad-Bhāgavatam* it is stated that time is the impersonal feature of the Supreme Personality of Godhead which is present in this world to remind us. We act so perky, well dressed, well fed, chattering our civilized language as we stumble through the forest with a million ideas in our heads. But we will soon pass. Most trees outlive us. Human superiority is to understand all selves are eternal spirit. We can receive education from the *Vedas* and the guru, and we can also see for ourselves the rotting log.

6: Moose

We met a moose shortly after we arrived, when there was still plenty of snow on the ground. Although he had no antlers, I think it was a bull moose, but the meeting was too brief to become well acquainted. He snorted outside the cabin, about fifteen feet away, and when I opened the door, he looked at me and Nimāi as if to say, "Who are you and what are you doing here in the land of wilderness?" He didn't show much fear or aggression. We watched each other for a while, and then he continued nosing around for edible weeds.

For people who live in this north country, a meeting with a moose usually means, "Hey, Brad, hand me the rifle." They plug him in the head. Good meat for winter. But do they really have to do it? They will scoff at my words. Granted that I don't know the hardship of a trapper or a northern homesteader. But God's law is the law for all. He who unnecessarily kills a creature (which means it is not done in service to God) will have to suffer karma in the future. A life for a life; you can't avoid it.

The moose I saw had a long hairy nose and big droopy lips dangling under his chin. Not very handsome. Patches of fur had fallen from his winter coat and he was awkward looking on spindly legs. But if the son says to the father, "Dad, your other son is so stupid and ugly looking. I want to kill him," the father will not allow. He will say, "Don't you dare! Just mind your own business, I'll maintain him." Our moose was a welcome sight at a time when we felt frightened in alien land. After seeing him, we felt less alone.

7: Spider

One cold day I sat for an hour and could see no moving creature, though I felt sure that many could see me. I could only hear birds. But when I looked at my notepad, I saw a small spider. He was tan colored and moving about with his many legs. But when I looked again, he'd disappeared. Most creatures are shy, and they want nothing to do with a human being. I don't blame them.

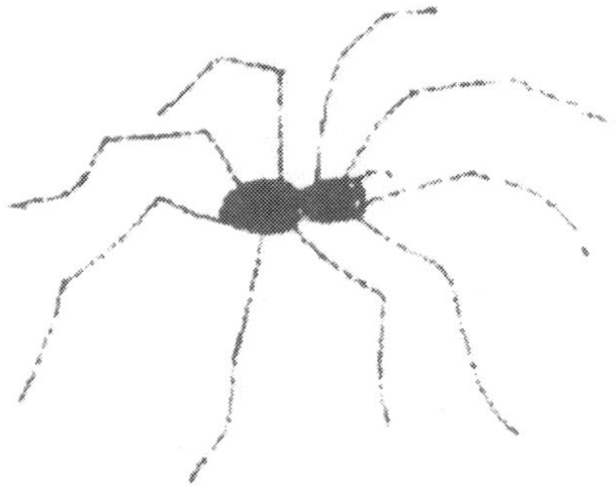

8: Bear

According to a booklet in the cabin, "An annoyed black bear can quickly kill a human." That got us going. Nimāi saw the bears first. But before I saw one, I often sensed them. I mistook a dark boulder or a stump for a bear. Even a blowing weed or a quick movement by a robin made me look up in expectation.

I remember William Faulkner's *The Bear* in which the bruin was a symbol for God —He who is unseen but is always watching. But Vedic literature teaches that the Supreme Lord Kṛṣṇa is our dearmost friend. For us the bear may be more of a symbol of fear of death.

When I actually saw the bear, I did not meet symbolic fear, but the real thing. I had to act. But what was right? Should I run, climb, or stand still? I had heard different advice. She was on all fours, round-backed, and with a cub alongside. I was sitting on a hill overlooking a steep ravine, and the bear started down the ravine from the opposite side. I decided it was better that she see me rather than walk on top of me, so I stood, cracking twigs. She stopped. I stood frozen with fear. Did I think of Kṛṣṇa? Yes—I could hardly stop from talking out loud to Him. But I waited for the bear—she was the object of my fascination. Then she saw me or smelled me. She must have known I wasn't fearless, and yet I was something tall and strange. She decided to give me the right of way and turned around, black and sleek on four claws, and started up the hill with junior behind her. They took their time and stopped once to look back, and then disappeared. It was a while before I settled down after my encounter with the king of these mountains.

Now I can join with the story tellers, "The time I met Blacky over a ravine." It wasn't Death. Or if she *was* death, she was only on a visit—"See you later."

9: Rocks and a Rock

How do you get to know a rock? The same way that you meet other objects or persons. There's a first meeting with some first impressions. A colorful rock catches your eye, whereas some rocks are nondescript lumps. Rocks that you see more often become part of your life. They seem to be the densest objects in the natural world. No human by himself can lift a very big rock. If hit on the head by a rock, your skull will crack before the rock does. But rocks aren't violent if you leave them alone; they very humbly and silently stay in their own place. During the day they heat up from the sun's rays and grow cold at night.

There was a grey-blue rock in front of the cabin. It was flat and about as big as my hand. On closer inspection I noticed that it was layered. The green sediment must have formed thousands and millions of years ago, maybe at the bottom of a pond or lake. Some clay and copper dropped ever so slowly through the water. And just as this rock may have been formed by the wearing down of a mountain, so it also is wearing down.

The tiny lichen which has attached itself to the rock is breaking it up, and so is the thawing and the freezing. The rock has been smoothed by wind and rain and is being worn down by time.

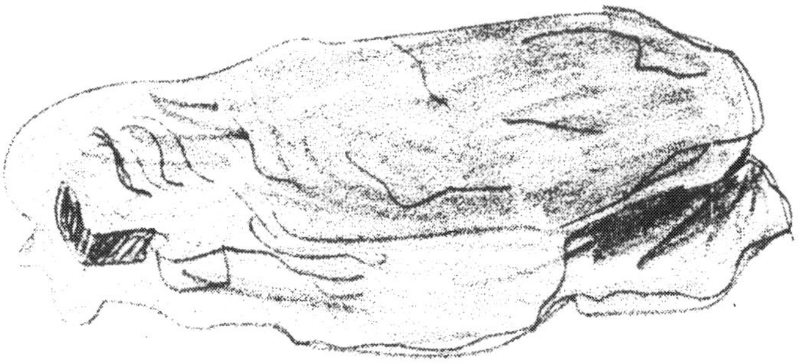

Why do we think we are better than a rock? At least in terms of longevity, we are just a flash in the pan. The rock has seen empires come and go, and many persons like us. The only reason a human being is special is because he has higher consciousness for self-realization. A human can break through the cycle of birth and death, but a rock can only wait.

10: Jet Trail

One day I quietly looked up and saw a shining object making twin jet trails high above. The sky was blue and the double lines of the white jet stream were very clear. Soon the engine could be heard, but not very loudly and only for a while. I thought of the nuclear doomsday movie, *"The Day After,"* which showed the white trail of an intercontinental missile leaving Lawrence, Kansas, while megaton nuclear warheads raced to the U.S. from Soviet Russia.

After five minutes there was no more jet sound. The jay became raucous. A junco twittered. The jet trails faded in the blue.

11: Trying to Figure It Out

Robins sang, "Cheer up, cheer up," and a winged Polly nose seed floated onto my head. But why is everyone a predator?

I admit there's a limit to communing and seeking brotherhood in the forest. It is all claw and fang, tramping and swooping down, killing by strangulation, bleeding to death, eating flesh, crunching bones.

Only in human life can you hope to comprehend this by hearing from the *śāstras*. The savagery of the woods is no worse than that of human civilization, which makes war and runs slaughterhouses. In fact, the "law" of humans is worse than the laws of the jungle.

Some days in the forest were like that: Confused about Kṛṣṇa's plan and finally realizing, I can't know anything on my own. I came back to the cabin and read *Śrīmad-Bhāgavatam.* Then in the dark we chanted while the wolves howled.

12: Creekside Birches, Rosehips, and Buttercups

It was a relief to wander into the birch grove. The trees were growing by a stream covered by snow and ice. We saw the red birch shoots. The older birches were sprouting buds like pussy willows. Growing among the new birches were little bushes of rosehips. They tasted like dry fruit with a small core of juiciness. By the same creekside, we found a bank where yellow buttercups were growing, the first flowers I saw in the mountains

The Supreme Lord's creation is vast and inconceivable, and souls are everywhere.

13: Chickadees

Some chickadees came close, singing *tseep-tseep* from the nearby evergreens. They were curious to watch a human being. I could hear the flutter of their wings and see their black round heads, white throats, and gray bodies. Before they appeared, my mind was off in a different direction, self-absorbed with lofty thoughts. The chickadees reminded me that I'm just one soul, and God is everywhere.

14: Sounds

The crow circled over the evergreen first, announcing big news. I noticed my first butterfly. Was that faint sound before sundown the beginning of the crickets? Sometimes it was hard to distinguish between silence and the pervading vibrations, because the silence in the mountains was full of space and time outdoors. A single fly buzzing, the flutter of passing wings, a crow caw—it was a game to figure out where the sounds came from. You heard a frog croak, but then the "croak" seemed to fly. Was that a woodpecker drilling? A long silence was broken by a blue fly at your ear.

Gradually I felt more at home with the sounds, and we added our own. But in the morning, when Nimāi and I chanted vigorously, nature stepped back and looked on.

15: Human Moods Versus Nature

In a birch grove I was often scolded by a red squirrel. I had heard him scold other animals, even when the animals were hidden from view. It was like a long, alarm-clock chattering. Sometimes he varied it with a *chuck chuck*, sassing me because I sat under "his" tree. Many birds also called out, either for mating or as a warning. As the weather warmed, I heard the creek bubbling under the old winter ice, and I frequently noticed something new, such as a big wasp nest hanging from a branch.

But sometimes when sitting alone, all of nature's displays only made me feel lonely. Nature was ultimately incommunicable and "dark," like the pictures in the *Bhagavad-gītā* which show the animals in the mode of darkness. The beasts in the jungle are in the lowest of the three worlds, the hellish animal species, where no one can hear about Lord Kṛṣṇa's name, fame, and pastimes. At times like that, I looked out at the trees and branches as if they were prison bars. "How long will we have to stay here?" I thought, "When can we return to temples and good cooking?" But I usually stopped myself from such depressing thoughts and turned to the sublime features of the wilderness. The unfriendliness was more my own mood than any mistreatment by Mother Nature. She had not asked me to drop down here. So, what did I expect?

If I want more intimacy, I should turn to Lord Kṛṣṇa. The wilderness was also open to me if I opened to it, instead of being miffed when the squirrel jeered at me, or when I stumbled over rocks because I walked inattentively downhill. Sometimes I remembered a relevant verse from scripture, such as:

> A person who has given up all desires for sense gratification, who live free from desires, who has given up all sense of proprietorship and is devoid of all false ego—he alone can attain real peace.
>
> —*Bhagavad-gītā, 2.71*

16: Ants

I watched the ants at a rotting stump on a hillside. They were large, with a red front half and a black, ball-shaped rear. They looked like they could give me a mean bite, and so I took care not to get too familiar with them.

I noticed that the ants leaving the stump were usually empty-handed, but some of those returning carried pieces of other insects. When you came close enough, the whole hillside seemed alive with moving ants. But once you stepped away for a few yards, they were hardly noticeable on a quiet sunny day. This reminded me of Śrīla Prabhupāda's comment when he flew for the first time, on his journey from New York to San Francisco in 1967. He said, "From the sky the houses look like matchboxes. Just imagine how it looks from Kṛṣṇa's point of view."

Sometimes when I felt morose because of our isolation from humans, I would go and crouch among the ants at the stump and watch the frenzy. That they were highly motivated was obvious, but the purpose of it all was never clear to me, or whether it was absolutely necessary for the ants to live that way in order to survive. Watching them used to cure me of a desire to once again take part in highway traffic at rush hour, or in the downtown pedestrian traffic during the morning and evening bustle.

While condemning materialistic civilization, Śrīla Prabhupāda used the phrase anthill civilization." "Both humans and ants build tall edifices," he said, "but if a man doesn't know of the soul and Kṛṣṇa, then despite his proud skyscrapers, his civilization is no more than a glorified anthill."

The hunter who was turned into a Vaiṣṇava by Nārada Muni stopped in his rush to Nārada to gently brush aside the ants in his path. Jaḍa Bharata did not want to step on ants, and so he incurred trouble for himself by not properly carrying the king's palanquin. Stepping on ants is also mentioned as one of the items of unintentional violence, for which a person must be purified by yajña. The Jains avoid it by walking with a broom before them. Vaiṣṇavas serve the Lord and chant Hare Kṛṣṇa to absolve themselves from unintentional violence.

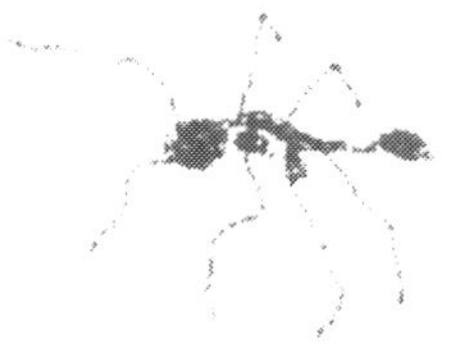

17: Movement

The closer you look at any square foot of forest earth, the more it comes alive. Here's a hole in the ground, an opening to some creature's house. Here are some tiny mushrooms, partly knocked over. The weeds are blowing slightly, but their whole bodies move from top to bottom. Specks of bright lichen have taken hold. If you had a microscope, you'd see much more. Everything is moving, nothing is still.

Into the quiet, the woodpecker's drill sounds as sharp as an electric tool. The sound reminds you that all here are predators and victims. Each plays both roles, hunter and hunted. These are nature's truths, not man's, no one can alter them. The more we enter this world, the more we think to get out of it.

18: Owls

When the moon was bright you could see him in the branches of a tree. The owl eats *only* meat. With his big eyes and facial discs, "the wise owl," is a fat, downy killer.

It depends with whom you empathize. Just as in a Hollywood movie or in a novel, when you enter the life of the leading character, you sympathize with him; his enemies become yours. So, in nature, every creature has its own children to raise and feed, and the parents have to work hard and long hours. From the wolves' point of view, they are not cruel or savage, just hungry. They have to track many miles and days before catching a moose. Still, my sympathies go to the moose. But then the moose ravages many living plants.

And so with these owls. If there are mice afoot tonight, no matter how careful they are, the swift, silent owl will see them with his enormous eyes and snatch them and eat them whole. Mother Durgā punishes us according to our *karma* and desires. As Nārada Muni warned Kings Prācīnabarhiṣat,

> My dear king, please see in the sky those animals you have sacrificed without compassion and without mercy in the sacrificial arena. All these animals are awaiting your death so they can avenge the injuries you have inflicted upon them. After you die, they will angrily pierce your body with thorns.
>
> —*Śrīmad-Bhāgavatam 4.25.7–8*

19: Ducks

Many species of ducks mix in the nearby lake. One black and white species is like a harlequin. He has a black head with a white half-moon in front of his eye. His sides are like bars of black and white. It seems as though nature "shoots the works" on the drake with little left to bestow upon his mate. Other ducks were redheads, black and white, and the brilliant, green-necked mallards.

It was like a men's sporting club, with only a few ladies along. There was swimming, diving, preening, and scratching. It was quite chilly by the lake, and the ducks reminded me of Prabhupāda's teachings about *acintya śakti*. Each species has its own potency, or *śakti* which is often inconceivable to another species. We tend to think that humans are superior to ducks and all other creatures in almost every way. But when you analyze it, they have their *śaktis* which are impossible for us.

Just to view the ducks for a few minutes turned my hands cold and my body started to shiver, and yet they were playing and diving in the cold, ripply water. I wondered whether the ducks were suffering in the cold. Sometimes Prabhupāda said that the animals are suffering— "Do not become like an animal that has to work hard day and night just to get its food." But at other times he described the animals as completely provided for by God and living without extraordinary endeavors. Both examples are true. The animals are provided for, and yet they suffer—but they don't know that they are suffering. Their greatest suffering is their lack of enlightenment. Their consciousness is so limited that they do not miss their lack of higher intelligence, and they have less sensitivity to pain. The humans have greater potential for becoming liberated, but also a greater tendency for neurosis and psychosis.

It looks like fun diving in the cold water and living in such an unpolluted environment. The ducks were cohabitating peacefully, taking only what they needed for food and not spoiling the land. They seemed innocent.

20: Sound

One day I met sound in the forest. I had ventured deeply among the trees and saw an owl fly from a branch and disappear. Then I stood still. My shoes and coat made no noise. I began to notice different levels of wind, higher and lower. Eventually I heard trees creaking and rubbing. Things rattling, things falling, then silence. As I became quieter, I heard my own pulse and heartbeat. After fifteen minutes, I uttered out loud, "Hare Kṛṣṇa" and heard it much better than usual. I cannot say that sound is a *person* whom I met, although we know from the Vedas that there are demigods in charge of everything. What I met was not a person but a world of quiet and of sound vibration that came when I quieted down and listened. The words made me reverent, a bit fearful and alert. The names of God came as a prayer. It is best to chant that way, instead of vibrations by a hurried person who was not practiced in hearing anything.

Try it yourself:

Hare Kṛṣṇa, Hare Kṛṣṇa, Kṛṣṇa Kṛṣṇa, Hare Hare
Hare Rāma, Hare Rāma, Rāma Rāma, Hare Hare

The manuscript of "Persons, Places, and Things I Met While in the Mountains," by Gauracandra Swami, ends here. He was writing them or thinking about them until the day we left. When I recently showed him what he'd done, he said, "Someday, I would like to go back there and meet Lord Kṛṣṇa through nature."

(Nimāi dāsa brahmacārī)

To be continued...

4

Chota's Way

Chapter 1

At the edge of a palm tree jungle, in a large open tent, three hundred mice and a few crows sat together to honor Choṭa dāsa on the occasion of his fourth birthday. They had erected a temporary altar with pictures of Śrīla Prabhupāda, Lord Caitanya, Lord Nityānanda and Rādhā-Kṛṣṇa. Choṭa sat to the left of this altar facing the audience, while a young field mouse stood making a speech.

"... And after quickly assimilating the rudiments of Vaiṣṇava philosophy from Prabhu Nimāi, our Choṭa Prabhu became—I think it is safe to say—the first pure devotee of the Gauḍīya-*sampradāya* to appear in the mice species!"

"No, not the first and not a pure devotee," said Choṭa, but the mice were cheering and didn't hear his mild protest. Even if they had heard it, they would have smiled at his humility. It was well known that Choṭa *was* the first mouse devotee who knew and exemplified the teaching of Śrīla Prabhupāda. There had been many mice living in the Hindu temples, but they had not become enlightened. Until Choṭa's arrival in Guyana a year ago, a mouse's life had simply been eating, mating, sleeping and defending. Now hundreds of mice had become devotees of the Lord, and they were eager to praise Choṭa for his part in spreading the Kṛṣṇa consciousness movement.

"Nor is Choṭa Prabhu *merely* a pioneer," said the speaker with a flourish of his paw. "He continues to lead us by his nectarean discourses from the scriptures. He continues to wipe out our forgetfulness of God. I know that Choṭa doesn't like to hear his glories, but we request that today he please allow us to speak from the heart for our own purification."

"Jaya! Jaya!" the mice cheered. Choṭa sat still with downcast eyes and a grave expression. The field mouse concluded his speech and placed a garland of lotuses around Choṭa's neck and shoulders. Choṭa took off the garland because he already wore four other flower garlands. He felt that he was being buried under lotus blooms. Now another mouse came to the dais and began an oration that was like a continuation of the previous one. Choṭa had told them that the whole birthday program shouldn't take more than half an hour, but they had been speaking now for a full hour, and the crowd was still attentive. Some of the crows had become fidgety and had walked off, but those who remained were listening intently.

"Choṭa's devotional talents are unlimited, so I will speak only to the extent I am able." The speaker was a lady mouse who was one of the main organizers of the children's schools. "As we all know, Choṭa has always been a very bold preacher, beginning with his dangerous forays into the walls of houses in North America. He has continued the same compassionate work among the mice of Guyana by going door to door in every town and village to spread Lord Caitanya's mission. He has also opened many temples and has been the prime mover in organizing a Vaiṣṇava movement among mice species, just like the worldwide movement of human Vaiṣṇavas. Choṭa has continued to do astounding things even in recent months. I refer to his breakthrough in learning how to read Prabhupāda's books. Whereas previously we were limited to learning by hearing whatever Choṭa had learned and passed on from Nimāi Prabhu, now it is possible that the whole world of Śrīla Prabhupāda's books may be open to us!"

The mice rose to their feet, raised their arms, and began cheering, *"Jaya* Choṭa Prabhu! *Haribol!* All glories to Prabhupāda's books!"

"Not only that," the *gurukula* matron continued, "but even more recently Choṭa Prabhu has done what we always thought was impossible. He has introduced Lord Caitanya's teaching to *other* animal species.

Truly Choṭa Prabhu is an empowered Vaiṣṇava just like the great *ācāryas* of the past. Who knows what unprecedented new discoveries and advances Choṭa will reveal to us in the coming days? Let us simply pray for the long life of our leader. Let him find us all always active and submissive to his directions!"

Choṭa felt uneasy hearing the praise, but his feeling was more than the usual humility. Something had been building within him for months. He hadn't thought that he could tell them, but now when he heard their expectations of him, he decided at least to hint indirectly at what was on his mind.

Choṭa addressed the crowd, "My dear friends and devotees ..." (He remembered what Nimāi had told him of how *ācāryas* responded when they were praised). "Whatever kind things you have said describing a Vaiṣṇava are not true of me. I am a fallen soul in a mouse body. But like all of you I have been fortunate to come into contact with the teachings of the pure devotee, His Divine Grace A. C. Bhaktivedanta Swami Prabhupāda, as passed down by his human followers and as contained in his books. And thus, we have all been engaged in chanting the Hare Kṛṣṇa *mantra.*" Choṭa thought, *Tell them that if they really love me they should allow me time to chant and read.*

"If there is any worth in my activities," said Choṭa, it comes from the enlightened *paramparā* teachings and loving guidance I have received from our beloved preceptor, Nimāi Prabhu. He was so patient and considerate that he was able to impart Kṛṣṇa consciousness even to subhuman species who are not usually able to receive higher learning. That is his credit. I have shared that with you, and you have submissively received it, and your lives have benefited. As Lord Kṛṣṇa says in the *Bhagavad-gītā,* even a little devotional service—such as a mouse might be able to perform—can save one from the greatest danger at the time of death. The danger is that in the next life we may be pushed into a still lower species of life with complete forgetfulness of God. So, my request is that you observe my birthday not by praising me, but by resolving that we shall all cooperate together to practice Kṛṣṇa consciousness and spread it. Let us dedicate all our energies to this goal."

The mice responded by beating on their *mṛdaṅga* drums and clashing their hand cymbals. The ladies made sounds of ululations with their tongues. Some of the devotees who had been cooking in an adjoining kitchen came to the doorway and peeked in to hear Choṭa's words.

Choṭa told himself, *Go ahead, tell them what's on your mind.* "I have one personal request," said Choṭa. "If I am actually to serve you and other living beings, then I have to be a fit devotee. But at present I am not fit. I do not have a taste for the most basic practices of chanting and hearing. So, I humbly request you to please allow me to pursue the basic *sādhana* of Vaiṣṇavism, of which I have so far not realized, not even a drop. Without this higher taste, all my activities are actually trivial and farcical. Please give your mercy in this very tangible and practical way so that one day I can actually become a genuine chanter and reader of Prabhupāda's books. Only then can I convince others to do the same."

Choṭa ended his speech here, and everyone was pleased with him. They asked him to be the lead singer for the *mahā-kīrtana.* He knew the mice like to chant for at least an hour, and he wasn't sure if he could last that long, but he would give it a try. Closing his eyes, Choṭa sang the introductory prayers to Śrīla Prabhupāda and the Pañca-tattva and then the Hare Kṛṣṇa *mantra.* He sang the first tune he had ever heard from Nimāi. Within moments, the mice were moving back and forth. Choṭa usually preferred a more sedate *kīrtana* where one could meditate on each *mantra.* The real purpose of chanting was to vibrate the holy name and to hear it, and not to get carried away by melodies or fancy steps. But when the dancers started smiling and inducing one another to step lively, and when the drummers beat their instruments with expertise and pleasure, it was infectious, and Choṭa wanted to join their spirit.

One mouse started a circular march around the whole tent area, and soon hundreds of mice were in motion and song. Then another group formed an inner circle within the first, and a few of the more celebrated dancers moved within that ring and began twirling and bending, inducing one another into more and more displays of graceful dancing. Because of his seniority and relatively old age, Choṭa wasn't expected to leap and cavort, yet he watched with appreciation. He wished he had their freedom from inhibition—and their springy legs. At least he could carry the tune, so he took responsibility for that, as loudly as he could. His mind and body were soon complaining, but Choṭa hoped to transcend difficulties. If all these younger devotees and even children and crows could be so absorbed in *kīrtana* for an hour, why couldn't he? "It's not boring," he thought, "it will destroy all boredom and complaints, if I can just enter and taste the holy names: Hare Kṛṣṇa, Hare Kṛṣṇa, Kṛṣṇa Kṛṣṇa, Hare Hare, Hare Rāma, Hare Rāma, Rāma Rāma, Hare Hare."

The ecstatic *kīrtana* was an indication of the health of the Hare Kṛṣṇa movement among the mice. Only a year ago very few were interested, but now wherever Choṭa and the devotees went in Guyana, mice enjoyed their chanting and many liked to take part. Devotee-mice had learned to make *mṛdaṅgas* and *karatālas* as well as to use some of their popular instruments like banjos, tinpot drums, and rhythm sticks. In this way they tasted the bliss of devotional service and fulfilled the desires of the *ācāryas* that all living beings, "even the worms, birds and beasts," become elevated in *bhakti*. Or as Śrīla Prabhupāda said, "Even a child can take part in chanting, or even a dog can take part in it and dance in ecstasy."

By mouse standards, the *kīrtana* for Choṭa's birthday celebration was a big one. The regular members all joined wholeheartedly, and some who rarely attended meetings had also come and plunged into the center of it. The giant *harināma* chorus attracted many onlookers including birds who jeered. A few crow *bhaktas* took up guarding the *kīrtana*, and they had to drive away an unfriendly hawk. They did this by circling him and harassing his flight.

"Anyway, it's stupid," said the hawk as he finally flew off.

"No, it's not," replied a crow. "*You* are."

Choṭa felt waves of fatigue and boredom, but then they went away. He began to embrace the *mantra* and appreciate how God was so great and kind to appear in His name. "This is just a shadow of the full, perfect name because I am not qualified," thought Choṭa, "but even this is *very* merciful." He felt the auspicious presence of the names and knew for sure that the chanters were pleasing the spiritual masters. It was not a matter of gauging one's symptoms, or even of meditating on them, but of just surrendering, crying out "Kṛṣṇa! Kṛṣṇa!" and singing against time and death.

Finally, the head cook approached Choṭa and humbly asked if the *kīrtana* could end soon because the feast was all prepared and hot. Choṭa had lost track of the time. It had been about one and a half hours. So, he increased the rhythm for five more minutes. The dancers became frenzied, and the holy name roared into the sky. Choṭa ended it, and they all sat down sweating and laughing and grinning. As Choṭa sang the song to Nṛsiṁhadeva, he also prayed that Nṛsiṁhadeva please protect all the mice and the movement from the attacks of demons and predators. Choṭa then stood up and announced, "As Śrīla Prabhupāda used to say, Chant Hare Kṛṣṇa and when you get tired—take *prasādam*!"

They sat in long rows. The servers entered the area carrying big pots and ladles. Freshly washed orange leaves and clay pots were placed before every seated devotee. There was a commotion of excited chatter, shouts, and laughter. The men sat down beside each other, and families sat with their children. The first servers to walk down the aisles carried rice and dropped a portion of it on each leaf plate. Then came the *dāl* bearers. By the time the *sabjī* carriers entered, Choṭa was loudly reciting the prayer for honoring *prasādam*.

"Śarīra *abidyā-jal*!"

The congregation responded with a mighty shout, "ŚARĪRA ABIDYĀ-JAL!"

"Joḍendriya tāhe kāl."

"JODENDRYA TĀHE KĀL."

When the formal prayer was finished, a devotee called out, *"Bhagavat prasādam ki—"*

And everyone responded, *"JAYA!"*

"His Divine Grace Choṭa Prabhu *ki*—"

"JAYA!"

And then the eating began in earnest. There was so much food that all the plates were heaped and spilling over.

"Hey, did you try the *sāmosas* yet? They're great!"

"Bhakta Mickey took six pieces of pizza!"

Aside from the regular devotes, many guests were present. Some animals came by just for the food and so got their first introduction to Kṛṣṇa's *prasādam*. The crows couldn't believe there was so much food! They kept looking around to protect their own plates until they realized that everyone had enough, and more kept coming!

There was a particularly nice vegetable preparation of eggplant and curd. Another favorite was fried *urad dāl baḍās* in a creamy yogurt sauce topped with tamarind chutney. There were baked Gaurāṅga potatoes with sour cream herb sauce, and broccoli with cheddar cheese sauce. Some devotees quickly finished their portions, but the servers came by again with seconds. All the preparations were popular, but especially the *samosās* with tomato chutney, the cauliflower *pakoras*, and the hot *purīs*. The servers didn't wait long before bringing out an array of sweet preparations: sweet rice, *gulābjāmuns, sandeśa, laḍḍus, barfi*, varieties of milk sweets and cakes.

Some of the preparations were carried on big trays by several mice. Servers had to wind their way carefully between the narrow rows of animals.

"Prabhu, could you please pick up your tail?"

Everyone was cooperative. The devotees who were serving were also enthusiastic, knowing that they too would get their chance to honor the *prasādam*.

Some devotees became talkative. Some were silent, absorbed in honoring *prasādam*. Some finished quickly and left. Others stayed long, relishing the event until the very end. Some became intoxicated and boisterous. There was praise for the cooks. The babies seemed to be tasting the food with all the parts of their bodies. Some of them began walking around dropping food, occasionally knocking over a cup of nectar, but no one seemed to mind. *Dhotīs* were loosened and legs stretched out to accommodate the excess *prasādam*. Some sat straight, but others leaned back on one paw, and a few even lay on their sides.

Choṭa sat at the place of honor, flanked by some of the senior devotees of Guyana. He was aware that many eyes were watching him, and he didn't want to appear voracious. But he was quite hungry and not satisfied to just nibble politely at his food. When he dropped his inhibitions, the devotees were pleased to see him eat as much as the others. Again, and again, the servers came by encouraging him to take another portion of eggplant *sabjī*, more hot *purīs*, another crisp *pakora*. Some palates are particularly fond of savory food, while others are inclined to sweets, but Choṭa was inclined to both—with a particular weakness for sweets. He refused to take more than one *gulābjāmun*, although he could have eaten two or three. After half an hour, he decided it would be good for him to stop eating and leave the feast scene. As he got up the mice cheered, and Choṭa realized that he had forgotten all his dissatisfactions. He was satisfied not merely from food, but from Kṛṣṇa's mercy. And he found it particularly pleasing to see hundreds of devotees and guests gathered before the altar pictures, honoring the Lord's *prasādam*.

Chapter 2

When Choṭa returned to his room, his cousin Yamala dāsa was waiting for him.

"Did you take the feast?" asked Choṭa.

"Yeah, but I could hardly enjoy it. I'm in such anxiety." Choṭa gave him a mat to sit on, but Yamala began pacing the room, fingering the beads in his bead bag. Yamala wore a team jacket with the letters "Lord Chaitanya's Army" printed on the back. He had been recruited along with Choṭa and Choṭa's big brother Arjuna, three years ago when all three of them lived as ordinary mice in the Rādhā-Dāmodara temple in Pennsylvania. They had been trained together in Kṛṣṇa consciousness by Nimāi and brought by him to Guyana where they were still the only American-born mice. They had each grown in different ways. Choṭa remained the spiritual leader while Yamala had blossomed into a dedicated and able manager, although less inclined to reading and chanting. He was respected among the mice devotees but was seen as rough and impetuous.

"Your brother Arjuna has gone nuts," said Yamala, staring at Choṭa. "He's blaspheming you and the whole movement. We have to stop him."

"What's he doing?" asked Choṭa. Choṭa wished Yamala would sit down, but there was no use asking him.

Yamala blurted, "He's gone around to all six of our temples preaching blasphemy and directly attacking you. He's become a demon. He says that Nimāi Prabhu was a flaky devotee, and so our movement is bogus because it's based on him as our Founder-Ācārya."

"Whoever said Nimāi was a Founder-Ācārya?" asked Choṭa. "I said ..."

"*I* know," said Yamala. "But they don't know. The devotees are getting bewildered. He's turning a lot of heads. So, *you've* got to do something right away to stop him." Something in Yamala's jacket pocket began beeping loudly. It was his emergency communicator signaling him to go to the nearest telephone and call his home number.

"I'll be back in a minute," said Yamala.

Choṭa sighed. Troubles weren't new to him. He usually took them as daily fare, knowing that "If you take on headaches, you'll become dear to the Lord." As Choṭa often quoted from Bhaktivinoda Ṭhākura, "Troubles that I encounter in Your service, my Lord, I will consider a great happiness." But on hearing this latest outbreak, Choṭa again felt his growing desire to be free of management. He wanted to let someone else handle it. Would these troubles never end? He felt his life slipping by, but he was not becoming a real devotee. Choṭa gazed out the window and saw devotees wandering leisurely, recovering from the big feast. More ceremonies—a dramatic skit and *kīrtanas*—were scheduled for the evening.

Yamala returned, talking. "That was Raṇcora dāsa in Berbice. They're all getting agitated by Arjuna. Now he's printed a leaflet and is giving it to the guests at the feast. He says that Nimāi is bogus and that you, Choṭa, are puffed up and want followers. You accept too much wealth. I'd like to haul off and belt Arjuna in the mouth. He's written some nonsense that you eat too much to be a spiritual leader."

Choṭa laughed, "At least that's true for today."

"It's not funny," said Yamala, and he walked up and down the small room, his whiskers twitching menacingly as he chanted an incoherent *mahā-mantra*. "Something has to be done to stop your brother."

"He's just peeved," said Choṭa, "because we have always called him 'Junior.' And he feels guilty, I think, that we've left our family and ..."

"Arjuna says that you are trying to take the credit for this movement, whereas actually it's all Lord Caitanya's mercy."

"That's true."

"He even tells some story that once you didn't want to get out of the van to go on *saṅkīrtana*, and he had to convince you."

"I don't remember that," said Choṭa. "I know I'm guilty of pride and things like that. But why should Arjuna attack the whole movement? We're all imperfect, even Nimāi is imperfect, and he always admitted that. We are imperfect, but we are repeating the perfect message from Śrīla Prabhupāda's books."

"Right!" Yamala cried, "And this is what you've got to tell them." The machine began beeping again in Yamala's jacket, but he ignored it. A mouse came to the open window and said that they were waiting for Yamala to come to rehearse his part as the Muslim Kazi in the dramatic skit.

"Tell them to wait," said Yamala. His pacing quickened like an animal in a cage.

Choṭa suddenly wanted to tell Yamala what he had been thinking, that he wanted to take time to improve his *sādhana*. Arjuna's criticism seemed to confirm for Choṭa that the most important thing he could do would be to somehow gain attraction for chanting and hearing. He hesitated to express it to Yamala, knowing that he wouldn't see the logical connection. "But if my credibility is being challenged," Choṭa thought, "the best response would be to make my spiritual life beyond challenge. As Prabhupāda used to quote, 'Caesar's wife should be above suspicion.' If I actually became a devotee with attraction to chanting Hare Kṛṣṇa and reading Prabhupāda's books, then my position would be beyond reproach. It would be a wonderful example to follow rather than a cause for fighting."

"Listen to this," said Yamala. "Arjuna says that animals cannot really understand the chanting. He has some quotes from Prabhupāda that Kṛṣṇa consciousness isn't for animals, only for humans, that the difference between humans and animals is that the human being can become self-realized and the animals can't. He says that the examples which Nimāi and you have given from Vedic literature are only rare exceptions. The examples of Lord Caitanya inducing the jungle animals to chant the holy names and of Śivānanda Sena being kind to a dog who then chanted Hare Kṛṣṇa for Lord Caitanya are all just exceptions. He says that what Prabhupāda actually taught is that the only thing you can do for animals is not to kill them and to give them *prasādam*."

"I don't agree," said Choṭa. "The main point is that we are not this body. As Kṛṣṇa says in *Bhagavad-gītā*, 'The humble sages, by virtue of true knowledge, see with equal vision a learned and gentle *brāhmaṇa*, a cow, an elephant, a dog and a dog-eater.' Yes, an animal taking to Kṛṣṇa consciousness is very unusual, but we can't deny the Lord's extraordinary mercy. Even an animal can take the mercy of the Lord, and that's the ultimate conclusion of the *saṅkīrtana* movement."

"I know that!" Yamala now came up close to Choṭa and tapped him on the chest with his paw. "But now you've got to tell them. We have to make vigorous propaganda against Arjuna Prabhu."

"I'll do the needful," said Choṭa. "But listen, Yamala, here's what I think. Our response to these criticisms should be to improve our spiritual lives. I want to take more time for chanting and reading. This is the leadership that is required, not just making counter-propaganda. I would like to work full time on my chanting and my study of Prabhupāda's books."

"What?" Yamala's mouth fell open in disbelief. "This is not time for weakness, Prabhu."

"You call a desire to chant and hear a weakness?"

"Yes. Remember in the *Bhagavad-gītā* when Arjuna wanted to retire from the battle? What did Kṛṣṇa do? He chastised him!"

Choṭa became quiet and listened.

"Chanting and reading is *bābājī* stuff," said Yamala. "We're preachers. And you're the leader. You can't retire. We've got to confront this menace. Call meetings. Make a tour. Go to Arjuna and tell him he has got to stop or else. Don't allow him even to visit the temples. He has to leave Guyana. Many mice are already bewildered by him, and you've got to tell them to do their regular work."

"I agree," said Choṭa in a subdued voice. "But there has to be a time—"

"This isn't a time for chanting and hearing," said Yamala. "Listen, I'd like to take time for that myself. I'm about a hundred rounds behind on my quota, and I haven't read a page in weeks. I'm not proud of that. But I know I have to fight so that our spiritual movement can be protected."

Choṭa began to speak, but Yamala cut him off. Yamala said, "As far as I'm concerned, chanting and introspection are luxuries, although I know they are the goal of life. There's no time for them now. We have to get out and fight. We're declaring war on *māyā*. You know Prabhupāda said, 'Work now, *samādhi* later.' So don't mind my saying so, Choṭa, but you're on the mental platform. As Kṛṣṇa's representative I'm telling you that it's your duty to go out there."

"Okay," said Choṭa. "I'll take action. I'll write a letter to the temple against Arjuna's propaganda. And I'll take a tour of all the temples."

"Now you're talking," said Yamala. The two mice embraced, and Yamala left to answer the call of his beeping communicator.

Choṭa told the devotees that he could not attend the dramatic skit or evening *ārati*. He sat down to write a letter against Arjuna's propaganda. Then he remembered that he had not finished his daily quota of sixteen rounds. He got up and began walking and chanting on his beads, but his mind was too agitated for even the slightest attention to the holy names. He tried calming himself, sitting on his bed, but then he felt sleepy. He wanted to go outside for fresh air, but he knew that wherever he went he would meet crowds of animals. So, he resigned himself to pacing the room, in the style of Yamala dāsa, and grinding out a few poor rounds of *japa*.

Choṭa woke at 2:00 A.M. the next morning. Although he usually rose from bed at 3:00 A.M., he felt impelled to get up and read *Śrīmad-Bhāgavatam* before the rush of events began. He had no strict reading program, and so he decided that any book by Prabhupāda would do. Prabhupāda himself had said that the books were just like sweet balls, and they would taste sweet no matter where you bit into them. Choṭa selected the *KṚṢṆA* book and began reading "Akrūra's Arrival in Vṛndāvana." It was such a nice meditation. Akrūra traveling to Vṛndāvana and anticipating seeing Lord Kṛṣṇa. At first Akrūra thought himself too materialistic to actually see the Lord, who is very difficult even for *yogis* to see. But then Akrūra said, "Enough of such thought! After all, even a fallen soul like me can have a chance to behold the infallible Supreme Lord, for one of the conditioned souls being swept along on the river of time may sometimes reach the shore."

Under lamplight in a quiet room, Choṭa read on. Akrūra was confident that the Lord would be merciful to him. Akrūra said, "I am going to see the Supreme Lord Viṣṇu, the reservoir of all beauty, who by His own sweet will has now assumed a humanlike form to relieve the earth of her burden. Thus, there is no denying that my eyes will achieve the perfection of their existence."

Choṭa paused and looked up thoughtfully from the page. Unless one regularly heard these narrations, how would it be possible to remember the form and activities of the Supreme Lord? And without remembering Kṛṣṇa, how was it possible to be a devotee? It was not enough just to "belong" to a movement or to wear a team jacket. As Akrūra had said, "All sins are destroyed, and all good fortune created by the Supreme Lord's qualities, activities, appearances, and words that describe these. Words bereft of His glories are like the decorations on a corpse."

Choṭa recalled how he had been given the gift of reading less than a year ago. Yes, it had been a *gift* from the Lord. Choṭa bowed down and placed his head at the base of the book. He prayed, "I thank you, Lord, for speaking to us through scripture. Despite my sinful body, which is not better than a poisonous snake like Kāliya, You have nevertheless allowed me at least to glimpse Your form and teachings through *Śrīmad-Bhāgavatam*. But now that You have given me the ability to read, please make it complete and reveal Your actual presence through the words."

Choṭa allowed his greed for reading Prabhupāda's books to fill him without guilt. He felt the conviction that Śrīla Prabhupāda was pleased with him and that he should not squelch his growing desires. Choṭa thought, "Hearing about Kṛṣṇa is the most important thing. Unfortunately, although the mice devotees are enthusiastic, they do not know yet of the importance of reading. They praise me for reading, yet they don't seem to do it themselves." Choṭa attempted to study further. But he found his attention span had been exhausted within ten minutes. So this was the predicament: Although he had been praised as the great leader of devotees among the animals, he did not deeply appreciate reading or chanting. And if the leader had no taste, what kind of example could he set for the followers? "Therefore," Choṭa thought, "even if no one else encourages me, I must find the means to concentrate on chanting and hearing." With mixed feelings, Choṭa closed the book and turned to *japa*. Now he could hear mice stirring; the little temple was coming to life. Soon he would have to face them.

Chapter 3

As requested by Yamala, Choṭa started at once on a tour of the country to counteract the propaganda of Arjuna. Choṭa held meetings in temples and visited people's homes, preaching Kṛṣṇa consciousness and answering challenges and doubts. For example, in Berbice, he was invited by a devotee-mouse, Mr. Apsara, who worked in a bauxite mill. Mr. Apsara and his wife, two sons, and two daughters had all been active devotees attending the local temple, but since hearing criticisms of Choṭa, they became somewhat standoffish. Still, they invited him to their modest house, and after a *kīrtana* and scripture reading, Mr. Apsara asked some questions.

He inquired in a polite and indirect way, but what he really meant to say was, "Is it true what they say about you, Choṭa, that your teacher wasn't a pure devotee and that you are also faulty? Are you proud? Are you too fond of sweets like they say?" Choṭa had been repeating the same philosophy where he went, that the criterion for speaking perfectly is to follow strictly the authority of guru, śāstra, and *sādhu*. Choṭa quoted statements by Śrīla Prabhupāda, such as, "I don't claim that I am a pure devotee or perfect, but my only qualification is that I am trying to follow the instructions of the perfect." And, "One may be a rascal number one from material estimations, but if he simply strictly follows whatever is said by Caitanya Mahāprabhu or His representative spiritual master, then he becomes a guru." But although he defended himself, Choṭa thought, *I shouldn't be doing this. Arjuna's criticisms of me are light compared to the real truth, which is that I don't love Kṛṣṇa and I find chanting His holy names a heavy chore. I am posing as a spiritual leader, but I don't realize anything that I read or say in my lectures.*

When Choṭa stopped speaking about himself and went on to defend the movement, he felt more conviction. Arjuna's handbill had stated that Śrīla Prabhupāda never expected animals to follow the four rules (no illicit sex, no meat-eating, no intoxication, and no gambling) and he never expected them to understand *Bhagavad-gītā As It Is*. It was more honest, Arjuna claimed, to admit this, to engage in animal propensities and stop the farce. In reply, Choṭa quoted many scriptural statements and attempted to prove that they were intended for all souls, including animals. If previously the mercy had not been extended to the animals, that did not mean that it could not be done now by the extraordinary grace of the Lord's empowered preachers. Rūpa Gosvāmī had said of Lord Caitanya, "You are the most munificent incarnation of God, and You are teaching the highest form of love of God in a way that was *never before so freely distributed*."

Most of the devotees who heard Choṭa assured him that they supported him and that he had turned the tide in his favor by his visit. But it was tiring going from place to place, sometimes hitching a ride on a train or walking or taking a boat from village to village. Yamala dāsa had formed a "Committee to Counteract Blasphemy," and they had given Choṭa his itinerary. He had to keep in touch with the CCB by phone calls and letters, and sometimes they assigned him new places to visit. Choṭa felt a sense of accomplishment in carrying out the duty, but sometimes it seemed futile to him. It was like superficial patchwork rather than an actual remedy. Choṭa had his idea of a deeper rectification both for himself and the movement, but whenever he had brought it up, no one seemed interested.

After spending a week in Crabwood Creek, Choṭa had to wait while the car went in for repairs. As soon as he heard of the delay, he decided to visit an old devotee-friend who lived in that town. So, he started out, with no assistant, to the house of Padma dāsa, who was a crow. Padma was the first crow who had been converted into a devotee of the Lord. Choṭa had met him in a park at a festival for vegetarians. (At that time the crow was not a vegetarian but was attracted by the garbage thrown out at the festival.) They had sat down together and struck up an acquaintanceship. After associating with Choṭa for a few weeks, Padma had decided to commit himself fully to the teachings of Śrīla Prabhupāda. Some of the mice devotees were hesitant to accept him at first, since crows were traditionally their enemies. Because Choṭa was personally so friendly with the crow (who later accepted the name Padma dāsa) and because Padma himself showed the symptoms of being a dedicated devotee, they begrudgingly accepted the fact that Kṛṣṇa consciousness could indeed be spread to animal species other than mice.

Choṭa and Padma had worked together lecturing at animal schools, which had also led to Choṭa's interest in learning to read. In fact, it was Padma dāsa's encouragement that bolstered Choṭa in his first difficult attempts to gain literacy. Padma was considered a serious and honorable devotee, but unfortunately, he had begun to backslide. His wife said that he sometimes smoked an intoxicant the locals called "weed." His health was not good, and he became very absorbed in taking health cures and in reading books on psychology with the aim of self-improvement. He seemed less interested in *bhakti-yoga*. Choṭa never deliberately abandoned his friend, but their ways began to part. Choṭa was intent in serving the purposes of the movement, and Padma began avoiding the association of devotees.

To reach Padma's house, Choṭa had to enter the crow neighborhood, which was somewhat risky. Hare Kṛṣṇa was a popular movement among mice, but only a very few crows had taken to it. Crows remained the enemies of mice, or at least they were always harsh and sarcastic toward them.

As Choṭa walked quickly down the garbage-littered street, crows called out at him from their front porches.

"Hey mouse! You lookin' to be a meal?"

"Hey mousey, you better get your face outta here before dark if you like breathing! Caw! Caw!"

Choṭa showed a faint smile but was very nervous as he kept walking ahead. The tense situation at least forced him to chant fervently in his mind, Hare Kṛṣṇa, Hare Kṛṣṇa, Kṛṣṇa Kṛṣṇa, Hare Hare, Hare Rāma, Hare Rāma, Rāma Rāma, Hare Hare.

Padma lived in a rundown, unpainted little house on stilts. Although almost all the crows on the block perched on their front perches or on their roofs, Padma was within his house, and Choṭa had to knock repeatedly on the front door. As soon as Choṭa was admitted, the two friends exchanged obeisances and a hearty embrace.

"How are you doing?" asked Choṭa, smiling.

"Okay," said Padma and he laughed. "Please come and in and sit down. What would you like, wheatgrass or carrot juice?"

"Oh, I'll just take some water if you don't mind."

Choṭa was glad to see pictures of Kṛṣṇa on the wall, but he noticed many different kinds of books on the shelves. *The Transparent Ego: How to Be Your Own Psychiatrist* was open on the table, and Choṭa picked it up.

"Is this any good?" Choṭa asked.

"Yes," replied Padma, "it's helpful. But not really."

"You look a little worn," said Choṭa. He was a bit shocked to see Padma so thin and without his black luster. Padma replied that he hadn't been feeling well; his back hurt him, he had indigestion, and he was feeling depressed.

"But I'm on a new diet, taking just wheatgrass and enemas. I think it will be good. I recommend it to you, too."

Padma was married and had a young daughter. His wife and daughter said, "Hello," but then allowed the two friends to talk in private. They sat on comfortable cushions, and Choṭa sipped at his water while Padma drank down some pills with wheatgrass juice.

"Do you still smoke?" asked Choṭa.

"Sometimes."

"I wish I could help you," said Choṭa. "But I know you don't want preachy talk. Remember though, how happy and effulgent you were when we were visiting schools together?"

Padma brightened, and they began to reminisce about better days.

"I always remember," said Choṭa, "how spontaneously you were attracted to Prabhupāda's books. You used to read by the hour. I think only because of your help was I able to learn myself."

Padma agreed that he had been happier when he was following the spiritual practices. At Choṭa's request, Padma tried explaining his mental predicament. He said one dilemma was whether to be more responsive to his family's material demands or more concerned with his own spiritual advancement. He spoke of feeling inadequate and oversensitive—everyone seemed to be against him, or even if they weren't, people were too loud and demanding. He had always been a misfit. It was a very psychological explanation, and Choṭa couldn't quite follow it. He sincerely nodded and encouraged Padma that the real solution was to take shelter of the Supreme Personality of Godhead.

Padma looked sincerely into Choṭa's eyes and asked, "How are *you* doing? I heard they were blaspheming you."

Choṭa confided to his old friend. "Yes, I'm being so-called blasphemed. But what they say is really true. Or even if the details aren't true, it's true that I'm not a qualified spiritual leader. The good thing about this criticism is that it makes me want to really improve myself. I'm hopeful that if I could just spend time chanting and hearing, I could make real progress."

"Sounds good," said Padma.

"But they won't let me do it."

"They?"

"Yamala and the devotees. They say my attempt to increase my *sādhana* means that I just want to be a *bābājī*."

"But what do you say?"

"I think the desire to increase *sādhana* is auspicious," said Choṭa. "In my case I think I crucially need it at this particular point in my life. Otherwise, the more people praise me and sometimes criticize me, and the more leadership I assume, the more it becomes a farce. Even the greatest active preachers sometimes took considerable time out for self-cultivation."

"Yes, of course. And what does Śrīla Prabhupāda say about this?"

"You know he often criticizes those who go alone to chant Hare Kṛṣṇa just to get some cheap reputation. But I don't think those instructions are an absolute condemnation of *bhajana*. I've been noticing that there are many references to great devotees—even Lord Caitanya—going alone, avoiding crowds, and seeking solitary places. I heard that Bhaktisiddhānta Sarasvatī Ṭhākura chanted alone for ten years before he began his mission, and Śrīla Prabhupāda did also when he lived in Vṛndāvana."

"Speaking of solitude," said Padma, "have you ever met the turtle who lives in the jungle? They say he's an accomplished hermit and mystic. Maybe he could tell you something about it first-hand. Anyway, if you feel so convinced, why don't you just spend more time chanting and reading?"

"Maybe I will," said Choṭa, and he began thinking aloud. "Maybe right now I'll take a three-day retreat. I'm supposed to be on this whirlwind tour to counteract propaganda. But I don't think anyone would notice if I just disappeared for a few days."

"Yeah, I think you should do it."

Choṭa and Padma had been together for two hours, but neither wanted to part. Choṭa agreed to stay for lunch. It was an all-raw meal of lettuce, sprouts, and a tomato. For dessert, there were grapes. After eating, they both rested a little while on blankets on the floor.

Choṭa then suggested that they could read together, which they used to do in the old days. Their method was that they would take copies of the same book and read aloud together. First Choṭa would read while his friend listened, and they would both make comments. With two copies of the *Bhagavad-gītā,* they began chanting and hearing. As Padma read, Choṭa became drowsy but then jumped to his feet. "I always do this!" He laughed. "This is what I want to cure." When Padma read the verses about one's mind being the best friend or worst enemy, he put the book down and spoke more about his mental troubles. Choṭa had observed over the years that Padma always had new problems—there didn't seem to be any end to them or any ultimate root, except for the explanations given in the *Bhagavad-gītā.* And Padma seemed to lack faith in the process of *bhakti* as a cure-all. Choṭa tried to encourage him. Together they looked up references about controlling the mind. And so they went on reading for an hour.

It was dark when Choṭa finally left his friend's house. Some crows hooted him, but he took it in stride and hurried back to the temple.

"Where were you for so long?" a devotee asked. "We were worried."

"I was at Padma's."

"Oh, him. He hardly ever comes to the temple anymore. He's in *māyā.* It's your mercy to go and see such a fallen person. But I don't know if he deserves your attention."

Choṭa wanted to say, "He helped me." But instead, he said, "Padma is an old friend. He's done a lot of service for Prabhupāda and Lord Caitanya. Maybe one day he'll come back. But even now, wouldn't it be funny if he were closer to God than we were?"

Chapter 4

Choṭa decided to take three days for a spiritual retreat. He phoned Yamala and told him he was exhausted from his tour and that he needed to rest. Yamala was suspicious at first, but when Choṭa lied saying that he had a fever and flu, Yamala agreed that he should rest. Choṭa confided in a few devotees at Crabwood Creek as to his actual activities. A friend lent him the use of a shack in the jungle, and a young field mouse named Bhakta Eddie volunteered to assist Choṭa by cooking. Choṭa was a bit skeptical whether Eddie would respect the solitude that he was seeking. But Choṭa wasn't ready to do it entirely alone, and so he agreed.

They arrived around 9:00 A.M., and Choṭa immediately began chanting *japa*. The shack was in the middle of a coconut grove where the trees were strong and gracefully bending, with bunches of green coconuts at the top. They could hear the rustle of big leaves and the gentle clacking of bamboo in the breeze. Many varieties of birds were singing—the yellow bird known as the bananaquit was most frequently seen flying and hopping about. A dappling of shade and sunshine created a pleasant effect, and Choṭa's spirits soared.

Choṭa thought of Śrīla Prabhupāda's profound but simple instruction on how to chant: Just pay attention to the words of the *mantra* and nothing else. Choṭa's intention was to serve the holy names without expecting a reward. He focused on the sound vibrations, but after half an hour, he realized it was going to be difficult to keep it up. He would have to go on chanting with little or no taste for it. He found himself inattentive in the extreme. It was as if the holy names were a signal for his mind to turn over plans and reflect on current topics or simply to go off anywhere in the universe at the speed of mind. He doubted whether being alone with *japa* as his main activity would actually enable him to improve.

Bhakta Eddie had been busy in the kitchen, but then he peeked out at Choṭa on the porch and asked if he could chant with him. Choṭa nodded in agreement. After a few minutes Eddie turned and said, "Choṭa Prabhu, may I ask you a question?" Choṭa nodded.

"I'm trying to understand," said Bhakta Eddie, placing his palms together in respect. "Didn't Prabhupāda say that he preferred to stay at a temple rather than a hotel and that he wanted to always be near devotees? So, whatever you are trying to do, shouldn't you be doing it in a temple?"

"This is a temple," said Choṭa. "See the tulasī plant? Do you know what a temple is?"

"I see," said Eddie, "but isn't the most important thing to associate with devotees? Shouldn't we just spend our time in the company of other devotees rather than relying on our own minds?"

Choṭa smiled. "Who's relying on his own mind? I've come here to rely on the holy names. Do you want to help me or not?"

"I'm sorry," said Bhakta Eddie, "I didn't mean to be offensive."

"It's just for a couple of days," said Choṭa. "Let's both chant." The two resumed their *harināma* in the jungle, but Bhakta Eddie's questions remained with Choṭa and added to his uncertainty.

He continued grinding out the *mahā-mantra* without taste or attention. But after a few hours, when it was near lunchtime and he was hungry, Choṭa began to beg for the holy name. It occurred to him, at least theoretically, that the holy name was the Supreme Lord Himself. Choṭa thought, "Please be with me as I chant Your names. Help me to surrender to this real work. Help me chant from the heart." His budding mood of prayer was interrupted by the lunch of *dāl* and rice, after which Choṭa felt heavy and went inside to sleep.

After an hour of rest, Choṭa woke suddenly to Bhakta Eddie's voice. Eddie was about a hundred feet away on the jungle path talking to a passerby mouse. Eddie and this mouse attended the same school, and so they talked for a while about teachers they knew and then about cricket matches and a girl mouse named Wanda who had won the spelling bee. The passerby said he wanted to be an engineer, and Eddie replied that he was undecided, although maybe he would like to become a lawyer. Choṭa sat up wondering why Eddie was wasting his time in a conversation which Choṭa found pointless. The idle talk forced him to see how much he had changed in his outlook. He sensed his own strong determination for spiritual achievement. Choṭa felt tempted with pride, and so he rose to his feet chanting loudly. He walked onto the porch as a hint to Eddie that he should break up his chatting.

The afternoon's *japa* was hard work, but Choṭa felt good about it. It was very humbling to see his inadequacy. He felt helpless to improve, but he chanted with faith in the process. When Eddie came onto the porch again and asked to join him in chanting Choṭa hoped he would not ask more questions. But after a few minutes of *japa*, Eddie turned and asked, "Choṭa Prabhu, could you help me?"

"What is it?"

"How can I control my mind? I have so many material desires."

"Just chant," said Choṭa.

"Is that all? Just chant?"

Choṭa switched abruptly from his own feeling of inadequacy to the role of a superior.

"Not *just* chant," said Choṭa. "Don't minimize the chanting. If we could actually just chant, then all our problems would go away. Chanting means that you're invoking the presence of God, and if God is with you, then your mind is controlled, material desires are gone, and everything is blissful."

"But I don't feel blissful," said Eddie.

"Yes, well neither do I. But at least I'm not eager for *material* bliss. We shouldn't be discouraged. And because we're not so advanced that we can *only* chant, Prabhupāda and the *ācāryas* have given us many duties. Sometimes we can chant, sometimes read, sometimes cook—whatever we like to do, but for Kṛṣṇa. That way we can always practice Kṛṣṇa consciousness. Is that all right?"

Bhakta Eddie nodded hopefully. He had more questions, but Choṭa asked him to hold them for now.

At dusk, the mosquitoes came out, and Choṭa and Eddie took shelter under mosquito nets. From across the river, they heard the strains of rock music. Choṭa chanted on his beads and noticed that subtle "muscles" in his mind were beginning to exert attention and to neglect unwanted thoughts. But it was strenuous. By 10:00 P.M., with a sense that he was chanting just to complete a quota, Choṭa pushed the counter beads indicating the completion of sixty-four rounds. And then he fell fast asleep.

For the second day of his retreat, Choṭa planned to concentrate on reading. Full sets of Prabhupāda's books were scarce in Guyana, and all he had was his own copy of the *KṚṢṆA* book. He woke early, turned on the light, and remained under the mosquito netting while Bhakta Eddie slept. Choṭa was hoping that his reading would not be like the drudgery of a schoolboy's homework. He hoped that Lord Kṛṣṇa would speak to him from the pages of Śrīla Prabhupāda's book. Before opening the book, he prepared himself to recognize that he was about to do something very special. He knelt down, offered a brief prayer, and then touched the *KṚṢṆA* book respectfully to his head. Opening the book at random, he settled at Chapter 45, "Uddhava Visits Vṛndāvana."

Choṭa knew that he was not qualified to be included in the intimate pastimes of Lord Kṛṣṇa, Uddhava, and the residents of Vṛndāvana. Kṛṣṇa and Prabhupāda were kindly allowing him to hear, but in a higher sense he was not really included. At certain points in the narrative, however, Śrīla Prabhupāda turned and spoke directly to Choṭa.

> Those who are in the most exalted position of devotional service and ecstasy can live with Kṛṣṇa always by remembering His pastimes. Any book of *kṛṣṇa-līlā*, even this book *KṚṢṆA* and our *Teachings of Lord Caitanya*, is actually solace for devotees who are feeling separation of Kṛṣṇa.

When Śrīla Prabhupāda included him in that way, Choṭa realized that actually he had never been ignored by Kṛṣṇa in His pastimes. The Lord was inviting him to take part. Kṛṣṇa was saying to Choṭa as well as to every willing reader, "Come to Me, I am the Supreme Personality of Godhead. Live with me always." This was the inspiration Choṭa had been seeking: a śāstric confirmation for his own desire to spend more time with Prabhupāda's books. As he read on, it happened again. Uddhava had entered the house of Nanda Mahārāja and was offered an honorable reception. Nanda inquired how Kṛṣṇa was doing in Mathurā and whether He remembered His father and mother. Nanda described some of Kṛṣṇa's uncommon activities to Uddhava and became so overwhelmed that he could not speak anymore. Choṭa read it as if observing from a respectful distance. But Prabhupāda included him:

> ...To remain always absorbed in Kṛṣṇa consciousness was the standard of the inhabitants of Vṛndāvana as exhibited by Mahārāja Nanda, Yaśodā and the *gopīs*. If we simply follow their footsteps, even to a minute proportion, our lives will surely become successful, and we will enter the spiritual kingdom, Vaikuṇṭha.

Choṭa read for half an hour and was still going strong when Bhakta Eddie woke up. Eddie tried chanting but again fell asleep. After another hour, Eddie roused himself again and said to Choṭa, "It's really tough being a mouse. Maybe I'll get a better body next time. Should I want a better body? What do you think?"

"Yes, you should want a better body," said Choṭa. "You should want a spiritual body so that you can dance and play with Kṛṣṇa. But even subhuman persons are spirit souls. We're more covered over. You shouldn't just lament and *wait* for a better body. What do you think?"

"I think that by Prabhupāda's grace and by your association I can chant Hare Kṛṣṇa even now. I just have to stay awake." Bhakta Eddie began slapping his cheeks and pinching himself. He tried chanting loudly, but after half an hour, both he and Choṭa were nodding sleepily under the dim naked bulb.

Later in the morning, when Choṭa was again feeling hungry before lunch, he had another successful reading session. He began it with his little ritual, bowing down before the book and telling himself that he was about to do something very special. He prayed for the ability to listen to the Lord. This time he read about Uddhava's delivering a message from Kṛṣṇa to the *gopīs*. When he came to Rādhārāṇī's transcendental madness in speaking to a bumblebee, Choṭa felt that it was way over his head. It was fascinating, yet he could not dare to think he was included in Her relationship with Kṛṣṇa. But when Uddhava read Kṛṣṇa's letter, it seemed to be addressed not only to the *gopīs* but to everyone. Kṛṣṇa informed the *gopīs* that they should not feel separation from Him because "separation between ourselves is impossible at any time, at any place or under any circumstance, because I am all-pervading." And then Śrīla Prabhupāda turned to Choṭa dāsa and said, "Not only the *gopīs*, but all living entities are always inseparably connected with Kṛṣṇa in all circumstances." Choṭa thought of the controversy whether subhuman persons could practice Kṛṣṇa consciousness. Here was another confirmation in his favor: *"Not only the* gopīs, *but all living entities are always inseparably connected with Kṛṣṇa in all circumstances."* Later in the chapter Prabhupāda confirmed it even more:

> The effect of taking up Kṛṣṇa consciousness is just like that of drinking nectar. With or without one's knowledge it will act. The active principle of Kṛṣṇa consciousness will manifest itself everywhere; it does not matter how and where one has taken his birth. Kṛṣṇa will bestow His upon anyone who takes to Kṛṣṇa consciousness without any doubt.

As Choṭa read on, he felt as if he were encountering waves from the spiritual ocean. He thought, "If I regularly give the best time to hearing

Prabhupāda's books, I'll be covered by continual, blissful waves, and gradually my sense of material life will diminish in place of *kṛṣṇa-kathā*. My faith will grow strong, and I'll want to spend more and more time with the books. But what if I like it so much, I get addicted and want to leave off other duties? Probably that wouldn't happen. I could both read and perform active duties. But even if I did become a madman addicted to hearing *Śrīmad-Bhāgavatam*, wouldn't Śrīla Prabhupāda be pleased with that? And wouldn't it be a good example for others?"

At the end of the second day, Bhakta Eddie's younger brother came and said that Eddie's mom wanted him to come home right away.

"Tell her you'll come home tomorrow night," said Choṭa. But then he saw that Bhakta Eddie was inclined to go home. He had had enough of the retreat.

"I think you'd better go," said Choṭa. "We don't want to disturb your mother."

"Yes," said Eddie. "It's been very, uh...transcendental. Thank you for letting me stay with you."

After dark, the sounds of the insects and animals made Choṭa nervous, but he felt that he was finally beginning to face himself.

On his third day, Choṭa decided not to cook but to eat only banana and coconuts that he could gather easily. He chanted and read the *KṚṢṆA* book, and his moods alternated between very elated and quite depressed. Sometimes he considered that he would like to live the rest of his life this way, but then he did not want to stay alone for even another hour. He reasoned that staying alone was an art which he knew nothing about. Perhaps he should go see that meditating turtle whom Padma dāsa had mentioned and learn more about how to survive in solitude. Finally, Choṭa decided not to stay another night on his own but to return right away to the temple.

Chapter 5

As Choṭa approached the temple building, he heard the sound of the bell ringing for evening *ārati*. He entered the room, and his nose twitched from the aroma of sandalwood incense. His eyes rested upon the sight of the Deities' picture being worshiped on the altar. He was glad to be back; it felt safe.

He had arrived just at the start of the evening *ārati*, which was usually attended by only one or two mice besides the *pūjārī*. The room was bare, just varnished floors and no furniture except for a wooden altar with framed pictures and candles. Choṭa stood close to the altar and carefully observed the brahminical movements of the *pūjārī*. The *pūjārī* touched the flame to the ghee wick and held the wick as an offering to the picture of Śrīla Prabhupāda. Choṭa watched as if for the first time. He felt appreciation for the steady attitude of this *pūjārī*, who he knew performed the same ritual four times a day with simple faith.

The room was dark except for the candle flames on the altar and one light bulb in the rear of the hall. An old lady mouse with a couple of grandchildren was in attendance, and she had left a bag of rice as a donation before the altar rail. They all stood quietly and watched, while a tape of Śrīla Prabhupāda singing Śikṣāṣṭakam played softly. Choṭa heard the cries of the insects and other animals in the jungle night, but it didn't make him nervous as it did when he was alone. He felt that he was receiving extra mercy.

After *ārati* Choṭa was bombarded with messages and confronted by persons who wanted to see him. Most urgent was a phone call from Yamala dāsa, who had been trying to reach him for two days.

"Don't ever go off to where there's no phone," said Yamala. "You have too many responsibilities to just disappear like that, even if you are sick." Yamala said that Arjuna dāsa and his sympathizers "have declared war on the movement."

Apparently, some of Arjuna's followers had gone to a temple but were not allowed to enter, so they pushed their way in and ate lunch without permission. They also took a drum from the temple, claiming it belonged to them. When they were leaving, there was a scuffle with the temple mice, and one was pushed down the stairs and sprained his ankle. Yamala said, "Choṭa Prabhu, you have to go personally to Arjuna and tell him to leave the country *or else*. No one can do this but you. Do you agree?"

Choṭa agreed to go see Arjuna. He traveled to the town where Arjuna lived and called at his house. As soon as they saw one another, the two brothers embraced.

"I've heard so many rumors," said Choṭa. "Tell me Arj, what is your actual complaint?"

Arjuna gave Choṭa a cup of water and gestured for him to sit on a wicker chair.

"My complaint," said Arjuna, "is that we shouldn't have left our home and our responsibilities to Mom and Dad."

"What?" said Choṭa. "Then why didn't you say so? Why the big smoke screen about Nimāi and how animals can't become Kṛṣṇa conscious?"

"Because you're so fanatical you wouldn't listen."

"No, I can listen. But maybe I am fanatical. Please forgive me. Anyway, if you felt that way about leaving Mom and Dad and everything, why don't you go back?"

"Do you think I should?"

"Yes," said Choṭa, "I think that would be best. And you could also apologize to them for me. But don't go with this idea that I forced you to leave home. You left them by your own free will."

A few of Arjuna's friends came into the room, but Arjuna asked them to leave "so we can talk in private."

"What did I know of free will?" asked Arjuna. "You just swept me away with your talks and promises. And then we had to go out in freezing weather in a van, *in a cage!* You call that free will?"

"I'm sorry," said Choṭa, "You're right, I was fanatical. I'm sorry."

"Yeah. If I go North, I'll need money," said Arjuna.

"No, you won't. Mice can travel as stowaways in boats."

'Yes, but I'll have to pay an agent to find the right boat at the right time."

"I don't have any money," said Choṭa.

"Yes, you do. The movement has money."

"But that's all for Kṛṣṇa."

"Then I'll fight you," said Arjuna.

"All right," said Choṭa. "I'll get you the money somehow. But you have to call off this 'war.'"

"Okay, okay."

After things were amicably settled, Choṭa and Arjuna went to the kitchen and cooked their lunch. Choṭa had heard rumors that Arjuna was no longer practicing devotional principles, but he was glad to see it wasn't true. Arjuna sang the Hare Kṛṣṇa *mantra* while they cooked, and he offered the food to pictures of the Deities. Friends from the neighborhood came by, and they all sat on the floor honoring *prasādam* off citrus leaves.

"We *did* have some good times together," said Choṭa "Admit it, Arjunajī."

"Yeah," said Arjuna, smiling over hot rice and *dāl*. "Remember that time when we tried to distribute *prasādam*, but the ghetto mice came and took it away? Then we met some albino mice who were very interested."

Arjuna's neighbors laughed and asked to hear more adventures.

"Tell them," urged Choṭa, "how Nimāi taught us how to chant."

"Oh yeah!" Arjuna recalled, "actually *you* taught us Choṭa. But I remember that one time Nimāi told us to cry out like a baby for its mother. When he said that, at first, I just squealed and squeaked, but then I learned to say the words: *Hare Kṛṣṇa, Hare Kṛṣṇa, Kṛṣṇa Kṛṣṇa, Hare Hare, Hare Rāma, Hare Rāma, Rāma Rāma, Hare Hare.*"

The very next day a big scandal was uncovered within the movement, and Choṭa was asked to rectify it. Two mice devotees who lived in the far south of the country came to Crabwood Creek and reported it. One of the female mice living in that southern temple had complained to her father that a male mouse living in the temple had seduced her into illicit sex. The father of this girl was a judge, and he became very disturbed. The accused male mouse was one of the managers for the temple, and the rumor was that he had had illicit dealings with a number of lady mice in that town, all under the pretense of engaging them in devotional service. The southern mice requested Choṭa to please come with them to meet the judge and at least explain that this was not the proper behavior for devotees, and that the offender would be punished. Choṭa would also have to meet the accused mouse, who completely denied the girl's story. Even while Choṭa spoke with the southern mice, Yamala dāsa phoned him—he too had heard news of the brewing scandal. Yamala said that it was the worst possible trouble that had ever happened. It could smear the movement as a sex cult and ruin their preaching. "But why me?" asked Choṭa. "Why do you all come to *me* with this?" Yamala replied that Choṭa was the only one capable of pacifying the judge, and the only one with enough spiritual clout to get the accused to break down and tell the truth.

"You should also interview the girls in the temple," said a devotee from the South. "Some of them are starting to admit that they fell down with this guy. But others still deny it, although we're not sure. But everyone respects you, Choṭa, because you're very pure. When they speak to you, we think they'll admit what they didn't admit to us."

Choṭa agreed to leave the next day if he could get a boat going south. But that night he couldn't sleep well. His three-day spiritual retreat seemed to have taken place long, long ago. As thoughts passed through his sleepless mind, Choṭa considered that maybe he should just go away from all this, leave Guyana, and go somewhere to chant and read. Of course, he couldn't just leave; that would be irresponsible. "Anyway," thought Choṭa, "I just proved that I am incapable of living alone. I couldn't even stay alone more than a single night. Even if I wanted to, I couldn't become a *bābājī* like that." Choṭa then recalled that Padma said a meditating turtle lived in the South, nor far from their temple there.

He decided that he could go see him and try to find out how to practice solitude. The idea of seeing the turtle became pleasing to Choṭa and gave him a new motivation for going south. Otherwise, his assignment brought him mostly disgust and aversion.

Choṭa took an animal ferryboat down the southern canal. It was a five-hour journey. The water was muddy brown and the scenery pleasant, but the crowded conditions on the boat and the behavior of the passengers made it a test of tolerance. There were many carts and wagons on board, and their drivers almost invariably smoked cigarettes. There were muskrats and frogs and a few sewer rats who exuded an obnoxious odor. At one point the passengers at the stern became alarmed when they saw an alligator in the water, but it turned out to be an alligator's floating corpse.

On the same trip with Choṭa were several mice devotees who were also going to the southern temple. These young devotees took the opportunity of the ferryboat ride to distribute transcendental literature to the passengers, although only a few were interested. Choṭa watched as a group of roaches and grasshoppers gathered around one of the book distributors and made inquiries. One of the mice pointed over to Choṭa and said, "He's one of the leaders," after which a few roaches crawled over and asked Choṭa some questions. When the mice devotees shared a simple lunch among themselves, Choṭa joined them. He was inspired to be with the younger preachers, and he thought, "How could I be planning to leave all of this? Even if I *did* leave to practice my vows in solitude, it wouldn't be a permanent thing, and it certainly wouldn't be leaving the movement or Kṛṣṇa consciousness." After lunch, when Choṭa sat to chant *japa*, he nodded off in sleep even while others were watching him. He cursed himself and thought, "How can I not take action to improve this?"

On arrival in the South, Choṭa allowed his companions to go ahead. He said he would catch up with them later. He then went looking for the mangrove swamp where he had heard the turtle lived. Crawling through dense thickets of shrubs and tropical evergreens, he came to the edge of a pond. The whole area was filled with tangled roots and crevices where animals lived. A mysterious looking moss hung down from the trees, and large birds, not all of them friendly, glided through the air and landed here and there. Choṭa asked himself why he was coming to see this turtle since he was not a Kṛṣṇa conscious devotee. It was all right, he told himself. He wanted to talk with a genuine solitary to get some questions answered, just as devotees sometimes consulted doctors or lawyers. He could use it as devotional service, and if the turtle said anything against Vaiṣṇava principles, Choṭa would reject it.

From the shore, Choṭa studied the surface of the pond until he noticed a certain slimy rock that looked like the back of a turtle.

"Turtle! O Turtle!" he called, but the rock didn't respond. A field mouse ambled over to Choṭa and looked him up and down. "Looking for the hermit turtle, eh?"

"Yes, can you help me?"

"It's not so easy," said the field mouse, brushing bits of underbrush from his shaggy coat. "He doesn't just come up and talk to anyone. He's very particular. They say he is over 130 years old. He's meditating, ya know."

This mouse is so ignorant, thought Choṭa, *that he doesn't know I am perhaps the most famous spiritual mouse in the world and that I have just been worshiped by 300 mice at my birthday party.* But Choṭa kept this to himself.

"Well, what do I have to do to get his attention?" asked Choṭa.

"I dunno. You might have to stay here for a long time."

"I can't do that," said Choṭa, and the other mouse huffed and shuffled into a crevice in the ground.

"Turtle!" Choṭa called out loud. "My name is Choṭa dāsa, and I have come to respectfully ask you a few questions. I'm interested in practicing solitude. I'm a student of *bhakti-yoga.* We read the *Bhagavad-gītā.*

I have heard that you are a great solitary. Also, in the *Bhagavad-gītā* the tortoise is mentioned honorably several times, as you may know." Choṭa felt somewhat silly because no one was there, but then the rock on the pond moved slightly, and Choṭa was sure that it was the turtle.

"Yes," Choṭa called out, "the *kūrma* is compared to the *yogi*: 'One who is able to withdraw his senses from sense objects, as the turtle draws his limbs within shell, is firmly fixed in perfect consciousness.'"

At these words the turtle lifted his head—it was a slimy head covered with algae, resembling a *yogi's* matted locks—and looked noncommittally in Choṭa's direction.

Choṭa continued, "There's also a verse in Vedic literature that states, 'By meditating only, the turtle maintains his offspring and so do I, O Padmājā!' I really do wish you would come over and let me speak to you for a few minutes, dear turtle."

With a swift movement, the turtle submerged and reappeared perched on a rock in the water just a few feet from Choṭa. The turtle was three times Choṭa's size. Its massive shell was covered with slime and chipped in a few places. Its legs were scarred, and it emanated a rotten odor. But Choṭa sensed that he was face to face with a genuine hermit.

"What do you want to know?" asked the turtle. "Anyway, there's nothing that I can put into words."

"I've become interested in solitude," said Choṭa. "For us devotees that means chanting Hare Kṛṣṇa and reading the Vedic scriptures. I heard that you have been practicing solitude for a long time. So, how did you decide you wanted to live alone and practice meditation?"

The turtle blinked. "You have to be called to it," he said. Choṭa waited for him to say more, but he was silent. Choṭa sensed that this was going to be a short interview, and so he had better be as direct as possible.

"How do you know if you're called?"

"Some know it from their earliest youth," the turtle said. "They find their way by instinct to the place where they will be alone. But some reach solitude the hard way, through suffering and disillusion."

"I don't understand," said Choṭa. "How do you get invited, or as you say, called."

"Look," the turtle said, "if you can't firmly decide for yourself, then you aren't called. Solitude can choose you, but you don't belong to her until you accept. Do you understand?"

Choṭa decided to keep asking questions and to think it over later.

"What was your main motive in becoming a hermit? Were you feeling that you just wanted to get away from it all?"

"That's not it," said the turtle. "Although God knows the turtle's life is full of suffering. Our mothers' eggs are always being destroyed by humans or eaten by animals. But solitude isn't separation from life. If you try to go alone merely to get away from people you don't like, you won't find either peace or solitude. I go alone not to escape from everyone but in order to find everything and everyone in God. In solitude I feel love for others and communion with them that I can't find when I'm just doing all the things the turtle crowd does. So for me it's not running from the world; it's my *place* in the world."

"Do other animals criticize you?" asked Choṭa. "Or do you criticize yourself? I mean, when you have doubts how do you justify this life?"

The turtle said, "Too much self-justification is just a distraction. Look, *everyone* is alone. What's the big deal? Why are you asking?"

Choṭa felt embarrassed that the turtle did not seem to consider his questions very intelligent. The advantage he had gained by his *Bhagavad-gītā* quotes was ebbing away. Choṭa thought that he had already learned something valuable, and he wanted to ask more. But before he could speak again, the turtle sniffed, and then both animals twitched on hearing something to their right. Two female turtles emerged from a thicket at the pond's edge and were entering the water. As soon as they entered, a big male turtle poked his head up from within the pond and floated nearby. Seeing the hermit turtle, the other male turtle stretched his neck and hissed.

The hermit turtle said, "He thinks that I am after the women, but I couldn't care less. Let's move over here."

After repositioning themselves at a distance from the mating scene, Choṭa asked, "Do you follow any particular teachings? What is your science of God or theology?"

"I would rather not discuss it," said the turtle. "The main thing is to practice. Isn't that what you want to know?"

"Yes," said Choṭa. "But you have to be practicing something worthwhile. Otherwise, you're just beating on an empty husk."

"But there can be too much talk of theology," said the turtle.

Again they were interrupted by noises. The intruding male turtle had gone into the marsh with one of the females, and he was mounting onto her back. But then another male turtle arrived, and the two males began to fight. One male tipped the other over on its back and then disappeared with the females into the water.

Choṭa asked the hermit, "Do you find yourself making spiritual advancement by being alone?"

The hermit turtle did not reply but gave a loud, smelly belch. Then he said, "I am usually unable to pray. I do my meditating work and generally I'm peaceful. All I have is my solitude. It's there. It's inescapable. It's everything. It contains God."

Choṭa was impressed, but he would have to figure out the meanings later. He wanted to ask, "Why don't you preach?" But he doubted that the turtle would know enough about it. And anyway, Choṭa thought, he's not my *guru*. Choṭa opted for an easier question. "Can you have an inner life," he asked, "without being physically alone?"

The turtle said, "Physical solitude is important. Learn to be alone. But it's the means to the end. Don't you at least have a room or some place where you can go set yourself free? If you have found such a place, be content with it. Go there and breathe. Return to your private place as soon as you can. That's all."

The turtle went under the water. Choṭa called him back but he was gone. Choṭa then, hurried off to join the devotees in the southern temple, without thinking much about what he had just seen and heard.

Choṭa's investigation threw him into a whirlpool of events for the next four days. He first went to see the judge whose daughter claimed she had been seduced. The judge was not unreasonable, but it took a long evening of sitting with him and answering many questions on the philosophy, practice, and organization of the mouse movement in Guyana. Choṭa assured the judge that there would be a thorough investigation, and if the culprit was found guilty, he would be punished. But the culprit denied his guilt, and so did the other women whom some said were in an illicit connection with him. Finally, after two days of almost constant interviews with women, one of them confessed to having had an illicit relationship with the so-called counselor for ladies. Choṭa gathered painstaking, overwhelming evidence, and the accused male finally admitted some of his guilt. He spoke remorsefully and asked to be given another chance. Choṭa ordered that the counselor be removed from his duties and sent to another place. He then went back to speak to the judge and everyone else involved until everyone seemed satisfied. After four full days, Choṭa thought he had done all that was possible, and he told the devotees that he would leave the next day and return north.

That same night, however, several hours after eating, Choṭa felt a pain in his stomach. He had had it for months, but now it hurt badly. It increased until he couldn't sleep, and the next morning he didn't feel like eating. The devotees phoned a friendly doctor who stopped by the temple to see Choṭa.

"You have the hurry-worry-curry disease," said the doctor. "It's an ulcer, the disease of modern civilization." The doctor said that he could give some medicines, but the only cure was to reduce stress.

"How do you do that?" asked Choṭa.

"Behavior modification," said the doctor. "Change of lifestyle, change of occupation."

Choṭa decided to stay an extra day in the South in order to rest. He was alone in his room, but he felt too tired to read or to put effort into *japa.* His stomach still hurt; it caused him more worry. By the afternoon, he began writing a report of his investigation to be sent to Yamala dāsa. Throughout the hectic activities, Choṭa had also been thinking, at least unconsciously, of his meeting with the meditating turtle. It had influenced him in a significant way, but his main conclusion was that only a senior Kṛṣṇa conscious devotee could help him.

Chapter 6

Choṭa decided to take a sabbatical, so he wrote a note and mailed it to Yamala.

> I am going to take a sabbatical for increasing chanting and hearing. I will do it for a year. I will keep in touch. Please don't be angry with me. I'm trying to improve myself to be a better servant. I'm sure you will all be able to handle things in my absence.

Choṭa didn't know exactly how he would live alone, but he hoped that the Lord in the heart would guide him. After all, it was God who provided for all living creatures, and so He would also provide for a mouse who sought to spend his full time in self-realization. Choṭa knew this fact theoretically, and he often recited it in lectures, but now he wanted to experience it. He especially wanted to experience Kṛṣṇa's loving presence as manifest in Vedic literature. Carrying a small suitcase, Choṭa hopped onto a fishing boat and went to the nearby Caribbean island of Tobago.

He went to the beach. There he saw banana and mango trees and coconut palms as well as nut-bearing trees and fresh ponds. Combing the hot beach for a few days, Choṭa came upon abandoned bamboo shacks and the ruins of a few small stone houses. He selected a shack located in a palm tree grove within sight and sound of the ocean surf. There he spread out his straw mat, fashioned a primitive bookstand from pieces of wood covered with a cloth, and decided to make the place his home.

He thought that one of the most important features of his new life should be privacy. A complete daily schedule of devotional activities was also important. Therefore, on his first day in the beach shack Choṭa sketched a plan for his daily routine. He would rise very early, by 1:30 or 2:00 A.M. He would chant in the quiet with the surf as the only accompanying sound. As early as possible, he'd start reading. Because Choṭa had left the security of his home and friends so abruptly, he hadn't been able to take many books, or amenities like a tape recorder. All he had was the *KṚṢṆA* book. He could get more books later, but he wanted to be satisfied with this one book, which was good enough for a great devotee like Mahārāja Parīkṣit. Choṭa planned time for chanting and reading as well as time for food foraging and for making efforts to locate Nimāi by letter. His only other long-term plan was to keep in touch with the boat agent, so that if and when he learned of Nimāi's whereabouts, he could go there without a long delay.

Choṭa's first reading session in his new hermitage was from the section, "Lord Kṛṣṇa Teases Rukmiṇī." He began to read it just as the sun came up on a balmy tropical morning. Bowing down before the book and praying that Lord Kṛṣṇa would speak to him directly through the pages, he sat back to read the pastime of the Lord. He had heard it before, but it always delighted him. How could the Supreme Lord be so light-hearted as to tease His pure devotee? How is it that He spoke not in defying words but with jokes to tell a dearest devotee that She was wasting her time by worshiping Him? Choṭa knew that Kṛṣṇa was being wonderful to speak to her like that. He was so intimate with Rukmiṇī that He wanted to see Her loving annoyance. It was His conjugal relationship with Her. Choṭa knew that he himself was trying to approach the Supreme Lord in the mood of reverent servant. He wanted to see Kṛṣṇa as the worshipable Godhead and guru and himself as the always reverent disciple. Rukmiṇī-devī also wanted to see the Lord as Her beloved master, but Lord Kṛṣṇa's desire was to joke in order to see Her shining beauty. Choṭa enjoyed reading the Lord's self-berating talk, because He used many of the jibes which non-devotees make about His character, such as His having two sets of parents, His bellicose spirit, His dancing with unmarried girls and then deserting them, and so on.

By testing His devotee directly, Kṛṣṇa seemed to turn everything upside down. When the Lord said, "I release you from devotional service.

You don't have to go through the trouble of worshiping me anymore," Choṭa wanted to cry out with Rukmiṇī, "No, Kṛṣṇa, I want You! I don't find fault in You!" But still Kṛṣṇa persisted in joking. He said that He was detached from loving relationships: "I actually have no love for You, though You loved Me even before our marriage." In response to these words, Rukmiṇī felt great fear and fell unconscious like a banana tree cut down by the wind.

As usual, Choṭa was able to keep up his interest only for about ten minutes, and then he seriously lagged. He knew that he should like the *KṚṢṆA* book, and he *did* like it. But he was covered by the lower modes of nature, especially sleepiness and mental restlessness. And Choṭa realized that so far, he only read with his tiny brain. He was not able to read from his heart. Still, he hoped that one stage would lead to another. Just as exterior solitude would lead to inner awakening, so his study of the *KṚṢṆA* book would lead to *bhakti*.

After a few days in his new home, Choṭa became acquainted with his neighbors. The quiet was regularly broken by the raucous cries of crows, who moved around the palm trees and on the ground nearby looking for food. When he heard the cry of the hawk, Choṭa stayed indoors and peeked timidly out the window until the hawk was gone. He often saw seagulls flying, and at the water's edge he saw sandpipers and tiny ghost crabs who lived in holes on the beach. Choṭa went for a dip in the ocean's wavelets each morning. Fortunately, he had picked a deserted stretch of beach, and so humans didn't come by often. When they did appear, they were a great disruption with their loud radios. On one occasion a man and a woman came right to the door of Choṭa's shack and looked in. Then they threw a bag of garbage and empty beer cans through the window which took Choṭa an hour to clean up.

One day a hermit crab scraped its way into the shack entrance. He was a strange looking fellow with an oversized claw, and he carried an abandoned snail shell on his back. Choṭa couldn't speak his language but indicated that he wanted privacy, and the hermit crab dragged itself away. But he continued to appear at the door almost daily. Choṭa soon discovered that a black bat hung from the ceiling of the *bhajana-kutir*. When he first saw it, Choṭa considered either stoning it or vacating the shack. But the bat slept quietly all day and was gone all night, so Choṭa decided to live with it. There were also the usual spiders and passersby, like the sideways-walking land crabs and dogs from whom Choṭa had to hide.

Choṭa was paid a visit by some friendly field mice. They were impressed to hear that Choṭa had traveled so widely. He explained about the chanting of Hare Kṛṣṇa, but they didn't want to know anything about it.

"I had a friend who once traveled to Trinidad," said a field mouse, "but I never before met anyone who has been to as many places as you have. Can you tell us more about Pennsylvania and all the places you have been?" Choṭa tried to satisfy them, but he made it clear that he had come to the beach for solitude. The field mice took the hint and mostly left him alone, although he and the field mice shared fruit that fell from the trees and often met at the water holes. The babies of the field mice also played at Choṭa's front door.

Choṭa had come to Tobago near the end of the rainy season. He had to endure a leaky roof, dark skies, and heavy winds. He attached a piece of plastic from wall to wall and stayed dry within one part of the room. As for bugs and mosquitos, it was pretty much the same as in his former home. So there were considerable flaws in his paradise, but on the whole, Choṭa remained encouraged. He spent his days virtually alone, faithfully following his *sādhana*. When he read the *KṚṢṆA* book, he felt that he was neither in Guyana nor Tobago, but in the spiritual world. He read in small doses, but they began to accumulate.

Choṭa's intensified attempt to worship Lord Kṛṣṇa in book form also brought out some of his latent misgivings. Lord Kṛṣṇa's superhuman activities were sometimes hard for him to believe. How could He have a billion family members? Were there actually demons with a thousand arms? From a mouse's point of view, it certainly seems fantastic to hear of Kṛṣṇa and Balarāma jumping eighty-eight miles from a mountain, or of Kṛṣṇa expanding into seven forms to wrestle with bulls and then marrying sixteen thousand princesses. Despite all the warnings given by Śrīla Prabhupāda in the *KṚṢṆA* book, Choṭa sometimes thought of the pastimes as "stories," or he wondered whether Kṛṣṇa was an ordinary man.

Choṭa dealt with these doubts soberly and knew them to be dangerous by-products of his untrained mind. He reread the preface and appreciated Prabhupāda's explanation that God is Bhagavān and all-powerful. As the Supreme Controller, He floats all the huge planets in outer space, and He expands as the inner guide within every living entity. So, if God appears in His original form to show us a small sample of His inconceivable opulences, by lifting Govardhana Hill or marrying 16,108 wives, why should we doubt? Choṭa had brought up the same doubts a year ago to Nimāi, who had told him the story of the frog in a well. The frog was visited by a cousin who had just seen the Pacific Ocean. When the cousin frog tried to explain the size of the ocean, the frog in the well could only compare it with his own experience of a tiny well. Yes, Choṭa reasoned, there are *many* things I have not experienced in this world, what to speak of other planets. Choṭa also fought his doubts by simply disregarding the empirical or speculative approach and by accepting *KṚṢṆA* book as scripture. The liberated *ācāryas* accepted Lord Kṛṣṇa as the Supreme Truth. Choṭa's doubts never went away completely, but they didn't overwhelm him. He tolerated them just as he tolerated the hermit crab coming to the doorway or the spiders dangling in midair.

Sometimes Choṭa also had doubts about his sabbatical for improving *sādhana*. One night he suddenly thought, "What am I doing here? Why have I left the devotees and my position in the movement?" But he learned to deal with this. He called it "the dissatisfaction factor." He had been dissatisfied that too much activity within the movement was taking his attention from *sādhana* and now that he was devoting full-time to his *sādhana*, he was also feeling dissatisfied. But did it mean that every time he felt dissatisfied, he had to run and change his whole environment? When he thought about it with a cool brain, Choṭa concluded that he was now doing the right thing. He was becoming spiritually stronger and gradually gaining an appreciation for chanting and reading. If he sometimes felt stabs of dissatisfaction, the real cause of that was his lack of Kṛṣṇa consciousness, and he would have to tolerate it.

Choṭa was not inclined to go anywhere, but he had to make a trip into town on business. He posted his letter to Nimāi and rented a mailbox without any difficulty. But when he went to the harbor to inquire about voyages, a seafaring rat tried to discourage him.

"You, a mouse, go aboard a ship?" The rat laughed. "Can you climb across a mooring rope?" Choṭa assured him that he could do it, and he walked halfway up the hawser to prove his point. Choṭa found a boat agent and was put on a list for departures to distant places.

"Where are you staying?" asked the agent, who was a house rat. When Choṭa said, "The beach," the rat gave a serious warning, "You better watch out for snakes out there. They could swallow you in a minute!" Choṭa decided not even to think about it and to just depend on Kṛṣṇa. He was glad when his chores were over and he returned to his shack by the sea.

Choṭa practiced prayer as he had never before done in his life. When he became nervous from sounds at night or when a dog came by, he prayed, "O Kṛṣṇa, please protect me." But even when he was peaceful, he tried to call out to Kṛṣṇa. He prayed before reading and when trying to remain attentive in his *japa*. Prayer was part of his *sādhana*. He felt that Lord Kṛṣṇa was inviting him to pray. Choṭa also realized (at least in a theoretical way) that he needed to call on Kṛṣṇa constantly. He tried not to limit his prayers to demands and blessings, but to listen to what the Lord wanted. If he could learn the art of prayer, he knew that he would not be so indecisive or dependent on others. But he was also afraid that the Supreme Lord might ask him to do things that he was not ready to do. Choṭa's prayer was not at all perfect, and yet he persevered. Every day he tried again. He always seemed to fail, but he always tried again.

His new life gave him scope for wholehearted *sādhana*, with few distractions. He noticed that he was attaining a state of steadily high consciousness. He relished peace and simplicity. He always anticipated reading yet another *KṚṢṆA* book section. And although in one sense his chanting didn't seem to improve, he was always filled with good intentions and eager to wake up in the middle of the night to begin chanting again. Sometimes all of nature seemed to be chanting Hare Kṛṣṇa and inspiring him with the presence of God. The ocean was an aid to meditation, and it hinted of the greatness of Kṛṣṇa. The rising and setting of the sun drew him into a natural worship of the "eye of God." He was grateful for the sea breezes and the rustling palm fronds and the fact that he was far away from industrial noise. He also increased his practice of physical obeisances whenever he could remember it. Although he didn't count them, he sensed that he was bowing down many times a day.

Chapter 7

Choṭa's appearance had changed. White hairs had begun to appear on his head. His fruit diet had made him noticeably thinner, and his fur was usually flecked with sand. To ward off the sunshine, he sometimes wore a piece of straw that he had found in the shack. Many saw him as another beachcomber. Neighbors who overheard him talking to himself thought he was eccentric. They didn't know what he was doing.

Choṭa's "talking to himself" began as part of his readings. Sometimes he read aloud from the *KṚṢṆA* book, and then he started speaking to his mind, asking Kṛṣṇa to please reveal Himself through the scriptures. At first, he spoke only a sentence or two, and then he went on for ten minutes or half an hour. He began thinking of the Lord as a highly respected friend to whom he could tell everything. He spoke as honestly as he could and tried to elevate his talk to give thanks and to praise the glories of the Lord Kṛṣṇa as described in the Vedic literatures. In Choṭa's prayers sometimes Lord Kṛṣṇa spoke—as Choṭa read His words from the *KṚṢṆA* book or remembered other words of the Lord—and sometimes Choṭa spoke. Choṭa prayed a while walking to the ocean, collecting fruit, or sitting alone in his hut. It enlivened him, and he noticed that it improved his *japa*. He no longer felt that *sādhana* was merely a chore. And he no longer felt that he was all alone.

One day while sitting and reading, Choṭa suddenly jumped from his seat at the sight of his cousin, Yamala, entering the shack.

"The jig is up Choṭa," said Yamala in a loud voice. "I've come to bring you back to your duties." Yamala was wearing his team jacket and sweating. He carried a heavy-looking suitcase. "You really picked an outpost! I had to *walk* the last mile. Got anything to drink?" Choṭa felt embarrassed at his meager shack and his sandy appearance. Then he noticed that behind Yamala was a mouse devotee named Paṇḍita dāsa. Choṭa guessed that Paṇḍita had been brought along to supply Yamala scriptural arguments against Choṭa.

"Please sit down," said Choṭa.

"No thanks," said Yamala. "But maybe *you* better sit down." Yamala looked around, displeased. "I can see," he said, "that you've deviated from Prabhupāda."

"Don't talk like that," said Choṭa, "or I'll ask you to leave. Why can't you accept that I'm different from you and not be so judgmental? Accept me as I am."

"Why should I accept you as you are?" said Yamala sharply. "That's bogus. There *is* such a thing as right and wrong, ya know. It's not that 'everything is one.'"

Paṇḍita dāsa said, "According to Rūpa Gosvāmi, if you practice *bhakti* without following the śruti and *smṛti,* then you're a disturbance."

"But wait a minute," said Choṭa, "I'm following all the rules. The first is to always think of Kṛṣṇa and never forget Him. All the other rules are maidservants to that." They were each speaking tensely and quickly.

"Read to him, Paṇḍita," said Yamala, "from the quotes."

Paṇḍita dāsa took out a sheaf of papers, but before he could read, the bat on the ceiling began squeaking. It was a high-pitched sound.

"What's *that*?" asked Yamala, and he stepped back in fear. "It's a bat! Choṭa!"

"This is too much," said Paṇḍita, and his mouth turned with disgust.

"Is he gonna come down?" asked Yamala.

"He's registering a complaint," said Choṭa. "He might come down if you're too noisy. So, calm down."

They sat down as Paṇḍita dāsa read aloud, "This is from Prabhupāda's purports in the *Caitanya-caritāmṛta.* He says, 'At the present moment we see that some of the members of ISKCON are intending to leave their preaching activities in order to sit in a solitary place. This is not a very good sign. It is a fact that Śrīla Bhaktisiddhānta Sarasvatī Ṭhākura has condemned this process for neophytes. The neophyte devotee must act and work very laboriously under the direction of the spiritual master, and he must thus preach the cult of Śrī Caitanya Mahāprabhu. Only after maturing in devotion can he sit down in a solitary place to chant the Hare Kṛṣṇa *mahā-mantra* as Śrī Caitanya Mahāprabhu Himself did."

"There are other quotes also," said Choṭa. "For—"

"It's no good Choṭa," said Yamala. "Listen, I love you. When I see other mice devotees deviate, it doesn't matter to me. But you! You're like my śīkṣā-*guru.*" Yamala's eyes filled with tears. "Please come back to your prescribed duties."

"'*Yad yad ācarati śreṣṭhas,*'" quotes Paṇḍita dāsa. "Whatever actions a great man performs, common men follow. And whatever standards he sets by exemplary acts, all the world pursues."

Choṭa became softened. "I appreciate what you're saying," he said. "But maybe you've got the wrong impression. I never said that I wouldn't go back to my duties. I'm just taking a sabbatical for a year, and I'm doing it in order to become fit to serve. As for the scriptures, Lord Kṛṣṇa has said that when a person practices self-realization he lives in a solitary place. Lord Caitanya Himself used to avoid large crowds. For example, when He went to Vṛndāvana He chanted the holy name at Imlitala by Himself."

"Are you Lord Caitanya?" asked Yamala. "Our quotes are heavier than yours, Prabhu. Give him another, Paṇḍita."

Paṇḍita dāsa read aloud, "'A devotee is not interested in so-called meditation in the Himalayas or the forest. Rather his interest is in the busiest part of the world, where he teaches people Kṛṣṇa consciousness. The Kṛṣṇa consciousness movement was started for this purpose. We do not teach one to meditate in a secluded place just so that he may show that he has become very much advanced in so-called transcendental meditation, although he engages in all sorts of foolish material activity. Rather, every member of the Kṛṣṇa consciousness movement is interested in going door-to-door to try to convince people about the teaching of *Bhagavad-gītā As It Is.*' That's from the Seventh Canto of *Śrīmad-Bhāgavatam*, Ninth Chapter, forty-fourth verse."

"Yes," said Choṭa, "Kṛṣṇa consciousness is for preaching. But what is preaching? For example, Śrīla Prabhupāda praises the Six Gosvāmīs as great preachers. The song says that 'they were very expert in scrutinizingly studying all revealed scriptures with the aim of establishing eternal religious principles for the benefit of all human beings. They're honored all over the three worlds because they are absorbed in the mood of the gopis.' And what did they do? They lived in Vṛndāvana and wrote. Also, Paṇḍitjī, I can quote back to you the same verse, 'What a great man does, others will follow.' Because unless we *practice* Kṛṣṇa consciousness what is there to follow? And Lord Caitanya stated that a devotee's behavior establishes the true purpose of religious principles.

It's because I do want to set a good example that I've been feeling like a hypocrite when I'm not really chanting or reading. I think that our whole movement needs more examples of devotees who go back to the basics. We are too much caught up in solving problems and worrying about money and public relations, at least *I* was too caught up. If you had given me time to practice my *sādhana*, I wouldn't have had to act in this extreme way to get what you should have given me gladly."

"I didn't know you were so stubborn," said Yamala. "Usually you do what I say. You've always been submissive to the wishes of the Vaiṣṇavas. This new stubborn spirit is, I think, on a lower platform. Look at you, you're as sandy as a beachcomber. Do you think Śrīla Prabhupāda would be pleased?"

Yamala sensed that he was wearing away at Choṭa's confidence but that it wasn't going to be a quick victory. Choṭa felt distraught, but at the same time he was aware of the etiquette in receiving guests.

"Why don't we just cool down," he said. "It's time to get ready for lunch *prasādam*. You both look hot and sweaty."

And so they agreed to break for lunch. In the mood of a temporary "cease-fire," Yamala and Paṇḍita went with Choṭa to bathe in the ocean. They sat uncomplainingly before a lunch of bananas and coconuts. Choṭa hoped that while eating they would speak on lighter topics, but Yamala took the occasion to speak of the latest troubles.

"The temple in the south," he said, "was destroyed by humans in a bulldozer. None of the mice devotees were hurt, but now they're spread out, mostly living with their parents. Some of them have also not been practicing as strictly as they were so we've got to get money to build again. If you were there, Choṭa, you could take collections."

"The real thing," said Choṭa, "is for the devotees to regain their spirit after the catastrophe. They have to associate with each other and support each other. Even if they stay home they can still chant, and they can meet together. The important thing is not to lose the spirit of enthusiasm. It doesn't depend on the building. If we're sincere, Kṛṣṇa will supply. Just like we've heard in Prabhupāda's life. When the devotees first went to London, they had no place. Prabhupāda told them to go on preaching, and then eventually they got a place and George Harrison helped."

"Well, then, you should be there to preach," said Yamala.

Choṭa replied, "I need to do what I'm doing, and I ask for your patience."

Yamala quickly finished his meal and began pacing back and forth while the others were still seated.

Yamala said, "Choṭa, your reputation is suffering. The mice devotees don't know where you are and what you're doing."

Yamala was pleased to see that these words struck home. Choṭa looked worried.

"Why don't you tell them nicely?" Choṭa asked. "Or let me write a letter for you to take back. But you're right, it wasn't very considerate of me. I'm sorry. Will you take back a letter?"

Paṇḍita dāsa said, "One who takes the position of spiritual leadership but does not deliver his dependents will go to hell. And here's another quote by Prabhupāda regarding preaching. It's in the *Caitanya-caritāmṛta*: 'Bhaktisiddhānta Sarasvatī says the spiritual master authorizes his devotees to preach, but those who are not advanced prefer to chant Hare Kṛṣṇa *mantra* in a solitary place. Such activities constitute a type of cheating process in the sense that they imitate the activities of such exalted devotees. Rather everyone should endeavor to preach the cult of Śrī Caitanya Mahāprabhu in all parts of the world and thus become successful in spiritual life. One who is not very expert in preaching may chant in a secluded place, avoiding bad association, but for one who is actually advanced, preaching and meeting people who are not engaged in devotional service are not disadvantages.'"

Yamala and Paṇḍita could see that they had weakened their opponent. At least he was not looking very happy.

Yamala said, "I can see that you're still sincere and that you want to do the right thing. We'll give you time to think it over. We're catching a boat back tomorrow, and I hope you'll go with us."

Yamala and Paṇḍita left to stay for the night at an animal hotel. For the rest of the afternoon, Choṭa's head was spinning. He couldn't read or chant. At night he couldn't sleep but only lay down while his mind replayed all that they had said and done. He felt violated.

The next morning before dawn, Yamala came by himself to the beach shack. He bowed down before Choṭa who immediately returned the obeisances.

"Please forgive me," said Yamala, "for acting roughly yesterday."

Choṭa was relieved to hear it, although he suspected this might be another tactic.

"I had a dream last night," said Yamala in a softer voice. "Before I took rest, I thought of what you had said about how a devotee shouldn't be a hypocrite. Then I had a nightmare that the messengers of death were after me. I woke up scared and with a strong impression that I should come to you and make a confession. But you must keep it confidential. A few times last year I was very agitated for sex, and ... I ... went ... to a prostitute. And still sometimes I practice self-abuse."

Choṭa's mind said, "I told you so," but he listened respectfully and tried to think of the best advice.

"I suppose you should get married," said Choṭa. "That's the Vedic solution. Also, if you can make your *sādhana* strong, you can fight *māyā* from any position. You know, Prabhupāda has described that the mind works in three stages: thinking, feeling, and willing. We can't avoid all thoughts of illicit sex, but we can make the deliberate effort not to let our mind progress into the stages of feeling and willing." They continued talking about the problem, and Yamala thanked him.

"Another reason I became so weak," Yamala said, "is that I've been working too hard. I think it was good for me to come here and see how you're living with so much attention to your spiritual needs. I couldn't do it myself. I see your point, but I have to do the needful for the movement. I'll die fighting on the battlefield of *saṅkīrtana* rather than become a *bābājī*. I mean, what if we all left like you did? Won't you please come back with us? We all need your help." Choṭa felt guilty and wavered.

"Give me a week more," he said. "I have a quota of reading that I want to finish."

"Okay," said Yamala. "We'll take your letter and read it to all the devotees. I admit that I've been badmouthing you to others. Please forgive me. Now I'll tell them that what you're doing is actually glorious. But I just think that your own spiritual advancement is a luxury at this stage. I'll tell the devotees you're coming back in a week."

Chapter 8

After they left, Choṭa tried to restore the sanctity to his life, but he felt that it was broken to pieces. Twenty-four hours passed, and he still couldn't force himself to open the *KṚṢṆA* book. He kept imagining Yamala telling the devotees, "Choṭa was in *māyā*, but we saved him." And he felt guilty that he had left Guyana to tend to his own spiritual needs. Instead of living in the present moment and concentrating on the words of the *mahā-mantra* and the scriptures, Choṭa's mind dragged him to other times and places: he saw Yamala walking into the beach shack, and he saw the faces of the devotees in Guyana, as in dreams. Hours passed in disturbed reveries.

Choṭa also lost his tolerance for the inconveniences of the beach: The sounds of baby mice at play annoyed him, and the fleas became unbearable. He thought about deadly snakes, and he became afraid of unfamiliar sounds.

Finally, he decided that he *must* reenter the *KṚṢṆA* book at once. He opened the book looking for a passage that would assure him that God is great and that we should hear His glories and serve Him. After a few moments, he stopped at a page in which the transcendental *surabhi* cow came to see Kṛṣṇa after the Lord had subdued the pride of Indra. Choṭa read, "The *surabhi* offered her prayers as follows:

> My dear Lord Kṛṣṇa, You are the most powerful of all mystic yogīs because You are the soul of the complete universe, and only from You has all this cosmic manifestation taken place. Therefore, although Indra tried his best to kill my descendant cows in Vṛndāvana, they remained under Your shelter, and You have protected them all so well. We do not know anyone else as the Supreme, nor do we go to any other god or demigods for protection. Therefore, You are our Indra, You are the supreme father of the whole cosmic manifestation, and You are the protector and elevator of all the cows, *brāhmaṇas,* demigods and others who are pure devotees of Your Lordship. O Supersoul of the universe, let us bathe You with our milk, for You are our

Indra. O Lord, You appear just to diminish the burden of impure activities on the earth.

Choṭa read it a second time aloud. He liked Surabhi's affection and the fact that Lord Kṛṣṇa alone was her protector. Choṭa thought that Lord Kṛṣṇa was also his protector. As He protected the descendant cows of Surabhi, so He would protect Choṭa's *sādhana*. Choṭa saw his practices of chanting and hearing as calves and cows in a field, and Kṛṣṇa was protecting them. Choṭa sighed—he had reentered the spiritual ocean. Once again, he felt that everything would come out well by the regular practice of reading.

After a single day of neglect, he had had to break through accumulated resistance. Old doubts and prejudices filled his mind again like cobwebs. But when he had persisted and read, he gradually had been allowed to enter the sacred presence. Choṭa also understood better that his attempt to read in a prayerful way and to enter a kind of dialogue with the Lord through the scriptures was really "shooting for the rhinoceros." Kṛṣṇa's *darśana* was not so easily attained. It was not wrong to read that way—it was ideal—but maybe unattainable for now. Choṭa humbly begged for the smallest crumbs of realization as he read the passage again, "We do not know anyone else as the Supreme ... Therefore, You are our Indra. You are the Supreme Father of the whole cosmic manifestation, and You are the protector ..."

Within a few days he had restored much of his former schedule, but he was convinced that Yamala dāsa's passionate association had made him unable to read and chant. He tried not to think of returning to Guyana or what would happen if he didn't go as promised.

Soon after, Choṭa had another visitor. It was Padma, the crow, who had flown from Guyana.

"Haribol, Choṭa."

"Padma! What a surprise!"

Padma looked different from all the vicious crows who fought on the beach. He was an enlightened soul—but today he looked very sad.

"Why have you come?" asked Choṭa. Padma began to speak, but tears welled from his eyes and rolled down his wan, black cheeks. He broke down sobbing. When he had calmed himself and Choṭa had given him a seat and a cup of coconut water, Padma managed to tell his tale of grief.

"My wife left me for another male crow," he said. "I never knew before what it meant to be 'broken-hearted', but now I feel an actual pain and emptiness in this region." He pointed to his chest with his right wing. "How could she have done this to me? What did I ever do to deserve this ultimate transgression?" He began crying again. "I can't eat. I cry all the time and just feel sorry for myself. But at the same time, I know it's like a lesson from life and from Kṛṣṇa. The knots of bondage built up in my heart from sex life have been severely weakened and bruised. I just want the miserable feeling to go away. So, I came to see you."

"I'm sorry to hear it," said Choṭa, "but sooner or later it had to happen. If not an embarrassment like this, then at least by the death of one of you. But your hurt feelings will gradually subside. Remember, millions of marriages break up every year, and people live through it. It's unfortunate, but it's an opportunity to reach out and increase your own relationship with Kṛṣṇa—He won't let you down."

"I gave up so many opportunities to follow the path of householder life," said Padma. "And now it's all ripped away, what little happiness I had. I'm still attached to her. It's crazy." Choṭa listened. He thought that was probably better than anything he could say.

"I'm sorry," Padma cried, "that I've strayed away from Kṛṣṇa consciousness. I think now I should move back into a temple. What do you think?"

"Could you really move into the temple?" Choṭa frowned. "You have so many bad habits. Shouldn't you go more slowly and carefully? You feel renounced now but—why don't you stay with me for a few days to chant and hear?"

Padma brightened. "That would be very nice. Thank you."

"But you have to stay busy here, or it will be *māyā*. Remember how you used to read Prabhupāda's books and memorize Sanskrit verses? Why not try that again?"

Choṭa suggested a day's outing. He knew of a "secret" waterfall up in the hills. They began by walking along the beach until they saw a stream merging into the ocean. A path alongside it led into the jungle. The palms and sand soon led into an open forest with banyan trees, breadfruit trees, and filtered shade. As they walked, they gained in elevation, gradually at first and then as the path became steeper, they climbed with more noticeable strain. The crow hopped ahead while Choṭa sometimes scampered or slowed down to a crawl. It became shadier and cooler. They began hearing more birds and less ocean. Twittering birds were close by, and occasional, louder calls came from further in the jungle. Now bigger trees towered over the medium range. Spanish moss trailed and ferns blanketed the forest floor. The two friends walked silently, sharing the refreshing sensations, the feel of water in the air, and the cool shelter of the trees.

By now the path was less trodden and it was harder climbing. They began noticing more—parrots and other brightly colored birds flying from tree to tree looking for the ripest fruits and the most fragrant flowers. Then they heard the waterfall. It was a sound like wind rustling leaves or heavy rain on a roof. The sound increased, and they quickened their pace in anticipation. The water in the stream rushed faster, bubbling around the rocks and under the bank. Finally, they broke into a clearing by a large pool and above was the fifty-foot-high falls. The whole area was brighter; the forest seemed to stand back admiring the cascades. The force of the waterfalls was broken by rocks jutting out into its path, and so although it was loud, it was not deafening. The pool was crystal clear, and the bottom pebbly with flat rocks around the edge. Choṭa and Padma began wading into the calm water. After the intense sun of the beach and the labor of climbing, it felt good swimming in the pool. After wading, they lay on the bank and Choṭa considered which fruits to eat. The sweetest ones were those lying on the ground, already tasted by the parrots. Choṭa gathered up some custard apples, bananas, guava, and mangos. They assembled a sumptuous fruit meal and offered it to Lord Kṛṣṇa with prayers.

Padma seemed to have temporarily forgotten his troubles. He turned to Choṭa and said, "You seem to be doing well here."

"I have to leave in one week," Choṭa replied.

"So soon?"

"Yamala convinced me to go back."

"Do you think it's right?"

"It's not enough time," said Choṭa, "I wanted to establish strong chanting and reading as a part of my life, so that when I go back, I can keep it up. If I go now just because he said so, it will be the same thing."

"Your ulcer may get worse," said Padma.

Choṭa laughed, "Yamala says the movement will collapse without me."

"It's true that your presence is important," said Padma. "But you can keep in touch by writing letters for now. And maybe you can invite some of the mice out here on Ekādaśīs so they can see you."

"Yamala would be afraid," said Choṭa, "that if they come out, some of them might not go back."

"Maybe you worry too much what he thinks," said Padma. "Yamala, Yamala, caw, caw."

"I'm not sure about myself yet," said Choṭa. "That's why I want to go and see Nimāi Prabhu, but talking with you also helps. I don't think I'll go back. I'm just a baby in spiritual life in terms of learning how to chant and read and pray."

Choṭa began to share some of his realizations with Padma. He told about his method of prayerful reading, and he remembered how he had been trying to converse with the Lord as a daily practice.

Choṭa said, "I also went and saw that meditating turtle that you recommended."

"Did he help?"

"Some. He said you have to be called to be a solitary. Anyway, I'm not going to be a lifetime hermit."

While the two friends made their way leisurely down the hill, Choṭa spoke yearningly of chanting and hearing the holy names.

"Chanting is so important," he said. "It cleanses the heart and enables you to stop committing the four sinful activities. But my problem is I don't *feel it*."

"Do you have to feel it?" asked Padma. "Isn't the holy name a fact whether you feel it or not?"

"Yes, but if you feel nothing at all, the *Śrīmad-Bhāgavatam* says your heart is steel framed."

That night, Choṭa and Padma read *KṚṢṆA* book together. The small shack was dark outside the glow of their candle. The towering figure of the crow barely moved, but the gray head of the mouse followed the words from line to line. Choṭa paused and looked up, "I enjoy reading Kṛṣṇa's teasing Rukmiṇī. Kṛṣṇa said that she should divorce Him because He was a vagabond unworthy of her." The mere mention of marriage turned Padma back into depressed feelings, but Choṭa hauled him back to *kṛṣṇa-kathā*.

"Let's read aloud this section where Rukmiṇī analyses each of the Lord's self-deprecating remarks and sees them as true praises of His glory."

Choṭa read:

> My dear Lord, Your statement that You do not act as an ordinary person with a particular aim in life is also perfectly correct. Even Your great devotees and servants, known as great sages and saintly persons, remain in such a state that no one can get any clue to the aim of their lives. Human society considers them crazy and cynical. Their aim of life remains a mystery to the common human being; the lowest of mankind can know neither You nor Your servant. A contaminated human being cannot even imagine the pastimes of You and Your devotees.

"Yes," Padma smiled, "it's interesting that she uses the word cynical. Nondevotees think we are cynical because we turn down the sense gratification activities that they pursue with so much passion. The other crows, for example, are always harassing *jīvas*—robbing eggs, killing babies. And they say *we're cynical!*"

Choṭa read on:

> My dear Lord, You have stated that marriage between persons equal in social standing, beauty, riches, strength, influence and renunciation can be a suitable match. But this status of life can be possible only by Your grace.

This passage hit too close to home for Padma. He began thinking again about his broken marriage, so they talked about it some more. Choṭa mostly listened.

"How could she do such a thing?" asked Padma. "I feel now like I'll never be able to meditate on Kṛṣṇa again, I'm so distracted. I suppose I should think about getting married again in the future, but my faith is completely blown. Is there any such thing as Kṛṣṇa conscious marriage in Kali-yuga or is it all pie in the sky? I tried to make her a devotee, where did I go wrong?" Padma was crying again, sniffling his tears. After a while, he blew his nose and said, "Anyway, let's hear more about Kṛṣṇa's marriage, not mine."

Choṭa read on:

> In the society of the servitors and served in Kṛṣṇa consciousness, one is not subjected to the pains and pleasures of material society, which functions according to sex attraction. Therefore, everyone, man and woman, should be an associate in Your society of servitors and served.

"I'd really like to be a servant in that society she describes," said Choṭa, "of the Lord and His servants. That's our Hare Kṛṣṇa movement. I really believe it's the best society there is, and I want to be a part of it. I haven't come out of Guyana to get away from it, you know."

"I know," said Padma, "you're trying to be an honest servant."

Padma took a turn reading:

> My Lord, You have stated that only beggars praise Your glories, and that is also perfectly correct. But who are those beggars? Those beggars are all exalted devotees, liberated personalities and those in the renounced order of life. They are all great souls and devotees who have no other business than to glorify You. Such great souls forgive even the worst offender. These so-called beggars execute their spiritual advancement in life, tolerating all tribulations in the material world. My dear husband, do not think that I have accepted you as my husband out of my inexperience; actually, I've followed all these great souls. I followed the path of these great beggars and have decided to surrender my life to Your lotus feet.

Choṭa cheered, "*Jaya* Śrī Kṛṣṇa and the transcendental beggars!"

"It sounds wonderful," said Padma. "I think the Lord may be turning me into one of those beggars. I hope so."

After two days, Padma thought that he should return to his place in Guyana. Choṭa accompanied him to the edge of the beach. Before he flew off, Padma grinned and embraced his friend.

Choṭa said, "It must be wonderful to be able to fly. And now you can do it for Kṛṣṇa."

"Yes," said Padma. "I am already thinking of how to arrange my life in that way. At least I'm one devotee who is glad that you have come out here alone to improve your *sādhana*. Your solid example has inspired me. Thank you." With a deft hop, Padma spread his wings and flew up. He was soon flapping over the ocean. His silhouette looked like a sleek jet plane, and Choṭa thought of Jaṭāyu, the king of the birds.

Chapter 9

The boat agent came to Choṭa's shack to inform him of a rare opportunity. A ship was leaving for New York, and Choṭa could go as part of a group tour.

"But the person I'm looking for," said Choṭa, "may not be in New York. He could be anywhere."

"From New York you can find out where he is, that's for sure," said the boat agent. He wanted to sign Choṭa up on the spot.

Choṭa's breast fluttered with emotion. He was happy on the beach, and yet he wanted to see Nimāi. If he stayed where he was, there would probably be another confrontation with Yamala.

"All right, I'll go," he said decisively. The agent began filling out the ticket.

"But there is one condition," said the agent. "You have to travel incognito and not reveal to the other passengers that you are a Hare Kṛṣṇa mouse."

"Why?"

"Because my boss is afraid it may hurt business. You know some people regard you all as a cult. Not *me!* I say, 'to each his own.' But the boss is afraid because this is a high-class human ship, and we mice have to be very careful. As I said, it's a tour group of twelve mice, and you'll be taking your meals together. It will only take five days, and you'll be in New York before you know it."

"All right, all right," said Choṭa. He was used to such ignorance. Although he didn't choose to go incognito, he thought it might be interesting.

Climbing aboard the freighter was easy enough, but when he joined the tour group in the cargo hold, he was expected to socialize. He introduced himself as a teacher in a boys' school and shook hands with the male and female passengers. When he entered the sleeping compartment, which he shared with two male mice, Choṭa felt that he had been plunged into hell. He considered jumping ship and returning to the beach shack. "I want to be alone!" Choṭa thought. "Why go to New York?" But he reminded himself that although his beach life was peaceful, he remained unsettled. He wanted to be alone to practice *sādhana*, but he also wanted to submit to higher authority. The idea of going to Nimāi and settling it once and for all was a comforting thought. If it took some austerity to reach Nimāi, he would have to accept it.

The first night at sea, the tour group met for an orientation meeting. There, to Choṭa's great surprise, he saw his brother, Arjuna!

The tour leader smiled, "You gentlemen know each other?"

Choṭa stammered that they were former school mates who had not met in quite a while. Like Choṭa, Arjuna was also incognito, but their eyes spoke to each other with happiness and relief.

Choṭa tried to get in the same room as Arjuna, but on the first night it wasn't possible. Choṭa was assigned to a tiny compartment along with two North Americans who had been vacationing.

"Did you go to the Merry Mouse Tavern in Tobago?" one mouse asked.

The other replied, "Yeah, I was there. I had to fight to keep the girls off."

"Yeah, man!" the first mouse replied. "I had three girls in one night. But there was a brawl, and I had to smash a guy's face in."

"Rum is real cheap," said the other. Both of them were carrying bottles of liquor in their luggage, and they placed them carefully on the floor.

Choṭa said nothing but sat on his bunk, while the two tourists—Hank and Chuck—struck up a quick friendship.

Chewing a scavenged cigarette butt, Chuck asked Choṭa, "What were you doing in Tobago?"

"I've been living down here for quite a while," said Choṭa. "In Tobago I was staying on the beach."

"Do you know the Beach Rat Lounge?"

"Naw," said Choṭa, "I don't care for that stuff."

"A teetotaler, huh?" Chuck winked at Hank.

Hank said, "Let's go forage for drinks in the human bar."

Choṭa soon turned out the light and tucked himself into bed. His roommates came back later, making noise and filling the compartment with the odor of tobacco. Finally, they fell asleep, and there was only the sound of snoring and the ship's engine reverberating through the bulkheads.

Choṭa sat up and started chanting the Hare Kṛṣṇa *mantra* in his mind. He pictured himself in a temple or on the beach under a sky filled with clean stars. But silent, mental *japa* seemed out of his reach. Even Lord Kṛṣṇa's friend, Arjuna, had said he wasn't able to think of the Lord in that way. Choṭa began making a whispering sound as quietly as possible, *Hare Kṛṣṇa, Hare Kṛṣṇa* .... His whispers proved effective. Although he felt unhappy and alone, his mind paid close attention to the *mantra*. He lost track of time. In the morning it seemed to Choṭa that he had stayed up all night in deep supplication of the holy names.

The first group meal was breakfast. They had assigned seats, and Choṭa was about six places away from Arjuna. When the waiter attempted to put bug sausages on his plate, Choṭa abruptly pushed them away. "No thanks, I'm vegetarian," he said. "I'll just have some fruit." Arjuna said the same, and a mouse at the end of the table also refused the meat.

"Well, you can give *me* meat," laughed a big muscular mouse. "They can have their rabbit food."

"Vegetarian, huh?" said the mouse beside Choṭa. "What's wrong with meat?"

"Meat is somebody's flesh," said Choṭa. "Humans kill animals just to enjoy a taste sensation. But a mouse—or a human—can actually avoid killing fellow creatures and still eat well."

"I'll second that," said the mouse at the end of the table. "We tend to forget what a piece of meat actually is. Besides the violence factor, meat isn't healthy."

"That's a lot of nonsense," said a female mouse.

"*I* know what meat is," said Choṭa's roommate Chuck, "and I don't care for your do-gooder meddling. Without meat in a mouse's diet, he becomes a wimp."

"Now, now gentlemen," said the tour guide, a fat fellow with a white fur belly. "Let's just drop the subject and enjoy our meal."

Choṭa noticed the lady mouse beside him saying a prayer of grace before she ate. The two devotees glanced at each other and nibbled at their fruit, surrounded by the odor of sausage, heavy munching, and common talk.

Choṭa and Arjuna managed to get reassigned to the same room, and the other vegetarian mouse was put in with them. As soon as Choṭa and Arjuna were left alone, they hugged each other with joy.

"O my dear Vaiṣṇava," said Arjuna. "Meeting a person like you is the perfection of one's eyesight. Touching your lotus feet is the perfection of the sense of touch. In the material world, it's very difficult to find a pure devotee of the Lord."

"I don't consider myself a Vaiṣṇava," said Choṭa, "but I'm sure glad to see you."

The two brothers spoke about where they were each going, but they were even more eager to talk about Kṛṣṇa. They had been through a night of bad association, but it had intensified their appreciation for

Kṛṣṇa and His devotees. Choṭa told Arjuna that he had stayed up all night chanting in whispers.

"I couldn't chant well," said Arjuna. "How can we hear each word when we chant? I'm real unhappy about that."

"We have to first recognize that we're not hearing the *mantra* very well," said Choṭa, "before we can try to hear better. So, if you are unhappy about bad chanting, that's not as dangerous as complacence. If we think, 'Well, I've always chanted my rounds in this way, and anyway, Prabhupāda said it's a gradual process,' then how can we improve?"

"But it *is* a gradual process, isn't it?" asked Arjuna.

"Unfortunately," said Choṭa, "it's a gradual process both ways—one can just as easily lose one's taste for Kṛṣṇa consciousness gradually. If we chant offensively, gradually we lose our desire to be a devotee, and we lose the ability and the desire to complete even sixteen rounds daily." Choṭa was carried away by enthusiastic realizations.

"I think that we are meant to control the mind," said Choṭa, "and fix it on Kṛṣṇa a lot more than we do. We're meant to hear, chant, and remember, and that's what I've been trying to do in my concentrated *sādhana.* Prabhupāda and Kṛṣṇa say it all the time: 'Our activities should be so molded that we can't help but think about Kṛṣṇa during the day.'"

"Yes," said Arjuna, "but the problem is that for many of us that mold has been broken. Just to survive we have to go to work, and we definitely get distracted from Kṛṣṇa. I think what you're doing is great, re-emphasizing the importance of remembering Kṛṣṇa always."

The two mice were standing close together gesturing, but they suddenly froze. The doorknob turned, and their roommate re-entered.

"It's a beautiful day," said the roommate. "You ought to go topside and see the ocean and the sky." It was painful to be cut off from their *kṛṣṇa-kathā*, but the two brothers sat down and made friends with their fellow mouse. He said his name was Bob and he was a language teacher. "I also write poetry," he said. The three spoke more of vegetarianism.

"They take it lightly," said Bob, "but meat is murder. Of course, for a carnivore it's hard to stop. But some ancient texts tell us that there used to be a time when even humans and animals got along amicably." Bob sat back in a chair and crossed his legs. He was a chubby, curly-headed rodent and seemed at ease in discussion.

"The solid basis of vegetarianism is nonviolence," said Choṭa. "And the basis of nonviolence is God consciousness because all creatures are sons or daughters of the Supreme Father, *therefore* we shouldn't kill."

"I don't believe in God," said Bob. "I think the idea of God as a person is something the humans have made up. Some of the humans speak of God, other cultures call it the Self or Buddha. I just think of it as Life."

"But if we don't believe in God," said Arjuna, "we're just materialists. Like Choṭa was saying, there has to be a spiritual basis for vegetarianism."

"What makes you think," said Bob, "that you have to believe in God in order to be spiritual? There were plenty of spiritual persons among the human atheists. Many of the Eastern teachers, and many poets, were certainly spiritual, but they didn't believe in God."

"What do you mean by God?" asked Choṭa.

"Some person," answered Bob, "like you said, the Father, the Supreme Being."

"Scriptures like *Vedānta* say that He's a person," said Choṭa, "but not a person like you or me. He has inconceivable potency, and everything comes from Him, including life and everything impersonal. God cannot be understood just by speculating about Him. He has to be understood from scriptures and then revealed in a devotee's heart."

"Hmmm," Bob mused, looking from one brother to the other. "Are you brothers?" he asked.

Choṭa and Arjuna replied together, "Yes." They wanted to tell him that they were devotees of Kṛṣṇa and the *Bhagavad-gītā*. But they remained incognito. Choṭa said a few more things in defense of pure theism, but if he couldn't talk about Kṛṣṇa, it would be impossible to go on. How could he explain God consciousness without finally referring to the teachings that he knew best, the authoritative *Vedas*? The question of the existence of God slipped away from their discussion. They found other things they had in agreement with Bob, and he showed them one of his favorite poems:

One instant is eternity;
Eternity is the now.
When you see through this one instant,
you see through the one who sees.

"Would you like a milk sweet?" asked Arjuna, bringing out a piece of *prasādam* he had brought from the temple.

"Mmmm! Thank you very much." The two brothers glowed with satisfaction as Bob munched on God's mercy and accepted a second one.

The three vegetarian mice continued to be a subject of conversation at the group dinner table, although everyone avoided angry disagreements. In particular, the behavior of Choṭa and Arjuna made people curious. Someone had noticed Choṭa walking alone in the passageways early in the morning saying something to himself. He was often seen reading an unusual book someone asked, "Do you belong to a secret society?"

"Sure," said Choṭa, "but if I told you it wouldn't be a secret anymore."

Someone else asked, "Why do you get up so early?"

"I was praying to God," said Arjuna, who tended to be too open for someone traveling incognito.

One day at lunchtime a lady mouse asked, "Is there some religious reason why you don't eat meat?" And so bit by bit, although they had tried to play the incognito role, the truth was uncovered: the two quiet mice, Choṭa and Arjuna, were followers of the Hare Kṛṣṇa sect. There was momentary surprise and some under-the-breath mutterings between some of the passengers, but in the end, it didn't make a great deal of difference. At least now no one bothered to ask them to go to the bar, and the females seemed less interested. But their roommate, Bob, was eager to know more.

"I should have guessed you were Kṛṣṇa devotees," he said, "when you gave me that sweet. May I ask you some questions?"

Choṭa and Arjuna no longer tried to hide. They wore *japa-mala* beads around their necks, and the *KṚṢṆA* book was displayed on a desk.

"I've been to your temple feast," said Bob. "I like it. But there's one thing I can't reconcile. I once overheard some of your people advising a student that he should quit school, leave home, and join the temple. Why do you do that?"

"It's not really our policy," said Arjuna. "Once a *brāhmaṇa* wanted to leave his home and join Lord Caitanya, but the Lord told him that he should stay home and chant Hare Kṛṣṇa and tell people about Kṛṣṇa.

"I see," said Bob. "I just have trouble accepting renunciation of the world wherever I find it. Even when I heard the Buddha left his wife, I always thought that his wife was more enlightened than he because she just went on with the regular business of life."

"But Lord Buddha was *also* enlightened for *leaving* the world," said Choṭa. "In Lord Caitanya's case, He left his wife in order to minister to the whole human—and animal—family. His wife, Viṣṇupriyā also became a glorious, renounced saint, who is worshiped by all Vaiṣṇavas."

"I see," said Bob. He didn't seem to agree with what they said, but he was interested and pleased to talk with them.

The brothers became bolder and began cooking and offering *prasādam* to a Deity picture in their room.

"Now that I know it's *prasādam*," said Bob, "I like it even more—although I don't believe in it."

"Now you know our secret," said Choṭa handing him a dish of hot *halava*. "What's yours?"

"Secret?" asked Bob. "Oh, I believe one thing on one day and something else another day. I think we're all bozos on the same bus. I believe in animal protection—I'm a charter member of Rodent's Rights. I believe in Life with all its beauty and terribleness, or I aspire to believe in it. I believe in Love. But I better not tell you some of the things I'm into," he laughed, "they're not proper for a monk to hear."

On the last night at sea, a party was held in the dining hall. Meat dishes and alcoholic drinks had been foraged from the human's restaurant—and special vegetarian plates for the three nonmeat-eaters. The mood was mellow. A world-traveling rat came and sang a folk song. Bob read some poems. Bob then asked the tour guide, "Could the two Kṛṣṇa mice sing their chant for us?" Choṭa and Arjuna launched into a *kīrtana*, and without knowing exactly what it was, most of the passengers joined in as if it were a community sing-along.

When the *kīrtana* was over, the passengers asked questions. Although the inquiries were more racy than reverent, Choṭa felt it was well worth it. "Their questions are glorious," he thought, "and to answer them properly is the proper duty of a devotee." At least for the time being the freighter-hell had become Vaikuṇṭha.

Afterwards, the devotees served sweet rice to the guests. Choṭa and Arjuna returned to their room in an ecstatic mood—and since Bob shared the room, he also shared their bliss. Choṭa and Bob exchanged addresses and promised to keep in touch.

As the ship pulled into a Manhattan pier, the mice shivered. Choṭa and Arjuna had been long-term residents of the South, and their natural coats were not thick enough for northern winter. But like everyone else, they had to clamber down the mooring rope. Many of the passengers were greeted by friends and relatives on the dock, but Choṭa and Arjuna were alone.

"Tell Mom and Dad that I'm all right," said Choṭa. "I used to think that they were demons, and I preached to you like that. So please explain to them that I'm sorry."

"Why don't you come with me?" asked Arjuna.

"Maybe later," said Choṭa. "We have different responsibilities, Kṛṣṇa wants you to fulfill our family duties, and I'm meant to serve the movement. So as two brothers we can share the duties. You're freeing me to preach, and I ..."

"Pray for me," said Arjuna. "Pray I don't fall into *māyā*."

"Hare Kṛṣṇa."

They parted on a city street. Choṭa began asking for the whereabouts of the New York Hare Kṛṣṇa temple, while Arjuna sought directions to Pennsylvania.

Chapter 10

Choṭa asked scores of mice, "Where is the humans' Hare Kṛṣṇa temple?" But they said they didn't know. Someone suggested, "Look it up in the Yellow Pages," but Choṭa didn't know how to do that. It was cold and dark, and the mice were busy in the struggle to survive.

One said, "Hey Mac, better get off the street before yuh get killed."

In a group of mice huddled around a hot laundry vent, Choṭa found an old one who had heard of Hare Kṛṣṇa. "Yeah, there was a book about it, the Swami who came to Manhattan. He came at an old age with no money. He was brave! I think his place was on the Lower East Side. Something like 26 Second Avenue." Choṭa thanked him and gave him the last of the *prasādam* he had carried from the boat.

Choṭa went underground and started downtown. He had never been in such a hellish place. Every few blocks he ran and hid as gangs of rats swarmed by. And he saw huge alligators! There was a deafening noise of trains screeching, and the ground shook as in an earthquake.

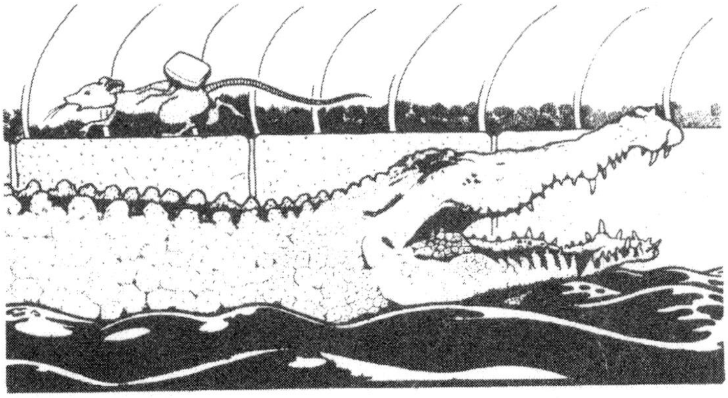

Choṭa nosed up through the opening in a sewer grate to see where he was—but that was even more frightening than below. Heavy cars and trucks rolled by shaking the earth. In between cars Choṭa caught a glimpse of buildings that were so tall you couldn't see their tops. And the humans were rushing everywhere. "Kṛṣṇa! Please protect me!" he gasped. He traveled on by instinct. He surfaced at First Street and Second Avenue, traveled in the dark shadows of the curbside, and finally reached Prabhupāda's storefront, at 26 Second Avenue. On the door was a sign:

PRABHUPĀDA MUSEUM AND CULTURAL CENTER
Kirtans MWF 8:00 P.M.

The hall was locked and dark, but Choṭa entered through the mail slot. In the aura of the streetlights, Choṭa looked around the interior of the storefront. It was a temple room with an altar at one end, an oriental rug on the floor, and pictures on the wall. One blow-up photo showed Śrīla Prabhupāda dressed in his robes with his hand in his bead bag, standing in the courtyard in front of a birdbath. Another picture frame held a printed "Notice" of rules for initiated devotees signed by A. C. Bhaktivedanta Swami on November 26, 1966. There were also paintings of Rādhā-Kṛṣṇa with a cow in Vṛndāvana and the Pañca-tattva of Lord Caitanya. A faint odor of incense pervaded the room.

Choṭa realized that he was in a sacred place. Nimāi had told him about 26 Second Avenue, the first temple where humans in the West had gathered to see and hear His Divine Grace Śrīla Prabhupāda. He had heard how they had wild *kīrtanas* here and how the hippies came and challenged Prabhupāda with their crazy theories. It was here that Prabhupāda calmly and strongly preached Kṛṣṇa consciousness and typed his own manuscripts on an old typewriter. He and his boys served Love Feasts on Sundays. They said that Śrīla Prabhupāda used to cut up an apple after *kīrtanas* and distribute it to his congregation. Once a derelict came in and gave Śrīla Prabhupāda toilet paper, and His Divine Grace accepted it as service. From here the devotees would walk to Tompkins Square Park where they all chanted. In those days they used to call Śrīla Prabhupāda "Swāmījī."

This was the place. Choṭa felt blissful just to be off the streets and away from the violence of the subways. Only a flimsy door and a glass window separated him from the outside, and yet it was quiet in here at Prabhupāda's lotus feet. Choṭa surmised that the devotees didn't live in this place, and so he had it all to himself. He circumambulated the room, bowing down before the pictures. But soon he felt fatigue, and so he curled up under a corner of the rug.

Choṭa dreamed that the lights were turned on and human devotees had entered the room from a back door. They wore fresh Vaiṣṇava *tilaka* on their foreheads. Some of them wore beards and street clothes, and one or two were dressed in yellow *dhotīs*. They brandished cymbals and a drum, and he overheard one of them say, "When the Swami comes." Then the front door opened and guests started arriving, taking their shoes off and sitting down in yoga style on the floor. Some of them also said "the Swami," and one said he wanted to "get high" from chanting and then Prabhupāda himself entered from the back door. Choṭa dreamed that he was watching him from a mouse hole in the wall where he had a vantage of the whole room. Prabhupāda was golden and looked very beautiful, and yet he was right there with all the young people, mixing in a friendly way. Swāmījī sat upon a dais, wrapped the cords of his hand cymbals around his fingers, and started the one-two-three rhythm. Soon everyone was chanting to a slow, sedate beat.

It was a *kīrtana* from the past, and Choṭa was allowed to join the audience. First the Swami sang with his steady, holy voice, and then everyone responded in tune. A few rose to their feet and moved back and forth, and then they started a stately, circular procession in the middle of the room. Swāmījī looked around the room making little nods with his head and closing his eyes when he chanted. Sometimes his eyes were closed in meditation, and then sometimes he opened his eyes to approve and conduct the worship. Choṭa felt that he had never been in such a deep, blissful *kīrtana.* Imitating the Swami, sometimes he too closed his eyes and sometimes opened them and swayed back and forth. He felt that not only his body was swaying to the music but that his soul was swaying, and the whole universe was swaying. Faces showed happiness as they swayed and danced, and it was perfect because the Swami was there conducting it all.

As the singing continued in waves of lead and response, Choṭa noticed many musical instruments, like flutes, a man in the back stroking the wires of a piano's insides, a man playing a bongo drum, someone a flute, another a guitar—and the Swami who opened his eyes approved them, and kept them all within the meditation on the holy names: Hare Kṛṣṇa, Hare Kṛṣṇa, Kṛṣṇa Kṛṣṇa, Hare Hare/ Hare Rāma, Hare Rāma, Rāma Rāma, Hare Hare.

Choṭa woke from his dream feeling sheltered and at peace. Drunken passersby made noise outside, and trucks rumbled, but it was on the other side of the door. "I'm safe," he thought, "if I can stay in the *kirtan*." And so he slipped back into a blessed sleep. When Choṭa woke again, although his body was tired, he rose up to practice his early morning *sādhana*. He thought of his schedule in the beach shack and how nice that had been. The boat trip had turned out to be exciting, but he had not found time to read Prabhupāda's books. Choṭa noticed an open book placed on a book stand in front of the altar. He went up to it, and in the light from the street he was able to make out the words. It was Śrīla *Prabhupāda-līlāmṛta, Planting the Seed.*

Choṭa began reading but then remembered that he wanted to say a prayer before beginning. Placing his head at the base of the book stand he whispered, "My dear Lord Kṛṣṇa, I want to read this book now with awareness that it is very special. Please reveal Yourself to me as I read, if that is Your desire. This is a book about Your pure devotee, Śrīla Prabhupāda. Let me read to appreciate and adore him and to give thanks to You, although I am unworthy."

The book was open to a section where Prabhupāda was lecturing in the Second Avenue storefront in 1966:

> This sound—*Hare Kṛṣṇa, Hare Kṛṣṇa, Kṛṣṇa, Kṛṣṇa, Hare Hare / Hare Rāma, Hare Rāma, Rāma Rāma, Hare Hare*—will cleanse the dust, and as soon as the dust is clear then, as you see your nice face in the mirror, similarly you can see your real constitutional position as spirit soul. In Sanskrit language it is said, *bhava-mahā-dāvāgni*. Lord Caitanya said that. Lord Caitanya's picture you have seen in the front window. He is dancing and chanting Hare Kṛṣṇa. So, it doesn't matter what a person was doing before, with sinful activities. If he is engaged in service, then he will be purified.

To focus better on the meanings, Choṭa read the same passage twice. He tried to hear Prabhupāda speaking through the book ... "Anyone can take to it. It doesn't matter where you happened to take birth. There is no bar for anyone."

"Just listen," Choṭa told himself, *"Prabhupāda is speaking to you if you'll just listen."*

> People are suffering for want of Kṛṣṇa consciousness. Therefore, each and every one of us should be engaged in the preaching work of Kṛṣṇa consciousness for the benefit of the whole world. Lord Caitanya, whose picture is in the front of our store, has very nicely preached the philosophy of Kṛṣṇa consciousness. The Lord says, "Just take my orders, all of you and become a spiritual master." Lord Caitanya gives the order that in every country you go and preach Kṛṣṇa consciousness ... We should not have any attraction for worldly activities, otherwise we can't have Kṛṣṇa. But it doesn't mean that we should be inimical to the people of the world. No, it is our duty to give them the highest instruction, that you become Kṛṣṇa conscious ...

Choṭa thought, "Here it is, the message for preaching, you can't avoid it." He read it again. Choṭa then turned directly to Prabhupāda in the book and said, "But Prabhupāda, does Yamala dāsa have to be the judge of what is preaching?" Choṭa read looking for strength and confirmation. He couldn't help but look for support of his own beliefs, but he wanted to look further, to be touched by the will of the Lord and Prabhupāda.

This time he read the story, told by Prabhupāda, of a thief who went on pilgrimage with friends. Prabhupāda said the story illustrated how habit was second nature. The man's habit was to steal at night, and so he got up and took his friends' baggage. But instead of stealing it, he just moved the baggage around. In the morning he told the travelers, "I am a thief by occupation, and because I have the habit to steal at night, I could not stop myself. But I thought, *I have come to this holy place, so I won't do it.* Therefore, I placed one man's bag in another man's place. Please excuse me."

The *Līlāmṛta* then described how as Prabhupāda was lecturing, an "old derelict" walked into the room with bathroom tissues for the toilet. Prabhupāda had laughed, but thanked his visitor, "Just see, it is a natural tendency to give some service." Choṭa thought, *It all happened here.* There was the dais where Prabhupāda sat, and there was the door to the toilet where the derelict had put the rolls of tissue. Choṭa again felt overpowered by sleep, and he lay down in front of the book stand.

Choṭa dreamed that Prabhupāda came and spoke to him from the dais. Humans were also there, but Prabhupāda turned to him.

Prabhupāda looked at him and said, "You too may chant Hare Kṛṣṇa."
Choṭa looked up and said, "But what shall I *do* Śrīla Prabhupāda?"

"That's all right," said Prabhupāda.

Choṭa woke. He accepted what Prabhupāda had said: *He wants me to chant, me and everyone.*

As the morning sunshine entered, the noises of the city increased, but Choṭa remained in the storefront. He chanted *japa*, sometimes sitting, sometimes walking back and forth. He was elated just to do it. And when he wasn't elated, he practiced and practiced.

In the early evening, human devotees entered the storefront. Choṭa ran into a hole and watched them. They turned on the lights, tidied the place, and then began a *kīrtan*. The music was sweet, with harmonium and expertly played *mṛdaṅgas.* About a dozen guests gradually arrived. Choṭa expected that there would be *prasādam,* and he was very eager for it. In fact, during the lecture given by a young man who quoted many verses from *Bhagavad-gītā*, Choṭa became distracted with hunger. By his highly developed sense of smell, Choṭa was well aware of the presence of Kṛṣṇa's mercy. When he noticed ladies carrying pots out of the storefront, Choṭa couldn't restrain himself. He ran after them into the courtyard and upstairs into Prabhupāda's old apartment. Choṭa looked quickly into the two main rooms, but he was drawn irresistibly into the kitchenette, where the ladies stood before the small stoves. "It's ecstatic to cook here," said a *mātājī*. "You can think that Śrīla Prabhupāda used this same stove. And in the other room the devotees used to sit every day for lunch, and Prabhupāda would serve them."

The ladies began to heat up some of the preparations they had cooked in their temple, and they placed them in pots on the floor before a table and picture in Prabhupāda's main room. As Choṭa watched from a concealed corner, he saw plate after plate, pot after pot assembled before the pictures of the Deities. There were whole wheat *purīs* cooked in *ghee.* In a bowl sat a big stack of fine *basmati* rice with peas and fried cashews. An open pot revealed a *sabjī* made of eggplant, tomato, chickpea, and spinach. Coming a little closer and standing on his toes, Choṭa noticed a pot of banana *halava* with golden raisins and coconut. He also saw cauliflower *pakoras* with tomato chutney. There was *burfi* made from fresh whole milk that appeared to have black walnuts added to it. And there was a big pitcher of nectar, which he guessed was made with buttermilk and orange juice with a touch of vanilla and with fresh strawberries floating on top. When all the preparations were gathered, the ladies left the room.

"This is my chance," said Choṭa, "but I must act quickly." He was about to dart ahead and eat, but then he caught hold of himself. How could he eat food that was not yet offered to Kṛṣṇa? Choṭa thought that maybe he could consider that it *was* offered since everything in Prabhupāda's apartment was holy. Or maybe they had already offered it in their temple before coming here. "I know!" said Choṭa, "I can offer it myself without waiting for the humans to offer." But before he had a chance to carry out his plans, the ladies came back, and he scampered out of sight. One *mātājī* bowed down and reverently said the prayers for offering *prasādam* to the Supreme Lord through the mercy of His pure devotee.

"Let's go downstairs," said one of the women, "we can catch the end of the *kirtan*, and then some of the *brahmacārīs* can help us bring the *prasādam* down."

Left along with the duly honored *prasādam*, the famished devotee mouse made a heartfelt prayer of thanks and dove into the pots.

Choṭa was interrupted, but he managed to come back again and again and eat when no one was looking. When he was fully satisfied, and visibly fattened, he waddled into a hole and thought of sleeping. But then he heard a devotee say, "All right, let's go back to Brooklyn." Choṭa had to make a quick decision. Should he stay on here in Prabhupāda's storefront or go with the devotees? If no one came here except for three nights a week, would he have to fast until then? The solitude would be delicious, and he had had such intimate dreams. But then he remembered his purpose. "I almost forgot!" thought Choṭa. "Living in Manhattan is so distracting! I came here to find out where Nimāi Prabhu is. I have to go to their temple and work on it." Choṭa jumped into a picnic basket of leftover *halava* and rode in the van with the devotees, who chanted Hare Kṛṣṇa all the way to Brooklyn.

Chapter 11

Choṭa didn't know what to expect when he arrived at the humans' Hare Kṛṣṇa temple. It was a huge building. He quickly found a mouse hole and entered within the walls. "I hope it's not like that city sewer," he thought. To his pleasant surprise, Choṭa found a mouse singing the Hare Kṛṣṇa *mantra* while mopping the floor in the hallway.

Choṭa ran up to him, "Haribol! I didn't know there were mice devotees here!"

"Whaddaya mean?" the mopper asked. He began wringing out his mop in a bucket.

"I—I thought," said Choṭa, "I thought I was the only one."

The mouse laughed. "You must be joking. There are devotees all over the world, aren't there?" The mopping mouse seemed young and inexperienced, so Choṭa asked in a patronizing tone, "Where did you learn about Kṛṣṇa consciousness?"

"From Śiva-jvara Prabhu."

"I don't think I know him," said Choṭa, and he began to feel uneasy. "Is he *here*?"

"His office is on the third floor in the inner level wall," said the mouse. "By the way, my name is Bhakta Joe. What's yours?"

"Choṭa dāsa." They shook paws, and Joe offered to bring Choṭa to the office of Śiva-jvara Prabhu.

On the second floor, Joe said, "This is the women's quarters." The door swung open and three female mice came out talking loudly. They carried books in a carrier with wheels just like the female devotees in Guyana. All this was uncanny to Choṭa. How could it be? By the time they reached Śiva-jvara's office, Choṭa had seen several more mouse devotees, and it seemed as if there might be many more. A plaque on the door said:

Śiva-jvara Prabhu
New York Guru of Mice

It was a well decorated office. Two mice sat on comfortable chairs. The larger mouse wore a silk saffron scarf around his neck, and Choṭa guessed that that was Śiva-jvara. There were shiny trophies on the cabinets, and Choṭa noticed a tank for dispensing drinking water. There were intercoms on the desk.

"Yes?" the mouse with the silk scarf looked up.

"Uh..." Choṭa suddenly felt awkward. "My name is Choṭa dāsa," he said. "I have just come from Guyana. I didn't know ..."

"Choṭa?" Śiva-jvara seemed to find the name familiar. "Are you *the* Choṭa?" He grinned, "Are you the original mouse-devotee Choṭa?"

This is more like it, thought Choṭa. "Yes!" he said, and he blushed.

"Please accept my humble obeisances," said Śiva-jvara. He scraped his chair back and bowed down to the floor. Choṭa also dove for the floor saying, "Please accept mine."

"Excuse me," said Choṭa, "but I just met a mouse mopping in the hall, Bhakta John or Joe, and he said that he had learned Kṛṣṇa consciousness from you. I'm very curious—could you tell me, where did you learn?"

"From the human devotee, Nimāi Prabhu," said Śiva-jvara, looking steadily at Choṭa. "From the same person you did."

Choṭa was visibly shaken. He could hardly believe it. *This will be hard to adjust to*, he told himself. But he smiled sociably as if he were only mildly interested.

"I never knew," said Choṭa. "It's quite a surprise for me. I feel like

Lord Brahmā in that story where he goes to see Lord Kṛṣṇa in Dvārakā. Do you know that one?"

"Yes, of course," said Śiva-jvara. "Lord Brahmā of this universe once went to see Lord Kṛṣṇa, but the Lord's doorman asked him, 'Which Brahmā are you?' Lord Brahmā thought that he was the only master of the universe.

Choṭa wanted to sit, and he also wanted to drink. But he couldn't presume. This Śiva-jvara seemed to be the big leader here. Choṭa's whole world had just turned upside down, and he didn't know what to expect.

"Please sit down," said Śiva-jvara. "Would you like a cup of water? Have you had *prasādam*? We're very honored to receive you here."

Choṭa sat down heavily in the chair. The pace of his recent adventure was making him over tense.

"So, what brings you to Brooklyn, Choṭa Prabhu?"

Choṭa replied, "I'm trying to find Nimāi Prabhu, and someone said that New York City was a good place for world communications."

"It is that," said Śiva-jvara. "Unfortunately, our Nimāi Prabhu is not considered an important devotee by the humans. They don't realize that he's empowered to teach mice. So we hardly ever hear anything about Nimāi. We sometimes listen in the walls to what the humans are doing, and we find out what's going on all over the worldwide movement. But they don't talk about Nimāi. Since you're here though, I could ask more mice to listen, and we'll try to get some news of him. You simply must stay at least a few days and speak to all the devotees. They would love to hear from you how you first met Nimāi Prabhu. And maybe you can go out on *saṅkīrtana* with us."

As Choṭa sat he continued to through big changes, the enormity of which only he could appreciate. *I suppose I should have considered such a possibility,* he thought to himself. *Nimāi is free to teach whoever he wants, and certainly Lord Kṛṣṇa is free. But I just didn't know. This must mean that I'm special only in Guyana.* Once he accepted it, Choṭa began to feel cheered at what he'd just learned. It was actually very good news. It was enthusing. The world was a friendlier, more liberated place than he had ever expected. The Hare Kṛṣṇa movement was spreading way beyond his power and control—and that was good! But it was also a fact—hard to accept—that Choṭa was not the only devotee in the world. He was only a tiny one among many.

Choṭa was given a private cubby hole where he could stay. Early the next morning, he joined about a hundred mice for *maṅgala-ārati*, within a large hall before an altar. They had *kīrtana* together, just like in Guyana. Śiva-jvara then addressed the assembled devotees and officially welcomed Choṭa Prabhu to New York. Śiva-jvara said, "Choṭa was the first devotee-mouse to hear Kṛṣṇa consciousness from Nimāi Prabhu. He will give a lecture tonight." The devotees cheered, and one hit the drum a few times. Śiva-jvara then said that there was a big mouse festival today at a cheese factory uptown, and all the devotee-mice were going. "We have a book table, and we will be distributing *prasādam*," Śiva-jvara said, "and I hope that Choṭa Prabhu will honor us with his presence. Will you come?" Choṭa nodded yes, although he resented being pressured in public.

The Brooklyn Mouse Temple, located within the walls of the human temple was the home of a fast-moving community. Choṭa was swept through the morning program, and before he had time to think about it, he was sitting with a dozen devotee-mice in the back of an underground cart, which roared uptown in the sewer. He was bewildered by the billboards and the tremendous numbers of rodents, bugs, and human beings everywhere. When they arrived at the cheese factory, Choṭa could hardly believe that they were expected to expose themselves in such a dangerous situation. Choṭa thought mice always avoided humans, but here they were right in their midst. He even saw a mouse corpse lying in the gutter, being picked at by crows. No one had told Choṭa what to do, but when he asked the mouse beside him, he said, "Don't let your tail get caught. Watch out for the buses."

And then they were on the street. Someone gave Choṭa a bag of *prasādam* and a cart of books. He stood alone. He cringed from the sound of a jackhammer, sirens from humans' cars, screeching brakes, and beeping horns.

"Excuse me, sir," said Choṭa as a mouse sped in his direction.

"Get lost, rat face," said the mouse, who grazed by Choṭa's shoulder.

Choṭa asked the next mouse, who replied, "I don't give to beggars."

He approached a group of mice sitting on a bench. Most of them waved him away, but one said, "I've got one minute. What's it about? Shoot."

"This is spiritual food," said Choṭa. "It's being introduced to mice for the first time in history. It's very tasty. And these books tell us revolutionary information, that we are not actually our bodies. We are souls. We can know this by chanting." Choṭa placed a book in his hands.

"Is this Hare Kṛṣṇa?" asked the mouse. "I've already got a religion. No thanks."

Choṭa bit his lip and asked for a donation.

"Donation? You *gave* me the book. Do you want me to call da cops?"

Choṭa looked imploringly at the other mice on the bench. A lady mouse said, "Why don't you do something useful?"

Choṭa wasn't used to being insulted, and he took it hard. He kept trying, but no one took anything from him. Only a few even stopped to hear him. He felt very cold and was shivering, and so he went inside a building. But it was too hot in the building so he came out again. He wanted to talk to another mouse-devotee but he had lost his way. Choked by fumes from the gigantic city buses, Choṭa staggered as big pieces of garbage blew into his face. Finally, he found the main hall where the devotees had their book table and decided to stay there. He sat beside an elderly female mouse who was distributing cups of nectar to anyone interested. The old female noticed Choṭa shivering and gave him a knit hat and scarf. She then requested Choṭa to tell her some stories of his association with Nimāi Prabhu in the old days.

Throughout the long day, Choṭa saw Śiva-jvara boldly approaching mice and other rodents. He got them to stop while he gestured and talked in an entertaining way. They listened to Śiva-jvara, gave him money, and took books and *prasādam*. Choṭa had gotten over his initial shock—the fact that other mouse-devotees did exist—and now he was appreciating the qualities of New York mice and noting the difference between them and the mouse devotees that he knew. He was impressed by Śiva-jvara's leadership and also by the respect that was offered to him by all the mouse-devotees.

At 7.00 PM., after a long day of *saṅkīrtana*, a hundred mouse-devotees gathered in the *kīrtana* hall of their temple to hear Choṭa dāsa speak. He was a bit nervous but mostly eager and confident. "Yesterday I discovered that I am not the only mouse to hear about Kṛṣṇa," he thought. "And today everyone saw that I can't distribute books on the New York City streets. But that doesn't mean that I can't tell great stories of the early days!"

"It all began one day several years ago," said Choṭa. Looking at the admiring faces in the audience, Choṭa felt proud. "I can't help it," he thought, "it's the truth. I was the first mouse-devotee to hear from Nimāi, *long* before Śiva-jvara heard."

"Nimāi Prabhu came up the stairs to his room," said Choṭa, "and I came out of a hole—and our eyes met. He said, 'What do you want, *prasādam*?' He wasn't like other humans. Something inside me made me respond and for the first time in my life. I spoke human English language. I said, 'What's *prasādam*?'"

"Then Nimāi began to instruct me," said Choṭa. As he spoke, Choṭa forgot his pride and became absorbed in pleasure. "Nimāi taught me about transmigration of the soul," said Choṭa, "at our very first meeting. He said all living beings are spirits souls, and they are all equal.

Only due to *karma* is someone in the body of a human and another in the body of a mouse. He told me about Kṛṣṇa, the Supreme Personality of Godhead. He said everything had to be learned on the basis of scriptures."

"But he wasn't teaching academic knowledge from *Vedas*. I asked questions, and we talked back and forth about the *qualities* of a devotee. The lessons came from life. For example, when we went out on traveling *saṅkīrtana* in the winter, me and the other mice lost heart, and Nimāi preached to us about surrender, and then we learned about prayer. One time, Nimāi—he was so humble—said that he thought preaching to mice was a small thing, and he was embarrassed by it. We encouraged him, and I repeated what I had already heard from him, how the Lord is pleased by any little service we do if the *bhakti* is strong. Under Nimāi's guidance, I developed the urge to preach. That's when we started going into the walls of the houses with *prasādam*."

Choṭa spoke and tasted nectar. He was aware that a talk like this could easily turn into self-praise, and he didn't want to do that. He knew that his audience was hankering for genuine talks of Nimāi and the beginnings of the Hare Kṛṣṇa movement among the mice. They wanted to hear of the ecstasies that were awaiting all sincere devotees, so Choṭa steered away from praising himself. If he spoke about himself, it was mostly as a blundering disciple.

After an hour Choṭa paused, and Śiva-jvara suggested that he could answer questions. Paws went up around the room. "Could you explain why it is that you were able to speak to Nimāi Prabhu and not to other humans?" The question was asked by a mouse with a penetrating look. In his one day in Brooklyn, Choṭa had observed that the mouse-devotees were more complicated persons than those in Guyana. In Guyana he had never been asked a question like that.

"I really don't know," said Choṭa. "If I tried to analyze it, it would be speculation. The fact that I was able to communicate at all was Kṛṣṇa's grace, and the fact that I could only communicate to one was also His grace. Is that all right?" The mouse who asked the question shrugged his shoulders. "I thought perhaps you could analyze it more," he said. Choṭa said he couldn't. "Does your ability to talk with Nimāi have something to do with your *karma* from a past life?" asked another intent devotee-mouse.

"Yes, according to the scriptures," said Choṭa, "but I don't know specifically in this case." He hoped the questions wouldn't all be like this. He looked around for someone with a less demanding expression and called upon the elderly lady who had given him a knit cap on *saṅkīrtana.*

She asked, "Could you tell us something about the movement in Guyana?"

Choṭa began telling it with zest. They had been smuggled into the country in a lunch box by Nimāi. They went on *padayātrā* along with the humans. Choṭa's own role was so central in the movement in Guyana that he couldn't help but take a boastful tone. But then in his mind he heard Yamala saying, "Yeah, Choṭa, and tell them that you walked out on it!" Choṭa stopped abruptly, as if Yamala were actually in the room. He continued describing it in a subdued way. They had recruited hundreds of congregational members, constructed temples, some of them had learned to read, and they had introduced it to a few crows. Neither Choṭa nor the audience had had enough, but Śiva-jvara drew it to a close. He said they could schedule another meeting for another night. Śiva-jvara also mentioned to the assembled devotees that Choṭa had come to New York in hopes of learning the whereabouts of Nimāi Prabhu.

"I told Choṭa that we sometimes listen in on the humans through the walls," said Śiva-jvara. "And I said that some of us could volunteer our time to do some listening on his behalf. Unfortunately, the human devotees, although they're more enlightened than other humans, have an improper estimation of Nimāi Prabhu. They don't understand how he's empowered to speak to mice, how he spoke to Choṭa and to me. So, although we usually hear news about other leaders, we hardly ever hear mention of Nimāi. That's their shortcoming. Anyway, if any of you have some time, please volunteer to do some wall-listening so that we can help our honored guest to accomplish his mission here in Brooklyn."

Chapter 12

Listening in on the humans was a simple process for the mice. There was a concealed mouse hole in the human president's office, and a mouse could sit there and snoop on anyone speaking with the temple president. Ārjavam dāsa, the temple president, saw men and women in his office almost all day long. And when he spoke on the phone, the voice of the person he spoke to was projected over a conference loudspeaker on his desk. Śiva-jvara told Choṭa that the mouse-devotees would help him by eavesdropping so that he could get news of Nimāi, but as it turned out, the mice were too busy to put in time at the listening hole. So Choṭa did it himself, several hours a day.

He heard many names and places but no mention of Nimāi. One day a devotee phoning from India mentioned the name Gauracandra Swami. Choṭa knew this was Nimāi's Gurudeva. The devotee said he was calling on behalf of Gauracandra Swami, who wanted his secretary to come and join him in Bombay. But before the message was completed, the line became full of static. The devotee in India said he would phone again, but so far, he had not, or at least not when Choṭa was listening, which was often.

As Choṭa watched Ārjavam, he developed a liking for him. Ārjavam heard everyone's complaints and tried to help, although he often couldn't do much.

Ārjavam didn't overeat or sleep too much, and Choṭa noted that when he had a few spare moments, Ārjavam would open the *Śrīmad-Bhāgavatam* and read—even if it was only two minutes—until the next interruption. He also chanted his rounds with strong feeling, and Choṭa even heard Ārjavam pray out loud a few times when he thought no one else was listening. Once he said, "O Kṛṣṇa! O Prabhupāda! What am I going to do? I can't do this service nicely. No one seems to be pleased with me, but please engage me in your service."

Among the devotees who frequently came to see Ārjavam were the treasurer, the *saṅkīrtana* leader, and the temple commander. The treasurer said that they had no money, and Ārjavam had to get more devotees out on *saṅkīrtana.* The temple commander said that no one was cooperating and threatened to quit. Then a devotee came in and told Ārjavam that he wasn't qualified.

"You're too soft," said the critic, "and if I may say so, you're too simple to be the temple president. My wife told me that you listen too much to your wife. Nowadays a temple president has to be like a top executive. My wife said that you ought to let someone else more qualified take over."

"I wouldn't mind." said Ārjavam. "But who?"

"Maybe I could do it," said the critic. Ārjavam suggested that he bring it up at the next meeting of the temple board. Ārjavam's wife came in every day at noon and gave him a cold plate of *prasādam*. She said that she wanted to move away from the city, and she told him of the women who picked on her. Several of the unmarried girls who were past thirty years old or even over forty, and who were very anxious to get husbands, regularly came by and asked Ārjavam if he had any prospects yet. Ārjavam seemed genuinely concerned for them, but he couldn't produce husbands, although Choṭa heard him phoning around asking on the ladies' behalf.

Ārjavam sometimes interviewed devotees who wanted to leave Kṛṣṇa consciousness. He listened to what they said and encouraged them to keep trying. He interviewed persons who wanted to join the temple and encouraged them, and he told them the rules. Sometimes at the request of the temple board, Ārjavam had to call a devotee in and give him or her an official reprimand. Ārjavam began these sessions with apologies and asked the devotee to please not take offense. The devotees would present him with ultimatums. For example, the cook came in and said, "I want to change my service so I can go out and preach." Ārjavam told him that it was a good idea, but that he should not do it until they found a replacement. He was often telling people to be patient and tempering extreme remarks such as the cook's saying, "I don't see the spiritual benefit anymore in feeding people."

One young devotee's parents came to see Ārjavam. They said that they liked the temple, but they wanted their son to become a doctor. When Ārjavam said he had no objection, the parents said, "He listens to you, so please talk some sense into him. He's just being rebellious, isn't he?"

By listening regularly, Choṭa noticed that Ārjavam was often misquoted and misrepresented by devotees in their arguments. But when Ārjavam himself heard the distorted reports, he often said nothing to correct it, or he did so gently.

One day while Choṭa was listening, but not very attentively, Vira dāsa, the temple commander, came in and asked permission to exterminate the mice. Choṭa jumped and began trembling. He was about to run away but forced himself to stay and hear it.

"They come at night and eat from the kitchen *bhoga*," said Vira, "sometimes even in broad daylight. The cooks are sick of it. So I'm just going to spread some strychnine all over the floor boards. I think there's a lot of them."

"It's better to keep everything clean," said Ārjavam. "Vaiṣṇavas are not supposed to kill. Remember the story of the hunter who was converted by Nārada into a devotee? He avoided killing even ants."

Choṭa was thrilled to hear a human preaching nonviolence. He poked his head out of the hole to see the effect of Ārjavam's words on Vira.

"But that's not practical," said Vira. "Once the mice get into a place, you can clean day and night, and they won't go away."

"Prabhupāda didn't like it," said Ārjavam. "I read that a devotee once asked him, 'Can we kill the rats, Śrīla Prabhupāda?' And Prabhupāda replied, 'No, you should be killed.' Prabhupāda said that the rats or mice were Māyā's agents sent to us when we don't keep clean. Can't we just have a *mahā*-clean-up? Maybe there's a nonlethal disinfectant we can use."

Ārjavam sounded determined. It was an issue that he felt strongly about. Choṭa wished he could help him with his arguments. He thought of one himself. What about the example of Śrīla Prabhupāda's father, who would put a bowl of rice out in the middle of his cloth shop at night so that the rats could eat it? Choṭa knew many quotes also, but he couldn't speak. His fate—and the fate of all the mice—lay in Ārjavam's hands.

"Nonviolent disinfectant? You mean like boric acid? The stuff doesn't work even on roaches."

"What about those Havahart mousetraps?"

"No," said Vira, "the mice are too clever for that. We've got to poison them."

"Prabhu," said Ārjavam, "you've got to think how to avoid killing. Think of the heavy *śāstric* statements against killing. We'll get karmic reactions. Even the *kṣatriyas*, who were allowed to kill animals, still had to atone for it. I recently read something in the Seventh Canto, and I think it mentions mice."

Ārjavam opened his desk volume of the *Bhāgavatam* and found a reference, which he read aloud:

> One should treat animals, such as deer, camels, monkeys, mice, snakes, birds and flies exactly like one's own sons. How little difference there actually is between children and these innocent animals.

"I believe it," said Vira. "But when the rodents get too offensive, even Śrīla Prabhupāda would allow killing them. I heard that the landlord at 26 Second Avenue wanted to exterminate, and Prabhupāda said it was all right."

Choṭa felt like screaming out, "*That's not the whole story*! *The landlord asked and Śrīla Prabhupāda said no. Then the landlord came back and insisted. But in this case, no landlord was insisting.*"

"Ārjavam Prabhu," said Vira, "the mice are even going on the altar and taking Rādhā-Kṛṣṇa's water and flowers. They crawl on the Deities. That's offensive, *sevā-aparādha,* and if we let the mice do this, this is also *sevā-aparādha* for us. You're the temple president, so you'll get the *karma*. The Deity is God, but it's up to God's devotees to protect Him against rodents and enemies."

"Yeah," said Ārjavam, and he seemed to be weakening. Devotees knew that Ārjavam was a soft touch, and if they just persisted long enough, he would change his mind.

"A temple president has to act as a *kṣatriya,* not just as a *brāhmaṇa,"* said Vira. "It's a war, isn't it? We're the devotees, and the mice are demons as far as I'm concerned. Lord Kṛṣṇa came to kill the demons and to protect the devotees. I've poisoned them before, but this time I just thought I'd mention it to you." Vira got up ready to leave.

"I guess this matter is your department," said Ārjavam. "But I think we should discuss it more at the weekly board meeting."

"That's okay with me," said Vira. But in the meantime, I'm going to wipe out the current batch of mice with some strychnine tonight. Thanks for your time, Prabhu," said Vira, as he left the room.

Ārjavam put a sign on his door, "Resting. Do Not Disturb." He sat at his desk, gently massaging his forehead. He then opened the *Śrīmad-Bhāgavatam*.

Choṭa came out of his hole and started climbing up the leg of the temple president's desk. He was acting under a strong instinctive drive. But because Choṭa was a highly developed mouse, he stopped for a moment to think. "If Nimāi could talk to other mice," Choṭa thought, "then I can talk to other humans." Choṭa reached the top of the desk and peered up at Ārjavam. He noticed that Ārjavam was a stockily built human with dark hair and kind eyes. Choṭa prayed, "Lord Kṛṣṇa, please help."

Ārjavam was surprised to see him. "Oh?" he said looking at the bewhiskered pointy face of the mouse. "Did you hear us plotting to kill you?" asked Ārjavam.

"Yes," said Choṭa, "and I wish to submit a plea on behalf of many devotees of the Lord that you please spare us."

Ārjavam was astonished to hear the mouse speak. He blinked his eyes several times and shook his head.

"It's real, Prabhu," said Choṭa. "By the grace of *guru* and Kṛṣṇa, a lame man can walk, a blind man can see the stars, and a mouse can speak."

"So be it," said Ārjavam. "But what can I do?"

"Give the order to spare us," said Choṭa. "The temple commander only gave arguments of why *demons* should be killed. But what you don't know is that there are a hundred mice living in this temple who are actually chanting Hare Kṛṣṇa and practicing *bhakti-yoga.* Living entities should never be killed, but especially devotees!"

"How is it possible?" asked Ārjavam. He and Choṭa were about three feet apart. Ārjavam seemed to accept it as another important interview. "Prabhupāda says that animals can't take to Kṛṣṇa consciousness, only humans."

"But sometimes they can," said Choṭa. "Lord Caitanya's mercy is expanding all over the world, thanks to Prabhupāda and his human followers. Even long ago Prahlāda Mahārāja told his demon friend, 'O sons of the demons, everyone including you, the *yakṣas, rākṣasas*, the unintelligent women, śūdras and cowherd men, the birds, the lower animals and the sinful living entities, can revive his original eternal spiritual life and exist forever simply by accepting the principles of *bhakti-yoga*.' That's in the Seventh Canto."

"I'm very impressed to say the least," said Ārjavam. "But from what Vira says the mice are getting very offensive. We can't just let them crawl on Rādhā-Kṛṣṇa and take the food offered to Them. It's one thing to give *prasādam* to the animals, but it's a different thing when the animals come and steal the food before it's offered or disturb the Deity worship."

"Just give me twenty-four hours and I'll stop all offensive behavior by mice," said Choṭa. "Don't let him kill us tonight. If we stop all offensive behavior, what reason is there to kill us?"

"I agree," said Ārjavam. "I don't know if anyone will believe me if I say I spoke with a mouse. But I'll try to stop it. I'll tell them to wait a day, and if the mouse offenses stop, then there's no need to kill."

"Thank you, Prabhu. Please accept my humble obeisances." Choṭa bowed and then scampered down the desk and into the mouse hole.

Choṭa rushed into Śiva-jvara's office and said, "Call all the devotees together at once! We're about to be poisoned by the humans!"

Śiva-jvara wanted to talk about it among the leaders, but Choṭa insisted that there wasn't a moment to lose. When most of the mice had hurriedly come together, Choṭa told them of the temple commander's plan to commit genocide on the mice using strychnine. The temple president of the humans, Ārjavam, did not agree to it, but it was likely to take place anyway tonight!

"I knew it," said Śiva-jvara, and he stamped his foot. "They call themselves devotees, but they're actually our deadly enemies."

A mother mouse cried out, "The children! They may have eaten it already."

"Let's get out of here," said one mouse to his friend—they had moved into the temple the day before.

"Hold on, Prabhu," said Choṭa, and he looked at the mice who were about to leave. "Let's depend on Kṛṣṇa. There is more danger outside the temple than inside."

"This report has to be investigated," said one of the analytically minded mice. "How do we know for sure that they have even got strychnine?"

"I seen it! I seen it!" said Bhakta Joe, the mopper. "I seen the temple commander putting boxes of it out on the shelf in the kitchen." Voices rose in panic while Choṭa tried to get their attention.

"I told you," said Śiva-jvara, "we should have discussed this in private."

"Just let me speak," said Choṭa. "We have a plan to avert this disaster."

Someone called out, "I know a plan! Let's send in a team of hit mice. They can defuse the strychnine."

"We have to do more than just run away or defuse the poison," said Choṭa. "I promised Ārjavam that the mice would stop stealing *bhoga* and would stop disturbing the altar of the Rādhā-Kṛṣṇa Deities. In return, he said that he would personally try to stop the poisoning."

"Why should we trust Ārjavam?" asked Śiva-jvara.

"If Kṛṣṇa consciousness is going to spread to all species," said Choṭa, "we have to cooperate with the humans."

"That's all right," said a voice from the rear of the hall, "but don't be sentimental."

Śiva-jvara finally agreed with Choṭa that mice should not go into the humans' kitchen to steal *bhoga* and should not go on the altar. He said that he would set up a twenty-four watch by guards who would make sure that no mice would break the rules.

Meanwhile, Ārjavam kept his side of the promise. He phoned the SPCA and asked about nonviolent means to restrict rodents. Their expert, "Trapper Dan," suggested putting Skippy peanut butter in a Havahart trap and then relocating the trapped mice several miles away. When Ārjavam said these mice didn't want to be relocated, Trapper Dan suggested spreading ammonia and said, "No need to kill them, they're just looking for food and shelter like anyone else."

Ārjavam confiscated the strychnine from the temple commander and placed it in his own closet. He also plastered up all the mouse holes, sprayed foam insulation into the cracks, and told Vira to wait a day to see if these nonviolent methods worked.

The next day Vira dāsa reported to Ārjavam that there had been no incidents. The flowers and water of Rādhā-Kṛṣṇa were unmolested, and no *bhoga* had been taken. Vira said that he had even set out some tasty *bhoga* just to tempt the mice and had placed flour around the area to detect the mice footprints, but none came, "It must have worked," said Vira.

When the mice saw that the strychnine had been put away and that the obnoxious but not lethal ammonia was spread around, they considered themselves saved from the disaster. Everyone praised Choṭa. The cooks made him cupcakes with carob icing and a cheesecake with the words, "Choṭa, *ki jaya*" printed in icing. Some devotees suggested that a brass plaque be made and engraved with Choṭa's name and a description of how he saved a hundred lives. Choṭa enjoyed the praise, but he said it was Kṛṣṇa who had saved them.

Choṭa felt too shy to go back to Ārjavam and thank him. He no longer possessed the intense inspiration that had driven him to speak to a human being. Choṭa thought that maybe his speaking to humans was something that was given to him on special occasions, and he shouldn't try to use it unnecessarily. And so he thought of another way to communicate with Ārjavam. When Ārjavam left his office to go to the bathroom. Choṭa slipped in and placed a piece of his cheesecake on the temple president's desk along with a note.

Dear Ārjavam Prabhu,

Deepest thanks from all of us. I will do my best to keep everyone off the altar and out of the *bhoga.*

Your servant,
Choṭa dāsa (the mouse)

After a few days, the mice became somewhat complacent about the new rules. Some of the mice guards began complaining of losing sleep. The praise of Choṭa as a great hero began to ebb away. When a devotee approached Śiva-jvara for money for Choṭa's plaque, some of the analytically-mixed devotees began to express doubts as to whether Choṭa had spoken with Ārjavam. Some doubted whether the humans had actually been planning to use strychnine. When Choṭa noticed his popularity fading, he thought it was probably a good thing. But he never doubted what had happened.

Chapter 13

About a week after the genocide threat, Śiva-jvara asked him if he would like to move to 26 Second Avenue. He could be in charge of a full-time preaching center for mice. Choṭa thought it was a wonderful idea. He was beginning to feel aimless in the Brooklyn temple, which Śiva-jvara had noticed. Since Ārjavam had blocked up the mouse hole in his room, Choṭa was no longer able to listen in for news of Nimāi. Neither could he fit in as just another member of Śiva-jvara's *saṅkīrtana team.* And he also didn't have the presence of mind, at least while in the crowded Brooklyn temple, to pursue his own chanting and reading. When Choṭa did spend one day reading *KṚṢṆA* book in his room, a mouse-devotee asked him, "Are you becoming a bookworm?"

Śiva-jvara explained exactly what he wanted at 26 Second Avenue. The storefront should be turned into a *saṅkīrtana* base for book distributors, with programs all day long for the public. Choṭa thought of Prabhupāda's original temple in terms of its sanctity—it was a *tīrtha.* It would be a good place to be alone, to recover one's own thoughts and *sādhana*. Choṭa thought, "If I can get close to Prabhupāda like I did that night, by reading and recalling his *kīrtanas*, it will be nice—and Śiva-jvara won't mind. There's no need to argue with him about our different styles." *But I wonder what Nimāi Prabhu would think of me being there?*

So Choṭa moved to the Lower East Side. He selected a corner of Śrīla Prabhupāda's writing room as his own living space. He would hold *kīrtana* on Tuesday, Thursday, and Saturday nights, which were the nights when the humans didn't use the storefront. Choṭa had heard of Prabhupāda's rooms within the Rādhā-Dāmodara temple in Vṛndāvana, India, and he hoped to arrange his quarters at Second Avenue in a similar way. He wanted to keep the atmosphere simple and quiet, with only one or two *brahmacārīs* living there. People could come and visit to see where His Divine Grace sat and where he worshiped, and they could take part in *kīrtana*. Choṭa would absorb himself all day in Śrīla Prabhupāda's books and activities, and impart some of it to the guests in the evening.

As Choṭa moved from room to room in Prabhupāda's apartment and when he went downstairs through the courtyard into the storefront, he tried to meditate on the presence of Kṛṣṇa and His pure devotee. He imagined how Prabhupāda might have seen the sunshine falling into the room with the dust motes in the air. He guessed where they might have bowed down and touched their heads to the parquet floor and where Prabhupāda walked with bare feet.

Choṭa knew Prabhupāda's daily schedule, and he followed it. He rose early and read at the time when Śrīla Prabhupāda had written his books. He honored *prasādam* at 8:00 A.M. and noon, and held *kīrtana* at 7.00 P.M. And to whomever he met, Choṭa spoke about Prabhupāda's mission and recalled the activities he had read of in the early New York days: "Prabhupāda sat over there under a picture of Kṛṣṇa playing a flute. He sat on that pillow just behind the little trunk which served as his desk. Prabhupāda wore a *khaḍi dhotī* and spoke on *Bhagavad-gītā* and *Śrīmad-Bhāgavatam* and *Caitanya-caritāmṛta* in his classes. Prabhupāda said that the chanting of Hare Kṛṣṇa cleanses the mind and brings transcendental pleasure—because Lord Kṛṣṇa is the reservoir of all pleasures. Everyone should take to Kṛṣṇa consciousness and make their lives sublime, there is no tax on chanting Hare Kṛṣṇa, and anyone can do it. Even a child can take part, even a dog can dance and chant in ecstasy."

In addition to hearing Prabhupāda speak through his books, Choṭa discovered Śrīla Prabhupāda's voice over the tape recorder. The human devotees kept a large collection of Prabhupāda's tapes, and it wasn't difficult for Choṭa to open a box, place a tape in the machine press the "play" button, and listen. After finishing a tape, he stored it back where he had found it.

Hearing Prabhupāda's voice was difficult at first. Hardly any of the mice were able to appreciate it. They preferred to hear Kṛṣṇa consciousness spoken by another mouse. "But if they tried to hear it," thought Choṭa, "they could do it." He thought of ways to encourage them. Even if one didn't have much time for sitting and listening, still one could push on a tape and hear even a simple sentence by His Divine Grace, and it was just like being there with him. Choṭa couldn't pay attention for long, either in reading or hearing, but he loved to press the tape machine and hear even a sentence like: "Now the thing is, unless I think of Kṛṣṇa, that He is an ordinary man, how could He speak to the sun-god, Vivasvān? But that sort of thinking is not bona fide. Because if you want to study *Bhagavad-gītā*, then you have to take the words from *Bhagavad-gītā*. The Lord is not like an ordinary man."

Only two devotee-mice had joined Choṭa at 26 Second Avenue. Their life was simple. They picked fruits and greens from the garbage thrown out by a grocer on First Avenue. After they washed it, it was quite fresh, and they offered it with prayers and ate their simple meals. Each mouse pursued his personal studies and greeted guests. Three nights a week they held *kīrtanas* and Choṭa lectured. Since only a few mice attended the lectures, Choṭa spoke informally, based on what he had been reading each day in the book.

One night they were joined by two Lower East Side mice who had been practicing Kṛṣṇa consciousness on and off for about a year. A small, dusty sparrow also came in and asked if he could attend. Choṭa began by recalling what he had just read in the *KṚṢṆA* book chapter, *The Rājasūya Sacrifice*. Choṭa explained that in Kṛṣṇa's pastimes He appears to be acting like a member of the human species, but Vyāsadeva and Śukadeva always point out that Kṛṣṇa is not actually a human being, but the Supreme Personality of Godhead. No one should think of Kṛṣṇa as an historical human being with limitations of a mortal creature. Neither should Kṛṣṇa's superhuman activities be thought of as imaginary stories.

"In this chapter," said Choṭa, "there is a nice example of Lord Kṛṣṇa being appreciated as the Supreme Truth. At the Rājasūya sacrifice they had to pick out a person to be worshiped first in the ceremony. Sahādeva began to speak in favor of Lord Kṛṣṇa, and this is what he said:

> No one can be equal to or greater than Kṛṣṇa in terms of time, space, riches, strength, reputation, wisdom, renunciation or any other consideration. Anything considered an opulence is fully present in Kṛṣṇa. As an individual soul is the basic principle of the growth of his material body, Kṛṣṇa is the Supersoul of this cosmic manifestation. All Vedic ritualistic ceremonies, such as the performance of sacrifices, the offering of oblations into the fire, the chanting of the Vedic hymns and the practice of mystic yoga, are meant for realizing Kṛṣṇa. Whether one follows the path of fruitive activities or the path of philosophical speculation, the ultimate destination is Kṛṣṇa; all bona fide methods of self-realization are meant for understanding Kṛṣṇa. Ladies and gentlemen, it is superfluous to speak about Kṛṣṇa, because every one of you exalted personalities knows the Supreme Brahman, Lord Kṛṣṇa, for whom there are no material differences between body and soul, between energy and the energetic, or between one part of the body and another. Since everyone is part and parcel of Kṛṣṇa, there is no qualitative difference between Kṛṣṇa and all living entities. Everything is an emanation of Kṛṣṇa's energies, material and spiritual.

Choṭa knew that if he read too much it would tax their small attention span. He tried to draw them into discussion.

"Can any of you think of other scriptural references," asked Choṭa, "where Kṛṣṇa is declared as the Supreme Personality of Godhead?"

The sparrow shook his head no. A mouse who was a bit chewy around the ears said, "Isn't the whole *Bhagavad-gītā* about that? Kṛṣṇa says He is the light of the sun and the taste in water."

One of the *brahmacārīs* said, "Among beasts I am the lion and among birds I am Garuḍa."

"Yes!" said Choṭa. "And Kṛṣṇa concludes that chapter by saying whatever you see in the whole world is just a spark of His splendor."

Two street mice entered the storefront through a recently enlarged hole in the door. They were rough-furred and unkempt. But Choṭa had come to learn that rough-edged mice could be thoughtful.

After listening for a moment, one of the newcomers asked, "Isn't Kṛṣṇa just a manifestation of God?"

"But if he's God," asked the unkempt mouse, "does that mean that all other teachings of God that don't mention Him as Lord Kṛṣṇa with a flute and so on are false?"

Choṭa sensed that the question was not asked as a challenge but as a natural doubt. He felt enlivened to answer, "The Vedic scriptures teach us," said Choṭa, "that there are many, many, manifestations of God. Some are in the group known as Viṣṇu, or God Himself, and some are manifestations of God in mortal beings, and they are called *jīvas*."

"I always thought," said the doubting mouse, "that although there may be manifestations, God is ultimately the whole universe, or The Spirit."

"Yes. God is the spirit, and He's the universe," said Choṭa, "but He's also the Supreme Person. The *Bhāgavatam* states: *vadanti tat tattva-vidaḥ*, God is present as impersonal spirit, and as God in the heart, but in His highest feature He is the Supreme Person, Kṛṣṇa."

The questioner became silent, as if he wanted to think over what Choṭa had said. Choṭa then went on to present another segment from his reading. It was a passage which showed that Kṛṣṇa was especially inclined toward His devotees. Choṭa wanted to show that it is not a contradiction for the Lord to be the Supreme Truth and yet to have a personal inclination for His devotees.

"Here's an example," said Choṭa, "of Kṛṣṇa's special affection for the devotee. It was spoken by Queen Kuntī in the Tenth Canto:

> For You, the well-wishing friend and Supreme Soul of the universe, there is never any illusion of "us" and "them." Yet even so, residing within the hearts of all, you eradicate the sufferings of those who remember You constantly.

Choṭa asked his audience for other examples of the same teaching.

No one replied, and so Choṭa quoted *Bhagavad-gītā* 9.29.

"So Kṛṣṇa is God," said Choṭa, "and yet He has special love for His devotees."

"How come He always appears as a human?" another mouse asked.

"He doesn't," said Choṭa. "He appears in all species. But in His original form of Kṛṣṇa, He's humanlike. Don't think He's just for the humans. In the spiritual world all kinds of liberated entities enjoy with Kṛṣṇa."

For about twenty minutes he had held their attention, and they continued to stay for a second *kīrtana* and cups of milk. As Choṭa sat up late talking with one of the guests (and overhearing other nice *brahmacārīs* talking to guests), he felt blissful. "This is New York preaching," he thought, "and in the same place where Prabhupāda used to preach." In his satisfaction, Choṭa had even forgotten about his dilemma which had made him leave Guyana. He forgot about his search for guidance.

One day an older mouse named Mother Candra arrived at 26 Second Avenue along with two younger female mice. Candra said that Śivajvara Prabhu had instructed them to live at the Second Avenue center and make it a base for going out to distribute books and *prasādam* to mice. Choṭa objected to their moving in.

"It's for preaching, Prabhu," said Mother Candra. "If we can do the austerity of going out to meet the people, you should be able to put up with us living in 'your' center. Do you have something against female mice?"

"No. I regard you as mothers," said Choṭa.

Mother Candra had orders from higher authority, and so there was nothing Choṭa could do about it. They moved in. Choṭa's place was within Śrīla Prabhupāda's apartment, and the new residents stayed in the storefront. Choṭa figured that it might not be so bad as long as they remained independent of his activities. But the very next day, one of the young females asked Choṭa if she could speak with him. He said that he could not see her alone, and so she brought her female friend. Choṭa set out three mats, and they sat in Prabhupāda's worship room in front of the picture of Lord Caitanya.

"How can I help you?" asked Choṭa.

The mouse named Bhaktin Janey blinked her long eyelashes and a tear emerged from the corner of her eye, "Mother Candra is very hard on us," she said.

"We're only mice," said the mouse named Durgā dāsī, "but we have to go out six days a week." Choṭa immediately felt sorry for them.

"We want to please Śiva-jvara Prabhu," said Durgā dāsī, "but we can't keep up the pace. The city is such a heavy place! Just yesterday a rat chased us for a whole block."

"And a street mouse tried to pull off my whiskers," said Bhaktin Janey, touching her face.

"It sounds very difficult," said Choṭa, glancing at them, then at the picture of Lord Caitanya, and then at the floor. "We all have austerities to face," he said, "but none of us can do what we're unable to do. I'll talk to Mother Candra on your behalf and see if we can arrange some relief for you."

"Oh, thank you, Prabhu," said Janey with a faint smile. "I knew you would understand. You seem so saintly."

When Choṭa approached Mother Candra, she was putting tiny sweet balls into individual bags for distribution on the street. Choṭa hesitated, not knowing whether to refer to Janey and Durgā as "girls" or "young mothers." He also disliked the fact that he was becoming entangled in their affairs.

"Mother Candra?" said Choṭa. "The devotees in your party came to see me, and they said that it's too hard for them to go out six days a week."

"Humph," said Mother Candra, and she sat back from her packing work. "If they don't complain about one thing, it's something else. Anyway, it's not *my* order. Śiva-jvara Prabhu said that they should go out six days, and we just have to surrender to it." Candra threw an open look at Choṭa. "Sometimes I also feel overworked," she said. "And I don't have a husband anymore to go to. But as Śiva-jvara Prabhu says, 'We're all like soldiers in the *saṅkīrtana* army. When we take on a little difficulty, we can alleviate untold sufferings of people we approach.'" Mother Candra convinced Choṭa that he should speak again to the young girls and urge them to do their prescribed duties.

"You're a better preacher than I am," said Mother Candra, "so you can change their minds."

The next day Janey and Durgā came again to see Choṭa, and Mother Candra accompanied them. He spoke the party line, but with sympathy.

"But we're not humans, you know," replied Bhaktin Janey, "we're limited."

"The real problem," said Durgā, "is not that we have to go out six days a week, but that we have to work eight hours a day."

"And the result of that" said Janey, "is that we can't chant all our rounds every day."

"No," said Choṭa calmly, "You *have* to chant your rounds every day."

"Śiva-jvara says we don't have to," said Bhaktin Janey.

"I don't think he said that," said Mother Candra. "He said ..."

Choṭa became annoyed. He decided to speak what he felt. "Lord Caitanya once praised Haridāsa Ṭhākura for being a good preacher and a well-behaved devotee. So, we can't give up either one. But if you don't have enough time to chant your rounds and you're so agitated, then what's the use? It would be better if you spent less time on *saṅkīrtana* and kept your *sādhana* healthy. We can't be fanatical. That's all I have to say about it. Is there anything else you want to ask me?"

"Why can't we sleep in beds of shredded paper?" asked Janey. "Why do we have to sleep on the floor?"

"Can't we eat cheese that's not offered to the Deity when we're out on *saṅkīrtana?"* asked Durgā.

"I can't answer these questions of policy," said Choṭa, and he stood up, indicating that the interview was over. "I'm not your authority, I'm just a tiny mouse. All glories to Prabhupāda."

Later that night, when Choṭa was alone, he had an impulse to look at himself in the mirror. It was something he hardly ever did. He crawled up on the bathroom sink and looked at his image. He preened his whiskers and turned his face to see it from a three-quarter profile. Then he combed his hair with his claw until he'd formed a part, as he'd seen some of the fancy New York mice do. He thought of Guyana and the inner turmoil that had forced him to come to New York, but somehow that all seemed distant. Images of the evening continued to linger in his mind.

Chapter 14

A few days later, six male mice arrived at the storefront. They said that Śiva-jvara had ordered them to start a daily lunch program at 26 Second Avenue.

"We already have lunch every day," said Choṭa.

"No, silly," said Rudra dāsa. "This is for the public. Śiva-jvara Prabhu wants it to be like a charity meal for any mice in the neighborhood who need it. It will be good publicity. And we'll give them *prasādam*, food offered to Kṛṣṇa.

Choṭa couldn't object, but he knew that such a program would completely change the atmosphere at Prabhupāda's storefront. He watched with misgivings as the mice moved in their pots and stores of grains. They sectioned off a part of the storefront as their sleeping space and also took over the kitchen and the worship room upstairs. Choṭa retreated to his corner in Prabhupāda's writing room and grumbled to himself. When Mother Candra complained to Choṭa about sharing space with the lunch program devotees, Choṭa reminded her that they were all meant to sacrifice for the higher cause. "Śiva-jvara wants to bestow mercy on the Lower East Side in the form of *prasādam*. And we should all try to cooperate."

For Choṭa, the storefront as a Prabhupāda-*tīrtha* had been demolished. But he tried to make the best of it. The one *good* thing he saw from the changes, was that there were now more devotees present for his evening classes.

Choṭa started giving classes on how to appreciate Śrīla Prabhupāda's tape-recorded lectures. Some of the mice thought animals weren't capable of comprehending the human voice, but Choṭa disproved that by his own example. Some admitted that hearing a tape by Prabhupāda might be possible, but like Sanskrit grammar or typewriting, it was too difficult to be any fun. So Choṭa coaxed them into it by playing a short segment of a tape and then discussing it. First, he told them some of the rudiments of good listening.

"It's like a reward for a day's devotional service, "he said. "Only those who please Lord Kṛṣṇa will be able to hear, not others. If you can't listen at first, just relax and open your inner ear. By this one act, hearing Prabhupāda, you can become completely Kṛṣṇa conscious and lose all fear. Prabhupāda says so."

"What do you mean by hearing with the inner ear?" asked Mother Candra.

"I mean don't listen like an animal," said Choṭa.

About fifteen mice were gathered around Choṭa, who stood poised by the recorder. Attendance at his classes was steadily increasing, and he was gaining a reputation as an interesting speaker.

"Okay, Prabhus, just listen," said Choṭa. "This is Śrīla Prabhupāda talking to some devotees in his room in 1969. He's telling how he himself was eager to listen to his spiritual master." Choṭa pressed down on the tape recorder with both paws, and the sound came on:

> My spiritual master said this boy hears very nicely, he does not go away. That first impression he gave to other Godbrothers. "I shall make him disciple." These very words he said. Actually I didn't follow him in the beginning. It was high philosophical speaking and I was a new boy. I could not follow him, but actually I was much glad to hear. I was simply asking,

> "When Guru Maharaja will speak?" And I will sit down and go on hearing. I'll understand or not understand. Others will disperse, I will not disperse. That was my qualification.

Choṭa pressed the pause lever and then sat back on his haunches.

"So what did Prabhupāda say?" Choṭa asked.

"I couldn't make it out," said Rudra dāsa, and others agreed with him.

"I heard some of it," said Bhaktin Janey. "He's saying that he wanted to please his spiritual master and all he could do was listen. That was his qualification."

"Very good," said Choṭa. "Anybody else?"

"He asked," said Durgā dāsī, "When Guru Mahārāja will speak? And his guru noted it."

"Yes, and how can we apply this to our own lives?" asked Choṭa.

A mouse named Willy spoke up. He was one of the regular but unkempt visitors to the storefront. "I've heard that hearing is one of the first principles in *bhakti*. Is that right?"

"Yes, it's called śravaṇam," said Choṭa. "Whereas in other yoga disciplines you have to practice difficult austerity, in *bhakti* you just have to sit like we're doing and listen. If we aren't listening to this tape, we'd be listening to something else like noises or nonsense talk. But when you listen to Prabhupāda or Kṛṣṇa and if you listen with devotion ..."

"Okay, Choṭa," said Rudra dāsa, "let's try again. Give us another segment." Choṭa pressed the "play" button:

> There was one first instance. At that time, I was not initiated. There was a circumambulation of the whole of Vṛndāvana. And so, although I was not initiated, I was one of the important members. I thought, "Let me go. What these people are doing circumambulating all over Vṛndāvana." So, I went to Mathurā, then I went to Vṛndāvana interior to a place known as Kośī. In that Kośī one of my Godbrothers declared that Prabhupāda is going tomorrow back to Mathurā. He will speak this evening. So anyone who wants to hear him they can stay, and others may prepare to go to the Śeṣasāyī temple. So although I was new, I did not want to go to the temple, I decided that I shall hear. At that time, I was so new that some of my important Godbrothers were sitting together like this, and I was sitting last. My Guru Mahārāja knew that this boy is new, everyone has gone except a few selected Godbrothers. So, he marked it that this boy is interested in hearing.

This time more mice had been able to understand it. Several of them raised their paws.

"Hearing is even more important than visiting the Śeṣasāyī temple," said one of the *brahmacārīs*.

"This shows that Prabhupāda was very special," said Rudra, "even in the beginning, and his guru noted it."

Choṭa let everyone speak what they had heard and understood. A lively conversation continued for twenty minutes. Then Choṭa played another section:

> So hearing is very important. Just like Arjuna heard from Kṛṣṇa. Because I was serious about hearing, therefore now I am serious about *kīrtanaṁ*. *Kīrtanaṁ* means speaking or preaching about the Lord. So one who is serious about hearing, he can become a future nice preacher. *Śravaṇam.* The next stage is *kīrtanaṁ* and that is development. If one has heard nicely, then he can speak nicely. *Śravaṇam kīrtanaṁ smaraṇam,* then the consciousness will automatically develop, unless your mind is concentrated and your consciousness is right you cannot rightly hear or speak.

Choṭa asked each person in the audience to say at least a few words on what they had appreciated from the tape. Then the sparrow, who hardly ever spoke when meeting, said, "I liked the sound of his voice."

"Isn't hearing Prabhupāda's tapes blissful?" asked Choṭa. "And it's easy. So let's try whenever we can to go on hearing. Don't think it's something boring or too difficult."

"It's not boring when you teach it," said Bhaktin Janey, "but by myself it's very hard."

After the listening session, all of the devotees and guests lingered for cups of milk. Some of them personally thanked Choṭa for the classes and asked, "When will you be speaking again?"

Choṭa's classes ran about half an hour over the scheduled time, and as a result, some of the mice went to sleep later than usual. Mother Candra reported this to Śiva-jvara in one of her regular visits to the Brooklyn temple. She also told Śiva-jvara that Choṭa had said that the *saṅkīrtana* females didn't have to work six days a week or eight hours a day if it was too difficult. This report disturbed Śiva-jvara, who wrote Choṭa a note:

The *saṅkīrtana* is more important than your classes. Don't

instruct Candra's party. I suggest you start attending our weekly board meetings in Brooklyn and learn our mood for preaching in the New York area. What about your search for Nimāi Prabhu?

Choṭa was sorry to read this and figured it was caused by a misunderstanding created by Mother Candra. He promised himself to see Śiva-jvara, but as the days went by, Choṭa became entangled with duties and didn't have time to leave the storefront.

The daily free lunch was well attended, although the crowd was a smelly and somewhat cynical group. It took the full-time concentrated efforts of six mice to gather food and cook and distribute it daily. In addition, it took them all afternoon to clean up the kitchen and storefront. After a few days, two of the lunch workers disappeared, and Choṭa was dragged into the work. He started cleaning up the storefront in the afternoon, since no one else did it. He hoped that Śiva-jvara would hear how he was trying to cooperate.

The female *saṅkīrtana* party proved to be a serious distraction for Choṭa. Mother Candra kept allowing the young ones to come and get counseling from Choṭa, although he asked her not to. Janey and Durgā took a special liking to Choṭa. They rendered little acts of service to him, such as putting flowers in a vase on his desk. Janey gave him a saffron scarf like the one Śiva-jvara wore. And they often asked him if there was anything they could do for him while they were out on *saṅkīrtana.* At first, Choṭa saw them as sentimental youngsters, although he appreciated their attentiveness in his classes. Then someone started a wild rumor that Choṭa had agreed to become the guru of Bhaktin Janey. When he thought about it later, Choṭa figured the rumor started with an answer he had given to Bhaktin Janey. She had asked if only human beings could be spiritual masters, and he had replied that according to the scriptures anyone who knew the science of Kṛṣṇa was qualified to be a guru. But Choṭa hadn't been thinking of it for himself. In fact, he had all along avoided the issue, even in Guyana. It was another one of those things that he wanted to consult with Nimāi Prabhu about, although he saw that Śiva-jvara was going ahead and accepting the title "guru" on his door. Choṭa figured that the rumor must have been spread by Mother Candra and that was how it reached Śiva-jvara.

Choṭa gave a class on the importance of reading Śrīla Prabhupāda's books and chanting one's daily *japa*. He began by what he thought was an important verse:

śṛṇvatāṁ sva-kathāḥ kṛṣṇaḥ
puṇya-śravaṇa-kīrtanaḥ
hṛdy antaḥ stho hy abhadrāṇi
vidhunoti suhṛt satām

Śrī Kṛṣṇa, the Personality of Godhead, who is the Paramātmā [Supersoul] in everyone's heart and the benefactor of the truthful devotee, cleanses desire for material enjoyment from the heart of the devotee who has developed the urge to hear His messages, which are in themselves virtuous when properly heard and chanted.

—*Bhāg.* 1.2.17

Choṭa spoke for a few minutes repeating what he had heard: The messages of Lord Kṛṣṇa are non-different from Him. Whenever somebody hears and chants God glories, Lord Kṛṣṇa is present in the form of the transcendental sound vibration. Therefore, it is very easy theoretically to directly associate with the Supreme Lord. It can be done at any time by anyone just by chanting and reading. The only problem is that people don't have a taste for hearing and chanting. Kṛṣṇa *wants* us to give up this material world of sin and reaction to sin—He wants to take us back to His eternal, blissful abode. But unfortunately, most of us don't want to go back to Godhead. Or even if we have a little desire, we're stuck with our sinful habits. But if we try to chant and hear, then by the grace of God, who is in everyone's heart, we get strength—Kṛṣṇa

Himself cleans our hearts, and we develop a taste for spiritual life.

"Let's talk about this problem," said Choṭa, "of not having a taste, and of neglecting *sādhana*."

The mice devotees knew that this was Choṭa's specialty, and when he spoke about it, it aroused their own desires for *sādhana*.

"What about the fact that we're only mice?" asked Willy. "How much is really expected of us?"

"By Lord Caitanya's grace," said Choṭa, "we've discovered that we can chant and hear. When Prabhupāda was here at 26 Second Avenue, he used to say that even a roach in the wall can hear the chanting. Prahlāda Mahārāja said to his friends that everyone including the demons, the birds, and all the lower animals, can revive their eternal spiritual life just by practicing *bhakti-yoga*."

"But how much?" asked Willy. "Do we have to follow a daily quota for reading and chanting?"

This was a touchy point for the devotees. Some had said the quotas that had been given to humans did not apply to animals.

"Our discussion should be how to achieve perfection," said Choṭa, "rather than trying to find a way to do as little as possible."

"My question," said Rudra, "is, what if your work is so demanding that you don't have time for the quota of chanting and reading?" Choṭa began to reply more openly, assuming that he was among friends.

"When I don't do my quota of chanting and hearing," Choṭa said, "I feel like a hypocrite. Our whole mission is to tell people to practice Kṛṣṇa consciousness. But if I don't chant and read, how can I tell others to do it? Aside from that, if I don't chant and read, I get agitated and I start resenting my work."

Choṭa's words struck chords in the others. Some of the mice began admitting their own lacking and asking help from Choṭa. Some of the mice felt defensive. A few weren't sure whether Choṭa himself knew the proper balance between *sādhana* and regular work.

"There shouldn't be conflict between work and *sādhana*," said Choṭa. "But sometimes there is. There's supposed to be a perfect system to follow, whether you perform your prescribed duties living in a temple or elsewhere. But that perfect system doesn't just work by itself. Each individual has to figure out his or her own balance. All I can say, speaking for myself, is that the more attention I give chanting and hearing, the stronger I become. And when I neglect it, I feel like I'm drowning. Also, it's not just the quantity that we do, it's the quality."

Even if some of the audience thought that Choṭa was going overboard about *sādhana*, they respected him and believed that he had a keen desire to chant and hear. But what Choṭa couldn't express to them, even as he spoke, was that his own *sādhana* was only a fond memory. He felt that he had exhausted his sincerity and that he was talking about a hearing he *used* to have. He felt empty while urging the others to be more serious about their *sādhana*. He felt the need to revive it again.

"What should you do if you get fried." asked Mother Candra, "from going too long without doing your minimum quota of *sādhana*?"

"You better get unfried," said Choṭa. "When an elephant is burning to death in a forest fire, his only relief is to get out of the fire and into the stream. We have to enter the stream of chanting and hearing. Don't remain fried, save yourself."

"Can't we think about Kṛṣṇa even while we work?" asked Bhaktin Janey. "If our work is devotional service, why can't we think of Kṛṣṇa all the time?"

"We should read and then work," said Choṭa, "and chant and then work. Or better yet, we should chant while we work and think of what we've read even while working. Yes, everything we do should be devotional service, and so we should act in a way to always remember Kṛṣṇa and not do things that make us forget Him."

The questions and answers ran on for an hour beyond the scheduled time. But no one complained. Despite his reluctance to speak as Vyāsa's perfect representative, Choṭa assumed the position. By doing so he was able to assert that everyone *could* keep a balance between work and *sādhana*. This satisfied most of the questioners in the audience. And if Choṭa's ideal balance was still beyond him, that didn't make the message less valid. After all, they had gathered not just to talk about their own shortcomings, but to hear from Śrīla Prabhupāda and Vyāsadeva.

Once again, the devotees lingered in the storefront and sat together to drink hot milk. While Choṭa was listening to more questions from two newcomers, the quiet sparrow who had attended all his classes came up beside him.

"I just wanted to let you know," the sparrow said, "that I appreciate these lectures. Especially tonight, I think I see a breakthrough for myself."

This confidential moment with the sparrow—who then hopped out of the storefront—made Choṭa feel that all his troubles were worthwhile.

When the cook quit, the entire responsibility for the daily lunch fell on Choṭa's shoulders—foraging, cooking, serving the guests, and cleaning up. The first day he did it, he was too exhausted to give a class at night.

"Tell Śiva-jvara Prabhu," Choṭa said to Mother Candra, "that I can't keep this up."

Bhaktin Janey brought Choṭa a cup of herbal tea and suggested that he take extra rest. Then she asked for more counseling.

"I think I know what my problem is," said Janey with a downcast glance. "I really need to be married, don't I?"

"Yes," Choṭa said, "that's the Vedic system."

"Mother Candra says I need to be protected," said Bhaktin Janey. She scratched her claws on floor in an idle gesture, as if she were drawing a pattern. Choṭa watched her. "What do you think?" she asked.

"Mother Candra is right," said Choṭa, "it's the Vedic system." He couldn't think of anything else to say but added, "So just be patient and Kṛṣṇa will fulfil your desires."

After that, Choṭa lost his ability to hear the holy names with attention. While fingering his beads and uttering the *mahā-mantra*, he either thought of his lunch program or Bhaktin Janey. Thoughts of Janey were especially overpowering. They weren't really thoughts, but heart tugs. Choṭa couldn't remember ever feeling like that before. She had invaded his room and his life in the form of flowers, tea, and other service. He wore the scarf that she gave him. Choṭa thought, "Unless I leave this situation, I will soon be in over my head."

"Where are you going?" asked Mother Candra as Choṭa walked out of the storefront.

"It's time to go forage," said Choṭa.

"Here's a note from Śiva-jvara Prabhu," she replied and handed him a white envelope.

Choṭa crawled warily down the gutter of First Street, towards First Avenue where the grocer left produce in the back alley. Stopping a moment beside a parked motorcycle, Choṭa opened the note:

> I heard that you are overwhelmed with the lunch program. It seems like an over-endeavor to me. I'm thinking to call back all the devotees to centralize preaching in Brooklyn. What do you think?
>
> Ys,
> Śiva-jvara dāsa
>
> PS. Nimāi Prabhu just arrived in Brooklyn.

Chapter 15

From the moment he read the note, Choṭa traveled as fast as he could to the Brooklyn temple to look for Nimāi. He couldn't find him in the men's dormitory or in the temple room. Choṭa then looked in the "boot room," a place used by the human devotees to store boots and out-of-season clothes. There he saw Nimāi Prabhu seated on the floor talking with Śiva-jvara. Choṭa's heart beat faster, and he was about to run forward, but he checked himself. He felt pain that he was not the only mouse devotee in Nimāi's life. He knew that he could go in and claim his own place beside Nimāi, but decided it would be better to go later when Nimāi was alone.

Choṭa waited patiently, and as Śiva-jvara began to leave the room Choṭa hid himself. But then Nimāi laid down on a pile of summer clothes and fell asleep. Choṭa watched and waited. He was surcharged with thoughts and feelings, which he tried to condense to the most direct and important questions. His desire to take direction from Nimāi had built to a pitch, but he didn't want to ruin his opportunity by incoherent ramblings. And so he rehearsed what he wanted to ask his beloved teacher. Choṭa felt relieved just to be near Nimāi. He watched and waited, making sure that Nimāi did not slip out of sight.

After an hour, Nimāi woke. As he sat up, Choṭa entered. When he saw that Nimāi recognized him, Choṭa jumped on Nimāi's knee and ran up to his shoulder. He nuzzled against his friend's ear, while Nimāi softly stroked his back.

"Choṭa, my little one …" said Nimāi.

"I've been waiting so long to see you," said Choṭa. "Always listening in to find out where you were."

"I also missed you very much," said Nimāi. "How have you been?"

Choṭa began to pour out what he wanted to say. He tried recalling his neat outline of questions but was unable to remain within bounds.

"I don't know where to begin" said Choṭa. "First, you should know that the movement of Kṛṣṇa consciousness among mice in Guyana has increased *wonderfully*, way beyond our dreams."

"*Jaya*! Tell me about it!" Choṭa had climbed upon a small box so that he was a little bit lower than eye level with Nimāi—just like they used to sit a year ago.

"Yes, I'll tell you everything," said Choṭa. "I've been really anxious to find you. That's why I've come to New York—to consult you about a personal dilemma I'm having. How long will you be here in New York?"

"I have to leave tomorrow to go to India," said Nimāi, "to join my spiritual master. I also want to tell *you* what I've been doing, although it's mostly that I've been in *māyā*, and my Gurudeva has been saving me."

"Leaving tomorrow?" asked Choṭa. "Then we'll have to talk right away. Or can I go with you to India?"

"Sure, you can come," said Nimāi. "We did it before." They both paused, silent.

"It was difficult when we traveled before," said Nimāi, "wasn't it? We can decide. But let's talk now, I want to hear *everything*."

"As the movement developed in Guyana," said Choṭa, "I received honor, and they regarded me as a big leader." Choṭa laughed. "Your Choṭa who couldn't even drink a *loṭa* of milk without spilling it. I accepted their honor as Kṛṣṇa's mercy, although I always made it clear that I was representing my authorities like you and your Gurudeva and Prabhupāda. But they regarded me as a special mouse, and it built up until some months ago at my birthday party, 300 mice held a big celebration for me."

"That's amazing," said Nimāi. "Are there mouse temples?"

"Yes," said Choṭa. "I'll tell you about it. But here's the thing—although they praise me, I don't actually have a taste for the most basic practices of Kṛṣṇa consciousness—chanting Hare Kṛṣṇa *mantra* and reading and hearing from Śrīla Prabhupāda's books. This is my problem. This year I've developed a strong desire to spend as much time as possible chanting and reading. I've learned how to read Prabhupāda's books. So when I read and chant, I feel like I'm entering into Kṛṣṇa's presence, which is what the śāstras say will happen if you hear submissively. Kṛṣṇa is in the holy name, and Lord Kṛṣṇa is in the *Śrīmad-Bhāgavatam*, which is as brilliant as the sun.

"But I think I want this *sādhana* so badly that my other duties seem too burdensome. It's like I have to make up for lost time, all the time in which I haven't read or chanted nicely. And my time of life is running out—even Mahārāja Parīkṣit spent his last seven days *only* in hearing *Śrīmad-Bhāgavatam*. But the mice devotees don't encourage me. They themselves don't chant or read hardly. They're more interested in active things. My cousin, Yamala, whom you remember, is now one of the responsible leaders, and he tells me that my intense interest in chanting and hearing is false renunciation. He says I'm becoming a *bābājī*, as if that's the worst thing possible. And so they make me feel guilty. But even if I try, I can't give up the conviction and craving for taking long periods of time to chant and hear. I even had to leave Guyana; I took a sabbatical. And now I'm coming to you. How can I give up my love for *sādhana*? And yet how can I give up my other duties?"

After Choṭa had gotten this much out, he was panting and trembling. He worried that maybe it all sounded completely inconsequential or incoherent.

Nimāi looked quiet and thoughtful. "Your problem is so spiritually advanced," said Nimāi, "that I don't think I can help. You've gone beyond me, Choṭa. You were always an advanced devotee, even from the beginning."

"That's not true," said Choṭa. "You were always my teacher, and so only you can solve my dilemma. I went to hear from a famous meditating turtle in Guyana, but I couldn't accept what he said as absolute. And, of course, when I hear from Yamala or from my friends, whatever they say I always think that only Nimāi can tell me, only when I hear from Nimāi can I trust it. Nimāi Prabhu, I want to do the will of Lord Kṛṣṇa and Prabhupāda. And *that's* why I've increased my practice of *sādhana*. Because the books say that we should do it as most important. And yet sometimes it seems to be *my* will. And there are many quotes by Prabhupāda that stress mostly active preaching. So is my desire for solitude a lack of surrender? But I can't surrender to someone like Yamala. I want to obey God."

"You are obeying God," said Nimāi. "I think you've become a very sanctified mouse. But you don't want to hear that, do you? It's only your humility that makes you think I can help you still. The fact is, Choṭa, all I know is what my Gurudeva has told me. But I'll try to help you. You've waited so long to ask me these questions, and I don't want to just reply with something off the top of my head. Let me think."

Nimāi glanced at his watch. "Oh! I've got to go downtown," he said. "I've got to put my passport in for a visa in order to get it out tomorrow."

At Nimāi's suggestion, Choṭa agreed to travel in a small box with Nimāi, so that they could stay together while Nimāi did his business in

Manhattan. At the Brooklyn subway station, Nimāi went to the end of the platform where it was deserted and started telling Choṭa what he had been doing.

"Basically, I fell into *māyā*," said Nimāi. "That's sort of my whole life story in Kṛṣṇa consciousness. I'm a testimony to the power of the material energy to bewilder someone even after he comes to practice spiritual life. You know, *māyā* tries to cover us and tell us to give up spiritual life. But if I ever become successful, my life will also be a testimony that the mercy of the pure devotee is the most powerful thing. Anyway, after I left you mice in Guyana, I felt I was really bereft because I was so attached to your association. I felt too unhappy to just go back to my regular place on the farm, because devotees used to tease me there. So I met a wandering devotee, Pūjā, and we went off to India together."

Nimāi stopped speaking as someone walked their way. The passerby gave him a strange look.

"And then what happened?" asked Choṭa from the box.

When they entered the subway car, Choṭa could see only little bits of light and bits of faces of many human beings and he felt the jolting and the screeching. He wondered how he had ever been able to endure long periods in a little box and travel by plane all the way to Trinidad and Guyana. Choṭa thought that maybe he had grown to be less flexible and less surrendered. He used to be able to jump into any little box just because Nimāi asked him. When the other mice in the box complained, Choṭa had always preached to them and remained cheerful. Choṭa thought that maybe his former surrender was also a kind of recklessness, or the innocence of a new devotee. At least now he didn't think he could stand being cooped up for long. Aside from the physical inconvenience, Choṭa's mind kept telling him that he had better things to do—more important devotional service to perform on behalf of Nimāi and Lord Kṛṣṇa—and *that* was why he couldn't tolerate sitting cramped in a box and just tagging along wherever Nimāi went.

When Nimāi reached his subway stop in Manhattan, he paused a few more minutes on the platform and continued his story. "We went to Vṛndāvana," he said, speaking to Choṭa in the box, "although I never really entered Vṛndāvana in proper consciousness. Still, I'll never forget it and I hope I can return someday to really render service there.

My whole problem is that I was acting independently. Anyway, I got very sick, then I went to some health cure place where I got affected by hearing Māyāvādī philosophy. I'm too embarrassed to tell you all the things I went through. You'd probably lose faith in me. But what finally happened in South India was that my Gurudeva came and rescued me, and he put me in his direct service as his servant."

"Then what happened?"

"We traveled together to many places, and I became purified hearing him preach and act as a pure devotee. Then when we were in Canada, we were together in a plane crash. We wound up in the mountains far away from any civilization, and we had to live there alone for five months. It was a very beneficial experience for me. I learned more about myself there in those few months than I did in years anywhere else. And I learned to trust my spiritual master. If you and I can stay together and I have time, I'd like to tell you more about it."

When Nimāi submitted his passport at the Indian Embassy, the office clerk noticed that he was carrying a pet in a box.

"What is that, a hamster?" he asked. "You can't take him with you to India."

"Of course not," said Nimāi. "I'm just keeping him with me for now. I'll be leaving him with a friend."

Nimāi told Choṭa he had to do some last-minute shopping, and so Choṭa banged around with him as they went into a store to buy a duffle bag. Then they went to an electrical store where Nimāi purchased an electrical transformer so that he could play his tape recorder on Indian voltage. In the electrical shop, Nimāi put down Choṭa's box while he wandered down an aisle to inspect the latest tape recorders with earphones. Nimāi had no tape with him, and so he put on the earphones and listened to a demonstration tape of the Moody Blues band. Absorbed in music, Nimāi didn't notice the store's watch dog, a big boxer, enter from the rear. The dog immediately sniffed Choṭa's presence and dove for the box. While the mouse squeaked, the dog knocked the box onto the floor with his massive paws and growled and bit into it. Choṭa felt the walls crashing in on all sides, and he felt the hard teeth and the drool from the dog's mouth. He uttered the holy names in fear of death.

The store owner grabbed the dog and pulled him back. "What have you got in that box?" he asked. Nimāi had finally noticed. He ran to the spot and picked up the crushed remains. The dog was still straining heavily at his collar and growling.

"It's a goddam mouse!" said the store man. "Get it out of here!"

Choṭa's body was not injured, but he was in a state of shock, like a human who survives the wreck of his automobile. Nimāi held him in his hands and apologized profusely. Choṭa told him that it was all right and not to worry, but he began to tremble. Only when they reached the privacy of the boot room in the temple did Choṭa relax the fearful tension of his limbs. Nimāi covered him with warm clothes and gave him a plate of *mahā-prasādam*.

"It's not your fault," said Choṭa. "I shouldn't have been born into the material world. Kṛṣṇa is giving me warning."

Nimāi stayed with him while Choṭa dozed. When he woke, they began talking again.

"The biggest surprise of my life," said Choṭa, "was when I learned that you had spoken Kṛṣṇa consciousness to another mouse, Śiva-jvara. I had thought that me, Yamala, and Arjuna were the only ones."

"I didn't exactly choose to do it," said Nimāi. "That was when I was passing through New York with Gurudeva. It almost happened once before when I was in South India. I guess it happens when Kṛṣṇa wants it to. He makes me tell one mouse about Kṛṣṇa and then that creature tells others. Śiva-jvara said that you also spoke to Ārjavam Prabhu here. I heard that you acted heroically and saved all the mice from poisoning."

Choṭa mumbled a modest reply.

"There's something I haven't told you so far," said Nimāi, "which I'd like to confess. In the months after I left you, I began gradually to deny our experience. There was no one I could talk to about it, and I knew people would think I was crazy if I told them. I've never really even discussed it thoroughly with my Gurudeva. So I began to think of it as part of my whimsical behavior for which people call me "Nimāi the Gnome" and other nice names. Although the time I spent with you was a revival of my spiritual life because I was able to serve you and assist you to become *bhaktas*, I gradually began to forget and even think that maybe it never happened. I didn't want to be seen as eccentric."

Choṭa heard him thoughtfully but returned to his central question. "Nimāi Prabhu, what should I do? Please tell me what Kṛṣṇa wants. Is it wrong to spend so much time alone chanting and reading? What should I do?"

"I don't know yet," said Nimāi. "Maybe we should go together to ask my Gurudeva. Or if you don't come with me, I could ask on your behalf."

It had become obvious that Nimāi and Choṭa could no longer travel together. It was too dangerous. And Nimāi now felt it was also an insult to Choṭa, as if he had nothing better to do than remain hidden in the dark of Nimāi's pocket. Choṭa had full faith in Nimāi. Nimāi was waiting before giving him answers to his questions, but Choṭa felt patient. Just by being near Nimāi, he felt spiritually peaceful. He felt confident that the answer would come, because he had submitted it earnestly to Kṛṣṇa's representative, and he was ready to follow whatever Nimāi said.

Chapter 16

Mice usually didn't attend the humans' *kīrtanas*, but since Nimāi was present. Choṭa went to watch. It was a Wednesday night, the best *kīrtana* of the week in the Brooklyn temple. Many devotees who lived outside gathered on this night with temple inmates, and the mood was "let's cook it up." Sweaters, shawls, and bead bags were doffed and placed to the side. Some had brought their own drums from home, and they tuned them even before the *kīrtana* began. A strong singer was selected, and the men with *karatālas* and drums moved in close to urge him on. As the Deities of Rādhā-Govinda looked on, the devotees sang the Hare Kṛṣṇa *mantra*, and some danced with abandon. Guests and the more reserved devotees backed to the walls, although sometimes a dancer would pull an onlooker into the middle. Although the large hall was not well heated, the singers and dancers began sweating. Some were dripping from the forehead, and their *kūrtas* were soaked. In the back beside Śrīla Prabhupāda's *vyāsāsana*, women danced holding hands and running back and forth in a row. When the lead singer lagged, he gave the microphone to a fresh singer, and in this way the *kīrtana* stayed strong for an hour.

As Choṭa watched he felt disappointed that he was not a human who could leap like that. The incense on the altar gradually wafted back to where Choṭa was, and he caught the scent of a feast. He was also aware of the odors of sweating bodies as well as the perfume of some of the women guests. He couldn't see the Deities clearly from a distance, but he could hear, and he felt the pounding of the dancers' feet.

When the *kīrtana* was over, it took about five minutes for devotees to calm down. Choṭa was happily surprised to see that Nimāi had been asked to give the *Bhagavad-gītā* lecture. He had never been chosen before, but since he had just come from his Canadian survival experience, which had been published in *ISKCON World Review*, the temple president had asked him to speak. Choṭa wanted to go forward and help adjust the microphone and put a cup of water within Nimāi's reach, but he contented himself to watch the others do it.

The verse for the evening was *Bhagavad-gītā*, Chapter Eight, verse six:

yaṁ yaṁ vāpi smaran bhāvaṁ
tyajaty ante kalevaram
taṁ tam evaiti kaunteya
sadā tad-bhāva-bhāvitaḥ

Nimāi read Śrīla Prabhupāda's purport, ending with the words, "Therefore, the chanting of Hare Kṛṣṇa, Hare Kṛṣṇa, Kṛṣṇa Kṛṣṇa, Hare Hare / Hare Rāma, Hare Rāma, Rāma Rāma, Hare Hare is the best process for successfully changing one's state of being at the end of one's life."

"In Prabhupāda's introduction to *Bhagavad-gītā*," said Nimāi, "he also refers to this Eighth Chapter verse. Prabhupāda says that if we are to remember Kṛṣṇa at the end of life, we have to do so by practicing during this life. But mostly our thoughts are in the material energy. So, the best way to transfer ourselves to the spiritual energy, says Prabhupāda, is to give up mundane literature and to absorb our thinking in the Vedic literature. That's why the sages have given us so many books, such as *Śrīmad-Bhāgavatam*, *Bhagavad-gītā*, and the *Caitanya-caritāmṛta*."

Choṭa's ears pricked up. He felt proud to see his preceptor lecturing before many senior devotees and guests. He knew that someone might see Nimāi's speaking manner as shy and a bit faltering, but Choṭa saw it as natural humility.

"So we have to practice chanting and hearing," said Nimāi, "while we are well, and then we can pass the test at the end of life. It is stated in the *Bhāgavatam*, *ante nārāyaṇa smṛtiḥ*, 'everything will be tested at the time of death.' Prabhupāda once stated that we have a type of disease, which is to think that we may live for a long, long time, as if for hundreds or millions of years. Or we think that we'll never die. We don't think that we're in a predicament like Mahārāja Parīkṣit, who heard that he had only seven days to live. But actually, our life is jeopardized, and so we should take the opportunity to hear *Śrīmad-Bhāgavatam* and to chant. Hearing and chanting are the main activities in *bhakti-yoga*, and they will cleanse the heart. So, no matter what else may be our prescribed duty, either within the institution or in our homes or business life, we should never minimize our attention to these basics of śravaṇaṁ *kīrtanaṁ*."

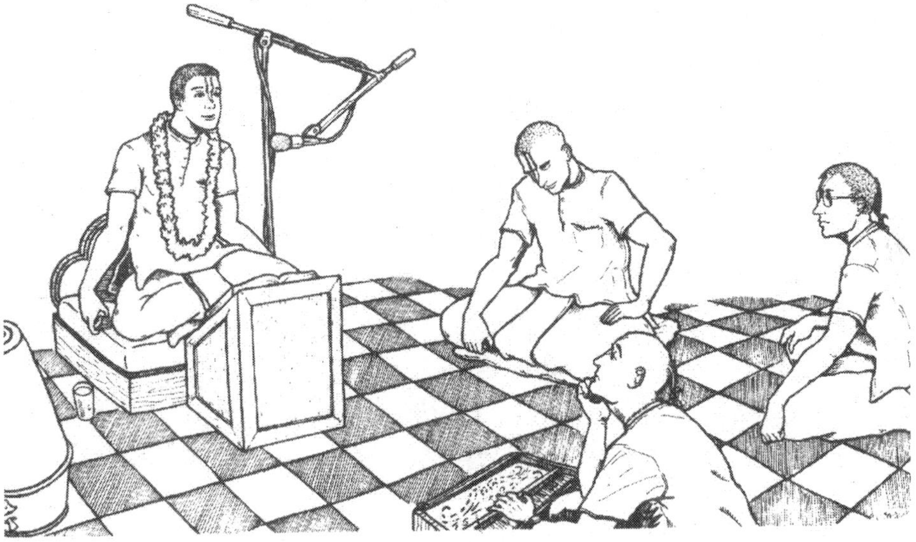

Choṭa listened with such rapt attention that he didn't notice how stiffly he held his back and that his tail was twitching. He took a deep breath and tried to relax. He had heard these themes and these exact words in other lectures, but when Nimāi spoke, it had a special influence over Choṭa. It confirmed that he had a spiritual link with Nimāi and that he could benefit very much by submissively hearing from him in *paramparā.* Choṭa was a bit distracted by a buzzing sound in the speakers, but it didn't really matter, because Nimāi was potent, and Choṭa's hearing was ideal.

"The most important quality of chanting is described by Lord Caitanya," said Nimāi, "in His *Śikṣāṣṭakam.* Although Lord Caitanya was the greatest scholar of His time, He wrote only eight verses, and they're all about chanting. Lord Caitanya says, *tṛṇād api sunīcena*: 'We should chant constantly by being in a very humble state of mind, thinking ourselves lower than the straw in the street.' And then Lord Caitanya, speaking as a conditioned soul, says that He cannot relish the taste of chanting because of committing offenses to the holy name.

Therefore, offenseless chanting is a way of life which we have to follow. We should remind ourselves every morning how to behave so that we don't commit the ten offenses to the holy name. This means to chant our *japa* nicely in the best possible time and condition and to associate with like-minded devotees who also speak and hear about Kṛṣṇa. As stated in the Śrī*mad-Bhāgavatam, satāṁ prasaṅgān mama vīrya-saṁvido / bhavanti hṛt-karṇa-rasāyanāḥ kathāḥ*: "In the association of pure devotees, discussion of the pastimes and activities of the Supreme Personality of Godhead is very pleasing and satisfying to the ear and the heart."

Choṭa knew that Nimāi was thinking of him. He thought that this lecture was for him, and he drank it in. It was what he had been waiting for. Choṭa prayed that Nimāi's lecture would go well.

When Nimāi asked if there were any questions, Ārjavam began speaking without raising his hand. "You spoke on the relationship between service and the importance of hearing and chanting. So hasn't Prabhupāda given us a balanced program of sixteen rounds of chanting and attending the *Śrīmad-Bhāgavatam* class for hearing, and that's all we need?"

Yes," said Nimāi, "but since the scriptures stress śravaṇam and *kīrtanam*, we should know that they don't happen automatically—we have to give them attention and devotion. As for the balance between śravaṇam, *kīrtanam* and other services, that may be different according to individuals. Prabhupāda has written that out of the ninefold practices of *bhakti*, one may favor particular ones—and that's according to one's individual taste. Each and every one of the processes is so powerful that if a person follows even a single one of them, he can achieve perfection. If we are unable to execute all these different types of devotional service, we must try to execute at least one of them."

Nimāi continued answering questions for about ten minutes. When some of the questioners challenged Nimāi, Choṭa became apprehensive. He felt a pinch of enmity toward the people who challenged, but he was relieved because Nimāi gave the right answers.

Nimāi ended by apologizing. He said there were many senior devotees present, and he hoped that they would forgive his presumption in giving the *Bhagavad-gītā* class and speaking. Someone then asked Nimāi if he could speak a little about his survival ordeal in Canada.

Nimāi replied that he had already used up enough time, and he was sure that everyone was eager to take the feast. This remark drew some cheers, which Nimāi took as his final cue to get down from the *vyāsāsana*.

Choṭa saw Nimāi merge into the crowd going to honor *prasādam*, and he knew he wouldn't get much chance to see him again. Choṭa ran to join the mice and tell them about Nimāi's speech, but most of them were busily engaged and didn't have time to hear him.

The next morning, immediately after *maṅgala-ārati* Nimāi caught sight of Choṭa and signaled that they should meet in the boot room. When Choṭa came before him, he saw that Nimāi was in a sober mood. They both felt sanctified from attending the *maṅgala-ārati* and from the *brāhma-muhūrta* hour.

"I'm ready now," said Nimāi, "to reply to your personal questions." Choṭa nodded and sat up straight.

"Don't be afraid to be yourself," said Nimāi. "If you are feeling strong desires to intensify your *sādhana*, don't suppress them. They're good desires. One may have to wait many, many lifetimes to have sure desires. So don't let your Godbrothers intimidate you by calling you a *bābājī* or whatever. You may not be exactly like them. I was trying to make this point last night in the lecture. We're each individuals, and even in the liberated stage everyone has a very particular *rasa* with Kṛṣṇa. So even now your "*rasa*" should be respected. But you have to start by respecting it yourself. Don't be guilty or wishy-washy. My Gurudeva once said that about me and all the trouble I got into in India—it was because I was too wishy-washy. Even my Gurudeva went through this soul-searching, and he still does, to find his own place in the Kṛṣṇa consciousness movement. When we were together in the mountains, he told me how he wanted to pray, just like you're doing. And Gurudeva wanted to start a Vaiṣṇava school, and he wants to travel and preach as a *sannyāsī*. He's doing all that now. But it's an important thing to recognize your way, and it has to come from within. Kṛṣṇa wants our *voluntary* service. I also realized that aside from what others might say or debate. I have my own relationship with my spiritual master. That way, my faith became stronger. Do you understand?"

"Yes, I understand," said Choṭa.

"But I don't think you should abandon your *prabhu-datta-deśa,"* said Nimāi. "Do you know the meaning of *prabhu-datta-deśa*?"

"Not really," said Choṭa.

"*Prabhu* means master," said Nimāi, and *deśa* means land. So *prabhu-datta-deśa* is the land, country, or place that has been given to you by the *guru*, or the Lord, where you should perform your service. You have a wonderful field in Guyana, which you have developed yourself, and now you also have followers there. I think it's your responsibility to continue there. If not forever, at least it should not be left prematurely, I don't think you should come with me to India. I believe that what I'm saying is what my Gurudeva would also say in your case. You don't have to run all over the world looking for places to hold retreats. You can chant and hear in your *prabhu-datta-deśa,* and the other devotees will learn to accept you. They may not be able to do it themselves, and they may not even approve of what you're doing. But they'll see. 'That's Choṭa's way. That's the way he's serving Kṛṣṇa.'"

"I think it is my way," said Choṭa, "but how can I be sure that it's Kṛṣṇa's way for me?"

"One way to know is by the symptom of satisfaction. When you serve Kṛṣṇa without motivation and without interruption, the symptom is *yenātmā suprasīdati*, you feel satisfied. As you feel deep satisfaction by this chanting and hearing, so you'll enter Kṛṣṇa's presence. Besides that, you are asking me and other devotees for confirmation. So you should go ahead and do it, Choṭa. Chant and hear to your heart's content, and at the same time help others. Help them to find their own best way to serve Kṛṣṇa. Just as you have particular tendencies and a kind of calling within Kṛṣṇa consciousness, so others may have a different one, and you have to help them find the strength to follow their own path. You said that you wanted to do Kṛṣṇa's will? So Kṛṣṇa says in *Bhagavad-gītā* that the best servant is he who preaches to His devotees. That should be part of your plan, because it's Kṛṣṇa's plan.

"I want to do that, Nimāi Prabhu," said Choṭa. "Recently I've been giving classes in the evening to the mice at 26 Second Avenue. But unless I get regular *sādhana*, I feel like a hypocrite. How can I preach chanting and hearing if I don't do it myself?"

"So do both," said Nimāi. "Just as Lord Caitanya said of Haridāsa, be well-behaved and preach."

Choṭa felt trust in what Nimāi was saying. He felt filled up with assurance. Because it was from Nimāi, Choṭa knew that he could follow these instructions and live by them.

"I feel satisfied now," said Choṭa. "I feel fixed. I want to go back to Guyana. I want to get involved again. But I'll take time, as much as I need—no matter what they say—to chant and hear."

Choṭa stole *prasādam* for Nimāi from the human's transfer tray. He had never done that for Nimāi before, but he dared to do it, and it made him think of Sudāmā, the poor *brāhmaṇa* friend who pleased the Lord by giving Him a small pack of chipped rice. Choṭa and Śiva-jvara scavenged enough *prasādam* for Nimāi's plane trip. Nimāi kindly accepted it, although he was distracted with last-minute travel arrangements. He had planned to get into the car with the *saṅkīrtana* devotees who were going to the airport to distribute books, but they had left without him. So he would have to go to Manhattan and take the train to the plane.

"How will we keep in touch?" asked Choṭa.

"It's difficult," said Nimāi. "We belong to different species, at least for now. But we're together in heart and instructions. If Kṛṣṇa wants, He can bring us together physically as well. Anyway, I'll probably see you in Guyana. Either my Gurudeva will go there and I'll go with him, or somehow I'll make it down to see you."

"Don't wait *too* long," Choṭa laughed. "We mice don't have a very long life-duration."

They parted at the front door of the temple. Nimāi flung his duffle bag onto his shoulder. It was heavy, and he staggered.

"You have no coat or hat," said Choṭa.

"I don't need it, I'm going to India," said Nimāi as he stumbled down the street. "Haribol, Choṭa!"

Choṭa wished that he could offer help, or that the human beings would drive Nimāi in their car, as they did with their *sannyāsīs* and temple leader. Choṭa stood watching on the temple step until Nimāi was out of sight. Then he turned back and waited for someone to open the door so that he could scoot inside.

Chapter 17

The day Nimāi left New York, Choṭa tried to leave by boat to Guyana. But the next departure was not for a week, and so Choṭa decided to use his time by going alone to chant and read. As he said good-bye to Śiva-jvara, he told him that Nimāi had encouraged him to take as much time as needed for chanting and hearing.

Choṭa went to an empty mouse hole in a garage on Long Island, which a friend had provided. There he planned a daily schedule for reading *KṚṢṆA* book and chanting *japa*. He no longer saw solitude as a frantic escape, but as a regular addition to his life. Neither did he expect that in two or three days he had to make a dramatic breakthrough in spiritual advancement. Solitude was a normal routine, like eating *prasādam* and breathing. It was a necessary replenishment for his hungry spirit. And so he took to it in a workmanlike, patient way, following the schedule of activities from morning until night.

Because of Nimāi's assurances, Choṭa felt more secure, not only about his solitude, but also in his relationship with Lord Kṛṣṇa. He still had to break through his mental inattentiveness, his tendency for sleepiness, and so many other bad habits, but beneath it all, he felt a simple peace and cheerfulness. There was no doubt about it—reading and chanting alone brought his attention into sharper focus. He *noticed* better what Śrīla Prabhupāda was saying in his books, and he was able to *hear* the Lord's names.

One day while reading, something caught Choṭa's attention in a special way. It was in the *KṚṢṆA* book narration of Lord Kṛṣṇa's visit to the poor *brāhmaṇa*, Śrutadeva. Lord Kṛṣṇa had expanded Himself into two forms in order to visit two very sincere devotees who lived in Mithilā. Thus, the Lord simultaneously went to the home of King Bahulāśva and a *brāhmaṇa* named Śrutadeva. The Lord also brought with Him many exalted sages who were all pure devotees. Śrutadeva was himself a pure devotee, described as "very learned" with no other desire than to be fully situated in Kṛṣṇa consciousness." Śrutadeva never took great pains to earn anything for his livelihood: "He was satisfied with whatever he could achieve without much endeavor, and somehow or other he lived in that way." While King Bahulāśva received Lord Kṛṣṇa and the sages in a very opulent and devotional style, Śrutadeva, because of his lack of money, was only able to offer the Lord and the sages simple accommodations, mattresses, wooden planks, straw carpets, and so on. But he welcomed them to the best of his ability. Śrutadeva's wife cooked rice and *dāl*, and Lord Kṛṣṇa's followers were very pleased to accept it, because it was offered with devotion. After his exalted guests were satisfied and sitting back comfortably, the *brāhmaṇa* Śrutadeva began massaging the lotus feet of Lord Kṛṣṇa and offering prayers.

As soon as Choṭa began to read the prayers of Śrutadeva, he became more alert:

> My dear Lord [said Śrutadeva], we can appreciate that not only today have You given me Your audience, but You are associating with all living entities as Paramātmā since the beginning of creation.

In his summary study comment, Śrīla Prabhupāda declared that "the statement by the *brāhmaṇa* is very instructive." Śrutadeva was praising the Lord for His entering into the material world as Lord Viṣṇu and sitting in a very friendly attitude in the heart of the conditioned soul. This means that every living entity from the very beginning has the Lord with him, and only due to mistaken consciousness does he fail to understand it. "When his consciousness, however, is changed into Kṛṣṇa consciousness, he can immediately understand how Kṛṣṇa is trying to assist the conditioned souls to get out of the material entanglement."

Although every word in the *KṚṢṆA* book is relevant and absolute, these words were particularly what Choṭa wanted to hear. He did not want to study the books looking for a reward, and yet he had a yearning in his heart—he wanted to know that Kṛṣṇa was his friend. So Śrutadeva confirmed it. And as Choṭa took it, *the Lord will be known by a devotee who goes alone to read the scriptures and who takes the time to be with Him*. Kṛṣṇa wanted this intimate union, and that was why He had to come into the heart of the *jīva*. As stated in the *Upaniṣads*, the Lord and the individual soul are like two birds in a tree, and the Lord is simply waiting for the *jīva* bird to turn to Him. Śrutadeva continued to pray:

> Thus, from the beginning of the conditioned soul's entering into the material world, You are his constant companion. When, therefore, the conditioned soul comes into contact with the pure devotee and takes to devotional service, beginning from the process of hearing Your transcendental pastimes, glorifying Your transcendental activities, worshiping Your eternal form in the temple, offering prayers to You and engaging in discussion to understand Your transcendental position, he gradually becomes freed from the contamination of material existence. His heart becomes cleansed of all material dust, and thus You gradually become visible in the heart of the devotee. Although You are constantly with the conditioned soul, only when he becomes purified by devotional service do You become revealed to him. For one who engages in Your devotional service and purifies his heart by constant chanting of Your holy name, You are easily understood as his eternal constant companion.

Choṭa took this all in a personal way, just like the encouragement Nimāi had given him. There was no doubt that Kṛṣṇa wanted us to be with Him but that He only reveals Himself to those who are purified, "by constant chanting of Your holy name" and by "hearing Your transcendental pastimes." This was the way to clean the heart and to know that Kṛṣṇa is with us, full of bliss, and that He is our protector. Kṛṣṇa would never be revealed, however, to the non-devotee, or to one who didn't take the time to be with Kṛṣṇa. Such a person only sees Kṛṣṇa as

Death, who comes to take away his misspent life.

"Yes," thought Choṭa, direct union with Kṛṣṇa is not only allowable, but Kṛṣṇa wants it. He wants us to turn to Him. And I want to do it."

Reading in an exalted mood, Choṭa soon came to the end of Śrutadeva's prayers. He then read Lord Kṛṣṇa's affectionate reciprocation with Śrutadeva. Prabhupāda wrote, "When He heard Śrutadeva's prayers of pure devotion, He was very much pleased and immediately caught his hands and addressed him." Choṭa very much liked the description of the Lord taking Śrutadeva's hands within His own hands. It was also mentioned that the Lord was smiling as He spoke. Choṭa envisioned the scene, and it seems that Kṛṣṇa was saying to Śrutadeva, "You know the truth about Me, and I also know about you. So now I will tell you something special."

> Dear Śrutadeva, all these great sages and saintly person have been very kind to you by personally coming here to see you. You should consider this opportunity to be a great fortune for you. They are so kind that they are traveling with Me, and wherever they go they immediately make the whole atmosphere as pure as transcendence simply by the touch of their feet. People are accustomed to go to the temples of God. They also visit holy places of pilgrimage, and by prolonged association with such activities for many days, by touch and by worship, they gradually become purified. But the influence of great sages and saintly persons is so great that by seeing them one immediately becomes completely purified.

Choṭa sensed that Lord Kṛṣṇa had changed the subject, both of Śrutadeva's prayers and also the mood of Choṭa's own reading. The Lord was saying something different than Śrutadeva. And although Śrīla Prabhupāda didn't say so directly, it appeared that maybe Lord Kṛṣṇa was restraining Śrutadeva's mood. Choṭa became a little surprised by Lord Kṛṣṇa's words, and he realized that the Lord is not a completely predictable person, but He is independent in whatever He speaks. So as Choṭa had listened submissively to Śrutadeva, he now listened to Lord Kṛṣṇa:

> My dear Śrutadeva, if a *brāhmaṇa* remaining self-satisfied, practices austerities, studies the Vedas and engages in My devotional service, as is the duty of a *brāhmaṇa*—or in other words, if a *brāhmaṇa* becomes a Vaiṣṇava—how wonderful is his greatness! My feature of four-handed Nārāyaṇa is not so pleasing or dear to me as is a *brāhmaṇa* Vaiṣṇava.

As Choṭa understood it, Lord Kṛṣṇa was saying, "Śrutadeva, you have praised Me, but what about these great devotees who are with me? Your attention has been exclusively for Me and not for these sages. Do not neglect them. Just consider their greatness." Since Choṭa had identified so personally with Śrutadeva's mood, he began to rethink whether something was wrong with that mood. Choṭa thought, "Have I neglected the sages? But what sages do I know? Does he mean the sages in *KṚṢṆA* book or all devotees, big or small? How should I honor them?"

> My dear Śrutadeva, you may therefore accept all these great saintly persons, *brāhmaṇas* and sages as my bona fide representatives. By worshiping them faithfully, you will be worshiping Me more diligently. I consider worship of My devotee to be better than direct worship of Me. If someone attempts to worship Me directly without worshiping My devotees, I do not accept such worship, even though it may be presented with great opulence.

Choṭa realized that he himself was supposed to be a sage, or a representative of Kṛṣṇa. Kṛṣṇa was saying, "Don't just stay in seclusion and worship Me, but be like the sages who are with Me, and travel to give Kṛṣṇa consciousness to others." That was why the Lord was diverting Śrutadeva's attention from Himself to the sages. One would praise the devotees and realize their greatness, which is that they go everywhere, to purify places and deliver others. They're not interested only in going alone for their own deliverance. Choṭa recalled that Nimāi Prabhu had also said this—the will of Kṛṣṇa is fulfilled by preaching. And now Lord Kṛṣṇa was also saying it as He held the hand of His pure devotee, Śrutadeva, and told him, "something special."

The message began to come through in whatever Choṭa read in the *KṚṢṆA* book. It made him more desirous to read and also increased his desire to share it. He began to think of all the preaching that he could do in Guyana when he went back. He remembered how his evening classes had been well received at 26 Second Avenue, and he resolved to speak like that every day to the devotees wherever he was. Choṭa also prayed to Kṛṣṇa that his periods of solitude would give him strength to do it. No one was going to rob him of his right to be alone with Kṛṣṇa, but he should share what he had learned with others.

When the week of solitude was finished. Choṭa reported to the boat bound for Guyana. It was another freighter. This time, however, he boarded as an ordinary mouse and not as part of a tour group. He didn't have to go incognito.

Appendixes

Glossary

ācārya – a spiritual master who teaches by example.

Ajāmila – devotee who fell down from spiritual life but was saved from hell at the time of death by chanting the holy name of the Lord, Nārāyaṇa.

anarthas – unwanted or unclean things in the heart.

ārati – a ceremony for worshiping the Lord with offerings of incense, ghee lamps, flowers, fans, incense, and other paraphernalia.

Arjuna – one of the five Pāṇḍava brothers; great devotee of Kṛṣṇa to whom He spoke the *Bhagavad-gītā*.

āśrama – the four spiritual orders of life: celibate student (*brahmācārya*), householder (*gṛhastha*), retired life (*vānaprastha*), and renounced life (*sannyāsa*); a dwelling place for spiritual shelter.

bābājī – one who retires from society to practice solitary prayer and meditation.

Bhagavad-gītā – literally, "Song of God", a discourse between Lord Kṛṣṇa and His devotee Arjuna in which Kṛṣṇa explains devotional service to the Supreme Lord as the ultimate goal of life.

Bhagavān – "He who possesses all opulences"; The Supreme Lord, who is the reservoir of all beauty, strength, fame, wealth, knowledge and renunciation.

bhajana – devotional song glorifying the Lord.

bhajanānandī – a devotee who performs his devotional activities in seclusion not attempting to preach.

bhakta – a devotee of Lord Kṛṣṇa.

bhakti – devotional service to Lord Kṛṣṇa.

Bhaktisiddhānta Sarasvatī Ṭhākura – spiritual master of A. C. Bhaktivedanta Swami Prabhupāda.

bhakti-yoga – linking with the Supreme Lord through devotional service.

Bharata Mahārāja – king who renounced his kingdom and became very advanced in spiritual life but became attached to a deer and thus had to take two more births before achieving liberation.

bhoga – foodstuffs not yet offered to Lord Kṛṣṇa.

Brahmā, Lord – the first created living being and secondary creator of the material universe.

brahmacārī – male celibate student; member of the first spiritual order of Vedic society

brahmacāriṇī – a female celibate student.

brahmacarya – celibate student life; the first order of Vedic spiritual life.

Brahman – The Absolute Truth; especially the impersonal aspect of the Absolute.

brāhmaṇa – one who is wise in the *Vedas* and can guide society in the spiritual teachings. According to the four occupational divisions or social orders of Vedic society, the *brāhmaṇa* is a member of the most intelligent class of men, the priestly order.

brahminical – "priestly"

cādar – long cloth wrapped on the body similar to a shawl.

Caitanya-caritāmṛta, Śrī – Kṛṣṇadāsa Kavirāja's biography of the life and philosophy of Lord Caitanya Mahāprabhu.

Caitanya Mahāprabhu, Lord – the incarnation of Lord Kṛṣṇa who appeared in West Bengal, India, in the 15th century to teach love of God by chanting His holy names, the Hare Kṛṣṇa *mantra*.

capātī – griddle-baked flat bread usually made of whole wheat flour and water.

cāturmāsya – the four months of the Indian rainy reason (from mid-July to mid-October), during which special vows for purification are recommended.

cāturśloka – the four verses of Śrīmad-Bhāgavatam (2.9.33–36) spoken by Lord Kṛṣṇa to Brahmā, which summarize the entire philosophy of Śrīmad-Bhāgavatam.

dāl – soup made from dried beans such as mung or *urad*.

dāsya – the devotional process of rendering service to the Lord; relationship with the Lord in the mood of servitorship.

Deity – an authorized form of the Lord made according to regulations in bona fide scripture in order to accept our worship.

dhāma – place of residence usually referring to a temple or the Lord's abode.

dhotī – a simple lower garment worn by men in Vedic culture.

Ekādaśī – a special fast day for increased remembrance of Lord Kṛṣṇa on the eleventh day of both the waxing and waning moon.

gāmchā – men's lower garment (usually similar in size to a towel) worn for bathing or in hot weather.

Ganges – holy river in India.

Garuḍa – the great eagle who is the eternal carrier of Lord Viṣṇu.

Gauḍīya *sampradāya* – the chain of spiritual masters coming from Lord Śrī Caitanya Mahāprabhu.

Gaura-Nitāi – (Deities of) Lord Caitanya and Lord Nityānanda, incarnations of Kṛṣṇa and His principal associate who taught love of God through chanting the Hare Kṛṣṇa mantra.

gopīs – Kṛṣṇa's cowherd girlfriends, His most confidential servitors.

goṣṭhyānandī – a devotee who preaches love of God as his primary devotional service.

Gosvāmīs, Six – the chief followers of Lord Caitanya Mahāprabhu.

Govardhana Hill – sacred hill in Vṛndāvana, India, where Lord Kṛṣṇa performed many pastimes.

Govinda – a name for Kṛṣṇa - "He who gives pleasure to the land, the cows and the senses."

gṛhastha – regulated householder life; the second order of Vedic spiritual life.

guru – spiritual master.

gurukula – school of Vedic learning for young boys and girls.

halava – food preparation made from grain (usually farina) roasted in butter, often with fruit or nuts added.

Haribol – literally, "Chant the holy name of Hari." Used as a greeting or exclamation among devotees.

Haridāsa Ṭhākura – great devotee of Lord Caitanya known as "Nāmācārya" or chief instructor of chanting the Lord's holy names: Hare Kṛṣṇa, Hare Kṛṣṇa, Kṛṣṇa Kṛṣṇa, Hare Hare / Hare Rāma, Hare Rāma, Rāma Rāma, Hare Hare.

harināma – congregational chanting of the holy names of the Lord.

Hiraṇyakaśipu – demon who conquered the universe and tried to kill his son, the great devotee Prahlāda. He was killed by the half-man, half-lion incarnation of God, Lord Nṛsiṁhadeva.

Hitopadeśa – one of the Vedic scriptures.

iṣ*ṭa-goṣṭhī* – discussions among Vaiṣṇavas about spiritual topics and the instructions of the spiritual master.

japa – chanting of the Hare Kṛṣṇa mantra individually on 108 beads.

jagad-guru – spiritual master qualified to instruct everyone in the universe.

Jagannātha Purī – holy city in India where Lord Caitanya performed many of His pastimes; location of major temple of Deity of Kṛṣṇa known as Lord Jagannātha.

Janārdana – a name of Kṛṣṇa, the original abode of all living beings.

jīva – living entity (the soul).

Kali-yuga – the Age of Kali. The present age characterized by the predominance of quarrel and hypocrisy; it is the last in the cycle of four ages and began five thousand years ago.

karatāla – hand cymbals used to accompany devotional singing.

karma – fruitive action for which there is always a reaction, good or bad.

Keśī – a demon who attacked the inhabitants of Vṛndāvana in the form of a wild horse, and was killed by Lord Kṛṣṇa.

khādī – homespun cotton cloth.

kīrtana – congregational chanting of the holy names of God.

Kṛṣṇa – the original name of the Supreme Lord (literally means "the all-attractive one").

Kṛṣṇadāsa Kavirāja – great devotee who wrote biography of Lord Caitanya Mahāprabhu entitled *Caitanya-caritāmṛta.*

kṛṣṇa-kathā – literally, "topics of Kṛṣṇa".

Kṛṣṇaloka – supreme abode of Lord Kṛṣṇa in the spiritual sky.

kṣatriya – a member of the administrative or protective class of men, the second order of Vedic society.

kūrta – upper garment worn by men in Vedic culture.

kuśa grass – auspicious grass used in Vedic rituals.

kuṭīra – place where one performs his spiritual practices in solitude

Kurus – the sons of Dhṛtarāṣṭra

laulyam – greediness to attain pure love of God.

līlā – pastimes of the Lord.

mādhurya (*līlā*) – relationship (or pastimes) with the Lord in the mood of conjugal love; the highest relationship of Kṛṣṇa, and His consorts, the *gopīs.*

Madhvācārya – thirteenth century Vaiṣṇava spiritual master who preached the theistic philosophy of pure "Dualism".

mahā-bhāgavata – a great devotee of the Lord.

Mahābhārata – history of greater India compiled by the literary incarnation of Kṛṣṇa, Vyāsadeva, which includes the *Bhagavad-gītā.*

mahā-mantra – "the great chant for deliverance": Hare Kṛṣṇa, Hare Kṛṣṇa, Kṛṣṇa Kṛṣṇa, Hare Hare / Hare Rāma, Hare Rāma, Rāma Rāma, Hare Hare.

mahājana – the Lord's authorized devotee, who by his teachings and behavior, established the path of religion.

mahātmā – literally, "great soul," one who is spiritually advanced.

mandir – temple.

maṅgala-ārati – the first auspicious worship service of the day, held around 4:30 A.M. in most temples.

mantra – a pure sound vibration that can deliver the mind from illusion.

māyā – (*mā*-not; *yā*-this) illusion; the external energy of Kṛṣṇa which allows the living entity to forget his original position as a loving servitor of the Lord, due to his own desires to enjoy separately from God.

Māyāpura - region where Lord Caitanya was born.

Māyāvādī – impersonalist or voidist adhering to the philosophy that ultimately God is formless and without personality.

mūrti – form of God or His pure devotee worshipped in the temple or at home.

nāmācārya – Nāmācārya Śrī Haridāsa Ṭhākura; literally, "teacher of the holy name."

Nārada Muni – pure devotee of Kṛṣṇa who travels throughout the universes in his spiritual body glorifying the Lord.

Nārāyaṇa – the Supreme Lord, who is the source and goal of all living beings.

Naimiṣāraṇya – sacred forest in north-central India.

Narottama dāsa Ṭhākura – Vaiṣṇava spiritual master in the disciplic succession from Lord Caitanya.

Nectar of Devotion – Śrīla Prabhupāda's scholarly and devotional translation of the Vaiṣṇava scripture, *Bhakti-rasāmṛta-sindhu*, written by Rūpa Gosvāmī.

Nṛsiṁhadeva – the half-man, half-lion incarnation of Kṛṣṇa who killed the demon Hiraṇyakaśipu.

padayātrā – a walking festival to distribute Kṛṣṇa consciousness.

Pañca-tattva – Lord Caitanya and His four principal associates, three of whom are His expansions (and thus also God) and one who is His pure devotee.

Pāṇḍavas – the five sons of King Pāṇḍu: Yudhiṣṭhira, Bhīma, Arjuna, Nakula and Sahadeva.

paṇḍita – a scholar.

Paramātmā – the Supersoul or the form of the Lord who resides in the heart of all living entities.

paramparā – a chain of spiritual masters in disciplic succession.

parikrama – walking tour of holy places of pilgrimage.

prabhu – literally, "master".

Prabhupāda, A. C. Bhaktivedanta Swami – Founder-Ācārya of the International Society for Krishna Consciousness.

Prahlāda – great devotee of Lord Kṛṣṇa rescued from his demoniac father by the half-man, half-lion incarnation of God, Nṛsiṁhadeva.

prākṛta-sahajiyā – pseudo-devotee who takes spiritual life cheaply and pretends to be on the highest platform of love of God.

prasādam – literally, "the Lord's mercy"; food or other items which have been sanctified by being offered to the Lord.

prema – pure love of God.

Pṛthu Mahārāja – an empowered incarnation of Lord Kṛṣṇa who demonstrated how to be an ideal king.

pūjā – authorized worship.

pūjārī – priest who serves and worships the Deity.

purī – bread deep-fried in ghee.

Rādhā-Kṛṣṇa – Lord Kṛṣṇa and His eternal consort, Rādhārāṇī.

Rādhārāṇī – the eternal consort of Lord Kṛṣṇa.

rākṣasī – she-demon.

Rāmānuja – an eleventh century Vaiṣṇava spiritual master who preached the theistic philosophy of qualified monism.

Rāmāyaṇa – history of Lord Rāmacandra, an incarnation of Kṛṣṇa, which was written by Vālmīki Muni.

rasa – one of five relationships between the Lord and His devotees:

neutrality, servitorship, friendship, parental affection and conjugal love.

rāsa dance – confidential pastime of the Lord and His topmost servants, the *gopīs*.

Ṛṣabhadeva – an incarnation of Kṛṣṇa as a devotee and king who gave important spiritual instructions to his sons and then renounced his kingdom for a life of severe austerity.

śabda pramāṇa – method of acquiring knowledge by hearing from authorized Vedic teachers.

sabjī – a spiced vegetable dish.

sādhana – regulated spiritual practices.

sādhu – a saintly person.

sādhu-saṅga – association with saintly persons.

sakhya – relationship with the Lord in friendship.

śakti – special potency.

śaktyāveśa avatāra – a special living entity empowered by the Lord with one or more of the Lord's opulences.

samādhi – total absorption in thoughts of Kṛṣṇa.

sampradāya – line of disciplic succession.

Sanātana Gosvāmī – one of the Six Gosvāmīs, chief followers of Lord Caitanya Mahāprabhu.

Śaṅkara – incarnation of Lord Śiva who propagated the impersonal Māyāvāda philosophy which maintains that there is no distinction between the Lord and the living entity.

saṅkīrtana – public chanting of the names of God, the approved yoga process for this age.

sannyāsī – one in the renounced order of life; member of the fourth spiritual order of Vedic society.

śānta – relationship with the Lord as a neutral worshipper.

śāstra – revealed scripture.

śāstric – instructions from the scripture.

sattvic – in the mode of goodness.

śikhā – the remaining tuft of hair on a Vaiṣṇava's shaven head.

śikṣā – instructions, instructing.

Śiva – partial incarnation of Kṛṣṇa who is in charge of the mode of ignorance and the destruction of the material cosmos.

śloka – Sanskrit verse.

śravaṇaṁ-kīrtanam – the devotional processes of hearing and chanting about the Lord.

Śrīla Prabhupāda – His Divine Grace A. C. Bhaktivedanta Swami Prabhupāda, Founder-Ācārya of the International Society for Krishna Consciousness.

Śrīmad-Bhāgavatam – Vedic scripture composed by Vyāsadeva to describe and explain Lord Kṛṣṇa's pastimes.

Śukadeva Gosvāmī – sage who originally spoke Śrīmad-Bhāgavatam to Mahārāja Parīkṣit just prior to the king's death.

sundara-ārati – the beautiful evening worship.

śūdra – one in the laborer class, fourth social order of Vedic society.

tapasya – austerity; accepting some voluntary inconvenience for a higher purpose.

tilaka – auspicious clay markings that sanctify a devotee's body as a temple of the Lord.

tīrtha – holy place.

tulasī – sacred plant dear to Lord Kṛṣṇa and worshiped by His devotees.

Upaniṣads – philosophical sections of the *Vedas*.

uttama-adhikārī – one on the highest stage of perfect devotion to the Lord who is unaffected by the material modes of nature.

Vaiṣṇava – devotee of Viṣṇu (Kṛṣṇa).

vaiśya – merchant or one who protects cows, third social order of Vedic society.

vāṇī – instructions of the guru.

vapuḥ – physical presence of the guru.

vartma-pradarśaka-guru – the person who initially shows one the path of Kṛṣṇa consciousness.

varṇāśrama – Vedic social system which organizes society into four occupational and four spiritual divisions (varṇas and āśramas).

vartma-pradarśaka-guru – the devotee who first introduces one to Kṛṣṇa consciousness.

vātsalya – relationship with the Lord as His parent.

Vedas – original revealed scriptures, first spoken by the Lord Himself.

Viśvanātha Cakravartī Ṭhākura – Vaiṣṇava spiritual master and commentator on *Śrīmad-Bhāgavatam* in the disciplic succession from Lord Caitanya Mahāprabhu.

Vṛndāvana – Kṛṣṇa's personal abode in the spiritual world; also, holy village where He appeared in India, which is non-different from the original Vṛndāvana.

vyāsāsana – seat of the spiritual master, who is the representative of Vyāsadeva (the original compiler of the Vedas.)

Yamunā – holy river in India where Lord Kṛṣṇa performed many of His pastimes.

Yudhiṣṭhira – eldest of the five Pāṇḍava brothers who Lord Kṛṣṇa established as emperor of the entire earth.

Acknowledgements

I would like to thank all disciples and friends who helped produce the past and present editions of Nimāi dāsa and the Mouse. The following GN Press staff members assisted with the production and printing of this second edition:

Ramila-devī dāsī
Nandarāṇī-devī dāsī
Baladeva Vidyābhūṣaṇa dāsa
Haridāsa dāsa
Kṛṣṇa-kṛpā dāsa
Kṛṣṇa-bhajana dāsa
Satya-sāra-devī dāsī
Lāl Kṛṣṇa dāsa

I especially thank Sthita-dhī-muni dāsa for his donation for the printing of this first single volume edition.

Satsvarūpa dāsa Goswami

Made in the USA
Columbia, SC
02 February 2024

45b0af0d-1e7a-4e72-8e08-29fc29cd6f3bR01